BATTLES OF DESTINY COLLECTION

VOL. THREE

JOY FROM ASHES

SEASON OF VALOR

AL LACY

Multnomah Publishers

BATTLES OF DESTINY, Volume 3
published by Multnomah Publishers
A division of Random House Inc.

© 2007 byALJO PRODUCTIONS, INC.
International Standard Book Number: 1-59052-947-2

Compilation of:
Joy from Ashes © 1995 by ALJO PRODUCTIONS, INC.
ISBN 0-88070-720-8
Season of Valor © 1996 by ALJO PRODUCTIONS, INC.
ISBN 0-88070-865-4

Cover Photography by Steve Gardner, www.shootpw.com

Multnomah is a trademark of Multnomah Publishers
and is registered in the U.S. Patent and Trademark Office.
The colophon is a trademark of Multnomah Publishers.

Printed in the United States of America

For information:
MULTNOMAH PUBLISHERS
12265 Oracle Boulevard, Suite 200
Colorado Springs, Colorado 80921

07 08 09 10 11 12 13 14 — 10 9 8 7 6 5 4 3 2 1 0

Novels by Al Lacy

JOURNEYS OF THE STRANGER SERIES:
Legacy
Silent Abduction
Blizzard
Tears of the Sun
Circle of Fire
Quiet Thunder
Snow Ghost

ANGEL OF MERCY SERIES:
A Promise for Breanna
Faithful Heart
Captive Set Free
A Dream Fulfilled
Suffer the Little Children
Whither Thou Goest
Final Justice
Not by Might
Things Not Seen
Far Above Rubies

Novels by Al and JoAnna Lacy

HANNAH OF FORT BRIDGER SERIES:
Under the Distant Sky
Consider the Lilies
No Place for Fear
Pillow of Stone
The Perfect Gift
Touch of Compassion
Beyond the Valley
Damascus Journey

MAIL ORDER BRIDE SERIES:
Secrets of the Heart
A Time to Love
The Tender Flame
Blessed Are the Merciful
Ransom of Love
Until the Daybreak
Sincerely Yours
A Measure of Grace
So Little Time
Let There Be Light

SHADOW OF LIBERTY SERIES:
Let Freedom Ring
The Secret Place
A Prince Among Them
Undying Love

ORPHAN TRAINS SERIES:
The Little Sparrows
All My Tomorrows
Whispers in the Wind

FRONTIER DOCTOR SERIES:
One More Sunrise
Beloved Physician
The Heart Remembers

DREAMS OF GOLD SERIES:
Wings of Riches
The Forbidden Hills
The Golden Stairs

A PLACE TO CALL HOME SERIES:
Cherokee Rose
Bright Are the Stars
The Land of Promise

Book Five

Joy from Ashes

Battle of Fredericksburg

For April, Chris, Andy, Anna Laura, Sundi, and B.J.—
the *greatest* grandchildren in the *whole world!*
What a joy to know that each of you has opened your heart to Jesus.
Thank you for being such bright spots in my life.
I love all of you more than you will ever know.

✳ ✳ ✳

PROLOGUE

When the controversy over States' Rights exploded into civil war on April 12, 1861 and the call for volunteers was sounded across the land, enlistment fever ran high. Yankees and Rebels alike feared that the war would end before they got a chance to fight. They had been charged by emotional oratory to expect a rush to the battlefield, a few days of excitement while killing men in the opposing army, and a triumphant, flag-waving return home.

Instead, the Civil War dragged on for weeks. The weeks turned into months, and the months into years. For every day they spent in actual battle, the soldiers of North and South passed weeks and sometimes months fighting such dull and unimaginative enemies as heat, cold, rain, snow, mud, dust, loneliness, homesickness, and irksome monotony. As one Yankee soldier put it, "War—except for the thrill of battle—is an organized bore."

Most of the men who volunteered for service did not seek to become professional soldiers. They were civilians who had temporarily answered the call to fight for their country. Few thought they might be killed in the fight. Their plan was to get the conflict over with and return to their normal lives. Yet over 600,000 of them would never see their homes again. Their bodies would lie in cold graves before the last shot in the awful, bloody war was fired. Hundreds of thousands would return home maimed, scarred, blinded, and missing limbs. What was supposed to be an exciting adventure altered their minds and bodies for the rest of their lives.

The recruits who answered the call of flag and country were no better prepared for the wearisome, everyday realities of military life than they were for the soul shattering shock of mortal combat. Few of them had ever tasted army camp food or slept under the stars or in a thin canvas tent for months on end.

Neither were they prepared for the harsh realities of the crude medical treatment that awaited the sick and wounded, for the horrid task of burying their comrades, sometimes by the hundreds, in common graves, nor for the grim, rat-infested, disease-ridden prisons that would hold the prisoners-of-war. (The story that unfolds in this novel will take you into one of those horrendous prisons.)

On July 21, 1861, the Confederates routed the Union army under Brigadier General Irvin McDowell, causing great shame and embarrassment to President Abraham Lincoln. The Yankee stragglers from the Bull Run battlefield had hardly caught up with their regiments when Lincoln ordered Major General George B. McClellan to Washington.

McClellan, who had studied engineering at West Point and had served on the staff of General Winfield Scott in the Mexican War, seemed to be a military leader of great promise. He had gained the attention of the War Department and President Lincoln early in the Civil War when he led in routing the Confederates at Beverly, Philippi, Romney, Middle Creek, Laurel Hill, and Rich Mountain in western Virginia in June and early July. The thirty-five-year-old general of the Department of the Ohio had helped build a strong rampart of Union support in that area, which ultimately resulted in the formation of the state of West Virginia.

McClellan had an unusual ability to organize men. Under the watchful eyes of President Lincoln and the War Department, he introduced strict military discipline to the regiments of easy-going recruits placed under his command, and soon had them functioning as hard-line soldiers. His men loved and respected him. He was small of stature and slight of build, and was affectionately referred to (out of his hearing) as "Little Mac." His cocksure bearing and self-sufficiency also garnered him the title, "Young Napoleon."

Answering President Lincoln's call, General McClellan arrived in Washington on July 25, 1861, and on July 27 was placed in charge of the army that had been commanded by General McDowell. For the next fourteen months McClellan was to dominate Union military action in the Eastern Theater and to build a large, smooth-working army.

There were two major Union campaigns during General McClellan's tenure as field commander of the Army of the Potomac: the Peninsular campaign in Virginia in the spring of 1862 and the defense of Maryland against General Robert E. Lee's bold invasion in the early fall of that same year.

The first campaign was the result of McClellan's insistence that the best defense of Washington was the destruction of the Confederate army, which occupied the 105-mile space between the two capitals, Washington and Richmond. Though there were some victories won in the Peninsular campaign, it failed to destroy the Confederate forces that stood in the gap. Lincoln and the War Department blamed McClellan because he seemed reluctant to move his army swiftly enough against the Rebels. When the president and the secretary of war ordered McClellan to hasten his attack, they encountered a reluctance they could not comprehend.

The second campaign produced the bloodiest one-day battle of the entire Civil War. The battle at Antietam Creek, near Sharpsburg, Maryland, was a Union victory, but in the eyes of Lincoln fell short of the victory it could have been had McClellan pursued and destroyed the Confederate army. Once again, McClellan had proven himself reluctant to strike while the iron was hot.

Lincoln's desire throughout McClellan's fourteen-month tenure as field commander was action, for which he often beseeched his commander. There had been a golden opportunity in the aftermath of Antietam (which took place on September 17) for the Federals to shorten the War dramatically by smashing Lee's weakened army. But McClellan had delayed, allowing Lee to escape into the Shenandoah Valley and reorganize and resupply his battered forces.

For some time, Lee had been operating with the nine infantry divisions of his Confederate Army of Northern Virginia unofficially grouped into two corps. These corps were under the command of his most reliable military leaders, James Longstreet and Thomas J. "Stonewall" Jackson. While Lee was regrouping in the Shenandoah Valley, the Confederate Congress approved Lee's corps organization and created the rank of lieutenant general, to which Longstreet and Jackson were immediately promoted.

An increasingly impatient Lincoln imposed a plan on McClellan—chase Lee southward immediately, moving the Union army along the eastern slopes of the Blue Ridge Mountains, remaining astride his supply lines. Press him, fight him, cripple him, then moved to Richmond and take it. Once the Confederate capital was in Union hands, the War would be short-lived.

Once again, however, McClellan moved his troops with slow deliberation. By the time they had inched their way south as far as Warrenton, Lee had positioned Longstreet's corps directly in McClellan's path. They were dug in and ready to fight. Lee's other corps, under Jackson, had remained in the Shenandoah Valley, posing a threat to the Union army's western flank.

A thoroughly disgusted Lincoln then called for his Army of the Potomac to pull back across the Potomac and wait for further orders. The orders arrived on October 6. McClellan was told by Lincoln through General-in-Chief Henry W. Halleck to cross the Potomac, pursue the enemy, give battle, and drive him south. This was to be done immediately before the wet fall weather came and turned the roads to mud.

McClellan sent a message back, informing Halleck that his army was in no condition to pursue and attack the enemy. Did Halleck—and the president, for that matter—not understand that he had requisitioned ammunition, shoes, blankets, and other indispensable articles shortly after the Antietam battle, and still they had not arrived?

While he waited for the needed supplies, McClellan worked on his campaign plan. He would lead his army across the Potomac and move them parallel with the Blue Ridge. They would swing around Gordonsville, then sweep toward Richmond from a westerly angle. With his men dressed and supplied properly, and his ammunition wagons loaded, he would have the troops and the guns necessary to take Richmond.

The needed ammunition and supplies arrived on October 25, and within two days, McClellan led his army across the Potomac toward Warrenton. Once again, his move was slow and deliberate. They reached Warrenton on November 7, and set up camp just outside of town.

Late that night, General McClellan was sitting alone in his tent, writing a letter to his wife by lantern light. There were footfalls outside his tent, followed by a voice asking if McClellan was presentable. Upon his invitation to enter, Brigadier General C. P. Buckingham appeared, followed by Major General Ambrose E. Burnside, both looking very solemn. After a moment of light conversation, Buckingham handed McClellan the order, of which he was bearer:

Headquarters of the Army
Washington, Nov. 5, 1862
General McClellan: On receipt of the order of the President, sent herewith, you will immediately turn over your command to Major General Burnside, and repair to Trenton,

New Jersey, reporting your arrival at that place by telegraph, for further orders.

H. W. Halleck, Gen.-in-Chief

McClellan read the order, then turned to Burnside with a slight smile and said, "Well, General, I hereby turn the command over to you."

When the Washington newspapers carried the story of McClellan's removal from command, Lincoln was quoted as saying he had replaced McClellan with Burnside because McClellan had the "slows."

As news of McClellan's dismissal spread amongst the troops, they trembled on the verge of mutiny. There had been great affection for McClellan amongst the men, and they were filled with anger. No other commander had ever so captured his soldiers, ever so entranced his followers. Violent invectives and denunciations were heard from the troops, along with threats of vengeance and mutterings of insurrection. Letters to friends and relatives at home denounced Lincoln's action bitterly.

On November 11, General McClellan was allowed to return to his troops to bid them farewell. A sadder gathering of men could not have been assembled. As McClellan passed in front of them, whole regiments broke and flocked around him. They begged him with tears not to leave them, but to say the word and they would storm Washington, demanding he be returned to their command.

A lesser general who was flanking McClellan shouted that he wished McClellan would put himself at the head of the Union army and throw the infernal scoundrels in Washington—including the president—into the Potomac River. Loud voices lended their agreement.

Government and military officials who stood by observing began to fear mutiny.

But their fears were quickly stifled. McClellan himself took control of the near-mob. With wise words he calmed the tumult and ordered the men back to their colors, reminding them of their duty. He told them they did not serve a man, but their country. They should perform as soldiers and follow their new commander, General Burnside. His words had their intended impact, and the men fell back into their places.

A short time later, McClellan met with his officers, telling them good-bye. There was not a dry eye in the assemblage. After grasping each officer's hand, "Little Mac" made a short speech in which he urged all of them to return to their commands and to do their duty to General Burnside as loyally and as faithfully as they had to him.

No military officer in the Civil War so resisted promotion as did Major General Ambrose E. Burnside. Three times in 1862, President Lincoln asked him to assume command of the Army of the Potomac. Burnside and McClellan had fought side-by-side on several occasions, and had been close friends for years. The man whose muttonchop whiskers eventually gave the name "sideburns" to the hair on the sides of a man's face demurred on the grounds that he was not competent to handle so large an army. He insisted that he was content to remain a subordinate under McClellan.

However, when Lincoln tendered his third offer, Burnside thought it over. The president was dead-set on removing McClellan as field commander. If Burnside did not accept the position, the command would go to a man he detested and distrusted—Major General Joseph Hooker.

Reluctantly, Burnside took command of the Army of the Potomac on the night of November 7, 1862, replacing his longtime friend. On the heels of his promotion came orders from General-in-Chief Halleck: "Report the position of your troops, and what you propose doing with them."

The dread with which Burnside faced his new responsibilities deepened with that order. He knew less than any other corps commander of the condition of his troops…and there was no time for him to learn. Lincoln wanted action, and he wanted it immediately. Delay had caused McClellan's downfall. Burnside found himself almost wishing he had let Lincoln give Joe Hooker the job.

President Lincoln had pondered his choices when seeking a replacement for McClellan, and faced the fact he had few men to choose from. The other eligible corps commanders all had disqualifying flaws.

Edwin V. Sumner, at sixty-five, was too old. William B. Franklin seemed too much embued with the same problem McClellan had. Lincoln's only other choice was Joseph Hooker, who was troublesome, cantankerous, and immoral. It was Hooker who brought prostitutes to his men to keep up their morale, and from this the women of that low profession garnered the name *hookers*.

Burnside, however, at the age of thirty-eight, was young and had proven his courage and valor on the battlefield. Though Lincoln wished Burnside had more self-assurance, he was the best available to replace McClellan. As often happened in the Civil War, Lincoln was forced to choose not the ideal man for the command, but the one who presented the fewest apparent liabilities.

Though handicapped with lack of self-assurance to meet the task before him, Ambrose E. Burnside attacked his problems vigorously. Within two days after taking command, he forwarded to Washington a bold new strategy for the capture of the Confederate capital. Instead of making a westward swing as proposed by his friend McClellan, Burnside would move his army rapidly southeastward from Warrenton to Fredericksburg, on the Rappahannock River.

Located forty-eight miles slightly southwest of Washington and fifty-seven miles due north of Richmond, Fredericksburg was considered by Burnside to be the doorway for his campaign to capture Richmond. In his message to Lincoln and Halleck, Burnside explained that by shifting toward the east, his army would stay closer to Washington and its base of supplies. It would also be on a more direct route to Richmond, for Fredericksburg stood on the main road midway between the two capitals. His plan was to outflank Lee's army, strategically placing his 130,000-man army between Lee's 78,000 troops and Richmond.

The key to Burnside's scheme was to have pontoon bridging equipment available when he arrived opposite Fredericksburg. With the floating bridges in place, Burnside's massive army could quickly cross the deep Rappahannock, take Fredericksburg before Lee could block them, then move south and seize Richmond.

Burnside knew that everything depended on speed. To streamline his operations, he proposed to reorganize his command by creating three "grand divisions" as he labeled them, each containing two corps, and each with its own staff. To command the grand divisions, he named three major generals: Sumner, Franklin, and Hooker.

The rest of Burnside's message dealt with the problems of supplying his enormous army. He requested thirty barges be loaded with goods and sent down the Potomac to a new supply base at Belle Plain, some ten miles northeast of Fredericksburg. He asked for additional wagon trains of ammunition and supplies, along with a huge herd of beef cattle, to move overland from Alexandria to the Rappahannock crossing. Most important was his request for enough pontoons to build floating bridges so he could get his army across the river.

Lincoln and Halleck were skeptical of Burnside's plan for capturing Fredericksburg on his way toward Richmond. Lincoln had tried for months to get McClellan to close in and fight the Confederate army, and now the new commander was proposing to skirt that army, seize Fredericksburg, then move on Richmond. Halleck threw up his hands and told Lincoln the decision to approve Burnside's plan was fully on the president's shoulders.

Glad, at least, to have a commander who was willing to put his army in motion, Lincoln approved the plan, adding in his message to Burnside, "It will succeed if you move rapidly; otherwise not."

The campaign was begun immediately. Under General Burnside's orders, Sumner's division led the way, setting off from the Warrenton camp at dawn on November 15, a day ahead of the other two divisions. Just after dark two days later, Sumner's advance elements marched into Falmouth, a small town situated on the north bank of the Rappahannock, less than two miles upriver from Fredericksburg. Franklin soon reached Stafford Court House, eight miles from Falmouth, and Hooker halted at Hartwood, just seven miles away.

Burnside seemed to be justifying the trust Lincoln had placed in him. In command for less than two weeks, he had concocted a campaign to seize and occupy the enemy capital, and his 130,000 troops now stood poised, ready to move on their first objective. Everything looked good. Fredericksburg and the hills beyond it were guarded by just four small companies of Confederate infantry, a cavalry regiment, and a battery of light artillery, diminutive at best against a force of 130,000. Longstreet's corps was bivouacked thirty miles away, at Culpeper, and Jackson's corps remained near Winchester in the Shenandoah Valley, a distance of sixty miles.

All Burnside had to do was get his army across the Rappahannock River, and the town would fly a Union flag. But there was one problem. The requested pontoons had not arrived. The Rappahannock was running rapid and riding high on its banks because of heavy rains up north. The water was very cold, even showing large chunks of ice. Burnside would be chancing the loss of men if he ordered them to swim across. He must wait for the arrival of the pontoons.

Fredericksburg, December 13, 1862

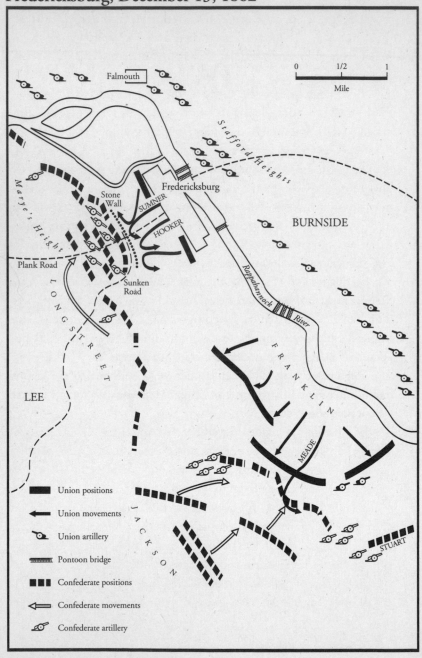

ONE

He stood alone outside his field tent, letting his gaze run the length and breadth of the long rows of tents that sheltered his corps from the weather. The night was cold and crisp, and the harsh, vagrant winds sweeping across the snow-crusted fields around Culpeper, Virginia, made him tighten his campaign hat and pull the lapels of his gray overcoat up around his neck.

The stars twinkled like diamonds above him and a half-moon hung sharp and clear-edged as though—on this night at least—a decorative afterthought of the Creator.

It was Sunday night, November 16, 1862. Lieutenant General James Longstreet watched the campfires along the tent rows winking in their struggle for survival, but shortly the winds would extinguish their flames and reduce them to glowing red embers.

Hands shoved into his overcoat pockets, the general pictured his fifty-eight thousand men asleep in their tents, taking their rest. Soon they would find themselves in combat again. The Federals were coming this way. Longstreet would know more what to expect when General Robert E. Lee arrived on Wednesday.

Longstreet had his own ideas. Abraham Lincoln had his sights set on capturing Richmond, the Confederate capital. But what route would the Federals take as they pressed toward their goal? If they came along the east fringe of the Blue Ridge, they would probably angle southeastward between Culpeper and Charlottesville in a direct line toward Richmond. If, however, they came straight south from Warrenton, they might first seize Fredericksburg, which would stand directly in their path.

Longstreet had made a wager with himself. Lincoln would order his new field commander, General Ambrose E. Burnside, to sweep down and capture Fredericksburg. Lincoln had replaced George B. McClellan as commander of the army of the Potomac because of McClellan's repeated reluctance to move his army quickly when Lincoln ordered action.

Two months earlier, General Lee had led his troops into Maryland, a move Longstreet had openly opposed. Lee and Longstreet were close friends, but the latter had argued against the bold invasion, saying it was foolish to cross into enemy territory when you were vastly outnumbered and outgunned. The Federals would launch a vicious attack simply because Confederate feet were making tracks on Union soil.

Once Lee, backed by President Jefferson Davis, affirmed that the invasion would take place as planned, Longstreet—soldier to the core—ceased to argue. But even as he followed Lee across the Potomac into Maryland on that fateful day in September, Longstreet was silently against it. The foolish scheme stuck in his craw and lay crosswise in his mind.

And now, as he looked back on it, Longstreet knew he had been right. The price paid in lives had not been worth it. The battle at Sharpsburg, Maryland, had left twenty-seven hundred Confederate soldiers dead along the banks of Antietam Creek, not to mention the nine thousand wounded, many of whom died of their wounds during the next three weeks. The Union had also taken six thousand prisoners.

Granted, the Federal forces suffered great losses, too. The Antietam battle had been the bloodiest one-day conflict since the War began. It would have been worse for the Confederacy, however, if McClellan had gone at the Rebel line as Lincoln had commanded.

The battle was a piecemeal affair. At no time did McClellan launch a concerted assault or even employ his reserves. Instead, he wasted his army's superior strength in a series of fragmentary attacks, using divisions and brigades instead of full corps.

Lincoln's grievance toward McClellan was that when he had the Confederates beaten, he did not follow through and destroy Lee's army. To have done so would, in Lincoln's mind, have spelled the end of the Confederacy. A full-fledged victory by McClellan would have left Richmond vulnerable to imminent capture. The Civil War would have ended.

Instead, Lee's army had escaped into Virginia's Shenandoah Valley and had been left in peace for two months. Lee brought in new recruits to replace those he lost on the banks of Antietam Creek, reorganized, and resupplied his forces.

For some time, Lee had been operating with his nine infantry divisions grouped unofficially into two corps under his top commanders—Thomas J. "Stonewall" Jackson and James Longstreet. In October the Confederate Congress approved Lee's corps organization and created the rank of lieutenant general, to which Jackson and Longstreet were immediately promoted.

In late October the increasingly impatient Lincoln imposed a plan on McClellan: Chase Lee southward, moving along the eastern slopes of the Blue Ridge Mountains and remaining astride his lines of supply. Press him, fight him if an opportunity presents itself...but *beat him to Richmond and capture it.*

Lee learned of Lincoln's orders from Confederate spies and immediately sent Longstreet's fifty-eight-thousand-man corps to Culpeper, placing them strategically in McClellan's path. He left Jackson's corps in the Shenandoah Valley, posing a threat if the

Federals came through there on their way to Richmond, rather than from Warrenton. When Lincoln was told by his scouts of Lee's clever move, he knew it had been possible because of McClellan's slow deliberation in marching his army. At this juncture, the Federal president made the decision to relieve McClellan of his command.

Word came to the Confederates on November 8 that on the day before, Major General Ambrose Burnside had been made commander of the Army of the Potomac.

Longstreet raised his eyes toward the star-studded sky and felt the smallness its great expanse always gave him. Though he made no claim to being a Christian, the rugged general was no atheist. God was up there somewhere, all right. He wondered if God cared about the thousands of men who lay sleeping in the fields. He reasoned that if God cared about them, He wouldn't have allowed the War to happen. There had been wars as far back as men have written their history. There always would be. The general had discussed the subject with an army chaplain one time. The chaplain had laid the blame for wars on Satan, the devil, who had inspired Cain to declare war on his brother Abel and shed his blood.

Longstreet wasn't sure what he believed about the devil, but he knew for sure that there was evil in the world.

The general lowered his gaze to the gurgling creek that flowed nearby, the silvery moonlight reflected on its surface. Longstreet drew in a deep breath and let it out with a sigh made visible by the frosty night air. His mind drifted to his wife and children. He knew they were warm and snug in their beds down in Richmond.

James Longstreet loved his family and missed them terribly. He hadn't seen them for over six months. "Maybe one day soon," he said aloud. "Maybe one day soon this war will be over, and we can be together again."

He wheeled about and entered his tent. He laid his hat on the small table that served as a desk and removed his overcoat, then sat down on the straight-backed wooden chair and removed his boots. He blew out the lantern and slid into his bedroll.

Sunrise the next morning came as no surprise. Longstreet was forty-one years old, and he had never known daylight to fail to come on schedule in all those years. He had recently read Charles Darwin's new book, *On the Origin of the Species by Means of Natural Selection*. Ignoramus. No, God was up there, all right. He made the whole universe and was keeping the earth in its orbit. No accident. Purpose and design in the universe by its Creator and Designer.

Longstreet left his warm bedroll and pulled on his boots. He could hear the activity of the camp as he shouldered into his overcoat and donned his campaign hat. He stepped out into the snappy morning air and filled his lungs. Men who milled about their tents nearby greeted him cheerfully. Though they smiled, he knew that behind those smiles were concerns about when and where the next battle would take place...and whether they would survive it.

Longstreet saw Corporal Ted Landrum hastening toward him from the cook's tent, carrying a tray of steaming food.

"'Mornin', General," grinned Landrum as he drew up. "Your breakfast, sir."

Longstreet smiled, opened the flap, and allowed Landrum to enter the tent ahead of him. Landrum placed the tray on the table and turned his boyish face toward the tall, full-bearded man. "Anything else I can do for you, sir?"

"No. Thank you, corporal. I'll set the tray outside when I'm finished. You can pick it up later."

"Yes, sir. Ah...General, sir...do we have any word yet about which route the Yankees may be taking?"

"Not yet. General Lee will be here day after tomorrow. Maybe he'll have something to tell us by then."

"Yes, sir. It's...it's just the waiting, sir. The men are jittery."

"I am, too," grinned Longstreet. "Guess we'll just have to jitter until the Yankees make their move, eh?"

"Guess so, sir," replied the corporal.

The wind had subsided some since sunrise, but it was still stiff and cold enough to make Longstreet keep his tent flap down. He was just finishing breakfast when he heard footsteps draw up outside, and a sturdy male voice call, "General Longstreet, sir?"

The general grinned to himself. A *familiar* sturdy voice. He picked up the tin cup that held one more swallow of coffee and said, "Come in, Major."

The flap opened and Longstreet looked up to see Major Layne Dalton enter, holding a small bundle of envelopes. "Mail boy at your service, sir."

The general set admiring eyes on the young major and downed the last of the coffee. Layne Dalton, an 1855 graduate of West Point, had served in the regular United States army as a lieutenant until the day after the Civil War began in April 1861, when he resigned from his post near Washington, D.C., and returned to his home at Fredericksburg, Virginia. A week later, he signed up in the Confederate army at Harper's Ferry, Virginia, and was taken in with the rank of lieutenant.

Shortly thereafter, Dalton was assigned to serve under Longstreet, and had served with him in several different divisions ever since. The rugged young officer had been at Longstreet's side in the First and Second Battles of Bull Run, Peninsular Battles, the Seven Days' Battles, and at the Battle of Antietam. He had distinguished himself under fire in every battle and had proven to be an able leader of men. Because of this, Longstreet had seen to it that he had been promoted to captain in July 1862, after the Seven Days' Battles, then had contacted Richmond after Dalton's outstanding valor at Antietam in September, recommending that he be promoted to major.

Longstreet chuckled at Dalton's sly humor and accepted the bundle of envelopes. "Thank you, mail boy. Anything interesting in this stack?"

Dalton grinned. "I believe you will find the one I placed on top to be of interest, sir. It's from Mrs. Longstreet."

The general's eyes sought out the handwriting on the top

envelope. It was written by the hand of the woman he loved, all right. He raised his gaze to the major and smiled. "I'll…ah…read it in private."

"I understand, sir. Sir…"

Longstreet's heavy eyebrows arched. "Yes?"

"Sir, I received a letter from *my* wife in today's mail, too. I…"

"Something wrong? Don't tell me Melody's having a problem in her pregnancy."

"No, sir."

"Thank God for that."

"Yes, sir."

"I can't remember when you first told me about it. How far along is she now?"

"Seven months. Doc Craig says she'll deliver about January 15."

"Well, I can see something's got you upset…something in her letter?"

"Yes, sir. Since we're only thirty miles from Fredericksburg, General, I need to ask your permission to make a quick ride home."

Longstreet's brow furrowed. "You seem a bit reluctant to tell me the content of the letter, Major. If I'm going to grant you time to ride to Fredericksburg, I'll have to know why you need it…and so will General Kershaw, since you're in his division."

Dalton cleared his throat, nodding. "Yes, sir. You see…my father-in-law, Jack Reynolds, is to stand trial for murder at the court-house in Fredericksburg tomorrow. The family needs me. Especially Melody. She's very close to her father, and if he's convicted, he will hang within a day or two after the trial."

Longstreet's expression froze, eyes unblinking. "Do you know the details?"

"Yes, sir. Melody wrote it all in the letter."

"Let me say right off that you have permission to go. But because of your rank, I'll have to know the details in case some unforeseen complications come up."

"I understand, sir. It's just that…well, a murder trial in the family isn't something a man wants to let out, even though I believe my father-in-law is innocent."

"I can sympathize with that, Major."

"Well, sir, it's sort of a long story, but I'll try to make it as brief as possible."

The general gestured toward a chair in the over-sized tent. "Sit down," he said. "I'll put this tray outside, then we won't be bothered over it, at least."

Once both men were seated, Major Dalton began his story.

The man Dalton's father-in-law was accused of murdering had been a long-time resident of Fredericksburg, Edgar Heglund. There had been bad blood between the Heglunds and the Reynoldses for over forty years—ever since Edgar Heglund, who was fourteen at the time, had shot and killed Jack Reynolds's dog claiming, mistakenly, that it had killed all of the Heglunds' chickens. From that time on, there was continuous trouble between them. When the two young men married and had families, the trouble did not subside.

Edgar and Ethel Heglund had five sons—Steve, Clyde, Everett, Keith, and George. Jack and Frances Reynolds had two children, Jack Jr. and Melody. As the years passed and the offspring of both families were growing up, the Heglund brothers—led by Steve—tormented Jack Jr. and Melody. Neither Edgar nor his wife ever disciplined their sons for their wrongdoing.

When they were in their mid-teens, Jack Jr. happened to run onto Steve without his brothers. Though Steve was somewhat bigger, Jack gave him a royal whipping. Steve ran to his parents and told them Jack Jr. and several of his friends had jumped him and beaten him up.

Edgar went to the Reynolds place with fire in his eyes, demanding that Jack Jr. and his friends be punished. Jack Jr. was there and said he had whipped Steve all by himself. Edgar went into a rage, called Jack Jr. a liar, and swearing, made a hostile move toward him. Jack Sr. stepped in and cold-cocked Edgar, breaking his jaw.

Things only grew worse between the families after that. Another Reynolds dog—this time Melody's—was shot one night, along with four of their horses. The culprits were never caught, but everyone in Fredericksburg knew who had done it. The town constable questioned the Heglund boys and their father, but they said they knew nothing about it. There was no evidence to convict them, so nothing could be done.

The next day, Jack Sr. bought four new horses and locked them up in the barn when evening came. About midnight, he discovered that the barn was on fire. Jack was able to get the horses out of the barn safely, but it burned to the ground. When Jack and the constable confronted Edgar Heglund and his sons, they claimed innocence. Ethel claimed her husband and sons were home with her at the time the fire was set. Jack called them all liars and warned them to leave his family and his property alone.

Several months went by without incident. Then Jack and Frances took their teenage son and daughter on a three-day trip to Richmond. When they returned, their house had been broken into. Cabinets were torn from the walls, the kitchen stove was filled with mud and manure from the corral, dishes had been shattered on the floor, and furniture all over the house had been destroyed. The worst thing of all was the destruction of Melody's piano.

At six years of age, Melody began to show her parents that she was properly named. Her inborn talent for music began to surface. The Reynoldses were poor—Jack was a cobbler—but they wanted their daughter's talent to be developed. They managed to scrape up enough money to pay for piano lessons, and their neighbors were nice enough to allow Melody to use their piano for practice.

They also began to put money away so they could buy their daughter her own piano. It took a long time, but they finally were able to purchase a used upright in Richmond, and presented it to her on her thirteenth birthday. Seven months later, the Heglund brothers destroyed the piano when they broke into the house.

Once again the town constable was called in, and this time he found incriminating evidence—a receipt from Fredericksburg's general store. Steve had made a purchase for the family and was carrying a copy of the receipt, which had his signature on it. Somehow while he was tearing up the Reynolds house, it dropped out of his pocket. When the constable confronted Edgar Heglund with the evidence, he had no choice but to call his sons before the constable. The youngest Heglund son, George, had not been in on it, but Steve, Clyde, Everett, and Keith had no choice but to admit their guilt.

The constable severely reprimanded the four brothers, then gave Edgar a choice—pay fully for the damage or have his sons face trial. The money was paid.

The constable warned the Heglunds to stay away from the Reynolds home and not to bother any of them at any time or any place. Another used upright was purchased for Melody, and the Reynoldses went on with their lives.

A couple of years went by with only hard looks between the two families when they met on the streets of Fredericksburg. Then in the spring of 1854, when Jack Jr. was nineteen, he didn't come home one night. His body was found washed up on the bank of the Rappahannock River the next morning. He had been bludgeoned to death with a heavy instrument and his body thrown into the river. Though the constable and the townspeople suspected Steve Heglund and his brothers, there was no hard evidence and no charges were brought against them.

The Reynolds family grieved over their loss, and knew in their hearts that the Heglund brothers murdered Jack Jr., but there was nothing they could do about it.

Footsteps were heard outside the tent, followed by the voice of Colonel Dwight Conley. "General Longstreet, sir…I'm sorry to disturb you, but we have a matter of utmost importance that only you can handle. It will only take a few moments."

Rising, the general answered, "Certainly, Colonel. Be right with you." He turned to Dalton and said, "Wait right here, Major. I'll be back shortly."

TWO

Major Layne Dalton was eager to be on his way to Fredericksburg, but there was nothing he could do but wait for the general to return. He would finish his story, then be on his way.

He sat on the chair, thinking about what Melody and her parents must be going through. With Jack Reynolds's life on the line, the waiting had to be excruciating. For several minutes, he dwelt on Jack's predicament, then his mind settled on the baby Melody was carrying.

Layne Dalton was sure his wife was going to give him a boy for their first child. He could feel it in his bones. If he was wrong and Melody was carrying a girl, he would love his little daughter every bit as much as he would love a son. But he desperately wanted a son. His own father had died when Layne was but two years old. The fact that he had never known the sweetness of a father-son relationship fired his desire to have such a relationship with a son of his own.

The major looked toward the tent flap. There was no sound of the general returning. He leaned forward with his elbows on his knees, then sat up straight and sighed. He pulled out the gold pocket watch his mother had given him when he turned thirteen. It had belonged to his father, who was a railroad man. The image of a steam engine was engraved on the back.

Five minutes after seven. The ride would take between two-and-a-half and three hours, if he kept his horse at a steady trot. He had hoped to leave in time to arrive home no later than ten, but he was going to have to settle for later.

Suddenly he heard voices. The voices grew closer, and the major thought he recognized General Longstreet's among them. He rose to his feet as the group of men approached the general's tent. Then they made an abrupt turn, and the volume of their chatter began to diminish. Dalton moved to the tent flap and looked outside. He could see the group of soldiers moving down a long row of tents. They were all enlisted men. The general wasn't among them.

The major went back to the chair and sat down. He thought once again of Jack and the heavy cloud hovering over him. He thought of the baby…and of Melody. How fortunate he was to have Melody Anne as his wife. In his heart, he hallowed the very first time he ever laid eyes on her. Suddenly he was back in Alexandria, Virginia, on that warm night in May 1858.

"Let's sit up front," Lieutenant Layne Dalton said to his best friend as he threaded through the crowd. "There are still some seats in the front row."

Lieutenant Jerry Owens was on Dalton's heels, holding the hand of Linda, who had been his wife for three months. Linda was having a hard time keeping up with her husband, holding onto him with one hand while lifting her long skirt with the other.

Dalton reached the front row of the center section and quickly claimed three seats in line with center stage. Out of breath, Linda sat down and the two men took seats on either side of her.

Jerry laughed as he looked past Linda and said to Layne, "You really like to get close to the action, don't you?"

"I always sit up front. That way I not only can hear everything clearly, but I can also see the expressions on the faces of the musicians and almost feel their heartbeat."

A young boy dressed in a sharp Concert Hall uniform came along in front of them. "Programs, folks? Ten cents."

"Sure," said Layne, reaching in his pocket. "One for each of us."

"Jerry and I can share one, Layne," Linda said. "We don't need two."

Jerry handed the boy two dimes before Layne could get his money out. "We'll take two, son."

As the boy walked away, Jerry handed his friend a program.

"You weren't supposed to do that," Layne said to the man who had been his fellow-classmate at West Point.

"And why not? You bought dinner and the concert tickets. Least I can do is put out a measly dime so you can have a program."

"I bought dinner and the tickets because I did the inviting," countered Layne. "It's your three-month anniversary, and I wanted to share it with you. After all, I was the best man at your wedding, wasn't I? The best man ought to treat the bride and groom on their three-month anniversary."

Jerry grinned. "You're amazing. Simply amazing."

Linda smiled and patted Layne's arm. "Sweet and amazing."

Layne responded with his famous crooked grin. "You just say that because it's true, Mrs. Owens."

Jerry laughed. "Sometimes she lies, Layne. *Amazing* you are...*sweet* you ain't! There were plenty of times at the Point when we bunked together that you were an old grump."

"Is that right? Well, I could tell Linda a thing or two about you."

"Now, boys," interjected Linda, "don't get into a scrap. This is a concert hall, not an arena."

Linda knew how much the young officers cared for each other, and that part of their fun was to make joking little digs.

"A scrap, honey?" chuckled Jerry. "It wouldn't last long enough to be a scrap. Layne couldn't fight his way through a wall of feathers! I'd put him out so fast, he wouldn't know what hit him."

"Hah!" reacted Layne. "If you and I got into it, there'd only be two sounds…me hitting you, and you hitting the ground!"

The tomfoolery ceased as quickly as it had started with the appearance of the orchestra members on stage. They took their places and began preparing their instruments for the concert. Violins, violas, cellos, and a bass viol were carefully tuned to the grand piano that stood to one side of the orchestra.

While the musicians prepared, Linda began reading the program. "Looks like we have several European artists here tonight," she said. "Two solo violinists…one from Germany, the other from Austria. We have a cellist from France, a flutist from Italy, and a singing group from Belgium. And we have talent from New York, Philadelphia, and—well, look here! We have one young lady who's from right here in Virginia."

Jerry leaned close and said, "Really? Let me see."

Layne was interested in who the local lady might be and looked at his program as Jerry read aloud, "Miss Melody Anne Reynolds of Fredericksburg. Piano soloist and songstress. Says she'll be on right after intermission."

"It's good to know we have some high class talent from Virginia," Layne said.

Jerry looked thoughtfully at his friend. "You know, Layne, when Linda and I got married, we agreed that within a month or two you'd be engaged. But you're not even seeing anybody, are you?"

Layne shrugged. "Not really."

"Well, you need to get with it before you end up a confirmed bachelor."

"I'm not worried. I just haven't found the right one yet."

Jerry turned to his wife and said, "Well, honey, looks like you and I are gonna have to get busy and dig up Miss Right for my pal, here. Married life is great, and I hate to see him missing out."

Layne turned mock-dismal eyes on his friend and said, "Did you say *dig* her up? No thanks."

"You and I don't need to play Cupid, honey," Linda told her

husband. "A handsome man like Layne won't have any trouble landing Miss Right once she walks into his life."

Jerry shrugged and said, "I guess you're right. But I don't know what you mean by *handsome*."

At eight o'clock sharp, the maestro appeared from the wings and walked to center stage. The crowd applauded while he took his place at the podium, bowed to them, then turned to face the orchestra and picked up his baton. The concert was under way.

After an hour and a half of delightful instrumentals and vocals, the intermission came. Layne and Jerry stood and stretched while Linda kept her seat.

"Well, it's been good so far," Jerry said. "I hope our little Virginia gal is as good as all those Europeans."

"I hope so too," Layne said.

They chatted about all manner of things for the next fifteen minutes. They were talking about their latest exploits at baseball when once again the maestro emerged from the wings and walked toward center stage. He bowed at the podium and allowed the applause to subside, then introduced the next performer as the Commonwealth of Virginia's own Melody Anne Reynolds. She would play a piano solo followed by a ballad.

Layne Dalton applauded with the rest of the crowd as Miss Reynolds appeared from the wings and moved to the grand piano. She was wearing a long-sleeved, floor-length black dress with a collar of white lace. Her dark-blue eyes glittered from the gas-powered spotlights as she smiled at the crowd.

For the next five minutes, the crowd was mesmerized by the skill, style, and talent of Melody Anne Reynolds. Enthusiastic applause and shouts of "Bravo!" erupted as soon as her lithe fingers brought the piece to a close. Smiling, she rose from the piano bench and bowed to her audience.

Layne was the first to his feet, and within seconds the entire audience was standing, applauding, and shouting their approval of the exceptional performance.

The applause slowly died out and everyone sat down. The orchestra began playing the introduction of the next number, and Melody Anne Reynolds walked gracefully to center stage. As she began singing a touching, sentimental ballad, Jerry stole a quick glance at Layne and smiled to himself.

Layne Dalton had never laid eyes on a woman who so stirred his senses. As she sang, Melody's gaze fell on Layne, who was sitting barely a dozen feet from her. For a fleeting moment their eyes met, and she smiled at him. Layne smiled back. Her warmth and tenderness swept like fire through him. He had never known such feelings before.

As Melody finished the last line of the song, her eyes fell on young Dalton again. She did not smile this time, but she did allow her gaze to lock with his a second or two longer than before.

Layne once again jumped up, applauding for all he was worth, and the whole crowd stood and applauded with him. Smiling, Melody bowed and walked off the stage. The applause continued, with voices shouting their approval of the outstanding performance. Melody came back on stage, took another bow, and disappeared once more. The maestro returned to the podium and the concert continued.

Jerry leaned past Linda and said, "You kinda like her, don't you."

Layne was staring toward the wings where he had last seen Melody and did not hear his friend.

"Layne!" pressed Jerry. "Hey, remember me?"

People around them were scowling at Jerry.

"Sh-h-h!" hissed Linda. "You're making too much noise."

Lowering his voice to a whisper now that he had Layne's attention, Jerry said, "You really like her, don't you."

"She's a very talented young lady," Layne whispered.

"And very beautiful, right?"

Layne met his gaze evenly. "Can't argue with that."

"How about if I introduce you to Melody Reynolds after the concert?"

Both Layne and Linda looked at Jerry wide-eyed.

"You know her?" Layne asked.

"How do you know her?" Linda queried.

"Please, folks," spoke up a man directly behind them. "If you want to talk, go out to the lobby."

"Sorry, sir," Jerry said. Then leaning past Linda, he said, "I'll introduce you to her after the concert."

Layne's heart seemed on fire. He nodded and smiled.

They settled down to enjoy the rest of the concert, and no more was said. As far as Layne was concerned, however, every instrument in the orchestra could have been playing a different tune. He was thinking only of Melody Reynolds.

Finally the last number was played and the audience gave its final enthusiastic round of applause. The maestro bid them all good night. Being down front meant that Layne and his friends would be the last to reach the lobby. Jerry and Linda were holding hands and walking just ahead of Layne as they slowly moved up the aisle.

Layne tapped Jerry on the shoulder and said, "Why'd you wait till Miss Reynolds was off stage before you told me you knew her?"

Jerry waved him off and replied, "Don't worry about it, my friend. Some things in life just have to remain a mystery. You just hold on. In a matter of minutes you and Melody will be acquainted."

Linda tried to get her husband to explain how he knew Melody Reynolds, too, but he avoided giving her a direct answer. Soon they reached the lobby, and Layne's eyes traveled to the greeting line. There was Melody Reynolds amid the European artists, smiling and warming people with her beauty and pleasant personality.

Jerry and Linda were still in front of Layne as they drew near. Layne's heart was drumming his ribs.

Jerry smiled at Melody and said, "That was a stunning performance, Melody. I'd like to introduce you to someone who enjoyed it more than anybody else in the hall."

"Pardon me," Melody said, tilting her head slightly. "Do I know you, Lieutenant?"

"Well, no, you don't. But I would like to introduce you to a young man who was hypnotized by your performance tonight." He motioned for Layne to move closer.

Layne did so, eyeing his friend with suspicion. Jerry laid a hand on Layne's shoulder and avoided Linda's you-conniving-rascal look.

"Miss Melody Anne Reynolds," said Jerry, smiling from ear to ear, "I want you to meet the man who without a doubt is your number one fan. Lieutenant Layne Dalton...Miss Melody Anne Reynolds."

Melody smiled warmly at the man whose dark, expressive eyes she had noticed while singing her ballad. She extended her hand and said, "Lieutenant."

Layne's blood was racing as he took the small hand in his own, did a slight bow, clicked his heels, and lifted it to his lips.

Linda elbowed her husband, saying with her eyes, *Look at that. When did you ever do that with me?*

Layne released Melody's hand and stood to his full height. "Miss Reynolds, this is indeed the greatest pleasure of my life."

"Why thank you, Lieutenant. You honor me."

I more than honor you, he thought. *I think I love you.* Aloud he said, "That was a stunning performance, Miss Reynolds. You truly are blessed with marvelous talent."

"You're very kind," she smiled. Then fixing the audacious Jerry Owens with steady eyes, she said, "Lieutenant Dalton, now that you and I are acquainted, maybe you would like to introduce me to your friend, here, and the charming lady with him."

"Of course," grinned Layne. "May I present Linda Owens and her brassy husband, Lieutenant Jerry Owens. The lieutenant and I were roommates at West Point, and up until a moment ago, he and I were best friends."

Melody laughed. "Oh, please. Don't let what the lieutenant did destroy your friendship. I'm...ah...I'm sure he meant well."

"I sure did, Miss Reynolds. You see, Layne's been awful lonely of late, and—"

"Jerry," cut in Linda, "why don't you just leave it where it is?"

The four of them laughed together, then Melody looked around and spotted a handsome couple standing nearby. "I'd like for you people to meet my parents."

Jack and Frances Reynolds had been watching and were delighted to meet the Owenses and Lieutenant Dalton. They chatted briefly, then Jack Reynolds turned to his wife and daughter and told them they should be returning to the hotel. As good-byes were being said, Layne moved close to Melody. "I meant what I said, Miss Melody. Meeting you has been the greatest pleasure of my life."

Melody blushed, dipped her chin, then raised her gaze to his. "Thank you, Lieutenant. I really don't understand why you feel that way, but—"

"Would...would it be all right sometime when I can get down to Fredericksburg...if I call on you?"

"Why, of course," she responded with a smile. "That would be nice."

The lieutenant was having a hard time breathing. "Good!" he managed to say. "What is your address?"

It was late in the afternoon two days later when Lieutenant Layne Dalton rode up in front of the Reynolds house in Fredericksburg. It was a warm day, and the windows were open. He could hear the sound of a piano, but could tell it was being played by someone other than Melody.

Layne noticed a buggy coming down the dusty street and recognized Jack Reynolds at the reins. He swung from the saddle, tied his horse's reins to the hitching post, and smiled at Reynolds as he drew up.

"Well, if it isn't Lieutenant Dalton!" exclaimed the cobbler. "Melody said you would be coming to call on her sometime, but I didn't expect it to be so soon."

"Well, I...ah...was able to get a pass from my company commander, sir. I have to report back by sunrise."

"You won't get much sleep, in that case."

"I don't mind, sir. If I can take Miss Melody to dinner and spend a little time with her, it'll be worth it."

Jack Reynolds liked the young lieutenant. He grinned and said, "You two hit it off real good, didn't you?"

"Well, I—"

"All Melody's talked about for two days is *you.*"

"Really?"

"Really. Melody's giving a piano lesson at the moment. Why don't you come on out back with me? I'll park the horse and buggy by the back porch, and you and Melody can use them to go to supper."

"Yes, sir," nodded Dalton, climbing on the buggy.

Reynolds drove the buggy to the rear of the house and hauled up at the porch. Frances was standing at the door, talking to a neighbor.

Frances was also surprised to see the lieutenant, but welcomed him and introduced him to Lizzie Springston, explaining that Lizzie's daughter was taking a piano lesson from Melody. Then Frances said, "Well, Lieutenant, I didn't expect to have this pleasure so soon. Melody's going to be pleased to see you. When the piano lesson's over, Melody and I will start supper. Won't be any trouble at all to put another plate on."

Layne glanced at Jack, then said, "I appreciate the invitation, ma'am, but with your permission, I'd like to take Miss Melody to dinner."

Frances frowned. "*Dinner?* I thought you told us the other night that you're a Virginian. Didn't you say you were born and raised over by Roanoke?"

"Sorry, ma'am. It was always *supper* to me until I entered the Academy. They taught us that army officers have to be refined…and to those Yankee professors the evening meal is *dinner.* I'll have to ask you to pardon my error."

Jack laughed. "Well, we'll pardon you this time, Lieutenant, but don't ever let it happen again!"

Everybody was laughing when suddenly Melody appeared at the kitchen door with twelve-year-old Melba Springston. Melba proceeded onto the porch, but Melody seemed frozen in the door frame, her hands affixed to either side. Her eyes were wide as she held them on the army officer.

Lieutenant Layne Dalton sidestepped Melba, a wide grin across his face, and said, "Hello, Miss Melody."

THREE

Melody Anne Reynolds had found her mind and heart fixed on the dashing young lieutenant since meeting him at the concert. She had dreamed of him both nights. She gave him a warm smile and said, "Hello, yourself, Lieutenant Dalton."

There was warmth in her eyes and music in her voice. Layne needed a few seconds to collect himself. "I…ah…I was able to get a pass from my company commander. I'd like to take you to din—to supper if it's all right with you."

"Why, I would be honored, Lieutenant."

"I don't know how well Fredericksburg is fixed for eating establishments, but you can choose your favorite place."

"All right. My favorite place is not very fancy, but it has great food. It's called Mabel's Café."

"Then Mabel's it is," Dalton said, smiling from ear to ear.

"Just hold on, now, Lieutenant," interjected Frances with a look of devilment in her eyes. "You said with *my* permission you would like to take my daughter out."

"Yes, ma'am."

"Well, I just want to make sure about what you're taking her for—dinner or supper."

"Oh, supper for sure, Miz Reynolds," Layne said in an exaggerated Southern accent.

Frances responded in kind. "All right. Y'all be sure you is going for *supper*, and y'all have my permission!"

There was laughter all around.

Layne and Melody arrived at Mabel's Café as twilight was settling over Fredericksburg. Melody found several friends at the café and introduced them to Layne. There were curious eyes and whispering lips all over the place while the happy couple enjoyed their meal and became better acquainted. They both were taken with the other, but discreetly did their best to hide it.

A high moon put a silver wash on the town as Layne drove the buggy through the streets toward the Reynolds home. Melody felt safe and secure with Layne and relished every moment with him. Though he was quite strong, he had treated her like a China doll all evening. Lieutenant Dalton was every inch a gentleman.

Layne pulled up in front of the Reynolds place where his horse was tethered at the hitching post.

"I'll walk you to the front door, Miss Melody," he said quietly. "Then I'll take the horse and buggy around back. Your father will probably want to come out and show me where he wants the buggy parked."

Before Melody could reply, Jack Reynolds came out the front door. "I'll put the horse and buggy away, Lieutenant," he called amiably. "Since its such a nice warm night, maybe you and Melody would like to sit out here on the porch swing for a while."

Melody's father had never made such a suggestion to any other young man she had dated. The gesture was not lost on Layne, either.

"I appreciate that, Mr. Reynolds," he said, smiling. "I won't stay long. I already told Melody I have to be back at camp by sunup."

"Yes," said Melody, "and I told him I feel guilty that he's going to lose a night's sleep just to see me."

"It's only forty miles or so from here to the camp. I just might get back in time to sleep an hour, maybe two. And if not, it's still been worth it."

Jack grinned and said to Melody, "You'd better treat this one real good, honey. He's the kind that'll make some young woman a real good husband!"

"Daddy!"

Jack laughed and said, "If you two'll climb down, I'll put horse and buggy away."

Layne jumped out of the buggy and helped Melody down. Jack led the animal toward the back of the house and said over his shoulder, "Come back anytime you can, son. Only next time, plan to eat here at the house. Between Melody and her mother, they whip up some lip-smacking good meals."

"I'll do that, sir," grinned Layne. "And thank you."

As the couple moved toward the porch, Melody said, "Lieutenant, I'm sorry for Daddy's remark."

"You mean about me making some young woman a good husband?"

"Yes. I don't doubt that you will, but it was inappropriate for him to say it like that. I love him with all my heart, but sometimes...well, his timing is bad."

Layne took Melody's arm to help her up the steps. "Miss Melody," he said, "please don't be embarrassed. His remark didn't bother me in the least. And besides, I hope he's right. I hope I will be a good husband to the woman I marry. I sure plan to, anyway."

Melody didn't know what else to say, so she started asking questions about Layne's childhood. He had already told her at the café that both of his parents were dead, and that he had no siblings.

Layne told her what she wanted to know about his childhood, recounting some humorous incidents. She enjoyed it and laughed repeatedly. The porch lantern and the silver moonlight illumined her features. He loved watching the toss of her head and listening to the melodic run of her voice.

All too soon it was time for him to go. Melody walked him to his horse, and the animal nickered as they drew up to the hitching post. Layne grinned and said, "That's right, ol' boy. She sure is."

Melody looked at the lieutenant quizzically.

"This horse and I talk to each other, Miss Melody."

"Oh? And what did he just say?"

"He said you're the prettiest young lady he's ever seen."

"Lieutenant, you...you overwhelm me. I don't know what to say. I—"

"Miss Melody, it isn't I who overwhelm you, it's the horse. He's the one who made the remark about how pretty you are. I simply agreed with him."

Melody loved Layne's sense of humor and his quick wit. He was the most interesting man she had ever met. She laid a hand on his forearm and said softly, "Well, you tell this fine animal I appreciate his compliment."

The touch of Melody's hand sent tingles through Lieutenant Dalton. "I'll tell him while we head for camp, Miss Melody."

"You can just call me Melody, Lieutenant. The *Miss* isn't necessary."

He gave her a lopsided grin. "All right, Melody. And you can just call me Layne. The *Lieutenant* isn't necessary."

Melody's heart was racing. "Thank you for the supper, Layne. And thank you so much for coming all this way to see me. Please come back again."

"I will."

"Soon."

"I will."

Layne's arms ached to hold her, but he forced himself to turn away. He untied the reins from the hitching post, looped them over his horse's head, and swung into the saddle. Just then the front door came open, and Jack and Frances stepped onto the porch. "Lieutenant," called Jack.

"Yes, sir?"

"Do you think you can get a pass for weekend after next? We're having a family get-together, and there'll be plenty of good food. Frances said she and Melody will cook whatever your favorite meals are for Saturday and Sunday both. And we've got a spare bedroom."

Layne looked down at Melody who was eyeing him with anticipation. "Since it's that far away, sir, I'm pretty sure I can get a pass. I'll be here mid-afternoon a week from Saturday."

"Wonderful!" exclaimed Frances, who was holding onto her husband's arm. "And what are your two favorite meals?"

"Well, ma'am," grinned Dalton, "I'd say one'd be cornbread and beans...and the other would be chicken-and-dumplings with black-eyed peas."

"You can plan on both," Frances assured him. "And you'll stay in our spare room?"

"That'd be fine, ma'am."

"Well, we'll just plan on it then."

"Yes, ma'am. Thank you."

"And I will look forward to it," spoke up Melody.

"So will I," nodded Layne. With that, he touched heels to the horse's flanks and rode away.

Lieutenant Layne Dalton waded his horse across the Rappahannock and headed north toward Alexandria. He visualized Melody's kindly face and sweet smile and let the sound of her voice resound in his mind. Truly she was the most captivating woman he had ever met. He was sure he was falling in love with her.

The anticipated weekend came, and Lieutenant Dalton happily immersed himself in the family gathering, meeting relatives on both sides of Melody's family. Conversation around the table on Saturday evening revealed that Hank Reynolds (Jack's older brother by two years) was taking his family west. Hank had learned of a huge gold strike near Virginia City and was heading out there to get his share of it. While wolfing down cornbread and beans, he tried to persuade Jack and Frances to pack up and go with them. Big money could be made in Nevada. The West was starting to boom, and people were moving out there to build new lives on the frontier. The way Virginia City was growing, Melody would be sure to pick up plenty of music students.

Jack laughed and said he would let Hank do the gold mining. He was a cobbler and would stay and run his cobbler shop.

Later that evening, after the dishes were done and the kitchen cleaned up, Melody gave a concert on her old upright piano, thrilling family members with her talent. But no one was thrilled as much as Layne Dalton.

There was another concert on Sunday night, and afterward Layne and Melody took a short walk together. In their parting moments at the hitching post, he came close to kissing her, but refrained. He knew how he felt toward her; he wasn't sure as yet how strong her feelings were toward him.

Because of planned military maneuvers, Layne was unable to visit Melody for several weeks. The first week of August he obtained a pass, and late on a Thursday afternoon, knocked on the door of the Reynolds house.

There were rapid footsteps on the inside, and when the door swung open, Frances smiled and chirped, "Layne Dalton! How are you? Come in! Come in!" Before Layne could utter a reply, Frances shouted, "Melody! Layne is here!"

From upstairs, Melody's voice called back, "Who's here, Mother?"

"Layne Dalton, honey!"

There was dead silence, then Melody appeared at the top of the stairs. She was in a plain cotton house dress, and touched it at the collar as she looked down at Layne and said, "I'm not dressed for receiving a caller, Layne. I hope you don't mind seeing me like this. I've been cleaning out some closets, and—"

"You look mighty good to me," he cut in. "Sorry I couldn't let you know any sooner. My commanding officer only granted the pass at supper time last night. I have to be back by sunup, so I rode as fast as I dared."

Melody bounded down the stairs and, to Layne's surprise and delight, into his arms. They held each other tight, then Melody rose up on her tiptoes and planted a tender kiss on his cheek. "It's so good to see you! I appreciate your letters, of course, but it's just not the same. Did you receive my last letter? The one about my picking up four new students all in one week?"

"It came just yesterday. That gives you what…fourteen students now?"

"Mm-hmm. And with the new ones I figure I'll have enough money to buy a new upright by Christmas."

"Christmas present for yourself, eh?" he chuckled.

"Yes! I'm so excited! This old one is really starting to show its age."

"Well, which is it this time, Layne?" Frances asked. "Home cooking or Mabel's?"

"If it's all right with your daughter, it'll be home cooking."

Melody turned to her mother and said, "If it's all right with you, I'll rush upstairs and make myself a bit more presentable, then come help you get supper on."

"You really don't need to make yourself more presentable on my account," Layne said. "You look mighty good just the way you are."

Melody dabbed at her hair. "You sure?"

"Positive."

Jack Reynolds came in just then from the back side of the house. He welcomed Layne with a smile and a handshake and asked how long he could stay. When Layne told him, Jack grinned at his daughter, then looked at Layne and said, "Sure glad you could show up, my boy. Melody's been pining around here, acting like a sick calf. This visit will perk her up for sure."

"Daddy! You shouldn't tell Layne things like that!"

"Why not?" Jack chuckled. "It's the truth."

"You men find a place to sit down," Frances said. "The sick calf and I will whip up some victuals."

"Mother!" said Melody, eyes wide. "You're getting as bad as Daddy!"

"You mean as *good* as Daddy," laughed Jack.

Supper was almost over when a knock came at the front door. Jack excused himself and went to answer it. He returned with a young couple, introducing them to Lieutenant Dalton as Walter and Harriet Smith. Melody got up from the table, embraced Harriet, and explained to Layne that the three of them had gone through school together. Walter had been a couple of grades ahead of them, but Harriet and Melody were in the same graduating class.

Layne shook hands with Walter and did a slight bow to Harriet, who smiled and said to her husband, "I like this man! He knows how to conduct himself in the presence of a lady."

"If I bowed like that every time you came into my presence, I'd have a chronic backache!"

Everyone laughed. Then Harriet said, "We didn't mean to interrupt your supper."

"You didn't, honey," Frances assured her. "We were just finishing up."

"We'll be on our way," Walter said. "We just wanted to come by and remind you that we're having revival services at our church all next week, starting Sunday."

"Oh, yes," said Jack. "You told us about it a couple weeks ago."

"We'd sure love to have you come."

"Well, we'll see about it," replied Jack. "Maybe we can make it on Sunday morning, at least."

"Good," grinned Walter. Then turning to Dalton, he asked, "Are you going to be here on Sunday, Lieutenant?"

"No, sir. I have to be back at camp by sunrise tomorrow morning."

"I see. Well, perhaps we can get you to visit our church some other time."

"Who knows?" chuckled Layne.

When the Smiths were gone, Layne said, "I've never been to a revival meeting. Have any of you?"

"Never have," Jack said.

"I think it might be interesting," said Melody. "I've heard that they usually have some lively music. I'd like to hear it."

"From what I'm told," put in Jack, "the preaching gets pretty lively, too. You know, that hellfire and brimstone stuff."

"I've heard some of that kind of preaching," Layne said. "My grandmother used to take me to a Baptist church in Roanoke when I was little. Scared me."

"Well, maybe a little scaring would be good for us from time to time," Frances said. She sighed, then slapped her hips with the palms of her hands, and said, "Jack, why don't you help me do the dishes and clean up the kitchen so these young people can have a little time together?"

"Okay, I volunteer," laughed Jack.

Layne looked at Melody and asked, "How about a small concert? Then we can take a walk."

Melody took him by the hand and led him into the parlor. She settled on the piano bench, and Layne leaned on the top of the old upright, looking down at her. Melody played three instrumental pieces, then began playing and singing Stephen Foster's "Beautiful Dreamer." Her eyes met Layne's and held them. Layne Dalton was smitten with love. He had to find a way to tell her.

"That was beautiful," Layne said when she finished the song.

Melody blushed, rising from the bench. "Sorry about some of the off-key notes. Some of the strings on this old piano won't hold true anymore."

Layne grinned. "I didn't notice the piano. I was listening to the beautiful voice of the beautiful lady."

"You're very kind, Lieutenant Layne Dalton."

"It's not kindness, Miss Melody Anne Reynolds. It's just factual speaking."

"You ready for that walk?"

He gave her his arm and said, "I'm ready."

They walked around the block four times, then entered the Reynolds's yard, mounted the porch, and sat on the swing. The porch lantern burned a few feet away by the door.

"Nice people, the Smiths," Layne said.

"Yes. Harriet is one of my closest friends. They're very kind and considerate people. Either one of them would go the limit to help someone in need. They're a perfect match."

"I can see that. They were made for each other."

"God does that, don't you think?" Melody said.

"Makes people for each other?"

"Mm-hmm."

"Yes, I suppose He does. Mom used to tell how she looked for her ideal man...you know, the man of her dreams. And Dad said he had done the same thing. They were very happy together."

"I wish I could have known your parents," Melody said.

"You'd have loved them. And they'd have loved you, too. You're easy to love, you know."

Melody wasn't sure how to respond. "Not always," she said quickly. "I can be crabby and mean sometimes."

Layne chuckled. "I can't picture that. But even if you were, I'm sure the man of your dreams would love you anyhow." He let those words settle in her mind, then said, "You do have a man of your dreams, don't you? I mean one you've pictured in your mind since you were a little girl?"

"Oh, of course." Layne was dangerously close to the very thing that had been on Melody's mind ever since they first met. "And you've had a girl of your dreams, I suppose?"

"Definitely."

Melody's throat constricted, but she had to ask. "This girl of your dreams...what does she look like?"

Layne adjusted his position on the swing so as to look Melody in the eye. "Well, she's exactly your height and build."

"Really?"

"Yes. And she has honey-blonde hair, deep-blue eyes, lovely white teeth, and a cute little nose exactly like yours."

"Really?"

"Really."

Melody licked her lips and blinked to clear the mist in her eyes. "May I tell you about the man of my dreams?" she asked.

"Of course."

"Well, if you looked in a full-length mirror, you could see exactly how tall he is, how he is built, what his facial features are like, the color of his hair, and the color of his eyes. And I'll tell you his initials, too, if you'd like to know what they are," she said with a tremor in her voice.

"Would…would they have *Lieutenant* in front of them?"

"Yes," she breathed.

Layne leaned close, and suddenly their lips were together in a soft, velvet kiss. When they parted, Layne embraced her and said in a half-whisper, "I love you, Melody. I fell in love with you the moment you walked out on that stage in Alexandria. I didn't recognize what it was, but it didn't take me long to figure it out. I've only grown to love you more ever since."

Melody reached up and stroked his cheek. "It took me a little longer to fall in love with you. It wasn't until after the performance, when we were so subtly introduced by your friend. And I've only grown to love *you* more ever since."

They kissed again, the fire of their newly confessed love burning between them, joining their hearts in a union of tender emotion.

Layne held Melody close once more. She was quiet within his arms, relishing his love. After a long moment, he said, "I'm afraid I've got to be going."

She pushed back gently so she could look in his eyes. "When will I see you again?"

"I'm not sure. It's liable to be several weeks."

She stroked his cheek once more and whispered, "I'll miss you terribly."

"I'll miss you terribly, too," he said, placing the tips of his fingers under her chin and bending down to kiss her again.

Holding onto his hand, Melody walked with him to the hitching post. His horse bobbed its head and nickered.

"That's right, boy," said Layne. "She sure is."

"Oh, you two!" Melody giggled.

Layne kissed her once more, then mounted. "My letters will keep coming," he said.

"Mine, too," she assured him. "I love you, darling."

"I love you, too. More than you will ever know. I'll let you know when to expect me again, once I know myself."

"I pray it'll be soon."

Layne smiled at her, then turned his horse and rode away into the night.

FOUR

A cool wind whipped across the Rappahannock River on Wednesday, October 6, 1858, as the Reynolds family pulled up to the dock at precisely 1:00 P.M. in their buggy. Neighbor Wiley Price and his three young, husky sons drew alongside them in their wagon.

"I'll be glad when this mystery is solved," Jack Reynolds said to Wiley.

"Me, too," nodded Price. "This young fella must have somethin' pretty big up his sleeve."

"I guess so," Frances said, "since he told Melody in the letter to have four strong men and a wide-bed wagon to meet the boat."

"How do we know who to contact?" asked Richard Price, the eldest son.

Melody held up the letter, which was open in her hand. "Layne says in here just to ask for Captain Elrod Dean. He's the boat's skipper and he'll tell us what item we're to unload."

"Well, here comes the boat right on time," Wiley said. "This mystery will soon be cleared up."

"It sure will," came a resonant voice from behind.

Everyone turned to see the speaker.

"Layne!" exclaimed Melody. "You didn't say *you* would be here!"

Layne dismounted and gave her his famous crooked grin. "I wanted to surprise you."

"Help me down. I want to greet you properly."

Layne stepped to the wagon, took hold of Melody, and eased her down. Melody stood on her tiptoes and kissed his cheek, saying with feeling, "It's so good to see you, darling! I've missed you terribly."

Layne glanced at Jack, who grinned and said, "She's told us all about it, my boy. Seems to me she can call you 'darling' all she wants."

"You're right about that, sir," grinned Dalton, hugging her close.

"All right, Lieutenant Dalton," said Melody, "we have our neighbors, the Prices, here with the wagon as you requested. I think it's time they know what it is they're going to have to load into their wagon."

"Oh, you do, eh?" Layne chuckled. "Well, they'll know shortly. Let's go onto the dock. I'll present a couple of papers to Captain Dean, and we'll soon be on our way."

There were people on the dock ready to meet family and friends as the big boat steamed up and crew members jumped onto the dock to secure it. A gangplank was laid between the boat deck and the dock. While passengers disembarked, Layne hastened across the gangplank, threading his way amongst them, and quickly found Captain Elrod Dean.

Moments later, four crewmen were wheeling a large wooden crate on dollies toward the dock. When Melody saw the crate, she looked at Layne and said, "What on earth?"

"I've arranged to have it unpacked right here," he said quietly. "Once it's out of the crate, it'll be easier to handle. Between the Prices and myself, we should be able to manage it."

When the crate had been wheeled onto the dock, the crewmen used small crowbars to begin carefully taking it apart. Soon the top of the crate was removed, then the sides were laid flat. Melody's hands went to her mouth and tears welled up in her eyes. Jack was muttering something to himself, and Frances was about to cry.

"Layne!" Melody gasped. "What have you done?"

Layne took her into his arms and said, "We'll take the canvas off once we have it in the house, darling. I figure with a little furniture rearranging, and removal of that old upright, it'll fit fine in the parlor."

Frances moved up to her daughter and Layne, and wiping tears, laid a hand on Layne's arm. "Layne... I hardly know what to say. This is so kind and generous of you."

"Layne, how can we thank you?" Jack said.

"No need to, sir," Layne replied. "I'm in love with your daughter. Presenting her with this instrument is a great pleasure."

"Any idea what it weighs, Lieutenant?" Wiley Price asked.

"I'm not sure," said Dalton, "but the salesman I corresponded with by wire in New York told me five strong men could handle it."

"Well, we're about to find out," Richard chuckled.

A half-hour later, the old upright piano was on the back porch, and under Frances's directions, the men were rearranging some of the furniture in the parlor to make room for the concert grand.

"That should do it," said Frances. "Now you can bring in the piano."

The women looked on as the grunting, puffing men carried the grand into the parlor and positioned it in place. Richard hurried out to the wagon and brought in the canvas-covered bench. He and his father unwrapped the bench while Jack and Layne removed the protective canvas from the piano.

As section by section of the expensive instrument was revealed, Melody "oohed" and "ahhed" at the beauty of its rich, dark wood. Last to be revealed was the keyboard. When she read the make of the piano just above the keys, she squealed, "It's a Steinway! A *Steinway!*"

Jack and Frances were at a loss for words.

Melody leaped at Layne, wrapped her arms around his neck, and planted a quick kiss on his lips. "Oh, Layne, you shouldn't have done it! But I'm glad you did!"

Everybody laughed.

"Congratulations, Melody," Wiley said. "That's the most beautiful piano I've ever seen."

"Thank you...and thank all of you for your help. It is deeply appreciated."

When the Price men were gone, Melody sat on the bench and said, "I know it'll need tuning after coming all the way from New York, but I've just got to hear its tone."

She played a few bars and looked up at Layne. "It's hardly out of tune at all!"

"That's because it's a Steinway, honey," Jack said.

"Oh, I know. Steinway's are marvelous instruments. Ever since I first played one at a concert in Washington a little over a year ago, I've dreamed of owning one. And now I do. Oh, Layne, how can I ever thank you? I love it! I love it! I love it!"

"I'll have Mr. Franks come by and tune it perfectly for you tomorrow, honey," said Jack.

"Thank you, Daddy," she smiled, still running her fingers lightly over the keyboard and smiling at Layne as she played "Beautiful Dreamer." "Mr. Franks won't like it that I now own a Steinway. He was making good money off us, coming by once a month to tune the old upright. Now, we'll only need him once a year...if that often."

"Ah, but you're creating more customers for him by getting more young people interested in playing the piano, my dear," put in Frances. "Mr. Franks is doing all right."

"I guess that's true," Melody nodded. Even though a few of the strings were slightly out of tune, she broke into a concerto and played it all the way through. When she finished, her audience applauded vigorously.

Melody rose from the bench and embraced the man she loved, thanking him one more time.

Jack said, "Well, I've got to get back to the shop. I left a note on the door saying I'd be back at three o'clock. It's almost three, now."

"Would you mind if I ride along with you, sir?" Layne asked. "I need to talk to you for a few minutes."

"You mean in the buggy, or do you mean you'll ride your horse alongside?"

"I'll just ride in the buggy, sir, if it's all right. I can walk back."

Melody and Frances had no idea what was going on, but listened quietly as Jack said, "You're quite welcome to ride with me, Layne. Let's go."

That evening after supper, Layne and Melody were in the parlor alone, sitting on a love seat. Two lanterns burned in the room, both turned low. In the soft light, Melody held his hand and said, "Darling, I don't mean to wear you out with it, but I want to thank you again for my wonderful piano. There are really no words to describe what it means to me. I'll never be able to—"

"Hush, my love," whispered Layne, putting the tip of his fingers to her lips. "You have thanked me quite sufficiently. In fact, just to see the look in your eyes at the dock when you realized it was a grand piano was thanks enough. I'm glad you're happy with it, and I hope it'll give you years and years of pleasure."

Melody stroked the side of his head and said, "You wonderful, wonderful man. I love you so much."

"And I love you, Melody Anne Reynolds," he responded, reaching into a shirt pocket. "In fact, I love you so much, I want your name to be Melody Anne Dalton." Melody saw the diamond engagement ring between his fingers as he added, "Will you marry me?"

Tears filmed her eyes, and as they spilled down her cheeks, she choked out the words, "Yes! Yes, I'll marry you!"

Layne slipped the ring on her finger, held it there, and said with emotion, "I now pronounce me the most blessed and fortunate man on earth."

They kissed, then embraced.

After a moment, Melody eased back to look into his eyes. "Oh,

I think I'll just explode! My beautiful Steinway…and now this," she said, holding up the hand that wore the ring. "It's almost too much!"

"I figure an eight-month engagement would be proper," Layne said. "What do you think?"

Melody silently counted on her fingers and replied, "That would make it a June wedding. Yes, that would be very proper."

"I checked the calendar. June 11 is a Saturday. How about June 11?"

"Sounds great to me." Melody paused a moment, then said thoughtfully, "I suppose since we're doing things properly, you should ask Daddy for my hand in marriage."

Layne grinned. "I already did. That's what I wanted to talk to him about when I rode downtown with him."

Melody looked at her engagement ring again. "Well, I guess he didn't object."

"Not in the least. He said he'd be glad to get rid of you."

Melody met his gaze and saw the look of devilment in his eyes. She cuffed his jaw playfully. "Layne Dalton, you scoundrel! Daddy did not say that!"

The happy couple laughed together, enjoyed another kiss, then Layne said, "Well, darling, I'd better be heading north. Sunrise must find me back in camp."

Neither the Reynolds nor the Dalton families had been church-goers, but on Saturday June 11, 1859, Layne and Melody had a military wedding at the Fredericksburg Community Church, where Walter and Harriet Smith were members. An army chaplain conducted the ceremony. Jerry Owens was best man, and Harriet Smith was Melody's matron of honor.

Layne had a sizable inheritance left him by his deceased parents, and used most of it to purchase a large two-story house next door to the Smith's.

There was no time for a honeymoon. Layne was given a three-day pass for his wedding and was due to report back at camp on Tuesday. On Monday, Wiley Price and his three sons were on hand to help move Melody's Steinway from the Reynolds house to the Dalton house six blocks away.

Layne, Jack, and the Price men loaded the piano onto the Price wagon, then Layne and Jack followed the wagon in the buggy through the streets of Fredericksburg.

Melody, her mother, and Harriet Smith were waiting on the front porch of the newly purchased house for the piano to arrive. When they saw the wagon coming down the street, they left the porch and met them as they drew to a stop in front of the house.

Layne wanted Melody to have a special music room in her new home. On the second floor near the top of the stairs was a large spare bedroom, and Layne had hired a carpenter to install double doors to the room to accommodate the Steinway. In front of the room was a wide landing that dovetailed into the hallway that led to two other bedrooms and the master bedroom.

Layne had told the Prices that he would need their help in moving a large bookcase in the new music room before they carried the piano inside and up the stairs. The women volunteered to stay outside with the piano while the men moved the bookcase.

"Melody," Harriet said, "aren't you afraid to have them try to carry your piano all the way up those stairs? I'd think you'd have chosen a downstairs location for your music room."

"I did," smiled Melody, "but that husband of mine said I needed a larger room than anything that's available downstairs. He wouldn't take no for an answer."

"I think maybe the man you married is going to spoil you rotten," put in Frances. "Your father spoiled you, too, but I think Layne's going to outdo him."

Melody laughed and started to reply when she saw five men on horseback coming along the dusty street. Frances saw her daughter's eyes grow cold and looked to see what Melody was glaring at. Her own eyes narrowed as Steve Heglund and his four brothers reined in at the wagon.

All five Heglunds had a churlish look about them, but the four younger ones together could not match the look in Steve's wide-set, thick-lidded eyes. There was a fixed snarl on his lip, and no one—not even Steve Heglund—could tell you the last time he had ever smiled. He carried a calloused spirit about him, and there was a hostile quality in his voice that always made him sound irritated. It was as though God knew beforehand how ugly the man would choose to be on the inside, so He gave him a face to match.

None of the Heglunds were large men, but they were muscular and known for provoking fights just for the fun of a good scrap. Of course, they only provoked fights when they outnumbered their opponents and felt sure they would come out the victors.

From his saddle, Steve looked at Melody and grunted, "I hear you're a new bride, blondie."

"Yeah," chuckled Clyde Heglund. "Word is you married some fancy-pants army officer."

"He's a lieutenant, yes, but he's no fancy-pants," Melody responded coolly. "Believe me, you don't want to get on his wrong side."

"He's inside the house right now," put in Frances, wanting to keep them at bay. "He'll be back out in a moment. It would be best that you boys move along."

Steve eyed the grand piano and ejected a low whistle. "So that's the ritzy piano he bought ya, huh? Must be true what I heard about your fancy-pants lieutenant. Lotsa money in the bank, eh? Pianos like this'n don't come cheap. Married yourself some money, didn't you, blondie?"

"My name is not blondie, and it's none of your business who I married."

"I ain't got much money, blondie, but if you'd tied the knot with me, you'd know what it was like to be married to a real man."

"I wouldn't marry you, Steve Heglund, if you were the last man on earth!"

Layne Dalton was just coming out the front door with the other men on his heels. His ears picked up the anger in Melody's voice and the name *Steve Heglund*. He concluded the five riders must be the Heglund brothers.

Wiley Price was first behind Layne, and when he saw the familiar faces, he half-whispered, "Trouble, Layne. It's the Heglunds."

"Yeah," Layne said. "Trouble for *them* if they're not careful."

Steve was not yet aware of the men emerging through the front door. He leered at Melody and blared, "You'd be better off married to me than to that fancy-pants lieutenant, honey!"

Layne was off the porch in a hurry. He rushed past the women and rounded the wagon. Before Steve could react, steel-like fingers had him by the shirt, yanking him from the saddle.

Steve hit the ground hard and the wind was knocked out of him. Layne stood over him, fists clenched, jaw set.

Clyde Heglund looked as if he was about to dismount. Wiley pointed at him and snarled, "You stay put!"

Clyde knew that Wiley meant it. He froze where he sat, eyes roving to his three brothers. Everett, Keith, and George were of no mind to tangle with Wiley Price and his muscular sons.

Steve struggled to his feet, gasping for breath and rubbing his left shoulder. There was murder in his eyes. "You just started somethin' I'm gonna finish, soldier!"

"You're not to call my wife *honey*! You got that?"

A devil's temper stirred behind the smoky color of Steve Heglund's eyes and changed the slant of his mouth as he said, "You're a newcomer here, soldier boy. Do you know who you're talkin' to?"

"I know exactly who I'm talking to! And if you think your name scares me, you'd better think again."

Keith Heglund feared what might happen if his oldest brother tied into Melody's husband. The Price brothers and their father might decide to take on the Heglunds, and make a free-for-all of it. The Prices were too tough to handle. Keith wanted no part of them.

"You're going to apologize to my wife for the way you were talking to her, and you're going to apologize to me for calling her *honey*," Layne said, "or I'm going to pound you into the dirt! Let's hear it!"

In spite of the pain in his shoulder, Steve clenched his fists and was about to go after the lieutenant. Keith, who was the most levelheaded of the clan, realized Steve hadn't noticed the Prices standing by. "Steve!" he shouted. "It ain't worth it! Look around you!"

There were five Heglunds and five men to face, even if Jack Reynolds stayed out of it, which he probably would not. Jack was getting on in age, but he was not the kind to back away from a fight. Steve knew the Prices were a tough bunch, and Melody's new husband looked like he could handle himself. Smart thing would be to eat humble pie and back off. There would be another day when he could catch this army man without the Prices around, then he and his brothers would pummel him good.

Steve looked at Keith, then at Clyde, Everett, and George. It was in their faces. They were not eager to get into a fight. He would use his hurting shoulder as an excuse to back out. He rubbed it again and said to Keith, "You're right, little brother. It ain't worth it. Especially since this soldier boy took me by surprise and injured my shoulder."

Steve turned to Layne and said, "You took advantage of me, pal, jerkin' me outta the saddle like you did. But next time—"

"My wife has an apology coming, Heglund!" roared Layne. "Let's hear it!"

Steve fixed him with a hard look, then turned to Melody and said, "I'm sorry for talkin' to you like I did."

Melody loved seeing Steve Heglund in this position. She held her mouth in a grim line as she nodded her acceptance.

"Now me," Layne said.

Steve Heglund regarded him dismally and ground his reluctant apology between his teeth. "I'm sorry for callin' your wife *honey*."

"Fine. Now, get on your horse and ride," Layne said.

Hatred for the army man churned inside Steve Heglund as he stepped in the stirrup and swung into the saddle. Barely moving his lips, he hissed, "There'll be another day, soldier boy."

"I didn't mean to take so long."

Layne Dalton was snapped back to the present. General James Longstreet had entered the tent and was sitting down at his table.

"What's that, sir?" Dalton asked.

"I said I'm sorry to keep you waiting. I didn't mean to take so long."

"Oh. That's all right, sir."

"Well, Major, go on with your story. You were telling me about the Heglund brothers getting away with murdering Melody's brother...and what led up to your father-in-law being accused of killing Edgar Heglund."

FIVE

Major Layne Dalton leaned forward on his chair and said, "Well, sir, when the Civil War broke out, all five of the Heglund brothers decided to join the Union army."

"The *Union* army?"

"Yes, sir. They agreed with Abraham Lincoln that secession was unlawful, and even though they're native Virginians, they would not side with the Rebel 'traitors.'"

The general pulled a cigar from his pocket, held it between his fingers, and said, "I can't understand how anyone could go against their home state. I could no more turn on South Carolina, Major, than I could turn on my mother."

"I feel the same way about Virginia, sir."

Longstreet bit the end off the cigar and said, "I guess you haven't taken up this nasty habit, have you?"

"No, sir."

"I won't offer you one, then."

"That's fine, sir."

The general took a wooden match from another pocket, struck it, and while the flame flared, said, "Proceed, Major." He then touched flame to the cigar and puffed it into life.

Layne Dalton did not like the odor of cigar smoke. He eased back on the chair to escape it as much as possible and went on. "Edgar Heglund was in agreement with his sons and put his blessing on their joining the Union army. There were other Fredericksburg citizens who agreed with the Heglunds, but the majority did not."

"Hurrah for the majority," Longstreet said.

"The Heglund brothers were talking some of Fredericksburg's other young men into joining the Federal side, and one day an argument got started at the town square and almost became violent. Jack Reynolds and Edgar Heglund did get into a fight and had to be pulled apart. Jack screamed at Edgar that he and his sons were the real traitors and that Edgar ought to pack up his wife and move north of the Mason-Dixon line.

"Edgar said that Fredericksburg was his home, and nobody was going to force him out of it. Other Union sympathizers agreed, and one man said it wouldn't be long until the North whipped the South into submission anyway, then the Southern sympathizers would be the ones in trouble.

"Well, the Heglund brothers left Fredericksburg and joined the Union army, as did several other young men from the town. The hard feelings between my father-in-law and Edgar continued to grow worse as time passed and this war grew older."

Dalton coughed and turned his face away as cigar smoke rolled into his face. Longstreet jerked the cigar from his mouth and said, "Sorry, Major. I'll just put this thing out." As he spoke, he ground out the cigar in his ash tray and dropped it in a bucket behind his chair.

"Thank you, sir," Dalton said. "So, to proceed, after the Antietam battle in September, we all got a few days to rest, and I returned home to see Melody. While I was there, I learned that Clyde Heglund had been assigned to serve as a guard in a Union prison camp somewhere. Nobody I talked to knew which one. Steve, Everett, and Keith, I learned, were serving in the Union Army of the Potomac...I think in General Burnside's division. George Heglund, the youngest, had lost a leg at Malvern Hill and had recently returned home."

Dalton pulled the envelope from his coat pocket once again and unfolded the letter. "In Melody's letter, sir, she says that on November 9, her father and George Heglund met face to face on a side street. Jack's story is that George stood there, balanced on his crutches, and reviled him for being a traitor. Jack lashed back that George's brothers had murdered his son. They had fooled the law, but he knew it was they who did it.

"George bit back, saying he hoped his brothers *had* killed Jack, Jr. My father-in-law went into a rage and shoved George to the ground. As Jack stormed away, George screamed that his father would get even with him."

Longstreet stroked his long, full beard. "So I suppose Edgar went after Jack."

"Yes, sir. That very night Edgar appeared on my father-in-law's doorstep demanding that he come out of the house. Melody says her mother was at our house at the time. Jack stepped out the door and found himself looking down the barrel of a revolver. Jack made a grab for the gun, and suddenly they were in a wrestling match. The gun went off, and Edgar collapsed with a slug in his midsection, and he died four hours later. Neighbors reported hearing the gun shot, but no one actually witnessed the incident."

"Too bad someone didn't see it," Longstreet said, "but since Edgar came onto Jack's property with his gun, I'd think any judge and jury would rule out murder."

"Well, sir, there's a complication. Turns out the revolver is Jack's."

Longstreet's brow furrowed. "I don't understand."

"Well, quite some time after the Heglund brothers tore up the Reynolds house, Jack discovered that his revolver was missing. He reported the missing gun to the town constable, and an investigation followed, but the Heglund brothers denied having stolen it. Fredericksburg has had two constables since the break-in, and according to what Melody says in her letter, the present constable cannot find any record of Jack's having reported the gun missing."

"So with no record of the report, it looks like Jack is lying."

"Yes, sir. Melody says that four credible witnesses have come forth who saw Jack push George to the ground and stomp away…and they heard George scream that his father would get even with him. Word around town is that the county prosecutor—whom everyone knows was a close friend of Edgar's—is going to say in court that Jack was waiting with his gun for Edgar to show up."

"Major, it doesn't look good for your father-in-law," General Longstreet said. "I hope somehow the truth will come out."

"Thank you, sir."

"I would give you longer," said the general, "but with the Yankees moving this way and another battle in the making, I must insist that you be back here by sundown on Wednesday. General Lee will be here that day, and he no doubt will have information we can act upon. We need to be ready to follow whatever orders he gives, which will, in all probability, see some kind of move on our part on Thursday. I need you here for that, as does General Kershaw."

"I understand, sir."

"I realize this only gives you time to be there for the trial…not for the execution, if it comes to that. But let's pray that Mr. Reynolds will be acquitted, and that there'll be no execution."

"Yes, sir," said the major, rising.

Longstreet took out an official-looking piece of paper with his name printed on it. Dipping pen in ink-well, he wrote out his order, signed it, and handed it to Dalton. "Show this to General Kershaw, then carry it with you."

Dalton saluted and said, "Thank you, sir. I'll be back by sundown on Wednesday."

Longstreet returned the salute and said, "God go with you."

The major smiled and headed for the tent opening. When he reached it, Longstreet said, "Give my best to Melody, Major."

"I will, sir."

Major Dalton headed for Brigadier General Joseph B. Kershaw's tent, which was near the rope corral where the horses were kept. He was moving at a brisk pace when he saw one of his favorite soldiers angling toward him from between two tents. Sergeant Richard Rowland Kirkland, though only nineteen years old, had repeatedly shown his willingness to do anything his superiors asked of him, no matter what inconvenience or danger it might bring upon him.

Kirkland was tall and slender, with dark hair and a thin, hollow-cheeked face. His slim, dark mustache made a sharp contrast with his teeth when he smiled. He was doing just that when he approached Dalton and joined him in his brisk pace.

"Good morning, Major Dalton," Kirkland said. "You seem to be in a hurry, sir. Is there something I can do to help you?"

"And good morning to you, Sergeant. I'm in a hurry because I have to make a hasty ride to Fredericksburg once I show my orders to General Kershaw."

"May I bridle and saddle your horse for you, sir? While you're talking to General Kershaw, I mean. That would speed up your departure once you've finished showing the orders to him."

"Yes, it would," Dalton said. "You know which horse is mine, don't you?"

"Sure do, sir. I'll have him ready to go in no time."

Kirkland veered off toward the corral and the major continued toward Kershaw's tent. The general was just coming out, in conversation with a pair of captains, as Dalton approached.

General Kershaw was a square-jawed, rugged individual, who was all business. He gave Dalton a tight smile and said, "Something I can do for you, Major?"

"Yes, sir," responded Dalton, unfolding the paper and handing it to the general. "General Longstreet said to show you this before I leave. He has given me permission to ride to Fredericksburg immediately."

The general, who was in his early fifties but looked ten years older, rubbed his heavy mustache while reading the order. He handed it back to Dalton and said, "Whatever your emergency is, Major, I hope everything will turn out all right. God be with you."

Dalton thanked him and hastened toward the corral to find Sergeant Kirkland leading his horse toward him, saddled and ready to go.

He took the reins from Kirkland and led the bay gelding toward the edge of the camp before mounting. "Thank you, Sergeant. You're a gentleman."

"Just want to be of help, sir," Kirkland replied, keeping pace with him. "Sir?"

"Yes?"

"I don't know if you recall, but you told me about your wife being pregnant right after you found out she was."

"Yes, I remember," nodded Dalton.

"Well, sir…you seem to be somewhat upset. Is…she having a problem with the pregnancy?"

"No. There is an emergency, but it is an entirely different matter."

"I'm glad for that, sir, though I'm sorry about the emergency."

"Thank you."

"Sir, when you told me about the baby, you were sure it's a boy. Do you still feel confident it's a boy?"

"Sure do."

"Have you and Mrs. Dalton picked out a name for him yet?"

"Sure have. Daniel Lee Dalton, after my favorite uncle."

"That's wonderful, sir. I sure hope little Danny will be a strong, healthy baby."

"Thank you, Sergeant," said the major, mounting his horse and settling in the saddle.

The November air was nippy as Major Dalton approached Fredericksburg. It was mid-afternoon and the sun was barely peeping from behind some low-hanging, long-fingered clouds.

Dalton greeted the Confederate soldiers on duty at the edge of town and rode straight for his house. People on the streets greeted him along the way. His heart quickened pace when he turned a corner and his house came into view. He hadn't seen Melody for nearly three months.

He wondered how big she would be by now. She had only said in her letters that she was losing her figure and hoped he would still love her. Silly girl.

Layne turned into the yard and rode toward the barn and small corral at the back. Though the windows of the house were closed, he could hear Melody playing her prized concert grand. He removed the saddle and bridle from the horse and made sure it had grain and water, then headed for the back porch. Melody's music could still be heard. He found the back door unlocked, entered the kitchen, and hurried through the dining room. As he approached the staircase, he noted that Melody was playing a hymn. He couldn't identify it, but he had heard it in church services when he was a boy.

The thrill of knowing he was about to see his wife and hold her in his arms had Layne's heart pounding as he bounded up the stairs. He reached the landing and ran his hand along the railing as he moved toward the open double doors of the music room. He adjusted his collar, making sure he was presentable, and stepped into the room.

Melody stopped playing, eyes wide, and breathed, "Layne! Oh, Layne!"

She slowly rose from the piano bench, but before she could take a step, Layne had her in his arms and was kissing her.

Tears touched Melody's cheeks as she awkwardly clung to her husband with the baby between them. They embraced for a long moment, then she eased back from him and brushed away her tears. She looked down at her bulging midsection and said, "I've really lost my figure, haven't I?"

Layne cupped her face in his hands, kissed her again, and said, "You sweet thing. I love you more than ever. You're going to give me a son."

She took hold of his wrists and asked, "You won't throw me away if it turns out be a girl, will you?"

Layne kissed her once more and said, "Silly girl. Of course I won't throw you away. I'll love a daughter as much as I would love a son…but I know it's a boy." He patted her stomach and asked, "You are taking care of yourself and little Danny Lee, aren't you?"

"Of course," she said, taking him by the hand. "Lets' go downstairs. Are you hungry?"

"A little. But I can wait till supper. Why don't we just go to Mabel's?"

"I'll be glad to cook supper for you, darling," she said softly.

"Not tonight, sweetheart. I don't want you working in the kitchen tonight. We'll just go to Mabel's. Okay?"

"Of course, as long as you don't think I'm being lazy."

"That'll be the day…when Melody Anne Dalton becomes lazy. I have to head back Wednesday in time to be at camp by sundown. I'll let you cook supper for me tomorrow."

"Oh, I'm so glad you could be here for the trial. It'll be such a help to all of us."

"I'm glad, too," he replied. "General Longstreet was very understanding. He would have let me stay longer, but General Lee is coming to the camp Wednesday. The Yankees are coming this way, and for sure, there's going to be a big battle. General Longstreet and General Kershaw need me there."

"I wish this awful war was over," Melody said with shaky voice.

"Yes, don't we all," Layne nodded.

They passed from the music room, crossed the landing, and stopped at the rail, looking down to the parlor and reception area below.

"How's your daddy holding up?" Layne asked.

"He's got a good grip on himself. Actually, Mother's the one who's having the hardest time."

"I can understand that. Any further developments since you wrote the letter?"

"No. Daddy's attorney says it doesn't look good, but he's working hard in the records department at the police building. He says if he can just produce evidence that Daddy reported the gun missing, it will put a whole new light on the trial."

"You'd think people in the police business would be more careful with their records, wouldn't you?"

"Yes. Time's running short, but we're trusting the Lord to take care of the matter. Daddy's innocent, and God knows it."

Layne was amazed to hear his wife talk of God in such a familiar way. It caught him off guard, and he could think of nothing to say in response.

They reached the stairs, and he put an arm around her as they began slowly descending the staircase. "I heard you playing a hymn when I came in," he said. "I've never heard you play church music before. I know I heard that hymn as a boy when Grandma used to take me to church, but I can't think of its name."

"'Amazing Grace.' John Newton's most famous hymn."

"Oh, that's right. I knew I'd heard it before."

They reached the bottom of the stairs. Layne released her from his strong arm, and she turned to face him. "Darling, I have something to tell you. I didn't put it into any of my letters because I wanted to tell you in person."

Layne grinned and said, "I know! Doc Craig says you're going to have twins!"

"No! No! Nothing like that," Melody giggled. "It's regarding the hymn I was playing. Come. Let's sit down here in the parlor, and I'll tell you about it."

When they were seated comfortably on a small couch, Melody turned to face Layne and laid a hand on his arm. A strange light danced in her deep-blue eyes as she said, "Darling, I know you remember that night a couple of years ago when Walter and Harriet had us over for supper and talked to us about our need to know Jesus Christ personally, to have salvation and forgiveness of our sins."

"Yes, I remember." A queasy feeling settled in Layne's stomach.

"Well, three weeks ago they had a revival meeting at Harriet's church, and she invited Mother, Daddy, and me to the meeting. And…well, darling, we responded to the preaching and received the Lord Jesus into our hearts. He has forgiven our sins and cleansed us in His blood. We're Christians now."

Layne could tell that Melody was on edge as she spoke, not knowing how he might react. He loved her too much to hurt her in any way. Though the news was a bit disconcerting, he smiled and said, "If this has given you and your parents peace and contentment, honey, I'm glad. Especially in the light of what your dad is facing right now."

"It most definitely has," she told him. "Like I said, we're trusting the Lord to take care of Daddy. Harriet came over and prayed with me last night about it. I just know the Lord will see that justice is done." Melody paused, then said, "My greatest concern now, darling, is that you come to know Jesus, too."

"Well, like I told you when Walter and Harriet talked to us a couple of years ago—my Uncle Dan taught me when I was in my teens that every man has to meet God in his own way. I wouldn't hurt your feelings for anything, but I have to be honest with you. The fanatical approach taken by the Bible-thumpers is just not my way."

Melody started to speak, but Layne took her hand and said, "Honey, I will never stand in the way of your faith, but as for me…I'll leave that part of my life just as it is."

Melody did her best to cover the disappointment in her voice as she said, "I bought myself a new Bible, darling…and I bought one for you, too."

Layne was thrown off balance, but managed to smile and say, "That's fine. Thank you."

"Your Bible is over there on the mantel. I would like for you to carry it with you when you go."

Layne made his way to the mantel and picked up the Bible. Melody had written a note to him on the flyleaf. He read it quickly and was touched by her well-chosen words. She was smiling at him when he looked back at her.

"You're the most wonderful woman in the world, Melody Anne Dalton. Thank you. I will carry this Bible with me everywhere I go."

"I've underlined several passages in the New Testament for you to read. The pages are identified with bookmarks. You'll see them."

"All right," he nodded.

"Darling, when you read those passages, you will see that no body comes to God in his own way. We must come to Him *His* way. The Scriptures I've underlined make this very clear and will show you the way. You will read them, won't you?"

"Of course," he responded warmly. "I want to make little Danny's mother happy. If my reading this Bible will make you happy, I'm more than glad to do it."

"Thank you," she replied, swallowing a lump in her throat.

After supper that evening, Layne left Melody long enough to go to the Fredericksburg jail and visit his father-in-law. Jack was elated to see him, and in the course of their conversation, told him of his new-found faith. Layne said he was glad for him, and that with the kind of faith Melody seemed to have, it wouldn't surprise him if Jack walked out of the courtroom tomorrow a free man.

By noon the next day the trial was over. The attorney's search in the police records had been rewarded just before midnight the night before. He found papers in an old dusty file cabinet giving proof that Jack had reported his revolver stolen a few months after the Heglund brothers had broken into the Reynolds home.

The jury agreed with Jack's attorney that Jack had no reason for reporting the gun missing if it was not so, and that he could not have foreseen nor premeditated the incident that took place on his porch. The jury believed that the Heglunds had stolen the gun, and that Edgar had carried it to the Reynolds house the night he was killed. Jack was acting in self-defense.

As the Reynoldses, the Daltons, the Wiley Price family, and Harriet Smith stood together in front of the courthouse, some of

Fredericksburg's citizens approached Jack, telling him they were glad justice was done. Others, who favored the Heglunds, turned up their noses and walked away.

Frances clung to her husband's arm, elated at how the Lord had answered prayer on Jack's behalf. Suddenly she saw Ethel Heglund coming their direction with George beside her, hobbling along on his crutches. During the trial, both Ethel and her youngest son had glowered at her across the courtroom.

"Ethel and George are coming," Frances whispered to her husband.

All eyes were on mother and son as they drew up. Ethel fixed Jack with hate-filled eyes and rasped, "The jury may have acquitted you, Jack Reynolds, but as far as I'm concerned, you murdered my husband!"

"Edgar carried my stolen gun to my house for one reason, Ethel. He was going to shoot me. You know it, George knows it, and the jury knows it."

"This ain't over, old man!" George railed. "My brothers ain't gonna take it lightly when they find out you murdered Pa! You're gonna be sorry, I'll tell you that!"

Layne moved close to George and said tartly, "Jack didn't murder your father, kid. It was self-defense, and you'd better make sure your brothers understand that."

"My brothers will see it just like me and Ma do…and they'll act accordingly." He made a half-turn on his crutches and said, "Come on, Ma, let's go. It stinks here."

SIX

Layne and Melody Dalton accompanied her parents to their home, and while the four of them were eating a light lunch in the kitchen, Frances said to Jack, "I think we just as well tell the kids right now, don't you?"

"No reason to delay it," he nodded.

"Tell us what?" Melody asked.

"Your mother and I came to an agreement about a week ago," Jack replied. "If I was acquitted—and thank the Lord He brought it to pass—we would pack up and head for Virginia City."

Melody's eyes widened. "Virginia City, *Nevada*?"

"That's right."

"Has Uncle Hank been writing you?"

"Yes, he has," Frances said. "Your daddy hasn't told you this, but his cobbler business has been hurting of late. Uncle Hank has written several times telling us that his gold mining business is prospering magnificently. In his last letter, he asked your daddy to come out and be his partner."

Concern etched itself on Melody's pretty face. She set worried eyes on Layne, then said to her father, "Nevada is a long way from here."

"I know, honey, but this is a once-in-a-lifetime opportunity. The war has hurt my business, with so many men away from Fredericksburg in the army…and with the looks I was getting from some of the townspeople today, it's only going to get worse. Becoming a partner with Hank will set your mother and me up for the rest of our lives. Can you understand that?"

Layne saw Melody's lower lip quiver. He took her hand and said, "When the war's over, honey, we can go visit them in Nevada."

Melody willed herself calm and looked at her mother, then at her father. "I understand. I'm glad for both of you. It's just that I'll miss you both so terribly."

"We'll miss you, too, honey," said Jack. "And we'd sure like to be here when our little grandbaby is born. But if I don't take Hank up on his offer soon, it'll be gone."

"I know, Daddy," Melody said, trying to smile. "We'll just have to pray that the Lord will one day let all of us be together again. Maybe when the war's over, Layne and the baby and I can live out West."

"That could happen," Layne said. "The Indian situation out there is going to warrant a number of forts. It'll take soldiers to man those forts."

"What I'm concerned about, now, honey," said Jack, "is this Heglund threat. They might decide to take out their wrath on you."

"I don't think so, Daddy. It's you they'll want. I doubt they'll bother me."

"Maybe I should move you elsewhere, Melody," Layne said. "I don't want that bunch to have any opportunity to harm you."

Melody patted his arm. "They're not going to harm me, darling. This is my home. I want to stay right here."

"You know them better than I do," Layne said tightly, "but if there's any chance—"

"I'll be fine. I have Harriet right next door, and plenty of other neighbors all around me. The Heglunds aren't going to come around our house, anyway."

"If they even so much as frighten you, this earth isn't big enough to hide them. I'll find them and make them wish they'd never been born."

Jack noted the resolute look in his son-in-law's eyes. "I believe you mean that, Layne."

"With everything that's in me, sir."

The next morning, Harriet Smith had Layne and Melody over for breakfast, knowing Layne would have to leave shortly and ride for the camp near Culpeper.

They discussed the war situation as they were eating. Layne lamented that he might not be able to see Melody again until after the baby was born, since the Union army was making moves toward further aggression against the Confederacy. There might be a whole series of battles before he could get back.

Harriet looked across the table at Layne and said, "I don't want you worrying about when the baby comes. So far, Melody's pregnancy has been quite normal, and we have no reason to believe she's going to have any complications. If for some reason Dr. Craig is not available when the time comes, I've had considerable experience as a midwife. I can deliver the baby."

Layne eased back on the chair and said, "Harriet, you don't know what it means to me for Melody to have such a good friend. My mind will be much more at ease knowing you're here to look out for her."

"It's my pleasure," smiled Harriet.

"And if you should see any of the Heglund brothers slithering around our house, send somebody for the police immediately, will you?"

Harriet laughed. "*Slithering* is a good word for a Heglund. Yes, Layne, I'll keep an eye out for the snakes."

When breakfast was over, Layne and Melody returned to their house for a few private moments before he had to ride out. They went to the music room, where by request, Melody played and sang "Beautiful Dreamer" for her husband.

When she finished, he leaned over and kissed her, and said, "I need to be going, sweetheart."

"Could you stay long enough for me to sing 'Amazing Grace' for you? I'd like for you to have the words ringing in your heart while you ride."

Layne cuffed her chin playfully and said, "If you play and sing it, I guarantee you the words will ring in my heart."

Melody played and sang "Amazing Grace" for her husband, praying in her heart that its message would take hold of him.

When she finished, they walked down the stairs together. Melody waited while Layne bridled and saddled his horse, then met him at the front porch as he led the animal from the barn. They held each other for a long moment, then shared a lingering kiss. Layne mounted to the sound of squeaking leather, then looked down at Melody and said, "Please keep writing me through Richmond, sweetheart. No matter where I am, the War Department will get the letters to me eventually. And send me a lock of little Danny's hair when he's born, okay?"

Melody replied through tears, "Yes. I will, darling. You won't forget to read your Bible?"

"No. I promise. So long, sweetheart. I love you."

"I love you, too," she said, choking out the words.

Melody Anne Dalton watched the man she loved ride away. "Dear Lord," she prayed, "keep him safe. And please bring him to Yourself very soon. I want Layne to be saved more than anything in the world."

Major Dalton rode into the Culpeper camp late in the afternoon on Wednesday, November 19. The shadows were long as he drew rein at the rope corral. When his feet touched ground, Sergeant Kirkland came running up and said, "Major Dalton, sir."

"Yes, Sergeant?" responded Dalton.

"General Longstreet told me to watch for you, sir. He wants you in town at the meeting house immediately. General Lee is there. They are meeting with all the officers in our corps. It's very important."

"All right," grinned Dalton, mounting up again. "I'll get right over there."

"How's Mrs. Dalton, sir?"

"She's doing fine, thank you."

"Things work out okay with the emergency?"

"Splendidly. Everything's fine."

"I'm glad, sir."

"Thank you, Sergeant."

The sun had dipped below the western horizon by the time Layne hauled up in front of the Culpeper Meeting House. He recognized General Lee's horse, Traveler, tied next to General Longstreet's and General Kershaw's animals. Two corporals at the door greeted him. While one opened it so he could enter, the other said, "You're just in time, Major Dalton. They're about to start."

Dalton moved inside and saw Lee and Longstreet standing before the other officers who were seated on backless benches at the front of the building. When Longstreet saw Dalton, he smiled and said, "Ah, Major Dalton. Glad you're here. We were just about to begin our meeting."

Robert Edward Lee knew Dalton. As the major drew up and saluted, Lee smiled and said, "Good to see you, Major."

"Thank you, sir. It's good to see you, too."

Layne admired the Confederate army leader. Lee's full head of silver hair and his ruler-straight military stance highlighted his air of dignity. The general looked tired. There were dark, pronounced circles under his eyes. Though he was only fifty-six years of age, he looked much older. Layne knew it was the price a military leader paid in war time.

Dalton spoke to the other officers and sat down among them. Some asked in hushed voices about his hurried trip home, but before he could explain, General Longstreet interrupted with a loud voice,

"All right, gentlemen, your attention, please. General Lee and I have been in discussion since he arrived here this morning. He has information for us, and wishes to address you at this time."

The officers all stood at attention and saluted their beloved leader.

Lee saluted in return, smiled, and said, "Be seated, gentlemen."

General Longstreet remained on his feet, standing a little behind and to the side of Lee as the silver-haired leader spoke in his slow, southern accent. "As you gentlemen know, on November 7, just twelve days ago, Abe Lincoln relieved George McClellan as commander of the Army of the Potomac and replaced him with Ambrose Burnside. I understand that for the first few days, there was almost mutiny amongst the Federal ranks because of it. Too bad it didn't happen." The officers laughed.

"I'm sorry about McClellan's departure. My years as a military leader have developed some kind of sixth sense within me that has helped me to divine an opposing commander's intentions. I found General McClellan to be extremely predictable, as you gentlemen know from some of our previous conflicts.

"I have feared that Lincoln would one day make a change and put in charge a man I did not understand. It is beginning to look like he's done it. General Burnside has me a bit confused. I have learned that in the past few days, he has formed his army into what he calls his three 'grand divisions.' Each division contains two corps, each of those with its own staff. Three major generals command the divisions...Edwin Sumner, William Franklin, and Joe Hooker.

"I learned day before yesterday from my intelligence people that General Sumner and his grand division departed from their camp near Warrenton on November 15, and are headed south. I have no word as yet on any movement by the other two Yankee divisions."

Major General Lafayette McLaws raised a hand.

"Yes, General McLaws," nodded Lee.

"What is your thinking about this move, sir? Are we looking at the beginnings of the thing we've feared most…Lincoln's move to capture Richmond?"

"I'm not sure, General. From the way Sumner's headed, I'm thinking that possibly General Burnside is intending to take his army to Alexandria, put it aboard ships, sail it to North Carolina, and begin an offensive there."

At that moment the door opened and one of the corporals said, "Pardon me, General Lee, but there's a courier here from Confederate intelligence. Says he has important news. Shall I send him in?"

"By all means," nodded Lee.

The courier hastened through the door, half-ran to General Lee, and handed him a sealed envelope, saying, "I brought this as fast as I could, sir."

"Good job, Corporal," smiled Lee. "Thank you."

Lee waited until the courier was gone and the door was shut, then removed a folded sheet of paper from the envelope and read it silently. He looked first at Longstreet, then at the group of officers and said, "Gentlemen, this throws a whole new light on the subject. I think, General McLaws, you were right. This just may be Lincoln's long-awaited drive toward our capital city. General Sumner has bypassed Alexandria, and late today marched his grand division into Falmouth."

General Lee set his tired eyes on Dalton. "Major Dalton, your home is in Fredericksburg. I'm correct, am I not? Falmouth is little more than a mile upriver from Fredericksburg."

"Exactly a mile-and-a-half, sir," responded Dalton, a cold ball of ice forming in his stomach.

Lee nodded, looked at the paper in his hand once more, then said to the group, "Intelligence also says that Franklin and Hooker are leading their divisions southward about a day's march behind Sumner. I can only interpret these moves in one way: the Union army is launching its campaign to move on Richmond! It *could* be a feint, but I'm inclined to believe they've set their Yankee minds on our capital city. Well, I can tell them this much—they're going to have a fight on their hands. The Army of Northern Virginia will be in battle position before they get a glimpse of Richmond's rooftops!"

There was a rousing cheer from the officers.

Lee turned to Longstreet and said, "General, I presume you have a map of Virginia in your tent?"

"Yes, sir," replied Longstreet, stepping closer.

"You and I will burn some midnight oil and meet back here with these men at sunrise."

When the meeting was dismissed and the officers were leaving the building, Layne Dalton approached Lee and said, "General Lee, sir, do you think Burnside will try to capture Fredericksburg on his march toward Richmond?"

"I don't know what to think, Major. If it were McClellan, I could tell you for sure he would want to capture Fredericksburg. But Burnside is untested. I just don't know what might be in his mind. He might bypass Fredericksburg, figuring he'll own it anyway if they capture Richmond. I know you're asking because your wife is there, and I certainly understand your concern. So let me say this…I am definitely going to prepare to defend Fredericksburg. I really wouldn't want to fight the enemy there, but we'll be prepared to do so if we have to."

"Yes, sir."

Lee noted the worried look in Dalton's eyes and said, "Let me add something here, Major."

"Yes, sir?"

"If we see that we have to defend your town, we'll evacuate every civilian to a safe place. Mrs. Dalton will be in no danger."

"Thank you, General. I appreciate your understanding my apprehension."

Lee smiled. "I have a wife, too, son."

General Longstreet was still standing close. Before Dalton turned to leave, Longstreet said, "General Lee, if this is indeed the Union's move to take Richmond, shouldn't you get General Jackson and his troops over here?"

"I can't afford to move Jackson's corps out of the Shenandoah Valley. At least not the better part of it. I fear that if I did, Burnside might turn some of his army that direction and we'd lose the Valley."

Longstreet did not always agree with General Lee's military strategy. To him, the Shenandoah Valley was in no immediate danger. Were the choice his, he would concentrate the entire Army of Northern Virginia between Burnside's Army of the Potomac and the Confederate capital. If Richmond fell, the Federals would have the Valley anyway.

Longstreet, however, would not argue with his superior, but said tactfully, "I'm glad you intimated, sir, that you might bring at least some of General Jackson's corps over here. Wouldn't it be wise to shift at least a few of his divisions east of the Blue Ridge so they would be closer at hand?"

Lee regarded his subordinate with careful eyes, and nodded slowly. "That might be a good move, General."

Having gained ground, Longstreet was feeling bolder. "And may I suggest, sir, that you bring General Jeb Stuart's cavalry brigade all the way over here? If Burnside is doing what we think, we're going to need more cavalry."

Lee pulled absently at an ear. "I'm sure General Jackson wouldn't mind sending us General Stuart. Let me think on it."

After a long night of study, pouring over the Virginia map with Longstreet at his side, Lee was ready to move his army. The two men slept barely over an hour and were up at dawn.

The officers grabbed a quick breakfast and gathered in the Culpeper Meeting House just as the eastern sky was turning a pinkish-yellow.

Lee wasted no time getting down to business. He laid out his orders to the officers, explaining that after a night of studying the situation, he felt General Burnside would probably try to capture Fredericksburg on his way to Richmond, since it lay directly in his path. Therefore, as much as he would rather fight the Federals some twenty-five miles farther south of Fredericksburg along the North Anna River, he would prepare to take his stand at Fredericksburg.

Two divisions would be sent out immediately from the Culpeper camp. One, under Brigadier General Robert Ransom, would move south along the Orange & Alexandria Railroad to a point just south of Fredericksburg. Dug in there, Ransom would be in a position to defend the town in case the Yankees decided to swing around and come in from the south.

The other division, under Major General Lafayette McLaws, would march directly to Fredericksburg, accompanied by Joseph B. Kershaw's brigade, William H. F. Lee's cavalry brigade, and James H. Lane's artillery. They would take defensive positions around Fredericksburg on the east, north, and west as directed by McLaws.

Lee explained that he was wiring General Stonewall Jackson to move a few of his divisions east of the Blue Ridge in order to have them closer to Fredericksburg if needed. He also would order Major General Jeb Stuart's cavalry to move down from the Shenandoah Valley and scout the enemy's movements along the Rappahannock River.

General Longstreet smiled to himself while Lee explained his strategy.

A cold wind came up as the assigned units moved out of the Culpeper camp, scudding heavy clouds across the sky that soon covered the rising sun. General Lee promptly sent his wire to Stonewall Jackson in the Shenandoah Valley and waited for confirmation that the orders had been received. In less than an hour, Jackson wired back that the designated divisions were preparing to move out, and that Jeb Stuart's cavalry would be headed toward the Rappahannock by 10:00 A.M.

The Confederate troops arrived at Fredericksburg in the middle of the afternoon on November 20. While they were setting up their artillery on the hills to the south and west of the town, and the cavalry and infantry were getting into position, Major Dalton stationed his infantry unit in the trees on top of Marye's Heights. Named for the family whose mansion nestled like a fairy castle in the woods near the crest of the main hill, Marye's Heights was the highest point on the hills that made a semi-circle around Fredericksburg.

Dalton's five hundred men were positioned alternately in small groups between the big guns and howitzers of the artillery. He was checking with Brigadier General James H. Lane to be sure Lane was satisfied with the protection his troops would offer his artillerymen when he saw Sergeant Kirkland coming toward him.

Lane eyed the way Dalton's men were positioned, pulled his overcoat collar up against the cold wind, and said, "Major, you've done a magnificent job. My men will appreciate the protection you're providing, especially if the Yankees come storming up these hills.

"We're here to do our job, sir," grinned Dalton. "We'll guard you like watchdogs."

"I don't doubt it," Lane nodded. "I've already thanked General Kershaw for giving you to us."

Sergeant Kirkland drew up, saluted both men, then said to Dalton, "General Kershaw asked me to come and tell you, Major, that you don't have to check with him again before going into town. He said when you're satisfied that your men know their positions, you can go ahead. He said to remind you that you can only be gone for an hour."

"Thank you, Sergeant," nodded Dalton.

As Kirkland hurried away, General Lane said, "I understand the people in town are pretty upset at the prospect of a battle taking place here."

"I'm not surprised," replied Dalton. "Even though they'll be evacuated before any shooting starts, they don't want their homes destroyed."

"You know someone who lives here?"

"Yes, sir. My wife."

"Oh? So Fredericksburg's your home."

"Yes, sir. My prime concern is for my wife's safety, but I'm also worried about my house. I asked General Kershaw earlier for permission to go into town and spend a little time with Melody. She's expecting our first child, and I want to comfort her as much as I can."

The general smiled. "Then be on your way, my friend. Don't let me delay you."

Melody was seated at the kitchen table with Harriet. They were kneading dough together and discussing the sudden occupation of the surrounding area by the Confederate army. Both women feared what a battle in their town would do to it.

There was a knock at the front door. Melody started to get up, but Harriet was quickly on her feet, saying, "You stay put, honey. I'll see who it is."

Harriet could make out Layne Dalton's tall, wide-shouldered form through the sheer curtains before she opened the door. Turning the key, she swung the door open, and said with a smile, "Hello, soldier. Melody was just saying if you were amongst the troops gathering here, you'd find a way to come and see her."

"I'd wade through a herd of wild elephants to see her," grinned Layne. "How are you, Harriet?"

"Just fine," she replied, closing the door behind him. "She's in the kitchen."

Layne laid his campaign hat on a table in the parlor, draped his overcoat over the back of an overstuffed chair, and headed down the hallway that led to the kitchen.

Harriet called after him, "I'll give you two a few minutes alone together."

Layne looked back and smiled, acknowledging her words, then stepped into the kitchen to find Melody standing by the table, arms open to receive him.

"Hello, darling," she sighed.

He took her in his arms, and they held each other for a long moment, then kissed warmly. He hugged her again, then sat her down at the table and eased onto a chair beside her.

"Oh, Layne, I've been so upset," Melody said. "There's going to be a battle right here, isn't there?"

"It's possible, honey," Layne said, taking both of her hands in his. "It looks like the Federals are beelining for Richmond, and as you know, Fredericksburg is right in their path. General Lee is watching them carefully. He'll see to it that the town is evacuated before any fighting breaks out."

"That's what everyone is telling me," she said, drawing a shuddering breath, "but what about our home? I've heard what those Yankees do when they capture a town. If they don't burn all the houses to the ground, they destroy everything in them and steal what they don't destroy. Layne, what are we going to do?"

"Our soldiers are rooting down all around here, sweetheart. We're going to do everything we can to keep anything like that from happening."

"Harriet and I have been praying together about it...but I have to admit that my faith is a bit weak right now."

"I appreciate Harriet looking after you. She's a gem."

"That she is," Melody agreed. "Where...where do they have you and your men?"

"We're up on Marye's Heights. Sort of bodyguarding an artillery unit. We'll have a real advantage from up there if the battle comes. High ground is always an advantage."

"Is the Marye family still in the mansion?"

"Yes. General Kershaw talked to them. They want to stay, even if the rest of the town evacuates. John Marye said if the high ground is an advantage for the army, it's an advantage for them, so they'll not leave."

"I'm glad you're on high ground," she said with strain in her voice. "Oh, Layne, I couldn't stand it if anything happened to you. I'll be so glad when this horrid war is over."

"Won't we all," he sighed.

Melody met his gaze with a tender look. "Darling, have you read any of the Bible passages I marked?"

"Only a few. I've been pretty busy. But I will as time allows."

They talked for a few minutes about Jack and Frances, wondering how far west they might be by now. Then Layne talked about the baby and how he was looking forward to the day he could hold little Danny in his arms.

The clock on the wall showed Layne he had ten minutes to report back to General Kershaw. He held Melody tight, kissed her, and said, "I'll see you again as soon as I can."

They spoke their love for each other, and as Layne was about to leave the kitchen, Harriet came in. Layne thanked her once again for the way she was taking care of Melody, and hurried away.

SEVEN

R ain began to fall from a heavy sky on the afternoon of November 20. At Culpeper, General Robert E. Lee received word that all three of Burnside's grand divisions were closing in on Fredericksburg. It was evident that he was going to have to fight them there.

Lee ordered General Longstreet to march the remainder of the troops to Fredericksburg and make ready for battle. The Rebels trudged through a heavy downpour and the deplorable mud that went with it. General Lee rode Traveler alongside General Longstreet in the lead, his head bent against the wind-driven rain.

When they arrived at Fredericksburg just before dark, the two generals had their tents set up atop Marye's Heights where they could enjoy a commanding view of the town, the river, and the surrounding terrain. Lee was jolted to look across the Rappahannock and behold a massive army. At the same time, a messenger arrived from Major General Jeb Stuart's cavalry brigade, which was moving southward along the Rappahannock. Stuart's message was that the Federals were setting up camp on the hills above the east bank of the Rappahannock at Fredericksburg. Stuart had learned that there were 130,000 of them.

Lee was upset over Confederate intelligence. Reports he had received within the past few days indicated that Burnside's three divisions might total as many as 75,000, but Stuart's figure had to be accurate, for the huge gathering of Union forces Lee could see across the river were much more than 75,000. His heart sank. He would have somewhat under 59,000 troops when Stuart's cavalry arrived.

Longstreet saw the look on Lee's face and said cautiously, "General, sir, shouldn't you send for General Jackson's corps?"

Lee's gaze was riveted on the Union army across the river. When he did not answer, Longstreet said, "General, sir?"

"I heard you, General," Lee drawled, still focusing on the enemy troops, who were fading from view in the gathering darkness. "I can't bring myself to leave the Valley vulnerable as yet."

Longstreet wanted to yell at him. Why couldn't Lee see that the Shenandoah Valley would be a lost cause if the Federals were not halted in their drive to Richmond? They needed Stonewall Jackson's remaining 19,000 troops desperately. But Longstreet knew better than to argue with his venerable leader.

The rain continued to come down in torrents all the next day. Lee stood outside his tent in the downpour and wondered why Burnside did not attack. It could not be the rain. Many battles had been fought in rainstorms. Why wasn't Burnside sending his massive army against the opponent they so greatly outnumbered?

Major General Ambrose E. Burnside paced like a caged lion in his tent just outside of Falmouth, Virginia, a mile-and-a-half upriver from Fredericksburg. Major Generals Edwin V. Sumner, Joseph Hooker, and William B. Franklin stood shoulder-to-shoulder, eyeing their upset and nervous leader. The rain pounded the tent, and water dripped from some of the worn seams along one side.

Few of the Army of the Potomac's officers had full confidence in their newly appointed leader. The three who stood in the tent and observed Burnside's feverish state of mind were wishing General McClellan was still in command.

Hooker and Burnside had never gotten along. They did not like each other, and everyone knew it. Beyond Hooker, however, there was no dislike for Burnside. Whatever his fellow officers and subordinates thought of Burnside's abilities, nearly all of them agreed that he had a captivating personality. Not only had he shown extreme courage, such as in the Battle of Antietam, but there was a certain brigandish air about him. The thirty-eight-year-old major general wore heavy muttonchop whiskers, a broad-brimmed hat atop his balding head, and carried his holstered revolver low on his hip.

The man chosen to replace McClellan smiled frequently, remembered names well, looked after the welfare of his troops, won friends with ease, and took orders in a gracious, submissive manner from his superiors. Hence, he accepted the commission as commander of the Army of the Potomac even though he did not feel qualified.

Burnside's new responsibilities had made him ill the first two days, but he attacked his problems vigorously, nevertheless, and on November 9 he forwarded to President Lincoln a bold new strategy for the capture of Richmond. He proposed concentrating his forces along the route southwest toward Gordonsville to convince Lee that the Federals intended to continue their drive in that direction.

Then Burnside would make a quick pivot and move his army rapidly southeastward from Warrenton to Fredericksburg, on the Rappahannock River. Burnside explained to Lincoln that by veering eastward while maintaining a southerly route, his army would stay closer to Washington and its base of supplies. It would also be on a more direct route to Richmond because Fredericksburg was on the main road midway between the two capitals. Burnside's plan was to cross the Rappahannock and capture Fredericksburg before Lee could amass enough men to stop him, then move south, seize Richmond, and bring an end to the bloody war.

Along with his daring scheme, Burnside requested of Lincoln

that thirty canal boats and barges loaded with needed goods be sent down the Potomac to a new supply base at Belle Plain, ten miles northeast of Fredericksburg. In addition, he wanted a wagon train of ammunition and food to move overland from Alexandria to the bank of the Rappahannock where he would gather his army, across the river from Fredericksburg. And most important, Burnside requested enough pontoons to build several floating bridges across the Rappahannock, which was now swollen and rising due to heavy rains up north. Without the floating bridges, he could not get his troops across the river to attack and seize Fredericksburg.

There had been little enthusiasm in Washington for Burnside's plan. Lincoln discussed it with General-in-Chief of the Union Army, Henry W. Halleck, and Halleck did not like it. He argued that the best route was to swing the Army of the Potomac westward to Gordonsville. This would bypass Fredericksburg and give a straight shot to Richmond southeastward, and avoid the need of pontoons and lumber to build floating bridges.

Wires had gone back and forth between Burnside and Lincoln, but in spite of Halleck's objections, Burnside held firm, insisting his plan was best. It would throw Lee off balance by making him think the Federals were going to take the Gordonsville route. Fredericksburg could be in Union hands and the Federal troops on their way to Richmond before Lee could raise a blockade.

Lincoln had been skeptical of Burnside's scheme, also. He had tried for months to get McClellan to meet the Confederate Army of Northern Virginia head-on, and now his new commander was proposing to skirt that army and simply move on the Confederate capital. However, Lincoln was so pleased to finally have a commander who was willing to put his army in motion that he approved the plan on November 14. His last words in the wire of approval were: "Your plan will succeed if you move very rapidly; otherwise not."

Burnside paced and fumed in front of his three division commanders, cursing the name of Brigadier General Daniel P. Woodbury, who was responsible for delivering the pontoons and bridge-building materials. General Sumner said, "Sir, I'm sure it's the rain that's holding General Woodbury up. It's just one of those things that nobody can control."

Face red with anger, Burnside said, "General Sumner, it's November 25! I ordered those pontoons on November 14, the same day I ordered the wagonloads of food, supplies, and ammunition. The wagons got here four days ago. They had to go through rain and mud, too. No, there's some bungling going on in this army, and somebody's head is going to roll!"

The sixty-five-year-old Sumner held his voice steady and said, "General Burnside, sir, experience has taught me not to speak out against fellow officers until I know the circumstances."

Burnside's face reddened the more. "May I remind you, sir, that the president and General Halleck will hold one man responsible for how this campaign goes? *Me!* If those pontoons had arrived when they should have, we could have made an easy thing of capturing Fredericksburg. Not now! Lee's got his forces dug in too well. I'll take it on the chin for it, but General Woodbury's going to be sorry he fiddled around getting those pontoons here!"

General Hooker, who had never covered his dislike for Burnside, snapped, "Seems to me, *sir*, you ought to take some advice from General Sumner, who was in a fighting uniform before you got out of diapers! You should hold your caustic comments until you learn why General Woodbury's late."

Burnside was about to lash back when a voice called from outside the tent, "General Burnside! Good news! The pontoons are here!"

Burnside moved to the flap, jerked it open, and set dark eyes on a sergeant who stood dripping in the rain. "Is the entire wagon train here?"

"Yes, sir."

"General Woodbury?"

"Yes, sir."

"You go tell him I want him at my tent immediately!"

"Yes, sir," saluted the sergeant, and hurried away.

Franklin, who was a few years older than Burnside, said, "Sir, I mean no disrespect, but you should at least hear General Woodbury out before you take any action."

"General Franklin, it's easy for you to stand there and tell me what I ought to do. But the responsibility for what happens here rests on my shoulders."

"I know that, sir," Franklin replied, clearing his throat, "but if you fly off the handle before you give General Woodbury a chance to explain, you could do yourself some real harm. You need the respect of your men."

"He's giving you sage advice, sir," Sumner said. "I know this delay has dragged wickedly across your nerves, but you must gain control of yourself and meet General Woodbury with conduct that becomes an officer of the Union army...especially the commander of the entire Army of the Potomac."

Burnside took a deep breath, ran both palms over his face, and willed his nerves calm. Then in a half-whisper, he said, "You're right, General. You're right."

"General Burnside!" came the sergeant's voice above the roar of the rain.

"General Franklin, will you open the flap and invite General Woodbury in, please?" Burnside said.

Franklin pulled back the flap and saw Brigadier General Daniel P. Woodbury leaning close to the tent beside the sergeant. Water was dripping off the brim of his campaign hat. "General Burnside asked me to invite you in, sir. Please enter."

Franklin thanked the sergeant and sent him away as Woodbury, a stately man in his mid-fifties, moved inside.

Woodbury saluted Burnside, acknowledged the presence of the other officers, then removed his dripping hat and said, "General Burnside, sir, I'm sure you're fit to be tied with the delay of the pontoons and the building material, but we got a late start, and the mud has been atrocious."

"I know about the mud, sir," said Burnside, "but what is this about a late start?"

"Well, sir, I did not receive the request for the pontoons and material from General Halleck until the eighteenth. I found out while we were loading the wagons that you had actually put in the order in a wire to President Lincoln on the fourteenth. I'm sorry, sir, but we got here as quickly as we could."

Burnside had no reason to doubt Woodbury's word. For some unknown reason, Halleck had delayed turning in the order. Was it because Halleck disagreed with his plan and deliberately held off turning in the order? Halleck was a proud bird. Maybe this was his way of getting back at Burnside for persuading the president to adopt his plan instead of Halleck's. Burnside would never know. There was nothing he could do about it.

"You're right, General," Burnside said. "I have been quite upset at the delay. It has allowed Lee to fortify himself on all the high places and in every nook and cranny of Fredericksburg. The delay is going to result in more Yankee blood being shed than would have been otherwise. However, it is apparently no fault of yours."

Burnside glanced at Sumner and Franklin, thanking them with his eyes for calming him down. He would not look at Hooker.

"Well, sir," said Woodbury, "if you're through with me, I need to get back to the wagons. We'll begin building the bridges immediately. I assume you plan to float them down the river to Fredericksburg for the actual crossing."

"Correct," nodded Burnside. "When can I plan to do so?"

"Well, sir, we should have the bridges built and ready for service in four or five days."

Burnside had hoped the work could be done quicker, but since the construction of floating bridges was beyond his experience or knowledge, he said, "Do your best to make it four, will you?"

"Yes, sir," Woodbury said. He saluted, spoke briefly to Sumner, Franklin, and Hooker, and was gone.

At nightfall on November 25, General Robert E. Lee learned of the arrival of the pontoons at Falmouth. Now Lee knew why Burnside had not attacked before. He called his commanders together and informed them that General Burnside was going to float his army across the Rappahannock. Lee admitted that he should have sent for General Stonewall Jackson and his troops earlier, and he wired Jackson while his commanders watched. Longstreet heaved a sigh of relief, hoping within himself that Jackson would arrive before the floating bridges were ready for use.

In the meantime, Jeb Stuart and his cavalry of a thousand had arrived. When Jackson's corps got there, the Confederates would have almost seventy-eight thousand men, leaving them still heavily outnumbered by the Federals.

General Burnside's army faced more problems and more delay. Southern civilians took refuge in old abandoned buildings across the river at Falmouth and began firing on the men building the floating bridges. The bridge-builders were unarmed and refused to work with bullets buzzing at them from across the river.

Burnside dared not pull large numbers of men from the camp across from Fredericksburg for fear that the Confederates might take advantage of the smaller force and make their own attack. Eager to get the bridge-builders back to work, Burnside had a few infantrymen fire at the civilians in the old buildings. The civilians were great in number, and for the most part were skilled marksmen. Though the return fire from the Yankee infantrymen limited their shooting, they continued to take their toll of Yankee lives, making progress on the bridge-building slow. Burnside was strung tight because of the further delay.

The weather turned colder as the days passed, and snow replaced the rain.

Stonewall Jackson had set a grueling pace for his troops, and they arrived at Fredericksburg in a heavy snowstorm late in the afternoon on November 29. The corps of more than nineteen thousand men was a welcome sight to the troops already at Fredericksburg. Lee quickly deployed Jackson's troops, sending Brigadier General Jubal Early's division to Skinker's Neck, some twelve miles down river, Major General Daniel H. Hill's division four miles farther down river to Port Royal. The division of Major General Ambrose P. Hill was deployed at a spot six miles southeast of Fredericksburg, and that of Brigadier General William B. Taliafero at a location four miles south of town. These four commands were to guard against any attempt by Burnside to cross downstream and outflank the Confederates. At the same time, Lee ordered Stuart's cavalry to fill in along the lines and on the semi-circle of hills at Fredericksburg, strengthening the ranks.

On December 8 the sky was cloudy, but no snow was falling. Lee, Longstreet, Kershaw, and Layne Dalton stood together, hats pulled low and heads turtled into their coat collars against the icy wind that whipped over Marye's Heights.

Lee set his gaze on the four-hundred-foot-wide Rappahannock below and said, "Word is that Burnside's almost got his floating bridges done."

"When do you plan to call for evacuation of the town, sir?" Dalton asked.

"When I know the blue-bellies are ready to make their move," replied Lee. "Most of the people down there have nowhere to go except the fields and the woods. I don't want to send them out there until I have to. This cold weather could be the death of a number of them if they have to stay away for long. This was one of the reasons I didn't want to fight the Federals here." Lee paused, then asked, "What about your wife, Major? Does she have some place to go? I'd sure hate to see her have to camp in the woods, carrying that baby and all."

"Yes, sir," Dalton nodded. "A widow in the church lives about three miles west of town. She's offered to let my wife and our neighbor stay with her until they can return home again."

"Good," said Lee. "I'm glad she has a place to go."

General Kershaw smiled at Dalton. "Sergeant Kirkland tells me you're pulling for a boy, Major."

"Yes, sir, I am. I'll love her if it's a girl, of course, but down deep, I just know it's a boy."

"I guess that's natural. Most men want a son for their first child. Of course, girls are mighty special, Major. Speaking from experience, I can tell you that a father and his daughter can develop a wonderful relationship. I've got two precious daughters, and I wouldn't trade what we've got between us for anything in this world."

The attention of all four men was drawn to a formidable figure lumbering toward them along the edge of the trees. As he walked, his eyes were fixed on the massive army camped on the hills across the Rappahannock.

"Good morning, General Jackson," Dalton said as the tall man drew near.

Jackson returned the greeting, then moved up beside Lee and once again gazed on the Federal forces across the river.

Thomas Jonathan Jackson, at thirty-eight, was one of the best-known generals in the Confederate army. He had been dubbed "Stonewall" for his extreme courage under fire at Bull Run, and led a corps of rough and rugged soldiers who would follow him anywhere.

"We'll have our hands full when they come across the river, General," Lee said.

Jackson pulled his collar up tight around his neck and nodded. "That we will, sir. We may not be as large as the Yankee force, but we'll see that those blue-bellies have their hands full, too."

"No doubt about it," Longstreet said.

Jackson looked down at Fredericksburg, shaking his head. "What a scene," he said. "Two mighty machines of destruction…and huddled between them the forlorn little town."

"War is a terrible thing," put in Kershaw. "Especially on civilians."

"When are you going to evacuate the town, General?" Jackson asked Lee.

"When I'm sure Burnside is ready to attack. As I was telling the others here, for the most part, those poor people down there have nowhere to go but the fields and the woods. I don't want to push them out of their homes until it's absolutely necessary."

"Certainly," nodded Jackson. "Not with snow on the ground, and as cold as the nights have been."

"Exactly. General Stuart has some men watching the progress of the bridge-building at Falmouth, and when they tell me that the bridges are on the water, I'll advise Mayor Tillman to move the people out."

"How long do you think it'll be?"

"From what I'm told by Stuart's spies, I'd say three days...four at the most."

Jackson rubbed his bearded chin and shook his head. "I hope the people of Fredericksburg have homes to come back to when this ordeal is over."

Dalton excused himself and made his way amongst the trees, speaking to his own men and artillerymen as he walked. He found a private spot a few yards from the gate of the Marye mansion, knelt beside a naked-limbed oak tree, and removed his hat. "Lord," he said, "I'm...not very good at this praying business, but I'm awfully worried about what's going to take place here shortly. Please...please let Melody and little Danny get out of town before those Yankees come. And I'd appreciate it too if You'd protect the house. With Melody's parents gone, she and little Danny wouldn't have anyplace else to live. I know I don't deserve for You to answer this prayer, but...would You for my family's sake? Please?"

EIGHT

A light snow began to fall during supper on the evening of December 8. After the meal, General Burnside crowded all of his generals and colonels into his spacious field tent and stood before them by lantern light.

"Gentlemen," he said with a tone of authority in his voice, "I've gathered you here to announce that the pontoon bridges will be ready for use in two days. I am setting the attack for Thursday morning, the eleventh. We'll float the bridges down the river under cover of darkness on the night of the tenth, and bring the troops across the Rappahannock and move on Fredericksburg at dawn."

Colonel Joshua L. Chamberlain, commander of the Twentieth Maine Infantry Regiment, raised a hand for recognition. Chamberlain, the thirty-three-year-old preacher-turned-soldier, was tall, handsome, and extremely bright. He was Phi Beta Kappa, Bowdoin College, Brunswick, Maine, and could speak seven languages fluently.

"Yes, Colonel," nodded Burnside.

"Do I understand correctly, sir, that you plan to send the whole force across the river, directly against Fredericksburg?"

"That's the plan."

"I don't mean to be argumentative nor disrespectful, sir," Chamberlain said cautiously, "but it is my understanding that you talked to your generals about crossing at other places on the river, spreading our troops out so as to make a wide sweep on the town and all those Rebel fortifications. Is this so?"

"Yes, Colonel. But I've changed my mind. Lee has spread his troops along the river southward and inland. By this I know he expects me to do just as I had planned earlier. I'm going to surprise General Lee by bringing the entire force—except for some reserves— head-on into Fredericksburg."

General Hooker's features registered his disagreement, and he spoke up without asking to be recognized. "Have you notified General Halleck of this change in plans?"

"Just this afternoon," Burnside nodded, fixing Hooker with a level stare.

"And have you heard back from him?"

"Not as yet."

"What if he doesn't reply?"

"Then I'll proceed as planned."

"I protest the idea! Have you seen the way Lee's got the whole area fortified? He's got the high ground on Marye's Heights, and it's loaded with artillery. They'll chew us to pieces if we try to cross the river into the teeth of those cannons. This is preposterous! You're out of your mind!"

Burnside fought to control his rage. "General Hooker, may I remind you that if the pontoons had arrived when they were supposed to, taking Fredericksburg would have been a snap! And may I also remind you that I didn't ask for this command. In fact, as you and these other men know, I tried desperately to avoid it."

"That's no excuse for sending troops into the teeth of those cannons and howitzers!" blared Hooker. "We need to attack from every direction!"

"You're forgetting something, General...and possibly you are too, Colonel Chamberlain. We have our own cannons and howitzers well deployed on Stafford Heights and the ridges below the heights. Our artillery will give cover as the troops cross those bridges."

"I haven't forgotten a thing," retorted Hooker. "But I am wondering if you wouldn't change your tactic if *you* had to cross on one of those bridges while the enemy is blasting them to bits!"

"May I remind you, sir," Burnside said through clenched teeth, "that I am commander of this army by order of the president of the United States of America? Your insolence is both an insult to Mr. Lincoln and unbecoming that of a major general of this army! You will hereby refrain from any more such outbursts, or I will have you put under arrest!"

Hooker cast a furtive glance at General Sumner, who gave him a solemn look and slowly shook his head.

When Burnside saw that Joe Hooker was silenced, he looked at Colonel Chamberlain and asked, "Since we have our own artillery on high ground on the east side of the river, Colonel, do you feel differently about my plan now?"

"Without seeming insolent, sir, may I speak my mind?"

"That's what I want you to do," Burnside nodded. "I ask only that you speak with the proper degree of respect, and not in the manner displayed here by General Hooker."

"Yes, sir. With all due respect, General Burnside, I feel that your logic in this matter is seriously flawed."

Burnside blinked. "Go on."

"Well, sir, General Lee apparently has not anticipated a direct attack on Fredericksburg because, as you have pointed out, he has spread his troops along the river southward and even inland. However, the exceptionally advantageous position his artillery and infantry occupy on the high points behind the town are probably the most formidable he could ever hope to find in any war anywhere. He has distributed his troops intelligently, taking care—in my estimation, at least—to provide for rapid lateral movement to counter any maneuver we might undertake. I believe we should cross the river elsewhere with our troops, let our artillery exchange fire with theirs, and spread our men out for the attack."

General Sumner, who stood flanking Burnside, moved closer to him and said, "What Colonel Chamberlain says, sir, makes sense. Besides, I have some other reservations about your plan."

"And, what are those reservations, General?"

"Well, sir, once we get the pontoon bridges floated down to Fredericksburg, we've got to link them together. That's going to take time. It can't be done in pitch-black darkness, so whether we have moonlight to work by or do it in broad daylight, Lee will have his sharpshooters blasting away at us. Our men will be sitting ducks."

"May I say something, sir?" asked Major General William Franklin.

"Yes," nodded Burnside, his face a grim mask.

"We've got other problems too, sir. I'm sure Lee will evacuate the town before we get there with the bridges. He'll have free access to any and all buildings to place snipers in. When our men move into Fredericksburg, they'll be open prey to them. Not only that, but whenever we show Lee that we're coming across the river with practically the entire Army of the Potomac, the divisions he has spread inland and down the river are within a short march of the town. We outnumber the Confederates, sir, but they've got position advantage all over us. Lee's no fool. He's ready for us. I strongly recommend we spread our men out for the attack as Colonel Chamberlain has suggested, and let them cross the floating bridges somewhere other than right at Fredericksburg."

"You gentlemen still don't see it, do you?" Burnside said, shaking his head. "Lee's outlying divisions can't fly. I still say by sending our entire force across the river at Fredericksburg, we'll surprise Lee, and we can occupy the hills and the town before he can bring anything serious against us. We outnumber them almost two-to-one. With the element of surprise, we can overwhelm them."

Burnside looked at Colonel Rush Hawkins of the Ninth New York and asked, "What do you think, Colonel?"

Hawkins pulled at an ear and was brutally frank. "If you make the attack as contemplated, General Burnside, it will bring upon us the greatest slaughter of the war. There isn't infantry enough in our whole army to take those troops nestled up there in the heights."

Hawkins and Burnside were close friends. Surprised that the colonel had taken this position—and irritated that he had—Burnside looked at Lieutenant Colonel Joseph H. Taylor, another close friend, and asked, "What do you think, Colonel?"

Equally forthright, Taylor responded quickly. "The carrying out of your plan will not be warfare, sir. It will be murder."

"What's going on here?" Burnside said in a rush of angry, biting words. "Am I to be surrounded by men who have forgotten their duty as officers in this army? Where is your sense of loyalty!"

Burnside looked over the faces of the group for some kind of support. All was quiet.

Then Brigadier General William H. French of the Fourth New York said with enthusiasm, "I'm in agreement with General Burnside! With the element of surprise and twice as many men, we'll have the battle won and Fredericksburg in our hands within forty-eight hours!"

The other officers stood silently exchanging furtive glances.

A determined look settled in General Burnside's eyes. He addressed the group of officers with gravel in his voice. "I have the backing and the authority of the president of the United States to lead the Union Army of the Potomac in the way I see fit. Therefore, the final decision lies with me. I realize that with the authority goes the responsibility. I am ready to shoulder both. We will proceed with my plan.

"The attack, therefore, is officially set for Thursday morning, December 11. On Wednesday the men will be issued three days' rations. The infantrymen will be issued sixty rounds of ammunition each. There are wagons positioned on top of Stafford Heights with plenty more food and ammunition if we need it before this battle is won.

"I remind you, gentlemen, that your duty as officers of this army is to back me in my decision and show me total loyalty. You are dismissed."

Mayor Donald Tillman sat on the edge of his bed as he removed his shoes and discussed with his wife the imminent attack by the Federal army. It was half past nine on Wednesday night, December 10.

Mrs. Tillman was sitting at the dresser, brushing her hair. "It can't be much longer till those horrible Yankees storm the town. Don't you think you should issue the evacuation order tomorrow? I'd hate to see the people—and us for that matter—trying to get out of town with cannonballs exploding all around us."

"I've got the townspeople on alert, dear," Tillman said, rising from the bed and carrying his shoes to the closet. "But, like General Lee, I hate to put them out in the elements till it's absolutely necessary. We've got your brother's house for shelter out there in the country, but most of our citizens will only have the sky for a roof."

"I understand," said Sarah Tillman, "but will you be able to move them out fast enough when the Yankees come?"

"I'm sure we'll have ample warning. General Lee said he will send word to commence the evacuation when his spies upriver report that the pontoon bridges are on their way. I've got several of the elderly men in town ready to be criers when the time comes. We should be able to get all eighteen hundred of us out of town in an hour or so."

"I sure hope so," Sarah sighed. "It would be terrible if—" Her words were cut off by a loud knock at the front door. "Who could that be at this late hour?" she said, looking at her husband.

"I'll find out," he replied, putting on his slippers.

Mayor Tillman hurried through the house, carrying a burning lantern, and opened the front door. Two men in gray uniforms stood before him. One was a sergeant, the other a corporal.

"Good evening, Mayor. I'm Sergeant Benson and this is Corporal Manfred. General Robert E. Lee sent us."

Tillman swung the door wide and said, "Come in out of the cold, gentlemen." The soldiers stomped the snow from their shoes and stepped inside.

Tillman gestured toward the parlor. "Would you like to sit down?"

"There really isn't time, sir," replied Benson. "General Lee wanted us to tell you that our spies reported to him about a half-hour ago that the Yankees are floating their pontoon bridges down river right now. Since there's no moon, they'll most likely begin to assemble them at daylight."

"I hope General Lee is ready for them," Tillman said.

"As much as possible, sir. He figures it'll take Burnside's engineers a couple of hours, at least, to assemble the bridge sections together. You should have plenty of time to evacuate the town if you start moving people out at daylight."

"We can handle it," nodded Tillman. "Tell General Lee we'll have the town evacuated by around seven-thirty."

Obscure light broke through a heavily clouded sky at 6:15 on the morning of December 11, 1862, but Fredericksburg and the area around it was shrouded in heavy fog. Ghostly mists danced and swirled on the cold surface of the Rappahannock River, making it extremely difficult for the Union engineers to see what they were doing.

Atop Marye's Heights, General Lee welcomed a messenger from Brigadier General William Barksdale, telling him that sounds coming through the fog on the river indicated that the Yankees were assembling their floating bridges.

At the same time, several of Fredericksburg's elderly men rode through the town, warning the people that the Yankees were coming. Evacuation began almost immediately.

The frightened people bundled up against the cold and began leaving their homes, bearing what food and portable effects they could carry. They made a pitiful procession, trudging through eight-inch-deep snow with nowhere to go but to the fields and the woods out of cannon range. There they would face the cold until the battle was over and they could return to their homes...if there would be any homes left standing.

Little girls carried their dolls and little boys took along one kind of toy or another. Young mothers carried their blanket-wrapped, crying babies in one arm, and food and diapers in the other. Some of the women with older children, or without any children at all, carried plucked chickens, flour sacks, and Bibles.

A handful of nurses from Fredericksburg's small hospital walked alongside horse-drawn wagons, speaking words of comfort to their patients who lay huddled under blankets. Some of the elderly were so feeble, they could carry nothing. They only hobbled and stumbled along in the slippery snow.

The evacuees had to cross a creek swollen with the winter rains and deadly cold. The icy wind sliced through their coats like frozen knives. Some of Jeb Stuart's cavalrymen went to the creek and ferried as many people as possible across on horseback. The line of shivering, dejected people stretched from the snow-laden streets of Fredericksburg to the creek.

At the Dalton house, Melody was upstairs in her bedroom with Harriet Smith, making preparations to leave. Melody's hands were shaking as she stuffed some garments into a small bag, along with a few toiletries and her Bible.

Harriet took hold of her hands and said, "Honey, we've committed our husbands and our homes to the Lord. There's nothing more we can do. Please get a grip on yourself."

"I'm sorry, Harriet. I should be stronger than this. I should be able to trust the Lord better."

"You're a young Christian yet, honey," Harriet said in a tender tone. "It takes spiritual growth to learn better how to lean on the Lord. But may I give you a brief word of encouragement?"

"Yes, of course."

"You trusted God's Word for your salvation, didn't you? I mean, you accepted by faith what the Bible said you had to do to be saved. Right?"

"Right."

"Then what you have to do now is learn to trust the same Book for your walk through this life. God expects you to do that. He says in Hebrews 11:6 that without faith it is impossible to please Him. We're saved by faith, and we walk by faith. Just as we completely trust the Lord Jesus to save us, so we must trust Him in the same way for our daily walk. We must cling to His Word by faith, for instance, when He says, *Be careful for nothing; but in every thing by prayer and supplication with thanksgiving let your requests be made known unto God. And the peace of God, which passeth all understanding, shall keep your hearts and minds through Christ Jesus.*"

Misty-eyed, Melody smiled weakly and said, "Harriet, I'm so glad the Lord gave me a friend like you."

Both women heard a door close downstairs. Harriet headed for the hallway, saying, "You finish up there. I have a hunch it's either your husband or mine."

When Harriet reached the landing, she saw Layne Dalton bounding up the stairs two at a time. "Hello, Harriet. Are you and Melody about to get out of here?"

"Yes. We're almost ready."

Layne moved past her and said, "I talked to Walter yesterday. He said he'd been able to come see you a couple times since he got here."

"Yes, and it sure was good to see him. Is the fog lifting off the river yet?"

"Not yet," Layne said over his shoulder as he preceded Harriet into the bedroom.

Melody was on her feet, arms open wide, as Layne embraced her.

"We were about to leave, darling," she said. "I'm glad you could come before we did."

"So Mrs. Shrewsbury is still expecting you, I assume."

"Yes. I'm so glad we have a place to go."

"So am I. I want you and little Danny to be warm and safe."

"We will be," she replied softly. "The Lord has been so good to give me Bertha Shrewsbury for a friend. She's a wonderful Christian, Layne."

"You told me Charlie Weymouth was going to let you ride his horse while he leads it to the Shrewsbury place. Is that still the plan?"

"Yes."

"Shouldn't he be here by now?"

"He was here a few minutes ago, but we weren't quite ready. He'll be back shortly."

"I want you out of here before that fog starts to lift. Burnside may begin shelling the town once he can see what he's shooting at."

Harriet picked up Melody's small bag and said, "I'll let you two kiss good-bye without an audience. Meet you downstairs."

When Harriet was out of the room, Layne and Melody shared a lingering kiss, embraced, and kissed again.

"I'll walk you down the stairs, honey," Layne said, "then I've got to hightail it back up the hill."

"Oh, Layne, I wish this horrible ordeal was over! I want you back home and in one piece!"

"I'll be fine, sweetheart. Come on."

Melody hesitated. "Layne, have you been reading your Bible...the passages I marked?"

"A little. I've been awfully busy."

Deep lines etched themselves across her brow. "Darling, you're going to face enemy guns out there. I want to know if...if something happens to you, that you'll meet me in heaven."

Layne took her hand and led her out of the room. "I'll be all right, honey. I've got to live through this so I'll be around to provide for both you and little Danny."

Together they descended the stairs. While Harriet stood by, Layne kissed his wife one more time, told her he loved her, and headed out the door. He leaped on his horse, waved at the two women as they stood watching him from the parlor window, and rode away. Within seconds, the house was engulfed in fog and disappeared from his view.

The major trotted his animal out of Fredericksburg and drew near the southern range of hills that skirted that side of town. At the base of the long, gentle slope that led up to Marye's Heights was a stone wall four-feet high. An old road ran along the outside of the wall.

Heavy patches of fog drifted on the wind across the hillsides, partially blocking the view of the Marye mansion high above. The open slope was rough and rugged and dotted with dozens of ancient oak trees. The summit of Marye's Heights was covered with a thick copse of oaks and heavy brush, giving ample protection for the Confederate infantry and artillery that waited there for the battle to begin.

As Dalton headed his horse through one of the wall's few openings and began the ascent, he peered through the mists at what he could see of the two-story mansion that stood like a defiant fortress at the crest. It was made of red brick in colonial style, having a central section with wide porch and four white pillars, and two one-story wings, making it a famous landmark fully visible on a clear day from anywhere in the valley.

On the semi-circle of wooded hills, the Confederates waited behind a continuous line of entrenchments, concealed by the thick underbrush. Most of Longstreet's corps made up the force on Marye's Heights.

The opposite bank of the Rappahannock River was closely lined by a range of commanding hills on which the Union artillery was posted. A greater part of Burnside's big guns, especially those situated on lofty Stafford Heights, bore down on the town, but nearly all of them were in a position to blast the level ground in the valley on the west side of the river.

When Major Dalton reached his post atop Marye's Heights, he saw a figure moving toward him through the drifting mists. It was

Sergeant Richard Rowland Kirkland, Dalton's self-appointed adjutant.

"Hello, Major," Kirkland grinned. "Did you get to see Mrs. Dalton before she evacuated?"

"Yes, I did," Dalton responded as he slid from the saddle.

"She doing all right, sir? Carrying the baby, I mean?"

"Yes, everything's fine."

"Well, you can thank the Lord in heaven for that, can't you?"

Layne Dalton was realizing more and more that he owed a great deal to the Lord in heaven. "Yes, I certainly can," he replied. "I certainly can."

Kirkland took the reins of Dalton's horse and said, "I'll take care of him for you, sir."

"Thanks, Sergeant."

Layne turned and looked toward the town below. He could barely make out the rooftops through the fog. Though he could not see the long line of evacuees, he was sure that by now Melody was on her way out of Fredericksburg. His heart was heavy for her. Carrying a baby, with her husband in the army and gone so much, was difficult enough, but now she was having to leave her home, wondering if it would be there whenever she returned.

Major Dalton found himself praying for Melody's safety, and for the baby's safety, too. When he ended his prayer with a sincere "Amen," he smiled to himself and headed toward General Kershaw, who stood talking to some of Dalton's infantrymen.

In a half-whisper, he said to himself, "I do believe Melody's faith is touching you more than you realize."

NINE

Harriet turned away from the parlor window while Melody remained to watch Layne ride away into the fog. "Be back in a minute," Harriet said, heading for the kitchen. "I need to make sure the back door is locked."

Lot of good it'll do if the Yankees want in, thought Melody as Layne vanished from view. She turned away from the window and placed one hand to the small of her back, the other to her forehead. With effort, she made her way to the stairs and slowly climbed to the landing. She steadied herself with the banister, then moved down the hall to her bedroom. She sat on the edge of the bed, still holding a hand to her head, and lay down.

"Melody!" came Harriet's voice from downstairs. "Where did you get to?"

"I'm upstairs in my room," Melody called toward the open bedroom door.

Harriet hurried up the stairs and down the hall. "Charlie will be here any minute, Melody." She drew up short when she saw her friend on the bed. "Are...are you all right?"

"Not really. I'm not feeling well. Something's happening inside me."

"What do you mean, *something?*"

"Just...well, pain. Low in the abdomen and in the small of my back. I feel a little lightheaded."

"You think the baby's coming?"

"I don't know. Maybe if I lie here a few minutes, I'll be all right."

"You lie there, all right, honey. I'm going to go get Dr. Craig."

"He may be already gone," Melody said.

"We'll find out. You rest. I'll be back as soon as I can."

Harriet had barely entered the hallway when someone knocked at the front door. She hastened down the stairs and opened the door.

Charlie Weymouth smiled and asked, "You ladies ready, now?"

Harriet's hand was at her throat and her face was pale. "Charlie," she said, "I need your help."

"What's wrong?"

"Melody...she may be going into labor. Would you see if you can find Dr. Craig? I'm an experienced midwife, but I'm not qualified to handle anything out of the ordinary. The baby isn't due for another month."

"I'm on my way," nodded the old man, wheeling and scurrying across the porch.

Harriet dashed up the stairs and into the bedroom. Melody was on her side, doubled up in a fetal position, gritting her teeth and grunting in pain.

"You just hang on, honey," Harriet said, laying a hand on her. "Charlie's on his way to find Dr. Craig right now. Shouldn't take long."

"Unless he's...he's already evacuated," said Melody through clenched teeth.

"Well, if Charlie doesn't find him, and that baby's coming, we'll just have to handle it between the four of us."

Melody looked up at her. "The *four* of us?"

"Mm-hmm. You, me, the baby...and the Lord."

* * *

Across the Rappahannock, General Burnside stood with his officers and peered through the fog at the engineers laboring to link the bridge sections together. Burnside had mixed feelings about the fog. It was slowing the progress with the bridges, but so far it had kept the enemy snipers from opening fire on the engineers.

A few yards from where the officers were collected, the Heglund brothers huddled together in the thick mist. They were part of Major General Edwin V. Sumner's division. Steve was a sergeant, and his two younger brothers were corporals. Word had spread among the Union troops that the exodus from Fredericksburg was under way.

Steve turned to his brothers and said, "I gotta make sure Ma and Pa and George get to safety."

"How you gonna do that?" asked Everett. "The bridges haven't been laid across the river yet. Besides, when they *are*, we're goin' to cross 'em into enemy fire. There ain't no way you can check on them."

"I got to," Steve argued. "I wanna see that they get out, and that they got someplace to go."

"They'll prob'ly do like most ever'body else and camp in the woods," Keith said. "What else is there to do?"

"I don't know, but I'm goin' over there right now and see for myself that they get out before our artillery starts to bombard the town."

"How you gonna get across?" asked Everett.

"Float on one of those old dead trees lyin' over there."

"Ain't nobody gonna give you permission to do that," insisted Keith.

"Well, I'm about to find out," said Steve, walking away. "I'll ask Captain Tweed."

Moments later, Steve found Captain Art Tweed standing on the bank of the river with some enlisted men, peering into the fog, trying to make out what kind of progress was being made on the bridges.

Steve saluted and said, "Cap'n, could I talk to you a minute?"

"Sure," nodded Tweed. He excused himself to the other men and walked a few paces with Steve. "What is it, Sergeant?"

Steve Heglund explained the situation to his captain, asking if he could go into Fredericksburg and check on his family.

Tweed looked at him like he had lost his mind. "Sergeant, your life wouldn't be worth a wooden nickel in there right now. That blue uniform would draw Rebel bullets like honey draws flies. And you sure can't swim the river. You'd never make it. You'd freeze up and drown before you got halfway."

"I can float across on one of those old fallen trees, sir," pressed Heglund. "With this fog, ain't no Rebel sharpshooter gonna see me."

"Sorry, Sergeant. Request denied. Every soldier must stay in his place. When this fog begins lifting, General Burnside is going to order us across those bridges in a hurry. Get back to your post."

"But, sir—"

"That's final, Sergeant!" snapped Tweed, and turned away.

Steve Heglund swore under his breath, calling the captain some choice names, and stomped back to his brothers.

"Wouldn't let you, would he?" Everett said.

"No, but I'm goin' anyhow. If anybody should ask where I am, make up somethin' about me havin' to go deeper into the woods for some reason you don't know about."

Steve persuaded his brothers to help him drag one of the logs into the river. Then he scrambled aboard, carrying a thick broken limb to use as a paddle. With much effort and a couple of near mishaps, he finally made it to the other side and onto the bank.

Furtively he made his way through the drifting fog, darting down alleys, cutting through backyards, until he came to the street where he had grown up. Ethel Heglund and her crippled son were just coming out the front door when Steve dashed across the yard. Mother and son were momentarily startled to see a man hurrying toward them through the mists.

"Ma! George! It's me, Steve! Get back into the house!" Steve said as he bounded onto the porch and urged them back inside.

"Oh, I'm so glad you've come," Ethel said. "We heard that General Sumner's corps was here, so we knew you and your brothers would be over there across the river. Are Everett and Keith all right?"

"Yeah, Ma, they're fine."

"How'd you get across the river? Them bridges in place already?"

"No, not yet. I floated across on a dead tree."

"You did *what?*" Ethel exclaimed.

"Where's Pa?" Steve asked. "Ain't he goin' with you?"

George and his mother exchanged pained glances.

"Your Pa's dead, son," Ethel said.

Steve's mind froze on her words. He shrank back as if she had slapped him across the face with a wet dishrag. *"Dead?"* he gasped. "When? How?"

"A month and two days ago," said Ethel. "On November 9. Jack Reynolds murdered him. Shot him dead."

"Jack Reynolds!" blared Steve, his throat tightening.

"Jack ran into George on the street," Ethel said. "They got to arguin', and Jack got real mad. He took advantage of George and shoved him down real hard. When your pa found out about it, he went over to the Reynolds place and invited Jack outside. He was gonna beat him up good for what he did to George. Jack come out of the house with a gun and shot your pa in the stomach. He died a little while later."

Cold, white fury filled Steve's eyes. "Did they hang him for it?"

George snorted. "Jury acquitted him. Said it was self-defense."

"Self-defense!" exploded Steve. "You mean he's runnin' free?"

"Sure is," George nodded, adjusting his position on the crutches.

"Well, he's a dead man now! Even if he's already evacuated, I'll find him!"

"He ain't here at all," said Ethel. "Jack took Frances and headed for Virginia City, Nevada, over three weeks ago. Joinin' his brother Hank in the gold minin' business."

Steve's eyes pinched back until they seemed almost hidden behind the hooded lids. "When this war's over, I'm goin' after Jack Reynolds."

Steve made sure his mother and brother were out of town and camped as comfortably as possible in the woods, then floated back across the icy Rappahannock and informed his brothers of their father's death. They felt the same fury as Steve and vowed to hunt Reynolds down after the war was over.

Dr. David Craig was packing medicines into a large suitcase when Charlie Weymouth entered his office and told him excitedly that Melody Dalton might be going into labor. Dr. Craig already had his horse hitched to his buggy. Passing the long line of evacuees streaming out of town, he sped to the Dalton house with Charlie riding alongside him.

Charlie waited in the hall outside Melody's bedroom while the doctor examined his patient with Harriet looking on. Harriet had made Melody undress and get in bed before the doctor arrived. As Dr. Craig finished his examination, he drew the blankets up to cover her again and said, "Melody, I believe you are simply experiencing false labor. No doubt it has been brought on by the stress of all that's going on around you. However, I advise you not to travel."

"But Dr. Craig, the Yankees are coming," Melody said.

"I know, and I wish I could tell you it would be safer for you to get out of town. But if you even so much as try to ride in a buggy or a wagon...much less sit in a saddle or even try to walk, you could go into labor quite easily. At this stage in your pregnancy, it could be very dangerous for both you and the baby. The only safe thing right now is complete rest. The pains you are having are warnings that things are not right. Further strain could be disastrous."

Melody's features were chalk-white. There was a desperate note in her voice as she looked at Harriet and said, "You must leave, Harriet. I don't want you vulnerable to whatever is going to happen here."

"Melody, I'm not about to go off and leave you here by yourself," Harriet said.

"But I've heard how vicious the Yankees can be. Who knows what they might do if they found you here?"

"Honey, I can't believe those Union soldiers would harm two helpless women…especially when one of them is about to have her baby, and the other one is there to care for her."

A spasm of pain caused Melody to draw her legs up, clench her teeth, and release a tiny whine.

"Doctor," said Harriet, "isn't there something you can give her for the pain?"

"Not safely. The pains will stop, I'm sure, once she settles down. Look…I'm sorry to make her stay here when she's so frightened, but there really is no choice. I think you're right. No Yankee soldiers are going to hurt two helpless women."

"Doctor," Harriet said, "would it be possible for you to stay here at the house? For the rest of the day, I mean? Just to make sure she settles down and the pains stop?"

"I wish I could, but I've had the town criers telling everyone that I'll be at the Ralph Jones farm in case they need me. I must go there immediately so they'll be able to find me."

"I understand, Doctor. If…if Melody should develop more problems, may I come for you?"

"Of course. Don't you hesitate. But again, I think if she can settle down, the pains will go away. See if you can get her to sleep."

"I'll do my best," Harriet assured him.

Dr. Craig looked down at his patient and said, "Please try to relax, Melody. The sooner you do, the sooner the pains will ease up. However, if they get worse and Harriet decides you need me, have her come and get me, okay?"

"Yes, Doctor. Thank you."

He reached down and squeezed Melody's hand. "You're welcome. It's going to be all right, young lady. It's going to be all right."

With that, Dr. Craig moved to the door and pulled it open. Harriet looked past him and saw Charlie Weymouth standing in the hall with his hat in his hand. "Thank you for bringing Dr. Craig,

Charlie," she said. "We both appreciate it."

"Is Melody gonna be all right, Doc?" Charlie asked.

"She'll be fine."

"Well, I gotta be goin' too, Miss Harriet," said the old man. "More people to help before the trouble starts."

"Thank you, Charlie," she said. "And God bless you."

Harriet watched the two men until they disappeared down the stairs, then moved back to the bed and said, "How about I fix you some hot tea, honey? Maybe that would help you to relax, maybe even go to sleep."

"Yes," replied Melody, smiling up at her friend. "Could I get you to rub my back first? It's really hurting."

"Of course. Roll on your side and I'll work on it."

"Doc?" Charlie Weymouth said as the two men passed through the front door of the house and closed it behind them.

"Yes?"

"I could hear pretty much what was being said there in Melody's room. I appreciate what you told them and all, but there's somethin' that's botherin' me."

"And what's that?"

"You didn't mention anything about what they should do if them blue-bellies cut loose with their cannons and start bombardin' the town."

"They won't do that, Charlie. What purpose would it serve? If they want to occupy the town, they sure don't want it in rubble and ruin."

"I don't think they want to occupy it very long, Doc. If they do get in here, they'll steal and plunder and probably do a lot of destruction just for meanness. And if you ask me, they'll also bombard the town just for meanness." Charlie paused a few seconds, then said, "If I'm right, those two sweet gals are in trouble."

"Well, let's hope you're not, Charlie," said Dr. Craig, climbing into his buggy. "Melody is in no condition to travel. Not even a little distance. She must stay in that bed and rest, or I'm afraid she'll lose the baby."

The fog began to lift about ten o'clock that morning. General Burnside was elated. He stood on the river bank and shouted encouragement to his engineers, who had already linked bridge sections more than halfway across the river.

Working unarmed, the Union engineers positioned the pontoons one at a time, moored them securely to each other, and laid the large sections of planking in place, lashing them firmly to the pontoons with heavy lengths of rope. Infantry and cavalry both must use the bridges to cross the river.

On the Confederate side of the Rappahannock, Brigadier General William Barksdale rode uneasily up and down the bank, inspecting his pickets and listening to the sounds of the Union engineers at work. From time to time, he could hear the engineers talking in undertones as they pieced their assault bridges together in the fog.

General Lee had ordered Barksdale's troops—the Thirteenth, Seventeenth, and Twenty-first Mississippi Regiments, three companies of the Eighteenth Mississippi, and a battalion of the Eighth Florida—to open fire on the bridge-builders once they could make them out through the fog. Barksdale had posted his sharpshooters in rifle pits and behind walls all along the river front. They were to stay in their positions and harass the Federal crossing until General Barksdale saw that it was too dangerous to remain there. They would then withdraw to the main Confederate lines.

At last Barksdale's vigilance was rewarded. The fog began to lift. He checked his pocket watch. Ten o'clock. He hurried along the bank, alerting his sharpshooters and telling them to open fire as soon as they had clear targets.

Barksdale stationed himself close to the bank in a stand of trees and waited. By 10:20 the fog was thin enough to make out figures moving on the floating bridge sections. He trotted his horse toward his line of men and shouted, "Open up on 'em, men! Give it to 'em!"

Barksdale fired the first shot as a signal for those along the line who could not hear his voice. There followed a roar of musketry. Men in dark uniforms fell into the icy water while others flattened themselves on top of the bridge sections, attempting to avoid the heavy fire.

On the heels of Barksdale's commencement of fire, General Longstreet, atop Marye's Heights, commanded his artillery to open up, sending a barrage of cannonballs amid the bridge builders.

On the Union side of the river, General Burnside swore and sent a command to his artillery atop Stafford Heights and along the flanking ridges. In reply, 150 Federal cannons opened their iron mouths with a thunderous roar, hurling a tempest into the sharpshooter lines along the west bank of the river.

Barksdale's men, however, were well protected. The general himself took shelter behind a large warehouse near the docks. Though a few of the sharpshooters were hit, most of them were untouched. To counter the Union artillery attack, Longstreet turned all his big guns on Stafford Heights. Soon it was an all-out artillery battle.

While the artilleries pounded each other, the Union engineers went back to work. Once more Barksdale's sharpshooters sent them scrambling for cover.

General Burnside stood amid the sheltering trees on the east side of the Rappahannock and ordered thirty-six guns brought to the river bank to blaze away at the Confederate sharpshooters. This drove Barksdale's troops back into hiding. Longstreet saw the Federal engineers working once again, so he directed several of his big guns on the bridge builders.

By now it was almost 1:00 P.M. A frustrated Burnside decided to retaliate by doing the thing he knew the Confederates feared most. He brought one hundred big guns to bear on the town itself.

As the heavy bombardment of Fredericksburg began, General

Hooker dashed up beside Burnside and shouted above the roar, "General, what are you doing? It isn't necessary to destroy the town! Nobody's shooting at us from there!"

Burnside marked Hooker with blazing eyes. "You don't seem to understand that this is war, General! I'll do whatever I have to in order to take the town! Now get back to your post!"

"But destroying it won't help you take it! Why not keep all the guns blasting at the river bank and Marye's Heights?"

"Because this will gall their guts!" snapped Burnside.

"But Fredericksburg is a part of our American heritage. Doesn't that mean anything to you?"

"Do the words *court martial* mean anything to you, Joe?"

Hooker set his mouth in a grim line, turned, and stomped away.

The Confederates on the hills looked down with a mixture of grief and wrath at the enemy's violent storm of destruction upon the historic old town. Fredericksburg, except for its church steeples, was still veiled in the misty fog that had left the river but settled in the town and surrounding valley.

The earth trembled at the deafening cannonade. The howling of the solid shot, the bursting of the shells, and the dismal sound of collapsing houses united in a dread concert of doom. Every heart of the thousands of Confederate soldiers yearned for revenge.

Blue-white clouds from the bursting shells appeared above the town, and from its center rose columns of dense black smoke from houses set on fire by the explosions. There was virtually no wind. The smoke rose in great pillars for five or six hundred feet before spreading outward in loathsome black sheets.

Atop Marye's Heights, General Lee stood with Generals Longstreet and Jackson, peering at the scene below through his field glasses. After several minutes, Lee lowered the glasses and said, "I fear there are not enough of us to prevent the Federals from crossing the river."

"It's inevitable, sir," said Jackson. "But we'll give them a fight they won't forget when they get over here."

"That we will," Longstreet said.

"General Jackson," said Lee. "Send word to General Barksdale that when the enemy starts across the river, he and his troops are to withdraw gradually while firing into their ranks. I want them to join your men at the base of this hill. I will leave it to General Barksdale's discretion just when to begin his withdrawal."

"Yes, sir," said Jackson, moving away to find a messenger.

"We'll still whip them, sir," said Longstreet. "We've got the advantage of position."

"You're right," Lee nodded. "General Ambrose E. Burnside is going to get a baptism of fire for his first battle as commander of Mr. Lincoln's army."

Some fifty yards from where Lee and Longstreet stood, Major Layne Dalton waited with three captains and their units of infantry under his command. They would go into action when the Yankees swarmed across the river and headed for Marye's Heights.

Dalton was heartsick over what was happening to his town and the damage that might be done to his house, but he took comfort in one thing: At least his wife and unborn baby were safe.

TEN

Harriet Smith sat in an overstuffed chair in a corner of the bed-room where Melody Dalton lay sleeping. Harriet had taken her Bible from a small canvas bag she had packed for her stay with widow Bertha Shrewsberry. She was reading Psalm 91, drawing strength for her own heart. Her eyes kept coming back to verse one and the note she had made next to it in the margin some years ago.

> *He that dwelleth in the secret place of the most High*
> *shall abide under the shadow of the Almighty.*

The note in the margin read: "Safety is not the absence of dan-ger, but the presence of God."

Harriet leaned her head back against the softness of the chair and whispered, "Dear Lord, only You know what is going to happen to us. Please help me to be strong for Melody's sake. And please help both of us to remember that Your presence is with us, no matter how great the danger. Please help me to—"

Melody stirred, rolled her head back and forth on the pillow, then went still.

Harriet had rubbed her back for about a half hour after Dr.

Craig and Charlie Weymouth left. It had helped to relax her. Then Harriet had gone down to the kitchen and made some hot tea. After drinking two cups of it, Melody became drowsy and had fallen asleep. She had been asleep, now, for well over an hour. The grandfather clock in the parlor had just struck a quarter to one.

Harriet would not disturb her. Melody needed the rest. They would have some lunch whenever the expectant mother woke up.

Harriet laid her Bible down and went to the window that faced her own house. Their street was deserted, and what she could see of the side street a quarter-block away was also deserted. She figured everyone was out of town by now. She stood there for some time, staring vacantly. Before turning away, Harriet ran her gaze over her house and said, "Lord, hasten the day Walter and I can live a normal life again."

Harriet turned from the window, cast a glance at Melody, and returned to the chair. Just as Harriet sat down, the chimes in the grandfather clock told her it was one o'clock. The pleasant sound had barely died out when there was a strange rumbling, like distant thunder. It came in a series of deep-throated noises—*pum-pum*—followed by shrill whistles and earth-shaking explosions.

Harriet sprang out of the chair and dashed to the same window she had looked out moments before. Beyond her own house, she saw sheets of flame and billows of smoke. The Federals were shelling the town!

The expression of horror that claimed her features looked back at her in a faint reflection from the glass. There were more shrieking shells and more explosions, each one seemingly coming closer.

Suddenly behind her, Melody sat bolt upright in the bed, screaming, "Layne! Layne!"

Harriet rushed to her and wrapped her arms around her, saying, "It's all right, honey! It's all right. I'm here."

"Layne's dead, Harriet!" Melody wailed. "A cannonball blew him to bits! It did! It blew him to bits!" Melody's entire body was quaking, and her skin was like ice.

"No, Melody!" Harriet cried. "You were dreaming. You were only dreaming!"

Melody drew a shuddering breath and looked around her, then at Harriet. "Layne is all right? He wasn't—?"

"No, sweetie," Harriet breathed, tenderly brushing loose strands of hair from her forehead. "It was just a dream."

A whining shell exploded less than a half-block away, followed by two more, shaking the house.

Melody gripped her friend hard. "The Yankees!" she gasped. "They're bombarding us!"

"Yes," Harriet nodded.

Another cannonball exploded, even closer. Melody's body jerked and her fingernails dug into Harriet's arms. Her eyes blazed in a mixture of anger and terror. "Those wicked devils! Why are they destroying the town? They'll kill us, Harriet! They'll kill us!"

Harriet prayed in her heart: *Help me, Lord! I'm scared, too! Please don't let her lose the baby. Give me strength to help Melody.* Suddenly to mind came Psalm 91:1.

"Melody!" Harriet said. "Listen to me! Psalm 91:1 says, *He that dwelleth in the secret place of the most High shall abide under the shadow of the Almighty.* We're under His shadow right now. He is here with us! Do you hear me, Melody? The Lord is here with us!"

"Yes—yes He is. I know He is." Melody took several deep breaths, trying to calm herself. Shells were shrieking and exploding all around them.

"Listen to me, honey," said Harriet, forcing steadiness into her voice. "I wrote something in my Bible years ago, right next to Psalm 91:1. Something our previous pastor said in a sermon: 'Safety is not the absence of danger, but the presence of God.' Think about it. Jesus is here with us right now. We're safer here with the shells exploding all around us than we would be anywhere else without Him. Do you understand?"

"Yes, I...I think so."

"Then we must trust Him to take care of us," Harriet said, squeezing Melody's arms.

Just then two Union cannonballs slammed into the Smith house next door, exploding in a huge fireball. The windows in Melody's bedroom shattered, spraying shards of glass all around.

Harriet let go of Melody and staggered to the window, crunching glass under her shoes. Flames licked around the edges of a huge hole in the roof amid billows of black smoke. Her lips parted to give voice to a heart-rending wail. Melody, trembling all over, threw back the covers and started to get out of bed.

Harriet heard her and pivoted. "No, honey!" she gasped. "Stay in bed!"

"But your house! Your house is on fire!"

"Yes," Harriet said, bursting into tears. As she rushed to Melody and threw her arms around her, another cannonball shrieked overhead. The two women clung to each other, expecting the missile to strike the Dalton house. It passed directly over the roof and struck a tree in the front yard of the house next door to the west. The tree exploded into a thousand pieces, branches and bark scattering every direction.

More shells whistled and whined around them, but were now striking farther west and to the north, across the street.

Tears streamed down Harriet's cheeks as she held Melody tight and said, "They're shooting beyond us, honey. The Lord is with us! He has protected us!"

"But your house will burn to the ground!" Melody sobbed. "Look at it! It's going up in flames!"

Harriet left her and went again to the window. "The front part of the house on the first floor isn't burning yet. Maybe I can still save some of our things!"

Fear filled Melody's eyes. "No, Harriet! Don't go in there!"

"I promise I won't take any chances," Harriet said.

"But if you go inside the house and it collapses, you'll be killed. No personal items are worth your life."

"I won't do anything foolish. If it doesn't look safe, I won't try it. Don't you worry. I'll be back to take care of you." With that, Harriet was out the door and moving down the hall.

Melody lay back down, pulled her knees up, and ejected a tiny mew of pain. She was hurting again.

For another full hour, General Burnside's artillery bombarded the town and the area just across the river where Barksdale's sharpshooters were positioned. In a full hour-and-a-half, the Federals fired five thousand shells into Fredericksburg. The explosions destroyed hundreds of houses, tore gaping holes in brick buildings, dug craters in streets, yards, and gardens, and toppled a great number of trees. But the vicious bombardment failed to kill or drive off Barksdale's men.

When Burnside gave command for the artillery to cease fire and the engineers to resume their work, the tenacious sharpshooters emerged from their shelters once more and resumed firing. The Yankee engineers were forced to leave off their work again and head for cover.

Burnside was beside himself with rage. Brigadier General Henry J. Hunt, who commanded the Union artillery, approached the angry leader and said, "Sir, those sharpshooters are too well protected. My artillery just can't dislodge them. May I suggest that you forget trying to connect the bridge sections, and instead, float the troops across the river on the sections? If we don't get our men in that town right soon, we may not ever do it."

Burnside was at his wits' end. The idea sounded plausible. It was worth a try.

"Good thinking, General," he said with a shadow of a smile on his lips. "I'll have some of the infantry shoot at the Rebel sharpshooters while the troops float across on the sections. We'll probably lose a few in the crossing, but as you say, if we don't occupy the town pretty soon, we may never do it."

Burnside gave the order to his officers and assigned teams of engineers to row the troops across on the pontoon sections. Volunteers from the Seventh Michigan, the Nineteenth and Twentieth Massachusetts, and Eighty-ninth New York were the first to clamber onto the makeshift assault boats and start across the icy Rappahannock.

It was just after three o'clock in the afternoon when the Federals began their daring crossing. General Barksdale's sharpshooters put them under heavy fire. One Union soldier was killed and several were wounded during the crossing, but all the floating sections made it to the other side.

The men-in-blue leaped ashore and formed ranks under the protection of the riverbank. Then they rushed into Fredericksburg via the nearest street. The swarm of Yankees was so great that before General Barksdale's sharpshooters could begin to withdraw, thirty of them were taken prisoner. Now more Federals were able to land safely, assemble their units, and push on into the town.

Barksdale knew it was time to withdraw his troops and join those of Stonewall Jackson at the bottom of the hills that led up to Marye's Heights. Barksdale led the withdrawal, his men firing at the approaching swarm of Yankees, retiring street by street through the burning town, hotly contesting every inch. Within a stretch of about fifty yards, the advancing Federals lost ninety-seven men, including several officers.

Finally, the Confederates reached the stone wall at the foot of Marye's Heights, where Jackson and his infantry drove back the oncoming Yankees, giving their comrades cover while they vaulted the wall and fell behind it, exhausted. The heavy fire of Jackson's infantry held the Union troops at bay, and as darkness crowded out the light of the dying day, the firing ceased.

General Barksdale's gallant troops had accomplished their mission superbly, holding up the crossing of the Union troops for the better part of the day. Atop Marye's Heights, General Lee stood amongst his officers, artillery, and infantry, and led in a rousing cheer for the sharpshooters.

General Lee removed his hat, ran his fingers through his silver hair, and looked down at the scene below. Flames licked away at houses, barns, sheds, trees, and commercial buildings all over the town. The flames made the billows of smoke an orange-red color, and their blazing light illuminated the low-hanging clouds that covered the cold, pitiless sky.

Lee took a deep breath and said to Longstreet, "General Barksdale and his men did a magnificent job today."

"That they did, sir," agreed Longstreet. "No one could have expected any more of them."

"This battle will probably produce a good many more heroes before it's over," mused Lee. "Our men have all done well, but there's one thing that gnaws at my insides."

"What's that, sir?" Longstreet asked.

Lee's words came grudgingly from his lips. "Fredericksburg is now in Union hands."

There was a deathly silence among the men within the sound of Lee's voice. In the grip of that silence, Major Layne Dalton looked toward the section of town that included his own neighborhood. Fire and smoke reached skyward. He swallowed hard, wondering if Melody would have a house to return to when the conflict was over.

Sergeant Richard Rowland Kirkland moved closer to Dalton and laid a firm hand on his shoulder. "I know what you're thinking, sir, and I'm sorry if your house is the source of one of those fires. But when this horrible war is over, you can rebuild again, like so many others will have to do. At least Mrs. Dalton is safe. She and little Danny are your future…plus however many other children the Lord gives you. It'll be all right, sir."

Dalton turned to look at Kirkland by the light that glowed from the burning town. "Thank you, my friend. You ought to be a preacher. You seem to have a knack for coming up with the right words at the right time."

"Of course, we don't know that your house *is* on fire, do we, sir?

Maybe the Lord in heaven just cupped His hand over it and spared it from those Yankee shells."

At the Dalton house, Melody lay in her bed, watching Harriet sweep up the broken glass by the light of two lanterns that burned in the room.

"I'm sorry you weren't able to salvage anything from your house, Harriet," Melody said with compassion in her voice.

"The heat was just too great for me to even think of trying to go inside," Harriet said, dumping glass into a wooden waste container from a dustpan. There were tears in her eyes as she added, "I know we can rebuild the house, but there's no way on earth we can replace so many things that were destroyed in the fire. Family things...old letters, picture albums, and the like. You know."

"Yes."

Harriet looked into Melody's eyes from across the room. "Any more pain?"

"Not much. Could I come and look out the window? I'd like to see what it looks like."

"The doctor told you to stay in bed. Complete rest. Besides, you don't want to see it. It's horrible."

"Yes, I do. It's my town, too."

"Oh, all right, but let me help you."

Harriet laid down the broom and dustpan and headed toward the bed. "Put your slippers on. There could be some little pieces of glass that I missed. I sure don't want to have to pick them out of your feet."

"Yes, boss ma'am," smiled Melody.

"It's good to see you smile."

"Can you give me one back?" Melody asked.

"How's this?" Harriet said smiling.

"Beautiful."

Together they went to the broken window and looked out on the burning town.

"Oh, how awful, Harriet!"

"I know. Dirty Yankees."

"Do you suppose they'll shell us again tomorrow? If they do—"

"I don't think so," replied Harriet, pointing down to the street. "Look."

Melody's eyes fell on men in dark uniforms moving about on a side street at the end of the block. "Looks like they've moved in," she said.

"Maybe we'd better lower these lamps so if they come down the street, they won't know we're in here."

"I...I think I'd better get back on the bed," Melody said.

After getting Melody situated on the bed, Harriet lowered the lamps, then said she would go downstairs to the kitchen and prepare them some supper. An hour later, Harriet carried a tray of hot food up the stairs and into the bedroom. She set it on the table next to Melody's bed, then returned to the landing and picked up the lantern she had left there. As she did, the ring of light flowed through the open double doors into the music room, and her eyes fell on the beautiful concert grand Melody loved so much. "Lord," she said, "hasten the day when Melody can play her piano again...in peace."

Harriet returned to the bedroom and pulled a chair next to Melody's bed. She gave thanks for the food and for God's protection, then they began to eat their supper.

"The Yankees will plunder the houses that aren't destroyed, won't they?" Melody said.

"I expect they will, unless General Lee fills these streets with troops."

"But from what Layne and Walter told us, our army is so vastly outnumbered that we won't be able to hold them back."

"Well, all we can do now is pray that the Lord will continue to protect us, Melody. He certainly kept those shells from striking this house today."

"That He did."

"God always knows what He's doing," Harriet said. "We don't always understand the way He does things, or even why He allows unpleasant things to happen in Christians' lives, but He never makes mistakes. This is where faith comes in. We must trust Him when things go our way...and when they don't."

Harriet left Melody long enough to go to the kitchen and wash the dishes, then returned to spend the rest of the evening in womanly conversation. Before retiring for the night, they read the Bible together and prayed for their safety and the safety of their husbands.

As dawn came on Friday, December 12, 1862, Generals Lee, Longstreet, and Jackson stood atop Marye's Heights and beheld the vast number of Union soldiers who now occupied Fredericksburg. The generals, believing that the town had been completely evacuated, agreed that in the face of the overwhelming odds, their best plan of action was to defend the high ground. No matter how many troops Burnside had at his disposal to throw at them, the Confederates had position advantage. They were going to make full use of it.

There was some early morning mist on the Rappahannock, but not enough to hinder the completion of the pontoon bridges. The sky cleared by five-thirty, and while the sun was rising, the Federals made ready to push the remainder of their infantry into Fredericksburg.

General Burnside pondered his next move while his troops moved across the wobbly, bouncing bridges a few at a time. Burnside chose not to send his men in large numbers for fear the Confederate artillery might cut loose on them at any time.

The Rebel bombardment, however, did not come. Burnside figured—and correctly—that Robert E. Lee would wait for the Union army to come against his well-fortified position.

The delay in getting all the Union infantry across the river and into Fredericksburg afforded the Yankees time to indulge in one of the Civil War's most disreputable ventures—wholesale looting. The evacuation of the town's civilians and the withdrawal of General Barksdale's sharpshooters left Fredericksburg wide open.

Though many houses and commercial buildings had been destroyed, and some were still burning, hundreds were intact. The pickings were easy, and what the wild, reckless Federals could not use, they demolished.

They broke into houses, splintering doors and shattering windows. They smashed mirrors, fine china, and alabaster vases. They ripped up bedding, dumped out the contents of dresser drawers, mutilated books, paintings, and draperies, and used axes and hatchets to chop up furniture.

Rosewood pianos and finely sculpted pump organs were dragged from houses and piled in the streets. The organs were burned and the pianos were employed as horse troughs, or wrecked by soldiers who danced on them and kicked the keyboards apart.

While the looting and destruction were going on, the Heglund brothers hurried to see if their house was still intact. When they turned the corner of their block, they saw men-in-blue doing their wicked work to houses across the street and to the one next door. They hurried inside and were relieved to find that nothing had been touched. Then they went back outside to convince their fellow soldiers not to harm it.

"You know what we oughtta do now?" Keith said.

"What's that?" asked Steve.

"Go over to the Reynolds house."

"Why?" asked Everett. "They don't live there no more."

"I know, but I'd like to tear it up anyhow."

"I'll go for that!" Steve said. "C'mon, let's go see what damage we can do!"

Moments later, they turned onto the block where the Reynoldses had lived and found that out of twenty houses that lined both sides of the street, only nine remained standing. The others were in rubble or had been burned to the ground. One of those completely burned was the house where Jack and Frances Reynolds had lived.

"Well, good riddance," Keith said. "I just wish this war was over so we could go to Nevada, find Jack, and make him pay for murderin' Pa."

"His day's comin'," Everett said.

Suddenly a wicked grin twisted Steve's mouth.

"What're you grinnin' about?" Keith asked.

"Speakin' of Jack," said Steve, "since this house he lived in is gone, how about his daughter's house? I think we oughtta see what's left of it. If there *is* anything left, we can finish it off."

Everett laughed. "I can't think of anything I'd rather do. Sure hope it's still standin' so we can have us some fun!"

ELEVEN

Melody Dalton was feeling somewhat better. After breakfast and a bath, she was sitting at her dresser in a heavy robe, looking into the mirror and brushing her honey-blonde hair. Harriet was making up Melody's bed, putting on clean sheets and pillow cases. Both were aware of distant shouts and laughter in the town, along with destructive-sounding bangs and crashes. Harriet had hung a blanket over the broken window, but cold air and noise were still getting in.

Melody's hands trembled as she looked at her friend in the mirror and said, "They'll be here sooner or later. Do you really think they'll leave us alone and not harm us or the house?"

"Like I said before, honey, those Yankees are human beings. I don't think they're going to cause any trouble here, especially when they see that you're carrying a baby."

"I hope you have a better understanding of human nature than I do," said Melody. "I've heard, as you have, what those Yankees have done in other Southern towns. They've—"

There was a sudden splintering crash downstairs. Harriet stopped what she was doing and said, "Sounds like we've got visitors. You stay here."

"It's the front door!" gasped Melody in a half-whisper. "They've broken into the house!" She jumped to her feet, dropping the hairbrush on the dresser.

Harriet paused at the door, fingers white against the frame. "Melody, sit down and stay there! I don't want you all doubled up in pain again!"

With that, Harriet hurried toward the staircase. She heard male voices speaking excitedly, and a sound of shattering glass. She peered around the corner.

Harriet's heart seemed to stop. Her skin crawled, and a chill ran through her. It was the Heglund brothers. Inching back, she swallowed hard, fought for breath, and looked again. There were no other Union soldiers with them. The Heglunds had come to the Dalton house alone. One of them had thrown a straight-backed wooden chair through a parlor window.

Steve picked up a vase and hurled it across the parlor. It struck a large full-length mirror, shattering both. Next he yanked a painting off the front wall and smashed it against a bookshelf. "Until I can get to Jack, I'll have to be satisfied tearin' up stuff that belongs to his daughter!"

"Feels good, don't it?" Keith said, grabbing the bookcase and tipping it over. It crashed to the floor, spilling books in three directions.

Everett picked up a chair and threw it against another window. The chair split apart and the window shattered. The curtain rod gave way and the drapes and sheers fell to the floor.

"Too bad Jack ain't here to see what we're doin' to his daughter's stuff!" Keith said, kicking over a small table. The unlit lantern it held crashed to the floor.

"Yeah!" Steve cackled, sounding like a wild man. "And it's Layne Dalton's stuff, too! I hate that smooth-talkin' Reb almost as much as I hate Jack Reynolds. I only wish he was here so I could tear *him* up!" He went to the parlor fireplace, picked up the poker, and moved to the center of the room where a beautiful chandelier hung from the tall ceiling. Swinging with all his might, he repeatedly struck the dangling glass prisms, splintering them into tiny pieces. Candles and candle holders scattered all over the room.

Harriet wheeled and hurried back down the hallway. Melody was at her bedroom door.

"How many of them are there?" she asked.

"Three, but these are no regular Yankee soldiers."

"What do you mean?"

Harriet took Melody by the hand, pulled her into the bedroom, and closed the door. "Come over here and sit down," she said, guiding her to an overstuffed chair in the nearest corner.

"What do you mean, they are no regular Yankee soldiers?" Melody asked as she eased into the soft chair.

"It's the Heglund brothers...Steve, Everett, and Keith!"

The names struck Melody like a triple slap in the face. Her features went dead-white. Her mouth quivered, and she compressed her lips to stop the quivering. The wicked Heglund brothers had murdered her brother. She had no reason to believe they would not murder her—and Harriet—too.

Melody was about to speak her fears when Harriet said, "I heard Keith say your father murdered his father. So they've been told the lie. Steve just said he hates Layne almost as much as he hates your father. It sounds like they're here to do all the damage they can."

Terror was a living thing in Melody Dalton's eyes. "Harriet," she stammered, "you know those three murdered my brother. If they find me here, they'll kill me, too! Maybe both of us!"

There were more crashing sounds downstairs.

"They'll come up here, Harriet!" Melody said, her whole body trembling. "There's no place for us to hide except the closets...and they're likely to look there for something to smash or break!"

"Look," Harriet whispered, "maybe the best thing is for me to put in an appearance before they come up here and find us. I think it'll sit better with them than if they find us hiding."

Melody's voice was hoarse with emotion, choked with the fear that chilled her blood. "Maybe, if Steve wasn't down there. But he's so wicked, I wonder if he isn't half devil!" There were more crashing sounds, followed by coarse laughter.

Harriet hugged herself, tightly gripping her upper arms. "Honey, we don't have any choice but to try. But first, let's get you back into bed."

Harriet helped Melody into the bed and covered her with a blanket. Steeling herself, she took a deep breath and said, "Here goes." Without looking back, she left the room and made her way down the hall, praying under her breath. She could hear two of the Heglund brothers in the back part of the house. The third was still in the parlor, calling to them with glee. She learned the source of his glee when she saw Everett using a bayonet to rip up Melody's over-stuffed couch.

Harriet clenched her fists against the icy dread that sought to claim her, then started down the stairs, her hand gliding shakily along the rail of the banister.

Suddenly Everett caught the movement out of the corner of his eye and stopped with the bayonet buried deep in the back of the couch. A bit stunned to see her, he blinked, then looked toward the kitchen where his brothers were demolishing dishes. "Steve! Keith! C'mere!"

Harriet continued to slowly descend the staircase with her heart drumming her rib cage.

When his brothers did not respond, Everett shouted, "Steve! Keith! Come in here!"

The noise stopped abruptly and Steve's voice filled the house, "Whattya want?"

"Come in here!" Everett repeated.

"What is it?"

"Come and see!"

Heavy footsteps were heard as Steve and Keith moved down the hall that led from the kitchen to the parlor. When they entered the parlor, they saw Everett looking toward the staircase with a wicked grin on his face.

"Well, what is it?" Steve snapped, turning to follow his brother's line of sight. When his eyes fell on Harriet, he halted in his tracks.

"Well, lookee here!" Steve sneered. "If it ain't ol' lady Smith! What're you doin' here? Don't you know ever'body's s'posed to be outta town?"

Harriet was four steps from the bottom. She stopped, and for a second or two remained immobile, holding her breath. Steeling herself again, she looked Steve square in the eye as he moved toward her, and said with a quiver in her voice, "I…am asking you to leave the house. Please. Right now."

"Why, Mrs. Smith, we can't leave here now. We've got a lot of things to do yet. Besides, why should you care? It ain't your house."

"Steve asked you what you're doin' here, lady," butted in Keith. "Why ain't you evacuated like ever'body else?"

Harriet's hand was still on the railing of the banister. She backed up a step and said, "Mrs. Dalton—Melody—is upstairs. Her baby is due next month, and she's been having some problems. She has been quite ill…and still is. Too ill to leave when everybody else evacuated. Dr. Craig said she would lose the baby if she tried to travel. I'm…staying with her to do all I can to see that she carries her child full term. I ask you again to please leave. She's had it bad enough with all the shelling yesterday. I appeal to your sense of compassion. Melody is very ill. Please don't do any more damage to her belongings."

Steve Heglund grinned wickedly, a demonic look in his eyes. "Now ain't that too bad? The daughter of my pa's murderer is sick. I think I'll have a good cry over ol' lady Dalton."

"Yeah, big brother," Keith said, "maybe we all oughtta shed some tears for her and her kid."

Everett snorted. "So Jack Reynolds's daughter is sick, eh? Well, maybe we can make her sicker! How about we go upstairs and tear up her bedroom!"

"Why, Everett," said Steve, waggling a finger at him, "you're not showin'—how did Mrs. Smith put it?—you're not showin' your sense of compassion. You know, like her old man showed for Pa when he gunned him down in cold blood."

Harriet backed up two steps and said, "Melody's father did not gun your pa down in cold blood. It was your pa who went after Jack...with the gun you three stole when you broke into the Reynolds house years ago. Jack was able to get close enough to wrestle him, and the gun went off, striking your pa in the stomach. The jury acquitted Jack of murder; it was self-defense."

Steve looked around at his brothers. "She ain't tellin' it like Ma and George told it."

"Well, who you gonna believe?" asked Everett. "This ol' biddy's lyin'."

"Sure she's lyin'!" gusted Keith. "She's Melody's friend, so naturally she's gonna lie to protect Jack's name."

"I'm not lying!" snapped Harriet. "Your pa went to Jack's house with the full intent of killing him. It backfired on him. And even if it wasn't so—even if Jack had murdered your pa—that wouldn't be Melody's fault. Why should she suffer at your hands for something she had no control over? Have you no decency at all?"

Again Steve looked around at his brothers. "Everett, you have any of that stuff?" he asked, grinning.

"What's that?"

"Decency."

"Naw. It don't pay to have none of that."

"Keith, you got any decency?"

Keith Heglund threw his head back and roared with laughter. "No, big brother, I ain't got none of that stuff."

Steve turned back to Harriet and noted that she had backed part way up the stairs. "Well, Mrs. Smith, it looks like we ain't got no decency. So I guess it's time we paid a visit to Jack's daughter."

Harriet wheeled and bounded up the stairs, lifting her skirt calf-high. Steve lunged after her, but lost his footing and fell on the stairs. His brothers were on his heels and fell on top of him. All three swore as they unscrambled. When they had gained their feet, Harriet had already reached the landing and was out of sight.

Harriet plunged into Melody's bedroom to see her frightened friend sitting up with the covers pulled tight around her neck, hollow-eyed and motionless. Harriet swung the door shut and looked for the key. There was none. "Melody, where's the key?" she asked.

"I don't know! There's never been a need to lock the door."

Harriet dashed to the overstuffed chair and began sliding it toward the door. But it was to no avail. The rapid footsteps of the Heglund brothers resounded in the hall, and suddenly the door burst open.

Harriet quickly placed herself between Melody and the three men. Her eyes were full of fire as she hissed, "Don't you dare touch her!"

Steve swore and struck her in the face with an elbow. Harriet stumbled and fell over the chair, landing on the floor.

Steve stood over Melody and said with a sneer, "I hate the name of Jack Reynolds, lady! You hear me? Your old man murdered my pa!"

Melody's insides tightened and she felt the baby move. Even her unborn child could sense the fear that was in her.

"Let me tell you who else I hate, lady. I hate that husband of yours. Since I can't get to *him*, I'll take it out on *you!*"

Harriet was on her feet again, steadying herself against the overstuffed chair. Melody glanced at her, then back at Steve Heglund as he loomed over her bed. "Get out of my house!" she said.

Steve looked around at his brothers. "Hear that, boys! The little lady with the big belly wants us out of her house!"

Harriet pushed her way between Steve and Melody's bed. "Big brave men, aren't you?" she said. "Oh, sure! You can threaten women! It would be a different story if Walter and Layne were here! You cowards—you'd be running like scared rabbits!"

Steve's mouth pulled down. He reached out and sank his fingers deep into Harriet's hair. He shook her head roughly and growled, "Get this into your skull, lady! I ain't scared of your husband or hers! And neither are my brothers!"

Harriet was doing her best not to let Steve know he was hurting her, but Melody knew he was. Her anger overrode her fear. Face blazing, she railed, "Let go of her, Steve Heglund, and get out of my house!"

Steve swore and threw Harriet to the floor, then slapped Melody's face with a stinging blow, flattening her on the bed.

"Atta boy, Steve!" laughed Keith. "Show 'em who's boss!"

Harriet scrambled to her feet, breathing hard, and pounced on Steve's back as she dug her fingernails into his eyes. Steve howled, but could not shake her loose. "Get her off me!" he screamed to his brothers.

Everett and Keith broke Harriet's hold and threw her to the floor. She went down in a heap.

Melody's voice rang with wild anger. "Leave her alone! Get out of my house!"

Steve slapped her again, flattening her on the bed as before. "Shut up, you!" he blared, rubbing at his stinging eyes.

She sat up again, her cheek bright red from the blows, and screamed, "You'll pay for this! Layne will beat you to a pulp for laying a hand on me!"

Everett and Keith stood by, waiting. They knew better than to make a hostile move before their older brother did. Steve swore at Melody, threw the covers back, and seized her by the arms. She fought him, but his strength was too great. He lifted her up and flung her across the room. Melody slammed into the wall, face-forward, the baby taking the full impact. She slid to the floor, dazed.

Steve stood over her, his teeth bared in rage. "So your fancy-pants husband will beat me to a pulp, will he? Well, let me give him somethin' to make him want me *real* bad!" As he spoke, he drew back his foot to kick her in the midsection.

Everett laid a hand on Steve's shoulder and said, "Wait a minute, big brother! You really want to get to her? I know somethin' better than kickin' her!"

"Yeah? What?"

Melody was crying in pain, and she could feel the baby squirming inside her. Blood appeared low on the front of her robe and began to spread.

"Remember that expensive piano Layne bought her?"

Steve grinned. "Yeah."

"Well, I noticed it in a room at the top of the stairs. I think it'd be heart-wrenchin' for Jack's daughter, here, to see that piano shoved through the balustrade and fall all the way to the first floor!"

"No-o-o!" Melody wailed. "Don't touch my piano! Ple-e-ase!"

"See, Steve?" Everett laughed. "I was right! It's gettin' to her already!"

"C'mon, Keith," Steve said, moving toward the door. "Let's fix that piano!"

"What about these women?" Keith asked, pausing beside Harriet.

"They ain't goin' nowhere! C'mon. Let's deal Jack's daughter some real misery!"

Melody crawled to her friend. "Harriet!" she wept. "They're going to destroy my piano!" Harriet was still too dazed to respond.

Melody whimpered as she crawled to the bed, gripped the bedstead, and painfully pulled herself to a standing position. She took a deep breath and stumbled to the door. She used the frame to steady herself, then made her way toward the music room, leaning against the wall. She could hear the Heglund brothers puffing and grunting in the room.

Melody was almost to the landing when she saw her prized piano roll through the music room door. Steve saw her bracing against the wall and said, "Watch this, woman!"

The Heglunds rolled the Steinway across the landing. It crashed into the banister, splintering it, and the front leg dropped over the edge, causing the strings to make a sharp, discordant sound. The piano slid slowly forward, then stopped, balancing dangerously.

Screaming at the Heglund brothers to stop, Melody groped her way to the landing and staggered toward Steve. In a mindless frenzy, she began beating on him with her fists. He cursed her and shoved her to the floor, then leaned against the piano. It was enough to tilt it over the edge. With a loud scraping noise, the Steinway slid off the landing and crashed to the floor below.

The Heglunds looked down and laughed.

Melody was on her hands and knees, weeping. Blood ran down her legs as she struggled to her feet and shuffled unsteadily to the edge of the landing. Tears stained her cheeks. For a long moment, she didn't move. She just stood there, staring down at her demolished Steinway with wide, disbelieving eyes. These wicked men had destroyed the most wonderful gift Layne had ever given her. A black wave of anguish surged through her. Releasing a wild, primal scream, she made a dash for Steve, intending to push him over the edge.

Harriet was now at the door of Melody's room, leaning on the frame. In horror, she saw Steve meet Melody's charge and shove her toward the edge of the landing where the piano had crashed through moments before. Melody clawed desperately at the broken banister and grasped a dangling length of railing for a second. Then it broke off in her hand, and she went screaming over the edge.

Melody landed on top of the piano, which stood at an angle. Her head struck the hard wood, knocking her unconscious. Everett and Keith drew up beside their older brother, who stood at the lip of the landing, looking down at Melody.

"Is she dead?" Keith asked.

"Naw, she's still breathin'."

"She's bleedin' pretty bad, though," Everett said.

"That's what she gets for her old man murderin' our pa. C'mon. We've done enough damage. Let's get out of here."

Harriet moved unsteadily down the hall. She reached the staircase and looked down at the horrid sight below. Melody had slid to the floor and lay in a heap beside the Steinway. The lower part of her robe was soaked with blood.

"Oh, dear God, no!" Harriet gasped as she started down the stairs.

When the Heglund brothers reached the street, a lieutenant on horseback came trotting toward them. "General Burnside is calling all the looters back to their posts. You men need to get back there as soon as possible."

"Yes sir, Lieutenant," said Steve, saluting.

The lieutenant nodded and rode away, looking for more looters.

Everett glanced back at the Dalton house. "What if she dies, Steve?"

The elder brother shrugged his shoulders and replied coldly, "So she dies. Pa's also dead, isn't he?"

"Her baby will die, too," Keith said.

Steve spit in the street. "So what? Just one less Dalton in the world. C'mon. We better get back to our posts."

TWELVE

Harriet Smith's head cleared quickly when she knelt beside her unconscious friend. Melody Dalton lay in a limp heap. Her mouth sagged open, and her breathing was shallow and irregular. There was a large bruise on the left side of her forehead that was swelling quickly and turning purple. This, however, was the least of Harriet's worries. The bleeding frightened her most.

There was no choice in the matter. Harriet was going to have to leave Melody and go for Dr. Craig. She straightened Melody out, then placed a pillow from the ripped-up couch under her head. From a linen closet down the hall she picked up several hand towels and used them to stay the flow of blood as much as possible. She then covered Melody with blankets. With shaking hand, she wrote a note telling Melody where she had gone in case she came to and found herself alone and lying on the floor. Then Harriet donned coat and scarf and dashed out the door.

The streets were deserted as Harriet ran westward toward the edge of town, the cold air assaulting her lungs. She glanced up and saw the Confederate artillery on top of Marye's Heights. They were ready for the full-fledged invasion that was coming.

"Oh, dear God," Harriet said, "don't let them start the battle till

I can get Dr. Craig. Please, Lord…let her be all right."

Harriet reached the outskirts of Fredericksburg and stopped to catch her breath. Coming toward her were several riders in gray uniforms. When they drew up, the leader touched his hatbrim and said, "Hello, ma'am. I'm Lieutenant Carlin. We're attached to General Jeb Stuart's cavalry. You really shouldn't be going into town. The Yankees have occupied it."

"I'm not going *into* town, Lieutenant," she gasped. "I'm *leaving* town."

Surprise showed on the young officer's face. "You mean you've been staying in town, ma'am?"

"Yes. During the shelling…and the looting."

"But, why, ma'am? Everyone was supposed to evacuate yesterday morning."

"Are you acquainted with Major Layne Dalton, Lieutenant?"

"Yes, ma'am. He's on Marye's Heights under General Kershaw."

"All right, then. Let me explain."

Once Lieutenant Carlin understood, he asked, "Where is Dr. Craig, ma'am?"

"He's at the Ralph Jones farm two miles southwest of town."

"All right. You go back to Mrs. Dalton. I'll send one of my men right now to fetch Dr. Craig. I'll send another up to Major Dalton and let him know what's going on."

Harriet thanked Carlin and headed back into town. She heard the lieutenant barking orders as she ran. Looking over her shoulder, she saw one rider head southwest away from town and another for Marye's Heights.

General Kershaw rubbed his stubbled jaw and said, "I'd like to let you go, Major, but this lull isn't going to last. The Yankees could attack at any minute."

"But, sir," argued Layne Dalton, "from what the sergeant said, my wife could be dying. Put yourself in my place. If it was your wife down there, wouldn't you want to go, no matter what?"

Kershaw nervously pulled at an ear. "Of course I would," he said. "But there are two reasons I'm hesitating. Number one, if the blue-bellies attack while you're en route, you could get killed real quick. Number two, I need you here to lead your men when the battle comes."

"Look at it this way, sir. What would you do if I went down in the midst of battle? You'd replace me with another officer, right?"

"Yes."

"Well, if the Federals launch their attack while I'm gone, put that man in my place. I'll get back here as soon as I can. As for the situation en route...I'll make sure I don't run into the enemy. Please, sir."

Kershaw sighed. "You drive a hard bargain, Major."

"I try, sir."

The general sighed again. "You're a good man, and this army needs you. Just be real careful, okay?"

A tight smile curved Dalton's lips. "Thank you, sir. I will."

Harriet knelt beside Melody, who had just started coming around when she returned to the house. The bleeding had subsided, for which Harriet was thankful. As she gave her friend water from a dipper, she told her that Lieutenant Duane Carlin had sent riders for Dr. Craig and Layne.

Melody looked up at Harriet and said with a tremor in her voice, "My baby's dead. I can't feel any movement."

"Now, honey, that doesn't mean the baby's dead. You're not moving right now, yourself. Both of you took the fall, and you're both a bit numb at the moment."

"I don't know what Layne will do if the baby dies, Harriet."

"Are you afraid he'll turn against God?"

"Yes. And not only that—I'm concerned about what he might try to do to the Heglund brothers. He could get himself killed."

They heard footsteps on the front porch, and the broken door squeaked open. Both women turned to see who it was.

"Layne!" Melody cried out.

Layne dashed across the parlor, knelt beside Melody, and cupped her pallid face in his hands. He kissed her tenderly.

"Doc Craig should be here soon," Harriet said, standing over them.

"I don't want Melody trying to talk," Layne said. "Can you tell me what happened? I can see that the Yankees have been here."

Harriet thought about not telling him it was the Heglund brothers who had been there. But she knew he had a right to know.

Before Harriet could speak, Layne said, "I see she's lost a lot of blood. Did you get the bleeding stopped?"

"As best I could. I don't think she's losing much now."

"And this bruise on her forehead…"

"Not a lot I could do for it. I soaked it with cold water."

"You're a gem, Harriet," he said. Then to Melody: "You and little Danny are going to be okay, honey."

Melody pressed her lips together and blinked her eyes slowly to signify her agreement. In her heart, however, she feared the baby was dead.

Looking back up at Harriet, Layne said, "Go ahead. Tell me what happened. Looks to me like Melody fell from up there."

Harriet told Layne the story as quickly and as accurately as she could, making sure he understood that it was Steve Heglund, not the other two brothers, who threw Melody across the bedroom and pushed her off the landing.

Layne was about to speak when Dr. Craig tapped on the partially open door and said, "All right if I come in?"

"Please do!" Layne exclaimed, rising to his feet.

The doctor gave Melody a quick examination as Harriet again explained what had happened. Dr. Craig rose to his feet, shaking his head, and said, "I've got to do a much more thorough examination, Layne. We need to get her upstairs on the bed."

"I'll carry her, Doctor," said Layne.

"Be very careful," warned the physician. "Her bleeding has almost stopped. I don't want it to start again. She could have some broken bones, too."

"I will," said Layne, bending over to pick her up.

He cradled Melody in his arms as he would a small child and carried her up the stairs. When Melody was comfortable on the bed, Dr. Craig said, "Layne, I need to ask you to leave the room while I work on Melody. I'll need Harriet to stay and help me."

"I understand, Doc. I'll be downstairs or out in the hall. Just call when you're finished."

Layne closed the door behind him and moved slowly down the hall toward the landing. He was feeling a mixture of emotions—wrath toward the Heglunds and icy fear for Melody and the baby. When he reached the landing, observed the broken banister, and looked down at the destroyed piano, his wrath increased.

Layne descended the stairs and assessed the damage in the rest of the house. His hands trembled with the desire to lay hold of the Heglund brothers, especially the brutal Steve.

Nearly an hour had passed and Layne was in the parlor placing books back in the bookcase. Out of the corner of his eye, he saw movement on the stairs. Dr. David Craig was descending slowly, a gray, dismal look on his face.

Biting his lower lip, the doctor reached the last few stairs, paused, and said solemnly, "I'm sorry, Layne. Melody went into labor right after you left the room. The baby's dead. It was a boy."

Dr. Craig's words were like fists striking Layne Dalton in the chest and stomach, leaving no breath in him. The blood drained from his disbelieving face. His mind was in a wild, maddening spin. He began to shake, every muscle and fiber in his body strung tight.

"It was the Heglund brothers who hurt my wife and killed my son, Doc," Layne finally managed to say through clenched teeth. "I'm going to—"

"Layne, listen to me!" cut in Dr. Craig. "Right now, Melo—"

"No! You listen to me! I'm going to kill all three of those…those wretched Heglunds, Doc! They're going to pay for what they did here!"

"Layne, listen to me! Right now Melody needs you! That baby was hers, too, and she's bearing the physical *and* emotional pain of its loss. You've got to calm yourself and go up there to her."

Layne drew a deep breath and got a grip on himself. "Okay…okay, Doc. You're right. I'll go up to her. But the day will come when I will make those murderers wish they'd never been born."

Dr. Craig took hold of the major's muscular arm and mounted the stairs with him. As they made their way upward, Craig said, "I'm sure you have to get back to your unit as soon as you can, Layne."

"Yes, sir."

"I'll take care of burying the baby."

"Thank you, Doc. I appreciate it."

When the two men entered the bedroom, Dr. Craig picked up the tiny bundle wrapped in a sheet and hurried out the door, saying he would return in a moment.

Layne eyed the bundle, biting hard on his lips. Then he moved toward the bed, where Harriet sat on the edge, holding Melody's hands.

"I'll leave you two alone," said Harriet, standing to her feet. "You need some privacy in your grief."

When the door closed, Melody set tearful eyes on her husband and said, "Darling, I'm sorry."

Layne stroked her cheek tenderly. "It's not your fault. Are you okay?"

"Yes. Dr. Craig says he can't find any broken bones."

Layne leaned over, wrapped her in his arms, and held her. They wept together for several minutes. When they drew apart, Layne sat on the edge of the bed, looking sadly into her eyes.

"I'll give you another son, darling. You'll still have your little boy," Melody said, drying her tears with the bedsheet.

Layne worked up a wan smile and was about to respond when Dr. Craig tapped on the door and said, "May I come in?"

"Yes, please do," Layne said.

"Sorry to barge in," the physician said, "but I do have to get back to the Jones place so others who need me can find me. As far as I can tell, Melody's all right, Layne. No broken bones. You can both be thankful that the piano came to rest at the angle it did. I believe it was the angle that helped break her fall. If she'd hit it flat, who knows how many bones she might have broken."

"That's something to be thankful for," Layne said.

"We all know there's a bloody battle pending," the doctor continued, "so I recommend you get these two women to Bertha Shrewsberry's place as soon as possible."

Dr. Craig mixed some powders, saying Melody would need something to sedate her and help ease her pain. Then Layne and the doctor left the house together. Layne returned shortly with an army wagon and drove the women to Bertha Shrewsberry's house in the country. Bertha received them gladly, and as Layne carried Melody, she led them to the room that would be Melody's for the duration of their stay.

Melody was a bit groggy from the powders administered by Dr. Craig, but she patted her husband's cheek as he gently laid her on the bed.

"You rest real good, won't you?" he asked.

"Yes," she said. "And I'll be praying for you during the battle."

Melody saw fire leap into her husband's eyes at the mention of prayer. She took his hand and said slowly, "Darling, don't let yourself become embittered toward the Lord. Our little son is in heaven now. He's with the Lord Jesus. There's no better place for him to be."

Layne gripped her hand tightly and looked out the window, staring vacantly at the setting sun.

"Layne, only those who put their trust in Jesus are going to heaven. If you want to see Danny there, you will have to turn to Jesus for salvation."

Layne Dalton was so filled with grief for his son and with hatred for the Heglunds that he barely heard her.

"Layne? Are you listening to me? Layne…?"

Slowly, Layne lowered his eyes to look at his wife. "One day, sooner or later, I'll have my vengeance on those filthy vermin!"

Harriet saw the fear that settled in Melody's eyes. She moved close to the vengeful man and said, "Layne, you could get yourself killed going after the Heglunds. God will make them pay for what they did."

"It's not up to God. It's up to *me*," Layne said.

Bertha Shrewsberry's house had a Bible in every room. Harriet picked the one up off the small table beside the bed and said, "Layne, let me show you something."

Layne was not interested in what Harriet was about to show him, but his gentlemanly sense of courtesy held him silent.

"Here," said Harriet. "Romans 12:19. The apostle Paul says, *Dearly beloved, avenge not yourselves, but rather give place to wrath: for it is written, Vengeance is mine; I will repay, saith the Lord.* Layne, God is saying that we are not to avenge ourselves…that vengeance is His. *He* will repay the wrongdoers."

Layne Dalton stood like a rock, not giving an inch. "I mean no offense to you, Harriet, but this is one time when vengeance will be *mine!*"

With that, he leaned over and kissed Melody on the forehead, the tip of her nose, and on the lips, and said, "I must get back to my post, sweetheart."

Melody tried to focus on his face as she said, "I'll be praying the Lord will bring you back safely. I love you, darling."

"I love you, too," he said. "Take care of yourself, won't you?"

"Yes."

Layne thanked Harriet and Bertha for their help, then drove away in the army wagon.

Darkness was falling as Layne approached the campfire where General Kershaw stood with several of his officers and enlisted men. Sergeant Kirkland spotted Layne first and dashed to him. "Hello, sir," he said, saluting. "General Kershaw told us about your wife. How is she, sir? And the baby?"

Dalton continued walking toward the campfire, face grim. "Not so good, Sergeant. I'll explain it to General Kershaw and you can listen."

"Ah, Major Dalton!" General Kershaw said as Layne drew up with Kirkland beside him. "I'm relieved that the hostilities didn't begin while you were gone, and I'm glad to see you back. How are Mrs. Dalton and the baby?"

Layne gave Kershaw a solemn look and said, "Melody is all right, but…but the baby…the baby is dead."

"No. What happened?" Kershaw asked.

With tears in his eyes, Layne quickly told what had happened. When he was done, the soldiers gathered close and spoke their condolences. Word was carried to the men of Dalton's unit, and they gathered to him, wishing to share their sympathy with him in his loss. While they were doing so, Generals Lee and Longstreet came along, and General Kershaw told them the story. They also offered Dalton their condolences.

General Kershaw then turned to General Lee in the presence of the men gathered near the fire and said, "What do you think, sir? What has held the Federals back from attacking? Do you think they will attack tomorrow?"

Lee had ridden out in early afternoon with General Stonewall Jackson to reconnoiter the enemy's position and to brace up Jackson's division for the impending attack. Jackson's troops would engage the Federals first, since they were positioned at strategic spots along the Rappahannock and at the stone wall that ran along the base of the hills that made up Marye's Heights.

Standing close to Lee was Major Robert Stiles, of Longstreet's division, a gifted writer who had chosen on his own to keep a log of the events at Fredericksburg. Stiles angled his paper toward the firelight and wrote as Lee spoke.

"The reason General Burnside didn't attack today was because he wasn't ready. However, I feel confident he will be ready by morning. My reconnaissance mission has erased any doubts whatsoever about where Burnside is going to attack us. By the way the Federals are positioned, I am sure they are going to try to turn our right side down there at Hamilton's Crossing with their artillery and cavalry...and come straight at us with the massive infantry they have assembled out there in the fields to the north. I have directed General Jackson to summon Generals Hill and Early and their brigades from their downstream positions. They must bolster the rest of General Jackson's division when the attack comes.

"We must be ready up here on the Heights to cover General Jackson's troops with cannonballs and bullets. I have an idea that stone wall down there is going to get a real blood-soaking before this is over."

Layne Dalton lay in his bedroll under the cold night sky and wrestled with his troubled emotions. He was concerned for Melody, that she recover from losing the baby. He wept for the loss of his little Danny. And his blood boiled with wrath toward Steve Heglund and the two brothers who dared assault his wife and property.

"God," Layne whispered, "I don't know why You let those...those men take the life of my little boy, but You did. I don't understand it. They tell me You're a good God...and I'm not saying You're not. You know every human heart, so I'm not telling You anything You don't already know. I think You should have kept Steve Heglund and his brothers out of my house this morning. But since You didn't, I'm going to get my revenge. *An eye for an eye and a tooth for a tooth,* Your Bible says. No matter how long it takes, I'm going to kill those slithering snakes for taking my son from me."

The cold night breeze blew over Marye's Heights, whining in the trees. It took Major Layne Dalton till nearly 3:00 A.M. to fall asleep.

THIRTEEN

Dawn came on Saturday morning, December 13, 1862, with a heavy fog hanging low on the Rappahannock River and on the battered, deserted town.

When Major Layne Dalton awakened amid the trees on Marye's Heights, he found Sergeant Kirkland sitting on the cold ground next to him. "How long have you been sitting there?" Dalton asked.

"Only about a half-hour, sir. I just wanted to make sure you were all right. Did you sleep okay?"

"Not too good," replied the major, sitting up and stretching his arms. "Took me quite a while to get to sleep to begin with, then I kept waking up."

"I can't say that I understand, sir, because I've never been a father, and I've never had a child die. But I want you to know that I sorrow with you in your grief."

Dalton stood and picked up his campaign hat, which lay close by. Like everyone else atop Marye's Heights, he slept in his uniform without removing his boots. He placed his hat on his head and gave Kirkland a weak smile. "You're quite a friend, Sergeant. I want you to know that I deeply appreciate your kind thoughts."

Both men noticed a small, slight figure in gray coming toward them. They recognized Private Benny Hay, who was in Dalton's unit and, like Kirkland, had taken a special liking to the major. Hailing from South Carolina, Hay was eighteen, small and frail, but he had shown great courage under fire in previous battles.

Hay saluted Dalton and nodded at Kirkland, then said, "Major Dalton, sir, I was on sentry duty last night when you came in, so I didn't know about your loss until after you had retired. I just want to say, sir, that I'm sorry about your little baby."

Dalton managed a slight smile. "Thank you, Private," he said softly. "I appreciate your taking the time to come and say so."

Hay turned and looked at the fog below. "From what I'm told, we'll be fighting the blue-bellies today soon's that fog lifts."

"I don't think there's any doubt about it," replied Dalton. "General Lee says this will be a bloody day."

"Well," spoke up Kirkland, "let's hope it won't be *our* blood."

"No sense worrying about it," said the major. "Worrying won't change a thing. Guess we'd better get our breakfast down. We're going to need all the strength we can muster here in a little while."

At ten o'clock, the sun was burning the last of the fog away, and both armies were set for battle.

Atop Marye's Heights, Major Dalton conferred with Generals Longstreet and Kershaw, then left to have a talk with his captains. As he walked along the edge of the trees, he came upon Major Robert Stiles, paper pad in hand, writing as he stood facing the massive force of the Army of the Potomac in the open fields to the north.

"'Morning, Major," said Stiles.

"'Morning, Major," echoed Dalton. "Writing about what you see, I presume."

"More about what I see in my mind than with my eyes at the moment," Stiles replied.

"May I take a look at it?"

"Certainly," nodded Stiles, and handed him the pad.

Dalton read it aloud. "We are about to enter into the arena of battle. I think of the gladiators of old, entering into the amphitheater in the presence of Caesar. *Morituri te salutamus!* 'We who are about to die salute thee!'"

Stiles looked into Dalton's eyes without a word.

"I'm afraid these graphic words are also portentous, Major," Dalton said. "Like General Lee, I think this is going to be a bloody day."

Before the fog lifted, the Confederates on the lofty hills around Fredericksburg could not see the force assembled in front of them, but they could hear a band playing, the muffled sound of troops in motion, the rumble of cannons and caissons being moved about, and the jingle of harnesses. Nerves were stretched tight.

General Robert E. Lee, as was customary for top military commanders, had retired to a relatively safe spot in the hayloft of the Marye barn. The door of the loft faced the stone wall at the bottom of the hill, giving Lee a perfect view of the town and the potential battle site.

General Jackson was at the lower elevation with his troops, standing near the four-foot-high stone wall. Outside the wall was the sunken road. It was a natural entrenchment and afforded protection for three thousand of Jackson's riflemen, arranged in ranks four-deep behind it. Lee had placed Longstreet's artillery and infantry on the heights above Jackson's infantry so the ground in front of the stone wall would be subjected to a murderous crossfire. Lee thought of what Longstreet's artillery chief had said earlier that morning: "A chicken could not live on that field when we open up on it."

Lee studied the men along the wall with his field glasses, picking out General Jackson. He smiled to himself. *Fitting*, he thought. *Dubbed "Stonewall" at the Bull Run battle, there he stands like a stone wall, preparing his men to fight the enemy at the stone wall!*

Lee let his gaze drift to the woods off to his right. There at the edge of the trees stood Longstreet. The command to commence fire for both artillery and infantry lay on his shoulders. Longstreet's command would set in motion a conflict that would cost many lives. Lee hated the thought, but this was war. Men bleed and die in war.

General James Longstreet felt fully the weight that lay on his shoulders. He knew the Union army would begin its advance soon at the command of General Burnside. Along with the advance of the foot soldiers and cavalry would come the command to open fire with the artillery socketed in the hills across the river.

Longstreet would have to trust his experience and his instincts for the proper moment to tell the men at his number one cannon when to fire the first shot, signaling the entire Confederate force to commence fire. Longstreet was of the "old school." He believed it best to let the advancing enemy get so close "you can see the whites of his eyes" before opening fire.

Longstreet took in the scene below through his binoculars. There were dazzling portions of snow on the surrounding fields. The sun forced its sharp light through the remaining patches of fog and intensified the reflections from fifty thousand bayonets. Interminable columns of infantry stood in ranks in the open fields. Longstreet could make out Union officers in dark-blue uniforms rushing from point to point.

Field artillery was whisked into position like so many children's toys. Rank and file, footmen and horsemen, small arms and field ordnance presented a sight to see.

Suddenly Longstreet heard a Yankee bugle and recognized its message. General Burnside, from his position on the opposite bank of the Rappahannock, had just given the command that would put the giant Army of the Potomac in motion. The dark-blue columns of infantry flowed toward the waiting Confederate lines like the massive waves of a steadily advancing sea.

Longstreet's attention was drawn to General Jackson, who now rode his horse to a small hill within a few hundred yards of Hamilton's Crossing, from where he would command his division. General Lee had ordered him to stay with the bulk of his men at the stone wall until the Federals began their attack. Jackson had a certain charisma about him that instilled in men the courage and the will to fight. The Rebels at the wall would need all the encouragement they could get.

Longstreet could feel the tension come alive in his men all along the lines atop Marye's Heights. They were waiting impatiently for the command to open fire. Too early.

The atmosphere on that cold winter's day was tight and fierce. From his position on the Heights, Longstreet's eyes were glued on the advancing army. It was a military panorama the grandeur of which he had never seen.

On they came, in beautiful rank and order, as if on parade—a marching forest of steel and hundreds of colorful regimental flags, contrasting with the dark blue of the uniforms and the dull russet hue of the wintry fields through which they marched. Somewhere in the midst of it all was a military band, the brass instruments sounding sharp and clear above the rumble of drums.

Suddenly it seemed that a tremendous thunderstorm had burst over Fredericksburg as three hundred Union artillery opened fire from Stafford Heights and its flanking hills across the river.

An instant howling of shot and shell hurled against the Confederate troops along the river and on the semi-circle of hills south and west of Fredericksburg. Scores of missiles crashed through the woods atop Marye's Heights, breaking down trees and scattering branches and splinters in all directions.

General Lee was on his feet, along with his aids, in the open door of the hayloft. The Yankee missiles were overshooting the Confederate artillery and infantry lines, but soon they would find the range. Lee wondered why Longstreet didn't give the command to commence fire.

General Kershaw dashed up to Longstreet, who was still peering through his binoculars at the sea of blue. "Sir!" gasped Kershaw. "Pardon me, but shouldn't we be firing back at those Yankee guns?"

"We will shortly," Longstreet said without removing the field glasses from his eyes. "They're still trying to find the range. We're safe for a few more minutes. I want to let those lines of infantry get a little closer before we start cutting them down, and I want to unleash all our fire power on the whole army of blue-bellies at the same time."

A Yankee shell whistled over their heads and struck in the woods behind them, exploding and felling a slender young oak.

"They're finding the range, sir," said Kershaw.

"Just need to get those blue-bellies down there in the fields a little closer, General," Longstreet said casually.

All along the Marye's Heights line, the men-in-gray hunkered down as missiles zoomed over their heads and exploded behind them. They were coming closer.

The men in Major Dalton's regiment were getting jittery. One of the riflemen called out from his position behind a tree, "Major Dalton! Do you suppose something is wrong with General Longstreet? Why isn't he giving the command to commence fire?"

"There's nothing wrong with him," Dalton shouted back. "He knows what he's doing. Just sit tight, everyone! We'll have more Yankees down in the first rush if we do it General Longstreet's way!"

The same kind of tension was mounting on the lower elevation, where Stonewall Jackson's division of infantry and artillery waited.

On came the men-in-blue, wondering themselves when the Confederates were going to open up on them. Meanwhile, their artillery across the river continued the cannonade with unabated fury, giving a background of fleecy, blue-white smoke to the animated scene.

General Longstreet, fully aware of the tension among his troops, continued to peer through his field glasses. Jackson's front cannons on the lower level were loaded with canister, and he wanted the Yankees close enough that the first burst of canister fire would take out several hundred.

"Come on! Come on, you blue-bellies!" he said in a half-whis-per.

General Kershaw knew the long-awaited moment was upon them. Wheeling, he ran back to his men, saying, "Get ready! He's about to give the command!"

The words were hardly out of Kershaw's mouth when Longstreet shouted the command to the signal cannon to fire.

Thunder rolled along the Confederate lines, sending deadly canister whistling and plowing into the dense columns of oncoming soldiers. The effect was devastating. Men were being blown in every direction, most of them dead before their bodies stopped rolling.

The rattle of musketry from behind the stone wall and atop Marye's Heights punctuated the deep roar of the cannons, filling the valley with an ear-splitting din.

The deadly accuracy of the Rebel artillery, backed by the sudden unleashing of thousands of muskets, seemed to paralyze the Union troops momentarily. Then in terror, they stampeded.

Confusion reigned for several minutes. It was a scene of blood, smoke, fire, and death. Soon, however, several Union batteries moved into position north and west of Marye's Heights. Together they fought back, concentrating tremendous fire on the Confederate positions.

Above the tumult could be heard the wild cheering of the attacking hosts in blue and the defiant, blood-curdling yell of the men-in-gray. The battle of Fredericksburg was under way in full force.

General Burnside had sent some five thousand footmen into the town the night before. He held them back for a while after the battle began, then sent word for them to pour out of Fredericksburg in close ranks and attack the Rebels behind the stone wall.

It was a horrible carnage. The Confederate artillery and musket fire that opened up as the Yankees emerged from the town was frighteningly lethal. Line after line of brave Union soldiers moved forward in strict order. Some leaned into the fearful crossfire as if advancing against a blizzard wind. They fell dead and wounded in droves.

Across the river, General Burnside stood amid a thick stand of huge oak trees and observed the wholesale slaughter of the first blue wave. Flanking him were Colonel Adelbert Ames and Lieutenant Colonel Joshua L. Chamberlain of the Twentieth Maine Regiment, a part of the Fifth Corps held in reserve on the east side of the river.

Colonel Ames, commander of the Twentieth Maine, was unhappy to be kept in reserve. He was a fighter, and he was eager to get himself and his men into the thick of it. Ames had been seriously wounded in the Battle of Bull Run a year-and-a-half earlier, and had received a Presidential Commendation for gallantry in that battle. He had done little fighting since.

Chamberlain, who was second in command of the Twentieth Maine, was likewise eager to get into the fight. His regiment had been held in reserve a few weeks earlier at the battle of Antietam and had seen limited action. The Twentieth Maine was champing at the bit.

Chamberlain turned to Burnside and said, "Sir, you have the entire Fifth Corps in reserve, here. I'm sure Colonel Ames will agree that in view of what's happening over there, our regiment is more than ready to cross the river and get into the fight."

"Whenever you're of a mind to send some of the reserves over there, sir, we'd sure like to be first," Ames concurred.

"I'll keep that in mind, Colonels," Burnside said. "We've just lost a lot of men, but I'm not ready to send any reserves as yet."

The Union troops behind the first charging lines stumbled over the dead under the scorching fire that was coming from behind the stone wall and the top of Marye's Heights. Long waves of men-in-blue pressed forward, firing their muskets. When one line halted to reload, another would move past them, overreaching their comrades' forward positions, trying gallantly to break the enemy line. Their only hope of success was to use their massive numbers to simply overwhelm Robert E. Lee's smaller army.

Huge clouds of smoke drifted over the plains, hills, and town as the firing increased. The roar was deafening. Shot and shell screeched in maddening sounds. The Confederates cannonballs came thicker and faster, dropping with uncanny accuracy into the midst of the tightly packed columns. It seemed that no Yankee could live through such firepower, but the endless waves kept coming.

At about 2:30 in the afternoon, Confederate cannonade set the high winter grass on fire at several points. The flames, quickened by a light breeze that swept down over the valley, spread rapidly in every direction. Agonizing screams and despairing cries came from the unfortunate wounded left lying in the path of the flames. They struggled vainly to flee. All over the burning fields they were crawling, stumbling, falling, overcome by pain and fire and smoke. They begged for help, but no one could help them.

At Bertha Shrewsberry's country house some three miles from the scene of carnage, the widow and Harriet Smith sat beside the bed where Melody Dalton lay. Melody was experiencing pain, but this was minor discomfort compared to the agony of soul she was feeling as the sounds of the distant guns rattled the windows of the house.

The women had spent much time in prayer together, and Bertha had also spoken many words of encouragement to Melody and Harriet concerning the hand of the Lord on their husbands. They discussed Psalm 91:1, and Harriet's note in the margin of her Bible: *Safety is not the absence of danger, but the presence of God.*

"We saw that when those Yankee shells were falling all around us," said Harriet. "Even though our house next door was hit and demolished, the Lord was with us."

"Praise the Lord for His sheltering hand," Bertha said.

Melody looked up from the pillow with tears in her eyes. "Bertha...Harriet..."

"Yes, honey?" said the older woman.

"Could we have another time of prayer right now? I want to ask the Lord not only for Layne's safety...but for Layne to come to Jesus."

The three women joined hands and prayed.

At about three o'clock, General Burnside decided it was time to send some of his reserves into the battle. Several of his units had almost reached the stone wall, but had been turned back. Burnside knew he could never hope to win the battle unless his army got past the wall and up the slopes to the top of Marye's Heights.

Burnside called his Fifth Corps officers to him and ordered that First, Second, and Third Brigades make ready to cross the river. The Twentieth Maine Regiment was part of the Third Brigade. Within minutes the three brigades of cavalry and infantry were lined up at the two pontoon bridges that bobbed in the water at the riverbank. A bugle trilled, and the Union troops started across the floating bridges.

It took Stonewall Jackson's and James Longstreet's artillery only minutes to see what was happening at the river. Quickly, they turned some of their guns on the bridges and opened fire.

They did not have the range at first. Some of the cannonballs fell short, exploding as they hit the river bottom and sending great gushers in every direction. Other cannonballs sailed just above the soldiers' heads. The waves caused by the exploding shells made the pontoons rock and sway. Men and animals struggled to keep their balance. The horses were wild-eyed with fear and fought their bits.

The entire Twentieth Maine was across the river before Lee's artillery began finding the bridges. The troops who had made it across made their way through the streets, their determined faces pointed toward the stone wall and Marye's Heights. When they reached the plains at the edge of Fredericksburg, they could see the terrible toll the Confederate artillery fire had taken—all around them were bodies and parts of bodies.

The fields spread before them were now a melee of mangled men and horses, living and dead, wreathed in powder smoke. Wounded soldiers, with the aid of others, streamed from the fields in search of cover. They yelled words of encouragement and warning to the men who had just come across the river.

The sun went down while what was left of Burnside's three fresh brigades slowly picked their way across the fields toward the stone wall. They leaped over fences, pushed through hedges, avoided the bodies of the dead and living, and joined their comrades on the front lines.

The battle went on briefly until muzzle flames shone in the gathering darkness. And finally the firing on both sides stopped.

FOURTEEN

A s darkness fell and the temperature dropped, a mist rose from the Rappahannock and was carried by an icy breeze across the land. The moon was rising, trying to force its silver rays through the mist.

General Robert E. Lee was at the crest of Marye's Heights, assessing the damage from the day's battle. General James Longstreet reported that many Confederate soldiers had been killed and wounded amid the trees atop the hill, and General Thomas J. Jackson reported many casualties among his troops on the lower level. His artillerymen and infantry that flanked the stone wall had suffered more than the riflemen behind the wall, though there were many men at the wall who lay dead and wounded. The cavalry stationed along the river bank had also sustained some casualties.

Major Layne Dalton stood near Lee, along with General Joseph Kershaw. They listened as Jackson described his casualties, and they could hear the moaning and crying of their wounded comrades.

Lee turned to Kershaw and said, "General, have your men carry water to the wounded back there in the trees, and see what they can do to alleviate their suffering."

"They're already doing that, sir," replied Longstreet.

Turning to Jackson, Lee said, "How about down below, General?"

"We're doing what we can, sir," said Jackson, "but we do have a problem. Many of our men fell over the wall after they were hit. We've probably got a couple dozen who are lying there wounded. The Yankees have a line not more than fifty yards from the wall. With what moonlight is filtering through the fog, any men I send over that wall would be perfect targets. I can't sacrifice men in order to give aid to the wounded."

The other officers who stood around could see the concern in Lee's eyes as the cries of the wounded carried up the slopes.

Major Dalton moved close to Lee and said, "Pardon me, General..."

"Yes, Dalton?"

"Sir, I think some of the cries are coming from wounded Yankees out there between the wall and that Federal line. Seems to me the Yankees are probably wanting to get help to their wounded as much as we are to ours. Would you give me permission to go down there and see if I can talk the Yankees into a truce so we can both get to our wounded?"

Lee frowned and said, "Truce, eh? You might get your head shot off while you're trying to talk those blue-bellies into it."

"I really don't think so, sir. I'm sure it's snipers they're worried about right now, too."

Sergeant Richard Rowland Kirkland and Private Benny Hay had brought more wood for the fire and heard Dalton's words to General Lee. They stood looking on as Lee ran his gaze over the faces of Longstreet, Jackson, and Kershaw and asked, "What do you men think?"

Each general agreed that the major should be given permission to proceed.

"All right, Major," Lee said. "Go down there and see if you can work out a truce. But be careful."

"I will, sir," nodded Dalton.

Just then Sergeant Kirkland and Private Hay moved up and Kirkland said to Dalton, "Major, sir…"

"Yes?"

"Private Hay and I would like to volunteer to go with you. Just in case those Yankees decide to take a shot at you."

Dalton grinned. "Sergeant, there are plenty of General Jackson's men down there. If any trouble starts, they'll pitch in."

"I don't doubt that, sir," said Kirkland, "but those are General Jackson's men. Private Hay and I believe there ought to be at least a couple of your own men with you."

Dalton looked at Lee, who smiled his approval.

"All right," said the major. "I'll take you two 'bodyguards' with me."

Moments later, the trio reached the bottom of the hill and approached the Confederate troops who huddled in the cold behind the long curved wall. Brigadier General Thomas Cobb of the Georgia Brigade saw them coming and moved to meet them.

"Is there something I can do for you, Major?" Cobb said, keeping his voice low.

"I'm on a special mission with General Lee's permission, sir. Sergeant Kirkland and Private Hay, here, volunteered to come with me. I'm going to try to talk the Yankees out there into a truce so we can get to our wounded men, and they can get to theirs."

"Jolly good idea," said Cobb, smiling. "I hope it works."

"Well, we're about to find out."

"We'll be ready to move over the wall if you can get 'em to agree to it, Major," Cobb called after him.

As they drew near the wall, Dalton bent low and said, "Keep your heads down. Those blue-bellies might start shooting if they see movement over here."

Dalton stooped down and peered over the wall toward the Federal troops, barely visible across the body-strewn field. The moans and cries of the wounded tore at Dalton's heart.

He cupped his hands to his mouth and shouted, "Hey, Yankees! Can you hear me?"

Calls for help came from the wounded. Beyond them, across the misty field, a voice answered back, "Yeah! We can hear you, Johnny Reb! You wanting to surrender?"

"Never! But I have a proposition for you. I'd like to talk to your highest ranking officer present. I am Major Layne Dalton, speaking under the authority of General Robert E. Lee."

"Most of our officers are farther back, Major," came the reply. "But if you'll hold on, I'll get the closest one."

"I'll stay right here."

Some three minutes passed, then a different voice came across the field. "Major Dalton...?"

"Yes!"

"I am Lieutenant Colonel Joshua Chamberlain, Twentieth Maine. What's your proposition?"

"I hear many of your wounded crying for help. We have the same thing here close to the wall. How about a truce until dawn to allow us to help our fallen men? Fair enough?"

"Fair enough," came Chamberlain's reply. "Speaking for Major General Burnside, the truce is on until dawn."

"Thank you, Colonel!"

"Thank you, Major! And give my regards to General Lee."

Moments later, Dalton stood before General Lee, announcing the truce agreement. Lee commended him for making it work and commanded Longstreet and Jackson to take advantage of the all-night truce and bury their dead.

Ghostlike figures of Yankee soldiers moved about on the open field in front of the stone wall, caring for their wounded and picking up their dead. The carnage suffered by the Union army was devastating.

Along the front of the wall, wounded Confederates were given water, then hoisted over the wall with caring hands and taken to the top of the hill for further care.

Confederate supply wagons carried picks and shovels to the Rebels who shivered in the cold night air, and hundreds warmed themselves by digging a common grave along the south side of the hills. The fog grew thicker by the time the long grave was deep enough, and though it was too dark to identify the dead, their gray-clad bodies were sadly placed in the grave and covered over.

The next morning was Sunday, December 14. Dawn came over a land covered with massive patches of fog, and with it, the end of the truce. On both sides, riflemen and cannoneers waited at their posts, and officers stood by to give their battle commands.

The day was only minutes old when the Union left opened up on the Confederate right near Hamilton's Crossing, where General Jackson was situated. The view from the wall and atop Marye's Heights was obstructed by the fog, but it soon began to lift, and the battle was underway in force.

From his perch in the door of the hayloft, General Lee was amazed to see the size of the force coming toward him. The immense army moved like a huge blue serpent about to encompass the Rebel force and crush it in its folds. The lines advanced at double-quick pace, and suddenly they opened fire.

The Union artillery cut loose from both sides of the river at the same time, and the command came from General Longstreet for the Confederate guns to unleash. Flame and smoke fringed Marye's Heights along its forward base, and death's dreadful work had begun once more.

The first wave of blue was repulsed after nearly thirty minutes, and the Union lines retreated, leaving their dead and wounded on the fields. From the stone wall and from the crest of Marye's Heights, the Confederate forces sent volley after volley after the retreating Federals.

Only a few minutes passed, then came a fresh wave of blue.

Confederate cannons, canister, and bullets cut great gaps in the Union lines, but it seemed their supply of new troops was endless. They just kept coming.

Lee studied the battle through his field glasses and scrubbed a shaky hand over his face. How long could his dwindling forces hold up against such overwhelming odds?

The fog soon dissipated completely, and under the cold winter sun, the battle continued in all its horror. As the bloody day wore on, the Union troops made indents on the Confederates that flanked the stone wall. Many Rebel prisoners were taken.

The repeated thrusts of the massive Union waves were slowly thinning Jackson's troops. General Longstreet studied the situation through his binoculars. He was not surprised when General Lee moved up beside him and said, "General, I think it's time to send some of this infantry on the hill down the slopes. One of these times, the Union thrust is going to overtake our men at the wall. They're going to need help."

"I was about to order just that, sir," Longstreet replied.

Lee returned to his hayloft, and within ten minutes, General Longstreet was flanked by Major Generals McLaws, Hood, and Anderson, as well as Brigadier General Kershaw. Together they observed ten thousand men-in-gray as they descended the slopes of Marye's Heights.

The first Rebel wave was within forty yards of the stone wall when the Federals suddenly created a wide breach in the Confederate line and poured over the wall with wild, blood-chilling yells. While many Yankees fell, the majority set their sights on taking the hill and raced up to meet the oncoming Rebels.

Union artillery that had been concentrating on the stone wall and the slopes above it suddenly went silent when they saw their own men scrambling over the wall.

Bayonets flashed and bullets flew when the two infantries met on the slopes. More Federals came from the woods and fields. The battle was fierce at the wall and grew worse up the slope as the Confederates tried to defend their hill and keep the determined Yankees from taking it.

Marye's grassy slopes were dotted with oak trees. Men on both sides used the trees as shields as they fired, reloaded, and fired again into the melee, cutting down enemy soldiers in the midst of bayonet and hand-to-hand conflict.

Hours passed as the battle continued, the Rebels holding the Yankees at about the halfway point. Suddenly a Union bugle sounded from somewhere outside the stone wall, and the Yankees made a hasty retreat toward the bottom of the hill. Weary, worn, and battered, the Rebels let them go and slowly began ascending the steep slopes toward the crest of Marye's Heights.

Just as the Yankees reached the wall, their artillery began to bombard the exhausted Rebels. Layne Dalton was two-thirds of the way up when suddenly his attention was drawn down the slope where Rebels were being blown into eternity. Even fallen, wounded Yankees were dying in the barrage.

Dalton's line of sight focused on young Private Benny Hay some eighty or ninety yards below, wandering in circles. His hands were outstretched and his face was blackened with powder. He was blind.

Dalton wheeled his mount and raced down the slope toward Benny. He intended to grab Benny's frail body and carry him to safety at the top of the hill. As Dalton drew near, the blinded Rebel soldier was stumbling toward a cluster of naked-limbed oak trees.

On the opposite side of the stone wall, the Union soldiers gleefully observed the rain of fire on the fatigued Confederates struggling to reach the crest of Marye's Heights. Among them were the Heglund brothers, cheering with the others as they watched the Rebels suffering and dying. They had spotted Layne Dalton earlier, and Steve was keeping an eye on him. When the major suddenly put his horse to a gallop and charged down the slope, Steve shouted, "Look, boys!

Looks like Dalton's gonna try'n rescue that Rebel up there by those trees!"

Dalton, jaw set with determination, dodged bodies dead and alive, Rebel and Yankee. He was almost to Benny Hay when a Yankee shell exploded at Benny's feet and killed him instantly.

Dalton skidded his mount to a halt beneath the oak trees where Benny met his death. Two more shells came shrieking out of the sky and burst into flames and smoke. One of them was close enough to send a load of shrapnel into the chest, neck, and face of Dalton's horse. The other exploded at the base of one of the large oak trees, toppling it.

The concussion of the dual explosions stunned Dalton. His mind was barely clear enough to react. He tried to avoid being pinned under the horse as it went down, but was unable to clear himself. The oak fell on top of horse and rider, and a limb struck the major's head, knocking him unconscious. He lay with one leg under the dead animal, covered with the branches of the tree.

From behind the wall, the Yankee soldiers prepared for another attack. Abruptly the Union bombardment stopped, and with a wild yell, the Yankees went over the stone wall, guns blazing.

Atop Marye's Heights, Longstreet ordered a fresh unit of Rebels out of the woods and down the slopes to meet the enemy. Within moments there was fierce hand-to-hand fighting once again. The fighting went on for about an hour on Marye's blood-soaked slopes. The Rebels were outnumbered by nearly two-to-one, and for a while it looked like they would be conquered. But they gallantly fought back until they began to drive the Yankees toward the stone wall. The tide was turning for the Confederates.

From a position General Burnside had taken on the second floor of a warehouse at the edge of Fredericksburg, he saw the fierce Rebel forces driving his army back. He immediately sent word to sound the retreat. He felt sure the Rebels were tired enough that they would draw back for rest. While he allowed his men to rest, he would bring up fresh reserves for a renewed attack. There were about two hours of daylight left. He wanted to hit them one more time before dark.

The lower inclines of Marye's Heights were covered with the wreckage of battle—dead men in blue, dead men in gray. Amid them were the wounded of both North and South, some moaning in pain, others crying out, shell-shocked, bleeding, and begging for water.

The Yankee soldiers implored their officers to do something for the wounded, but were told nothing could be done. If they tried, the Rebel sharpshooters would pick them off. Some argued that they should negotiate another truce, and a request was sent to General Burnside. But the general refused, saying they must hit the Rebel forces on Marye's Heights one more time before dark. As much as he disliked the situation, he could not allow time to help the wounded Yankees.

High above on Marye's Heights, the Rebels prepared for another assault, knowing Burnside was not through. He wanted the victory and would send his massive forces yet again.

Sergeant Richard Rowland Kirkland stood at the edge of the trees, looking down at the wounded men sprawled on the slopes. Their cries for water gripped his heart. Unable to stand it any longer, he went to General Kershaw and said, "Sir, I would like permission to take water to those poor men."

Kershaw shook his head and said, "No, Sergeant. I can't let you do that."

"But, sir, listen to them!"

"I hear them, son," Kershaw replied, his voice strained. "But those blue-bellies will come charging up here again shortly. You'd only get caught in a crossfire and be killed. I can't let you do it."

"What if I carried a white flag as a sign of truce?"

"No. They might think the white cloth signified surrender."

Kirkland looked toward the suffering men and said, "Then I'll go without the white cloth and take my chances. I can't stand to hear those pitiful cries and not do something about it."

Kershaw let his eyes roam over the carnage and said, "All right, Sergeant. Go ahead. But the instant those Federals start coming toward that wall, I want you up here on the double! You understand?"

"Yes, sir," Kirkland said, and hurried away.

Kirkland strapped on as many canteens as he could carry and headed down the slope. He was some thirty yards below the crest, drawing near the first line of wounded men, when Union rifles from below began to bark. Bullets chewed sod all around him. Ignoring them for the cries of the wounded, he dropped beside the first man he came to, which happened to be a Yankee. He could hear General Kershaw shouting at him from above, commanding him to return immediately. The bullets continued to whiz past his head, but paying them no mind, he said, "Here, my friend. Let me give you some water."

The Yankee ran his gaze over Kirkland's gray uniform and smiled grimly. Rolling his tongue in a dry mouth, he choked, "Th-thank you, Sergeant."

The sun was dropping low in the sky. Down on the plain, the Yankee officer who had commanded his men to commence fire saw what Kirkland was doing and gave a loud, sharp command for the firing to cease. The Federals looked on with amazement, realizing that the man-in-gray was giving water to one of their comrades.

"Well, God bless 'im!" someone said.

"Amen!" said another.

General Burnside's adjutant hastened up and asked the officer what was going on. Without a word, he simply pointed to the scene halfway up the hill.

Troops on both sides looked on in awe as Sergeant Kirkland moved from man to man—whatever the color of his uniform—giving him water to help relieve his suffering.

On Marye's Heights, General Lee stood amongst his officers and smiled as he beheld Kirkland through his binoculars. "What courage!" exclaimed Lee. "He ignored those Yankee bullets as if they were no more than common houseflies buzzing around him."

Lee lowered the binoculars and turned to Major Robert Stiles, who was furiously writing notes on his paper pad. "Major Stiles."

"Yes, sir?"

"While you're writing about this tremendous deed, I want you to dub Kirkland, 'The Angel of Marye's Heights.'"

Stiles grinned broadly, nodding. "Yes, sir. I like that. The Angel of Marye's Heights." As he spoke, he wrote the words in large capital letters.

On the opposite side of the stone wall, General Burnside, curiosity aroused, appeared among his men and looked on the touching scene before him. At that moment, Kirkland was kneeling beside a Union lieutenant.

"I've never seen the like," Burnside said. "That young sergeant is some kind of man."

"The man's an angel, sir," a nearby corporal said.

"I hope he lives through this battle," said Burnside. "I hope he lives through the war. Somebody ought to write a story about him...call it 'The Angel of Marye's Heights.'"

FIFTEEN

Down slope in Sergeant Richard Rowland Kirkland's path, a mortally wounded Rebel private named Ewan Simms was sprawled on the brown winter grass a few feet from where Major Layne Dalton lay unconscious. Dalton's lower body was under the horse's shoulder, and the dead animal's head rested on his chest. The horse's blood was on his face and neck.

Simms had seen Dalton race down the hill to rescue Benny Hay, and had watched the cannonballs kill Hay and bury Dalton beneath the horse and fallen tree. Simms's midsection had been badly torn by shrapnel, and he knew he was bleeding to death. His strength was gone. He could barely move his head. Concerned for Dalton, he turned his face toward him and called in a hoarse, weakened voice, "Major! Major!" When the unconscious major did not respond, Simms assumed he was dead.

Moments later, Sergeant Kirkland knelt beside Simms, took one look at the gaping wound, and realized the man was not long for this world. They knew each other well. "Hello, Ewan," he said softly. "I have some water for you." Simms gritted his teeth in a spasm of pain, then opened his mouth and drank.

While pressing the canteen to the dying man's lips, Kirkland looked around to locate the man he would visit next. The fallen oak with the dead horse beneath it caught his eye. His heart leaped in his breast when he peered through the branches and recognized the bloody face of Layne Dalton. "Major Dalton!" he gasped.

"The major's dead, Richard," Simms said. "I saw him go down."

Kirkland was stunned. Leaving Simms for a moment, he moved to the spot and stared down at Dalton beneath the horse and tree limbs. He began to weep as he returned to Simms, feeling a deep sense of loss. He had loved the major very much. He would miss him.

When Simms had his fill of water, he thanked Kirkland, and the sergeant moved on. Wiping tears, Kirkland went to another fallen comrade a few steps away, then moved on to a Yankee corporal some fifty feet or so from where Simms lay.

Simms was praying silently when suddenly he heard a weak moan from under the fallen oak. His vision was clouding, but he could see Dalton's head rolling slowly back and forth. Simms twisted himself with effort until he could see Sergeant Kirkland kneeling beside the Yankee corporal. He tried to call out, but his voice was too weak to be heard. He rolled onto his stomach, wincing with pain, and began crawling toward Kirkland, whose back was toward him. When he had inched his way about six feet, he saw Kirkland rise and go to another wounded Yankee farther down the slope. He tried desperately to call out, but could hardly make a sound.

Simms crawled on, ignoring the pain and using every ounce of his remaining strength to reach Kirkland. He made it another ten or twelve feet, but could go no further.

"Richard, the major is still alive!" he gasped in a hoarse whisper...and died.

Layne Dalton almost came to consciousness, then slipped back under and lay still.

From their position some fifty yards on the other side of the stone wall, the Heglund brothers looked on and assumed Dalton was dead when they saw the Rebel sergeant turn away without trying to give him water.

"I'm glad he's dead," Steve said. "The only thing I'm sad about is it wasn't me who killed him."

Everett and Keith looked at him and caught sight of their older brother's inordinate cruelty, an insidious and fleeting manifestation. It flitted over his face like some shadowy creature from its lair, revealing itself in its subtle wickedness.

Heavy clouds were gathering in the sky, covering the sun as it went down, while Sergeant Kirkland finished giving water to his final sufferer.

General Burnside sighed as he tore his gaze from Kirkland and looked at Generals Franklin, Sumner, and Hooker, whose curiosity had also brought them to the unusual scene on the slopes of Marye's Heights. "No time for another attack, now," he said. "Best thing for us to do is negotiate another truce and bring down our dead and wounded. We'll attack again in the morning."

When Sergeant Kirkland arrived at the top of the hill, he received a rousing cheer from his comrades. Generals Lee, Longstreet, and Kershaw met him, shook his hand, and commended him for a job well done. Then Lee asked, "Sergeant, we saw Major Dalton go down under that oak out there. Are we to assume that he is...dead?"

Kirkland's eyes filmed up as he nodded and replied solemnly, "Yes, sir. He's dead. His horse is dead, and he's lying underneath it. What I could see of him was awfully bloody. The shrapnel must have torn him up real bad."

Hundreds of Rebel soldiers gathered around Kirkland to express their appreciation for his heroic deed. Those who had seen Major Dalton's attempt to rescue Benny Hay talked about it in Kirkland's presence, expressing their deep sorrow at the loss of the major.

The Federals called for a truce, and it was agreed upon by the Confederates. The truce—as on the previous night—would end at dawn.

As darkness fell under a cloudy sky, both armies began carrying their dead and wounded from the battlefield. The Federals dug a common grave in the open field north of the stone wall, and the Confederates merely extended the one they had dug the night before.

As Steve Heglund and his brothers went over the wall to do their part in picking up Union dead and wounded, Steve said, "You know, it's so dark out here, we could get Dalton's body, and the stinkin' Rebels would be none the wiser. If we hurry, that is."

"What would we want with Dalton's body?" asked Keith. "You wanna stuff it?"

Steve peered at Keith in the dim light. "Not a bad idea, but what I really want is the privilege of dumpin' him in the ground. What's the matter with buryin' him in a Union grave?"

"Nothin' as far as I'm concerned," replied Keith. "Just so he's buried."

"C'mon," whispered Steve. "Let's go!"

Men of both armies were busy all over the hill, picking up the wounded first and carrying them where they could get at least a measure of medical attention. They would pick up the dead later.

The Heglund brothers reached the fallen oak, and together, rolled it off horse and rider. They were about to pick up Dalton when they saw him roll his head and heard him moan.

"Steve! He's alive!" Keith said in a hoarse whisper.

"Sh-h-h-h!" hissed Steve, looking around to see if anyone had heard. None of the soldiers nearby showed any sign of having heard Keith's outburst.

Everett bent low over Dalton and said, "I think he's semi-conscious. I don't think he knows what's goin' on, though."

"Fate is with me!" Steve said, whispering excitedly. "Now I get the privilege of killin' the dirty skunk myself!"

"You can't shoot him right here," Keith said.

"You ever hear of strangulation?" Steve hissed.

"That man alive?" The Heglund brothers were startled by the voice of Union Captain Eldridge Bonebraker.

Steve was trying to think of how to answer when Dalton moved his head and ejected a low moan.

"Yes, sir," replied Steve. "He's...uh...he's a Rebel major, sir. Don't you think we ought to take him prisoner?"

"Not if he's hurt bad. We don't need to use up our medical supplies on enemy officers."

"What if he's not hurt bad, sir?"

"Then take him prisoner," said Bonebraker, walking away. "But you better find out real quick, or his pals will be on your back."

The Heglunds worked Dalton free from the weight of the dead horse and went over him quickly. When they could find no wounds, except for a bad bruise on his head, they picked him up and carried him toward Burnside's warehouse headquarters where many Rebels were being kept as prisoners.

"I heard General Burnside say that all prisoners from this battle will be taken to the Federal prison at Point Lookout," Steve said.

"Yeah?" said Everett, surprised. "You mean Dalton is gonna be in the prison where Clyde is servin' as guard?"

"I'd like to kill him here and now," Steve growled, "but since Captain Bonebraker might be checkin' on him, guess I'll have to let Clyde find a way to work out an 'accident' for him at the prison."

Point Lookout, Maryland, was some sixty miles southeast of Fredericksburg on Maryland's southern tip, and had been chosen by General Henry W. Halleck as the prison where Burnside would deliver the Rebels he captured in the present campaign. The unconscious Confederate major was laid out in the warehouse, along with some two hundred other prisoners.

Because of his exhaustion, Sergeant Kirkland was not part of the "pickup" party on the Marye hillsides. No one in the Confederate Army of Northern Virginia was aware that Major Layne Dalton's body had not been picked up nor buried by men in gray. Generals

Lee, Longstreet, and Kershaw assumed he was buried along with all the other dead Rebel soldiers.

At eight o'clock that night, General Burnside met with his three commanding generals and ordered them to get as accurate a count as possible on the number of dead and wounded. When they came back two hours later, they stunned Burnside with the figures.

The Federals had buried nearly thirteen hundred men, but in addition to over nine thousand who were wounded—many of whom would eventually die—they as yet could not account for another seventeen hundred men. By the yellow light of the two lanterns that glowed in Burnside's makeshift warehouse office, Sumner, Franklin, and Hooker noted the sickly look that etched itself on their commander's face.

Burnside swallowed with difficulty, ran trembling fingers over his balding head, and said weakly, "Gentlemen, this is a sad situation."

"I think *debacle* is a better word than *situation*, General," Hooker said dryly. "But I sure agree it's sad. You and your tactics have cut a massive hole in the Union Army of the Potomac. Why don't you just admit it? You're bullheaded pride has cost us better than twelve thousand casualties!"

"Because this is a time of battle and great strain on all of us, General Hooker, I will not act as I would otherwise on your insolence." There was fury behind Burnside's shadowed eyes.

"Act however you want, sir," Hooker countered, "but if you'd listened to these two gentlemen and me, there would be thousands of men going back to wives, sweethearts, and parents from this encounter who now will never see them again."

Burnside saw the same attitude in the eyes of Franklin and Sumner, who remained silent. Drawing a short, sharp breath, he ran his gaze over their solemn faces and said, "That will be all for tonight, gentlemen."

"What about tomorrow?" pressed Hooker, rising to his feet.

"We will attack again," Burnside replied tartly.

Joe Hooker shook his head and walked away. Sumner and Franklin exchanged puzzled glances and followed Hooker, not looking back.

Monday morning, December 15, 1862, came with heavy clouds and a driving storm of sleet, snow, and freezing rain. Soldiers on both sides endured the elements, but there was no fighting.

Sumner, Franklin, and Hooker appeared at Burnside's makeshift office and asked to meet with him. Burnside, who looked as if he had not slept, welcomed them and sat down with them, asking what they wanted to see him about. All three said emphatically that the Union army should pull out before the weather cleared, and go back to Washington.

"Sir, it isn't just the three of us," General Hooker said. "We hear the men talking everywhere. Officers and enlisted men alike are blaming you for what has happened to us here, saying that General Lee has outsmarted you. The men are demoralized, and you will kill thousands more if you send them into battle when this storm clears."

Burnside shook his head and said, "You gentlemen and the men of this army are correct. This debacle is my fault. I laid awake all night thinking about your stinging words, General Hooker. I had them coming. I am telling you gentlemen now, I will tell the entire Army of the Potomac shortly…and I will admit it to General Halleck and President Lincoln. History will lay the blame for this awful beating at my feet…and that is where it belongs." He drew a deep breath, let it out slowly, and added, "We will wait until dark this evening and withdraw."

General Hooker left his chair and moved toward Burnside, extending his right hand. Burnside rose, met it, and gripped the hand firmly.

"Sir," Hooker said with feeling, "I admire a man who has the courage to face his mistakes and admit them. I may not like you, but I admire you."

"We'll leave it at that, sir," nodded Burnside stonily. "Now, let's make plans for our graceful withdrawal."

The storm continued all day, and the freezing rain became sleet late in the afternoon. After dark, the dispirited Union troops began their evacuation, crossing the Rappahannock on hastily repaired pontoon bridges that had been covered with mud and straw to muffle the sound of feet and hooves.

Major Layne Dalton, fully conscious and, except for a bad headache, unhurt, was put in a train of wagons and headed east. The prisoners would be ferried across the Potomac River to Point Lookout, Maryland, and locked up in the Federal prison.

Layne's mind went to the wife he loved and adored. He wondered how long it would be before he would hold Melody in his arms again...if ever. He knew that prisoners died by the hundreds in prison camps—Northern and Southern. Filth and disease took their toll.

Dalton was unaware that the Heglund brothers had captured him. Neither did he know that Steve Heglund had persuaded his division commander to let him and his brothers go along as guards on the prison-bound wagon train.

The weather cleared during the night, and the Confederates awoke on Tuesday morning expecting the Union forces to attack, their minds set on squashing the smaller army and taking Marye's Heights. To their surprise, they found that Burnside's entire Army of the Potomac was gone.

An elated Robert E. Lee spoke to his troops, commending them for whipping the Federals in spite of the overwhelming odds. Then waving to thousands of cheering soldiers, he rode off the hill with a cavalry escort and headed for Richmond.

The remaining generals met on the porch of the Marye house to make plans for getting their four thousand wounded to hospitals. Sergeant Richard Rowland Kirkland made his way up to the steps, and when General Longstreet saw him, he paused in what he was saying to the others and asked, "What is it, Sergeant?"

"Pardon me, sir," Kirkland said, saluting, "but it is important that I speak to General Kershaw."

"Of course," Longstreet said, swerving his gaze to Kershaw. "We'll excuse you for a few moments, General."

Kershaw nodded and descended the steps. "What is it, Sergeant?" he asked.

Kirkland's features were serious. "Sir, Major Dalton—God bless his memory—told me where his wife is staying. I would like your permission to go and tell her of the major's heroism and death on the battlefield."

"Of course, son," the general said. "It's very thoughtful of you. I know you and Major Dalton were close friends."

"Yes, sir."

"Tell you what—would you give me a couple minutes to write her a message?"

"Certainly, sir."

The slender young sergeant, now known as "The Angel of Marye's Heights," waited while Kershaw produced a small note pad from an overcoat pocket and used a pencil stub to hastily offer his sympathy to Melody Dalton. He used a second page to eloquently word his feelings about the major's gallantry and courage in dying to save a fellow-soldier's life.

When Kershaw finished, he folded the two pages and placed them in Kirkland's hand. "Tell her my love and prayers are with her, Sergeant."

"Yes, sir," said Kirkland.

Bertha Shrewsberry and Harriet Smith were working at the kitchen table, making a new dress for Melody Dalton. It was just after nine o'clock, and the morning sun was slanting through the east kitchen window.

The two women were discussing the fact that they had not heard the sounds of war since Sunday. They wondered if the battle was over.

Tears were in Harriet's eyes as she said, "Oh, Bertha…how much longer can this war go on? I do so long to have a normal life again."

"I know, dear," said Bertha, reaching across the table to give Harriet's hand a motherly pat. "I'll be so glad when this awful bloodshed and killing is over…and our men can come home again."

Harriet was about to say something else when a knock at the front door stole her words. "I'll get it," she said to Bertha, who had started to get up.

Harriet hurried to the door. When she opened it, her eyes took in the horse tied to the hitching post at the porch, then she looked into the face of the youthful soldier whose silhouette stood out sharply against the sunlit snow on the ground behind him. "Yes, Sergeant?"

"I believe this is the home of Mrs. Shrewsberry," said the tall, slender man.

"Yes, it is."

"And Mrs. Dalton is staying here, right?"

"That's right," replied Harriet, a cold feeling capturing her stomach. The sergeant's eyes told her there was bad news.

"Ma'am, my name is Richard Kirkland. I was in the battle at Fredericksburg."

"Do you mean the battle is over?"

"Yes, ma'am."

Harriet's heart was thudding. "I'm Harriet Smith, Sergeant. My husband, Walter, is in General Jackson's division. Do you know him?"

"No, ma'am, I don't. I can understand your anxiety, though. For your encouragement, all I can tell you is that we did not suffer near the casualties that the Union did. I…I certainly hope your husband is all right."

"Thank you," Harriet said, then swallowed hard. There was a quavery edge to her voice. "Please don't tell me you're here to tell Mrs. Dalton something's happened to Layne."

"Yes, ma'am. I...I was Major Dalton's adjutant, ma'am." Kirkland choked on the words. "He and I were very good friends."

"Is...is he dead, Sergeant?"

"I'm afraid so, ma'am."

"Harriet," came Bertha's voice from behind as the older woman drew up, "why don't you ask the young man in?"

Harriet's hand went to her mouth. "Oh! I'm sorry, Sergeant. It's just that...well, this news—"

"I understand ma'am," said Kirkland.

Harriet stepped to the side, widening the opening of the doorway. "Please come in."

Harriet looked at the widow. "Bertha, did you hear what he told me?"

Bertha's face reddened and moisture gathered in her eyes. "Yes. I heard you say, Sergeant—"

"Kirkland, ma'am. Richard Kirkland."

"I heard you say that you were Major Dalton's adjutant and close friend."

"Yes, ma'am."

"Did...did he suffer?"

"No, ma'am. He was killed instantly by an exploding shell."

A quivering hand went to Bertha's temple. "I'm glad for that, but oh, my. Poor little Melody."

Harriet put an arm around Bertha's shoulder.

"Is Mrs. Dalton here?" Kirkland asked, removing his cap.

"Yes," nodded Harriet, "but she hasn't been feeling well. She lost her baby, and seems to be having some complications."

"I know about the baby, ma'am. Major Dalton told me. If you don't think I should tell her right now, I can come back later."

The two women looked at each other.

"I wish she never had to hear this horrible news," Bertha said, "but it isn't right to withhold it from her, even though she's not feeling well."

Harriet was fighting tears. "You're right. It's going to be an awful blow, but it must not be kept from her."

Kirkland's features were gray. "Since you want me to go ahead, could I do it now? I...I'd like to get it over with. This is going to be the hardest thing I ever did in my life."

"Of course, Sergeant," Bertha replied, touching his arm. "Let Harriet and me go to her room and see if she's awake. If not, we'll awaken her. Is it all right with you if we stay in the room while you tell her?"

"I want you to," said Kirkland.

Sergeant Kirkland laid his cap on a nearby table and took off his overcoat as the women disappeared from the parlor. There was a large mirror on the wall to his right. He looked at his own image. The face looking back at him was edged with a graven somberness. It was a face that had grown considerably older in the last two days. Harriet returned, her features as gray as his, and said, "She's awake. All we told her was that a Sergeant Richard Kirkland is here to see her, and that you are her husband's adjutant. She suspects that something is wrong. I'll have to let you take it from there."

"Yes, ma'am."

Harriet led him down the hall and into Melody's room. Melody was sitting up in the bed, looking peaked and weak. Cold dread was evident in the lines of her face and in her eyes as she looked at him and waited for him to speak.

Kirkland's heart was racing, pounding so hard he could feel his pulse throb in his temples. "Mrs. Dalton, I'm Richard Kirkland."

"Yes. Harriet told me. You're my husband's adjutant?"

"Yes, ma'am. I've come to tell you...that the major—"

"No!" gusted Melody. "No! Layne's not dead! Please don't tell me he's dead!"

Harriet was standing by the bed on Melody's right, and Bertha was on her left. Both women sat on the edges of the bed and laid their hands on her shoulders and arms.

"Yes, ma'am. He was killed on Sunday, ma'am. But he died a h—"

"No-o-o!" screamed Melody, throwing her head back and forth in disbelief. "No, it can't be! Layne's not dead! Not my baby and my husband, too! No! No! No!"

Harriet wrapped her arms around Melody, holding her tight. Bertha leaned close, stroking her face as Melody broke into uncontrollable sobs.

It took some fifteen minutes for Melody to cry it out and grow calm. While the two women held her, she wept silently for several more minutes, then looked up at Kirkland with red, swollen eyes. "The battle at Fredericksburg is over, Sergeant?"

"Yes, ma'am. The Yankees pulled out last night."

Melody sniffed. "How...how did it happen?"

"It was on the hill at Marye's Heights. The Yankees came in such great numbers that they finally broke through our defenses and started up the hill. There was hand-to-hand fighting for hours. Then suddenly the Yankees pulled back, and their artillery started bombarding us."

Melody broke for a moment, cried a little, then got hold of herself again. "Go on, Sergeant."

"When the bombardment started, ma'am, the major and I were about two-thirds of the way up the hill. All of a sudden he looked down the hill and saw Benny Hay groping his way blindly amid the exploding shells. The major raced his horse down the hill to rescue him."

Melody closed her eyes, bracing herself for the words that would tell her exactly how her husband had died.

"Just before the major got there, ma'am, a shell exploded in front of Benny. More shells struck a second or two later. One or both of them took the major's life. He...he died a hero, Mrs. Dalton, a real hero. He gave his life trying to save the life of Benny Hay."

Melody took the hands of her two friends in her own and squeezed them hard.

"Dear Jesus," said Bertha, "help her. Give her strength, Lord, as only You can do."

"What about burial, Sergeant?" Melody asked. "Is there someone I should contact?"

"It's already been done, ma'am," Kirkland said softly. "We had to do a mass burial at the south base of Marye's hill."

She nodded silently, biting her lips.

Kirkland pulled the folded slips of paper from his shirt pocket. "I have something from General Kershaw, ma'am. He asked me to give you this and to tell you that his love and prayers are with you."

"Thank you, Sergeant," she said, accepting the papers and managing a faint smile. "You've been so kind to come all the way out here and tell me about my husband. I'll never forget it."

"I will admit, Mrs. Dalton, it's been the hardest thing I've ever done. I loved the major, and because of that, I wanted to be the one to break it to you. God bless you."

When Kirkland was gone, Melody read General Kershaw's note and cried again. Her two friends sat with her, offering every bit of comfort they could give her.

"The hardest part of all this is…that Layne died without the Lord," Melody said shakily.

Harriet squeezed her hand and said, "Honey, we don't always understand God's ways. We don't know why He let Layne be killed…but haven't we prayed that He would bring Layne to Himself?"

"Yes."

"You gave Layne a Bible to read, and you witnessed to him of your own salvation. Perhaps the Holy Spirit dealt in Layne's heart and brought him to Jesus before he was killed."

"Yes, let's hope so," nodded Melody, silent tears streaming down her cheeks. "I do so want to see my darling husband in heaven."

Only a few minutes had passed when Walter Smith showed up on the Shrewsberry doorstep. He and Harriet had a happy reunion, thanking the Lord that Walter had been spared in the battle. Walter had heard that Layne was killed, and offered his sincere sympathy to Melody.

Walter had gone home to find his own house demolished, but reported to Melody that hers was still intact. Melody invited the Smiths to move in with her until the war was over and they could rebuild their own house.

Walter returned to his division under Stonewall Jackson, and Harriet moved in with Melody.

During the next few days, Melody continued to have problems as a result of losing the baby. Dr. David Craig was summoned, and after examining Melody, he told her that she had sustained permanent injuries and would never be able to bear children. Dr. Craig explained that the pain she was having would subside as she healed, and within a couple of months, she would be fine. He expressed his condolences over Layne's death and spoke words of comfort.

By the middle of February, Melody was feeling fine again and announced to Harriet that she was going to move to Virginia City. With Layne gone, she needed to be with her family.

Harriet understood, though she told Melody she would miss her terribly. Melody said the Smiths could live in her house until theirs was rebuilt. By then she would know more what direction her life was going to take, and would decide about selling the house. They would keep in touch by mail.

SIXTEEN

No issue during the Civil War stirred such passions or inspired such deep-seated bitterness as the prisons of both sides. When the War began at Fort Sumter in April 1861, neither side made immediate preparation for the incarceration and care of prisoners. Southerners believed they would wear down the Yankee resistance to their secession in a very short time, and the hostilities would be over. Northerners expected to subdue the Rebels easily within three months, and return to their normal course of life.

Neither side expected to hold great numbers of prisoners. So unprepared were they that there was no coherent policy for the handling of prisoners. There was not a single military prison above or below the Mason-Dixon line capable of holding more than a handful of men.

Fortunately for both sides, there was little action—therefore comparatively few prisoners taken—during the remainder of 1861. In the East, the only battle with significant numbers of prisoners taken was in July at Manassas, which yielded some thirteen hundred Federal prisoners and only a handful of Confederates. In the West, the only major action was at Wilson's Creek in Missouri, where the tally of prisoners taken by both sides was barely over three hundred.

These were manageable numbers, and neither side as yet felt pushed to develop extensive prison systems. Most of the captives were held in a few tent camps. The thirteen hundred Federals taken at Manassas were spread all over the South, giving little if any problem to the Confederacy.

As the War dragged on, however, and bigger battles produced thousands of prisoners on both sides, Presidents Lincoln and Davis began to push government leaders to make room for them.

Prison camps were hastily developed and immediately jammed with captives. It soon became apparent that they were insufficient to handle the legions of prisoners being brought in. In prisons both North and South, meager rations, bad water, poor sanitation, and drafty tents or buildings brought on scurvy, dysentery, pneumonia, a host of other diseases…and death.

The unsanitary conditions also drew rats by the thousands. With food so scarce and the absence of adequate protein, prison rats were staple fare.

No matter what they ate, prisoners learned to gobble their food for fear it might be seized by other hungry inmates. Vicious and sometimes deadly brawls exploded over a few morsels of spoiled meat or vermin-infested rice.

In late 1862 the worst Confederate prisons were Castle Pinckney at Charleston Harbor, South Carolina, and prisons at Danville and Belle Isle, Virginia. The three most disreputable Federal prisons were at Johnson's Island, Ohio, Camp Douglas, Illinois, and Point Lookout, Maryland.

Point Lookout Prison consisted of several poorly built barracks to house noncommissioned men, and a few better-built barracks to house Confederate officers. The officers' barracks were also kept cleaner, and the officers were given better food and boiled water. The prison was situated on a barren, swampy bit of land at the mouth of the Potomac River where it emptied into Chesapeake Bay.

The sixty-mile trip from Fredericksburg to Point Lookout took three days. The wagon train of prisoners and guards was led by Captain Eldridge Bonebraker. On the morning of the first day—December 16—Major Layne Dalton sat in a rear corner of a wagon bed, facing forward. His head was still aching, and his thoughts were fastened on Melody. Would she know he was taken as prisoner, or would she think he was dead?

Captain Bonebraker and two lieutenants were the only ones in the train on horseback. There were three sergeants, five corporals, and twenty-four privates to drive and guard seventeen wagons, holding a total of 221 prisoners. The Heglund brothers avoided Dalton during the night, not wanting him to know they were in the train.

The sky was clear and the air was cold. As the wagons moved slowly eastward toward the Potomac, the Confederate prisoners rode in silence, each man absorbed in his private thoughts.

Layne Dalton huddled against the cold in his overcoat, thinking about Melody and his little son. A Union private was walking along-side the wagon, rifle-in-hand. Their eyes happened to meet, and the youthful private said, "Major, I saw what you did on Sunday…riding hard to rescue that soldier who had been blinded. I know we're ene-mies, but I recognize courage when I see it. That was a commendable thing for you to do."

A voice familiar to Dalton came from behind: "Private, are you fraternizing with the enemy?"

The private and Dalton turned to see Steve Heglund. "No, Sergeant," the private replied. "I was just commending him for his courage."

"Well, let's not be commendin' lowdown Rebel scum for nothin'. You hear me?"

"I hear you, sir."

"Just move on up to the next wagon," clipped Heglund. "I'll walk beside this one for a while."

When the private obeyed, Steve kept pace with the wagon, leaned close, and said, "You know who captured you, Dalton? It was me! Everett and Keith and me found you sleepin' like a baby under that dead horse and those tree limbs."

"Congratulations," Dalton said dryly. "You're a big brave soldier."

Heglund leaned even closer and dropped his menacing voice to a whisper so no one else could hear it. "You're a dead man, Dalton! My brother Clyde is a guard at Point Lookout. He'll get you, one way or another. I'd take care of you right now, but Captain Bonebraker frowns on murder. But you get this in your craw—Clyde'll get you, and you'll be just as dead!"

Seconds later, Everett and Keith drew up beside their older brother and sneered at Dalton. Steve called the private back, and the Heglund brothers moved out of Dalton's sight.

When the wagon train arrived at Point Lookout late in the day on December 18, the sky was spitting snow, and a cold, biting wind was coming off the bay. The Confederates from the Fredericksburg battle learned that there were already some six thousand prisoners housed on the Point. The enlisted men were ushered to their barracks, and the officers were taken to the small cabin that was the office of the prison commandant, Major Allen Brady.

Dalton was the highest-ranking officer amongst seven captured at Fredericksburg. Brady, a coarse and hard-faced man, stood them before him and explained that they had better quarters and would receive better food and water than the enlisted men. He then went over the prison's rules, and made sure they understood that any man who tried to escape would be shot. They were then ushered to one of the officers' barracks and placed in their cells.

Dalton was placed in a small cubicle with two bunks, but had no cell mate. The next morning, the officers in his barracks ate their breakfast together, then were sent back to their cells. They were told that they could not go outdoors until they had been there a week.

At breakfast, Dalton had learned that the prison camp covered some twenty-eight acres. Except for about a hundred yards of beach at the very tip of the Point, the camp was enclosed by an eight-foot-high stockade fence. The prisoners knew that any man who tried to swim in those icy waters would drown before he could ever reach land. In warmer weather, guards were posted at the water line to make sure no prisoner tried to swim for it.

Eight feet inside the perimeter wall and the one-hundred-yard stretch of beach was a built-in deterrent to escape—an ominous cordon called the "dead line." It consisted of short wooden posts topped with a single rail. The frail structure was no physical barrier, but the prisoners were forewarned of the consequences of venturing beyond it. Guards were instructed to call out a warning to a prisoner who approached the line. If he stepped over it, he would die in a hail of bullets.

Dalton learned that some fifty men had been shot to death beyond the "dead line." In all, some fifteen hundred prisoners at Point Lookout had died from wounds, dysentery, scurvy, pneumonia, typhoid, cholera, consumption, or being shot down in escape attempts.

Dalton also learned that Clyde Heglund was Sergeant of the Guard under Major Brady. Layne knew that as head guard, Clyde would be in a good position to carry out Steve's threat and have him killed. He would have to stay alert at all times.

When it came time for Steve, Everett, and Keith Heglund to leave the Point and head for Washington to report to General Burnside, Clyde told them he had an idea. He had three guards who had been wanting to return to active duty. He would go to Major Brady and suggest that he let those guards have their wish, and put his three brothers in their place. Not only would it keep all four brothers in one place, but it would put them in a position to work together to kill Layne Dalton.

Clyde Heglund presented his proposal to Brady. The prison commandant liked the way Clyde led the guards and handled the prisoners. He was sure Clyde's brothers would fit in nicely. He wired Washington immediately, and the exchange was approved within a day.

As the days passed, Layne Dalton wondered how the enlisted men stayed alive. The food he was eating was horrible, and what he was getting was better than what they were getting. Many of the officers had bad colds because there was little or no heat in the barracks. Dalton knew it had to be worse in the enlisted men's barracks. Every day he heard of men who were dying of pneumonia and from various other causes.

On Dalton's sixth day in the camp, Steve Heglund visited him and told him of the appointment he and his brothers had received as guards. He did all he could to intimidate the Confederate major and warned him to stay on guard. One day soon, Steve would have the joy of killing him.

On day seven, Layne was allowed to go outside after breakfast and mingle with the other Confederate officers near their barracks. He was talking to some of the men who had been with him at Fredericksburg when he happened to glance across the compound at another group of Confederate officers and saw his old friend Jerry Owens. Layne had lost track of Jerry when he had been assigned to the Trans-Mississippi Department of the Confederacy in late 1861. Layne excused himself and headed toward the other officers.

A guard stepped in front of him and asked curtly, "Where are you going, Major?"

"I just spotted an old friend of mine over there," Layne replied, pointing. "Any harm in my talking to him?"

"I guess not," the guard conceded. "The officers in both barracks often talk to each other."

"Thanks," nodded Layne, and broke into a run.

Jerry saw him coming and hurried to meet him. They came together and embraced. Then, as they gripped each other by the shoulders, Jerry said, "I'm sure sorry to see you in here, Layne, but I sure am glad to see you!"

"No more glad than I am to see you!" said Layne. "So you're a captain now."

"And you're a major!"

"That's what they tell me. How long you been here?"

Jerry explained that he had fought under General Van Dorn in the battle at Pea Ridge, Arkansas, on March 7 and 8. He was captured, and at first had been taken to Johnson's Island Prison in Ohio. The prison was filling up beyond capacity, so the Yankees transported him and four hundred other prisoners to Point Lookout.

The presence of his old friend lifted Layne Dalton's spirits. He asked about Linda and learned that she and their eight-month-old daughter were living with her parents.

"And how's Melody?" asked Jerry. "You got any younguns yet?" Jerry saw the sadness flit across Layne's face. "Layne, is something wrong?"

"You remember the Heglunds."

"Yeah. How could I forget? Especially since I have to look at Clyde every day. I guess you know we've got all four of them here now."

"I'm afraid so."

"So tell me what's happened."

Layne explained how the three Heglund brothers had forced their way into his house during the looting of Fredericksburg, and what Steve had done to Melody, which resulted in the stillborn child. Layne told him of taking Melody to Bertha Shrewsberry's house for safety, and that as far as he knew, she was doing fine.

"It's gotta be hard for you, not being able to go to her," Jerry said.

Layne nodded. "If I can just survive this place," he said glumly. "I know I haven't seen the worst of it, but what I've already seen is pretty disheartening. And even if I don't die of some disease, the Heglund brothers have a grave planned for me—threatened to kill me."

"They're fully capable of it, too," Jerry warned. "There was a young lieutenant in here named Hyman Stanton. Clyde got it in for him, and he ended up dead. Murdered. Made it look like some of the other prisoners did it, but everybody in here knows it was Clyde."

Layne shook his head. "Those Heglunds never seem to get

caught. What about Brady? I detect that he's a hardhead, but is he for murdering prisoners?"

"You're right about him being a hardhead, but he won't put up with the guards killing prisoners unless they're trying to escape. Last spring one of the guards killed a Confederate captain just because he didn't like him. Brady executed him."

"Really?"

"Yeah. He doesn't mind giving prisoners a good beating, but that's where he draws the line. He seems to have a special feeling toward officers. That's why we have it better here than the enlisted men."

"Isn't right," mumbled Dalton, "but there's nothing I can do about it."

"I feel the same way." Jerry ran his gaze to the officers in Layne's barracks and asked, "Who's your cell mate?"

"Don't have one."

"Oh? Neither do I."

"No? Any possibility Brady might let us share the same cell?"

"Maybe. We could ask for an appointment with him, but the best way is to do it through a chaplain in my barracks."

Dalton's eyebrows arched. "They've even taken a chaplain prisoner?"

"Name's Captain Michael Young. He's from Roanoke. Brady likes him. I think Captain Young could talk him into letting us bunk together. Come on. He's in the barracks. Let's go talk to him."

The two friends found Chaplain Young in his cell reading his Bible. He was in his late thirties and had been a pastor in Roanoke before the War. He and Layne took a liking to each other immediately. Young was sympathetic to their idea and went to Major Brady with their request. Brady granted it, and within the hour Layne had moved into Jerry's cell.

Young stood in the doorway of the cell while Layne adjusted his cot. Jerry took advantage of the moment to tell the chaplain about the Heglunds causing the death of the Daltons' unborn child and of their threat to kill Layne.

Young was touched by the story. He stepped into the cell as Layne was taking note of the Bible on Jerry's cot and said, "Major, let's sit down and talk for a moment."

"Certainly," Layne said.

The chaplain sat beside Jerry and looked across the small cubicle at Layne. "Do you understand, Major, that your little son is in heaven?"

"Yes, sir. Melody told me that. She's…well, she's a regular church attender. She believes in God and knows a lot about the Bible."

"I'm very happy to hear that." After a brief pause, he said, "From what I just heard about your being captured, it sounds like Melody must believe you're dead."

"It would seem that way to me, sir," said Layne. "If I'm not on the dead list, I'm sure on the missing list."

"Poor girl. This has to be hard on her, especially after losing the baby."

"Yes, sir."

"These Yankees won't let us get word to anybody on the outside, Major, so there's no way she can learn that you're alive. There's one thing we can do, though. We can ask the Lord to comfort her and give her strength in His own wonderful way until such time as this horrible war is over, and you can go home to her. Could we pray together for her?"

Layne Dalton, battle hero and leader of soldiers, was thrown off balance by the chaplain's request. "Uh…sure," he replied. "I…I appreciate that."

When Chaplain Young brought his prayer to a close, Layne was surprised to hear Jerry add an "Amen." He thought about the Bible lying on Jerry's cot, and wondered if his old friend had done the same thing Melody had.

Young smiled at Dalton and said, "You told me about Melody's faith in the Lord, Major, but you didn't tell me about your own. Are you a Christian?"

Layne felt his face heat up. He hoped it wasn't showing. "Well, I, uh…I was taught by my favorite uncle as a child that every man has to find God in his own way."

"No offense to your uncle," said Young, "but we have to come to God *His* way, not ours."

Layne remembered someone saying that to him before. Was it Melody?

"Seems my wife said something like that to me, sir. She also gave me a Bible and underlined several passages for me to read, but it was in my saddlebags when those Yankee shells put my horse and me down."

"The Yankees have provided me with several Bibles," Young said. "Would you like to have one?"

"Why, uh…yes. That would be nice. I appreciate that, Chaplain."

Young hurried back to his cell and returned with a Bible. He gave it to Layne, saying he had previously marked some passages and urged Layne to read them.

When Young was gone, Jerry told his old friend that only two weeks before, the chaplain had led him to Christ. Jerry then opened Layne's Bible and read aloud some of the passages the chaplain had marked. When he had read to him for some ten minutes, Jerry urged Layne to turn to the Lord, also.

Layne was nursing a deep-seated grudge toward God, but kept it to himself. He told Jerry he would think about it.

Each cell in the officers' barracks was allowed a kerosene lantern. That night, as they sat on their cots by the yellow glow of their lantern, Layne followed in his Bible as Jerry read Matthew's account of the crucifixion. Jerry saw that his friend was deeply touched by it, and decided to read the Mark, Luke, and John accounts, also. Jerry would let the Word of God do its work in Layne's heart. He closed his Bible and did not comment.

Later, when the guards had checked to make sure all cell doors were locked and all lanterns were out, Jerry lay in the dark and said, "Layne, now that the guards are out of the building and no one can hear us, there's something I want to tell you—I'm working on an escape."

"You are? By yourself?"

"Yep. Have to. The escape is going to be from this very cell."

"What do you mean?"

"Under my cot you will find the floorboards loosened in a section large enough to crawl through. I've been digging a tunnel for the past seven months. The back wall of the barracks, which is the back wall of our cell, stands just twelve feet from the fence. Did you notice the barracks was that close to the fence?"

"No, I didn't."

"It's slow-going, but by working a few hours almost every night these past seven months, I've dug back about ten feet. I figure that in another three months, I'll be out of here. Now, of course, *both* of us will be going."

"How are you digging? With your fingernails?"

Jerry chuckled. "I found a chisel that was probably used when this barracks was built. It was in the dirt near the side wall. So, using the chisel, I've chipped away a little at a time. I stuff the loose dirt in my pants pockets and throw it down the holes in the privies each morning."

"Owens, you're a genius."

"I know."

"You haven't told any of the other officers?"

"Wouldn't do any good. The door's always locked at night, and that's when the escape will have to be made. I couldn't take anyone but a cell mate with me. I don't see any reason to tell the others."

"So you crawl down in there, light the lantern, and dig away, eh?"

"That's it."

"Well, if you'll show me how you've been doing it, I'll take a turn at it right now."

The new year came, and the two cell mates continued to make progress on the escape tunnel.

Some time during each day, Jerry led in Bible reading. He had finally figured out that his friend was bitter toward God over the death of his son. Layne often talked about Danny and what it would have been like if the boy had lived. Though Layne did not let on to Jerry, the Bible reading was doing something in his heart.

On January 27, two Confederate corporals and three privates tried to escape from the prison, and were shot and killed.

The next day, Steve and Clyde Heglund approached Layne Dalton when he was alone outside the barracks. "Unusual for you to be alone, Dalton," Clyde said. "Where's your buddy, Owens?"

"Inside," said Dalton, fixing him with hard eyes. "He's got a cold. Thought it best not to come out in this frigid air."

"You know what I wish, fancy-pants Major?" Steve said.

"I don't really care," Layne replied levelly.

"Well, I wish *you* would try an escape like those boys did yesterday. I'd love to shoot you down like a mangy dog!"

Dalton eyed him steadily. "And nothing on this earth would make me feel so good as to wring the neck of the coward who beat up my wife and killed my unborn baby!"

Steve was about to retaliate when Clyde said in a quick whisper, "Look out! Brady's comin'!"

Steve looked across the compound and saw the commandant moving their way. Scowling at Dalton, he hissed through his teeth, "I'll get you, fancy-pants! I'll get you!"

With that, Steve and Clyde strolled away, leaving Dalton with a fiery-red face. Layne wheeled and entered the barracks before Major Brady drew near. His wrath was hot and his breathing erratic. He imagined how good it would feel to get Steve Heglund's throat in his hands. *An eye for an eye...*

As he was gaining control of his emotions, the Bible words

Harriet Smith had quoted to him came to mind: *Vengeance is mine; I will repay, saith the Lord.* He headed down the corridor for the cell he shared with his best friend. "But the vengeance should be *mine!*" Layne whispered. "It was *my* son he killed!"

The weeks passed and Layne Dalton continued to be appalled at the atrocities of the prison. Men died almost every day because of the squalor and lack of sanitation. When he discussed it with Michael Young, the chaplain could only say that the Southern prison camps were worse.

Time and again, all four Heglund brothers dealt Dalton misery whenever Major Brady was out of sight, hoping he would retaliate and they could kill him and claim self-defense. Fortunately, each time Jerry was with him and restrained him from making a fatal mistake.

Near the end of February, Steve Heglund drew up to Dalton when Owens was elsewhere and made a ribald remark about Melody. Dalton struck him, knocking him down, and had to be pulled off him by other guards. Unbeknownst to Heglund, Major Brady happened to be near and witnessed the whole thing. Dalton was confined to his cell for a week for striking Heglund, but Heglund was reprimanded severely by Brady for inciting the trouble.

On March 1, Dalton was in his cell alone during the afternoon, lying on his cot and wishing he could be working in the tunnel. Footsteps sounded in the corridor, and Steve Heglund's face appeared at the little window in the cell door.

Layne looked up, saw him, and said, "On your way, baby-murderer. There's nothing going on in here that's any of your business."

Steve looked up and down the corridor to make sure no one was in sight, then pressed his face close to the opening and said, "You know what, Dalton? I'm glad I knocked your ol' lady off that landin'…and it made me real happy to find out that your kid died. One less Dalton in the world! Somebody oughtta pin a medal on me!"

The stinging words were too much. Dalton thrust his right hand through the opening and grabbed the man's throat. Heglund made a gagging noise and tried to break the hold with both hands, but the angry major's thumb and fingers were like spring steel.

Heglund struggled to free himself, but Dalton held on with wild determination. Heglund was turning blue and his eyes were rolling back in his head when suddenly two guards entered the corridor.

"Hey!" blared one as they both ran down the corridor.

It took both men to break Dalton's hold and save Heglund's life.

A quarter-hour after the guards had carried Steve Heglund out of the barracks to revive him, Dalton heard footsteps again. This time he looked up from the cot to see Major Allen Brady at the door.

"Major Dalton," Brady said tightly, "I must reprimand you for what you just did. I could have you flogged to within an inch of your life. You understand that?"

Dalton rose from the cot and moved up to the door. "I know that," he replied, looking Brady square in the eye.

"But I'm not going to, Major Dalton, because I've observed how Mr. Heglund has badgered you. Some kind of grudge between you two?"

"Yes, sir. He beat up my wife in the Fredericksburg occupation. She was eight months pregnant, and the baby died. That's murder in my book."

Brady held Dalton's hard gaze, blinked, and said, "I'm sorry. There's nothing I can do about that. But I will order the sergeant to stay away from you."

"Well, keep his brothers away too, Major. There's trouble between me and the whole family."

"I'll talk to them, but you understand I can't keep them from their duties, only from speaking to you unnecessarily or doing anything else to rile you."

"Fine. Just so they leave me alone."

SEVENTEEN

On March 4, 1863, one of the officers in the cell next to Layne Dalton and Jerry Owens died of pneumonia. He also had a severe case of diarrhea. Colonel Byron Merrick, the surviving officer in that cell, was sick with a bad cold, and it appeared he might also be coming down with pneumonia.

The camp physician lived and had his practice at Lexington Park, Maryland, some twenty miles north of the Point. Dr. Alex Campbell came once every couple of weeks to do what he could for the sick and dying prisoners, but they were still dying an average of one per day.

Each of the officers' barracks had an eating area at one end. Meals, which were cooked in a shack nearby, were brought in by the guards. At breakfast on the morning of March 5, Steve Heglund was among the guards who delivered the meals to Layne Dalton's barracks, which housed some sixty officers.

Jerry Owens sat across the long table from Layne Dalton as Heglund laid a crude wooden tray before each of them and said, "I was sure sorry to hear about your neighbor dyin' yesterday, fellas. That's the way it goes in this place. Men are dyin' just about every day. Never know who'll be next, do we?" Heglund grinned wickedly and walked away.

During the day, Layne and Jerry talked about their tunnel. As best as they could figure, they were about six inches past the stockade fence. Just two more feet, and they would be free men.

At supper that night, Steve Heglund made sure he was the guard to carry the trays to Dalton and Owens. He said nothing when he set them down, just grinned maliciously and went on delivering trays with the other guards. The barracks door was closed and locked as the guards moved on, and the officers were about to begin eating when a large rat skittered under a table.

"Rat!" yelled one of the men, and jumped to his feet.

Within seconds, all the officers were up. Layne grabbed a broom that stood in one corner and, with grim determination, set out to corner the rat and kill it. One officer kicked at the rat as it ran toward him, then reversed directions. Finally, Layne cornered the rat and killed it with a few strokes of the broom handle.

Dalton and Owens disposed of the rat, then returned to their table and sat down to their meals. Without thinking, Jerry sat down where Layne was moments before. Layne eased down on the bench opposite him, grinned, and said, "I think we're sitting in each other's places, but I guess it doesn't make any difference. It's the same slop on that tray as this one."

"Guess so," Jerry chuckled, picking up the fork from the tray.

The meal was about halfway through when Jerry suddenly laid down his fork, clenched his teeth, and gripped his midsection.

"What's the matter?" asked Layne.

"Cramps," Jerry grunted, his face losing color. "Kind of dizzy, too."

Layne stood up, went around the table, and took hold of his friend by the shoulders. "Come on, I'll help you to the cell. You need to lie down."

"Yeah," Jerry nodded, struggling to rise while clutching his stomach. "This isn't good. I…I really am sick."

Layne spoke to the other officers at the table. "Better call the guards. Dr. Campbell should still be on the grounds. I heard somebody say he was staying to eat supper with Major Brady."

While two men banged on the door, shouting for the guards, Jerry Owens went from white to deathly gray and collapsed on the floor.

Layne knelt beside him and said, "Hang on, Jerry. We'll get help for you."

Jerry spasmed violently, thrashed about on the floor for fifteen or twenty seconds, then lay still. He closed his eyes, expelled one tremulous breath...and died.

Two guards came through the door and stood over Layne Dalton as he knelt beside his dead friend. Chaplain Michael Young knelt on the other side.

Young looked up and said to the guards, "He's dead. But I want Dr. Campbell to check the body. From what I saw, I think Captain Owens got some kind of poison."

While one guard was running after the doctor, the chaplain moved to the table and began to pick through the food on Jerry's plate. "Seems to me the captain must have gotten the poison from this food. He was perfectly fine until he had eaten about half of it." His eyes widened. "Major Dalton, come here, please."

Layne bent over the plate, and Young used the fork to separate out a number of tiny yellowish-brown seeds. "What do you make of these?" Young asked.

"Looks like the stuff they put out in those little tins to kill the rats."

"Rat poison. Put in there rather hastily, I'd say. Whoever did it didn't have time to make sure all the seeds were completely mixed into the rice and gravy."

Some of the other officers closed in, wanting to see for themselves. Dalton stood back, his mind in a whirl, and knelt once again beside the body.

Major Brady entered the room, followed by Dr. Campbell.

Layne stood over his dead friend while Campbell examined the body and asked questions.

When Layne finished his description of Jerry's agonizing death, he said, "We believe he was poisoned, Doctor. Wouldn't you say so?"

"Sure sounds like it," nodded Campbell. "We'll have to check with the cooks. Something poisonous got into his food, all right." He looked around and asked, "Anyone else having similar symptoms?" The men shook their heads.

"Doctor, Chaplain Young has something to show you," Layne said.

Young was still standing at the table, keeping guard over Jerry's plate. He made eye contact with the physician, then said, "Tell us what you see here, Dr. Campbell."

Campbell bent low and examined the diminutive seeds Michael Young had separated from the rice and gravy. "Mm-hmm," he said, standing to his full height and setting his gaze on Major Brady. "The captain was poisoned on purpose, Major. These are *nux vomica* seeds."

"What's that?" Brady asked, moving close and looking down at them.

"You use rat poison here in the camp, I believe."

"Yes. We put it in tins in all the barracks and other buildings. This place has quite a population of rats."

I could name you the biggest one, Layne thought. He knew exactly what had happened.

"*Nux vomica* is the poisonous seed of an East Indian tree, Major," said Campbell. "*Strychnos nuxvomica*."

Brady's eyes widened. "Strychnine?"

"Yes. As used in rat poison. In a very short time, it kills anything or anybody that eats it. Somebody purposely put rat poison in the captain's food."

Brady wiped a shaky hand over his face. "I'll have to talk to the cooks. Somebody in this place has some answering to do."

"I can tell you who that somebody is, Major," Layne Dalton said.

Brady swung his gaze to him and raised his eyebrows. "Now, Major, you must be careful with any accusations. I—"

"It's really quite simple, sir. Everybody here knows that Steve Heglund hates me with a passion…and I haven't tried to hide the fact that it's mutual."

"Now, Major—"

"Ask these men who were sitting at this table. It was Steve Heglund who delivered our trays to us. The poison was meant for me."

Brady started to speak again, but Layne cut him off. "Before any of us had taken a bite, a big rat came in here. We were all running around, trying to corner it and kill it. When the rat was dead, we sat down again to eat. Jerry unwittingly sat in my place, so I sat down in his."

"I'll question Sergeant Heglund," the commandant said evenly.

Layne shook his head. "Won't do any good. He'll deny it. Unless some honest guard testifies that he saw him put the poison in, he's going to get away with it."

Major Layne Dalton was right. When questioned, Steve Heglund denied putting the rat poison in the food. Since no one would testify they had seen him do it, the matter was dropped.

The next day, before Dalton was let out of his cell for breakfast, Dr. Campbell entered the barracks to check on Byron Merrick in the next cell. Merrick seemed to be doing better, but Campbell left him some medicine for his cold.

When the doctor was gone, Dalton and Merrick conversed through the wall for a few minutes, then the major looked up to see Steve Heglund peering at him through the small window in the cell door.

"So they're gonna bury your partner this mornin', huh?" Heglund said, keeping his voice low.

Layne left the wall and moved to the door. A dark stain of red started low on his neck and crawled up into his scowling face. "You'll get yours one day, Heglund!"

"Yeah? Well, it won't be *you* who gives it to me, fancy-pants!"

"Well, if it isn't, maybe it'll be God Himself!"

Heglund pursed his lips and huffed, spraying saliva. "There ain't no God, Reverend Dalton. Don't preach to me!"

"You'll find out when you take your last breath."

"Well, let me tell you this, darlin'…you'll draw your last breath a long time before I take mine. I'm gonna see to that!" His voice was still a sibilant whisper as he added, "Missed you last night with the rat poison, but sooner or later I'll put you in your grave." With that, he walked away and left the building.

Layne skipped breakfast. His grief over Jerry's horrid death had stolen his appetite. While the others were eating, Chaplain Young came to the cell, sat down with Dalton, and said, "Major, I know you're hurting inside because your friend died the death that was meant to be yours."

"Yes, you're right. And I'm hurting because his murderer is getting away with it."

"Well, let me say first that he *won't* get away with it. The Bible says vengeance belongs to the Lord. Sometimes God's wheels turn slow, my friend, but they do turn. Let Him deal with Steve Heglund."

Layne wanted to object, but he knew it would accomplish nothing.

"What I came by for," continued Young, "was to comfort you with one fact."

"Yes, sir?"

"Jerry was a Christian, Major. His faith was in the Lord Jesus Christ for his salvation. Jerry's in heaven, and I'm sure by now he's even met your little Danny. They're both in the sweet presence of Jesus. Don't wish either one of them back. To come back to this earth after one glimpse of the wonderful, shining face of Jesus would make this old world seem mighty dark."

"Yes, sir," Layne nodded, biting his lower lip

"You about ready to let the Lord into *your* heart, Layne?"

The biggest thing in Layne Dalton's life, other than his love for Melody, was his hatred of Steve Heglund. His meager knowledge of Scripture and his observance of Christians combined to tell him that if he received Christ into his heart, he would need to lay aside his desire to seek revenge. Layne Dalton did not want to stop hating Steve Heglund; his entire being longed for revenge.

"Not yet," he replied, meeting Young's steady gaze. "I'm still thinking about it, and I'm still reading my Bible."

"Well, just don't wait too long. If you die like you are, you'll never see Jerry or Danny again."

Every night, Layne Dalton worked on his tunnel. His desire to see Melody was stronger than his desire to get even with Steve Heglund. That could come sometime later. His arms ached to hold the woman he loved, and he longed to see her face. Besides, he wanted her to know he was alive and well. What a surprise she would have when he showed up!

As the weeks passed, Byron Merrick took a turn for the worse. He spent most of his time in his cell, lying on the cot. He could be heard coughing and wheezing all through the long hours of the night. Dr. Campbell visited him and gave him what medicine he could, but Merrick grew steadily worse.

On the night of April 2, Layne Dalton was working in his tunnel by lantern light. It was about 10:30. He would work till midnight, which he figured would put him inches from freedom. Tomorrow night he would break through the six to eight inches of sod above the roof of the tunnel, and head for home.

Colonel Merrick lay on his cot, getting sicker by the minute. His lungs were hurting, and he was feeling dizzy. He needed to take some of the powders Dr. Campbell had left him.

Merrick sat up on the cot and fumbled in the pitch-black darkness for a match on his small table. Finding the match, he groped for the lantern and removed the glass chimney. He struck the match and touched the flame to the wick, then raised it high enough to get enough light and blew out the match. He stood up to go for the powders, which were on the chair near the door.

When Merrick got to his feet, a coughing spasm came over him. He staggered, bumping the table. It rocked, and the burning lantern wobbled dangerously, scooted a few inches, and fell to the floor. Merrick's head went into a spin, and he passed out, falling on the cot.

Kerosene spilled in a wide pool across the wooden floor, and the flame quickly followed its path. The old wood used to construct the barracks was tinder-dry. In no time at all, the flames swept across the floor in a fiery sheet and began climbing the walls and the door.

The intense heat awakened Byron Merrick. He ejected a wild scream and began beating at the flames. Merrick's scream was heard throughout the barracks, and within minutes the place was filled with guards. The flames had spread from Merrick's cell to those on either side, and were licking up the walls and spreading to the doors.

Major Brady was on the scene, shouting for the guards to get the prisoners out of their cells and away from the building. Brady knew the old wood would go up in a hurry. All he could do was get the Confederate officers out before they burned to death.

By the time the guards reached Merrick's cell, he was writhing in flames on the floor. The door was ablaze. There was no way to get him out. The two men in the adjacent cell were yelling for help as the guards struggled against the intense heat to get the door open.

Layne Dalton was at the extreme end of his tunnel when the fire broke out, and at first he was unaware of it. But when he heard Merrick's screams and the shouting of the guards, he backed his way out of the tunnel and pushed his head through the opening under his cot. The cell was filled with smoke, and he could hear Steve Heglund saying, "I don't see him in there, Clyde!"

"He's gotta be in there! You just can't see him for the smoke!"

"Well, why ain't he screamin' to get out?"

"Maybe the smoke's overcome him."

"Well, in any case…he's stayin' in there!" Steve growled.

Layne decided to let the Heglund brothers think he was trapped. He coughed loudly and rolled on the floor from under the cot, crying, "Help me! Let me out!"

The flames had worked their way around the corner and were licking at the door frame. Layne looked through the smoke at Steve and Clyde and screamed, "Hurry! Open the door!"

The Heglund brothers laughed above the shouting of guards and prisoners and the roar of the fire. Everyone was too busy to pay any attention to them.

Steve pushed his face close to the small window in the door and said, "Well, darlin', I told you I'd get you! *Too bad we couldn't get to Major Dalton, Major Brady. Tch. Tch. We're sure sorry that nice Rebel officer had to die because his door was on fire and we couldn't get it open.*"

"Please!" Layne wailed. "Please don't leave me to burn to death! Let me out!"

Steve sneered at him and said, "Tell you what, fancy-pants major—I'll lie for you and make it sound to your sweet little wife that you died a brave man."

"No!" coughed Layne. "Please! Let me out!"

"Good-bye, ol' pal," Steve said. "Tell the devil hello for me!"

As the Heglunds turned away, Dalton cried, "You dirty rats! I'll come back from the dead and get you!"

Steve and Clyde laughed and disappeared. Dalton dived into the tunnel.

Guards were working frantically to get all the Confederate officers out of the barracks. As the two Heglund brothers left Dalton and headed down the corridor, they came upon Chaplain Michael Young, who was at his door, waiting for someone to let him out.

"Ah," said Young as the Heglunds drew up, "I knew someone would come pretty soon."

The corridor was thick with smoke. Steve and Clyde coughed and looked at each other. A guard came running down the corridor. He paused, blinked at the smoke that smarted his eyes, and said to

Clyde, "We've got them all out of the west end, Sergeant."

"Good," nodded Clyde. "Keep at it."

"Will do," said the guard, and hurried on.

The sounds of shouting men and roaring fire were all around them. Steve moved through the smoke and put his face close to the opening in the chaplain's door. "You look a little worried, Reverend," he said. "Gettin' warm in there?"

"Come on, open the door!" Young replied.

Steve laughed. "Well, now, whaddya know! The man of God is scared of the fire! I think Clyde an' I will do to you what we just did to your friend, Dalton. We'll just find it impossible to get the door open."

"You left Major Dalton in his cell to burn?"

"Yeah. And now it's your turn, man of God." He laughed. "Where's your God now? Seems to me if He exists, he'd be here to rescue you. Too bad. Hope you toast up real nice. *We're real sorry, Major Brady. Just like with Major Dalton, we couldn't get Chaplain Young's door open. It was just too hot to handle!*"

Clyde was laughing, too.

"You'll never get away with it!" Young shouted. "Other guards will come along before the fire reaches me!"

"You forget, holy man," Clyde said. "I'm the Sergeant of the Guard. As long as I'm standin' here actin' like I'm tryin' to get you out, I can keep the guards runnin' elsewhere. Nobody'll know the difference. Like Steve said, where's your God right now?"

"The chaplain won't need Him this time!" came the loud voice of Major Brady from behind them.

The Heglund brothers wheeled about to see the smoke-wreathed forms of the commandant and four guards whose rifles were aimed at them, hammers cocked. The two sergeants were quickly disarmed, and Young's door was opened.

"You're under arrest!" Brady said in an angry voice. "We heard every word! From your own mouths, you've condemned yourselves. Major Dalton's cell is an inferno now, and you'll face the firing squad for murdering him and for what you were about to do to Chaplain Young!"

Brady told two of the guards to take the Heglunds and lock them up in one of the shacks. While the rest of the building was being cleared, the guards moved Steve and Clyde across the fire-lit compound at gunpoint. Everett and Keith were together outside the blazing building, watching several guards throw water on the adjacent barracks to keep it from catching fire, and saw their brothers come out of the building with two guards holding guns on them.

"What's going on here?" Keith said to Everett.

"I don't know, but whatever it is, we gotta stop it," Everett said, cocking his rifle. "C'mon."

As the two guards ushered Steve and Clyde up to the door of one of the shacks, the other two Heglund brothers came up behind them, guns leveled, and Everett said, "Hold it right there!"

Surprised, the guards looked around to find ominous black muzzles pointing at them.

"Don't interfere!" said one of the guards. "Your brothers are under arrest."

"For what?" demanded Keith.

"Murder, and attempted murder."

"Drop those guns!" Everett said.

The guards complied, and the Heglund brothers locked them in the shack. Then they dashed to the corral, stole four horses, and rode away into the night, laughing because they had succeeded in killing Layne Dalton. They laughed even more when Steve told how Layne had said he would come back from the dead and get them.

Once they were a safe distance up the bank of the Potomac, the brothers agreed that they must wait until the war was over to return home. Steve thought of Jack Reynolds and felt a renewed desire to go after him for killing their father. He knew where Reynolds was, and he knew they needed to put plenty of distance between themselves and the Union army. He suggested to his brothers that they head west to Virginia City, Nevada, and kill Jack Reynolds.

EIGHTEEN

Major Layne Dalton worked his way northward through the back woods of Union territory for two days and was able to find a secluded spot on the bank of the Potomac River across from Coles Point, Virginia. By night, he floated across the river on a dead tree and quickly passed through Coles Point.

Outside of town the next morning he approached a farmer, told him his story, and was given a good horse and saddle. He headed northeastward for Fredericksburg, taking the back trails. After he had seen Melody and spent a few days with her, he would report in at Richmond and advise the Confederate army that he had been taken captive at Marye's Heights. His heart thrilled at the thought of holding Melody in his arms.

Dalton also thought of Steve Heglund and his brothers. Some day, he told himself, I'll find those four and make them pay. As he made the promise, Harriet Smith's voice resounded in his head, and Chaplain Michael Young's voice seemed to blend with it: *Vengeance is mine; I will repay, saith the Lord.* But God was too slow with His vengeance. Steve Heglund should have already received his just due for killing Danny.

Fredericksburg was still in a shambles as the major rode into town about nine o'clock at night. What few people were on the streets only saw a gray-clad rider by the dim street lamps, but no one recognized him or paid him any mind.

His heart drummed his ribs as he mounted his own front porch and knocked on the battered door. He heard footsteps inside and braced himself. When the door opened, he was looking into the wide eyes and gaping mouth of Harriet Smith. He knew the Smith house was in ruins, and seeing Harriet there did not surprise him. He figured she was living with Melody and happened to be nearest the door when he knocked.

He removed his hat, smiled and said, "Hello, Harriet."

It took Harriet several seconds to find her voice. "Layne! We thought you were dead!"

Layne stepped inside and closed the door behind him. "I figured that's what you and Melody would have been told. Where is she? How's she feeling?"

"She...she's not here, Layne. But the last time I saw her, she was feeling quite well."

"Not here?" he said, surprised. "Where then?"

"Well, when she was told that you were killed, she went into deep mourning. It was really rough on her, especially with the problems she had after losing the baby."

"Harriet, where is she?"

"She's in Nevada with her parents. Virginia City."

A hollow feeling settled over Layne. Melody was over two thousand miles away. He scrubbed a hand over his eyes and said, "Of course. With me dead, she would want to be with her parents."

"Yes."

"You spoke of problems after losing the baby. You mean something in addition to what she was experiencing the last time I saw her?"

"Well, it was all related. She finally got better, but Dr. Craig told her that she'd never bear any more children."

"She...she can't ever have children?"

BATTLES OF DESTINY

220

Harriet's hand went to her mouth. "Oh, Layne, I'm sorry! You shouldn't have learned that from me."

Layne's heart felt as though it were made of cold lead. Steve Heglund had not only murdered his unborn son, he had made Melody incapable of ever giving him another one.

"I'm going west," Layne said. "But what if she finds and marries another man before I get there?"

Harriet shook her head and patted Layne's arm. "Not the way she was grieving over you. She told me she would never marry again. You have nothing to worry about there."

"I hope you're right."

"You haven't told me where you've been, Layne. Prison camp?"

"Yes. Point Lookout, Maryland. Rotten place. Long story on how I escaped. Don't have time to tell it. What about the house?"

"Melody said Walter and I could live in it until we get ours rebuilt. Said we'd keep in touch by mail, and she'd make up her mind about selling it later."

"Guess we'll leave it at that for now. I'll head for Nevada tomorrow. Just keep it to yourself that you saw me, okay? As long as the Confederate army thinks I'm dead, I'll leave it that way till I can get to Melody. She has a right to know I'm alive and to see me. After that, I'll come back, surprise General Lee, and get back into the War."

"I think you're doing the right thing," agreed Harriet. "I won't breathe a word to anybody."

"Thanks. Walter all right?"

"Yes. Thank the Lord he made it through the battle here without a scratch. He's in Richmond."

"Tell him hello for me. You'll hear from us once I get to Virginia City."

"Will do. You want to stay here tonight? I can go down the street to Susanne Eckley's."

"I'll just sleep out in the barn," he replied. "Got a horse outside. He and I will do fine in the barn. That way you won't have to go to all that trouble."

"You're very kind. How about a nice hot breakfast in the morning?"

"Sounds good to me!"

Layne had some money stashed in a secret place in the house. He took the money and rode westward out of town, wearing civilian clothes and a pair of western-style boots he had owned for a couple years.

He made his first stop at a small town on the east side of the Blue Ridge Mountains, where he bought a rifle, a revolver, holster and gunbelt, ammunition, bedroll, and a small supply of food. He also bought a map, and in a hotel room that night, mapped out his route.

Dalton would travel west through Cincinnati, Ohio, on to Springfield, Illinois, then to St. Joseph, Missouri. From there he would cross the Missouri River into Kansas and head straight west for Denver. He would cross the Rocky Mountains, pass through Provo City, Utah Territory, and ride across the great desert of Nevada into Virginia City, which was only a few miles from the California border.

The Heglund brothers had chosen almost the same route to Nevada. After stealing guns, ammunition, civilian clothes, bedrolls, and food in Virginia, they headed west through Columbus, Ohio, and from there across Indiana to Springfield, Illinois. They arrived at St. Joseph, Missouri, on April 30, unaware that the man they believed to have perished in the fire at Point Lookout Prison was only a day behind them.

Traveling by horse and buggy, railroad, commercial wagon train, and stagecoaches, Melody Dalton arrived in Virginia City, Nevada, on April 9, 1863. Her parents were shocked to see her, and were saddened to hear that their son-in-law had been killed and that Melody had lost her baby.

Jack Reynolds had done well in his partnership with his brother and had built a large two-story house. Melody would have an up-stairs bedroom at the front, overlooking the wide street that also gave her a view of the towering Sierra Nevada Range to the west.

Melody immediately began looking for a job. Jack told her she did not need to work, that he would provide for her, but Melody said she wanted to pay her own way and that she needed to stay busy. A job would help keep her mind off of Layne.

Within a week, a waitress job opened up at a local café, and Melody took it. Her father warned her that many of the miners who frequented the café were obnoxious and foul-mouthed and would be hard to deal with. But Melody was determined to make her own liv-ing and to pay her room and board, so she told him she would deal with them the best she could.

And deal with them she did.

It wasn't long until every miner in town knew he was to keep his distance from the beautiful young Civil War widow. She was chained to the memory of her husband, and aimed to stay that way. Soon they also learned that she was a Christian, and came to respect her. Melody enjoyed her job and seldom had to fight off advances from unruly men.

Her worst times were when she lay in her bed alone at night. Memories of her life with Layne came like a flood, and though she treasured them, they made her miss him more and long to be in his arms. A night did not pass without tears soaking her pillow.

Often Melody dreamed of Layne and awakened in the middle of the night with her heart breaking for want of him. Sometimes ugly thoughts would stab her mind, as if Satan were trying to tell her that Layne had died lost. She would begin praying, and with it came peace about Layne's spiritual condition when he died.

On the night of April 30, Melody dreamt that Layne was alive, and they were together with Danny. The War was over, and they were frolicking in the yard of their home in Fredericksburg. Little Danny looked just like his father, with the same dark, curly hair and chocolate-brown eyes.

In the dream, Layne was on all fours and Danny was laughing, riding on his daddy's back. Layne was whinnying like a horse and acting as if he was trying to buck his little son off his back. When the ride was over, Layne lifted Danny up and hugged him, then stood him down and took Melody in his arms. Their lips came together in a magic kiss—

Suddenly Melody was awake and sat bolt upright in bed. She heard a heart-wrenching wail echoing in the room, then realized it had come from her. The bedroom door flew open, and both parents entered. Jack was carrying a lighted lantern.

Melody began to weep.

Frances moved to the bed and wrapped her arms around her daughter. "Another one of those vivid dreams, honey?"

Melody clung tight to her mother. "Yes. Oh, Mother, it was so real! Layne and Danny were playing together, then Layne took me in his arms and—oh, it hurts so much to know I'll never see Layne and little Danny this side of heaven. I miss them so much!"

"I know, sweetie. I know," said Frances, embracing her and patting her back.

Jack set the lantern on the bedstand and said, "Let's pray. I want to ask the Lord to ease the pain in your heart, darlin', so you can get back to sleep."

On the evening of May 6, 1863, Major Layne Dalton rode into Marysville, Kansas, and boarded his horse with the local hostler. He ate supper at a small café, then entered the lobby of the Jayhawker Hotel and approached the desk. "Got a room for a tired man?" he asked the middle-aged clerk. "Been on the trail all day."

Layne noticed that the man's face was battered and swollen, and his lips were split.

The clerk tried to smile past the stitches in his lips. "Sure do, mister. Have a nice clean room just waiting for you. Please sign the register there. How long will you be with us?"

"Just one night. Have to move on tomorrow morning."

As he was signing the register, Layne heard the lobby door open and close, followed by footsteps.

"Howdy, Les," came a friendly male voice. "What in the world happened to you?"

Layne laid the pen down and turned the register back to the clerk.

Les Cummings set friendly eyes on the newcomer and said, "I got beat up last night, Avery."

Layne waited patiently while Cummings told of four men who had registered at the desk the night before. They checked in about suppertime, then left the hotel. When they returned around ten-thirty, they were drunk. There were two ladies in the lobby at the time, and the four drunks began talking to them in a ribald way and using foul language. Cummings had reprimanded them, and one of the men went behind the desk and beat him into unconsciousness. When he came to, the four men were gone. The two women and the town marshal were there, looking down on him as the doctor worked on his battered face. The four men had left town in a hurry.

Three times in telling Avery his story, the clerk had used the name *Steve* for the man who beat him up. As he mounted the stairs and entered his room, Layne wondered if brutality just went with the name *Steve*. His mind, of course, went to the man he hated so passionately, who was probably finding some other poor Rebel officer to pick on at the prison by now.

After traveling steadily for two more days, Layne rode into Smith Centre, Kansas. Hardly had he turned his horse onto Main Street when he picked up that everybody in the town was talking about the bank robbery that had taken place there that morning.

Layne listened to a conversation at an adjacent table while he ate his supper and learned from a man who had been in the Smith

Centre Bank that there were four robbers. They were ugly, filthy-mouthed men, and the one who seemed to be their leader had pistol-whipped the bank president.

Layne suspected that the four men who robbed the bank were no doubt the same four men who had caused the trouble at the Marysville Hotel. He told himself that the leader who pistol-whipped the bank president was no doubt the Steve who had beat up Les Cummings.

Steve. The name made his stomach go sour. He pictured the repulsive face of Steve Heglund and renewed his vow to make him feel every ounce of his smoldering revenge.

On May 10, Dalton was riding into Oberlin, Kansas, at sunset, and his attention was drawn to a dozen or more riders coming toward him from the west end of town. They hauled up in front of the marshal's office and were met by a host of townspeople, who were all asking the same thing: Had they caught the bank robbers?

Layne's ears perked up as he guided his horse to the hitch rail close by and dismounted. He saw by the sign over the office that the marshal's name was Jed Rice.

Rice had left his horse and was standing on the edge of the boardwalk as he raised his hands and shouted for silence, "Everybody quiet! I'll explain if you'll get quiet!"

The rest of the posse stayed in their saddles as the babble of voices settled down.

"No, we didn't catch 'em," Rice said. "They gave us the slip."

"You mean you're gonna just let 'em go?" came a voice from the crowd. "They not only cleaned out the bank, but they killed Mack Henelt!"

"We did all we could," Rice said, "but we can't follow 'em forever. These men have jobs to work and businesses to run. I don't dare be out of town very long. That would leave Oberlin with no law at all. You don't want that, do you?"

The people began to talk among themselves. None of them wanted their marshal gone from town for any length of time. There were no government lawmen to pursue the robbers, and there was no militia. All army men were occupied with hostile Indians or fighting in the Civil War.

"We understand, Marshal," spoke up an elderly man. "At least we got one of those dirty killers. If he lives, we'll have the satisfaction of hangin' him!"

"You mean he's still alive?" Rice asked, eyebrows arched in surprise. "Doc told me before we rode out he'd prob'ly be dead time we got back."

"Just barely hangin' on, from what I'm told, Marshal," spoke up another man.

"I'd swear those four are brothers," said Rice, running his gaze over the faces of the crowd. "Anybody know if Doc's got a name outta the wounded one?"

"His name's Keith somethin', Jed," put in a portly man standing near him on the boardwalk. "Leastwise I heard one of 'em call him that when he took Mack Henelt's bullet."

Layne Dalton could not believe his ears. There were four robbers. They appeared to be brothers. The meanest one was named Steve. One of them had been shot during the bank robbery, and his name was Keith. The coincidence was too much.

Layne's scalp tingled. Could it really be the Heglund brothers? But they were at the Point Lookout Prison. Or were they? If this really was not coincidence, what were the Heglunds doing in Kansas? Where were they headed?

There was only one way to settle this. Marshal Rice was saying something about going to the doctor's office to check on the wounded robber. Layne would follow him.

The posse dispersed to put away their horses, and the crowd broke up. Just as Marshal Rice was approaching the door of Dr. Efram Pennock's office, Dalton called from behind him, "Marshal Rice!"

The marshal halted, looked over his shoulder, and said, "Yes, sir? Do I know you?"

"No, you don't, but I need to talk to you before you go in there."

Rice was congenial and allowed the stranger to explain why he needed to take a look at the wounded bank robber. Layne held nothing back. As briefly as possible, he told Rice the whole story.

The marshal, a stout man in his late fifties, said, "Well, Major, I don't blame you for wantin' to see that Steve Heglund pay for what he did. His brothers, either, for that matter. But on the other hand, I don't like to see you takin' the law into your own hands."

"Marshal, I heard you say that you and the posse couldn't spend any more time chasing these outlaws. There isn't any other law west of the wide Missouri who's going to bring them to justice. So what's wrong with me going after them?"

Rice saw the stubborn set to Dalton's jaw and the dogged look in his eyes. "Well, let's go in here and see if this Keith fella is the one you've got in mind."

Dr. Pennock's nurse, secretary, and receptionist was his wife, Erline. She looked up from the desk and smiled as they entered. "Hello, Marshal. I imagine you're here to see about the wounded outlaw. Who's your friend?"

"Name's Layne Dalton," Rice said. "Mr. Dalton, this is Erline Pennock, Doc's wife."

"Glad to meet you, ma'am," Dalton smiled, touching his hat.

"Is he still alive?" asked Rice.

"Yes. My husband's with him now. I don't think he'll make it through the night, though."

"It's important that we both see him. May we go in?"

"Let me ask the doctor," Erline said, rising from the desk.

While Erline was out of the room, Layne asked for the details of the robbery and shooting. Rice told him that while all four robbers were inside the bank, a teller named Mack Henelt had pulled a gun from a drawer in his cage and shot the one who now lay in the clinic. The others gunned Henelt down, ran to their horses, and galloped away. Rice added, "I think they left him because the bullet was in the center of his chest. No way they could take him with them. They figured he was done for."

Erline returned and told the two men they could go in. As Rice and Dalton moved through the door, they saw the wounded man on the examining table, and Dr. Pennock standing over him. Pennock motioned with his head for them to come to the table. It was Keith Heglund!

Keith's languid eyes focused on Dalton and went suddenly clear. His already pale features turned flour white, and his mouth flew open.

The doctor saw the reaction. He was about to speak to Dalton when Keith gasped weakly, "No, it can't be! Doctor, it's a ghost! Help me!"

"I told Steve and Clyde I'd come back and get them, Keith," Dalton said. "Where are they headed?"

The dying man's whole body shook violently as his eyes bulged with terror. "D-Doctor, do something! I'm...I'm dyin'! I know it! I'm lookin' at a dead man!"

"Jed, what's this all about?" Pennock asked.

"I'll tell you later," Rice replied. Turning to Dalton, he said, "Looks like he's your man, all right."

The major nodded, then set piercing eyes on Keith. He leaned closer and said, "Some brothers, eh, Keith? Ran like scared rabbits and left you to hang. They need to pay for deserting you, Keith."

Keith Heglund could do nothing but stare in terror at the man he thought had burned to death in the barracks at Point Lookout.

"Keith," Dr. Pennock said, "you aren't going to live long enough to hang. That bullet is touching your heart. It's a miracle you're not dead already. But if I try to take it out, you'll die instantly. You're losing blood, and there's nothing I can do to stop it. You will die before morning. If you can help these men stop your brothers from killing others, you ought to do it."

"The man's making sense, Keith," Layne said. "Where are they headed?"

Keith licked his lips, still wary of Dalton's presence, not knowing what to believe about him. "Could...could I have some water?"

Dr. Pennock gave him a drink. After he had taken his fill, Keith ran his frightened gaze to Dalton and licked his lips again. "They're headed to...to Virginia City."

A cold hand clutched Layne's heart. "To kill Jack Reynolds." It was a statement, not a question.

Keith nodded.

Rice turned to Dalton. "You told me your wife is in Virginia City with her parents. Is Jack Reynolds her father?"

"Yes, and I've got to catch up to them before they get there. They'll kill Jack, and probably my wife and my mother-in-law!"

Keith coughed in a strained, choking manner. "Layne...I...I'm sorry about...the baby." His eyes rolled back in their sockets. He coughed weakly again, and his chest went still.

"He's gone," said Pennock, feeling for a pulse in the sides of Keith's neck and finding none.

"Well, at least you got an apology from one of them," said Rice.

"I'll get more than that from the others," Layne said.

The three brothers rode hard into the night. When they were a safe distance from Oberlin, they found a wooded area next to a small stream and made camp. With the camp fire throwing flickering shadows on their faces, they ate pork and beans and drank whiskey.

"Too bad we had to leave him there," lamented Everett.

"Yeah," agreed Clyde.

"No choice," said Steve. "We'd have been caught and hanged if we'd stayed around tryin' to take him with us. When I saw that big hole in his chest, I knew he wouldn't make it. No doubt he died right away. Ain't nobody can live with a .45 slug in his ticker."

"Well, at least we showed that posse how stupid they are," Clyde said.

"Yeah," Steve laughed. "Only bad thing was we didn't get to blow none of their heads off."

"Stupid as they was," Everett said, "they're almost as bad off now as they'd've been if they'd got their heads shot off."

The Heglunds had a good laugh, finished their meal, and turned in early. They wanted to make sure they had a good head start just in case the Oberlin posse tried a second time to catch them.

Layne Dalton rode out of Oberlin at the crack of dawn. He grinned to himself. Jed Rice had not said another word to him about not taking the law into his own hands.

"Well, God," he said as the Kansas prairie stretched out before him to the west, "You got ahead of me with Keith. He did taste of Your vengeance, didn't he? But I'll take care of the other three myself."

NINETEEN

The Heglund brothers were finding that robbing banks was quite lucrative. They had done it at first merely to fill up their empty pockets as they rode west. Though they lost Keith, it did not deter their avaricious appetites.

They crossed the border into Colorado Territory on May 12, and on May 14 robbed the bank in Byers, killing two bank em-ploy-ees. As they galloped away from Byers on the rolling plains toward Denver, Everett's horse stepped in a gopher hole and went down with a broken leg. Everett was thrown hard, but was only bruised. He climbed up behind Clyde, and they continued on toward Denver.

The sun was almost touching the western horizon when they spotted a small herd of cattle grazing in a pasture near a shaded house, barn, and outbuildings. In the corral were several saddle horses, along with a few head of cattle.

"Well, boys, think I can find me a good animal in there?" Everett said.

"If you don't, it's because you're blind," chuckled Clyde.

"Ranch looks small enough there shouldn't be any ranch hands to contend with," said Steve. "Looks like the rancher and his wife there on the porch."

"Should be easy pickin's," Clyde said.

The Heglunds turned into the yard, riding through the long shadows of the tall cottonwoods that surrounded the buildings. The rancher said something to his wife and rose from the bench where they were sitting. His wife remained seated.

The rancher was a tall, slender man. He tilted his straw hat to the back of his balding head, smiled, and said, "Howdy, gents. Somethin' I can do for you?"

"Yeah," Steve nodded, pulling his horse a little closer to the porch. "My brother Everett here lost a good horse back the trail a ways. Stepped in a hole and broke a leg. Had to shoot it. We noticed some nice-lookin' horses there in your corral. We'd like to let Everett pick out the one he likes."

The rancher shook his head, grinning innocently. "Sorry, gents. None of those horses are for sale."

"What's your name, mister?" Steve said.

"Cashman. Floyd Cashman."

"Now Mr. Cashman, I guess you don't hear too good. Who said anything about buyin' 'em?" As he spoke, Steve pulled his revolver, cocked it, and leveled it on Cashman's chest.

"N-now, wait a minute!" the rancher gasped. "What's going on here?"

Mrs. Cashman rose from the bench and gripped her husband's arm. "Floyd, don't argue with them! If they want a horse, let them have it."

"Now there's some real sound advice, Mr. Cashman," Steve said. "Better listen."

"Do you know the penalty for horse stealing in these parts, mister?" Cashman boomed.

Steve aimed his gun at the rancher's face and roared, "Do you know the penalty for givin' me trouble?"

"Floyd, please," begged his wife. "Let them have a horse. He's going to kill you if you don't!"

"All right," Cashman sighed. "You can have the gray roan gelding."

Steve shook his head. "Everett'll take the one that suits his fancy, along with the bridle and saddle of his choosing. Now you two just mosey over there and sit down on that bench. Be real nice and quiet, and you'll be rid of us before the sun's all the way down."

Everett slid off Clyde's horse and made his way to the corral. Steve and Clyde sat their horses and trained their weapons on the Cashmans.

Everett opened the corral gate and moved in behind the split-rail fence. The cattle and horses stared at him and began stirring about. He was a strange body with a strange smell. Some of the animals moved around the back corner of the barn to a part of the corral Everett couldn't see. He was unaware that around that corner was an ill-tempered, long-horned bull.

Everett could see six horses—three stallions, two mares, and a gelding. The gelding was a bay with bald face and four perfect white stockings. He decided he would take the bay unless he found something he liked better around the corner.

The horses and cattle moved away from him as he headed for the back corner of the barn. When he reached it, he saw more cattle and horses, but the bull was blocked from his view by two black stallions. Everett liked the look of the stallions and began moving toward them.

"C'mere, boys," he said, holding out his hand. "Easy. I just want to take a look at you."

The stallions parted and dashed around him. Suddenly Everett was standing face-to-face with the bull. It gave him a menacing look, snorted, and shook its head.

Everett's blood ran cold. There was fifty feet of open space between him and the bull. Could he make it to the fence, about the same distance away, before the beast got him? Everett wanted to call out to his brothers, but he feared the sound might cause the bull to charge.

He felt riveted to the spot, as though he were standing in two feet of solid ice. He had to get away from the bull, but he would have to move very slowly.

He tried to slide one foot, but it barely moved. His body responded to his will only grudgingly. Icy sweat was trickling down his back.

The bull snorted, shook its head again, and pawed dirt.

Everett's heart was pounding like a mad thing in his chest. Ever so carefully, he moved a few inches to his right. The massive beast shook its head again, throwing a string of white saliva on the ground. Its eyes shone like angry coals. This strange man had dared enter its domain. It grunted, and Everett was sure it was about to charge. He glanced at the fence. It seemed no closer than before.

The bull lifted its head and bellowed. It was now or never. Everett sprang to his right, stumbled, caught himself, and bolted for the fence.

But he was too slow.

The bull roared and charged. As if in a nightmare, Everett's legs would not respond to the panic driving his mind. He let out a whimper of terror as he strained toward the safety of the fence. He knew he would not reach it in time. His knees gave way. As he struggled to right himself, the maddened bull hit him full force.

At the house, Steve and Clyde had heard the bull's snorting and bellowing, but only sent casual glances in that direction. When a wild scream pierced the air from the other side of the barn, they exchanged startled glances, wheeled their horses about, and galloped toward the corral.

Both brothers vaulted the fence and ran toward the back corner of the barn. When they reached it, the sight before their eyes startled and sickened them.

The bull—horns crimson with blood—had just dumped Everett on the ground and was about to spear him again. As Steve and Clyde opened fire on the massive beast, it lifted Everett over its head, shook him violently, and tossed him aside. Everett's lifeless form landed hard and rolled several feet, arms and legs flailing like a rag doll.

The pain from the bullets intensified the bull's rage. It turned with fiery eyes toward the source of its affliction and charged.

"The head!" shouted Steve. "The head!"

Both men fired as fast as they could, emptying their guns at the charging beast. Finally the bull's knees buckled, and it went down no more than a dozen feet from the backtracking brothers. They made sure the bull was dead, then darted to the spot where Everett's body lay in a crumpled heap.

"Man, what an awful way to die," said Steve, shaking his head. "Come on. Let's get him outta here."

Together, Steve and Clyde carried Everett's body from the corral. As they passed through the gate, they saw that the Cashmans were nowhere in sight. Movement down the road caught Steve's eye. Several ranchers had heard the gunfire and were coming to investigate.

"We gotta get outta here!" Steve gasped.

"What about Everett?" Clyde said, focusing on the oncoming riders.

"Leave him! Let the rancher bury him! Let's go!"

On the morning of May 15, Major Layne Dalton rode along the fence that led to the Cashman ranch house and spotted the rancher in a nearby field, standing knee-deep in a rectangular hole. There was a shovel in his hand and the body of a man lying close by.

Layne dismounted, wrapped the reins around the top pole of the fence, and hopped over. The rancher saw him coming and ceased digging, leaning on the shovel. He watched the approach of the stranger carefully, but showed no alarm.

Drawing up, Layne set his eyes on the mangled corpse and recognized Everett Heglund. "Mornin', sir," he said, nodding at the rancher. "My name's Layne Dalton. I'm trailing a gang of killers through these parts. Brothers named Heglund. I was going to stop and ask if you had seen them, but I don't need to ask now."

"They came in here, put guns on my wife and me, Mr. Dalton. They were going to steal one of my horses. Said this guy's horse had broken a leg farther back on the trail."

"Yeah, main reason I stopped. Yours is the first ranch from the spot I found the dead horse." Layne looked at the corpse. "I'd say Everett here died a pretty violent death."

"He went into the corral to steal a horse, and my bull gored him to death. The other two killed the bull."

"And rode on."

"Yep."

"You and your wife all right?"

"Yes, thank God."

"Well, I'll get back on their trail."

Back in the saddle, Layne pointed the horse's nose west. *Well, God, looks like You got there ahead of me again. But I want Steve and Clyde for myself—especially Steve.*

Layne Dalton trailed Steve and Clyde Heglund through Denver and over the Rockies toward the Utah Territory border, about twelve hours behind them. Layne pushed his horse as hard as he dared and was encouraged to find that he was gaining on them as they neared the Utah line.

On June 3, Dalton rode into Grand Junction, Colorado Territory, just after noon. A crowd of people was gathered in the street in front of the Rocky Mountain Bank. Layne suspected that the Heglunds had been there and robbed the bank. He hauled up at a hitch rail near the bank, slid from the saddle, and approached the crowd, which was formed in a circle in the middle of the broad, dusty street. Layne was tall enough to see over many of the heads. A man with a badge on his chest was lying in the dust.

The town's marshal was down with three bullets in him, and a doctor was kneeling at his side.

"What happened?" Dalton asked a young man who stood beside him.

"Bank robbery. Two gunmen held up the bank. Someone saw them go in with their guns drawn and notified Marshal Walls. He got there just as they were coming out, and they put him down."

The young man's words were barely out of his mouth when a woman's wail sliced through the warm air. Cries of alarm came from the crowd as the doctor stood up, shaking his head. The men in the crowd wanted a posse to go after the robbers, but without the marshal to lead them, none of the men would attempt it. There would be no posse.

"How long ago did this happen?" Layne asked, turning to the young man.

"About twenty, twenty-five minutes."

The major's heart leaped in his breast. They were now less than a half-hour ahead of him!

Dalton hastened to his horse and swung into the saddle. He was glad there would be no posse. He wanted the Heglunds for himself. He trotted the horse to the west end of town, then put it to a gallop.

The Heglund brothers rode hard for the first half-hour out of Grand Junction. Their treasury was growing. They now had two large canvas sacks stuffed full of money, tied to Steve's saddlehorn. They slowed to a walk to give their horses a breather.

"You really don't think they'll send a posse after us?" Clyde asked, looking over his shoulder.

"Nope," Steve said. "We put the marshal down. Town doesn't seem big enough to need or afford a deputy. Most townsmen won't try to put a posse together on their own. We won't have a problem with anybody from Grand Junction."

After a few minutes of silence between them, Steve glanced at Clyde and said, "Really upset over Everett and Keith, ain'tcha?"

"Yeah, but I been thinking of somethin' else too."

"What's that?"

Clyde paused, ran a finger under his nose, and replied, "Do you suppose somethin's doggin' our tracks because of what you did to Dalton's wife and kid and what we did to Dalton himself...and what we're plannin' to do to Jack Reynolds?"

"Somethin' like what? *God?*"

"Well, there's *somethin'* out there…or up there. I dunno. But it's like somethin' unseen might be followin' us, and is gonna make us pay."

"Melody's old man murdered Pa! The law let him get away with it, but we ain't! He's got it comin'. Don't you be frettin' about some kind of God gonna have retribution on us."

"Well, don't you think it's strange the way Keith and Everett were alive and healthy till we put ourselves on this journey to kill Jack?"

"Hey, Keith got in the way of a bullet! Happens every day."

"I don't think it happens every day. And look how Everett went out—that ain't somethin' that happens every day, Steve, and you know it. I tell you, we've been jinxed or somethin'."

"Aw, c'mon, Clyde, don't go nuts on me now! What happened to our brothers just *happened*. I'm tellin' you there ain't no God out there or *up* there. Ain't no jinx, neither."

"Well, maybe it's Layne Dalton!"

Steve pulled rein, stopping his horse, and glared at his brother. "Don't tell me you believe he's come back from the dead to get us! Those were just words of spite from a dyin' man. Nobody comes back from the dead!"

"Then what're ghosts?"

"Ghosts!" Steve laughed. "You know what ghosts are? Just figments of dumb people's imaginations. I'm tellin' you, nothin' and no one is doggin' us. Now come on, let's move."

The Heglunds were following a wagon trail that led into Utah. Some ten minutes later, they started down a gentle hill and saw a buggy off the side of the road. It was a one-horse vehicle, but there was no horse. As they drew abreast of the buggy, they saw a middle-aged man on the ground near the tongue. An arrow protruded from his left shoulder. He was conscious and holding a bandanna at the base of the arrow to stay the flow of blood.

The Heglunds halted their horses and looked down at the man, who raised his head painfully and said in a weak voice, "Help me...please."

"Sorry, pal, we ain't got time," Steve said. "We're in a hurry."

As they rode away, Clyde said, "Maybe we shoulda helped him. Did you notice the Bible on the seat of the buggy? He was prob'ly a preacher."

"I didn't notice no Bible," grunted Steve. "And if he's a preacher, all the more reason to leave him just the way he is."

Layne Dalton couldn't be sure it was the Heglunds, but he had spotted two riders ahead of him several times after leaving Grand Junction. The hilly country took them from his sight periodically, but the last time he had seen them some five minutes earlier, they had topped a rise, then disappeared on its other side.

Galloping the horse for all it was worth, he soon reached the rise and thundered over its crest. He saw a buggy sitting off the side of the trail, and noted that it had no animal harnessed to it. Seconds later, he spotted the man lying near the buggy's tongue and skidded his mount to a halt.

The arrow protruding from the man's left shoulder caught his eye as he leaped from the saddle. He knelt beside the wounded man, saying, "I didn't realize there were hostile Indians about. I'll take you into Grand Junction. I know they've got a doctor."

"Thank you," the man replied, running his tongue over dry lips.

"Here, let me get you some water."

Layne gave the wounded man water from his canteen, then examined the area where the arrow had entered. "I've never seen an arrow wound, sir, but I've seen lots of bullet wounds in the Civil War. I think you'll be all right. By the way, I guess I should introduce myself. My name's Layne Dalton."

"Pleased to meet you, Mr. Dalton," the wounded man said weakly. "I'm Reverend William Cady. I'm pastor of the Presbyterian church in Grand Junction. I was heading home from a visit to an ailing member of the church when a band of Utes came at me. They shot me and took my horse. Utes have been on the prowl lately."

Layne thought of the Heglunds. He wanted desperately to catch them before they reached Virginia City, but the preacher's life was at stake. There was no choice but to take him to the doctor. He broke the arrow off close to Cady's body, loaded him on his horse, and headed back to Grand Junction.

Night had fallen by the time Reverend Cady was bandaged up and ready to go home. His wife had been summoned to the doctor's office, and when Layne was about to leave and get a hotel for the night, the Cady's invited him home for supper and to stay in their guest room. He gladly accepted.

Supper was eaten in the parlor at the Cady home, where the preacher could lie on a sofa and take his meal. Mrs. Cady and the major sat nearby at a small table.

When the meal was over and Mrs. Cady was washing dishes in the kitchen, Layne sat in a chair next to the sofa and chatted with the preacher. Cady asked Layne where he was going, and Layne decided to tell him the whole story.

"I hope you find your wife and her parents doing well when you get to Virginia City, Major," Cady said, "but I'm concerned that your vindictive spirit toward this Steve Heglund and his brother will dry you up inside. I'm pulling for you to stop them from killing your father-in-law, and all, but I've seen vengeance get down deep into a man's soul and destroy him."

"I'm not going to let that happen, Reverend," Dalton smiled. "But I *am* going to catch up to those two and—"

"Kill them?"

Layne adjusted himself nervously on his chair. "I'm going to save my father-in-law, and perhaps my wife and mother-in-law, from being murdered, sir. There's some vengeance mixed in here, I'll admit, but they've got to be stopped before they reach Virginia City, and there's no one going to do it but me."

Cady studied him for a moment, moving his wounded arm in its sling to a more comfortable position. "There's a whole lot of vengeance in there, son. And since you say there's no one to stop them but you…what if you keep stopping to help people like me? Then who's going to protect your family from the Heglunds?"

Layne's mouth pulled into a thin line. "I just won't be stopping to help anyone else."

Cady grinned. "I can read people, Major. It isn't in you to ignore someone who's in trouble."

"Okay, okay. I know what you're driving at."

"Oh?"

"Yes. You preachers have your way of sneaking up on us. What you're about to say is that God can stop the Heglunds. Right?"

"Well, from what you told me, it wasn't you who took out Keith or Everett."

"No, you're right about that."

"Then who did?"

Layne knew the answer, but chose to skirt it. "Could have been God, but it might just have been circumstances."

"Maybe, but I doubt it. You told me your wife is a Christian, and your in-laws, too."

"Yes."

"So they're God's children. He watches out for His own, Major."

Layne had nothing to say.

"What about you, son?" Cady proceeded. "Since you haven't told me that you're a Christian, I assume you're not."

"Every man has to come to God in his own way," Layne said stubbornly, knowing that philosophy was about to get shot down again.

Cady called for his Bible and explained the gospel to Layne, pointing out that the only way to the Father is Christ Himself. Layne knew that the Lord in heaven was breathing down his neck. Nearly everywhere he went, someone was there to correct his lame philosophy and confront him with the gospel.

Cady took Layne to the cross from a half-dozen different directions, then closed his Bible. "Decision is yours, son. You can go on turning Jesus away, or repent, receive Him, and settle this thing."

Layne wanted desperately to unleash his vengeance on Steve Heglund, and he knew that things would change in his heart if he became a child of God. He held on with the tenacity of a bulldog. "I'm not ready, Preacher," he said, shaking his head. "I have to have more time to think about it."

"Well, let me ask you something? You say you're not ready to turn to Christ…are you ready to die?"

"I really need to get to bed, sir," Layne said, rising to his feet. "I have to ride out of here before dawn."

The Cadys saw to it that Layne Dalton had a hearty breakfast before he rode away from their house and out of their lives. They both thanked him for saving William's life and said they would pray for the safety of Layne's family in Virginia City…and for Layne to turn to the Lord before it was too late.

The major was ten miles west of Grand Junction when dawn's gray light appeared on the horizon behind him. He had to push hard to make up the time he had lost the day before. Worried that he might not catch the Heglunds in time, Layne started to pray, almost without thinking about it.

"God, I'm…in a pickle here. You know I couldn't just leave that poor man lying there with the arrow in him. So I…well, I've got to ask a favor of You. You know what those men are planning to do. Somehow You've got to—"

Layne Dalton gripped the reins till his fingers hurt, shook his head, and said, "What are you doing, Dalton? What right have you to ask your Maker for anything when you continue to turn your back on Him?"

Scolding himself changed nothing except to keep Layne from continuing his prayer. He would have to catch up to the Heglunds and stop their murderous scheme on his own.

By the time Steve and Clyde Heglund reached the town of Duchesne, Utah, near Indian Canyon, their horses gave out. Both were limping badly when they carried their riders into town.

"Let's hope we can find us a couple of good horses real fast," Steve said. "We're gettin' close enough to Nevada that my trigger finger is developin' an itch."

They spotted a sign along the town's main thoroughfare that read: *Jasper's Stable—Horses Bought, Sold, Boarded, Curried.*

"See that?" Steve said. "We'll get rid of these nags and be on our way!"

They dismounted and entered the tumble-down office to find an elderly man sitting at a crude desk made of wooden crates. "What can I do fer ya, gents?" the old man asked.

"We need to buy a couple good horses," said Steve. "We ain't poor, so don't waste time tryin' to sell us some broken-down nags."

"Wish I even had some broken-down nags to sell," the old timer said. "I ain't got a horse of any kind. The Uintahs came into town a couple nights ago and stole everythin' I had. No-good Indians, anyhow!"

"You mean you don't have any horses at all?" Clyde pressed him.

"That's right."

"Now, wait a minute!" said Steve, bending down to the level of the hostler's face. "My brother and I both saw two horses in your corral when we were comin' in here. Don't lie to us!"

"I ain't lyin'. Them's mine and my son's. We had 'em at home when them Indians come into town. I can't sell you those."

Steve whipped out his revolver and cracked the old man on the head with the barrel, sending him to the floor. Steve looked down at him and said, "We weren't wantin' to *buy* your horses, mister. We were just wantin' to make a trade!"

Jasper's son didn't show up while the Heglunds switched saddles and bridles. The old man was just coming around when they rode away, leaving their worn-out horses in the corral.

Layne Dalton rode into Duchesne the next day, his own horse worn out and hardly able to carry him. Entering the stable office, he found Jasper with a bandage on his head. Jasper told him about the Indians stealing the stable's horses a few days earlier and about the two men who yesterday had clobbered him on the head and stolen his horses. Layne knew who the two men were.

It took Layne half a day to locate a good horse he could purchase on a ranch several miles north of Duchesne. Once the deal was made, he was on his way west, headed toward Provo City.

He rode hard, feeling almost as if God was against his saving Jack Reynolds's life. *If not*, he thought, *why all these delays?*

TWENTY

I t was a hot day in late June when the Heglund brothers robbed the bank in Stillwater, Nevada Territory, some sixty-five miles east of Virginia City. The saddlehorns of both their horses were laden with canvas bags stuffed with money.

Three days earlier they had robbed the bank in Eureka, Nevada, and the following day the bank in Austin. Steve had not noticed that a bag hanging from his saddlehorn had *Bank of Stillwater* emblazoned on it.

Layne Dalton knew he was once again drawing close to the Heglunds when he arrived in Stillwater just two hours after they had robbed the bank. He watered his horse good, filled his canteen, and pushed on westward.

When night fell he wanted to keep going, but his horse was tiring, and he dare not push it too hard. He stopped beside a small stream and camped for the night.

Just nine miles ahead, the Heglunds camped on another stream about seven or eight miles from Virginia City. They would have their revenge on Jack Reynolds tomorrow, June 30, 1863.

✳ ✳ ✳

On the afternoon of Monday, June 29, Hank and Jack Reynolds waved good-bye to their families from the Wells Fargo stagecoach as it pulled away from the stage office in Virginia City. As joint-owners of the Reynolds Mining Company, they were off to Sacramento to negotiate the purchase of a gold mine in the High Sierras. The entire trip would take them a week.

That evening, Frances Reynolds and her daughter had supper together, then spent a couple of hours in Bible study discussing how a good God could allow evil in the world.

Later, lying in bed in the dark, Melody found sleep eluding her. Memories of Layne came to mind, one after another. They were still so fresh and her need for him so great that she began to weep uncontrollably, crying out his name over and over.

Soon there was a knock at her bedroom door. "Yes, Mother?" she said, sniffling, and using the sheet to dab at her wet face in the dark.

The door squeaked open. "Having another one of those bad nights, honey?"

Melody sniffed again. "Yes. I'm sorry I disturbed you."

A lantern burned on a table in the hall. Frances left the door open and sat down beside her daughter on the bed. They embraced, and Melody said, "Oh, Mother, I miss him so much…so terribly, terribly much."

"I know, dear," Frances said softly. "I know. I realize I can't fully enter into your grief because I've never lost your father. I shudder to think what it would be like if I did. And if I had the power to ease the pain in your heart, I would."

"I know you would, Mother," sniffed Melody, drawing a shuddering breath. "But we mortals can only go so far, no matter how much we love each other."

"That's right, honey. Jesus is the only one who can really ease your pain."

"Yes, and He does most of the time. Maybe sometimes He lets the pain come back to my heart so I'll draw closer to Him. I do pretty well with it, but sometimes I just have to have a good cry."

"And this is one of those times."

"I saw a little boy in town today, probably about four years old. He looked so much like Layne must have looked when he was that age—same dark, curly hair and eyes so brown they were almost black. I…I guess laying eyes on that cute little boy, and seeing how much he looked like Layne, made me want my little Danny so bad."

"Where'd you see him?" Frances asked.

"In front of the sheriff's office. You know that new deputy who came to town a week or so ago?"

"I've heard people mention him. His name's Wes something. Can't think of his last name. I haven't seen him yet, as far as I know. What about him?"

"Well, the deputy was talking to Sheriff Wyler, and the little boy was holding onto the deputy's hand. I figure he's probably the deputy's son."

"We'll have to make it a point to find out where they live and pay his wife a call. Maybe take her a meal or something."

"That would be nice. I'm sure it would help her feel welcome. Besides, I'd like to meet that little boy. Maybe even get to hug him." Melody's eyes filmed up.

"Oh, honey," said Frances, taking her in her arms again.

"I'm sorry," Melody said. "It's just that…knowing that even if Layne was alive, I could never have another child—"

Melody's body shook as she broke into heavy sobs.

"Go on, sweetheart," Frances said softly. "Cry it out."

Birds were singing in the trees to welcome the new day. Dawn had come, and the eastern sky was already growing pink.

Clyde Heglund rolled over in his bedroll, glanced at the birds flitting amongst the branches of the cottonwoods that lined the small brook nearby, then looked at his brother.

Steve's sleepy eyes focused on Clyde. "Go on back to sleep," he said. "Since we're only an hour's ride or so from Virginia City, let's take it easy this mornin'."

"All right by me. Just so this is the day we give it to Jack Reynolds for killin' Pa."

"We will, little brother. We will."

Layne Dalton awakened to find a slight hint of gray streaking the eastern horizon. According to his map, he was within little more than two hours' ride of Virginia City if he kept his horse at a steady trot.

He downed hardtack and beef jerky with water, then quickly saddled his mount and headed west. He almost implored the God of heaven to let him find the Heglund brothers before they could get to Jack Reynolds, but the guilt he carried on his conscience for the way he had kept the Lord from his heart and life would not let him go to Him for help.

Steve and Clyde Heglund lazily settled into their saddles and trotted away from the stream toward Virginia City. The sun was already giving promise of a hot day. The land about them, though furnished with a few streams, was mostly barren. Cottonwoods grew along the streams, but in the brown maw of the Nevada desert lay sun-bleached rocks and boulders amid patches of catclaw, rabbitbush, and cacti of various sizes and shapes.

They saw smooth-skinned salamanders sunning themselves on hot rocks, along with their scaly lizard neighbors. There were signs of the desert night creatures in the soft sand, and periodically they noticed a diamondback rattler slithering among the rocks.

Bald, sun-scorched mountains lay on either side of them as they followed that westbound trail through scattered clumps of brush and cactus. Soon they were climbing a steep slope onto a rugged hog-back. When they reached the crest, the jagged scars of two canyons stretched their shadowed length before them into the rocky terrain to the north.

The Heglunds found themselves staring at a range of rugged peaks, the sun magnifying the magnificent shapes into which centuries of wind had carved them. They descended the hogback and began to skirt the towering range. After several hours, they were riding once again on level ground among thick patches of scrub oak. Broken boulders, as though thrown down and smashed by some massive giant and his sledgehammer, were strewn about them.

"Look, Steve!" Clyde was pointing due west. "See it?"

"Yeah. Virginia City. Looks to be about five miles or so, wouldn't you say?"

"Yep. I can feel it in my bones. Pa's gonna do a somersault in his grave when we gun down Jack Reynolds!"

Suddenly Clyde's horse began to limp.

"Hold it, Steve," he said, drawing rein.

Steve's mount had already carried him a few yards ahead. "What's wrong?" he asked as he hipped around in the saddle.

"My horse's limpin'. Right foreleg."

"Well, see about it."

Swearing, Clyde dismounted.

"Could just be a rock," Steve said, leaning on his saddlehorn and patting the money-filled bags that hung there.

Clyde leaned over and hoisted the horse's right foreleg. Neither Clyde nor the horse saw the diamondback coiled on a rock shelf inches from his face.

"That's what it is," Clyde said loud enough for his brother to hear. "Got a big ol' stone wedged in between the shoe and the hoof."

Suddenly the snake struck. The horse gave a terrified whinny, shied, and bolted away. Clyde fell to his knees, letting out a blood-curdling scream. There was a look of stark terror in his eyes as he threw a hand to the snakebite on his cheek.

Steve was frozen to his saddle, gaping, appalled, as his brother screamed like a madman. Clyde's shrill cries evolved into "Steve! Ste-e-ve! Help me! He-e-lp me-e!"

Steve gave a shudder of revulsion. He feared snakes, and the sight of the diamondback slithering away sent waves of horror mixed with nausea through his body.

Clyde fell flat on the sand, still screaming Steve's name and writhing in pain and terror.

Steve finally went into action. He leaped from the saddle, grabbed a long-bladed knife, and dashed to his brother. Dropping to his knees, he seized Clyde's flailing hands and shouted, "Clyde! Clyde! Listen to me! I've got to lance the bite and suck out the venom. Lie still!"

"Steve, don't let me die!" he cried, trembling. "Don't let me die!"

"Hold still!" blared Steve, wielding the knife.

The sting of the sharp knife made Clyde wince and cry out, but he held as still as he could. Blood streamed down his face as Steve bent low and worked feverishly to suck out the venom.

Deputy Sheriff Wes Domire and his four-year-old son were enjoying a few hours together, allotted in kindness by Storey County Sheriff Chuck Wyler. Domire had rented the team and wagon from one of Virginia City's hostlers so that he and his son could see some of the country around their new home.

The boy was on the seat beside his father when Domire spotted a lone horse off the side of the trail. It wore saddle and bridle, which made him wonder what had happened to the rider. Seconds later, he spotted a second riderless horse about a hundred yards farther up the trail near a large boulder. And he saw a man on his knees, bending over a man who lay flat on his back.

If someone was in trouble, Domire wanted to be of help. He also realized there could be danger. "Son, I want you to climb back in the bed of the wagon and lie down flat," he said, patting the boy on the head.

"Why, Daddy?"

"I've got to stop up here and talk to a couple of men. I'm not sure what I'll find, so I want you down and out of sight. Don't even raise your head until I tell you to, okay?"

"Yes, sir," replied the boy, hurrying to obey.

When the child was flat in the bed next to the seat, Domire headed for the two men and said, "Don't make any noise, either, son."

"I won't, Daddy."

"Promise?"

"Promise."

"Good boy."

Steve Heglund glanced over his shoulder at the wagon and team as it came to a halt. At the reins he saw a dark-haired, clean-shaven young man wearing a broad-brimmed hat.

As the man was climbing from the wagon seat, Clyde let out a piteous wail. "Somethin's happenin' to my eyes! I can't see good! Don't let me die, Steve! Don't let me die!"

Steve cast another glance at the wagon and saw its driver moving his direction, then turned his attention back to Clyde. "It'll be all right," he assured him. "It'll be all right."

As Wes Domire strode toward the two men, his eye caught the canvas money bags tied to Steve's saddlehorn. He saw *Bank of Stillwater* on one of the bags and suspected he had come upon a pair of bank robbers. He lowered his hand over the butt of his Colt .45 and proceeded slowly.

Steve looked back at the approaching man and saw the sun glint off his badge. He didn't know why a lawman would come after them in a wagon, but the moment was too tense for deliberation.

Clyde's whining filled the hot air as Steve—his body turned so that his gun was out of the lawman's sight—slowly drew his gun and cocked the hammer. He noted that the lawman was holding his hand in ready position over his gun butt. The man was almost in point-blank range; there was only one thing to do.

"My brother just got bit by a rattler and—" Steve cut off his own words as he brought the gun to bear and fired, hitting Wes Domire in the midsection.

The deputy's instincts had his weapon out of the holster, but it slipped from his fingers when he jack-knifed from the impact of the .45 slug. His knees buckled, and he went down.

Steve kicked the deputy's revolver out of reach and was about to put a bullet in Domire's head when Clyde began to gag and choke, his face turning deep purple.

Quickly, Steve knelt over him. The venom was assaulting Clyde's brain, throwing him into convulsions. Steve's mind was spinning. There was nothing he could do for his brother. Clyde was going to die. There could be other lawmen in the area who might have heard the shot. He looked down at the deputy, who lay in a heap, barely moving.

Panic set in. Steve had to get out of there. Holstering his gun, he dashed to his horse and swung into the saddle. Without looking back, he galloped to Clyde's horse, relieved it of the money bags that hung from the saddlehorn, and sped away toward Virginia City. He had enough money to live like a king anywhere he chose. Maybe California. He would decide on that later. The main thing now was to have his revenge on Jack Reynolds.

In the wagon, the frightened little boy raised his head over the seat of the wagon. When he saw his father lying on the ground, he cried, "Daddy!" and went over the side.

His father was lying in a fetal position, clutching his midsection. Blood was running through his fingers.

"Daddy!" cried the boy. "That bad man shot you!"

"Yes," Domire said through his teeth, struggling to rise. "I've got...to get into the wagon...find the doctor."

"Come on, Daddy, I'll help you."

Though the four-year-old's strength was small, Wes Domire was glad for it as he made it to his feet and staggered to the wagon. "You go ahead and get in, son," he said. "I need to lean on the wagon a minute before I...try it."

"I'll help, Daddy," insisted the lad.

"No, son...I'll do it. Just get in so we can move out as soon as I'm in the seat."

While the boy was using the spokes on the left front wheel to climb up to the seat, Domire heard hoofbeats coming from the east. He turned to see a lone rider skidding to a halt. The rider slid from his saddle, glanced at the man on the ground, then hurried to the deputy, whom he could see was shot.

Layne Dalton saw the badge on the wounded man's chest and said, "I heard shots and came as fast as I could. Did the other one get away?"

"Yes," Domire nodded. "I'm sure these men are bank robbers. The other one had a money bag with the Stillwater bank's name on it."

"They're more than bank robbers. They're cold-blooded killers. I've been on their trail for a long time."

"Are...are you a lawman?"

"No. I'll have to explain later. Here, let me help you into the back of the wagon. We'll get you into town as fast as we can."

Layne picked the lawman up like he would a child and carefully lowered him into the wagon bed. When he had made him as comfortable as possible, he looked at the white-faced little boy. "This your daddy, son?"

"Yes, sir," replied the child, his eyes teary and his lips quivering.

Dalton picked him up, held him close, and said, "We'll get your daddy to the doctor."

The child hugged Dalton's neck, then said, "I want to ride back there with Daddy."

"Sure," said Dalton, setting him on the floor of the bed.

"Right in the belly, is it?" he said, looking down at the wounded man.

"Yeah. Went through my belt buckle."

"Can you hold the wound closed?"

"I think so."

"Okay. Let me check on Clyde over there and we'll go. What's the matter with him? I see blood on his face."

"The other one said he'd been bitten by a rattler."

Layne rushed to Clyde, who lay still, barely breathing. When he saw where the snake had bitten him, he knew the man was a goner.

"Clyde…"

The dying man looked up with languid eyes and focused on the speaker. His eyes widened in fear. He found his voice and choked, "It…can't…be!" He grimaced and stopped breathing. His sightless eyes stared at the cloudless sky.

Well, God, Layne said, turning away, *You got ahead of me again. And You've given me another delay. I know I'm a no-good sinner, but I'm asking you anyhow—please don't let Steve get to Jack…or the women.*

"He going to live?" the deputy asked as Layne tied his horse to the rear of the wagon.

"He's dead. I'll leave his body for the buzzards."

Layne noticed that the boy had eyes and hair the same color as his. A sharp pain lanced his heart. Would his little Danny have looked as much like him as this little boy did?

Layne climbed into the seat and took the reins in hand, then looked over his shoulder and said, "I didn't ask your name, Deputy."

"Wesley. Wesley Domire."

"Well, Deputy Domire, I'd like to put these horses to a gallop, but I'm afraid all the hard bouncing would do you more damage than taking a reasonable pace."

"Just go easy," replied Domire. "I'm losing blood, but not as fast as when I was first shot."

"We'll get you there," Dalton said, and put the horses into motion.

As they moved slowly toward Virginia City, Domire asked about Dalton's pursuit of the bank robbers. Since there was time, Layne began his story from the time the Heglund brothers murdered Melody's brother. When he told the part about his unborn son's death, he swallowed hard and said, "We were going to name him Danny."

"Really?"

"Yes, sir."

"Well," said Domire, "Dannys are special boys. I guess I didn't tell you, this little guy's name is Danny."

Layne looked over his shoulder, forced down the lump in his throat, smiled and said to the youngster, "With that name, you *have* to be special." Layne then finished his story, bringing Domire up to the moment.

"I'm sorry about this situation, Major," the deputy said. "If you weren't waylaid by getting me to the doctor, you would be breathing down Steve Heglund's neck by now. I hope something happens to keep him from your father-in-law."

"Me, too." Layne paused a moment, then asked, "Do you and your wife have other children besides Danny?"

The wagon hit a hard bump, and Domire gritted his teeth in reaction to the pain.

"There's only Danny and me, Major," Domire managed to reply. "My wife, Laura, died giving birth to him four years ago."

"Oh. I'm sorry."

"Thank you. Danny and I arrived here just eight days ago from Fresno. Sheriff Wyler is planning to retire at the end of this term, and he contacted me, asking if I'd come and take the job as his deputy. He says that with his recommendation, I'll be voted in as Storey County sheriff, hands down."

"Sounds good," Dalton said over his shoulder. "Main thing right now is to get you to that doctor."

When Layne drove the wagon into Virginia City, Wes Domire had taken a turn for the worse; he was losing blood fast. The deputy directed Layne to the doctor's office.

They pulled up in front of Dr. Jacob Meyer's office, and people on the street watched as Layne helped Danny down, then carried the wounded deputy into the doctor's office with Danny following.

Someone on the street said, "I'll go get the sheriff!"

A crowd began to collect in front of Dr. Meyer's office. Word was spreading fast that the new deputy had been brought in, wounded and bleeding, by a stranger.

Layne was ushered quickly into the examining room and laid Domire on the examining table. Then he stood by, holding little Danny Domire in his arms while the doctor made a hasty examination of the wound.

Wes's pain was growing worse. With teeth clenched, he did his best not to cry out. The small boy looked on, fearful for his father. Layne held him tight, patting him and speaking soft words of encouragement.

Teeth still clenched, Domire looked up at Dr. Meyer. "What do you think, Doctor?"

Meyer glanced at his nurse on the other side of the table, then replied, "You've lost an awful lot of blood, Deputy. An awful lot."

"More than I thought, I guess."

The doctor did not comment.

"Daddy," the boy said, fear written all over his face. "I want you to be all better!"

Layne patted him, squeezing him tighter.

Dr. Meyer raised his eyes to Layne, and he saw the sadness there. Little Danny's father was not going to make it.

TWENTY-ONE

Steve Heglund rode up to the Reynolds Mining Company office and left the reins looped over his saddlehorn. If he found Reynolds in his office, he would make sure the man knew he was killing him for murdering his father, then gun him down. He would bolt for his horse and ride away, knowing he had paid Jack Reynolds in full for murdering his father.

Hard-faced miners were milling about the grounds, some carrying mining tools. As Heglund approached the log building, a miner was headed straight for him.

"Say, could you tell me where I might find Mr. Reynolds?" Steve asked.

"I don't know whether you mean Hank or Jack, but both of 'em are on their way to California. Sacramento."

Heglund's countenance fell. "Oh. Do you know when they're expected back?"

"About a week."

"That long, eh?" said Steve, rubbing the back of his neck.

"Ed Dorrenson is in the office. He's the office manager. I don't know what you need, but he can probably help you."

"Oh, uh...no...I need to see Jack. Thanks."

"You bet," said the miner, and went on his way.

Heglund cursed under his breath. All he could do now was hole up in one of Virginia City's hotels and wait. He would get the most expensive room in town, stash the money in the room, then get himself a good hot meal.

Layne Dalton stood in Dr. Jacob Meyer's office with Danny Domire in his arms. Sheriff Chuck Wyler stood beside him.

The wounded deputy could see it in Meyer's eyes. He was in real trouble. Looking up at him, he said, "Doctor, don't...don't hold back on me. It's bad, isn't it?"

The nurse turned and walked away, knowing there was nothing more that could be done.

The doctor nodded grimly. "It *is* bad. When the slug chewed through your belt buckle, it carried myriad little metal slivers with it. The slug's lodged next to your spine, and it really tore up your insides I—"

"I'm losing a lot of blood, aren't I?"

Meyer cleared his throat. "Yes. You're hemorrhaging badly."

"There's nothing you can do?"

The physician's features were ashen. He moved his head back and forth slowly and spoke with a dry tongue. "No."

The child in Dalton's arms understood that his father's condition was serious. "Daddy!" he cried, reaching for him. Layne lowered the boy and let him wrap his arms around the deputy's neck.

Wes embraced his son. His voice came out cracked and broken. "Danny. Danny, I love you."

"I love you, too, Daddy. Please be all right."

The dying man held his boy for a long moment. There was blood on the child's shirt and pants as his father eased him back, saying, "Let Major Dalton hold you again, will you, son?"

Danny reached for the man he had come to trust in a very short time.

"I'm sorry, Wes," Sheriff Wyler said. "So sorry."

Wes Domire lifted his gaze to the man who held his son. Danny was clinging to his neck. "Major…"

"Yes?"

"I…I have to ask you a monumental favor."

"You name it," Layne nodded.

Wes licked his lips. "I told you…Danny and I have only been here a little more than a week. I…hardly know anyone in town."

"I understand."

"I have no family anywhere. Since…since your Danny died…would you and your wife take my Danny and raise him as your own son? I…can see that he already loves you and trusts you."

Layne Dalton's mind was awhirl. None of this seemed real. He didn't know what to say.

"He can even have your name…if you wish."

Danny was weeping, not understanding his father's intent. Layne was fighting tears of his own. He thought of Melody. He knew she would love Danny and would be happy to become his mother.

Layne's throat kept constricting on him. He turned to Wyler and asked, "Sheriff, is there some legal process here?"

"No," Wyler replied, shaking his head. "This is the Wild West, Major. If you're of a mind to comply with Wes's request, Doc and I can stand as witnesses to it. We'll even sign a paper to that effect, if you'd like. That way, nobody could ever give you a problem about it. You can make his last name Dalton officially, if you wish."

The child had his face buried against Dalton's neck, soaking it with his tears.

"Maybe we'll make it Daniel Domire Dalton."

"You…will do it then, Major?" asked Wes.

"Yes. Before you and these witnesses, I am adopting this boy in the name of my wife, Melody, and myself. I promise…we'll give him a good home."

Wes Domire smiled, then his face twisted with pain.

Dr. Meyer bent over him, then turned to Layne and whispered, "Take the boy into the waiting room."

As Layne headed for the door with Danny in his arms, the boy extended an arm back over Layne's shoulder, crying, "Daddy! Daddy!"

The nurse stood up from where she was sitting in the waiting area as man and boy entered. "Is he…"

"Not yet, but real soon."

Nurse and major tried to keep Danny's mind occupied by talking to him about things he liked to do, what kind of animals he liked, what his favorite foods were.

Less than five minutes had passed when doctor and sheriff passed through the door, faces glum. Dr. Meyer said quietly, "You have a new son, Major."

Layne picked the boy up. "I need to know how to get to the Reynolds Mining Company office, and how to find Jack Reynolds's house."

"I can direct you to both," Sheriff Wyler said, "but before you go, I want some answers. About all you told me was that a bank robber had shot down my deputy."

"That's right," Layne nodded. "Wes said the one that shot him rode away in a hurry."

"Did he give you a description of him?"

"No."

"Then Wes's killer is going to get away scot-free."

"He'll get his sooner or later, Sheriff."

Shaking his head, Wyler said, "You told me in there that you're Jack Reynolds's son-in-law."

"That's right."

"Melody's your wife?"

"Yes, and I need to go find her, Sheriff. You said you'd tell me how to find the mining company office and Jack's house."

Wyler provided both quickly.

Layne decided to go to the mining company first, and hoped he wasn't too late. The sheriff stayed on his heels as Dalton carried the boy outside. The crowd was still there looking on.

"You go ahead," said Wyler. "I'll tell the crowd about it."

As Layne placed Danny on the wagon seat, the boy said in a frightened voice, "I want to go see my daddy."

"I'm sorry, son. Your daddy had to go far, far away, and he can't ever come back. I'm your new daddy now. And you've got a mommy, too. You're about to meet her. We'll take good care of you, I promise."

Somehow the four-year-old knew he was loved by this man he had only met earlier that day. He didn't understand where his daddy had gone, but he had picked up enough to know it was something that could not be helped. He would miss him. There was a bright spot for Danny, however. He was going to have a mother! The boys and girls he knew in Fresno all had mothers. He had wanted one very much. Now he would.

Layne rolled the wagon onto the Reynolds Mining Company property and hauled up in front of the office. Miners were busily moving about, laughing and talking amongst themselves. Surely if anything serious had happened to Jack, the atmosphere around the place would not be like this.

Layne entered the office, taking Danny with him. He was greeted by a rather chubby man, who winked at the four-year-old and said, "Fine-looking lad you have there, mister. Looks just like you."

"Thank you," Layne grinned, meaning it with all his heart. "I'm looking for Jack Reynolds."

"He's not here right now. I'm Ed Dorrenson, office manager. Is there something I can do for you?"

"Will he be back soon?"

"Be about a week. He and Hank left for Sacramento by Wells Fargo stage yesterday afternoon."

Relief washed over Layne Dalton like a cool, refreshing ocean wave. Jack had left Virginia City while the Heglunds were still on the trail. But where was Steve now? Had he found out where Jack was going? Would he follow him to California to kill him?

"Say, has there been anyone else in here asking about Jack's whereabouts today?"

"Not that I know of, and I'm the guy they'd see to find out. Why?"

"Oh, nothing really. Well, I guess I'll catch Jack when he returns. Thanks."

"May I tell him who was looking for him?"

"Can't let you do that. It's a surprise. I'm from back east. See you again sometime."

"Sure."

"Could you tell me where the Wells Fargo office is?"

"This end of town, right on Main Street. Can't miss it."

"Thanks again."

Ten minutes later the wagon pulled away from the Wells Fargo office and headed into town. According to Sheriff Wyler's directions, the Reynolds house was at the other end of Virginia City. The Fargo agent had added more relief to the major's mind. Steve Heglund had not been there asking any questions about yesterday's Sacramento-bound stage, or about Jack Reynolds himself.

Steve must not be following Jack to California. But where was he? He must be somewhere close by. Somehow, after his reunion with Melody, Layne would find him.

Layne's heart was pounding with anticipation as he drove through the business district on his way to his beloved Melody. He kept an arm around Danny, who sat beside him, and began to pray.

God, I don't understand how You work. But then, I guess I'm not supposed to. Chaplain Young told me once that You hold the keys to death. Nobody can die unless You say so. And when You have a set time for somebody to die, nothing can keep them alive. You allowed Wes Domire to die, and You allowed me to find him and Danny and drive them into town. And now...now I have a little son—named Danny. You took my unborn son to heaven, but You have given me this one to love and to raise. Thank You. I know Melody will love this little fellow as much as I do already. And God, about my salvation, I—

Suddenly Layne's line of sight fell on a familiar face.

It was Steve Heglund! He was coming out of the plush Sierra Madre Hotel, headed for his horse, which was tied at the hitch rail.

Before checking into the hotel, Heglund had tied the horse in the alley at the rear of the building. Once he had his room key, he used the back stairs to transport the money bags to his room on the second floor. That done, he brought the horse to the street and returned to the room to count his loot.

Heglund was now going to take the horse to a stable down the street, then make a tour of the stores.

The flame of vengeance inside Layne Dalton fanned into full force at the sight of his mortal enemy. He yanked back on the reins, stopping the wagon in the middle of the wide, dusty street. At the same instant, Heglund's gaze settled on the man in the wagon with the small boy at his side.

Steve could not believe his eyes. Was he hallucinating? Layne Dalton was dead, burned to death in that tinder box of a barracks at Point Lookout. Could it be his ghost? No! Steve Heglund didn't believe in ghosts. But how could this be?

Steve's pulse raced. He felt an icy hand against the back of his neck, then it moved over his scalp, making it tingle. His eyes seemed to fill his whole face as Layne quickly lifted Danny over the seat and told him to lie flat on the bed. Steve would get over his shock, and when he did, a shootout was inevitable.

Layne was right.

Heglund's arms and legs had gone leaden upon first sight of the man he thought he had killed. It was Layne Dalton, all right, not some ghost. Steve was about to face off with flesh and blood!

Layne let go of Danny and clawed for the gun on his hip. Heglund went for his, but Layne was ahead of him, rising to his feet in the wagon box. Just as Layne dropped the hammer, one of the horses moved a step, jerking the wagon. The slug hit Heglund in the right shoulder, spinning him around and jarring the gun from his hand.

Layne's shot frightened the team, and they jumped a step, throwing Layne off balance before he could get off a second shot. The brief respite gave Heglund time to grab for the gun with his left hand. Just as his fingers were about to close on the butt, Layne got off another shot, though he was still a little off balance. It plowed a furrow through the crown of Steve's hat, missing his scalp by an inch.

The team lurched forward at the sound of the second shot, again unbalancing the vengeful major.

Suddenly Heglund realized that it was the shoulder on his gun-hand that was hit. He wouldn't stand a chance now, shooting it out with Dalton. People were milling about on the busy street. Dalton would not dare fire at him if he could put people between them.

A surrey was parked by Heglund's horse, and it was loaded with a large family. Heglund hurried to his horse, and though his shoulder was on fire, managed to swing into the saddle.

Dalton stood in the wagon box, steadying himself for another shot, when he saw his prey stagger to the horse and mount up. Layne saw that the family in the surrey—eyes bulging at what they were witnessing—was in his line of fire. Helplessly he watched the man he hated gallop away on a street busy with vehicles and riders.

Within seconds, Steve Heglund had ridden out of sight, south-ward.

People on the street were gawking wide-eyed as Layne pulled the wagon to an open spot near the boardwalk. He jumped out of the vehicle and grabbed Danny, whose face showed the fear that had him in its grip.

Layne spoke soothing words to the boy, then spied a portly, middle-aged woman standing in the door of Myrtle's Dress Shop, gawking like the rest of the people.

Layne rushed to the woman with Danny in his arms. "Ma'am, do you run this shop?"

"Yes, I own it. I'm Myrtle Roberts."

"Take care of Danny for me, will you? I have to go after that man."

Myrtle took the boy in her arms. Layne assured Danny he would be back shortly, then made a dash for his horse and rode southward like the wind. He had lost nearly five minutes.

Steve Heglund galloped south out of Virginia City, looking back as he pushed the animal beneath him as fast as it could go. Blood ran down his arm from the shoulder wound, which burned like fire. The blazing sun bore down on him, and sweat streamed into his eyes.

Heglund knew Layne Dalton would be coming. He had to throw him off his trail and find a place to hide. He also had to get the wound tied off somehow, so he wouldn't bleed to death.

Layne Dalton. How he hated the name! What kind of man could escape from a blazing inferno? All four Heglund brothers had reined their stolen horses to a halt on the crest of a hill that night and had looked back at the burning barracks just in time to see it collapse and throw up billows of flame and smoke. There was no way a mortal man could have lived through that.

Heglund was unarmed. There was no way to simply haul up and ambush Dalton as he came riding after him. He had no choice but to find a safe place to hide.

Heglund's hasty escape southward was taking him through rugged country, a devil's playground of tall rock formations, jumbled boulders, sandy arroyos, squat cacti, sagebrush, and tumbleweeds. He held the reins with his right hand, gripping the wounded shoulder with his left. The desert sun was a ball of fire and seemed to have picked him out to torture.

The galloping horse carried him down into a low draw, then climbed the sandy slope on the other side. Just as horse and rider topped out, Steve saw a dark opening in the side of a rock-edged knoll. It was a low-ceilinged cave, large enough to contain him, judging by what he could see. The area around the knoll was laden with huge tumbleweeds.

Steve Heglund had his hiding place. If he crawled into the shallow cave and camouflaged the opening with tumbleweeds, Dalton would ride on by and never know he was there. Once the hated Rebel had given up the chase and headed back for Virginia City, Steve could make good his escape.

Steve slid stiffly groundward and took another look toward the north. No sign of Dalton. He would come, all right. No question about that. But he wouldn't find Steve Heglund.

Heglund moved to the horse's back side and gave it a hard slap on the rump. The animal leaped with a start, then galloped down the gentle slope southward.

Steve gathered loose tumbleweeds that the wind had driven against the knoll and dragged them to the small cave. He clutched the prickly weeds and backed into the opening. It was cooler inside, and he liked that. He wriggled further back until the tumbleweeds fit nice and snug and cut out most of the brilliant sunlight.

There was no way Layne Dalton or anyone else was going to find him in here. He was safe. All he had to do was wait. Soon he could emerge from his little hiding place, sneak back into town under cover of darkness, retrieve his money, and go on his way. Once his shoulder was better, he'd come back to Virginia City. He would kill Jack Reynolds, and if Layne Dalton was still around, he'd kill him too. In fact, if Dalton was no longer around, he'd track him down and shoot him in the back.

He needed to give attention to his bleeding shoulder. The bullet had passed on through, for which he was glad. No lead poisoning. He pulled a large bandanna from his hip pocket and started to wrap it around the wound. His position on his belly was awkward, so he rolled onto his side. As he shifted, he found that there was a little more room further back in the cave.

He was inching his way back when he heard a chorus of hisses, accompanied by the unmistakable buzz of diamondback rattles.

Steve Heglund's blood turned to ice. His heart froze, then thawed and banged his rib cage. His breath was rasping in his ears.

Suddenly countless pairs of deadly fangs were striking flesh, from legs to chest.

He couldn't scream. He tried, but the sound was locked in his throat. He thrashed toward the mouth of the low-ceilinged cave, arms waving wildly in spite of the bullet wound.

The sharp, fiery stings kept coming.

Desperately, Heglund clawed at the tumbleweeds, trying to get out. But his strength was already draining away. He could barely lift a hand. It seemed the snakes would never stop striking.

His brain was fogging up. His throat was getting tighter. He couldn't get a breath. A black curtain was descending over him. A scream tried to wrench itself from his throat, but it wedged there and died.

And the snakes kept striking…striking…striking.

The hot wind seemed to scorch his face as Layne Dalton gouged his horse's sides to get all the speed the animal could give. He kept hoping to catch a glimpse of Steve Heglund off in the distance, but there was nothing but sunlight glaring off rocks, boulders, and sand.

The land was level for a while, then began to undulate. At one point, the galloping steed carried Dalton into a low draw, then sped up the sandy slope to its crest. A dark spot at the bottom of the gentle slope before him caught the major's eye. It was better than a mile away, but he thought it was a horse. Only seconds had passed when he was sure it was a horse. Moments later, he drew up to the riderless horse he had seen Heglund hop on back in town. There were drops of blood on the saddle and on the horse's coat.

Where was Heglund?

Layne rode back slowly, leading Heglund's horse and looking for some sign of the killer's departure from the trail. His eyes darted back and forth, taking in the gullies, rocks, and boulders where the killer could be hiding.

Layne figured if Heglund had been carrying a spare gun in his saddlebags, and was able to use it, he would have tried to ambush him by now. He was most likely down somewhere, unable to function well because of his wound.

Layne was almost to the crest of the long slope when suddenly he saw drops of blood on the stones and sand on the side of the trail. They led to a rock-edged knoll where a pile of tumbleweeds was strangely collected against its side.

Dismounting, gun-in-hand, Dalton moved slowly to the spot where the blood drops stopped. He saw, then, that Heglund had crawled into a small opening and pulled the weeds up to hide himself.

"Heglund!" he called, backing away at an angle with his gun pointed at the cave's mouth. "Come on out of there!"

Nothing.

"Heglund! You're wounded…bleeding! I can out-wait you!"

Nothing.

If the man had a gun, he would have fired it by now.

Layne moved up to the side of the cave and pulled the tumbleweeds away. The sight that he saw turned his stomach.

Steve Heglund's hands were outstretched, his fingers curled. His eyes appeared lidless, bulging from their sockets. His mouth was locked open in a silent scream of death.

Slithering over the dead man's legs and lower body were dozens of diamondback rattlers, their tongues darting silently in and out.

TWENTY-TWO

n empty feeling came over Layne Dalton as he mounted his horse, took the reins of Heglund's animal, and started back toward town at a slow walk.

For months, he had lived for one thing: to unleash the flame of his vengeance on the Heglund brothers, especially Steve. But not one of them had felt even a spark of it.

The God of heaven had kept him from fulfilling that yearning. It had been exactly as Harriet Smith and Chaplain Michael Young had pointed out from Scripture: *Vengeance is mine; I will repay, saith the Lord.*

Layne's mind drifted back to the day they buried Jerry Owens at the prison. "So they're gonna bury your partner this mornin', huh?" Steve Heglund had sneered at him.

"You'll get yours one day, Heglund!" Layne had fired back.

"Yeah? Well, it won't be *you* who gives it to me, fancy-pants!"

Layne's retort came strong from the recesses of his memory: *"Well, if it isn't, maybe it'll be God Himself!"*

As he rode toward Virginia City, Layne's words echoed through his mind over and over: *Maybe it'll be God Himself! God Himself! God Himself!*

Suddenly Layne felt as if his heart had burst into flame. It was a consuming fire, burning to the very depths of his soul.

Hot tears blinded his eyes, but at the same time they were washing away his spiritual blindness. He had caught glimpses of God's hand in his life the past several months, but now he could see clearly. The vengeful flame that had burned in his heart would have made him a murderer if the Lord had not taken control. He knew full well he would have killed any of the Heglund brothers as quickly as he had tried to kill Steve in front of the Sierra Madre Hotel.

Layne understood at that moment that the main reason God had taken control was in answer to Melody's prayers. She wanted him to be saved, and now he could serve his new Master unhindered by the consequences that would have been his to carry the rest of his life.

The rugged soldier and war hero veered the horses off the trail into the shade of a patch of scrub oak, slid from the saddle, and fell to his knees in the sand. He cried out in repentance of his sin to the Christ of Calvary, calling upon Him for salvation.

As he wiped tears, aware of the great relief in his heart, the new man in Christ thanked the Lord for saving him and for the way He had worked in his life. Then, settling in the saddle, he rode toward town.

Layne Dalton would take Danny Domire Dalton to Melody and show her that God's providential hand had allowed Steve Heglund to give them another Danny. Layne would take his wife and son back to Virginia and report to General Robert E. Lee for further duty.

The sun was touching the western horizon as the major drew up in front of Myrtle's Dress Shop and dismounted.

Danny was sitting at a small desk, drawing pictures on paper with a pencil when Layne entered the shop. Myrtle was standing over him, speaking in soft tones.

Both Myrtle and the boy looked up as Layne came in.

Danny jumped off the chair and ran to him with open arms.

Layne picked him up, hugged him, and asked, "Were you a good boy, son?"

"He sure was," Myrtle said. "No problem at all. Did you catch up to that man?"

"Yes, I did. Everything's fine. I want to thank you for taking care of Danny for me. May I pay you for it?"

"Not on your life," Myrtle laughed. "We had a good time, didn't we, Danny? He even helped me make some sales."

"Oh, really?" Dalton said as he moved toward the door with the lad in his arms. "Maybe Danny will share his sales commission with me."

Myrtle laughed, walked them to the door, and told them to come see her again. Layne thanked her once more and headed for the wagon. The door closed behind them.

Layne had already tied both horses to the rear of the wagon. While they drove to the stable by the light of the setting sun, Layne explained that Danny would now have a new home with a mommy to cook meals and wash clothes for him. He also assured Danny that his new mommy would love him very much, even as his new daddy did.

Layne returned the team and wagon to the hostler who had rented them to Wes Domire, and gave Steve Heglund's horse to him.

Back on the street, as the lowering sky was going from orange to deep purple, Layne placed the boy in his saddle and swung up behind him. Danny twisted around to give him a hug.

"Would it be all right if I call you Daddy? I love my other daddy, but he's gone far away and can't come back."

A lump lodged in the major's throat. He swallowed hard and said, "You sure may, son. You sure may."

After another hug, the little boy settled in the saddle, facing forward.

Layne's heart was racing. Next stop, the Reynolds house and a big surprise—no, two surprises—for Melody Anne Dalton.

"Well, Danny, let's go see your new mommy!" Layne said, clucking at the horse to put it in motion.

EPILOGUE

he conflict at Fredericksburg, Virginia, put more men on the
field of battle than any other military confrontation in the
Civil War. A few days after the battle, the vital figures were released by both sides.

Union losses were: 1,284 killed, 9,600 wounded, 1,769 missing
or captured...a total of 12,653 casualties.

Confederate losses were: 595 killed, 4,074 wounded, 653 missing or captured...a total of 5,322 casualties.

These figures were the greatest source of embarrassment to the
United States government since their terrible rout by the
Confederates at the first battle fought at Bull Run. Most embarrassed
was Major General Ambrose E. Burnside. It is reported that on their
way back to Washington, the badly whipped Yankees were formed
up in a review at the camp near Falmouth, Virginia. Commanding
officers rode up and down the ranks, waving their caps and swords in
an attempt to rouse a cheer for their chief commander, but all they
could elicit were boos and catcalls.

While Southern newspapers praised General Robert E. Lee and
his outnumbered Army of Northern Virginia, the Northern newspapers denounced Burnside for his "shameful bungling," and even

castigated Abraham Lincoln for firing General George McClellan and replacing him with "Bungler Burnside."

The war correspondent for the *New York Tribune*, A. D. Richardson, talked with General Burnside after the battle and left a record of the interview:

> I was not present at the battle but returned to the army two or three days after. Burnside deported himself with rare fitness and magnanimity. As he spoke to me about the brave men who had fruitlessly fallen, there were tears in his eyes, and his voice broke with emotion. When I asked him if anyone else was responsible for the slaughter, he replied, "No. I understand perfectly well that when the general commanding an army meets with disaster, he alone is responsible, and I will not attempt to shift that responsibility on anyone else."
>
> Burnside was, at least, great in his earnestness, his moral courage, and perfect integrity.
>
> Every Union soldier knew that the Battle of Fredericksburg had been a costly and bloody mistake, and yet I think on the day or the week following it, the soldiers would have gone into battle just as cheerfully and sturdily as before. The more I saw of the Army of the Potomac, the more I wondered at its invincible spirit which no disasters seemed able to destroy.

As we now know, Richardson's words were portentous. Perhaps the "invincible spirit" he wrote of was instilled in the Union army by their commander-in-chief, Abraham Lincoln, who wrote an open letter to the Army of the Potomac immediately after their return to the Washington camps. It read in part:

> Although you were not successful, the attempt was not an error, nor the failure other than accident. Condoling

with the mourners for the dead, and sympathizing with the severely wounded…I tender to you, officers and soldiers, the thanks of the nation.

The courage with which you, in an open field, maintained the contest against an entrenched foe, and the consummate skill and success with which you crossed and recrossed the river in the face of the enemy, show that you possess all the qualities of a great army which will yet give victory to the cause of the country.

Lincoln's faith in his army proved legitimate, for the victory was the Union's at Appomattox Courthouse, Virginia, on April 9, 1865.

At Marye's Heights during the Fredericksburg battle, thousands of soldiers on both sides looked on in awe as nineteen-year-old Confederate Sergeant Richard Rowland Kirkland carried water to the wounded men of the Union and the Confederacy. Both armies thereafter hailed him as the "Angel of Marye's Heights."

Kirkland was fatally wounded in the Battle of Chicamauga on September 20, 1863, at twenty years of age. His name was remembered in Fredericksburg, and after the War a street in that city was named in his honor.

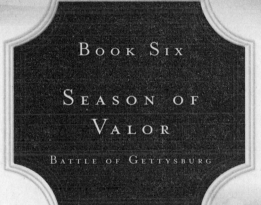

BOOK SIX

SEASON OF VALOR

BATTLE OF GETTYSBURG

A special word of appreciation to my good friend and Christian brother, Bruce Droullard of Readfield, Maine, who was so kind to supply me with vital information concerning Joshua L. Chamberlain and Bowdoin College, which I used in this book. Thank you, Bruce!

✷ ✷ ✷

To my little sister,
Patty Perkins,
who will always have a special place in her big brother's heart.
I love you more than you will ever know.

✳ ✳ ✳

PROLOGUE

G eneral Robert E. Lee's Army of Northern Virginia had shown itself to be a superb fighting machine at Fredericksburg, Virginia, in December 1862 and at Chancellorsville, Virginia, in May 1863 by decidedly defeating the Union Army of the Potomac in both bloody battles.

Lee was fully aware that there was trouble within the Federal army. President Abraham Lincoln was having a hard time finding the right man to command his Union forces.

Although Major General George B. McClellan had turned back the Confederates in the Antietam battle in September of 1862, Lincoln was unhappy with McClellan's reluctance to move against the enemy with haste when needed.

After the bloody Antietam confrontation, Lincoln decided to relieve McClellan of his command. He replaced him with Major General Ambrose E. Burnside on November 5, 1862. Burnside immediately made plans for moving his army toward the Confederate capital at Richmond.

Lee was in Burnside's path at Fredericksburg. Burnside made a series of tactical blunders in the Fredericksburg battle, and although his forces outnumbered Lee's by fifty-two thousand men, the

Confederates whipped the Federals soundly. The morale of the Army of the Potomac sank to the lowest point since the war began.

When Burnside and his haggard men returned to their camps near Washington, D.C., in late January 1863, the general's career as commander of the Army of the Potomac came to an inglorious end. Lincoln chose Major General Joseph "Fighting Joe" Hooker as his new leader. But Hooker's defeat at Chancellorsville in May immediately put him on Lincoln's "doubtful" list. Lincoln made no move to replace him, but watched him closely.

General Lee, still basking in the glory of his victory at Chancellorsville, well knew that the victory had little more than postponed the day when Lincoln's army would again make a move on the Confederate capital. To seize and occupy Richmond was Lincoln's ultimate goal. Lee could either retire to Richmond and stand a siege or take the initiative and invade Union territory.

The considerations that had prompted Lee's invasion into Maryland in September of 1862—a drive that was blocked at Antietam—still remained valid. A successful invasion of the North might bring diplomatic recognition from England and France. There could very likely be foreign intervention on behalf of the Confederacy against the Union.

Such a victory, in Lee's mind, would also encourage the antiwar Democrats in their agitation of Lincoln's administration to force Lincoln to end the war under terms reasonably favorable to the Confederacy.

There was another reason Lee wanted to invade the North—the chronic shortage of supplies in the South. Lee's troops were operating in a war-ravaged region partly occupied by the enemy. It bothered him that he was unable to provide adequate food and clothing for his men and forage for the Confederate horses.

Pennsylvania was Lee's target. The rich farmland of that state would provide the food and forage, and while his army was laying hold on Pennsylvania's resources, the people in the South would have time to stockpile supplies.

On May 14, after Hooker's withdrawal from Chancellorsville, Lee went to Richmond to discuss his plan with President Jefferson Davis and the Confederate cabinet. The Confederate leaders were uneasy about such a move, but Lee had a magisterial power about him, and the group finally approved his proposal.

On Monday morning, June 8, 1863, Lee arrived at Brandy Station, a whistle stop on the Orange & Alexandria Railroad a few miles north of Culpeper. Most of his Army of Northern Virginia was camped around the station. The Virginia sun shone down brilliantly from a clear blue sky.

Major General James Ewell Brown Stuart, Lee's chief of cavalry, had made preparations for a cavalry review for the supreme commander. In late afternoon, Stuart's cavalry mounted up. Lee looked on proudly as twenty-two cavalry regiments wheeled into a long column of fours in response to a bugle signal.

At that moment three Federal cavalry divisions, flanked by two infantry brigades, were only three or four miles away and moving toward the camp. The Union force had been sent by General Hooker, whose intelligence service had reported Stuart's recent move from Fredericksburg to the Culpeper area. Hooker's command was to "destroy the Rebel cavalry."

The Federal commander, General Alfred Pleasonton, decided to hide his troops in the woods and attack at dawn. When he began the assault the next morning, Pleasonton was surprised to find more than Stuart's cavalry in the camp. The hard-fought battle resulted in 866 Federal casualties and 523 casualties on the Confederate side. Pleasonton led his men in retreat, and General Hooker was in trouble with President Lincoln for ordering the ill-advised assault.

Things grew worse between Lincoln and Hooker, and on June 28, Hooker was relieved of his command and replaced by Major General George Gordon Meade.

The Brandy Station battle turned out to be the opening clash of a campaign that would come to a bloody climax just outside the small Pennsylvania town of Gettysburg. To that quiet farming community, the giant armies of blue and gray would be moved like pawns on a chessboard as if by some mysterious, inexorable hand of destiny. *Gettysburg* ... destined to be the bloodiest battle in the War Between the States.

You and I are about to embark on a journey into the lives of the people of both North and South who were touched by the Battle of Gettysburg, which has had more books written about it than any other Civil War battle. Most of those books are historical and documentary. Only a few novelists have undertaken the task of combining history with fiction to tell the story of Gettysburg. To those few—and with a little fear and trembling—I add this work of history-linked-with-fiction.

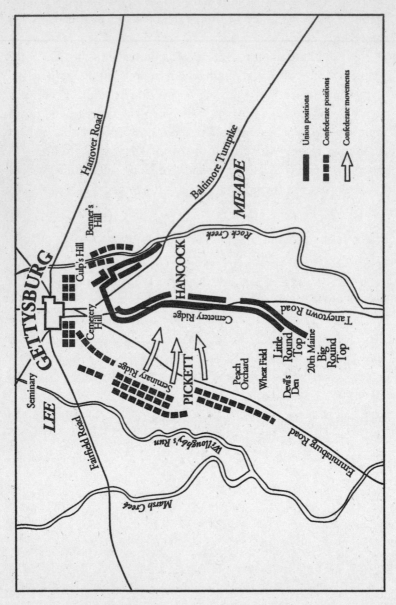

BATTLE OF GETTYSBURG
JULY 1-3, 1863

ONE

The lowering sun cast long shadows across the creek as Mike O'Hanlon strung his last sucker on the line, smiling to himself. A catch of five wasn't bad in less than an hour. The fish were biting pretty good today.

He picked up his fishing pole, laid it on his shoulder like a soldier would his rifle, and climbed the steep bank lined with towering elms. It was mid-April in Maine. The air still had a nip to it, and the leaves were just now coming out on the trees and bushes. Even the grassy fields about him still had a slight tawniness. New England had experienced a hard winter that year of 1853, especially the northeast corner. The temperature had plummeted to near-zero on several occasions, and stayed there sometimes for days on end.

Mike was glad spring had finally arrived. He was tired of winter. Fishing was no fun when you were freezing. And besides, spring always brought May, and on the thirtieth day of next month he would turn fifteen.

He topped the bank and stepped onto the country road. He looked briefly toward Brunswick, which lay some six miles to the south. His home was northwest of where he stood about a mile and a half. He was about to cross the road and angle through the fields

SEASON OF VALOR

toward home when he happened to glance up the road and saw Shane Donovan chopping wood beside the Wimberly's woodshed. Mike was surprised to see Shane at the elderly couple's place. He usually headed for home right after school to do his regular chores.

Shane was so intent on his work that he didn't see Mike coming up the road. As Mike drew nearer, he noted the old man standing in the door of the woodshed, looking on. Mike was rather spindly, and he marveled at the strength of his best friend. Shane could split logs as well as most men. Of course, knowing how was also an asset. Shane's father, Garth Donovan, was a lumberjack, and had started his oldest son working with him regularly when he turned ten.

Calvin Wimberly saw Mike turn into the driveway and called to him from the door of the woodshed. Shane turned to look at his redheaded friend and glanced at the string of fish.

"How many you got there?" he asked with a smile.

"Five. They were biting good this afternoon." Mike glanced at Mr. Wimberly, then looked back at Shane. "It's sure nice of you to chop wood for Mr. and Mrs. Wimberly."

"I'm happy to do it," Shane said. "Mr. Wimberly's been having some arthritis trouble in his shoulders, so I came by on my way home from school to chop up enough to last them a while."

"And I sure do appreciate it, too," Mr. Wimberly said.

"Nice to have the weather finally warming up," Shane said, looking Mike square in the eye. "After all, it's the twelfth of April."

"Yeah," Mike said. "Sure is nice. I can get more fishing in."

Shane hoped his mention of the date would bring a "happy birthday" from his friend. Mike knew Shane's birthday was April 12, but hadn't even mentioned it at school.

"I imagine you can't wait till Sunday," Mike said. "Probably seems like a long time, huh?"

Shane gave him a blank look. "I'm not sure I know what you're talking about. I mean…I enjoy being in church and hearing the Bible taught, if that's what you mean."

"You know what I'm referring to."

"Sorry, but you're going way over my head like Mr. Olmstead sometimes does in Sunday school class."

"You miss Joshua Chamberlain too, eh?"

"Of course. It isn't that I dislike Mr. Olmstead. He's a fine man and a solid Christian…but he shoots in the clouds sometimes. Mr. Chamberlain just has a way of making the Bible real clear."

"Well, let me make myself clear. I was talking about Ashley Kilrain."

"Ashley Kilrain? What about her?"

"What about her? C'mon, Shane, you can't fool me. I saw how she was looking at you during church service. She may only be thirteen, but she's awfully pretty!"

Shane blushed, ran his fingers through his thick, wavy hair, and said, "Aw, she doesn't have eyes for me…and she wasn't looking at me on Sunday, either."

"Well, I'm not blind. Besides, I'm not the only one who noticed it. Moira was sitting right by her, and she mentioned it to me after church on Sunday night."

"So Shane's got a girlfriend, eh?" Calvin Wimberly said. "With a name like Kilrain, she's bound to be Irish too."

"Oh, she's Irish all right, Mr. Wimberly," Mike said. "She's got beautiful reddish-brown hair, eyes as blue as the Irish Sea, a slight droop to the corners of her Irish eyelids like meself…and that fresh-scrubbed look with the rosy cheeks like all the girls in good ol' Dublin!" Pausing, he cocked his head and asked, "But you know who she is, don't you?"

"Of course. I was just funning Shane. Who in these parts doesn't know the Kilrains? After all, I'm wearing Kilrain-O'Hanlon shoes this minute!"

Ashley's father, Donald Kilrain, was co-owner of the Leprechaun Shoe and Boot Manufacturing Company in Brunswick, and Mike's father, Lewis O'Hanlon, was the other owner. Both men had come to America with their families in 1842 and established the company in Brunswick. Their fathers were co-owners of a company with the same name in Dublin. The fathers had provided financing for their sons to go to America and establish the new company. They had chosen Maine after reading about it in American magazines. They had made the right choice. The company was doing well, and the Kilrains and O'Hanlons were becoming wealthy.

Ashley and her sixteen-year-old sister, Moira, attended the Lewiston Finishing School for Girls in the town of Lewiston, some fifteen miles north of Brunswick. The sisters lived in a dormitory and came home on the weekends.

"Well, anyway," Mike said, "I sure wish it was me Ashley had eyes for instead of you, my friend!"

"Michael, Ashley Kilrain doesn't have eyes for me. But if she did, it'd be because she likes older men."

Mike gave him a bland look, then said casually, "Oh, yeah. It's your birthday, isn't it?"

"Yes, it is. A man's best friend shouldn't forget—"

"But that doesn't make you an older man. I'll turn fifteen on May thirtieth. You're only forty-eight days older than me!"

Shane laughed. "Yeah, *sonny*, and don't you forget it!"

Mike raised his fishing pole back to his shoulder and started toward the road. "See you at school tomorrow, grandpa!" he called.

Shane watched him go, then picked up the ax. Ten minutes later, he finished the chopping job. He carried the wood into the woodshed, hung the ax on nails provided for it on the wall, and said, "There you are, Mr. Wimberly. I'll be by to check on you in a few weeks. Have some more wood hauled in, and I'll chop it for you."

Calvin Wimberly pulled his wallet from his overall bib and said, "I figure a job like you just did is worth at least three dollars, Shane, so I'll make it five for good measure."

"Oh, no, Mr. Wimberly. I did that job because I wanted to be a help to you. I don't want any pay."

"But…"

Shane walked away and called over his shoulder, "I'll be by in a few weeks. See you then!"

The sun had just set, leaving its golden glow on the western horizon. Shane knew his parents would be wondering where he was if he didn't get home soon. He hopped a fence and started running across a large field toward home. It was a four-mile jaunt through fields and woods of picturesque farmland.

Shane was about halfway home when he spotted black smoke roiling skyward from the farmhouse of a young widow named Elsa Brainerd. Shane sprinted toward the burning house and saw Elsa near the front porch, beating flames off her dress. Two of her three children were with her, screaming in terror.

Terror was in Elsa's eyes as she looked up and saw Shane. He dropped to his knees and finished beating out the flames with his hands. Tears streamed down the widow's cheeks as she cried, "Shane! My baby is in the house!"

Shane looked toward the house. The front door stood open, and the smoke that billowed out the door and flattened against the ceiling of the porch was tinged with red flame. The windows on the bottom floor were closed, but angry flames licked against the panes and thick smoke was turning them black.

"What room is Darlene in?" Shane asked.

"The upstairs bedroom in the far east corner! The fire must have started in the kitchen. The back doors and windows are worse than these. The only possible way I could see to get inside was the front door. But look at it! No one can get in there now!"

Shane scanned the yard, looking for something he could use as a shield to get him through the flame-filled door. His eyes fell on a heavy blanket on Elsa's clothesline. Not far from the clothesline was a small corral next to the barn where a horse and a cow stood looking on. Inside the corral, butted up against the split-rail fence, was the stocktank, full of water.

"Oh, my baby!" Elsa wailed. "My baby! I should never have left her!" A trembling hand went to Elsa's mouth as Johnny and Melissa clung to her, their little faces frozen in masks of terror.

Shane ran to the clothesline and grabbed the blanket. He hopped the fence, plunged the blanket into the water, then made a mad dash for the front porch. Elsa shouted something to him, but the roar of the fire drowned out her words. He wrapped the dripping blanket around him and plunged through the door.

The house had a vestibule with a door to the parlor off to the right, another that led to a hallway straight ahead. The kitchen was at the end of the hallway, which was a blazing inferno. To the left was the staircase. Shane's eyes smarted from the smoke, but he saw that the stairs were just beginning to catch fire. Lambent flames played lightly across the first few steps, but the staircase was not yet blocked.

The heat was unbearable. Shane had a fleeting thought that he was glad he was going to heaven when he died. He bounded up the stairs. Smoke was thick in the hall. As he hurried through the heavy cloud toward the bedroom, he suddenly realized that his pantlegs were on fire. Quickly he lowered the wet blanket around his ankles and calves to smother the flames.

He could hear baby Darlene crying and coughing in the bedroom at the end of the hall. He ran through the door and saw the tiny crib in the corner. He bent over the weeping infant and wrapped her in the wet blanket.

He picked her up and hurried out into the hall. The smoke was thicker yet. He pressed his face into the blanket, drew a deep breath, and ran toward the stairs. He was almost there when he saw that the flames had swept across the stairs to the wall and climbed higher.

The staircase was now blocked.

Outside, Elsa Brainerd held Johnny and Melissa close to her, weeping and praying. A sheet of flame now covered the front door.

Melissa's attention was drawn to the road. "Mama!" she shouted. "It's Mr. and Mrs. Cox!"

Elsa's closest neighbors were Wayne and Betty Cox, who were in their late fifties. Apparently Wayne had just arrived home in the family wagon. He had the team at a full gallop, and the wagon bounced furiously. Betty hung on for dear life.

Behind them Elsa saw George Frye on his horse, riding hard, and another wagon coming at top speed from the opposite direction. It was her neighbors to the south, Carl and Sadie Nelson. Their eighteen-year-old son, Jerry, was in the bed of the wagon, standing and bending over between his parents, gripping the seat. His hat flew off just as Elsa looked back at the burning house.

George Frye raced to the opening in the Brainerd fence that served as a driveway. Pounding hooves raised a cloud of dust as he rounded the corner and beelined for the house. He slid from the saddle before his horse even stopped.

"Elsa! Where's the baby?"

"Upstairs in my bedroom!"

Frye took one look at the flames filling the front door and windows and said, "I'll run around back! Maybe there's a way I can get in. Where's your bedroom located?"

"You can't get in the back either," she said, wiping tears. "Shane Donovan is in there already…but I'm afraid something's happened to him. There's no way out."

"You mean Garth's boy?"

"Yes! I tried to go in and get Darlene, but my dress caught fire. Shane came running up and beat the flames out, then grabbed a blanket and ran into the house to get Darlene."

Both wagons rolled to a halt as Frye looked back toward the inferno. "He'll never get out now," he said with a quaver in his voice.

The Nelsons and Coxes jumped from the wagons and hurried toward Elsa and George.

"Elsa!" Wayne Cox said. "Betty told me you left Darlene home when you came over. Is she—is she—"

"Yes!" Elsa sobbed, clinging to her other two children. "Shane Donovan is in the house too! He went in to try to rescue her!"

The two women each put an arm around Elsa and one of the children. Sadie Nelson's hand went to her mouth.

"How long's he been in there?" Wayne asked.

Elsa's shaky fingertips touched her cheeks. "I'm not sure. Maybe seven or eight minutes."

"Dad, how about you letting me climb up on your shoulders?" Jerry asked. "If I could get up on the porch, maybe I could break a window and get inside. If Shane made it to the second floor, he might—"

The glass in an end window over the porch roof shattered. Every eye turned to see a foot kicking at the glass to clear the shards off the edge of the window. Then Shane crawled through the window, bearing the small bundle.

"Oh, thank the Lord!" Elsa said. "He's got my baby!"

Smoke lifted off Shane's clothing as he hurried to the edge of the porch and shouted, "Mr. Cox! Pull your wagon up close! I'll jump in the back!"

George Frye rushed up to the edge of the porch and said, "Just drop her down to me, Shane!"

"No, sir! It's too far down. No offense, sir, but I can't take the chance that between the two of us, we might let her fall. Please! Just give me a wagon to jump into!"

Wayne Cox was already to his wagon and climbing up to the seat. He grabbed the reins, gave them a snap, and guided the reluctant horses toward the blazing house. Both animals nickered in protest, but he snapped the reins again and shouted at them. They danced nervously as Wayne pulled the wagon directly under where Shane stood. The heat was intense and the roar deafening.

Shane hugged the baby close and jumped. When he landed in the bed of the wagon, he rolled onto his back and shouted, "Go!" The nervous horses were glad to trot away to cooler air. Everyone rushed to the wagon as Wayne pulled to a stop.

Elsa was first to reach the wagon, arms outstretched. Shane smiled as he leaned over and placed the baby into her mother's arms. With shaky hands, Elsa unwrapped the blanket, tears flowing, and looked at the infant, who was whimpering.

"Oh, Mommy's precious baby!" Elsa said, hugging her to her breast. "You're all right! You're all right!"

Johnny and Melissa jumped with joy. Shane swung down from the wagon bed, tiny tendrils of smoke still lifting from his clothing.

Elsa continued to weep as she stretched one arm toward him. "God bless you, Shane! God bless you! How can I ever thank you?" She hugged his neck tight, then released him.

"That was a wonderful thing you did, Shane," Betty Cox said. "You're a brave young man!"

"That's for sure!" Jerry Nelson said.

The others joined in, heaping praises on the fifteen-year-old boy. Shane scrubbed a palm across his sweaty, smudged face and said, "Any one of you fellows would've done it. I just happened to be here first."

"I'm not sure I would've had the courage to plunge through those flames," Jerry said, "even with a wet blanket. You did a wonderful thing, Shane. I'm sure little Darlene will cherish your name when she grows up…and for the rest of her life."

Again Elsa used one arm to embrace Shane around the neck. He felt her warm tears on his face as she said, "I'll always be so grateful to you, Shane."

The sun had gone down and twilight was slowly falling over the countryside. Standing in the brilliant light of the huge fire, the three men decided to soak the roofs of the barn and other buildings in case the sparks that were flying about should fall on them. Betty Cox invited Elsa and the children to stay with them until a new house could be built. She told her husband that she would go ahead and take Elsa and the children home.

Jerry offered to take the Nelson wagon and run Shane home. Weary from his ordeal, Shane took him up on it.

TWO

P oor Mrs. Brainerd," Jerry Nelson said as he guided the wagon along the road toward the Donovan place. "As if it wasn't bad enough losing her husband. How will she ever afford to build another house?"

"By herself, she never would," Shane said. "But she's not alone. The Lord knows that she and her children need a house to live in. He'll give it to her in His own way and in His own time. You'll see."

Jerry turned and looked at Shane in the gathering darkness. "I wish I had your kind of faith, my friend. There's not a trace of a doubt in your voice as you say that."

"David said, 'The Lord is my Shepherd. I shall not want.' The Shepherd takes care of His sheep, Jerry. He doesn't promise to give us everything we want, but He does promise to supply the needs we have. You're a young Christian yet. You've been saved how long now?"

"Since October. Six months."

"You'll learn as you grow older in the Lord. God keeps His promises. One way or another, Mrs. Brainerd will get her new house."

They were nearing the Donovan place and saw a wagon pulling

out of the driveway onto the road, heading their direction.

"Uh-oh," Shane said. "That'll be Pa. No doubt he's coming to look for me. When he comes home from the lumber mill, he expects me to have the chores done."

Jerry chuckled. "Well, I'm sure when he finds out what delayed you, he'll not be angry."

"I'd say you're right. Sure hope so, anyway."

The darkness made it hard to distinguish much more than silhouettes as the two wagons drew abreast.

"Mr. Donovan!" Jerry called out. "I've got Shane here. I was just bringing him home."

Garth Donovan pulled rein, stopping at the same time Jerry brought his wagon to a halt. Shane could make out his younger brothers in the back of the wagon. Patrick was eleven, and Ryan was nine.

"What's kept you, son?" Garth asked, a touch of anger in his voice. "You should've been home from school nearly three hours ago."

"Well, Pa, I stopped to chop wood for Mr. Wimberly. His arthritis is bothering him a lot, and he can't swing an ax without a lot of pain. I figured on doing my chores before supper, but I—"

"Maybe you shouldn't have tried to chop it all at once. I commend you for the deed, Shane, but you've had your mother and me worried. Why didn't you just cut up half the pile today and do the other half tomorrow?"

"Well, Pa— "

"It would've helped to have let your mother know you were planning to cut wood, Shane. I try to let you have some free rein with your time, but I don't want this kind of thing to happen again."

"Pa, I wasn't planning on it. I walk right by his house on the way home from school. He was out there trying to chop the wood as I came by and…well, when I stopped to say hello, I could see the pain in his face. I took the ax from him and told him I'd finish the pile. But you see, Pa— "

"Shane, I commend you for taking over the job for Mr. Wimberly. I want you to be that kind of boy. But shouldn't you have considered your parents? Didn't you realize we would be worried?"

"Pa, the job wasn't that big. I—"

"Come on and get into the wagon. We've got to get home. Thank you, Jerry, for picking him up."

"Sir…" Jerry said.

"Yes?"

"Sir, Shane is trying to tell you that something else came up that detained him."

"Something else? What, may I ask?"

"Go ahead, Shane. Tell him."

"Well, Pa, Mrs. Brainerd's house was on fire, and I had to stop and help her."

"Her house was on fire?"

"Yes, sir."

"So that's where those smoke clouds were coming from! I hope she and the children are all right."

"They're fine. Mr. and Mrs. Cox are taking them into their home till a new house can be built. They lost everything."

"We'll have to see what Elsa and the children need. I'm sure other neighbors will want to help, too."

"I'm sure they will," Shane said, jumping out of the Nelson wagon. "Thanks, Jerry. See you tomorrow at school."

There was a lengthy pause as Shane settled on the seat beside his father, then Jerry said, "Mr. Donovan…"

"Yes, Jerry?"

"There's…ah…there's something Shane hasn't told you. About the fire, I mean."

Garth looked at Shane, then back toward Jerry. "What's that?"

"Well, sir…your son is a hero. He rescued Mrs. Brainerd's baby girl. She would've died for sure if Shane hadn't gone into the house to get her."

There was a brief moment of silence, then Garth said, "Is that right, son? You went into a burning house and rescued the Brainerd baby?"

"That's exactly what he did, Mr. Donovan," Jerry said. "Your son risked his own life to save little Darlene Brainerd."

There was another moment of silence, this time a little longer. Then Garth turned on the wagon seat and wrapped his arms around his oldest son. "Shane, thank God you're alive! Are you all right, son? Did you get burned?"

"I think I might peel some skin, and my hair and eyebrows might be singed a bit. But I'm okay."

"Oh, thank You, Lord," Garth said. "Thank You for taking care of my boy! And thank You that little Darlene is all right!"

"Well, I guess I'd better head back," Jerry said. "Pa and Mr. Frye and Mr. Cox are soaking the roofs of the barn and sheds so they don't catch fire."

Garth again thanked Jerry for bringing Shane home, then turned the wagon around in the road.

"Shane, I want to tell you how proud I am. And I'm sorry, son, for not letting you get your story out."

"It's all right, Pa. You were just trying to tell me how I should've done things. You didn't know."

Garth swung the wagon into the yard and drove it to the barn.

"You boys go on in and wash up. I'm sure your mother's got supper about ready. I'll be right behind you."

Shane slid off the seat and his younger brothers hopped to the ground. As they walked toward the house together, Patrick said, "You really are a hero, big brother!"

"I just did what had to be done, that's all."

Shane headed for the rear of the house, intending to enter the kitchen from the back porch. As usual, lantern light could be seen flickering in all the windows on the lower floor. Suddenly there was movement on the back porch.

"Shane, are you all right?" Pearl Donovan called out.

"Yes, Ma. I'll explain why I'm late at the supper table."

"Boys, do me a favor and go through the front door, please."

Shane was puzzled by the unusual request, but said, "Sure, Ma," as he guided his little brothers toward the front of the house. Patrick and Ryan eased back to let Shane enter the house first.

Shane stepped into the large parlor and nearly jumped out of his skin when two dozen voices shouted, *"Surprise!"* then began a rousing rendition of "Happy Birthday." They all applauded when they finished.

Shane was pleased to see so many friends from church and school. When he saw Mike O'Hanlon's smiling face, he realized why his best friend hadn't said anything about it being his birthday. He let his gaze roam over the happy young faces, and his heart almost stopped when his eyes landed on Ashley Kilrain.

Shane had not told anyone how he felt about Ashley. He thought she was the prettiest girl he had ever seen. Not only that, but she was sweeter than any girl he had ever met, and she was a dedicated Christian. Ashley Kilrain, in Shane Donovan's estimation, was the epitome of Christian femininity and gracefulness. He loved her long, thick auburn hair, and her soft, rosy cheeks and deep-blue eyes were enough to take his breath.

And now she was looking straight at him, smiling warmly.

Pearl Donovan had positioned herself off to one side, standing with her husband and other two sons. It took her a moment to notice that Shane's shirt and pants were scorched, and that the hair at his forehead was singed. She leaned close to Garth and whispered, "What happened to Shane?"

"I'll tell you and everybody about it right now." Garth moved to the center of the parlor and said, "Listen, everybody. There's something you need to know."

When it got quiet, Garth looked at his oldest son and said, "Shane, as you can see, we planned a little surprise party and dinner for you. Your brothers and I had a scheme all worked out to get you off the place for about a half hour while your friends arrived and parked their wagons and buggies out behind the barn. You just unknowingly kept us from having to put our scheme into action."

Shane grinned, shook his head, and let his eyes brush over Ashley Kilrain's face. "Some schemers, all of you," he said.

"Now I want everyone here to know why our son was late and why his clothes are scorched," Garth said.

There was a low murmur among the group, then Garth told them of the fire at the Brainerd home and that Shane had risked his life to rescue the Brainerd baby. When the whole story had been told, everyone looked at Shane with admiring eyes. It seemed to Shane that Ashley Kilrain's eyes held the most admiration. There was a stillness in the house as the group realized how close their friend had come to death.

Pearl Donovan wept as she rushed to her oldest son and wrapped her arms around him. "Oh, Shane, I'm so proud of you! I'm so thankful to the Lord that you're still here to celebrate your fifteenth birthday! And I'm so glad that little Darlene Brainerd's life was spared!"

There were some amens among the group, and several spoke out, sometimes two or three at a time, showering the young hero with praise. Shane's features flushed with embarrassment.

"You're all very kind, but really...I'm no hero. I just happened to be the first one on the scene and did what had to be done. Any of you would've done the same thing."

"Takes a lot of courage to do a thing like that," Hector Donaldson said.

"That's right," agreed another. "A whole lot of courage!"

Pearl saw that her son was becoming increasingly embarrassed. "Well," she said, "we'd better eat or our supper will get cold!"

Shane was placed at the head of the main table, and his father sat at the other end. Three other tables were crowded into the parlor-dining room area.

Ashley was seated at the main table, next to Pearl, who sat across the corner from her husband. From time to time during the meal, Shane let his eyes stray to Ashley, feeling a strange warmth whenever he looked at her.

When the meal was over, it was time for games. The favorite was "Musical Chairs," which was played enthusiastically while Pearl played the piano. Even Garth joined in. After nearly an hour of games, it was time for Shane to open his presents.

When all the gifts had been unwrapped, Pearl, Patrick, and Ryan came from the kitchen carrying cakes—Pearl a large chocolate cake with lighted candles, and the boys smaller cakes. Everyone sang "Happy Birthday" again, and Shane easily blew out the fifteen candles. There was laughter and applause, then they all ate cake while mingling and chatting.

Shane made his way amongst his guests, thanking them for coming and for their gifts. He purposely saved Ashley till last so he could spend more time with her. She was talking to Hector Donaldson and a girl named Patricia Reynolds as he drew near. Patricia said a few more words to Ashley, then she and Hector excused themselves and walked away, joining a small group close by.

Ashley gave Shane a coy smile and said with a hint of Irish brogue, "I sure am thankful to the Lord that He protected you in that burning house, Shane. I know you've heard it already tonight, but you *are* a very courageous young man."

"You're very kind, Ashley, but I really don't think *courageous* is the right word to describe me. Maybe *determined* is the word. I was very determined to save that little baby's life, but to tell you the truth, I was scared to death."

Ashley smiled and said, "That's why I used the word *courageous*. Courage doesn't mean without fear. It means doing what has to be done in spite of your fear."

"Really?"

"Yes, really. You're a very courageous young man, Shane, and I'm proud to know you."

"And I'm proud to know such a smart girl who's also the prettiest girl I've ever seen in my life and I'm wondering why you're not in Lewiston at school since you only come home on weekends and this is only Tuesday."

While Shane was taking a breath, Ashley giggled and said, "Thank you for the kind words, Shane. The reason I'm here and not at school is because I wanted to come to the party. Daddy came and picked me up after school this afternoon. I didn't want the other kids in the youth group to be at your birthday party without me."

Shane wasn't sure Ashley meant that she wanted to be there for *him* or for the socializing. He hoped it was because she wanted to be there for him. He was trying to think of something else to say when he noticed Mike O'Hanlon looking at him from across the room. Or was he looking at Ashley?

Shane was about to ask how her Uncle Buster was when Ashley said, "I suppose you're going to the church picnic a week from next Saturday."

Shane struggled to free his tongue while the Irish lass held his gaze with her own. "Well, yes, I...I'm going to the picnic. Would...would you be my date?"

Ashley sucked in a tiny breath and said, "Why, I'd be delighted to go as your date, Shane. I'm honored that you would ask me. I mean that."

Shane's heart was pounding so hard he wondered if Ashley could see the front of his scorched shirt move.

"The honor will be all mine, Ashley. May I come by and pick you up in our family wagon? *With* my parents and little brothers, of course."

"You may," she said. "The picnic's at noon. What time should I expect you?"

"I'd say about a quarter till, if that's all right."

"I'm sure that will be fine."

"Then it's a date!" Shane said.

Moments later, the guests piled into the wagons and drove away. Shane kept his eyes on Ashley until she was swallowed by the night.

Only Mike O'Hanlon remained. He had made arrangements to spend the night with his best friend, and Shane was happy to have him. They had often stayed at each other's homes over the years. Shane's second-story bedroom was large and equipped with two three-quarter beds.

Shane had been dying to share his good news with Mike ever since the party was over. Finally alone with his friend, he lay in his bed with his arms behind his head, looking toward the dark ceiling.

"Mike…"

"Yeah?"

"I sure am glad Ashley likes older men."

"Oh? Why's that?"

"Because when I asked her to be my date at the church picnic, she accepted!"

There was a brief moment of silence. Then Mike said, "Hey, that's great, old man!"

There was a smile in Mike O'Hanlon's voice, but the darkness hid the grim form of his lips.

THREE

On Sunday morning, the bell in the tower of the First Parish Congregational Church in Brunswick was ringing as people came to the services in buggies, surreys, carriages, wagons, on horseback, and afoot.

The story of Shane Donovan's heroic deed had spread all over Brunswick and the surrounding farm area. When the Donovan family arrived in their wagon, people crowded around to commend the fifteen-year-old boy for his courageous act and to ask questions about it. Shane was not yet accustomed to his newfound fame and found all the attention embarrassing.

While he was answering questions, Shane saw the Kilrain carriage pull into the churchyard. Ashley was wearing a new hairstyle under her small plumed hat, and she was smiling at him. He hoped the new hairdo was for him.

In the Kilrain carriage, Donald and Mavor sat together on the front seat, along with Donald's brother, Vivian Kilrain. In the second seat, Moira sat beside her younger sister, while eleven-year-old William and nine-year-old Harvey rode in the third seat.

Vivian, at forty, was a year older than Donald, and a widower. He hated his first name and insisted that everyone call him Buster.

He was short and muscular, and his carrot-red hair and ruddy complexion gave him the look of a man with a quick temper. Buster Kilrain had served as a soldier in the Army of Ireland before coming to the States to work in the Leprechaun Shoe and Boot Manufacturing Company. Everyone in the family adored Uncle Buster.

The Kilrains pulled up and parked beside the Donovans. Shane was still surrounded by curious people, but while he talked to them, he looked at Ashley. She gave him another smile. Shane was about to excuse himself to go help Ashley from the carriage, but Uncle Buster beat him to it.

The Donovan boys, being the same ages as the Kilrain boys, hurried off to their Sunday school classes together. The rest of the family members greeted one another. Shane finally was able to politely break away from the curious ones and hurried to talk with Ashley. Before he could get to her, Buster clapped him on the shoulder.

"Well, Shane me boy, sure and if ye didn't go and become a hero! I think what ye did was grand and quite unselfish. Me compliments to you."

Shane grinned shyly and said, "Thank you, Uncle Buster."

A surrey pulled up next to where they stood, loaded with the Calvin Stowe family.

"Hey, Shane," Calvin said, "we heard about the fire at Elsa Brainerd's and about what you did. God bless you for being such a brave young man!"

"Thank you, sir," Shane said.

Calvin Stowe was professor of rhetoric at nearby Bowdoin College, a Christian liberal arts school. Harriet, his wife, had already made a name for herself with her novel that had been published two years previously. *Uncle Tom's Cabin* was creating quite a stir both above and below the Mason-Dixon line.

As Shane was speaking with the famous author, Wayne and Betty Cox pulled up in their wagon with Elsa Brainerd and her children aboard. Little Darlene was wrapped in a blanket and held in her mother's arms.

The crowd moved toward the Cox wagon, wanting to talk to Elsa and get a look at the baby. Shane stood back, looking on. He was glad to let Elsa and her baby girl have the limelight. As the people spoke to Elsa, Shane heard her say, "Yes! Praise the Lord for His protective hand on my baby…and praise the Lord for Shane Donovan! He's the bravest young man I've ever known."

Later, the choir opened the morning worship service with a rousing song, then two congregational hymns followed. At the close of the second hymn, the pastor, Dr. George Adams, rose from his chair on the platform and went to the pulpit. Adams, a distant cousin of John Quincy Adams, was a tall, stately man. Though he was only in his early fifties, his hair was silver.

Dr. Adams gave his normal announcements, then said, "My brothers and sisters in Christ, I believe that by now all of us have heard about our dear sister, Elsa Brainerd, losing her house in a fire this past Tuesday."

Shane Donovan was sitting between Mike O'Hanlon and Ashley Kilrain. He tensed up, hoping the pastor would not say anything about him having rescued the Brainerd baby. He heaved an inward sigh of relief when Dr. Adams proceeded to ask the people to sacrifice in a special offering for Elsa and her children. He said that if everyone would go the extra mile for the widow, they could raise enough money to build her a new house. There were scattered amens in the crowd, and the offering plates were passed.

While the money was being counted, Dr. Adams introduced twenty-four-year-old Joshua Lawrence Chamberlain, an 1852 Phi Beta Kappa graduate of Bowdoin College who was now studying for the ministry at Bangor Theological Seminary. While a student at Bowdoin, Chamberlain had been music director at the church, and he was now engaged to Frances Adams, the pastor's adopted daughter. Frances—better known as Fannie—was the church organist.

In the pulpit, Dr. Adams spoke highly of Chamberlain and told the crowd how proud he and his wife, Sarah Ann, were that Joshua would one day be their son-in-law.

Shane and Mike set admiring eyes on the handsome seminary student who during his college years had been their Sunday school teacher. His slim, muscular frame lacked an inch and a half of reaching six feet, but he had a way of carrying himself that gave the impression he was taller. His face was long and slender with prominent cheekbones and deep-set, gray-blue eyes under heavy brows. His hair was dark brown, and he was clean-shaven.

The congregation sang another hymn, and during the last stanza, one of the ushers hurried to the platform and handed the pastor a slip of paper. Dr. Adams read it and smiled.

When the hymn was finished, Adams stepped to the pulpit and said, "Friends, the Lord has worked in hearts here this morning in a marvelous way. I did not suggest any kind of a figure that it would take to build a house for Elsa Brainerd and her children, but I discussed it yesterday with Clyde Domire, who you all know is in the construction business. Brother Domire estimates that it will cost about four thousand dollars for the materials. He has already volunteered to build the house for no cost."

Elsa Brainerd, who sat between Melissa and Johnny with baby Darlene in her arms, began to weep. Betty Cox was seated next to Melissa. She reached over and patted Elsa's arm, saying, "The Lord takes care of His own, honey."

Elsa nodded, biting her lips and wiping tears.

"Mrs. Adams and I did some figuring the past couple of days," the pastor said. "We think the house can be furnished for about eight hundred dollars with another six hundred dollars needed for clothing and shoes."

Sarah Ann Adams was seated in the choir behind her husband. He heard her whisper, "George!"

He asked the audience to excuse him momentarily and went to his wife. She whispered something to him, and he nodded, then returned to the pulpit.

"My wife reminds me that there were toys burned up in the fire, as well as furniture and clothing. We had figured them in our total, but I forgot to mention them just now. You men know how wives are—sticklers for details!"

Laughter swept through the crowd.

"Anyway, Sarah Ann and I figured the grand total needed to start Elsa and the children over again—the cupboards stocked with groceries, too—would be around fifty-five hundred dollars."

The congregation waited in eager silence as the pastor looked back at the slip of paper, smiled broadly, and said, "My brothers and sisters in Christ...in checks and cash, a total of six thousand one hundred dollars was in the offering, with a few notes promising an additional thirteen hundred and forty-four dollars to be given in the service tonight. How do you like that? A total of over seven thousand four hundred dollars!"

The crowd cheered and applauded, many shedding tears. Elsa wept for joy. The Coxes both took her into their arms, reminding her how much she and her children were loved.

When the crowd noise subsided, a man stood and said, "Pastor, I'm volunteering my labor to help build the house."

That was all it took to trigger the same response throughout the congregation. Elsa cried the more, overwhelmed with the generosity of the people and the goodness of the Lord.

At the organ, Fannie struck up a song of praise. The pianist blended in, and the music director stood and led them all in singing praises to the bountiful God of heaven.

Dr. Adams then returned to the pulpit and opened his Bible. Shane heaved another secret sigh of relief. He wouldn't have to endure any more embarrassment. The pastor hadn't said a word about Shane's act of courage in rescuing the baby.

"This morning," the pastor said, "I want to speak to you on the subject of courage."

Shane swallowed hard, blinking in disbelief. Mike elbowed him, and Ashley gave him a smile.

Dr. Adams began his sermon by explaining that courage was not the lack of fear, but the wherewithal in a person to perform a necessary task in spite of fear. He then took his congregation into the Scriptures, giving biblical examples of courage. He showed that the supreme example was the Lord Himself, who set His face as a flint to go to the cross, knowing He would be forsaken by His Father while suffering the fire of God's wrath, the onslaught of the devil, and the fierceness of the jaws of death. Yet because He loved a lost world of condemned sinners, Jesus went to the cross with undaunted courage in spite of all He faced at Calvary.

After citing other examples of courage in the Bible, Adams took his audience to the three Hebrew children in the book of Daniel who went into Nebuchadnezzar's fiery furnace rather than bow before the golden image and deny their God. Shadrach, Meshach, and Abednego acknowledged that God might not deliver them, but showed their courage by going into the flames in spite of their fear.

Shane Donovan wanted to slide off the pew and hide on the floor when Dr. Adams used his act of courage as a closing illustration. Adams showed that in spite of his fear, Shane demonstrated courage by going into the blazing inferno after little Darlene Brainerd at the risk of his own life.

When the service was over, Shane was again surrounded by people who wished to congratulate him. His parents, Ashley, and Mike stood by looking on. They smiled at each other, seeing how embarrassed Shane was at being the center of attention.

The crowd around Shane had begun to diminish when he saw Joshua Chamberlain approaching him with Fannie Adams on his arm. Shane smiled broadly at Chamberlain, spoke first to Fannie, then extended his hand to Chamberlain.

"It's good to see you again, Mr. Chamberlain," Shane said.

"Thank you, Shane. I'm honored to be able to shake the hand of such a courageous young man."

"Well, thank you, sir. But I'll be glad when everyone can just forget about this whole incident. I don't much like being compared to

Shadrach, Meshach, and Abednego. What I did wasn't anything like what they went through."

"Perhaps not, but commendable all the same."

"Mr. Chamberlain, Pastor Adams didn't mention a wedding date. When are you and Miss Fannie planning on getting married?"

"We haven't set a date yet, Shane. We both feel the Lord would have us finish our education first. Fannie is making plans to go to New York City to further her music studies, and I'm going to continue preparing myself for the ministry at Bangor."

Shane saw that his parents and younger brothers were heading toward their wagon. "Well, sir, I hope I get to see you again sometime soon."

"Who knows? I'm sure one of these weekends I'll be back...even if Fannie's in New York."

They shook hands again, and Shane joined his family at the wagon.

The following Saturday, Shane and Ashley had their date at the church picnic. They paired up for games and entered the three-legged race, the pie-in-the-face contest, and the egg-tossing competition. That day drew them closer together.

Over the next several months, they spent more time together, making sure they always sat side by side in Sunday school class and in the church services. Shane became more and more attached to the pretty Irish lass.

In late spring, Moira Kilrain graduated from the Lewiston Finishing School for Girls and married a young man from Portland, and they made their home in that city.

When summer rolled around, Shane worked ten hours a day, six days a week at the lumber mill with his father. In the evenings and on Sunday afternoons, he was allowed by his parents and Ashley's to visit her at the Kilrain home. He was often invited for meals by Mavor, and became well-liked by the family. Uncle Buster had a special liking for Shane, for they had become fishing partners, squeezing in fishing time after work hours and before supper.

Elsa Brainerd's house was finished by early July. The entire community gave her a housewarming, adding kitchenware she needed and some things for the bedrooms.

Mike O'Hanlon worked eight hours a day during the summer at the shoe factory, learning the business. His father and Donald Kilrain had promised to make him a partner after he graduated from college. Half of his work was doing manual labor in the shop, and the other half was spent in the office learning the management end of the business. Mike was bright and industrious and was catching on fast. He and his best friend saw each other very little during the summer.

They were both glad for school to start so they could be together more. Mike noticed, though, that Shane sorely missed Ashley on the weekdays when she was in Lewiston at school.

In late September, a lumberjack who worked under Garth Donovan was accidentally killed on the job. Garth had often talked to him about the gospel, but the tough, foul-mouthed lumberjack turned a deaf ear. The accident took him instantly. The man died in his unbelieving state.

Dr. George Adams preached the funeral, which was attended by a great crowd of area residents. His sermon was loaded with gospel, and many unbelievers were converted, including several teenagers. The tragedy also served to draw the teenagers of First Parish Congregational Church closer to the Lord and to each other. Ashley, Shane, Mike, and their friends in the church youth group took the newly saved teenagers under their wings to help them grow in the Lord.

On April 12, 1854, Pearl Donovan surprised her oldest son by springing another birthday party and dinner for him, with his friends from church as guests. All of the teenagers who had come to Christ after the lumberjack was killed were there.

Pearl placed Shane at the head of the table again, with Ashley on the corner to his left. Next to Ashley sat a pretty brunette. Shane leaned over and said to Ashley, "I assume this young lady is a friend of yours."

"Yes, she is. Shane Donovan, I would like you to meet Charolette Thompson."

Charolette smiled and offered her hand. As Shane took it, she said, "Ashley has told me so much about you, Shane. I feel like I already know you."

"Charolette and I have been friends for some time," Ashley said. "She's going to stay at my house this weekend and come to church with us."

"Wonderful," Shane said. "It will be nice to have you at church, Charolette. And thank you for coming to my party."

"I'm glad to be here."

"Has everyone else met her?" Shane asked Ashley.

"I introduced her around while we were waiting for your daddy and brothers to bring you home."

Garth Donovan stood at his end of the table and asked Mike O'Hanlon, who was seated across from Ashley, to lead them in prayer. After he had prayed and everyone began to eat, Mike asked Charolette where her home was and where she knew Ashley from.

"I was born in Ireland," Charolette said with a smile, "but Father brought our family to America when I was ten. He opened a general store in Lewiston. My parents put me in the Lewiston Finishing School for Girls the following year, and that's where I met Ashley. We've become close friends."

"I see," Mike said. "Well, I'm glad you could come to the party for the old man here."

Charolette laughed at Shane's feigned protest.

"Everyone here has been so nice to me. I guess you all go to the same church?"

"We're in the youth group together."

"Well, I'm looking forward to visiting there on Sunday."

***

On Sunday morning, to everyone's surprise, Dr. Adams had invited a guest speaker to fill his pulpit. He had been over to Bangor that week and had heard his future son-in-law preach in chapel. Adams was surprised at the eloquence and maturity Joshua Chamberlain had gained since his term as music director at First Parish, and he invited him to preach both Sunday morning and evening.

Ashley and Shane sat together, as usual, with Mike sitting on Shane's other side. Charolette Thompson sat next to Ashley. During the congregational singing, Ashley noticed that Charolette was unfamiliar with the songs. Her heart went out to her. Charolette was such a sweet girl, but had been raised in a home where neither God nor His Son were ever considered.

Ashley knew that Charolette's mother had died of consumption a little over a year ago, and that her father gave her little of his time. He was too busy running his store to pay attention to his daughter. The only thing he did was pay her bill at the school and tell her to stay there on the weekends…he didn't need her around the house. On more than one occasion Ashley had found Charolette weeping in her dormitory room, missing her mother and feeling all but abandoned by her father.

As a female soloist prepared to sing just before the sermon, Ashley leaned close to Shane and whispered, "Pray for Charolette. I think she's almost ready to come to Jesus." Shane reached down and squeezed her hand.

Dr. Adams introduced Joshua Chamberlain after the solo, and when he opened his Bible and began to preach, Mike and Shane looked at each other and smiled. They were amazed at how much his speaking had improved since he had taught them in Sunday school. He was a good speaker before; now he was excellent.

With his heart on fire for Jesus Christ, Chamberlain preached a powerful gospel sermon, warning sinners of the wrath to come and giving them the crucified, risen Christ as the only refuge. When it came time for the invitation, and the crowd was standing and singing, Ashley looked at Charolette from the corner of her eye and saw that she was weeping. She leaned close and said, "Charolette, would you like to respond to the invitation? I'll go with you."

Charolette nodded, wiped tears, and said, "Yes!"

Ashley took her friend by the hand and led her down the aisle. Others went forward also. There was great rejoicing throughout the congregation for those who were coming to Christ.

Ashley stayed with Charolette while the pastor's wife counseled her. When the service was over, the two girls embraced and wept. Charolette thanked Ashley for caring enough to talk to her so many times about salvation. Many of the teenagers in the youth group gathered around Charolette, rejoicing with her in her new-found faith.

During the following year, Charolette Thompson visited the Kilrain home on several occasions, staying over weekends and attending church. She became well-acquainted with the young people in the Sunday school class. She was growing in the Lord and becoming an avid student of the Bible. Though Shane's heart was fixed on Ashley, he found Charolette charming and a joy to be around. She had a vibrant sense of humor and a sweet spirit.

FOUR

S hane Donovan was now seventeen, but since Ashley Kilrain was only fifteen, her father would not allow her to declare herself Shane's steady girlfriend. Donald and Mavor Kilrain wholeheartedly approved of Shane, but they had decided that their daughter could not enter into that kind of relationship until she was seventeen. Though Shane and Ashley had not declared that they were steadies, everyone in the church knew it would be that way once Ashley was old enough.

In late April 1855, First Parish Congregational Church held another picnic on a Saturday afternoon. Shane rode to the picnic in the Kilrain carriage with Ashley, her parents, her brothers, and Uncle Buster.

It was a bright, sunlit day with only a few puffy white clouds drifting in the Maine sky. The picnic was held on the church property, which had open fields of grass fringed and dotted with trees.

Some four hundred people came. Elderly folks sat on chairs in the shade. Young mothers tended to crying babies and tried to keep up with their older children. Some men played horseshoes while others stood around and talked. Many of the women collected in groups to talk also. There were frequent bursts of laughter. Children ran about, laughing and having a good time. Boys with bugs in their hands chased girls, and the girls screamed.

Barry Flanders, a young man who had come into the church earlier in the year, brought Charolette Thompson to the picnic, and Mike O'Hanlon brought Minnie Weatherton.

The first organized competition was the teenagers' three-legged race. Shane took Ashley by the hand, looked around at their friends, and said, "C'mon everyone, let's race!"

"I can't, Shane," Barry said. "I twisted my knee yesterday, and it's still giving me a lot of pain."

"Did you have a doctor look at it?"

"No. Ma says I'll have to if it doesn't get better by Monday."

"I hate to see you miss out on the fun, Charolette," Shane said.

She smiled. "It's all right. I'll enjoy sitting here with Barry and watching the rest of you."

A good-sized crowd, including the pastor and his wife, gathered to watch. Nine teenage couples entered the race, which consisted of four heats. The race was a distance of fifty yards, so there would be a ten-minute rest period between heats.

Mike and Minnie lined up next to Shane and Ashley. Mike grinned at Shane, then looked at Minnie and said, "We'll put these two in our dust."

Minnie giggled, got a firm grip on Mike's arm, and said, "I'm ready!"

The start signal was given, and the race began. Mike and Minnie stayed abreast of Shane and Ashley until forty feet from the finish line when Shane and Ashley pulled ahead, along with two other couples.

Just as they crossed the line, Ashley stumbled and went down, taking Shane with her. From the ground, they turned to see who had stayed in the competition with them. Mike and Minnie were among the couples who qualified for the next heat.

As Shane started to get up, Ashley howled, gritted her teeth, and said, "I think I turned my ankle."

"Really? Does it hurt bad?"

"Enough to take me out of the race. I'm sorry, Shane."

Shane grinned. "Silly. There's nothing to be sorry about."

"But now you'll be out of the race."

"It's all right, Ashley." Shane began to untie the rope that held their ankles together. "It's not that important."

When the rope was loose, Shane helped Ashley to her feet. "Here, lean on me. We'll go over to the bench where Barry and Charolette are and watch the rest of the race with them."

Mike and Minnie saw them and asked what had happened. After Shane told them, Mike kidded Ashley, saying she knew that he and Minnie would eventually beat them, so she turned her ankle on purpose. They all had a good laugh as they moved off the field to rest.

Donald and Mavor Kilrain, along with Uncle Buster, were waiting at the benches for them, having seen Ashley fall. She assured them it was only a slight twist. Satisfied that she was all right, the parents rejoined the other couples they had been talking with.

The three men who were officiating came up and asked about Ashley, wanting to make sure she had not been hurt seriously. When they learned that the injury was minor but enough to take her out of the competition, one of them said, "You were doing real good, Shane. You've still got about six minutes. Maybe you can find another partner."

Ashley turned to Charolette and said, "Do you suppose Barry would mind if you entered the race as Shane's partner? I hate to see him eliminated because of me."

"Of course I wouldn't mind," Barry said. "How about it, Charolette?"

Charolette looked at Barry, smiled, and glanced at Shane. "Would that be all right with you?"

"Sure, as long as Barry doesn't mind," Shane said. "I've got a feeling you'd be a good partner."

Charlotte looked at Ashley. "Honey, are you sure you don't mind the love of your life being tied to me?"

Ashley smiled. "You're my best friend in all the world, Charolette. I'm not worried about that."

"You're a dear," Charolette said, patting her arm. "I really am happy to get into the race, but I'm sorry it has to be because of your ankle."

"It'll be all right in a day or two," Ashley said. "Better hurry. The second heat is about to begin."

Shane gave Ashley a tender look and said, "Thanks. Charolette and I will do our best to win."

There was cheering on the sidelines as the second heat got under way. Shane and Charolette seemed perfectly synchronized as they ran, and came in first. Mike and Minnie came in on their heels.

By the time the third heat was finished, the two couples left for the final heat were Shane and Charolette, and Mike and Minnie. During the rest period, Mike chided his best friend, saying he and Charolette didn't have a chance.

"Oh? And just what makes you think so?" Shane said.

"'Cause you're the old man here, my friend. You just won't be able to hold up. Too bad Charolette had to get stuck with a nineteenth-century Methuselah!"

They had a good laugh together, and soon lined up to the sounds of a shouting crowd, ready to run the final heat. The start signal was given, and the race was on.

The race was neck-and-neck for nearly thirty yards, then Shane and Charolette began to edge ahead. When they were within ten yards of the finish line, Mike and Minnie were three strides behind.

"What's the matter young whippersnapper?" Shane called over his shoulder. "You gonna let this old man and his partner beat you?"

Mike shouted back a retort, but because of the noise from the crowd, Shane couldn't tell what he was saying. Shane and Charolette crossed the finish line first, and both couples fell on the grass, laughing. While the ankle ropes were being untied, Shane asked, "Now, what was it you shouted back at me, ol' pal?"

"I said you were ahead because that youthful girl was carrying you!"

The four of them laughed again, and the boys helped the girls to their feet. The grand prize was a huge watermelon. The crowd cheered the winners again, then the officials began preparing for a footrace between teenage boys.

"I don't suppose I could interest you in entering the next race, Shane, seeing as how you're so old and tired," Mike said.

"We'll see who's old and tired."

Shane called to his father to come and take the watermelon off his hands. Garth was there in seconds, offering his congratulations to Shane and Charolette and his condolences to Mike and Minnie. He hurried back to Pearl, carrying the prize.

Shane smiled at Charolette and said, "Thank you, young lady, for helping this old man win the race."

"Oh, you're welcome, Shane. The pleasure was mine."

Minnie and Charolette headed for the benches and found that Ashley was alone. Barry had gone to get them some lemonade. Minnie offered to get some for Charolette and herself, saying it should be her task since she lost the race. Charolette laughed and told her to hurry back as she sat down beside Ashley.

"How's the ankle feeling?" Charolette asked.

"It's not hurting quite as much, but it does seem to be swelling a little."

"Honey, I envy you."

"What do you mean?"

"To have such a fine, handsome, Christian boy like Shane interested in you—you're truly fortunate."

Ashley sighed. "You're right. He's a wonderful young man. I hope as we grow older that the love between us grows and deepens so we can marry. I can't think of anything more wonderful than being married to Shane Donovan."

When the picnic was over, Charolette watched Shane and Ashley ride away together in the Kilrain carriage. Lord, if You have another boy in this part of the world like Shane Donovan, would You bring him into my life?

A caravan of buggies, surreys, and wagons from Brunswick made the fifteen-mile trip to Lewiston for graduation day at the finishing school in late May 1855. Ashley Kilrain and Charolette Thompson graduated, both being sixteen, which was the average age for girls to graduate from the school. Fifty-seven other girls graduated at the same time.

It was hard for Charolette to observe families of the other graduates congratulating them. She was the only one whose mother was missing. Her father, Alfred Thompson, had come to the graduation and stood beside his daughter as friends offered their congratulations. Charolette introduced them to him, but he was cool and showed little interest in them.

Alfred excused himself for a few minutes and walked away, and Charolette began to cry. Ashley saw it, went to her, and wrapped her arms around her. Mavor saw the two of them together and came to see what was wrong. Charolette wiped tears from her cheeks and drew a shuddering breath. She was about to reply when Pearl Donovan walked up and asked if there was a problem. Ashley released her hold on her best friend, and Charolette explained with quivering lips and shaky voice how desperately she missed her mother and wished she could have lived to see her graduate.

The two mothers embraced her at the same time, speaking words of comfort. As they were doing so, Alfred Thompson returned.

"What's the matter?" he asked. "What happened, Charolette?"

"I...I miss Mama, Papa. I wish so much she could have been here to see me graduate."

"Well, she's gone, Charolette, and there's nothin' we can do about it. You ready to head for home?"

"I guess so."

"Then let's go."

"What plans do you have now that you've graduated, honey?" Mavor asked.

"I'm going to find a job, Mrs. Kilrain," she said, sniffing and dabbing at her tears with a hanky Pearl had just placed in her hand. "I'm going to look in Portland first, since it's the largest town around."

Mavor looked at Alfred and said to Charolette, "Your father has a thriving business, I understand. Doesn't he have a spot for you in his store? That way you could stay at home."

"C'mon, Charolette," Alfred said. "Let's get goin'."

Charolette's brow furrowed as she looked at the women and Ashley with fear in her eyes. She thanked them for being so kind to her, told Ashley she would see her as soon as possible, and hurried after her father, who was already heading toward the graveled lot where the vehicles were parked.

She was about to catch up to him when she saw Shane Donovan running toward her across the school lawn. She stopped and forced a smile as he drew up. From the corner of her eye, she could see her father untying the reins of the horse that pulled his carriage.

"Charolette," Shane said, "I saw that you and your father were leaving, and I wanted to ask if you'll still be coming to church on Sundays."

"I'll come whenever I can arrange a ride. I'll be looking for a job in Portland, and if I find one, I won't be able to come to Brunswick very often. I'll just have to see how the Lord works things out."

"Well, I'll be praying that He'll fix it so you can still come to church. I figured your dad would give you a job in the store."

Charolette glanced at her father, who was climbing into his carriage.

"Papa says it's better if I live and work elsewhere," she said, a trace of a tremor in her voice.

"Oh. Well, you'll be keeping in touch with Ashley, I'm sure."

"Of course."

"Good. Then we'll know how things are going for you."

She glanced again at her father, who was now settled on the seat, glaring at her. She hurried toward the carriage and looked back at Shane. "See you Sunday if I can."

Alfred Thompson scowled at his daughter as she climbed into the carriage. He said something Shane could not distinguish, but whatever it was hurt her, for her shoulders slumped and her head dropped forward. She didn't look back at Shane as the carriage rolled away.

Shane hurried to the others and said to Ashley as he drew up, "Poor Charolette. Her father really treats her bad."

"I know. He's downright mean to her."

"He needs some man to take him out behind the barn and give him a good whipping."

"Now, Shane," Pearl said, "you shouldn't talk that way. No matter how he treats Charolette, he's still her father."

"I know, Ma, but that doesn't give him the right to mistreat her. She's a sweet girl. Did you know she's going to be looking for a job in Portland?"

"Yes, she told us," his mother said.

"Well, if she finds one, she won't be coming to church much, if at all. I asked her if her father couldn't give her a job in his store. She told me he said it's better if she lives and works somewhere else."

"I asked Charolette the same thing in front of him, Shane," Mavor said. "He didn't even respond. Poor girl. Somebody needs to take her in and give her a home and some love."

The next Sunday, Shane Donovan and Ashley Kilrain were standing in front of the church building before Sunday school, chatting with other young people. Elsa Brainerd pulled her wagon up close to where they stood, smiled and said, "Hello, Ashley...Shane."

They greeted her, and Shane stepped up to help her out of the wagon while Johnny and Melissa hopped out of the back. Shane then reached onto the seat and picked up two-year-old Darlene, who smiled at him and said, "Unca Shane!"

"That's my girl!" he laughed, kissing her cheek and holding her close.

"She loves you a lot now, Shane," Elsa said, "but when she finds out what you did for her, she'll love you even more. I'll probably tell her about the time she turns five, so I can be sure she'll understand."

Shane kissed Darlene's cheek again and handed her to her mother. "I don't mind you telling her. Just don't make me sound more important than I am."

Elsa smiled at him, then hurried inside the church with her children.

Just then Ashley pointed to the street and said, "Shane, look!"

It was Charolette Thompson. She was driving her father's carriage, alone. Charolette raised a hand of greeting and pulled rein. When the carriage stopped, Shane stepped up, offered his hand, and helped her down. Charolette felt a tingle all over when she placed her hand in Shane's.

No, Charolette, she said to herself. Ashley is your best friend, and Shane belongs to her.

Ashley rushed to Charolette and embraced her. "Your father actually give you permission to drive here?"

"Well, not exactly. He got married last night, and he and my new stepmother are taking a two-day cruise down the coast. He didn't say I couldn't take the horse and carriage, so here I am."

"New stepmother!" Ashley said. "You haven't told me your father was seeing someone."

"It all happened real fast," Charolette said as they started toward the church together.

"Do you like her, Charolette?" Shane asked.

"I don't really know her. She…"

"She what?" Ashley said.

"Well…I…I guess I'd better not talk about her."

Ashley stopped and looked her best friend in the eye. "You're upset, aren't you? This new stepmother of yours…what's her name?"

"Ethel."

"Well, this Ethel…she doesn't like you, does she?"

Charolette cleared her throat nervously. "Well…I—"

"You don't have to say any more," Ashley said. "I knew it just by the look in your eyes."

"We'd better get inside, girls," Shane said, "or we're going to be late."

Charolette sat in Sunday school and barely heard the lesson. She was upset over her father's marriage, but even more, she was overcome with guilt because of her feelings toward Shane Donovan. While Chester Olmstead taught, she prayed inwardly, O Lord, forgive me. I shouldn't be having these feelings for Shane. You know I've been struggling with this attraction for him for several weeks. And You know I love Ashley and would never try to come between them. Please help me to smother these feelings. Please, Lord!

Charolette Thompson was unable to find employment in Portland, so her father reluctantly let her help in the store. She and her new stepmother did not get along well. Ethel seemed to resent Charolette's presence in the home and at the store. Alfred allowed Charolette to use the horse and carriage on the weekends so she would be out of the house. He knew she was spending them with Ashley Kilrain and going to church on Sundays.

Donald and Mavor were glad to have Charolette in their home and came to love her more as the weeks passed. Charolette said little about her new stepmother, but Ashley and her parents suspected that the reason Alfred allowed his daughter to spend the weekends with them was because neither he nor Ethel wanted her around.

Charolette continued to struggle with her feelings toward Shane Donovan. Whenever she was near him, she prayed that the Lord would send the man he had chosen for her life's mate into her life. The love between Shane and Ashley was deepening before

Charolette's very eyes, and though she rejoiced for Ashley, it was painful to watch. Until the Lord helped her to get over him, Shane had Charolette's heart. She vowed she would never let it show. If only there was another Shane Donovan!

One Monday morning in late July, Buster Kilrain happened to be at his brother's house. Buster knew of the unhappiness Charolette was experiencing at home. When she drove toward home after breakfast, Buster said to Donald, Mavor, and Ashley, "Poor Charolette. The likes of her misery is tearin' me heart out. She deserves some happiness. She ain't gonna find it as long as she has to live in that home and work in that store. How can her own father treat her like that?"

"I don't know," Donald said, "but something's got to be done for her."

"Well, I'd let her come and live at my house, 'ceptin' it wouldn't be proper for me and her to be livin' under the same roof. Besides, then she wouldn't have a job at all."

Donald spoke again. "Tell you what, family. I've been thinking there's no reason Charolette couldn't live with us. She's got her own room on the weekends. Why not just let it be her room all the time?"

"Oh, Daddy!" Ashley said. "That would be wonderful!"

"You know I'd love to have her," Mavor said. "But she still wouldn't have a job."

"Well, I think I've got that figured out too," Donald said. "Matilda Owens is leaving the factory to get married and moving to Bangor with her new husband. We're going to need someone to replace her. With her sweet personality and bright countenance, Charolette would be perfect for the receptionist's job."

"So what's our next move, dear?" Mavor asked.

"Well, we'll ask Charolette if she wants what I've just proposed…and if she does, the next thing will be for us to go and ask her father if he'll let us have her."

"I don't think we'll have a problem on either count, Daddy," Ashley said.

"I'll talk to Lewis about offering her the job. I'm sure he'll be agreeable to it. But since he's half-owner of the company, we always discuss this kind of thing. Then we'll talk to Charolette this weekend. If she likes our proposal, we'll go talk to her father."

Tears welled up in Ashley's eyes, and she wrapped her arms around her father. "O Daddy, this is the answer to my prayers! I've been praying so hard that the Lord would get Charolette out of that miserable situation. I know it's going to work out. I just know it!"

FIVE

Upon arriving at the factory that morning, Donald Kilrain entered Lewis O'Hanlon's office and explained Charolette Thompson's unhappy situation and his desire to hire her as the new receptionist. Lewis's heart went out to the girl, and he agreed that they should offer her the job.

The following Saturday evening, Charolette was again at the Kilrain home for supper. Donald offered thanks for the food, and everyone began to eat. After a few minutes, Donald looked at Charolette and said, "We're sure glad you can spend your weekends with us."

"Why, thank you, Mr. Kilrain. You've all made me feel so welcome here."

"As far as we're concerned, you're family," Ashley said, her heart pounding with excitement.

Charolette's eyes filmed with tears. She laid her fork down, looked around at the family, and said, "It's so kind of all of you to let me be a part of your family on weekends. I can't tell you what it means to me."

"Charolette," Donald said, "how would you like to be part of the family every day, not just on weekends?"

"I...I'm not sure what you mean, sir."

"I mean that I've talked it over with everyone at this table, and we're offering to let you come and live with us on a permanent basis if you so desire."

"Well, I— "

"Let me explain something before you speak. We know that you tried to find a job in Portland because your father and stepmother want you out from underfoot, so to speak. But you weren't able to find a job, so you're living at home and working in your father's store."

"Yes, sir," she said.

"We have a receptionist's job opening at the factory in a few days. I've talked it over with my partner, and he's in full agreement that we offer the job to you. We have no doubt in our minds that you can handle it with a little training. If you'd like to come and live with us and take the job, all you have to do is say so. The next move will be for Mavor and me to talk to your father about it. From what I know about the situation, I believe he'll let us have you. So…tell us what you think."

Charolette used a napkin to dab at her eyes, then said with a quavering voice, "I…I'm so overwhelmed, I can hardly speak. Yes! I would love to come and live here. And yes! I would love to have the receptionist's job. Papa will gladly let you take me off his hands, I can assure you."

Ashley broke into joyful tears, dropped her fork, and wrapped her arms around her best friend. "Oh, Charolette, I'm so happy! I've got a sister again!"

The family rejoiced together for several minutes, then made plans for Donald, Mavor, and Charolette to drive to Lewiston after church Sunday night to talk to Alfred Thompson. If all went as expected, they would load her belongings in the Kilrain carriage and move them into their home.

Alfred Thompson sat in his living room with Ethel beside him and said without emotion, "Sure, you can take her, Mr. Kilrain. She and my wife here don't get along too good. Besides, since Charolette got into that church stuff over there at Brunswick, she gives me the willies with all that holy talk." He paused, pointed a stiff finger at Donald, and said, "And don't you start in on this Jesus stuff. I don't want to hear it, and neither does Ethel."

Donald and Mavor were sitting together on a small couch. Charolette was on a hardback chair next to them.

Charolette rose to her feet and spoke softly. "I'll get my clothes and things, Papa, and we'll be on our way."

"Fine," said Thompson, also standing.

Moments later, Charolette's belongings were in the Kilrain carriage. Alfred and Ethel stood at the door in the soft rays of the porch lantern and looked on. Charolette stood beside the carriage and looked back at them. The Kilrains stood beside her as she said in a quiet voice, "Good-bye, Papa."

Thompson had his arm around his wife. He nodded stiffly, but said nothing.

"Don't bother to drift back this way, girl," Ethel said. "We won't be here. I've been tryin' to get your pa to sell the store and move to Chicago. With you gone, it'll be easier to get him to do it."

Mavor bit her tongue. She wanted to tell Alfred and his wife what she thought of them, but didn't. She put her arm around Charolette's shoulders and said, "Come on, honey. Let's take you home."

When the carriage pulled away into the night, Charolette was sitting between her new parents, weeping. She did not look back. Mavor wrapped her arms around the girl, held her close, and said, "I'm sorry, sweetheart. I don't know how a father could treat his daughter like that, but we'll make it up to you."

Charolette laid her head on Mavor's shoulder. "May I call you Mama, Mrs. Kilrain?" she asked, sniffling.

"You sure may."

"And you can call me Papa," Donald said.

It was almost ten-thirty when the Kilrain carriage swung into the driveway of the stately home. The Kilrains were surprised to see the O'Hanlon carriage parked in front of the house.

"What do you suppose this means?" Mavor asked.

"I don't know," Donald said, "but we're soon going to find out."

Donald halted the carriage next to the O'Hanlon vehicle, and with Charolette between them, the Kilrains hurried onto the porch. The door came open before they reached it, and Ashley stepped out into the soft orange glow of the porch lantern. They could see the O'Hanlon's standing just inside the door, somber looks on their faces.

Ashley looked at Charolette, then at her parents, and asked, "How did it go?"

"She's ours, honey," Mavor said. "We have her clothes and things in the carriage. But...what's wrong?"

"Come on inside," Ashley said, putting an arm around Charolette. "Lewis and Maureen have some bad news."

"What do you mean, bad news?" Donald said.

"Lewis will tell you, Daddy."

They moved inside the house and saw that Uncle Buster and Mike O'Hanlon were also there.

Mavor ran her gaze over their somber faces and asked, "Well...what is it?"

Lewis suggested that they sit down. When all but himself were seated, he explained that they had just received a letter from the post office. It was marked *emergency*, and had arrived on the ship from Ireland that morning. The postmaster had delivered it himself about an hour ago.

Donald's father, Marcus Kilrain, and Lewis's father, Jacob O'Hanlon, had gone hunting together nearly a week ago. Somehow Jacob had stumbled, and his gun went off. The bullet hit Marcus in the head and killed him. Alice Kilrain had sent the letter to ask for help. Jacob O'Hanlon was in a bad mental state and wanted Donald to move his family back to Dublin to take his father's place. Jacob would not be able to handle the factory alone. Alice was also pleading with Donald to return and take over the factory. She desperately needed him and his family with her.

A cold dread settled over Ashley. How could she bear to climb aboard a ship and leave for Ireland, knowing she would not be coming back? It was hard enough knowing she had lost her grandfather, but if the family returned to Ireland, she would lose Shane, too.

Mavor took her husband by the hand and said in a tight voice, "Darling, I don't think we have a choice. Your mother needs us…and the factory needs you. Jacob is going to need your help."

Donald looked at Lewis. "Maybe it should be you who returns to Ireland. You could be a great help to your father."

"I'm sure I could, but it's better that there not be two O'Hanlons running the business. Best to keep it one O'Hanlon and one Kilrain. Besides, it's your mother who's been widowed. She needs you and your family, Donald."

"Lewis, I'll do all I can to help you here," Uncle Buster said. "I've been around long enough that I can handle some of the management details and problems that come up."

Lewis smiled. "I'm sure you'll be a great help, Buster. I'll be glad to have you in that position."

"I'd like to help you in the management end, Pa," Mike said, "but I'm still too young and inexperienced."

Lewis laid a hand on his shoulder. "You'll be a real asset someday, son. But you're right. You need to get your college education and a few more years on you first."

Lewis's attention went to Charolette, who was holding onto Ashley, her features pale and her eyes shadowed with fear. "Charolette…"

The girl's gaze found his eyes. "Yes, sir?"

"Did your father give his consent to let you come live with the Kilrains?"

"Yes, sir, he did. All my things are outside in the carriage."

Lewis cleared his throat. "I want to tell you, dear, that the job is still yours. Maureen and I discussed the fact that if your father did give permission for you to live with the Kilrains—and they decided to move back to Ireland—you would either have to go back to your father, or you'd need another home."

"Yes, sir."

Lewis looked at Maureen. She walked across the room, laid a hand on Charolette's shoulder, and said, "Honey, we want you to know that you're welcome to come live with us. We have a large house. You'll have your own room, even as you do here."

Ashley turned to her and said, "Charolette, I'm sure my parents would take you with us to Ireland."

"Of course," Mavor said.

"We will if you want to go with us," Donald said.

Charolette tried to smile. "Thank you. I appreciate that. But with my father here in America, I—well, I just want to be where he can find me if he ever needs me. I so desperately want him to be saved, and if the Lord brought something into his life that would break down his stubborn will, I would want to be here for him."

"We understand," Mavor said. "And more than anything, we'd all love to see him come to the Lord."

Ashley hugged her best friend and said, "Oh, Charolette, I hate to go away and leave you!"

Mavor wrapped her arms around both girls. "You can write to each other. And who knows? Maybe Charolette can come to Ireland some time and see you."

Ashley nodded, but her throat ached and she couldn't speak.

Mavor squeezed Charolette and said, "You can stay here until we leave for Ireland, or I'm sure the O'Hanlons will let you move in with them right away."

"Yes," Maureen said. "Whatever you prefer, Charolette."

Charolette turned to Maureen, glanced at Lewis, then said, "Thank you both so much for opening your home to me. I appreciate it more than I could ever tell you...but I'd like to stay with Ashley as long as I can."

"We understand," Maureen said.

Charolette thanked Donald and Lewis for giving her the job, then the men went outside to carry in her belongings.

Ashley held onto Charolette's hand, but her mind went to Shane. A sick dread settled in her stomach. Her mother had invited Shane for dinner tomorrow night. Ashley would have to tell him that she and her family were moving back to Ireland. Not only did she dread telling Shane, but she wondered how she could face life without her dream of one day becoming Mrs. Shane Donovan. With an ocean between them, their lives could never be molded together. Ashley wished she was old enough to stay in America…but wishing couldn't add one day to her age, much less two or three years.

The next day, Shane left work at the lumber mill early enough to bathe, change clothes, and make it to downtown Brunswick before the stores closed.

Jeweler and clockmaker Hans Dinkler looked up from his worktable when the bell over the door signaled that a customer had entered the store.

"Ah, Shane Donovan!" said Dinkler looking over the thick spectacles on the end of his nose. "Goot afternoon. Vat can I do for you?"

"Hello, Mr. Dinkler. I…ah…I want to buy a necklace for someone very special."

The wrinkled old man smiled, raised his bushy eyebrows, and asked, "Vould her initials be A. K.?"

Shane grinned sheepishly and nodded. "Yes, sir."

"You going to marry that girl someday, eh?"

"Well, Mr. Dinkler, we…ah…haven't discussed that possibility. Her parents won't let us even be steadies yet, which I understand. But once we are, I'll bring the subject up with Ashley."

"Ah, that's a good boy," said Dinkler, tilting his head down to look at Shane over his spectacles. "I think these young peoples get married too soon these days. It is vise to vait until they are older."

"Yes, sir."

"Is it Ashley's birthday, Shane?"

"No, sir. I just want to show her how I feel about her, so I thought I'd give her a necklace."

"That is very thoughtful of you, my boy." Dinkler moved to a glass case at the end of the counter. "Look at vat I have here."

The case was laden with jewelry of all sorts—pocket watches, rings, necklaces, brooches, cameos, earrings, bracelets, and ladies' timepieces.

"Many to choose from, Shane. Vat price is your limit?"

"None, sir. I've saved for this. I want Ashley to have something real nice."

"Mmm." Dinkler nodded and reached under the glass for a necklace on a delicate gold chain. A heart-shaped locket adorned the chain. Engraved on the locket was a male hand and a female hand in a tender grasp of love.

Shane's eyes lit up. "Yes!" he exclaimed. "That's it exactly!"

"Now, son, this is rather high-priced. If you vant, I could let you pay me half now and half at a later time."

"How much is it, sir?"

"Vell, it is fifty dollars, my boy. Is too much?"

"Oh, no, sir. I'll take it."

Moments later, Shane left the store, carrying the necklace in a black velvet box with a white satin lining. His heart raced with excitement. This would convey to Ashley what he felt for her until the day he could put an engagement ring on her finger.

Shane would not consider proposing marriage until he and Ashley were older and he was making a good living. He would graduate from high school next spring at eighteen, then enroll at Bowdoin College. His dream was to be a professor in a Christian college and teach such subjects as history, English, and Bible. He would like to teach right there at Bowdoin someday, and go home every night to his beautiful wife.

At the Kilrain home, Ashley and Charolette were busy in the kitchen helping Mavor get supper ready. The dining room table was set, and savory aromas from the kitchen filled the house. Donald was in the parlor with his sons discussing their upcoming move to Ireland.

"It's Shane, Papa," William said as he looked out the front window.

Donald stood and said, "Now remember…don't say anything to Shane about our moving back to Ireland. Your sister wants to be the one to tell him."

Donald waited until Shane mounted the front porch, then opened the door before he could knock. "Good evening, Shane. Step inside and get a whiff of what's coming from the kitchen."

Shane drew a deep breath and said, "Mmm-mm! Smells good enough to eat!"

"That's what the boys and I have been thinking. Right, boys?"

William and Harvey both nodded.

Donald gestured toward the kitchen. "Well, gentlemen. I think the ladies are about ready for us. Let's not disappoint them!"

They entered the kitchen, and the women welcomed Shane. He was surprised to see Charolette, though he greeted her warmly. Ashley quickly explained that Charolette had come to live with them, and Shane said he was pleased to hear it.

During the meal, Shane could tell something was awry, though every member of the Kilrain family did their best to hide it. When he noticed that Ashley was absently picking at her food, he turned to her and asked, "Are you all right?"

"Of course," she said, forcing a smile. "Why do you ask?"

"You're not eating, and you seem preoccupied."

"Oh," she said, stabbing a bite of beefsteak with her fork. "I've just got a lot of things on my mind." She placed the meat in her mouth, forced another smile, and chewed.

"Is one of those things on your mind unpleasant?" he asked.

Ashley looked at her mother.

"Shane," Mavor said, "we've had a bit of bad news from Ireland."

"Oh?"

"Yes," Donald said. "My father was killed in a hunting accident."

"Oh, I'm very sorry, sir."

"We would have told you upon your arrival, but Ashley was going to tell you after the meal. She plans to have a talk with you."

Shane glanced at Ashley. "I'm very sorry about your grandfather. Please forgive me for—"

"There's nothing to forgive. How could you have known?"

"Well, I knew something was wrong, but I didn't have to stick my big nose in and start asking questions."

"It's all right," Ashley said. "You were just showing concern."

"How did it happen, sir?" Shane asked, looking again at Donald.

"Hunting accident. He was shot accidentally by Jacob O'Hanlon, Lewis's father."

"Oh, how terrible. This must be awfully hard on the O'Hanlon's too."

"You can imagine how they must feel, especially Jacob and his wife. They've been friends of my parents for as long as I can remember."

"Will you be going back to Ireland for a while to be with your mother?"

"Ashley," Mavor said, "maybe you and Shane should go on out to the front porch for your talk. Charolette and I will do up the dishes."

"I can wait if Ashley wants to help, ma'am," Shane said.

"No, that's all right. Charolette and I discussed it this afternoon. You two go on now."

Ashley took Shane's hand and said, "Come on. Let's go out on the porch."

Charolette prayed silently that the Lord would help Ashley as she broke the news and that He would ease the pain in Shane's heart when he heard it.

Donald had lighted the two porch lanterns just after supper, and they gave off a soft yellow glow across the front of the large house.

When Shane and Ashley stepped outside, she led him to the porch swing. The summer evening was warm. The aroma of honey-suckle was in the air, and the crickets were giving their nightly concert.

Shane felt the small bulge in his coat pocket as they sat down on the swing together. He wondered whether to give Ashley the necklace before she brought up whatever it was she wanted to talk to him about or wait until after. On impulse, he decided to give the necklace to her first. It would make the rest of the evening sweeter, no matter what subject was in the offing.

Ashley's mind was racing. How would she begin? She was hoping that Shane would ask what she wanted to talk about. Instead, she saw him reach into his coat pocket and pull out a small black box. Her gaze went from the box to his sky-blue eyes.

"Before we have our talk, there's something I want to give you," Shane said.

Ashley looked at the box again. "O Shane, you shouldn't be buying me gifts."

"This is more than a gift," he said, casting a glance toward the door to make sure they were alone. "This is my way of telling you…that I love you, Ashley."

Ashley's heart skipped a beat as he placed the velvet box in her hands. Her eyes found his as she said in a half-whisper, "I love you too, Shane."

She looked back at the box and slowly felt along its edges.

"Well, go ahead," he said. "Open it."

She drew back the lid, and the lantern light shone on the exquisite locket and delicate chain. Tears filled Ashley's eyes and spilled down her cheeks.

"O Shane, it's beautiful! I…I don't know what to say!"

"You see the clasp of those two hands? Just say that we'll never let go of each other. That we'll always be together. Ashley and Shane…forever."

SIX

Ashley Kilrain's throat tightened. The pulse throbbed in her temples. Tears flowed like miniature rivers down her face as she tried to find her voice.

She took the necklace from the box and held it close to her heart, her head down. For a long moment she wept quietly. The only sound was when she drew a shaky breath.

Shane put an open hand under her chin, tilted her head up, and asked, "You like it, don't you?"

She looked up at him through a wall of tears and nodded. Suddenly it all gave way and she blurted, "Shane, I love it, but we can't ever have each other! My family is moving back to Ireland, and I have to go with them!"

Shane felt as though he had been punched in the stomach. He stared at Ashley, paralyzed in a swell of disbelief and horror. "But you can't leave me! I'll…I'll talk to your parents. We'll work out a place for you to live here. Ashley, I can't let you go! I—"

"There's no choice, as Ashley said, Shane," Donald Kilrain said from the door.

The couple looked up to see Donald and Mavor move together onto the porch.

"I'm sorry to interrupt," Donald said, "but there's no reason to let your conversation follow the path it's taking."

Shane rose to his feet. "Mr. Kilrain, I love your daughter. I can't just let her sail out of my life!"

Donald and Mavor moved closer as their daughter wiped away tears and left the swing.

"Son, Ashley is still shy of sixteen. We cannot, and we will not, return to Ireland without her. You're only seventeen yourself. You both have plenty of time to fall in and out of love a dozen times before you find your life's mate."

"Neither of you are old enough to be in the kind of love that you build a marriage on," Mavor said. "There's a lot of maturing needed before that day comes."

"Mr. and Mrs. Kilrain," Shane said, "I love and respect you both. I would never do anything to cause a problem in your home. It's just that…this has hit me like a runaway coach. I do love your daughter very much—at least as much as a seventeen-year-old can. And the thought of her sailing across the Atlantic thousands of miles is more than I can bear. I—we will never see each other again. I hope you can understand how we feel."

Donald placed an arm around Shane's shoulder as Mavor folded a trembling Ashley in her arms.

"Shane," Donald said, "you're a fine young man, and a fine Christian. Mavor and I have allowed this relationship between you and Ashley to go on because we both love and admire you. You're certainly the kind of young man we want our daughter to marry. But I'll say again, you're both too young to be marriage-serious about each other. The Lord has seen fit to allow my father to be killed. He knew we'd have to return to Ireland when that bullet took my father's life. He has a plan for your life, Shane, and for Ashley's. As painful as it is right now, the two of you must allow Him to work it out. Does that make sense?"

"Yes, sir. But no matter what happens, sir, I'll always love her."

"I understand that's how you feel right now, son. And I wouldn't expect you to feel any other way. But God will make everything just right for both you and Ashley. And if He wants you two together, He can span the thousands of miles of ocean and bring you together again. He's able to perform His will, miles of ocean or not."

"Yes, sir," Shane said, his voice quavering.

"Daddy?" came a weak voice.

"Yes, honey?"

Ashley opened her hand and held the chain and locket so both parents could see it. "May I keep this? Shane just gave it to me."

"I gave it to her before I knew about the move," Shane said. "I wanted her to know how I feel about her. I wanted her to know that I never wanted us to let go of each other."

Tears welled up in Mavor's eyes, and her lower lip trembled.

"May I keep it, Daddy? Please?" Ashley said.

"Honey, I think not," Donald said. "Shane needs to save it for the young woman God has for him."

"Sir," Shane said, "even if the Lord has someone else for me…I couldn't give it to her, now that I've given it to Ashley."

"He's right, dear," Mavor said. "I think Ashley should be allowed to keep the locket. It will always be a token of her friendship with Shane."

Donald was silent for a moment, rubbing his chin in thought. "Well, okay."

"Thank you, Daddy," Ashley said, letting go of her mother to hug her father's neck.

"I think I'd better be going," Shane said.

Mavor hugged him. "Just stay close to the Lord, Shane. He'll work His perfect will in your life."

"Yes, ma'am, I'll stay close to Him. Right now, I don't understand why this has happened, but I'll stay close to Him."

Ashley was wiping tears again. Shane looked at her, then at her father.

"Mr. Kilrain, I've never held Ashley close before…but in your presence, sir, I'd like to embrace her."

"You have my permission," Donald said.

Shane looked deep into Ashley's eyes for a brief moment, then folded her in his arms. "I love you," he said. "I always will."

"I will always love you too, Shane."

Biting his lower lip, Shane released Ashley. He told her he would come by to see her the next evening, then he bid her parents good-night and left quietly.

Donald Kilrain put an arm around his daughter, and they followed Mavor inside where William, Harvey, and Charolette stood together, their faces reflecting their concern for Ashley.

Donald gave Ashley a hug and said, "Everything will be all right, honey. You'll see."

Mavor spent a few minutes consoling her, then Ashley said she wanted to go to her room. Charolette asked if she could go with her, and Ashley consented. When they moved into Ashley's bedroom and the door was closed, Charolette took her into her arms and held her while Ashley wept.

"I couldn't help but overhear about the locket," Charolette said. "May I see it?"

Ashley opened her fist, took hold of the chain with her other hand, and let the heart-shaped locket dangle in front of Charolette's eyes.

Charolette held the locket between her fingers and said, "Oh, it's beautiful. How thoughtful of Shane!"

"Before I told him we were moving back to Ireland, he said the clasped hands meant we would never let go of each other. And now—"

Ashley burst into heavy, heart-rending sobs. Charolette held her tight and spoke in low tones, trying to comfort her. Even so, Charolette envied Ashley. She had the love of the young man Charolette could not get out of her heart.

Shane Donovan and Ashley Kilrain spent as much time together as possible during the next two weeks, their hearts aching. The Kilrain house sold quickly, which was a relief to Uncle Buster. He would have had to oversee the sale and handle all the paperwork if it had not sold before his brother and family sailed for Ireland.

On Saturday, August 18, 1855, the church had a going away picnic for the Kilrains. They were to embark from Portland Harbor on Monday.

When the dreaded day arrived, many friends from First Parish Congregational Church gathered on the dock to bid the Kilrains good-bye. Buster Kilrain was there, along with the O'Hanlons, the Donovans, and Charolette Thompson. The Kilrains' daughter, Moira, was expecting her first child any day, but was having some complications and had been in bed for a week. Her husband would not leave her side. Donald, Mavor, and their children stopped in Portland to see them before heading for the harbor.

The huge ship loomed over them, and people filtered past the group to mount the gangplank and go aboard.

Shane and Ashley stood apart from the others, while good-byes were being said. Ashley was wearing the locket Shane had given her.

Mike O'Hanlon walked up and said, "Please forgive my butting in, but I want to tell Ashley good-bye." Mike hurt for Shane, but he felt his own pain, knowing he would probably never see Ashley again. "I…I'll miss you, Ashley."

"I'll miss you, too, Mike," she said, giving him a sisterly embrace. "Thank you for being such a good friend to me."

"You're welcome. I hope you have a real happy life." Mike blinked against the tears that flooded his eyes as he stepped away.

Ashley looked up to see Charolette standing next to Shane. She opened her arms to her, and the girls wept as they held each other tight. When they let go of each other, Charolette turned to Shane with tears streaming down her face.

"Shane, I'm sorry this terrible thing had to happen. I've been praying for you and Ashley, that the Lord's will be done in your lives."

"Ashley and I have talked a lot these past two weeks, Charolette. We've committed ourselves to His will. As much as it hurts right now, we must let Him have His way in our lives."

"That's a beautiful way to put it, Shane," Charolette said, smiling through her tears.

It was almost time for the Kilrains to board the ship. Mike and Charolette moved away to give the young couple their last few moments together.

Ashley held the locket between her fingers and said with tremulous voice, "Shane, even if the Lord doesn't have us for each other, you will always be a very special person in my life. I will love you in a special way, and I'll keep this locket forever."

"And you will always be a very special person in my life, Ashley. I will always love you in a special way, no matter what."

Ashley's parents walked up and Donald said, "Honey, we have to board now."

Ashley nodded, excused herself to Shane, and ran to Uncle Buster, embracing him. She loved her uncle very much, and told him so. She then hurried to each friend who stood on the dock, gave them a quick hug and a few parting words.

Donald and Mavor told Shane how much they thought of him, and expressed their gratitude for the mature way he was accepting their leaving.

When Ashley returned, she drew close to Shane and said, "Well, I guess it's time to say good-bye."

Shane looked at Donald and Mavor and said, "Mr. and Mrs. Kilrain, may I have your permission to kiss your daughter good-bye?"

"Certainly, Shane," Donald said.

The lips of the young pair touched briefly and discreetly, then Shane stood aside and watched Ashley walk up the gangplank with her parents and younger brothers. He felt as if his heart would burst.

The Kilrains were the last to step aboard, and the ship's shrill whistle blew as one of the crew closed the railing gate and the massive vessel began pulling away. The passengers stood along the railing, waving to those they were leaving behind. People on the dock wept, shouted, and waved back.

Mike and Charolette stood close to Shane, who thumbed tears as he watched the ship move out of the harbor toward the Atlantic Ocean. Almost unaware of their presence, he watched until the ship became a dot on the horizon, then vanished from sight. Mike drew up on one side of him and Charolette on the other, each putting an arm around him.

Day after day, Ashley stood on the deck of the ship with the ocean breeze brushing her face and fluttering her long auburn hair. She held the locket between her fingers and prayed for Shane, asking the Lord to watch over him. Her heart seemed to break as she thought of the good times they had enjoyed together and remembered the dream she had of one day becoming Mrs. Shane Donovan.

The ship arrived in Ireland on September 6, having stopped in a few seaports along the way.

Donald Kilrain took command at the Dublin factory, and the family settled in, caring for Grandmother Kilrain. When they had been in Dublin a week, Ashley wrote to Shane. She told him she was still wearing the locket and would always have a special love for him in her heart.

Shane thought of Ashley continuously, praying for her…and longing for her presence.

Charolette had settled in with the O'Hanlons and loved living in their home. She also loved her job at the factory. And she looked forward to seeing Shane at church on Sundays and Wednesday nights. Each time Shane and Charolette talked, Shane found that his admiration for her was growing. Though he had no idea how she felt about him, he often called her his "sweet little friend."

In mid-September, Bowdoin College began its fall semester with a few new instructors. Among them was Joshua Lawrence Chamberlain, who had attained his master's degree and had joined the faculty to teach logic, theology, rhetoric, and Greek.

Fannie Adams had finished her schooling in New York and was back on the organ at First Parish Congregational Church. Sunday morning, September 16, was the first time Chamberlain had been in the church in several months. His future father-in-law had asked him to sing just prior to the sermon.

Shane and Mike were sitting together, with Charolette and some other girls from the youth group on the same pew. Shane was on the aisle, Mike was next to him, and Charolette was next to Mike, wishing she was next to Shane.

When Joshua Chamberlain stepped to the pulpit, ready to sing John Newton's "Amazing Grace," Shane whispered to his friend, "When I go to Bowdoin next year, I'm going to take every class he teaches!"

At the organ, Fannie began to play the introduction to "Amazing Grace." Joshua lifted his voice above the sound of the organ and said, "Friends..."

When Fannie realized he wanted to say something before he sang, she lowered the volume, but kept pumping and playing.

"Friends, many of you have wondered if Fanny and I are ever going to get married. Well, let me be the first to tell you that we have set a date for the wedding. We'll be married right here on Friday, December 7, this year."

There was an immediate chorus of amens and some applause from the congregation. Fanny then raised the volume, skillfully went into the introduction, and played while her fiancé sang. There were more amens as the song was finished and Chamberlain stepped away from the pulpit.

After the service, Joshua Chamberlain spoke with Shane and Mike. Charolette looked on as the two young men congratulated him on his coming marriage and talked of days gone by. While they chatted, Chamberlain's attention drifted to the pretty brunette who stood near. He finished something he was saying to the boys, then smiled at the girl, and said, "Hello, Charolette."

Charolette was surprised that Chamberlain remembered her name, and her face showed it. "Hello, Mr. Chamberlain. How nice of you to remember me. After all, it's been a year-and-a-half!"

"Has it really been that long? Well, anyway, I recall your name because you opened your heart to Jesus when I was preaching. That makes you special."

"Thank you, sir. I'll never forget that sermon."

Fannie came off the platform, greeted the young people, and whisked her fiancé away for Sunday dinner at her parents' home. When they were out of sight, Charolette turned to the boys and said, "My what a memory! He must have a brilliant mind."

"That he does," Shane said. "He received many honors at Bowdoin and at Bangor Seminary, and he's also mastered seven foreign languages."

"Seven! Really?"

"Really. He knows Latin, German, Old Testament Hebrew, New Testament Greek...ah, let's see...Latin, German, Hebrew, Greek...and Italian, Arabic, and Syrian. That's seven, isn't it?"

"I think so," Mike said. "Pretty impressive, huh?"

"I should say," Charolette said.

"Like I told Mike," Shane said, "I'm going to take every class Mr. Chamberlain teaches when I go to Bowdoin. He's a great teacher and a great Christian."

"So you're going to Bowdoin?" Charolette said. "I didn't know that. What do you plan to study?"

"I'm going to major in education. Two of Mr. Chamberlain's courses will fit into my major, and I can take Greek and theology as electives. I've already checked. I want to teach in a Christian college someday. In fact, I'd like to teach at Bowdoin if the Lord will let me."

"I think that's a wonderful ambition, Shane. I hope it works out for you." Charolette then turned to Mike and asked, "How about you? What are your plans?"

"Oh, I'm going to Bowdoin, too. I'm going to major in economics to prepare for the partnership my dad and Mr. Kilrain are going to give me when I get out of college."

"So one day you'll be my boss!"

"That's right. And then, girl, you'd better watch your step!"

Shane received Ashley's letter the first week of November. He was thrilled to learn she was still wearing the locket. That night he answered her letter, telling her he still carried her in his heart and missed her very much. At church the next Sunday, Shane told Mike and Charolette about the letter. Charolette also had received a letter from Ashley. She said Ashley was missing Shane a lot and spoke of missing her other friends, too.

During the next four months, Shane and Ashley exchanged three more letters. Shane detected that Ashley was settling into life in her home country, and though in the letters she spoke of her special love for him, she said no more about the locket. He began to read between the lines. Ashley had resigned herself to the fact that they would never see each other again, a fact Shane was slowly resigning himself to as well.

On Shane's eighteenth birthday, the youth group gathered at the Donovan home for a party. Shane noticed that Mike O'Hanlon had Betty Helms, the newest girl to join the youth group, with him.

After the meal, and during cake time, Shane saw Betty talking with some girls. He slipped up beside Mike and said, "You've sure got a knack for latching on to the pretty ones."

Mike grinned and said, "Don't get any ideas, pal! Besides, you're still tied to Ashley."

"Only in memory, my friend. I'll never forget her, but we both know we'll never be together again. We've resigned ourselves to it."

Mike was serious for a moment. "Well, I'm glad you're able to face the situation honestly, though I'm sure it must be hard to accept." Then a grin curved his lips. "But if you're thinking of shining up to Betty, forget it. She doesn't go for you old duffers!" Even as the words were coming from his mouth, Mike found his heart longing for Ashley.

Shane turned to see Charolette standing behind him.

"What are you smiling about?" he asked with a chuckle.

"You two," Charolette said.

"What do you mean?" Mike asked.

"You're forty-eight days apart in age, and you talk about one being old and the other being young."

"Well, we've gone on like this for ages, Charolette," Shane said.

"Doesn't change a thing," Mike said. "Betty still likes younger men!"

"Well, I like older men," Charolette said before Shane could give his usual retort.

The look in Charolette's eyes startled Shane. He found himself really noticing her for the first time. He had never seen what a beautiful person she was…inside and out.

"Thank you, Charolette," he managed to say. "I'm glad you prefer older men." He paused, then smiled. "I like your hair. It's a new style for you, isn't it?"

"Why…yes."

"I mean, I always like the way you fix your hair, but this…well, it really looks terrific on you!"

SEVEN

As the weeks passed into months, Shane Donovan found a growing attraction for Charolette Thompson. But he had promised his love to Ashley, and he felt guilty over his feelings for Charolette.

Charolette was maturing into a beautiful young woman and into a strong Christian. Though she was warm toward Shane, she did not reveal the deep love she had for him. Her daily prayer was for God to have His perfect will in both of their lives.

Shane continued to work with his father in the lumber mill and steadily put on stature and muscle. He graduated from high school in the spring, and when fall came, he enrolled at Bowdoin College. Though taking a full load, he earned money for his schooling by working after classes and on Saturdays in the lumber mill.

He often thought of Ashley and heard now and then through Mike O'Hanlon of things taking place in the Kilrain family in Dublin. Grandpa O'Hanlon still had not gotten over the hunting accident, and Donald Kilrain was having to carry the load in running the factory.

On one occasion, Mike told Shane that Mavor Kilrain had mentioned in a letter to his mother that Ashley was now dating several young men. Shane felt a stab in his heart at that news, but he knew it was only right that Ashley date other young men.

Shane was superbly happy in college, especially getting to sit in Joshua Chamberlain's rhetoric, logic, theology, and Greek classes. The young instructor had been elected to professorship by the college board of directors just before the fall semester. He replaced Calvin Stowe, who had gone to teach in another college.

The friendship between professor and student blossomed. Chamberlain found young Donovan to be his best student and spent extra time with him. Chamberlain saw exceptional character in Garth and Pearl Donovan's oldest son, recalling Shane's heroic deed in risking his life to save the Brainerd baby when he was barely fifteen years old.

Charolette was thrilled that without fail, Shane found her and sat by her in the young adult Sunday school class and in all the church services.

On Sunday, October 12, 1856, Dr. George Adams announced proudly to the congregation that he and his wife were now grandparents. Fannie had given birth the night before to a beautiful baby girl, Grace Dupee Chamberlain. Joshua, who was in the choir, received applause, and the crowd had a good laugh when he stood and took a bow.

After the service, Charolette was at Shane's side as he approached Chamberlain and said, "Congratulations, Professor, on your new daughter."

"Thank you, Shane."

"Did you want a girl, Professor?" Charolette asked. "Or were you hoping for a boy?"

"Neither Fannie nor I cared which it was, just so the baby would be normal and healthy. And she is, praise the Lord."

"I can't wait to see her, sir," Shane said. "Does she look like Mrs. Chamberlain?"

"I'll say she does! Has Fannie's coloring through and through. I mean, skin, hair, and eyes."

"She has to be beautiful then," Charolette said. "Mrs. Chamberlain is such a lovely lady."

"Why, thank you. My sentiments exactly." Chamberlain paused, then said, "And you're becoming a stunning young lady yourself, Charolette. Has Shane taken notice?"

While Charolette blushed, Shane said, "Yes, I have, sir. I sure have."

Professor Joshua Lawrence Chamberlain's class schedule had him teaching theology the last hour on Monday, Wednesday, and Friday. On the Monday after the announcement in church of little Grace's birth, the professor mentioned in theology class that Christians can know the perfect will of God for their lives if they stay close to God and wait patiently for Him to reveal it to them.

When class was dismissed, Shane approached the desk as the professor was placing papers into a valise. Chamberlain looked up, smiled, and said, "Something I can do for you, Shane?"

"I think so, sir."

Chamberlain laid the papers and valise down, giving young Donovan his full attention.

"Well, sir, you mentioned in class that a Christian can know the perfect will of God for his life if he stays close to Him and waits patiently for Him to reveal it."

"That's right."

"Could you expand on that for me?"

"All right." Chamberlain gestured toward a straight-backed wooden chair that sat next to a far wall. "Grab that chair and sit down."

Chamberlain eased onto his own chair and picked up his Bible. When Shane sat down across the desk from him, Chamberlain said, "Get your Bible out and turn to Romans 12."

Shane flipped pages quickly and soon had the Bible open to the designated passage.

"All right," the professor said, "read me verses one and two."

"'I beseech you therefore, brethren, by the mercies of God, that ye present your bodies a living sacrifice, holy, acceptable unto God, which is your reasonable service. And be not conformed to this world: but be ye transformed by the renewing of your mind, that ye may prove what is that good, and acceptable, and perfect, will of God.'"

Shane looked up at his professor, and Chamberlain said, "It does say we can prove what the perfect will of God is for our lives, doesn't it?"

"Yes, sir."

"Now, there are some prerequisites to finding God's will. To sum up what both of those verses say, we're to be wholly dedicated to the Lord. We're to be living sacrifices, serving the Lord with everything that's in us. And if we are, we won't be conformed to this ungodly world system that is anti-God, anti-Christ, and anti-Bible. And you know that's the attitude of this world because Satan is the god of this world, according to Second Corinthians chapter four."

"Yes, sir."

"All right, then. In order to know the perfect will of God, we must be devoted to Him, living all the way for Jesus, and walking according to the Word of God."

"I understand that, sir."

"All right. Now, there are some things about God's will for us that are stated flat and plain in Scripture. Let's turn to First Thessalonians 4."

When both had found the passage, Chamberlain said, "Look at verse three. 'For this is the will of God, even your sanctification, that ye should abstain from fornication.' You already know that sanctification is being set apart by God for service. And down in verse seven, Paul wrote, 'For God hath not called us unto uncleanness, but unto holiness.' So God tells us that His will is that we live clean and serve Him."

"Yes, sir."

"There's another plain statement here in First Thessalonians. Look at chapter five, verse eighteen."

Shane flipped the page and found the verse. "'In every thing give thanks: for this is the will of God in Christ Jesus concerning you.'"

"That verse plainly tells us that God's will for every Christian is that we give thanks to Him for whatever comes along in our lives…the good and the bad, the pleasant and the unpleasant."

Shane grinned. "That's not always easy to do, is it?"

"No, it's not. But it is God's will that we do. Now, as for particular circumstances in our lives, God will reveal His will. He said He would. However, He seldom gets in a hurry to reveal it to us. He wants us to learn some patience along the way, and He wants us to keep coming back to Him…so He usually delays revealing His will. Go to the twenty-seventh Psalm."

Shane flipped pages again. "Got it."

"All right. Read me verse fourteen."

"'Wait on the LORD: be of good courage, and he shall strengthen thine heart: wait, I say, on the LORD.'"

"Let the word *wait* sink in."

"It already has."

Chamberlain chuckled. "Now, turn over to Psalm 37 and read me the first part of verse seven."

"'Rest in the LORD, and wait patiently for him.' So I not only need to wait, but I need to wait patiently."

"You're catching on. Now let's look at one more verse—Psalm 62, verse five."

"'My soul, wait thou only upon God; for my expectation is from him.'"

"So when we wait patiently for the Lord to do anything in our lives, we can expect Him to come through for us. Right?"

"That's what it says, sir."

"Now, there's another prerequisite—prayer. The Lord wants us to come to Him in prayer and ask for His guidance. Turn to John 14."

When Shane had located the chapter, Chamberlain said, "Read

me verses thirteen and fourteen, and note that it is Jesus speaking."

"'And whatsoever ye shall ask in my name, that will I do, that the Father may be glorified in the Son. If ye shall ask anything in my name, I will do it.'"

"Okay, now look across the page at 15:7 and read me that."

"'If ye abide in me, and my words abide in you, ye shall ask what ye will, and it shall be done unto you.'"

"There's plenty more," Chamberlain said, "but that's probably enough for now. Let's sum it up. We are to be living sacrifices, serving God and living holy lives while following His Word and seeking Him in prayer. And when we ask Him to reveal His will to us, and wait patiently for the answer, He will show us."

"Sounds reasonable," Shane said.

"Now…one more thing. *How* does the Lord show us His will? This is the key to the whole thing."

Shane grinned again. "I'm listening."

"Okay. Philippians 4, verses six and seven. Read it to me."

Shane eagerly turned pages, found the passage, and read: "'Be careful for nothing; but in everything by prayer and supplication with thanksgiving let your requests be made known unto God. And the peace of God, which passeth all understanding, shall keep your hearts and minds through Christ Jesus.'"

"Note especially the 'everything by prayer,' the thanksgiving, and the making of your requests known to God. And note too that with this comes the peace of God. When your heart and mind are at peace, there is no disturbance, right?"

"Yes, sir."

"All right. One more passage—Colossians 3:15. Go ahead and read it to me."

"'And let the peace of God rule in your hearts, to the which also ye are called in one body; and be ye thankful.'"

"Notice that Paul says to let the peace of God *rule* in your heart."

"Yes, sir."

"As we seek to know the will of God for our lives, and follow the things we've already seen from Scripture, then as we aim ourselves toward what we believe might be God's will for us, there will be a disturbance in our hearts if we are aiming the wrong way. It takes a close walk with the Lord to be able to recognize this, but the peace of God will rule in our hearts if we let it. Notice Paul said, 'Let the peace of God rule in your hearts.' We have a choice whether to let it rule or to refuse to let it rule. So if we aim only in the direction that gives us peace, we'll know we're following God's will for our lives."

"That's beautiful, sir," Shane said. "So when we know we're walking right before the Lord, and we pray and wait patiently, the Lord will give us peace in our hearts when we aim correctly or disturb our hearts if we aim wrong. If we're aiming wrong but keep heading in various directions until we get peace, we'll know when we've discovered His perfect will in our lives. The peace of God will rule and give the proper direction."

"Sounds to me like you've got the picture, my friend. Do you mind me using myself as an example?"

"No, of course not."

"Well, right now I'm seeking God's will for my life…and that of Fannie and the baby, of course. As you know, First Parish licensed me to preach better than a year ago, and I've preached in several churches in Maine, filling pulpits when the pastors have been away or been too ill to preach. What you don't know is that four different churches have issued me calls to be their pastor. Each one seemed quite inviting, but I just couldn't get peace about accepting any of them."

"Well, I'm glad of that, sir. I love sitting under your teaching."

"Thank you, Shane. Anyway, in spite of those tempting calls to pastor, I have absolute peace in what I'm doing here at Bowdoin. Maybe one day the Lord will put me in a pastorate, but right now I know He wants me right here teaching."

"I hope He leaves you here at least until I graduate, sir." Shane rose from his chair. "Thank you for your help."

Chamberlain stood up behind his desk. "You're very welcome."

Shane turned to leave, and Chamberlain said, "Shane..."

"Yes, sir?"

"Shane, you and I are friends."

"Yes, sir."

Chamberlain rubbed the back of his neck. "This, ah…this session we've had about knowing the will of God…I don't mean to be nosy, but does it have anything to do with your relationships with Ashley Kilrain and Charolette Thompson?"

"Well, sir, to be honest, it's the very reason I was asking about knowing God's will."

"I thought so. Look, Shane, I've been observing you and Charolette together since I moved back to Brunswick. Are you letting Ashley stand between you and Charolette?"

"Well, sir, I…I might be…a little."

"But you think enough of Charolette that you're wondering what God's will is concerning her in your life…and concerning Ashley."

"Yes, sir. You might put it that way."

"May I tell you my own thoughts about it?"

"Yes, please do."

"Shane, Ashley is out of your life now…for good. From what Mike has told me, the Kilrains expect to remain in Ireland permanently."

"That's right. But…there's a problem, sir."

"Do you want to tell me about it?"

"Well, it's just that even though it appears that Ashley will never be coming back to America, I…I made her a promise."

"Yes?"

"I promised that I would always love her, and I don't want to go back on that promise."

Chamberlain grinned a crooked grin and laid a hand on his student's shoulder. "My friend, you can always have a special place in your heart for Ashley. She was your first real girlfriend, right?"

"Yes, sir."

"That makes her special. But Shane, life must go on. Since the Lord took Ashley out of your life, He must have someone else for you. Shane Donovan needs to have his eyes and heart open for the woman God has for his life's mate. Since we've gone this far, and you know I care about you, Shane, I want you to open up and tell me how you really feel about Charolette."

Shane blinked and scrubbed a palm across his brow. "Well, sir, until recently I hadn't really noticed her as anything but a friend. But now I see her as a warm, beautiful, sweet Christian woman. I mean…she's really a wonderful person."

Joshua Chamberlain still had his hand on Shane's shoulder, and now he grinned from ear to ear. "Remember yesterday morning at church when we talked about the baby? Well, while you were saying something to me, I noticed Charolette looking at you."

"You did?"

"Yes. And I saw that certain look in her eyes, Shane. The girl loves you."

Shane blinked again. "Really? You think so?"

"I know love in a woman's eyes when I see it. Now, let me give you some sound advice, and I'll let you go. From this moment on, you should notice more about Charolette's being—how did you put it?—a warm, beautiful, sweet Christian woman. And I believe you added the word wonderful, too."

"Yes, sir. She's all of that, and more."

"Then accept my advice, Mr. Donovan, and take more notice!"

"I will, sir. I promise. I surely will!"

Shane Donovan and Mike O'Hanlon did not get to see each other often after they entered Bowdoin College. Mike's economics major placed him in different classes than his best friend's education major, and their jobs kept them busy and apart most of the time. Mike worked every hour he could at the shoe factory, and Shane's off-hours kept him busy at the lumber mill. What little spare time Shane could squeeze free, he spent with Charolette.

Shane showed more interest in her than he ever had before. Charolette soaked it all in, longing for the day Shane would say he loved her. When it came, she would tell him how long she had been in love with him.

Shane and Mike chanced to meet one evening in mid-November at a college social function. Mike had a girl with him Shane had not yet met. Her name was Marie Welton. She was from Augusta and in her first year at Bowdoin.

Charolette was with Shane. During the evening, Charolette and Marie became friends, and when they went to powder their noses, Mike asked if Shane was falling for Charolette. Shane told him about his counseling session with Professor Chamberlain some three weeks previously. Though he would always have a special love for Ashley, he admitted he had a growing attraction toward Charolette.

Mike casually said that Mavor Kilrain had written his mother again, and the letter had carried no news about Ashley's social life. Shane drew in a deep breath and said that Ashley had probably found her a steady young man by now. This time, it was Mike who felt a sharp pang in his heart.

Shane found Charolette on his mind continuously, whether he was in class, on the job, or doing homework in his bedroom. He was even having dreams about her. He began to use a pet name for her in the privacy of his mind. The only other person who knew about the name was the Lord Himself, for when Shane prayed for Charolette, he called her Charly.

In the last week of November, the Brunswick town council sponsored a concert at the town hall. Many of Bowdoin College's faculty and students attended. Shane and Charolette sat with Joshua and Fannie Chamberlain, and both couples fully enjoyed the evening.

When the concert was over and they were putting on their hats and coats, Joshua said, "I know you two walked to the concert, but Fannie and I will be glad to drive Charolette to the O'Hanlons and you to your home, Shane. It's a bit nippy out there."

Shane smiled and said, "We really appreciate the offer, Professor, but we came dressed warm enough to walk. It gives us a little more time together."

Chamberlain put an arm around his wife, winked at Shane, and said, "You know what, Fannie? I think Shane has finally noticed what a lovely young lady Charolette is."

"I've been noticing that for some time, sir. It's just that I've been noticing it a whole lot more lately!"

Fannie laughed. "Well, keep your eyes open!"

"Don't worry about that, ma'am. Charolette is so pretty, when I'm with her, I don't even blink!"

Charolette blushed, but inside she was reveling in Shane's words. The Chamberlains excused themselves, saying they had some people to see, and the young couple left the town hall and moved down the street arm-in-arm.

As they walked, Charolette looked up at Shane by the soft glow of the street lamps and said, "That was a nice thing for you to say."

"What was?"

"About not even blinking when you're with me."

"Well, it's the truth. Almost, anyway."

They came to a side street that led to the O'Hanlon home. Charolette noticed something in the shadows in front of one of the houses in the middle of the block.

"Shane...?"

"Yes?"

"I saw something up there."

"Where?"

"Right up there." She pointed with her free hand. "It's like someone is skulking, or something."

"Don't worry, you're safe with me. Probably just someone out for a walk, like us."

A street lantern on the corner at the far end of the block gave off enough light to throw a glow part way toward the middle of the block. The lantern at the corner behind them did the same. Charolette clung tightly to Shane as they drew near the dark void in the middle.

Suddenly, four figures appeared from behind a large oak tree and headed toward them.

"Shane," Charolette said with fear in her voice.

"It's all right, honey. Just keep walking."

The word *honey* did not escape Charolette's notice in spite of her fear.

There was enough light that Shane could see they were about to face four young toughs. The air was cold enough that their breath showed in small gray-white clouds.

As they drew abreast, one of the toughs bumped Shane, knocking him against Charolette and almost causing her to fall.

"Watch where you're going!" Shane said. "You almost knocked the lady down!"

The one who had bumped Shane stepped up close, putting his nose only inches from Shane's. He released a string of profanity, then said, "What are you gonna do about it?" The other three made a circle around them.

The tough's language lit Shane's fuse. "You're going to apologize to the lady for filling her ears with your foul language!"

"Is that right? And who's gonna make me?"

"You're looking at him!" Shane said.

The others laughed, and the tough cocked his fist, saying, "Let's see how you like the looks of this, buster!"

EIGHT

Shane Donovan ducked the flashing fist.

The young punk had no idea who he was dealing with. Shane was now six feet tall and weighed a solid, muscular one hundred eighty pounds. Though he never looked for a fight, it was not in him to avoid one if it was forced on him. He was no novice at fisticuffs.

When the hissing fist passed harmlessly over his head, Shane stayed in his crouch and sent a hard right to the tough's jaw. It caught him flush, staggering him. Shane followed with the other fist to the soft flesh under the man's ear, and dropped him to the ground.

The other three leaped for Shane, swearing at him. Charolette felt totally helpless. There was nothing she could do but stand there and pray.

Shane caught the closest tough with a blow to the nose, but the other two struck him on the side of the head twice in succession, and he felt his knees buckle. He managed to stay on his feet, but another fist banged him on the temple, and lights flashed inside his head. He felt himself falling. He could hear Charolette crying out, screaming for the toughs to leave him alone.

Two of them were on him now, pounding him wherever they

could find a spot. Shane was on his back, using his arms and legs to try to fend off his attackers, with little success. Then he caught a glimpse of Joshua Chamberlain's buggy parked in the street. Fannie was climbing out to join Charolette, and the professor was swinging a roundhouse punch at one of the toughs. Fist met jaw, and the tough went down. Another one lunged at Chamberlain and was dropped with a stiff punch. Two of the punks were on the ground, and the other two took off running.

Shane got to his knees, then slowly stood. He wiped a hand across his mouth and found it crimsoned with blood. The professor was standing over the two toughs who remained. Shane saw that one of them was the leader—the one who had started it all. His jaw appeared to be dislocated, and blood ran from both nostrils.

Shane stood over him and said, "Either apologize to the young lady for your language, or you're going to get a lot more of what you've been getting."

The beaten tough looked up in the dim light and said in a mumbling sort of way, "My jaw is broke. I...I can't make it work."

"You can say that much, you can tell her you're sorry."

The tough looked toward Charolette, who stood by the Chamberlain buggy with Fannie. "I'm sorry, miss. I apologize for swearing in your presence."

"You satisfied, Shane?" Chamberlain asked.

"Yes, I'm satisfied."

"Okay, then," Chamberlain said, "you two hightail it out of here!"

As the toughs hurried away, Charolette ran to Shane. "You're bleeding, darling! Here, let me see if this will help."

Charolette pressed her hanky to Shane's bleeding lip, the word *darling* reverberating in his ears.

Shane turned his head, causing Charolette to stop dabbing at his lip for a moment, and said, "Professor, I'm sure glad you showed up. I'd have been a bloody pulp by now if you hadn't."

"Oh, I didn't show up to help you, Shane," Chamberlain said.

"You didn't?"

"No. I didn't want to see those men get hurt bad, so I figured if I pitched in, they'd take off before you really put some damage on them!"

Shane laughed in spite of the pain all over his body.

"So I assume this started over that punk using foul language in front of Charolette," Chamberlain said.

"It actually started when they came along and bumped Shane on purpose," Charolette said. "They were looking for trouble. When Shane reprimanded the one who bumped him because it almost caused me to fall, he swore at Shane and asked him what he was going to do about it. Shane told him he owed me an apology for using that kind of language in my presence…and right about then, the punk swung at him."

Chamberlain smiled and said, "You're to be commended, Shane. It's a gentleman's duty to protect a lady's ears from foul language. I want to commend you for your courage."

"I didn't think about being courageous, Professor. I just did what a gentleman ought to do. The odds made no difference."

"Well, a lot of fellows would've backed off," Chamberlain said. "I'm proud of you. Come on, get in the buggy. Fannie and I will take you both home."

"If you'll just take us to O'Hanlons, sir, that'll be fine. I can walk home from there."

The Chamberlain buggy rolled through the dark streets of Brunswick, and soon pulled up in front of the O'Hanlon house. The porch lantern was giving off a yellow glow. Shane thanked the Chamberlains for the ride and helped Charolette from the buggy. They stood and waved at the professor and his wife, then stepped up on the porch.

"Now that we have better light," Charolette said, "I want to take a good look at that lip."

Shane looked into her eyes. She held his gaze for a second or two, then focused on the cut.

"Looks like the bleeding's completely stopped."

"You're a good nurse."

A smile curved her lips. "And you're a good protector. You've got some pretty bad bruises on your face, but there's no blood. Does the lip hurt?"

"A little. Charolette, I…"

"Yes?"

"Well…whenever I had a cut as a boy, Mom always kissed it, saying a kiss would make it better."

"If I kissed your cut lip, would that make it better?"

"Oh, I'm sure it would."

Charolette's soft lips touched his ever-so-carefully. When their lips parted, Shane held her close. Charolette laid her head on his chest and tried to calm her runaway heart.

"Charolette…"

She drew back and looked into his eyes. "Yes?"

"I can't hold it back any longer."

"Hold what back?"

"The fact that I have fallen head-over-heels, mind-heart-and-soul in love with you."

Charolette's eyes brightened with a sudden rush of tears. She drew in a quick breath and said, "Oh, Shane! Shane, I'm in love with you too!"

Shane folded Charolette in his arms and held her tight. She clung to him for a long moment before saying, "Shane…what about Ashley?"

"She'll always have a special place in my heart, Charolette. She's a dear friend, but I'm in love with you. The Lord meant us for each other. I love you, my sweet Ch—Charolette. And I always will."

Shane had almost revealed the pet name he had secretly given her, but decided to keep it a secret. He let her move back so he could look into her eyes, and said, "I realize marriage has to be a ways off yet, but I just as well get it all out. I want you to marry me when the time is right."

She raised up on her tiptoes, kissed him sweetly, and said, "Yes, darling. When the time is right, I will marry you. Just knowing that you love me and want me to be your mate for life is enough to keep me going. O Shane, I love you so much!"

And their lips met softly again.

Garth and Pearl Donovan were elated when their son announced that he and Charolette were officially courting. They loved the girl and had known for some time that she had eyes for Shane. The O'Hanlons rejoiced with their house guest when she told them of the courtship.

Mike said he was happy for them and that the Lord always did things just right. In private, Shane asked Mike if he had heard anything about Ashley lately, and Mike said he had not. He added, however, that a letter had come to his father, advising him that Grandpa O'Hanlon's mental depression over the hunting accident had improved and he was back at the factory, helping Donald Kilrain carry on the business.

As the days passed, the love Shane and Charolette had for each other grew deeper and stronger. Every time they were together, he found her more loving and more lovable, and thanked God for giving him such a wonderful young woman.

One cold night in the third week of December, they were leaving the college campus in the Donovan buggy after attending a Christmas program. They were bundled up under a heavy blanket, and Charolette was clinging to his arm. The sky was clear and a three-quarter moon cast its silvery spray on the snow-covered ground.

Charolette looked up at Shane and said in a half-whisper, "Oh, darling, I love you so much!"

Shane smiled at her. "And I love you, Charly."

Charolette sat up straight. "What did you call me? Charly?"

Shane cleared his throat nervously. "I guess I might as well confess. I've called you Charly to myself for quite a while."

"How do you spell that?"

"C-H-A-R-L-Y. Why?"

"Because my mother used to call me that, and she spelled it the same way."

"Well, if you rather I didn't think of you as Charly, I won't do it anymore."

"Oh, no! I think it's sweet of you. I want you to think of me that way, and from now on, I want you to call me Charly."

"Really? You don't think it sounds, well, too masculine?"

"Please. It will mean more to me than you'll ever know because you came up with it without knowing that's what Mom called me."

"Okay. If you want, I'll have Pastor Adams say, 'Do you, Charly, take this man to be your lawfully wedded husband?'"

"No, I just want you to call me that."

"All right. Charly it is."

The horses hooves were muffled by the blanket of snow that covered the ground as the buggy approached the O'Hanlon house.

"About your mother, Charly..."

"Yes?"

"How old was she when she died of consumption?"

"Thirty-three."

"Awfully young."

"Yes, but I have many fond memories of her."

"But not many of your father, I take it."

Charolette was quiet for a moment, then said, "Not many."

"But you still love him, don't you?"

"Of course. He's my father."

"Would you like to go to Lewiston and see him?"

"I'd love to. If he's still there. Ethel was trying to get him to sell the store and move to Chicago."

"But you don't know any more than that?"

"No. I haven't had any contact with him since the day he so gladly gave me over to the Kilrains."

"How about I take a little time off work and drive you over there on Saturday?"

"Would you really?"

"Of course. The Bible tells us to honor our father and mother. No matter how poorly he's treated you, he's still your father. Who knows? He might even be glad to see you."

"Maybe. But I can guarantee you Ethel won't be."

"We'll just ignore her," Shane said.

On the following Saturday afternoon, it was snowing lightly when Shane and Charolette emerged from the store her father had owned. The new proprietor explained that he had bought the store from Alfred Thompson the last week of November. He had no idea where they went. They had talked about Chicago, but three or four other places were often spoken of too—Minneapolis, St. Louis, and one or two he couldn't recall.

As the couple climbed into the buggy to head back for Brunswick, Shane saw the pain in Charolette's eyes. "I'm sorry, honey," he said. "I know you wanted to see him."

"Yes, but there's something worse than not getting to see him. I have no idea where they went for sure…and now I have no way of ever reaching him with the gospel. My mother died without being saved. I don't want the same thing to happen to him. I talked to him about Jesus many times, but he always turned a deaf ear."

"I guess all we can do now is pray for him. The Lord knows where he is, and He can send someone to witness to him."

"Thank you, darling, you're right. We'll pray just that way."

Christmas fell on a Thursday in 1856, and the O'Hanlons invited Buster Kilrain and the Donovans to Christmas dinner late in the afternoon. Buster had been with the O'Hanlons that morning when the gifts were opened, and Shane and Charolette had been at both places for the opening of gifts. Shane had a special gift for Charolette, but kept it a secret until it was almost time for dinner.

Charolette was busy in the kitchen, helping Maureen and Pearl. The men and children were in other parts of the house. Charolette was cutting freshly baked bread at the cupboard when she saw Shane enter the kitchen. She smiled at him as his mother said, "We'll be ready to eat in about ten minutes, son."

"I know, Mom," Shane said, heading toward Charolette. "I want to see my girl alone just before we eat. Charly, can we talk in the sewing room for a couple minutes?"

"Of course. Just give me a minute to finish cutting this bread."

"Sure smells good," he said, drawing a breath through his nostrils.

When Charolette laid the knife down, Shane took her by the hand and led her to the sewing room at the end of the hall on the ground floor. Shane closed the door, slid his hand into his pocket, and said, "I have a special present for you."

Charolette cocked her head, frowned, and said, "What is this? All presents for this Christmas have already been opened."

"Not all," he said, holding a small ring box for her to see.

Everyone was gathering around the table when Shane and Charolette appeared in the dining room. Her dark eyes flashed with happiness as she held up her left hand and said, "Everybody please notice!"

Pearl spotted the ring first and gasped, "Oh, how beautiful!" Then she threw her arms around the girl and began to weep.

Garth was second to embrace Charolette, telling her he was so happy that she would one day be his daughter-in-law. Uncle Buster was next, planting a kiss on her cheek and congratulating Shane on getting such a wonderful girl. The children followed Uncle Buster, then Lewis O'Hanlon hugged her and told her she had become like a daughter to him. Mike wrapped his arms around his best friend, congratulating him, then kissed Charolette on the cheek.

Lastly, Maureen tearfully congratulated the couple, hugged Shane, then took Charolette into her arms. "I knew this was coming sooner or later. I'm already dreading the day you leave our home. I feel the same way Lewis does—you're just like a daughter to me. We're going to miss you terribly!"

Charolette thanked her, hugged her good, and then all sat down to eat.

That night at bedtime, Mike was alone with his mother in the kitchen. The rest of the family was upstairs, getting ready to retire for the night.

Maureen took her son in her arms and said, "Michael, I have to confess something."

"What's that, Mom?"

"Well, I had entertained hopes that you and Charolette would fall in love, and I could have her for my daughter-in-law. She's such a precious girl. I love her so much."

Mike patted his mother's cheek and said, "The Lord already has one picked out for me, Mom…one that you'll love even more than you love Charolette."

The following Sunday, Dr. George Adams announced the engagement in the morning service, and by Monday morning, word had spread to the college. Everyone was happy for Shane and Charolette. God's hand was on them, without a doubt.

NINE

The winter of 1857 was hard, and spring was late in coming. But by the first week in May, it finally was out in full bloom. Graduation took place at Bowdoin College two weeks later, and school let out for the summer.

Shane and Charolette were often asked if they had set a wedding date, but they had not. Because Shane's part-time income was low and he had tuition to pay, he and Charolette agreed they should wait until he had graduated from college and obtained employment. Then they would marry. He would work on his master's degree a little at a time after that.

Fall came, then winter.

One day in early January of 1858, Lewis O'Hanlon visited Garth Donovan at the lumber mill and asked to see him for a few minutes. When the two friends sat down behind a closed door in Garth's office, Lewis said, "I've heard a rumor, and I want to know if it's true."

"A rumor? About what?"

"About you having made a deal with your employer to buy him out."

Garth grinned. "Now where did you hear that?"

"Your wife. Actually, I didn't hear it from her own mouth, I heard it from Maureen. Pearl told her to keep it under her hat, so I'm the only one she's told. She also said that Shane doesn't even know it…that you're planning to surprise him with the news just after the sale takes place."

Garth smiled warmly and nodded. "That's it. I've got something in mind, but I didn't want to tell him until it becomes a reality."

"And that is?"

"Those sweet kids are so in love…and it's obvious that the Lord has them for each other. They want to marry, but just can't see their way clear to do so."

A pleasant grin worked its way across Lewis's face. "So when Daddy Donovan becomes his son's employer, the boy gets a raise in pay."

"You're pretty smart for an Irishman. I want that boy to finish college…even get his master's degree if he wants it. But I'd like to see those two go ahead and get married. They're both mature for their age, and I know they can handle it."

Lewis threw his head back and laughed.

"What's so funny?" Garth asked.

"I'm having a good time realizing that great minds run on the same track."

"How so?"

"Garth, my friend, I've had this same thing going through my mind…and when Maureen told me about you're deal to buy the mill, I figured to come and talk to you about giving Shane a substantial raise so those two can get married."

It was Garth's turn to laugh. "I have a feeling that isn't all you came to talk to me about. You're going to give Charolette a raise too, aren't you?"

"You know me too well, Garth. But yes—that girl is voluntarily handling more and more work, and she deserves a good raise. Before I decided what 'good' is, though, I wanted to see if we couldn't put our heads together. So when does this sale take place?"

"In five days—January 12."

The two men discussed what income they thought the young couple would need while Shane completed his education, and agreed on the raises they would give to meet that need.

Lewis made a note on a slip of paper drawn from his coat pocket, and said, "All right, my friend. When will you tell Shane you're the new owner of the lumber mill, and that he's getting a raise?"

"On the morning after I sign the papers."

"Okay. I'll tell Charolette about her raise the same morning, but I won't mention a thing about the raise you're giving Shane. We'll just let nature take its course. Okay?"

"It's a deal."

The two friends shook hands and parted with a warm glow deep inside them.

"You what?" Shane gasped at the breakfast table on Wednesday morning, January 13. "You bought the mill?"

Patrick and Ryan looked on with bulging eyes and gaping mouths. Pearl smiled to herself.

"But Pa," Shane said, "that means you're my employer! My boss!"

"That's right, son. And it means something else."

"What's that?"

"It means that as your employer, I'm giving you a raise in pay."

Shane glanced at his mother, then said to his father, "You are? May I ask how much of a raise?"

"Triple what you're making now."

"*Triple?*"

"That's right. Starting today."

"Hallelujah! Now I can put more money aside for when Charly and I get married!"

"That's good thinking, son." Garth looked across the table at his wife. "Don't you think so, Mother?"

"Yes, it sure is. It's wise to have a good financial foundation when entering marriage. Not everyone can, of course, but it makes that difficult first year so much easier."

It was midmorning the same day when Lewis O'Hanlon came from the rear of the factory and passed by Charolette's desk on his way to his office. Without breaking stride, he said, "Charolette, when you have a minute I need to see you."

"I can come in right now if you wish," she called after him.

"Fine," he said, turning and smiling at her.

Charolette picked up her notepad and pencil and hurried to meet her boss. He gestured for her to enter the office ahead of him, then closed the door as she took a seat in front of his desk. He rounded the desk and sat down.

"Busy morning?"

"Yes, sir. I've been going over those orders from New York and Boston as Uncle Buster asked me to do. We're picking up a lot of new business in both cities."

"Great. That's what we like to hear."

Charolette held pad and pencil ready to take down whatever instructions he had for her.

"Now," Lewis said, "I want to talk about you, my dear."

"Me, sir?" she asked, eyes wide.

"Yes. Charolette, I cannot tell you how pleased I am with your work. Everybody in the factory appreciates you, especially Uncle Buster and me."

"Why, thank you, Mr. O'Hanlon. I appreciate your saying so."

"In fact, I appreciate you and your fine work so much that I'm going to double your salary."

"You...you're going to *double* my salary?"

"You heard me right. From your first day on the job, you've gone beyond your own responsibilities and taken on work that you saw needed to be done. I like that. It shows me what you're made of. You certainly are going to make Shane a wonderful wife."

"Thank you," she said shyly. "But Mr. O'Hanlon, you're already paying me well...let alone the fact that I'm living in your home, getting free room and board. You really don't have to give me this raise."

"Charolette, Maureen and I are delighted to have you living in our home. We've both expressed it before, and I'll say it for both of us again—we're going to miss you terribly when you and Shane get married. By the way...any date set yet?"

"No, sir. We plan to wait until Shane is out of college and working full time."

"But that's still more than two years away for his bachelor's degree, let alone if he goes for his master's."

"I know, but our finances won't allow us to marry any sooner."

"This raise won't help that situation?"

"Oh, yes, it'll help. I'm just not sure how much. I'll see what Shane says when I tell him."

"We're not trying to get rid of you, you understand. I just hate to see you have to wait so long to get married."

Charolette was smiling from ear to ear. "Thank you, Mr. O'Hanlon. Your confidence in me means more than I can ever tell you. And this raise is appreciated very, very much. I can't wait to tell Shane!"

That evening, Shane knocked on the door of the O'Hanlon home, eager to tell Charolette about his father's purchase of the lumber mill and the tripling of his pay.

The young couple had previously set the evening for a date, and because the weather was so cold, the O'Hanlons told Charolette that she and Shane could spend the evening together in the library, which had its own fireplace.

Mike opened the door, smiled and said, "Why, Shane, how nice of you to come and see me!"

Shane moved through the door and removed his hat. "I hate to break your heart, friend, but it isn't you I came to see."

Mike took Shane's hat, coat, and scarf. "I'll make it through this devastating disappointment somehow."

Shane cuffed him playfully on the chin. "She in the library?"

"I'm here," came Charolette's voice from the winding staircase that ended in the vestibule where the two young men were standing.

Charolette was wearing a black dress with white lace trim on the high neck and at the ends of the sleeves. Her raven-black hair was done in an upsweep, topping out in tiny ringlets that dangled onto her brow. Shane moved to the bottom of the stairs and gave her his hand as she reached the last step.

"You look splendid this evening, Miss Thompson."

"Why, thank you, Mr. Donovan."

"What's with all this formality?" Mike asked.

"Private stuff," Shane said, giving him a mock scowl.

"I guess I know where that puts me. See you two later."

"Thanks for the warning," Shane said.

Mike laughed and disappeared down the hall that led to the kitchen.

"I've got some real good news to tell you," Shane said.

"Oh? Well, it so happens I've got some real good news for you, too!"

Hand-in-hand, they moved down the hall and entered the library. The fireplace was crackling and giving off welcome warmth.

"Mike built the fire for us," Charolette said, leading Shane by the hand to the love seat that stood near the fireplace.

"Bless him," Shane said.

As they sat down, Charolette said, "Tell me your good news, darling. Then I'll tell you mine."

Shane took both of her hands in his, and with a lilt in his voice said, "My father just worked a deal with Mr. Throckmorton."

"The man who owns the lumber mill?"

"Yes. Mr. Throckmorton is retiring, and he's making it possible for Pa to buy the mill. They made it official yesterday."

"You mean your father is now owner of the mill?"

"Yes. And this morning at breakfast, he told me he's giving me a raise in pay starting today. And get this—it's triple what Mr. Throckmorton was paying me!"

Charolette's mouth dropped open. *"Triple!* Really?"

"Yes! Now we can set a date for our wedding! We can put a good amount of money away for a year or so, then we'll be in good financial shape when we get married."

Charolette placed her hand to her throat. "O Shane, this is wonderful! Praise the Lord!"

"Yes, praise Him! It is wonderful, isn't it. Now what's your good news?"

Charolette adjusted herself on the love seat, looked deep into Shane's eyes, and said, "I got a raise too!"

"You did?"

"This morning, Mr. O'Hanlon called me into his office and told me how pleased he is with my work. He's doubling my salary as of today!"

Shane hugged her. "Honey, that's wonderful!"

"Yes! Isn't the Lord good?"

"Yes, He is. He sure is."

Charolette eased back from his arms, put a hand to her chin, and looked at the floor.

"Something bothering you?" Shane asked.

"Oh, no." She raised her eyes to meet his. "It's just that—Shane, did your father mention our wedding when he told you of the raise?"

Shane thought a moment. "No. But when I said this would allow us to put more money aside, both he and Ma agreed it was a wise thing to do. Why do you ask?"

"Well, after he told me about the raise, Mr. O'Hanlon asked if it would make it possible for us to get married sooner. It's like—"

"Conniving?"

"I guess you could call it that."

"Seems so. I've got a feeling Pa and Mr. O'Hanlon got together and put these raises together so we could get married sooner."

"I think you're right. Mr. O'Hanlon sure seemed curious to know if it would affect our plans."

Shane was shaking his head in wonderment. "I just said that my raise would let us marry in a year or so, but now I'd say if we planned it right, we could get married in six months. What do you think?"

"Well, I would say we could get married even sooner with this much money coming in. But if we waited six months, we'd have a solid financial foundation under us. I agree. Let's drop it from a year to six months!"

Shane took Charolette in his arms and whispered, "I've got an idea. Let's get married on your birthday."

"My birthday?" she said, pulling back to look him in the eye. "You mean it?"

"Of course."

"O Shane, that'd be wonderful! I'll become your wife and turn nineteen on the same day."

The young couple went to the O'Hanlons and thanked them for conniving with Garth Donovan to give them both raises so they could get married sooner than they had planned. And Shane took Mike aside and told him that since the wedding date had now been set, he wanted to know if Mike would be his best man. Mike was elated and agreed.

It was announced at the church and at the college that the wedding was set for June 14. Friends expressed their joy to the happy couple.

In March, news came from Ireland that Lewis O'Hanlon's father had died suddenly of heart failure. There were brothers and sisters there who could care for Lewis's mother, but Donald Kilrain was asking for help in managing the company. There was no one at the factory in Dublin who had enough knowledge of policies and procedures to step into Jacob's spot. Because Mike had been working some in the management end of the business in Brunswick, Donald requested that he come and fill his grandfather's shoes until a new man could be trained for the job. Donald explained in the letter that the experience would be invaluable to Mike, even though he would have to drop out of college for a while, probably no more than a year.

Mike was eager to go. The experience would be a great help to his career, but the main reason he wanted to go was to see Ashley Kilrain. He was sure if she had found a steady beau, it would have been mentioned in one of Mavor's letters.

Lewis prayed for several days about Donald's request and discussed it with Maureen and Mike and Buster Kilrain. Nine days after the letter had arrived, Mike was called to his father's office at the factory.

When Mike entered the office, he found Uncle Buster there, too. He closed the door behind him as Lewis said, "Come and sit down, son." Lewis waited for Mike to sit before proceeding. "Mike, all of us have been seeking the Lord's guidance concerning Donald's request. He needs to have an answer soon, and Buster and I have decided that if you really want to go, we should send you."

Mike's eyes lit up. "You can put it down and draw a line under it, Pa—yes, I want to go!"

"Well, you can thank Uncle Buster for the opportunity, son. I'm pretty dependent on you here, but he says he'll work extra hours to make up for your absence."

"Thanks, Uncle Buster," Mike said. "I know I'll learn a lot working in the Dublin factory."

Buster's Irish eyes twinkled. "Sure, and don't I know that, me boy! And somethin' else."

"Yes, sir?"

"It'll also put ye a whole lot closer to little Ashley too, eh?"

Mike's countenance crimsoned. His eyes flicked to his father.

Lewis grinned. "You aren't fooling anybody, son. It's been written all over you since you found out Shane and Charolette were sweethearts. Be sure to tell Ashley hello for Buster and me."

Lewis and Buster had a good laugh at Mike's expense, then serious planning began. Mike would sail for Ireland as soon as possible.

On the following Sunday, Shane and Charolette were walking toward the church from the parking lot when they saw the O'Hanlon carriage pull in. Mike waved, calling for them to wait. They stopped and greeted him as he drew up.

"Shane, I need to talk to you right after church," Mike said.

"You want this private, or is it all right if Charly hears it?"

"It's fine if she hears it. But it's important. We'll talk right after church, okay?"

"Sure. Right after church."

The cold March wind blew through the naked trees that surrounded the church grounds as Shane and Charolette stood near the O'Hanlon carriage, greeting people as they passed by. Mike hurried toward them, having stopped to talk to Pastor Adams at the door. Charolette pulled her coat collar up to fend off the biting wind.

"I'm sorry to hold you up," Mike said, "but I have to tell you, Shane, that I won't be able to be best man at the wedding. I'm really sorry about it, but it just won't be possible."

Though everyone at church knew of Jacob O'Hanlon's death, no one knew of Donald Kilrain's request for Mike to come and help him.

"I know there has to be a good reason, Mike," Shane said.

Mike then told them he would soon be leaving for Dublin, and why. "I hope you understand, Shane. You too, Charolette."

Both assured him they understood, but were sorry he wouldn't be there for their wedding.

"How soon are you leaving?" Shane asked.

"This evening. The ship sails at six-thirty."

"Whoa, you weren't kidding when you said you were leaving soon. I'm sure going to miss you, friend. A whole year!"

"We both wish you the best, Mike," Charolette said. "We certainly will miss you." She paused, then said, "I envy you."

"Why's that?"

"You're going to get to see Ashley. I still miss her so much."

"I'll be sure to greet her for you."

"Do that. And tell her she owes me three letters. I haven't heard from her in a long time."

"Will do."

"Greet her for me too, will you?" Shane asked.

"Of course. And I'll tell her that your wedding is planned for Charolette's birthday. She'll be happy to hear that. Well, I guess I'd better head for home. I've still got some packing to do."

Shane and Charolette embraced Mike and told him they would be praying for him and looking forward to his return.

On Sunday evening, March 21, 1858, Mike O'Hanlon boarded the Ireland-bound ship with mixed emotions. He would miss his family and friends…but he was going to see the girl he loved.

The next morning, he pulled his cap low, turned up his coat collar, and walked to the bow of the ship. He stood there with the cold wind biting at his face and squinted against the bright sunlight that reflected off the choppy surface of the Atlantic. The bow of the ship rose and fell in the rough waters, and a light spray struck him in the face.

He lifted his eyes heavenward and prayed, "O Lord Jesus, You know what has been in my heart for so long. I have loved Ashley since she was twelve years old. You've never taken that love out of my heart." The ship's bow went low, then raised high, sending a heavy spray on Mike, but he only tightened his grip on the rail. "Dear Lord, You know that I never let on to Shane nor to Ashley because I never would have come between them. But now…now You've given Charolette to Shane, and here I am—within Your plan—on my way to Ireland. Lord Jesus, I can't look into Your great mind, but could it be possible that my love for Ashley has remained so strong because You have chosen her for me? That You have…or will…put the same kind of love in her heart for me? Lord, I pray that it will be so."

TEN

Mike O'Hanlon arrived in Dublin on April 6, 1858. Since there had been no time to send a letter to Donald Kilrain once the decision had been made, Mike himself would be Lewis O'Hanlon's answer to Donald's request.

Mike rode into town on a freight wagon owned by a Dublin merchant named Padriac O'Dwyer, who knew the Jacob O'Hanlon family. He also knew the Kilrains and had seen Donald on several occasions since he and his family had returned to Dublin.

Mike knew the Kilrain's address from the letters that had come from Mavor. O'Dwyer knew the neighborhood well and was kind enough to drive young O'Hanlon right up to the door. Mike thanked him, swung down onto the cobblestone street, and lifted his luggage off the wagon. He carried the four pieces to the door of the large, luxurious house two at a time. The house had a tile roof and was constructed of brick, which only the wealthy could afford. The other homes in the area were also expensive-looking.

Mike rapped the knocker on the door. Light, rapid footsteps preceded the rattle of the latch, then the door swung open. It was Ashley. Her face lit up when she recognized the young man who stood on the porch.

"Mike! Oh, thank the Lord you're here!"

Even as she spoke, she wrapped her arms around him. Mike hugged her too, then held her at arm's length and said, "You're a sight for sore eyes, Ashley! Is everybody in the family all right?"

"Yes, but they'll be even better when they see you! Come in. Daddy just got home. They're all in the library at the back of the house."

Mike set his luggage in the wide entrance hall, then followed Ashley as she led him by the hand to the library. When she led him through the library door, the entire family reacted with surprise, and delight, to see him. Donald and Mavor said he was an answer to prayer. William, who was now sixteen, and Harvey, who was now fourteen, shook his hand warmly.

Mavor and Ashley then hurried to the kitchen and started preparing supper. Donald sat Mike down and told him that somehow he knew Lewis would grant his request. He had already rented Mike an apartment near the factory and had set up his late grandfather's office for him.

The two of them discussed Mike's new job until the meal was ready. At the table, Donald thanked the Lord for bringing Mike safely to them, thanked Him for the food, and they began to eat.

Everyone fired questions at Mike one after the other. When business and family questions had been answered, there were inquiries about different people and what was going on at the church and in town.

It was Donald who asked the inevitable question. After taking a sip of hot tea, he looked at Mike and said, "And how about your friend Shane Donovan? He's in college, I understand. How many girlfriends has he got?"

"Well, sir, you're right. Shane is in college. Doing quite well scholastically. He's become a close friend of Professor Joshua Chamberlain. I guess you knew Mr. Chamberlain was back teaching at Bowdoin."

"Seems someone mentioned that in a letter. Fine man."

"That he is, sir. Shane has only one girlfriend though—that pretty Charolette Thompson. In fact, she's more than a girlfriend. They're now engaged to be married."

Mike noticed a slight bobbing of Ashley's head and a twitch at one corner of her mouth.

"Oh, really?" Mavor said. "That's nice. They're both such fine young people."

"They're getting married on Charolette's birthday…June fourteenth."

He saw Ashley's hands tremble slightly, but she smiled and said, "Oh, that's wonderful. I'm so glad for them. They both deserve to be happy."

"Charolette said to tell you, Ashley, that you owe her three letters. She very much wants to hear from you."

Ashley swung her eyes to her mother. "I know I owe her two. Didn't I answer the one that came last fall?"

"I thought you did," Mavor said. "Maybe it went astray. International mail does that a lot."

"Must be what happened," Ashley said. "I'm just sure I sent that letter. Anyway, I'll write her right away. I've been neglectful in answering the other two letters, and I need to ask her forgiveness."

"She still talks about you a lot, Ashley," Mike said. "I know it'll mean a lot to hear from you."

"I love her dearly and I miss her a lot. It…it's nice that they can be married on her birthday. Too bad you won't be there for the wedding."

"Shane asked me to be his best man. Wish I could've done it, but someone else will have to wear those shoes. I've got a feeling he'll ask Professor Chamberlain."

"How about you, Ashley?" Mike asked, trying to sound as casual as possible. "Any serious boyfriends in your life?" His heart seemed stuck in his throat as he waited for her reply.

She smiled and said, "Nobody special, Mike. I've met and dated several young men, but finding someone who's really dedicated to the Lord is like trying to find a needle in a haystack."

"It's the same with Christian girls. I've dated several who are in First Parish Church. Nice girls and all but not as dedicated as…as you, for instance."

Ashley's features tinted. "I…I just feel that if a person is going to live for the Lord, they should go all the way and give Him their best."

"My sentiments exactly," Mike said. "It's a girl with that kind of dedication that I've been waiting for the Lord to bring into my life."

"And He will," Mavor said. "You're such a fine boy, Mike. I'm sure the Lord has a wonderful girl picked out for you."

Mike couldn't help but look at Ashley. Their eyes met, and she gave him a sweet smile.

Professor Chamberlain dismissed his rhetoric class and was going through papers on his desk in preparation for his next class when he became aware of someone standing over the desk. He looked up to see Shane Donovan smiling down at him.

"What can I do for you, Shane?"

"I was wondering if I could have a few minutes with you sometime today, sir."

"Sure. How long do you need?"

"Not more than five minutes, sir."

"How about right after lunch? Right here?"

"Fine, sir. See you then."

Shane was waiting in the hall after lunch when Chamberlain arrived. The professor commented that Shane was always punctual. He opened the door and gestured for his favorite pupil to sit down in front of the desk, then took his seat behind it.

"All right, Shane, what can I do for you?"

"Well, sir, you're aware that Charolette and I are going to be married on June fourteenth."

"Yes, and I imagine you're starting to get some butterflies."

"Yes, sir. I guess that's to be expected."

"Happens to the best of us. But I don't imagine you came to see me to talk about butterflies."

"No, sir, I came to ask a favor of you. I'd like for you to be my best man in the wedding."

Chamberlain's eyes mirrored the surprise Shane's words brought. It took him a few seconds to reply. "Why, Shane, I would be honored to be your best man. Highly honored."

"The honor will be mine, sir. This will make Charolette happy too. Thank you!"

Shane stood and offered his hand. Chamberlain rose and met his grip.

"Just let me know about wedding practice and all that," Chamberlain said.

"I will, sir. And thank you again."

The next day, Shane was the first to arrive for Greek class. He greeted Chamberlain, who was writing Greek conjugations on the chalkboard. Chamberlain laid the chalk down and walked up to Shane.

"When I got home yesterday afternoon, I told Fannie that you had asked me to be best man in your wedding. She said she wanted to prepare a meal for the wedding party on the day of the rehearsal. It would be at our house afterward. Is that okay?"

"That's awfully kind of her. And yes, that would be great. Thank her for us, will you?"

"I will."

That evening, Shane told Charolette of Fannie's offer, and the bride-to-be was elated. When Sunday came, both Shane and Charolette expressed their appreciation to her, as did Garth and Pearl Donovan.

As the wedding date drew near, Shane and Charolette's love for each other continued to grow. They found a small cottage to rent in

Brunswick and began fixing it up like they wanted it.

They talked together about their home and their desire that it would glorify the Lord Jesus Christ. They would teach their children the Word of God and worship together as a family in the church. They agreed to follow the Bible's instructions for disciplining their children.

They decided that since they were doing well financially, Shane would enter graduate school after he received his bachelor's degree. They would not start their family until he had his master's degree and had a steady teaching job. They both hoped the job would be at Bowdoin College.

"I want to follow in the footsteps of Joshua Lawrence Chamberlain," Shane said.

Charolette smiled and said, "You really love that man, don't you?"

"Charly, I would lay down my life for him."

"I hope you don't ever have to do that."

Charolette's birthday—and thus the wedding day—fell on Monday in 1858. On the previous Friday, Shane and Charolette were eating supper in a small Brunswick Café. As they were finishing the meal, Shane noticed a "cat-that-ate-the-canary" look in Charolette's eyes.

"What do you know that I don't?" he asked, cocking his head at her.

"What do you mean?"

"You know what I mean. It's written all over your face. Come on, out with it."

"Well, I've been dying to let you in on it, but I decided to wait till we were through eating."

She dug in her purse and pulled out an envelope. Shane could tell it was addressed to Charolette in feminine handwriting.

"Who from?" he asked.

"Ashley. You remember that I got a letter from her not too long after Mike had gone to Ireland? All she said in that letter was that it was good to see Mike again."

"You told me that."

"Well, wait till you hear this. Do you want me to read it to you or just tell you what's in it?"

Shane eased back on his chair. "Why don't you just tell me what's in it while I sit here and enjoy the view?"

Charolette blushed. "Oh, Shane. You say the sweetest things."

"I just speak the truth, me lady. Go ahead. Tell me what's in the letter."

"All right. Are you ready for this?"

"How can I answer that? I don't know what's in it."

"Well, Ashley says that she and Mike have fallen in love, and they are engaged!"

"No kidding?"

"No kidding. The wedding is set for this coming December tenth."

Shane remembered the special love he and Ashley had promised each other and felt a warm glow spread through his chest. The Lord had guided their lives and provided them with the mates He had planned. Shane loved his Charly with everything that was in him and was superbly happy with God's choice for him…but the little red-headed lass who had been his first love would always have a tender place in his heart.

"Well, I'm mighty happy for them," Shane said, "but I wonder how they fell for each other so quickly. I sure never noticed anything but friendship between them before."

"Well, God works in mysterious ways sometimes."

"Would've been great if we had been able to have a double wedding," Shane said.

"Yes, that would have been nice. But at least we'll get to see Ashley again. Mike will be bringing his bride home to Brunswick with him."

***

The wedding rehearsal was held on Sunday afternoon, June 13, after which Fannie Chamberlain fed the wedding party, their mates, and their children in the Chamberlain home. During the meal, Shane and Charolette had eyes only for each other.

Dr. George Adams looked on with joy. In his many years of pastoring, he had counseled a great number of couples prior to their wedding. Other than his own daughter and Joshua Chamberlain, he had never seen a couple so in love. In his heart, he thanked God and prayed that their love would grow deeper and stronger all their married lives.

The wedding took place the following evening at the First Parish Congregational Church. The building was packed.

Charolette was a strikingly beautiful bride in her long white-lace-on-white-satin dress with lengthy train. It had a high neck and sleeves that came to a heart-shaped point at her wrists. On her head was a coronet of white lace from which flowed a delicate veil. The crowd looked on with admiration as she walked down the aisle on the arm of Lewis O'Hanlon to meet her groom.

There was pain in Charolette's heart because her father had deserted her and her mother was not alive to see her take her vows. But the pain eased with each step she took toward the man she loved so deeply.

The ceremony was beautifully done, with the Lord Jesus Christ highly honored. Fannie Chamberlain played the organ. In addition to being best man, Joshua Chamberlain sang two solos, one before the bride started her procession and a prayer song while they knelt at the altar just before the pastor pronounced them husband and wife.

The happy bride and groom took a five-day honeymoon in Portland, staying at a hotel and sailing on the Atlantic Ocean. On the last day, they were in a sailboat, drifting with the wind. Charolette was reading Harriet Beecher Stowe's *Uncle Tom's Cabin,* which she had purchased in a Portland bookstore. She had wanted to read it for a long time, but especially so since she had met the author and gotten to know her before the Stowes moved away from Brunswick.

Shane was reading a Portland newspaper and had come across an article telling of trouble in Washington between politicians of northern and southern states over states' rights and slavery.

Charolette noted the concerned look on his face and asked, "What is it, darling?"

"Oh, this slavery issue and states' rights. They're having a heated battle in Congress about it."

"That's what this book's about…slavery. Mrs. Stowe is completely opposed to it. I didn't have to read very far to figure that out."

"Well, so is God," Shane said. "He never intended for one human being to treat another as chattel. If the evolutionists were right, it would be different. They say we're all animals, so humans could be bought and sold like we do cattle and horses and hogs. But God created man in His own image. We didn't evolve from apes. Human beings are not to own one another."

"You're right about that. Slavery is not of the Lord. I hope those politicians get the issue settled before it grows worse. I hate to see Americans at odds with each other."

Shane folded the newspaper and dropped it on the deck of the boat. "Well, if they don't get it settled pretty soon, the battle won't be with words. It'll be with guns. The plantation owners will stir up big trouble if they think they're going to lose the right to own slaves. There's no way they'll just lie down and let their slaves be taken from them. There'll be a bloody war. Can you imagine Americans killing Americans on blood-soaked battlefields?"

"No, I can't."

The next Sunday the newlyweds were back in church, and on Monday they were back at their jobs. As the weeks passed, they found married life sweet and precious with the Lord at the center of their home.

In early September, Shane was given the teenage Sunday school class, and Charolette worked with him as helper. She also did whatever counseling was needed with the girls. The Donovans were full of joy serving the Lord.

College classes began the second week of September, and the weight of study and work was once again on Shane's shoulders. He was glad to have Joshua Chamberlain for three courses.

In Dublin, Ireland, one night in mid-November, Mike and Ashley were alone in the parlor of the Kilrain home, talking of their future. Then the subject turned to family and friends in America.

They were sitting side-by-side on a small couch, facing the blazing fireplace. In the flickering light from the fire, Mike noticed that when they talked of Shane and Charolette, Ashley became visibly nervous. He took hold of her hand and felt it trembling.

"Sweetheart, what's wrong?"

The other hand trembled also as she put it to her mouth.

"Mike, there's something I have to talk to you about."

"Must be serious. You're shaking."

"It is."

"Tell me about it."

She freed her hand from his and stood up.

"Wait here. I'll be right back."

When she returned, she was carrying a small black velvet box. She sat down beside him and opened the lid, displaying a gold necklace adorned with a heart-shaped locket. It was engraved with a male hand and a female hand in a tender grasp of love.

"I recognize that," Mike said. "Shane gave it to you. I remember you wearing it a lot."

"Darling, you know that I love you with all of my heart, don't you?" Ashley said.

"Next to the fact that Jesus loves me, it's the biggest, most wonderful thing in my life. I have to keep shaking myself to make sure I'm not dreaming."

Ashley laid a hand on his cheek and said, "Thank you. Just so you know without a doubt that I love you and I want to become your wife. My greatest desire is to live the rest of my life with you."

"I know that, sweetheart," he said, squeezing her hand. "Now, what about the locket?"

"When Shane gave it to me, we made a promise to each other. We promised we would always have a special love for each other, even if the Lord did not plan for us to marry." Her voice quavered as she proceeded. "Mike, I'm in love with you and you alone. The Lord meant us for each other. That's a settled fact between you and me. But...I still have fond memories of Shane. And I have a special love for him, though not like the love I have for you. Can you understand that?"

He smiled and squeezed her hand again. "Of course I can. I've got a special love for him myself. He and I are best friends. We always will be. What you're asking is, can you keep the locket, right?"

"Yes. As a token of the friendship between Shane and me. But if you want me to get rid of it, I will."

Mike folded Ashley in his arms, kissed her tenderly, and said, "Sweetheart, I'm glad you and my best friend have fond memories of each other. That doesn't bother me at all. And you know why?"

"Why?"

"Because Shane is madly in love with Charolette, but most of all, because I know you love me. It won't bother me at all if you keep it. I want you to."

"Thank you," she said, putting the locket back in the box and closing it. "I'll keep it...but I won't wear it."

Ashley laid the box on a lamp table next to the couch, and they began talking about all the good times they would have with Shane and Charolette when they returned to Brunswick. Ashley said how wonderful it would be to see them and that she hoped she and Charolette could become closer friends yet.

On December 2, a box arrived on a ship from America. Inside were wedding gifts from Shane and Charolette, Uncle Buster Kilrain, and Garth and Pearl Donovan. There was nothing from Mike's family because they were coming for the wedding and bringing their gifts with them.

The wedding took place as scheduled on December 10.

The previous October, Donald Kilrain had hired a new man with experience in the shoe and boot manufacturing business to train for management. Mike understood that the new man would be ready to take over his job by the end of March.

The newlyweds made plans to return to America the first week of April.

ELEVEN

Saturday, April 16, 1859, was a cool, cloudy day. The wind whipped across Casco Bay as the big ship swung off the Atlantic Ocean and headed due west for Portland Harbor.

Mike and Ashley O'Hanlon stood together on the starboard side and, like several hundred of their fellow passengers, squinted against the wind trying to pick out familiar faces in the crowd that waited on the dock. Ashley's long auburn hair kept blowing across her face, blocking her vision. She swept it back and held it there. Only seconds later, she pointed and said, "Mike, there they are! See them?"

It took Mike a moment to find his parents, Buster Kilrain, and Shane and Charolette Donovan, but when he did, he began to wave excitedly.

The ship swung in line with the dock and began to slow. Soon crewmen were tossing ropes to men on the dock, and two massive anchors on heavy chains were lowered into the water. Moments later, the gangplank was lowered, and passengers lined up to rush down to friends and loved ones.

Mike kept an arm around his wife as they descended the gangplank, then released her to hurry into his mother's arms. Shane and Charolette remained slightly aloof to give the O'Hanlons and Buster

Kilrain time to reunite with the newlyweds. Shane, who had been holding Darlene Brainerd, put the six-year-old down and said, "Even though you don't remember Miss Ashley, you can give her a big hug. You remember Mike though, don't you?"

"Yes, sir. He's your goodest friend, isn't he?"

"You've got that right!"

When Buster and the O'Hanlons had been sufficiently greeted, Mike and Ashley looked toward Shane and Charolette. Mike embraced Charolette. Shane and Ashley stood a few feet apart, not quite sure what to do. Their hearts were pounding, and they both seemed frozen on the spot. Then Ashley opened her arms and rushed to Shane, who held her close. She raised up on her tiptoes and kissed his cheek, saying through her tears, "Hello, Shane. It's wonderful to see you again!"

"It's good to see you. You look great. And you've grown up!"

Ashley backed off a step, cuffed him playfully on the upper arm, and said, "What do you mean? I was grown up before I left here!"

Shane laughed, then Mike wrapped him in his arms and hugged him tight.

"Good to see you, old pal!" Mike said. "And I do mean old! Forty-eight days of it."

Shane laughed. "You won't ever let anything die, will you?"

"Not that, my friend. Never! And let me tell you something."

"What's that?"

"I just saw Ashley kiss you on the cheek."

"You did?"

"Yes, I did. And I want you to know that you're the only man outside the Kilrain family I will allow her to kiss!"

"Well, that makes me one privileged bloke, doesn't it?"

"You'd better believe it."

Charolette and Ashley held each other close and mingled their tears of joy.

"Oh, Charolette, I've missed you so much. It's wonderful to see you!"

"It's so good to see you," Charolette said. "I'm never going to let you go away again!"

"I'm so glad for you and Shane. Are you as happy as I suspect you are?"

"Oh, yes, and even more! The Lord has given us such a precious love for each other. You and Mike too, right?"

"Mike's a wonderful husband. We're so much in love."

When the women had finished their embrace, they turned to see Mike hugging little Darlene. Ashley looked at Shane and said, "I wouldn't have known her if Mike hadn't told me who she was. Isn't she a doll?"

"That she is," Shane said. He then took the six-year-old by the hand and led her to Ashley. "Darlene, this is Miss Ashley. She's a very special friend of mine and Aunt Charolette's. How about a big hug for her?"

Darlene gave Ashley a hug, then moved back to Shane and took his hand. "She's pretty, Uncle Shane. I like her."

"Miss Ashley likes you, too. I can tell."

Ashley smiled down at Darlene. "I sure do, honey. You're a very special little girl."

"Shane, has she been told?" Mike asked.

"Yes. A few months ago, Elsa asked if we could come to the house. She felt Darlene was old enough to be told. It was quite a moment."

"I'll say it was," Charolette said. "She put a hug on Shane's neck that night like I've never seen before."

"And Charly cried a bucket of tears," Shane said.

Darlene's bright eyes danced as she looked at Ashley. "Uncle Shane saved me from burning up in the fire when I was a baby, Miss Ashley."

"Yes, I know. I remember when it happened."

"I love him very much. I would have died if he didn't come in the house and get me. I saw you kiss Uncle Shane. You love him too, don't you?"

The child's words tilted Ashley a bit off balance. "Why, of course I do. Your Uncle Shane and I have been friends for a long time."

"Darlene has adopted Shane and me as aunt and uncle," Charolette said. "She comes and stays with us quite often. Sometimes we have her sister and brother with us, too. Darlene stayed with us last night, so we brought her with us to meet you."

Innocent blue eyes looked up at Ashley. "Are you and Mr. Mike going to live with Uncle Shane and Aunt Charolette?"

"No, sweetie. We'll be staying with Mr. Mike's parents until we can get a place of our own."

It took the newlyweds only a few days to find a small cottage, which happened to be in the same block where Shane and Charolette lived. The two couples spent a great deal of time together, including riding to church on Sundays and Wednesday nights. They also attended church social functions together and spent time with other young couples, including Professor and Mrs. Joshua Chamberlain.

During off-work hours for Charolette, she and Ashley sewed together, making themselves dresses. Their friendship deepened, and the love they had for each other grew stronger. Like their husbands, they were the very best of friends.

One day in September, when both husbands were in school, the two young women were sewing at the kitchen table in the O'Hanlon cottage. They chatted about several things as they worked, then the conversation turned to their husbands, their courtships, and how happy they were in their married lives.

Charolette brought up the relationship Ashley and Shane had had when they were younger and expressed her joy that they could still be such good friends.

"Did you ever have any serious boyfriends before you fell for Shane?" Ashley asked.

"Oh, I had one when I was twelve. His name was Billy Burton." Charolette laughed. "He gave me a cheap little ring to show how much he cared for me. I've still got it, in fact."

"Really? Does Shane know?"

"Oh, yes, but he doesn't care. It's no more than a friendship thing."

There was no conversation for a few minutes, then Charolette said, "My mentioning of the ring Billy gave me just reminded me of that locket Shane gave you—the one with the two hands clasped. Do you still have it?"

"Why, yes I do. Mike took the same attitude toward it that you say Shane took about Billy Burton's ring. I wanted to keep it for the sentimental value it holds." She paused a moment. "Charolette, does it bother you that I still have the locket?"

"Oh, of course not. Not at all. Life in this world gives us enough bad memories. I'm glad you and Shane have some good ones."

"Mike and I are looking forward to being here for dinner tomorrow night. I know you were wanting to have the Chamberlains over before Fannie has her baby. It was awfully nice of you to invite us, too."

"I wouldn't think of inviting them and leaving you two out. Besides, when I invite you, I always get help in the kitchen!"

By March of 1860, the states' rights–slavery issue had heated up. The people of the South were bowing their necks against Northern politicians and newspapers who were speaking out against slavery.

In early April, Joshua Chamberlain addressed the dual issue of states' rights and slavery in his theology class. Though he spoke out against slavery, he expressed his wish that somehow the matter could be settled without violence.

A day later, Chamberlain entered the administration building a few minutes before first hour. Bowdoin's president, Dr. Leonard Woods, was standing in the hall in front of his office, talking to one of the science professors. Woods caught Chamberlain's eye and raised a hand for him to stop. Woods said some final words to the science professor, who then turned and walked away.

The president was a small man with narrow-set eyes that some people said could bore holes through a brick wall. He set those eyes on Joshua Chamberlain.

"Good morning, Professor."

"Good morning, Dr. Woods."

"I have word that you have spoken out on the slavery issue in your theology class."

"Yes, sir."

Woods's normally turned-down mouth curved upward into a wide smile. "I like what I hear. Seems you've got a good handle on this thing."

"Well, thank you, sir. I just felt that since the Bible makes it clear that God is against slavery, the theology class would be a good place to bring it up."

"Excellent, my boy. Tell you what...starting next Monday, I want you to take the next five chapel times and lecture on the subject to the entire student body and faculty."

"I'd be happy to do that, Dr. Woods."

"Good. I'm against slavery from the bottom of my feet to the top of my head, son. I want the students and the faculty of this college to hear what you have to say."

"All right, sir."

"I'll make arrangements for a short song service so you can get right to it. And I want you to speak an hour each time, Monday through Friday. You have enough material, I presume."

"I believe so, sir."

"Good. I want you to close each session with prayer, Professor. I'm sure I don't need to tell you to pray that Abraham Lincoln gets elected in November."

"Fannie and I are already praying that way."

"And well you should. We need to ask the Lord to let the issue be settled peacefully, but we all know that if Mr. Lincoln gets into the White House, slavery will be done away with in this country. By you're public prayer, you'll give an example to everybody on this campus of how to pray between now and November."

"I get the picture."

"And I'll be there on the platform, smiling while you're lecturing and shouting amen when you're praying. About half the people on this campus are old enough to vote, Joshua, and we want them to vote right, don't we?"

"We sure do, sir."

"And all of them are old enough to pray, and we want them to pray right, don't we?"

"Yes, sir."

Woods gave Chamberlain a pat on the back. "Better hurry now, or you'll be late to class. Can't have the professor arriving late to class now, can we?"

"No, sir," Chamberlain said, and darted down the hall.

Bowdoin College's chapel had been built in 1855. It was one of the earliest examples in the United States of German Romanesque architecture. It was a large stone building with twin towers which tapered to sharp spires that pointed boldly to the heavens. In addition to an ample auditorium to provide space for the college's daily chapel assemblies, it housed a huge library, an art gallery, and several meeting rooms.

On the Monday President Woods had designated for Chamberlain's lectures, students and faculty headed for the chapel from the other campus buildings shortly before eleven o'clock. Bibles and notebooks were in their hands. Chamberlain and the president walked together from the administration building, flanked on both sides by students. Other students greeted Woods and Chamberlain as they entered the chapel and headed for the platform.

After one rousing hymn, prayer, and a few announcements, Dr. Woods stood in the pulpit and explained that he had changed the normal program for chapel for that day and the rest of the week because he had asked Professor Chamberlain to bring hour-long lectures on the subject of states' rights and slavery.

There was a warm round of applause for Chamberlain as he stepped to the pulpit. He opened his Bible and directed his hearers to Exodus 1. "This book opens," he said, "with the children of Israel held in slavery by the Egyptians and their Pharaoh. Verse eleven says, 'Therefore they did set over them taskmasters to afflict them with their burdens.' They were *slaves*, my friends. God's earthly people were held in captivity as slaves. Now God allowed them to be taken into slavery as a disciplinary act for their sins, but He did not leave them there. God is against slavery. When the time of discipline was over, He delivered them from slavery. On the night of the Passover, He set them free. And we hear Moses say in chapter thirteen, verse three, 'Remember this day, in which ye came out from Egypt, out of the house of bondage; for by strength of hand the LORD brought you out from this place.' The Lord, I say, is against slavery. He brought them out of the house of bondage.

"And if you know the book of Exodus, you know that the reason Pharaoh continued to resist God and set himself to hang onto his slaves was for the purpose of *free labor*. This is exactly what we've got going on below the Mason–Dixon line today. The wealthy plantation owners and the big businessmen who make money from cotton and other crops planted, cultivated, weeded, and harvested by slaves are determined to keep those slaves and fill their pockets with more and more wealth. This isn't right!"

There was a chorus of amens from the audience.

Chamberlain then closed his Bible and read from news-papers—both Northern and Southern—showing his hearers what was being said about states' rights and slavery. With each pro-slavery article, he quoted additional Scriptures that made it clear God never intended for one human being to own another. When he read the articles that stood for abolition, he lauded the writers, saying they were correct in their thinking.

The hour passed quickly. Professor Chamberlain closed in

prayer, asking God to put a man of righteous character in the White House who would abolish slavery.

The next day Chamberlain opened his lecture by reading more Scripture and reminding his hearers of the Scripture they had considered the day before. He read more newspaper articles from both sides of the slavery issue.

"Now, ladies and gentlemen," he proceeded, "our founding fathers laid the foundation of this country on clear biblical prin-ciples. We will shoot ourselves in the foot if we stray from those principles.

"Furthermore, the United States was founded as a Union of one people. Our founding fathers did not vote themselves into a people. They recognized and declared that they were *already* a people. Therefore, I think of the people in the singular, as did our fathers. The people living in the states constitute the people of the United States. We all form one indivisible Union. This country and its land belongs to us all...and we to it.

"As you have heard from the articles I've read from Southern newspapers, there is talk in the South of a secession from the Union and a forming of the Confederate States of America. This would be an attack on our foundation as an indivisible people and nothing less than treason! If secession comes, it will be war on the Union and the Constitution. Such unthinkable conflict will bring untold damage, harm, and injury to this people, no matter on which side of the Mason–Dixon line they live."

Chamberlain was filled with emotion and had to stop and gain control of himself. When he resumed, he said, "It is apparent to the Southerners that if Abraham Lincoln is elected president in this coming election, it will be a death knell to their way of life. We must pray for this death knell, for slavery is an abomination to Almighty God. We must earnestly pray for Mr. Lincoln's election, and at the same time, pray that God will somehow keep this conflict from becoming a bloody war with fathers killing sons, sons killing fathers, brothers killing brothers...and worst of all, Christian brothers killing each other across fields of battle!"

Each day, Joshua Chamberlain stirred the emotions of students and faculty alike, giving them more Scripture refuting slavery and laying before them examples of dangerous attitudes being formed in the South. With deep emotion, he closed each session by calling for every one of his hearers to be in earnest prayer for the nation.

With war clouds hanging heavy over the nation, Shane Donovan graduated in May 1860, receiving his bachelor's degree in education. As planned, he soon signed up for the one-year master's program.

The national election was held in November, and Abraham Lincoln was elected president of the United States. Southern political leaders considered Lincoln's election the final affront in a long series of provocations that had pushed their states to the brink of secession. Ironically, it was the Southern political leaders themselves who had split the Democratic ticket, thus insuring Lincoln's election as a Republican.

The United States did not remain united very long.

In December, a secession meeting was held in South Carolina, and that state seceded from the Union. Others were seriously contemplating it. Lincoln hoped to bring the Southerners back, and in the weeks that followed, worked hard to do so. He did not want civil war.

While the war question festered, Shane labored hard on his studies, while working at the lumber mill and giving Charolette as much of his time as possible. There was also the Sunday school class, which he taught faithfully every Sunday.

By the end of his first semester, Shane was number one on the dean's list in the graduate school. When his name appeared on the president's report, he was summoned to Dr. Woods's office at the close of the school day. The president's secretary ushered Shane into the office, and Dr. Woods rose to his feet behind the desk and gave him one of his rare smiles.

"I was told that you wanted to see me, sir," Shane said.

"That's right, my boy," Woods said, rounding the desk and extending his hand. "I want to be the first to inform you that you are number one on the dean's list in the graduate school. I know the kind of work load you carry, working at the mill for your father. And you're a married man with responsibilities at home. To have achieved these grades, you have to be a master of your time. Congratulations."

"Thank you, sir. I'm determined to be a college professor, as you know, and I want to be as good a professor as Mr. Chamberlain."

"You're well on your way, I'll say that."

Shane cleared his throat nervously. "Sir, since I'm here, may I tell you something that's on my mind?"

"With a mind like yours, you sure can! What is it?"

"Well, sir, I have a big dream. Nothing could make me happier than to teach right here at my alma mater after I receive my master's degree. Would…would you consider my application?"

Woods laid a firm hand on Shane's shoulder and smiled again. "Let's consider the job applied for, son. I happen to know that there will be an opening in the faculty next fall that's right down your line. I'll tell you right now. The job is yours. We'll work on the details next spring."

"Thank you, sir!" Shane said, shaking the president's hand. "Thank you very much! My wife is going to be very happy when I tell her about this!"

TWELVE

By February 1, 1861, six more states had pulled out of the Union: Texas, Florida, Mississippi, Georgia, Alabama, and Louisiana. The seven states were in agreement. Northerners were interfering with the Southern practice of "that particular institution," *slavery.* The seceding states drew up a proclamation, which stated in part: "The people of the North have denounced as sinful the institution of slavery; they have permitted the open establishment among them of abolition societies, and have united in the election of a man to the high office of President of the United States whose opinions and purposes are hostile to slavery."

Even though he had not yet taken office, the president-elect continued to work at trying to bring the Southerners back to the Union; President James Buchanan stood by and did nothing. Lincoln pled with Buchanan to meet with Confederate leaders and do all he could to break down the barriers between the Northern and Southern states. Buchanan turned a deaf ear.

Lincoln then began to contact individual congressmen, attempting to persuade them to negotiate with Southern leaders. Some of them made a few feeble efforts, but they were ineffective.

On February 8, delegates from the seven seceded states met at

Montgomery, Alabama, and founded the Confederate States of America. The next day, the congress of delegates elected Jefferson Davis as their president. Among the plans made to protect the security of their new nation was the seizure of the coastal forts and navy yards in the southern harbors. Jefferson Davis immediately bolstered his military forces to make these seizures a reality.

On March 4, 1861 Lincoln took the oath of office. His inaugural address made his position on secession crystal clear as he spoke to the Southerners: "In your hands and not in mine, is the momentous issue of civil war. No state, upon its own mere action, can lawfully secede from the Union. I shall take care, as the Constitution itself expressly enjoins upon me, that the laws of the Union be faithfully executed in all the states. The power confided to me will be used to hold, occupy, and possess the property and places belonging to the United States government."

Davis's forces had moved swiftly, and by the time Lincoln was inaugurated, only two Southern forts remained under the Federal flag—Fort Sumter at Charleston, South Carolina, and Fort Pickens at Pensacola, Florida. The Union commanders at the forts that were now in Confederate hands had given up and left without a fight, feeling that holding their positions was not worth the risk of civil war. President James Buchanan had concurred, agreeing that they should lay down their arms and peacefully surrender their posts.

At Fort Sumter, however, tension grew between the militant citizens of Charleston and the small Union force stationed there. Major Robert Anderson, Union commander at Sumter, was determined to hold the fort.

Spring came, and along with green grass, budding trees, and flowers came ominous clouds of war.

On Saturday morning, April 13, Shane and Charolette Donovan were sitting at the breakfast table. Shane was in his work clothes, ready to head for the lumber mill. Charolette was still in her robe and slippers, enjoying a second cup of coffee.

Shane had the previous day's edition of the *Brunswick Times* spread before him, and he was shaking his head.

"What is it, darling?" Charolette asked.

Shane raised his eyes to meet hers. "Charly, it's not looking good at all down South. Real trouble is brewing at Fort Sumter."

"The citizens making threats to take the fort?"

"Much worse. Jefferson Davis has General Pierre Beauregard commanding a group of warships at Charleston Harbor. They've got the fort surrounded, and on Thursday, Beauregard demanded that Major Anderson and his men evacuate the fort. Major Anderson has refused to give in. He's willing to stand and fight."

"If Beauregard fires on the fort, we'll be at war, won't we?"

"Yes, we will."

Shane folded the newspaper, laid it on the table, and shoved his chair back. As he stood up, Charolette set down her coffee cup and rose to her feet. She moved to him, and they kissed long and fervently. Shane took his work hat off a peg, dropped it on his head, and the two of them walked to the front door of the small cottage, each with an arm around the other. Shane opened the door, kissed her once more, told her he loved her, and headed across the porch.

The walk to the mill was only about a half-mile. When he was almost to the corner, he turned and looked back. Charolette always watched him from the porch until he passed from view. He waved, and she waved back, throwing him a kiss. He was starting around the corner when he saw a crowd gathered three blocks away near Brunswick's business district. Mike O'Hanlon was running toward him from the same direction.

Shane broke into a run, and as the best friends drew abreast, Mike gasped, "Shane, it happened!"

"What happened?"

"The Confederates bombarded Fort Sumter yesterday, and Major Anderson and his men fought back! We're at war with the

Confederates! The message just came on the telegraph to the *Brunswick Times* from Washington. Their employees are on the streets shouting the news."

Shane's face went white. "I knew it. Charly and I were just talking about it. I told her Major Anderson wouldn't back down."

"Makes me feel sick all over."

"Yeah, me too. The Stars and Stripes are under fire by Southern traitors. Well, guess I better go tell Charly."

Another telegraph message arrived at the Brunswick newspaper late that afternoon, informing them that Fort Sumter had been under heavy fire since dawn that morning, but Major Anderson and his men were still holding firm.

The editor of the *Brunswick Times* ordered his staff to prepare a special edition, putting the story under bold headlines on the front page. The edition was on the streets and in the hands of Brunswick's citizens by 7:00 P.M.

More news came on Sunday, and was spread by word of mouth, since the newspaper offices were closed. The editor had stayed at the office all day to receive any word that might come from his sources in Washington.

By midday Monday, April 15, news had come to the people of Brunswick that in order to save the lives of his men, Major Anderson had surrendered Fort Sumter to General Beauregard on Sunday. The old flag had been hauled down and was in the hands of the traitors.

The first-hour class at Bowdoin College was canceled, and all students, faculty, and college employees gathered solemnly in the chapel. President Leonard Woods stood before the crowd and told them the latest news. With dejection in his voice, he said, "I have asked our Professor Joshua Chamberlain to address us on an impromptu basis in this dark hour. I have the utmost confidence in Professor Chamberlain and feel that he is best equipped to speak to us at this time."

Woods stepped back from the pulpit and gestured toward Chamberlain. "Professor..."

Chamberlain stepped before the crowd, cleared his throat, and said, "Ladies and gentlemen, I am an American. I love my country, and if some transatlantic force were to attempt to invade these sacred shores, I would be among the very first to take up arms against it."

There was a chorus of amens from the crowd.

"We have all been stunned to learn that the Confederacy has been so bold as to fire on United States property. We do not yet know if there are casualties amongst Major Anderson and his men, but I pray none have been killed or seriously injured. By this deplorable act, the flag of the nation has been insulted, the honor and authority of the Union has been defied, and the integrity and existence of the people of the United States of America have been assailed in open and bitter military attack. If I know our president as I think I do, this kind of aggression will not be taken lightly. Mr. Lincoln will call for retaliation. Civil war is inevitable."

Both men and women were wiping tears. Chamberlain turned to the president, who sat behind him on the platform.

"Dr. Woods, I believe the best thing we can do at this point is to break this crowd up into small groups and have a session of prayer. We must ask God to give wisdom to President Lincoln and our national leaders."

Woods stepped to the pulpit, laid a hand on Chamberlain's shoulder, and said to the crowd, "Let us do as our esteemed professor has suggested."

A cloud of gloom hovered over Brunswick, Maine, as well as over the entire Union. People moved about in every hamlet, town, and city as if they were in a daze.

On Tuesday, April 16, news came that President Lincoln had issued a plea for seventy-five thousand men to enlist in the Northern army. The Confederacy must be put down, and Lincoln felt if he could add that many volunteers to the existing U.S. army, victory could be achieved within three months.

Over three hundred men from Brunswick enlisted, including several single upperclassmen of Bowdoin College. They were lauded by President Woods for their patriotism and were told that upon their return, special classes would be held so they could catch up with their studies.

The volunteers from Brunswick were scheduled to join several hundred other volunteers from the state of Maine at Portland to be transported by ship to an undesignated port in Maryland. They would then march to a military camp set up near Washington, D.C.

All Maine volunteers were to board the ship at Portland Harbor on Saturday afternoon, April 27, at 4:00 P.M. Brunswick's volunteers were set to march out of their town at 9:00 A.M. for the twenty-one-mile hike to Portland. Brunswick's town council put the word out that all the town's citizens and those of the surrounding area should gather on Brunswick's main street to give them a proper send-off.

The crowd gathered, with many waving American flags as the volunteers assembled to begin the march. The street was lined with cheering people of all ages. Every business had closed for the occasion, and all employees were expected to be on hand.

The Bowdoin College band joined with the Brunswick High School band to play a military march. Flags waved and the people cheered as the Maine Volunteers marched southward out of the town, carrying what guns and ammunition they owned.

When they had passed from view, the crowd dispersed, with the people discussing the war and agreeing that it would be over in less than three months.

Joshua Chamberlain, Shane Donovan, and Mike and Lewis O'Hanlon were talking together. Chamberlain rubbed his heavy mustache and said, "I'd like to be going with them. It would feel good to pay those Rebels back for what they did to Fort Sumter."

"Me too," Shane and Mike said together.

"Time you gentlemen could make it to Washington, it would all be over," Lewis said. "I think Mr. Lincoln is right. Won't take long to put those traitors down on their knees begging for mercy."

"I'm sure you're right, Mr. O'Hanlon," Shane said. "But I'd like to be there to see and hear it."

Graduation day at Bowdoin College came the third week of May. Shane received his master's degree, and the next day he was given a contract as instructor in first-year English, world literature, and American history for the next school year.

Late in May, visions of a quick end to the war began to vanish. There was news every day of Confederate resistance, resulting in skirmishes between Union and Confederate forces in many parts of Virginia. Before the month had ended, President Lincoln called for forty thousand more volunteers.

In June there was a bloody battle at Rich Mountain, Virginia, and the Confederates took a solid whipping. People of the North were again optimistic that the war would be ended inside of three months.

But news of more skirmishes came, not all of them victories for the Union. Northerners once again began to wonder if victory was going to be as simple as had been thought at the outset of the war.

Then came devastation. In mid-July, a fierce, bloody battle took place near Manassas, Virginia, along Bull Run Creek. The Federals were handed an embarrassing rout. The Rebels had come on so strong that hundreds of Yankee soldiers fled in panic from the battlefield.

The Union army returned to Washington like whipped dogs with their tails between their legs. There was no question that the War Between the States was going to last much longer than the Federals had figured.

There were more minor battles and skirmishes from Virginia to Missouri in August and early September, and the Southerners held strong.

When school opened in mid-September, Joshua Chamberlain

was first to welcome Shane Donovan to the faculty. Shane was thrilled with his position, but was playfully harassed by Mike O'Hanlon about really being the old man.

As October came, President Lincoln called for more volunteers. Many volunteer regiments were forming in Maine and heading south to get into the war.

One Sunday afternoon in early October, the young Donovans and the young O'Hanlons were at the Chamberlain home, where they had eaten Sunday dinner. While the women were in the kitchen doing dishes and cleaning up, the Chamberlain children took naps. The men were in the parlor, discussing the Civil War.

"I don't know how much longer I'll be able to stand this," Joshua Chamberlain said. "It's hard to sit here in Maine and read about what's going on down south. I feel like it's my duty to join up and do my part."

"That's exactly how I feel, sir," Shane said. "I hate the thought of leaving Charly, but the longer this conflict goes on, the more I want to get into the thick of it."

"I don't want to leave Ashley, either," Mike said. "But there's a job to be done, and I should be in a blue uniform doing my duty."

"I don't have any military experience," Shane said, "but I could learn. I'm pretty good with a musket when it comes to hunting deer."

"Same for me," Mike said. "I've killed many a deer, but I've never carried a gun with the intent of killing human beings. But that's the way it has to be in war."

"I'd have to learn, too," Chamberlain said. "The only military experience I've had is a couple years at military academy in my teens. My brothers went there, too."

"I remember you mentioning your brothers back in the days when you taught our Sunday school class," Shane said. "You have three, if memory serves me. And…one sister?"

"Good memory. I'm the oldest. Horace came next, when I was six. Two years after that, Sarah was born. That was 1836. Then John, and the baby is brother Tom—Thomas Davee. He still lives at home near Brewer with our parents. He's thirteen years younger than I. Just turned twenty."

"They all live in the Brewer area?" Mike asked.

"Actually, Horace and Sarah live in Bangor with their families. John is still single. He lives in a small house between Bangor and Brewer."

The women entered the room, and the men stood up. When the ladies had seated themselves next to their husbands, the men sat down.

"Just when do you gentlemen plan to join the Union army?" Fannie asked.

"Oh, we don't have any plans," Joshua said. "We were just saying we'd like to get into the fight."

"So we heard. We weren't sure if this was just man talk, or if you were making plans we were going to hear about sometime soon."

Ashley laid a hand on her husband's arm and said to the group, "I hate the thought of Mike having to go off to war, but it will be his duty—and the duty of many thousands more—if this war isn't ended soon."

"That's what frightens me," Fannie said. "I know Josh's father has always wanted him to be a soldier. There are many soldiers amongst his ancestors."

"Well, I'm not going to be signing up unless it becomes a necessity," Joshua said.

"Me either," Shane said. "For right now, at least, I'm going to stay here and teach."

When the Donovans arrived home after church on Sunday night, Charolette began to fix them a light snack in the kitchen. Shane was seated at the table, and Charolette was at the cupboard, slicing bread, with her back to him.

"Shane...?"

"Yes, my love."

"The thought of sending you off to war puts ice in my blood. I can't bear to think about it. Oh, I hope it will be over soon."

Her back was still toward him, and tears had surfaced. She felt strong arms slide around her, and he kissed the back of her neck. She laid the knife down, turned, and wrapped her arms around his neck.

"Honey, I have to ask you," Shane said. "If this war does go on and more soldiers are needed...how would you take it if I signed up?"

There was a long silence.

"Darling, thousands of wives have already had to send their husbands off to that awful war. If...if you come to the place where you feel you should put on a uniform, how could I selfishly ask you not to go? I will back you all the way, Shane. Not without a heavy heart, you understand, but I will stand beside you in your decision."

Shane kissed the tip of her nose and said, "Sweetheart, you're the greatest wife a man ever had. I love you so. I would lay down my life to protect you from the Confederates if they invaded our land."

Charolette kissed her husband soundly and said, "Shane, I love you more than I ever realized a woman could love a man."

On Monday, at the Leprechaun Shoe and Boot Manufacturing Company, Lewis O'Hanlon was at his desk when he looked up to see Buster Kilrain standing at the office door, which was open.

"Top o' the mornin' to you, Lewis," Buster said. "Got a minute?"

"Sure. Come on in."

Buster approached the desk and said, "I've got something heavy on me heart, Lewis. I need to talk to you 'boot it."

"Of course. Sit down."

Buster took a seat in front of the desk and said, "Well, me friend, it's 'boot this here Civil War. As you know, ol' Buster Kilrain was a soldier in the Irish Army. I've seen combat and have a couple scars on me body to prove it."

Lewis leaned on the desk, looked Buster in the eye, and said,

"Buster, you're in your late forties. Let the younger men do the fighting. Besides, with the new contract from the government to produce thousands of boots and shoes for the army, I need you here worse than McClellan needs you on some battlefield."

"But Lewis, the army needs me fightin' experience. So I'm a little past forty-five. Men are signin' up who are in their seventies. If we don't get this war won, you'll be makin' shoes and boots for Rebel feet…at the point of a gun."

Lewis eased back in his chair, sighed, and said, "How about giving it a little more time? Let's see what happens the next few months, okay? I understand an old soldier wanting to get back into uniform, but let it ride a little longer. Please? I really need you here."

Buster rose from the chair, grinned, and said, "All right, me friend. Since it's you askin', I'll give it a little longer."

"Thank you. Now if things turn for the worse in the war and needing to fight really gets under your hide, come and talk to me again."

"I surely will. You can, ah, bet your boots on it. Pardon the pun."

THIRTEEN

W hile the Civil War proceeded in the South, the name of
Dwight Lyman Moody, a Congregational preacher from
Northfield, Massachusetts, was on the lips of Christians all
over the North.

The twenty-four-year-old evangelist had been converted to
Christ out of religious skepticism at seventeen years of age while
working as a shoe salesman in Boston. Moody was now making his
home in Chicago, and was holding great evangelistic crusades in the
larger Northern cities, seeing thousands coming to the Lord Jesus
Christ for salvation.

Moody was closing out a series of evangelistic meetings in his
hometown of Northfield on Friday, October 25, and Dr. George
Adams had him scheduled to preach at First Parish Congregational
Church in both morning and evening services on Sunday, October
27.

Placards on the walls of the church and of the main buildings at
Bowdoin College announced Moody's coming. There was excitement all over the Brunswick area, and Christians invited lost loved
ones and friends to the services to hear the fiery young preacher.

When the big day arrived, the stout-bodied evangelist thrilled the standing-room-only crowds with powerful, straight-forward Bible preaching both morning and evening. Over a hundred citizens of Brunswick and the surrounding area responded to Moody's impassioned pleas to come to Christ.

After the Sunday evening service, many people stood in line to meet Moody and shake his hand. He was at the front doors of the church vestibule with Dr. and Mrs. Adams, and the line stretched all the way down the center aisle of the large auditorium to the platform. The Chamberlains, the Donovans, and the O'Hanlons were in the middle of the line, which was moving very slowly. They understood why by the time they reached the vestibule. Dwight L. Moody was a warm and personable man. He took time to ask each person if they were saved. If anyone answered no, Moody quickly turned him over to the pastor, who had counselors standing by to take him aside and lead him to Christ.

Ashley leaned close to Fannie and said, "Looks like your father knew that Mr. Moody does evangelistic work at the door, too."

"Yes. Papa hurried him away this morning, but Mr. Moody insisted on meeting the people at the door tonight. I heard Papa telling the counselors before the service this evening to be ready for this."

When the Chamberlains finally reached the evangelist, he greeted the children first, then shook hands with Fannie and Joshua.

"Pastor's daughter, eh?" Moody said, while shaking Fannie's hand. "I love preacher's kids. How long have you been saved?"

"Since I was eleven, Mr. Moody. And what a joy to know Jesus all these years!"

"Amen!" Moody then gripped Joshua's hand and asked, "How about you, preacher's son-in-law? How long have you been saved?"

"Since I was sixteen. I got saved up in Bangor under preaching just like yours."

"Praise the Lord!" Moody said.

Moody also questioned the Donovans and the O'Hanlons as he shook their hands. He was happy to know they could give solid, clear-cut testimonies of their salvation.

"Mr. Moody, I'm one of the instructors at Bowdoin," Shane said. "Are you going to be preaching in chapel tomorrow?"

"Sorry, but I can't. Dr. Woods asked me to, but I have to catch a train in Portland early in the morning. I'm now doing extensive work with the Young Men's Christian Association in Chicago, and I have to be there for a meeting Tuesday morning."

"Well, sir, I'd love to hear you some more. That was great preaching today. The Lord bless you."

"And may He bless you too, Mr. Donovan."

The three couples went to the Chamberlain home, where Shane and Mike played with the children while the women prepared a snack. Grace and Wyllys were fed, then put to bed.

While the couples were eating, the discussion turned to the Civil War. President Lincoln was calling for more volunteers.

"The war is a long way from over unless some miracle takes place," Fannie said. "Our husbands must do their part if it drags on much longer. I'd like for us to ask the Lord to give us wives the grace we'll need if our husbands have to enlist."

"I'll vote for that," Charolette said.

"Me too," Ashley said, taking a tight hold on Mike's hand.

Fall turned to winter, and severe weather set in. Maine winters were notoriously cold and snowy, and January 1862 was worse than normal. While the people of Maine battled the elements, the Civil War went on in the South. President Lincoln called for yet more volunteers, and more regiments formed in Maine and headed for Washington by railroad from Portland.

One day in late March, Ashley stood by as Dr. James Holladay—family physician of both the Donovans and the O'Hanlons—sat on the bedside of Charolette Donovan, listening to her lungs with a stethoscope. Her face was pale and drawn. Holladay finished listening and dropped the twin prongs of the stethoscope around his neck.

"What do you think, Doctor?" Ashley asked.

Charolette put a hand to her mouth, coughed three times, and set her eyes on the physician.

"Her cold is better. I'd be worried if it wasn't after seven days. Her lungs are not nearly as congested as they were a week ago, and her temperature is almost down to normal. I'm a little concerned that the cough medicine I gave her hasn't done a better job relieving her cough, though." He pulled a dark-colored bottle from his black bag and looked at Charolette. "Let's put you on this. I think it'll work better than the other." Holladay rose to his feet and stuffed his stethoscope in the bag.

"You've been here with her every day, haven't you?" he said, turning to Ashley.

"Yes, sir."

"You're a very good friend, I'll say that."

"I'm her best friend, Doctor. And I'll be here every day until she's on her feet and feeling well again."

"I'll be back to check on you in another week," Holladay said to Charolette. "Of course, if the cough doesn't get better, let me know. I expect, though, that this new medicine will clear it up."

The front door was heard to open and close.

Charolette coughed again and said, "That'll be Shane."

Still in his heavy overcoat and hat, Shane appeared quickly at the bedroom door, smiled at his wife, then at Ashley, and said, "Hello, Dr. Holladay. How's she doing?"

"Her lungs have cleared up a lot, Shane, but her cough is still bad. I'm changing her cough medicine, hoping the new stuff will help her."

"Good. I want her out of that bed real soon." He winked at Charolette. "Ashley's been cooking for us every day since Charolette got sick, and I don't know how Mike makes it eating that horrible stuff all the time."

Ashley laughed and cuffed him playfully on the shoulder. "If I'd left the cooking to you, Charolette would be in her grave by now!"

The doctor chortled, shouldered into his coat, and clapped on his hat. "I'll leave the fighting to you two. I'm a man of peace."

In mid-April, the Chamberlains invited the Donovans and the O'Hanlons to their home for supper. Joshua's brother John had stopped for a couple of days to visit the family before leaving Maine for Washington, D.C.

As they sat at the supper table, Shane looked at the younger Chamberlain and said, "John, the professor tells me you graduated from Bangor Seminary last year."

"That's right."

"So what are you doing now?"

"I've been doing supply preaching in churches all over Maine. Many are those Josh has gotten me into because he knows the pastors. I haven't settled just what part of the ministry the Lord wants me in yet, but with the war on, it's hard to settle on anything. I've been praying about signing up with one of the Maine regiments, and I was about to do that a couple of weeks ago when the Lord opened a door of special service for me."

"Oh, what's that?" Mike said.

"Have you heard of an organization called the Christian Commission?"

"Can't say that I have."

John ran his eyes over the group. "Any of you?"

Every head was shaking no.

"Well, it's fairly new. By the way, Josh, you need to tell Dr. Adams about it. We need the church's support."

"So this Christian Commission you're going to tell us about is funded by support from churches?" Joshua asked.

"Mostly, yes. We do have some wealthy people in Bangor who send us money."

"What does your Christian Commission do, John?" Charolette said.

"We go to the battlefields and tend to the physical and spiritual needs of the soldiers. We distribute Bibles and Christian literature, along with what fruit we can lay our hands on. We write letters home for wounded men who are unable to do so…and just work at cheering up the troops."

"So you're on your way south to the battlefields?" Ashley asked.

"That's right."

"Will you be in danger?" Charolette asked.

"You might say so. Couple of our men have been hit with shrapnel when cannonballs have hit close. We even had one shot by a sniper. Only got a slight wound, though."

Charolette started to speak again, but went into a coughing spell and left the table. As she went to a back room, John looked at Shane. "She have this cough very long?"

"No, just a few weeks. Started with a cold. The cold's gone, but the cough isn't. Nothing the doctor gives her seems to work. He says she'll just have to wear it out."

"I'm afraid it's going to wear her out first," Ashley said. "I can tell she's lost some weight."

"You fellows ought to join the Commission," John said. "Good way to serve your country."

"I think it's fine if that's what the Lord puts on your heart, John," Joshua said. "But if I join anything, it's going to be the Union army. I want to fight those Rebels."

"Me too," Shane said.

"And me," Mike said.

Charolette returned to her place at the table and said, "Forgive me, all of you. I just can't seem to get rid of this miserable cough."

"There's nothing to forgive, Charolette," Fannie said, reaching over and patting her hand. "We've all had coughs. We know you can't help it."

The Civil War continued, and there was no end in sight. The Confederate army had taken a greater toll on the Union troops than any of the military leaders of the North had ever dreamed. General Robert E. Lee was proving to be an able leader, and he had some hardy and intelligent leaders under him, such as Thomas J. "Stonewall" Jackson, James Longstreet, and Pierre G. T. Beauregard.

At the same time, President Lincoln was having problems with his military leadership. There was conflict between Lincoln and his top general, George B. McClellan. In Lincoln's way of thinking, McClellan was not aggressive enough. McClellan insisted that he was simply a careful tactician who moved methodically in order to lose as few men as possible.

On July 1, 1862, Lincoln issued a plea to the governors of the Northern states for 300,000 more men to enlist in the Union army. Governor Israel Washburn of Maine filled the state's newspapers, asking for volunteers to fill the state's quota of eight regiments. Each regiment would be "one thousand strong," according to the governor.

Joshua Chamberlain could stand it no longer. His conscience was bothering him more and more. Other men had left their families to serve their country, and it was time for him to get into the fight.

But first, he must obtain a leave of absence from the college. The board of trustees, willing to part with a few men for the Union's cause, was giving leaves of absence quite readily to instructors. It was different with those of professor status. A man of that stature was more important to the college than to the military.

There was, Chamberlain knew, a legitimate way for him to obtain the leave. After two years of pressure and persuasion from President Leonard Woods and the board of trustees, Chamberlain had agreed to give up his professor of rhetoric position and take the chair of professor of modern languages of Europe. The trustees had offered him a great inducement: a two-year leave of absence to travel Europe whenever he chose, expenses for his family to travel with him, plus regular salary and a $500 bonus.

Chamberlain had planned to take the leave of absence beginning in the fall of 1861. But the war came, and he decided to put off the trip till the war was over. Now, he still had the leave coming, and though there would be no salary or bonus, he could lawfully be gone for the two years. Certainly the war would be over by then. He would talk to Dr. Woods about it.

Chamberlain was sure he could quickly raise the "thousand strong" needed for a regiment. He knew Shane and Mike were on the verge of enlisting, and so was one of his favored students, a single man named Ellis Spear. Ellis had spoken to him on several occasions about enlisting, the last time just two days ago.

And then there was his brother Tom who had come to see him and his family in late June. Tom was also on the verge of enlisting. With Shane, Mike, Ellis, and Tom eager to go to war, they would be good recruiters. With their help, and the help of others who would catch the fever, he was sure he could put a thousand men together in a matter of weeks.

Dr. Woods and the trustees agreed to the leave of absence on July 13. The next day, Chamberlain wrote to Governor Washburn offering his services to the army. Within two days, he had a favorable answer from Washburn and an invitation to come immediately to Augusta and see him. The letter stated that Washburn was pleased at Chamberlain's personal enthusiasm and was encouraged that he felt he could collect enough men for a full regiment.

During the two days it took to hear back from the governor, Chamberlain had told Fannie his plan and received her backing. He also told Shane, Mike, and Ellis and sent a wire to Tom. Charolette and Ashley gave the same backing to their husbands that Fannie had.

By the afternoon of the second day, Joshua Chamberlain's recruiters had done their work, and over a hundred of his present and former students stated that they were ready to sign up in his regiment.

With the letter in hand, Chamberlain rode a fast horse to Augusta and was warmly welcomed by the governor. Washburn offered Chamberlain a colonel's commission and command of the regiment. Chamberlain was flattered, but told the governor he did not feel qualified since he had no military experience. He would rather start lower under a man who had combat experience and learn soldiering from him.

Washburn told him perhaps he could get Colonel Adelbert Ames to head up the new regiment. Ames, a Regular Army officer and Mainer from Rockland, had been seriously wounded at the Battle of Bull Run in July of 1861. He had now recuperated and was desirous of returning to the war. Washburn would contact him. The governor asked Chamberlain to keep working in the meantime to recruit men for the regiment, which Chamberlain assured him he would do.

Tom Chamberlain arrived in response to his brother's call and went to work with Joshua, Shane, Mike, Ellis, and several other men to sign up more recruits. While other Maine regiments were being put together, those who backed Chamberlain worked the hardest. Each new man contacted several others. Proud and patriotic Maine men, eager to serve their country and their state, signed up—farmers, clerks, lumbermen, storekeepers, lawyers, builders, school teachers, fishermen, merchant sailors, and college and seminary students.

Two days later, Governor Washburn summoned Joshua Chamberlain to his office in Augusta. When Chamberlain entered his office, Washburn shook his hand and said, "Well, Professor, I've got good news. Colonel Ames has signed up. He'll be your commander, and he's elated to be part of a Maine regiment."

"Good! I'm happy to hear it. And you'll be glad to know, sir, that we now have over four hundred men signed up. The recruiting is going well."

"Excellent, Lieutenant Colonel Chamberlain! You're doing a great job."

Joshua's eyes widened. "Lieutenant colonel, sir?"

"That's right. At least you will be officially in another few days."

"Why, thank you, Governor. I figured I might be made a captain, but you surprise me."

"You recall, my friend, that I was willing to make you a colonel, but you disqualified yourself. Since you'll be second in command under Colonel Ames, you should be a lieutenant colonel. I'll be appointing other officers according to how well they do in signing up men for the regiment."

"That's a fair way to do it, sir."

"I've got men working at the moment on a training camp for all the new Maine recruits," Washburn said. "It's on farm land just east of Portland. The farmer is Glenn Mason. He has generously offered to let us use twenty acres for training purposes, so I'm going to call it Camp Mason. Colonel Ames is going to take charge of the camp, as well as being commander of the Twentieth Maine."

"The Twentieth Maine, sir? That's our regiment?"

"Yes. You'll be traveling south with the Sixth, Seventh, Eleventh, Sixteenth, Seventeenth, Eighteenth, and Nineteenth regiments to give those Rebels their due. We're getting boots and shoes from the Leprechaun Company there in your town, and we've got caps and uniforms being hastily made by several clothing manufacturers. The men will have to train in their own clothes and footwear, but we should have sufficient uniforms and footwear by the time all the regiments are ready to head south."

"Sounds like we've got the wheels rolling, sir."

"Have to. We've got to do our part to give President Lincoln the troops he's calling for. We've got to put those Rebels down and end this awful war."

"Yes, sir. I'd like to get it over so all of us can go on with our lives."

"Well put, son. Check back here with me next week…Tuesday, let's say. By then we should have the grounds at Camp Mason ready, and Colonel Ames can begin his training program."

* * *

Charolette Donovan sat in Dr. James Holladay's office, with her husband beside her. She had almost gotten over the cough, but now it was coming back.

"So what do you think, Doctor?" Shane asked. "She doesn't have a cold this time."

"The only thing I can figure, Shane, is that about the time she would've gotten over the cough from the cold, we entered pollen and mold season. Her cough is from an allergy, or maybe from several allergies. When we get into fall and the first frost comes, this cough will clear up, I'm sure."

"I hope you're right, Doctor. She's really suffering with this thing."

"I just got some new cough syrup in. Comes highly recommended by the American Medical Association. It's got nothing habit-forming in it, but I believe it'll relieve the cough a great deal and ease the pain in her lungs."

Training for the Maine troops began at Camp Mason on August 14. Colonel Ames was a tall, slender, dark-haired man of twenty-six, and a graduate of West Point. He was all business, and military through and through. He immediately laid down strong disciplinary measures and began whipping the men into shape. Ames's military demeanor made the men all the more eager to fight Rebels. Their enthusiasm gained momentum as new recruits reported for training camp every day.

The married men from Brunswick returned home at night, traveling back and forth in wagons. On a Friday evening in the third week of August, Shane Donovan slid out of the wagon, told the other men he would see them the next morning, and wearily made his way toward the front door of his cottage. It had been a hard day.

Before he reached the porch, the door came open, and

Charolette appeared, smiling at him with love in her eyes. It bothered Shane that she was so pale, though the latest cough medicine Dr. Holladay had given her had helped. It also bothered him that she had not gained back any of the weight she had lost.

"How's it been today?" he asked as he took her in his arms.

"How's what been?" she asked, kissing the tip of his grimy chin.

"You know…the cough."

"Oh, maybe a little better." She kissed his dirty chin again.

He laughed. "Honey, you'll get mud in your mouth doing that."

"So?" she said, kissing his grimy cheek this time. "It's your mud, so it's precious mud."

"You're silly," he said, and planted a kiss on her lips. When he released her, he grinned and said, "You ought to see your face. I put a big ol' smudge on it."

"Then I'll never wash it off." She turned her head away and covered her mouth as she coughed.

After Shane had bathed and combed his hair, they ate supper together.

"Does Colonel Ames still have you teaching men how to handle a musket?" Charolette asked.

"Mm-hmm. Tomorrow he's going to begin teaching us how to fight with bayonets."

"Oh, how awful! Shane, I don't like this. I wish this war was over. I can't bear to think of you out there on some battlefield with some Rebel trying to kill you with a bayonet. That's even worse than the idea of bullets flying."

"It's all part of it," he sighed. "War is war. Colonel Chamberlain told me that Mike and Tom and Ellis and I are going to start learning how to fire handguns."

"Really? Why?"

"Because officers wear handguns, and it looks like the four of us are going to be made officers because of how many men we've recruited."

"Well, I'm proud of you. How many men are signed up now?"

"As of yesterday morning, there were nine hundred and four. I know some more came in today, but I didn't hear any final count. We'll have our thousand strong in a few more days, I'm sure."

Charolette suddenly grew quiet. Tears filled her eyes, and her lips began to tremble.

"Aw, sweetheart," Shane said, leaving his chair. He rounded the table and put his arms around her. "Don't cry, Charly." He kissed her cheek. "I'll be home from that ol' war before you can bat an eye. Then we can go on with our lives. I'll be back teaching, and we'll have us a passel of little Shanes and little Charlys running all over this place."

FOURTEEN

The Maine recruits at Camp Mason began to receive heavy shipments of shoes and boots on August 18. Uniforms and caps started arriving in Portland by train on August 22, the same day the Twentieth Maine Regiment attained its "thousand strong." Colonel Ames placed the continuing influx of men into other regiments.

The hot August sun beat down on the camp as men were being drilled at one spot, while at other locations, they were learning hand-to-hand combat and musketry, and young officers were being trained with handguns.

Lieutenant Colonel Joshua Lawrence Chamberlain had caught on to bayonet fighting quickly and was now instructing new recruits in the art. Chamberlain worked with each man about ten minutes at a time. He stopped to rest a few minutes every half hour, then was back with a bayoneted musket in his hands, training another man.

During one half-hour break, he moved within the shade of a tree, took a deep draw on a water jug, and sat down. He was just leaning his head back against the trunk when he saw the stout form of a man with carrot-red hair standing over him.

"Top o' the mornin' to you, Colonel," Buster Kilrain said.

"It's afternoon, Buster." Chamberlain said.

"Aye, so 'tis," Kilrain said, glancing at the sun. "Anyway, nice to see you."

"Just what are *you* doing here?"

"Now, what do ye think a soldier would be a doin' at an army camp, me friend? I'm gettin' ready to go to war."

"You are, huh?"

"Aye."

"And what regiment did they put you in?"

"Well, they haven't yet, y'see. In fact, your commander doesn't even know I'm here. I figured to see you first."

"Buster, are you sure you want to do this?"

"Sure as God in heaven made little green apples."

"And Lewis O'Hanlon turned you loose to join the army?"

"Aye. With a little persuasion, ye understand."

"But you're what—forty-eight years old?"

"Forty-*seven,* I'll have ye know. They're signin' 'em up lots older than me all over the U.S."

"But not in Maine. The oldest man in our outfit is forty-five."

"So? What's two years? An' I bet I c'n whip any one o' them forty-five-year olds. Probably c'n whip 'em all at the same time."

Chamberlain laughed. "Okay, you've convinced me. Go on and tell Colonel Ames you want in."

"But, I don't want in just any regiment. I want in yours."

"We already have our quota, Buster. We were told to sign up a thousand, and we did. A 'thousand strong,' just like the governor said."

Buster leaned down low, looked the lieutenant colonel straight in the eye, and said, "Now, Joshua, you're the second in command in the Twentieth. With that much power, certainly ye c'n make it a thousand-and-*one* strong."

"Well, I could probably swing it."

"And somethin' else."

"Yes?" Chamberlain rose to his feet.

"I've got army experience. Plenty of it."

"Yes, I know."

"Now, I was a sergeant when I mustered out o' the Irish army. Seems to me like I ought to be a sergeant in this army, don't it to you?"

"Well, I'll see what I can do. Come with me." They walked together across the grassy field toward Colonel Ames's tent.

"Son, don't take this wrong," Buster said, "but you look a bit clumsy out there a-teachin' them boys bayonet fightin'."

"Really?"

"No offense, now, but you're goin' at it with your feet too close together…and y'need to hold the musket with your left hand closer to the muzzle."

"So you're experienced at bayonet fighting, are you?"

"Aye. Ye might say that."

Vivian "Buster" Kilrain was inducted into the Maine militia, assigned to the Twentieth Regiment at Joshua Chamberlain's request, and made a sergeant by Colonel Ames on the spot. Twenty minutes later, Chamberlain was sitting in the shade of his favorite tree watching Buster train the young recruits in bayonet fighting.

With sweat pouring off him, the forty-seven-year-old Irishman glanced at the man in the shade and said, "Me and me big mouth!"

The rest of the boots and shoes were there by August 27, and the remaining uniforms and caps arrived the next day. Governor Israel Washburn set departure date for Saturday, August 30. He had notified the railroad several days earlier to be ready on the last weekend of the month. The governor was assured that several trains would be at Portland, ready to haul the troops. One of the trains would have ample flat-bed stock cars to carry the horses the army was providing for the officers.

Among the officers appointed by Governor Washburn were Captain Ellis Spear, Captain Shane Donovan, Lieutenant Mike

O'Hanlon, and Lieutenant Tom Chamberlain.

While the officers were at the tent where their uniforms were to be fitted, Mike leaned close to Shane and said, "So you outrank me, eh, captain? I didn't think you came up with that many more recruits than I did."

"Well, tell you what, sonny…Governor Washburn and Colonel Ames took something else into consideration."

"Oh? And what was that?"

"They know that older men are much more mature than younger men, and can handle a higher rank and the tough decisions that go with it."

Mike grabbed his stomach and said, "I think I'm going to be sick!"

The training camp was quiet on Friday, August 29. Those men from farther upstate had already told their families good-bye, and sat around now in the shade, talking in low tones. Those men who lived close enough to spend the day with their families did so. Though they were eager to get into the fight, there was a good deal of sadness.

At the Chamberlain home, Joshua packed his gear, then played with the children for a long time. When they went down for their naps, he sat with Fannie on the parlor couch and held her in his arms. They talked of old times and of their plans for the future. They hoped that this time President Lincoln had enough troops to swarm the enemy and bring surrender. They prayed that Joshua would be home soon and that life would return to normal.

At the O'Hanlon home, Mike and Ashley spent the day reminiscing about their childhood and marveling at how the Lord had brought them together as husband and wife. Ashley did her best to maintain her composure. She did fine until late in the afternoon. They were standing at the parlor window watching the sun drop below the treetops on the west side of the street. Mike was behind her, with his arms around her. He heard her sniffle and felt her body stiffen.

"Now, I thought we agreed there wouldn't be any tears," he said, turning her around to face him.

"I knew when I agreed to it, I wouldn't be able to keep from it. O Mike, I'm so scared!"

"Now Ashley, we've got to trust the Lord in all of this. He never makes a mistake. If He should let a bullet—"

"No!" she said, placing a trembling finger to his lips. "Don't talk like that! You've got to come home to me, Mike. You've just got to! God knows I need you."

"Then, just leave me in His hands as I go to war, as I must leave you in His hands here at home."

Ashley's entire body shook as she clung to her husband and sobbed as if her heart would shatter.

Shane and Charolette Donovan sat on the back porch of their cottage, holding hands and enjoying the shade from a pair of oak trees that hovered over the yard. For hours, they had talked about the loneliness they would both experience until Shane came home again. Charolette promised to pray for him many times every day, asking the Lord to keep him safe. Soon they grew quiet, each with their own thoughts, and continued to hold hands.

As the sun slowly set, a cool breeze tufted Charolette's long black hair. She smoothed it with her free hand, then coughed suddenly, using the hand to cover her mouth. Concern showed in Shane's eyes as he looked at her.

"I hate to go off and leave you with that cough still bothering you."

"Don't worry about me," she said. "I'll be all right. Soon as the first frost comes, I'll get over it."

"I hope you're right. You still don't have your color back."

"Well, I'll be rosy-cheeked and sassy next time you see me. Just wait and see."

At eleven o'clock on Saturday morning, August 30, 1862, the eight new Maine regiments did a dress parade on the streets of Portland, with spectators there from ten counties.

The people of Brunswick were out in great numbers to observe the Twentieth with a mixture of pride and enthusiasm. Colonel Adelbert Ames had placed the Twentieth Regiment in front of the others when they formed the parade. He and Lieutenant Colonel Joshua Chamberlain rode their horses just ahead of their regiment. Behind the Twentieth and in front of the Nineteenth, which followed next, was the Bowdoin College band.

It was a thrilling sight for all Mainers. The regiments were gloriously arrayed in snappy caps of dark blue with dark-blue uniforms that had shiny gold buttons and brass belt buckles. The officers wore crimson sashes and swords. Their revolvers and gunbelts would be issued, along with new rifles and ammunition for all the troops, when they arrived at the armory in Washington, D.C.

Chamberlain was resplendent astride the beautiful stone-gray stallion the army had provided him. Silver oak leaves denoting his rank gleamed from the gold-edged, light-blue shoulder straps of his dark-blue uniform. A leather belt, with fittings that held his shiny officer's sword and scabbard, wound around his waist and was fastened by a gilt and silver buckle.

The men of the Twentieth Maine admired Colonel Ames, but they admired their lieutenant colonel even more. There was something about Chamberlain's carriage and deportment that instilled confidence in them as they headed for unknown fields of battle.

The parade finally led to a spot in the center of Portland where Governor Washburn waited with the congress of the state of Maine. Fannie Chamberlain, Charolette Donovan, and Ashley O'Hanlon were in the crowd. The three wives held on to each other and wept when the eight thousand men in uniform raised their right hands and followed Governor Washburn as they took their oath of allegiance to the United States of America.

The trains were ready at the Portland depot a block away. The soldiers walked slowly to the depot, many of them accompanied by friends and family. The Chamberlains, the Donovans, and the O'Hanlons found private spots for a few last moments together before the trains pulled out.

Shane held Charolette close and said, "Charly, I love you so much. Please take care of yourself."

"I will, darling," she said. "Don't worry about me. I'll be fine. Just hurry home to me…and don't ever forget that in my heart I'll be right there beside you every minute. I love you, my precious husband, more than mortal words could ever express."

Shane squeezed her tight, then they kissed long and tenderly.

The three wives stood together with tears streaming down their faces as the train that bore their husbands chugged out of the station.

During the next week, Ashley often paced the floor of the cottage, praying and weeping. Lewis and Maureen knew she was having a difficult time and asked her to come and live with them, but she politely turned them down. She felt closer to Mike when she was in their house.

At the Leprechaun Shoe and Boot Company, Charolette had her moments each day when she had to leave her desk and find a private spot to cry. Along with it, she coughed sometimes until her throat was sore. She returned to Dr. James Holladay, who examined her and assured her that the cough was the result of an allergy. It would clear up when the first frost came and took the pollen and mold out of the air.

By the second week, Charolette and Ashley agreed to trade off staying at each other's homes for the night. In the evenings they read the Bible and prayed together and wrote letters to their husbands…letters they wondered if Shane and Mike would ever receive.

"Where you from?" an idling sailor yelled to the new soldiers marching through Boston from the railroad station to the docks of Boston Harbor. Local residents, who had seen many an inexperienced regiment tramp the city's narrow streets on its way to war, turned to watch.

"We're from the land of spruce gum and buckwheat cakes, friend!" a Maine lumberjack-turned-soldier in the Twentieth Maine shouted back.

Everyone laughed, then an old man in the crowd lifted his cane, swung his hat, and called for three cheers for the men of Maine. "Hip, hip, hooray!" rang pleasantly in the ears of Adelbert Ames and Joshua Chamberlain as they sat astride their horses.

A woman cupped her hands to her mouth and shouted at Chamberlain, "Show ol' Bobby Lee who's boss, will you, handsome?"

Chamberlain smiled at her and lifted a hand.

The Maine regiments reached the wharves of the busy Massachusetts port and were told they would be placed aboard separate ships for their journey to Alexandria, Virginia. The Twentieth was placed aboard the U.S. steamer *Merrimac*. A smaller craft would follow, carrying their horses.

A great crowd of well-wishers had gathered on the docks. As the *Merrimac* began to pull away, the men of the Twentieth saw the arrival of a new regiment of Massachusetts soldiers, dressed in their new uniforms. One of the Massachusetts soldiers stood on the edge of the dock and shouted to the men on the *Merrimac*, "Three cheers for Old Abe and the Red, White, and Blue!"

The men of the Twentieth responded loudly, cheering their president and Old Glory. By the time they were out of the harbor, they were all hoarse from shouting. They were going to the war, and just in time, too. People on the streets had handed them newspapers full of news of a Union defeat at a second battle of Bull Run on August 29 and 30. They were saddened by the news and determined to help turn the tide.

Four days later, as the *Merrimac* carried the men of the Twentieth Maine up the wide Potomac after passing through the southern tip of Chesapeake Bay, the captain showed them George Washington's home at Mount Vernon. The place inspired such awe that many soldiers removed their caps in respect as they floated by.

It was midday when they arrived at Alexandria. Union officers who met them told Colonel Ames that the Twentieth Maine would become part of Third Brigade in the First Division of the Fifth Army Corps, Army of the Potomac under General Daniel Butterfield. They were to make camp on the bank of the Potomac for the night, and would march into Washington the next day, where they would have guns and ammunition issued to them. They would march on to Fort Craig, Virginia, seven miles outside of Washington. The other Maine regiments were attached to different brigades as they landed in Alexandria.

It was hot and humid as the men of the Twentieth did what they could to make themselves comfortable under the trees that lined the river's banks. Mike O'Hanlon was about to sit down under a tree with Shane Donovan and some other men when he noticed a string of boats steaming their way northward toward Washington. It was what he saw on the boats that captured his attention.

"Shane, look!" he said.

Shane and the dozen or so men close by looked at Mike, who was pointing to the boats. "They've got wounded soldiers and…and *dead* ones on those boats."

Other Maine soldiers had seen them too, by then. All stood gaping as they beheld five boats with wounded men-in-blue lying on the decks. Six boats followed with lifeless forms covered with blankets and sheets.

Buster Kilrain stepped close to Mike, who was now sided by Shane. He sighed and said to both of them, "A hard sight for men who've not yet seen combat."

"Do you ever get used to sights like that, Uncle Buster?" Mike said.

"No, son. Never. It's all a part of this thing called war, but ye never get accustomed to seein' your pals bloodied, maimed, and killed."

Shane put an arm around Mike's neck, locked it snugly in the crook of his arm, and said, "I couldn't stand it if anything happened to you, Mike. You're like a brother to me. We've both got to come through this thing alive."

"I pray we do," Mike said with tears in his eyes. "But…if either of us should be killed, at least we know we'll see the other one in heaven. Thank God we're saved, Shane."

"Yes, praise the Lord for that."

As they prepared to march into Washington the next morning, the men of the Twentieth Maine saw more boats steaming up the Potomac from the south. As with the boats the day before, they were carrying dead and wounded Union soldiers to Washington from the Bull Run battlefield. The sight of them left a solemn feeling with the men from Maine.

They reached the armory in Washington at mid-morning and were issued brand new Enfield rifles and forty rounds of ammunition. The officers were given new Navy Colt .45 revolvers, gunbelts, and as many rounds. Equipped with their weapons, the "thousand-and-one strong" regiment marched through the city toward Fort Craig. The officers rode their horses.

Washington was alive with the military—squads of cavalrymen on their hardy mounts, battery horses pulling big cannons through the streets, wagon trains of supplies, and soldiers any direction one cared to look.

By way of Long Bridge across the Potomac River, the regiment marched seven miles, without a rest break, to join its assigned brigade at Fort Craig, Virginia. For the new recruits, it was a difficult march. Each man was wearing new boots and burdened with his personal possessions, heavy new rifle, and ammunition.

Footsore and weary at the end of the march, the Twentieth joined General Daniel Butterfield and his Third Brigade, First Division, Fifth Army Corps, Army of the Potomac.

There were five veteran regiments camped at the fort from Michigan, New York, and Pennsylvania. They had fought at the second Bull Run battle, and were battle-scarred, worn, and sharply reduced in numbers. They welcomed Colonel Ames and his thousand men warmly.

On September 12, the First Division, Fifth Corps moved out of Fort Craig, and the Twentieth Maine began its first long march. The soldiers of the Twentieth looked down from Arlington Heights to see the blue columns of troops preceding them across the Potomac, followed by artillery, cavalry, and rattling supply wagons. Bands played and sunlight glinted off the burnished rifle barrels.

Chamberlain was at his commander's side, the two of them making a handsome pair sitting erect on their mounts. The men of the regiment marched in a long column, their new uniforms and accouterments contrasting with the worn and sometimes blood-stained uniforms of the veterans. The latter marched with renewed vigor and confidence, their morale bolstered by the thousand men of the Twentieth Maine.

They arrived exhausted at their designated Union camp on the banks of the Monocacy River two miles from Frederick, Maryland, on September 14. While settling in at the Frederick camp, the men of the Twentieth Maine heard their first sounds of war. Distant cannons thundered as elements of the Union army battled the Confederates for possession of three South Mountain passes.

The next morning, orders came for the Twentieth Maine, along with other units, to move out. Robert E. Lee's army was assembling near the small Maryland town of Sharpsburg, and must be met head-on.

Signs of war were all about them as they marched. Wounded soldiers of both armies lay along the roads, and fresh mounds in the fields showed where the dead had been buried. They marched through Turner's Gap, the main pass through South Mountain, and saw more signs of battle. Debris was everywhere, giving evidence that cannonballs had blasted houses, barns, sheds, trees, bushes, animals, and humans.

Deeper in the pass lay unburied bodies of soldiers killed in battle. Some lay with their sightless eyes staring at the sun-filled sky above. All of the bodies were bloody, and some were bloated, turning the stomachs of the men of the Twentieth, who had yet to fire a shot in combat.

At one point, Joshua Chamberlain looked down from his horse and saw a dead Rebel soldier sitting with his back against a tree. There was a New Testament clutched solidly in his stiff fingers. Chamberlain turned to Ames and said, "Just a boy, sir. Probably not more than sixteen or seventeen. I hope he knew the Author of that little Book in his hand. If he did, I'll meet him in heaven someday."

Ames, who made no pretense of being a Christian, mumbled something indistinguishable, and they rode on.

At noon on September 16, 1862, the Twentieth Maine—along with the other units that had been marching with them—joined Major General George B. McClellan's massive Union force a short distance from Sharpsburg.

A bloody battle was about to begin.

FIFTEEN

The Twentieth Maine Regiment camped on the south side of the road that led to Sharpsburg, just outside the small village of Keedysville. Across the way to the north, the sloping grassy meadows were thick with blue-uniformed men, horses, and equipment. Sporadic musket fire could be heard beyond the tree-lined crest of the slopes. Word was that General Joseph Hooker's brigade had crossed Antietam Creek and established itself there under sniper fire, making preparations to attack General Robert E. Lee's left flank the next morning.

A stiff wind whipped up while the reinforced Army of the Potomac made ready to face the Army of Northern Virginia on Union soil. Dark clouds began to form, and soon covered the Maryland sky.

The men of the Twentieth Maine observed as General George B. McClellan met beneath a cluster of oak trees a few yards away with Major General George W. Morell, commander of First Division, and Major General Daniel Butterfield, commander of Third Brigade of First Division. The three generals were in deep discussion.

The men of the Twentieth were amazed to see that General McClellan was of such small stature. They knew he was called Little

Mac, but none had realized he was barely five feet tall.

As they stood looking on, one of the Mainers commented, "It would take two of him to make a good-sized man."

"Tell ye what, soldier," Buster Kilrain said. "Don't judge a man by his size. Sometimes giants come in small bodies. From what I know, these men who have fought under General McClellan see him as just that—a military giant—much as the Frenchmen who fought under Napolcon Bonaparte saw *him*. You're goin' to be fightin' Rebels with the small man as your supreme commander. Learn to respect him for what he is on the inside, not the outside."

The soldier's face flushed and he said nothing more.

Captain Ellis Spear looked around at his fellow officers and said, "I wish we'd had more time for training. Our infantry can barely march in rudimentary formation, let alone quickly load and fire the new Enfields with any precision."

"Maybe that's what they're talking about over there," Mike O'Hanlon said. "Maybe General Butterfield is asking General McClellan to hold us in reserve, since we have no combat experience."

Colonel Adelbert Ames was standing close by and heard his officers talking. "I think not, Captain O'Hanlon," he said, stepping closer. "If Third Brigade is ordered into battle tomorrow, no regiment will be left out. Our men will just have to do the best they can…and while they are, they'll be getting valuable experience."

The wind eased some, but rain began to fall. It rained softly for the rest of the day and into the night. The men of the Twentieth Maine lay in their tents, finding sleep hard to come by. They wondered what part their regiment would have in the coming battle. And each man wondered if he would be among the living when September 17, 1862, was history.

The rain stopped about an hour before dawn, and the sky began to clear. Captain Shane Donovan had slept little. His thoughts had been on the battle at first, but in the last couple of hours, he concentrated on Charly, praying for her and thinking about her health.

Dawn came and with it the sudden sound of musketry and cannon, announcing the advance by General Hooker's brigade on Lee's left flank. Men scrambled about in the Twentieth Maine's camp, making ready under Colonel Ames's orders to be prepared to move out if the command came from General Morell through General Butterfield.

The sounds of battle beyond the crest of the meadows grew louder and more pronounced as the sun put in its appearance, and shortly thereafter, word came to Colonel Ames to push the Twentieth Maine to the top of the tree-lined ridge and wait in reserve.

A quarter-hour later, the Mainers, along with a few other units, were lying low in the wet grass atop the ridge, nerves taut. They watched as General McClellan sent his army to clash with the gray-uniformed invaders along the banks of Antietam Creek.

As the sun rose higher, the deadly spectacle unfolded in bloody panorama. Thousands of soldiers charged and countercharged each other out of the woods, over cornfields and meadows, amid the deep-throated boom of cannons and the rattle of muskets. Victims were falling like flies beneath the blue-white smoke that formed in shapeless clouds over the field of battle. High-pitched Rebel yells punctuated the deafening roar, along with the shouts of the men in blue.

Shane Donovan lay in the grass between Lieutenant Colonel Joshua Chamberlain and Mike O'Hanlon.

"Colonel, have you ever wondered how you'll do when you're in the middle of a battle like that?" Shane asked.

"You mean if I'll have the desire to turn and run?"

"Something like that. A man can't know what he's made of until he faces the test."

"I think every man wonders just how he'll react when he's facing enemy gunfire."

"I sure do," Mike said. "I hope I don't turn coward and run."

"You aren't going to run, Mike," Chamberlain said. "You'll do just fine."

"I sure hope so, sir." Mike thought of Ashley and told himself he could never look her in the eye again if he showed himself to be a coward in combat.

Chamberlain raised up and ran his gaze over the rest of the Twentieth. Every man except Colonel Ames and Sergeant Kilrain was asking the same question, he told himself.

The battle dragged on, and some of the units held in reserve on top of the ridge were called into the conflict. The men of the Twentieth Maine waited.

The battle raged and the hours passed. Just before 4:00 o'clock, a rider galloped up the slope and found Colonel Ames, who was talking to the leader of a unit from Michigan some thirty yards from where his men sat in the grass under the trees. The rider spoke to Ames, pointing westward, then rode back down the slope. All eyes were on Ames as he hurried to where his officers were clustered.

Ames ran his eyes over the men—who were now on their feet—and said, "We've got orders from General McClellan to move two miles due west. General Franklin's troops are facing heavy opposition near there. General Butterfield says General McClellan wants us on hand for Franklin. We'll probably be called into action to support him."

The Twentieth Maine made a hard run for the designated spot, carrying their guns and ammunition. Only Colonel Ames went on horseback. The word once more was *wait*. They watched the battle rage, and could not believe the carnage taking place before their eyes. The battlefield was littered with dead and wounded soldiers and animals. Ames's regiment was appalled at the sight, but remained ready to charge into the fight when the order came.

Ellis Spear stood next to Joshua Chamberlain and said, "Colonel, I don't know how much more my nerves can stand. I think the rest of our unit is feeling the same way. Look at them."

Chamberlain ran his gaze along the line, observing faces. There was no question that their nerves were raw.

"I'm feeling the same way," Chamberlain said, "but there's

nothing any of us can do about it. General McClellan is on top of this thing. We have to trust him."

Suddenly, the same rider came galloping toward them.

"Look!" one of the men shouted. "That messenger's coming back! We're going into the fight, men! We're going to kill us some Rebels before the sun goes down!"

"We'll have to hurry," cried another. "The sun'll be down in half an hour!"

Every man in the Twentieth was on his feet, ready to go. Colonel Ames stepped up to meet the rider as he skidded to a halt, saluted and said, "Colonel, sir, General Butterfield sent me to tell you he just got orders from General McClellan."

"Yes?"

"You are to return the men to where you were earlier, sir. On the ridge. You are to wait there until you receive further orders."

Ames saw the dejection among his men. He lifted his voice so that all could hear. "Men, this is all part of being soldiers! I know you would rather fight than wait, but we must follow orders. We're to return to the ridge where we were before. Let's move out!"

Darkness had not quite settled over the land when the Twentieth reached the ridge. The sight that lay before them wrenched their stomachs. Thousands of bodies in blue and in gray lay in the fields, on the meadows, and along the creek banks, their silent forms offering a grim portent for the soldiers of the Twentieth Maine.

Orders came shortly for Ames's troops to return to the road where they had set up camp. Their hearts were torn as they marched in the darkness and heard the cries of wounded and dying men all around them.

During the night, General Robert E. Lee picked up his wounded and stealthily marched his army back into Virginia under cover of darkness. Lee's divisions had been severely battered by McClellan's reinforced army.

The next morning, word came to General Butterfield from General Morell to march Third Brigade through Sharpsburg and onto the north bank of the Potomac, where they were to await further orders. Morell warned that they should be alert for any Rebel troops that might have been left behind to safeguard the escape of the battered Confederate army. Colonel Ames passed the warning on to the men of the Twentieth Maine.

Word came down the line as the troops prepared to move out that McClellan's division leaders had tried to persuade him to chase Lee's crippled army down and destroy it. McClellan had refused to discuss it with them further, saying such a pursuit would do no good. It was reported that General Franklin had warned McClellan that President Lincoln would be furious if he bypassed the chance to wipe out Lee's army when it was so vulnerable. McClellan had turned a deaf ear.

As Third Brigade marched out, Ames and Chamberlain were riding side by side. Behind them on horseback were Captains Spear and Donovan and Lieutenants O'Hanlon and Chamberlain.

Ames was heard to sigh and say to Chamberlain, "McClellan's failure to pursue could be his undoing. I agree with Franklin. The president is not going to like it one bit when he hears about this."

With the other units of Third Brigade, the Twentieth Maine marched across yesterday's contested ground. Sprawled, heaped, crumpled bodies in blue and gray lay everywhere, interspersed with dead horses, overturned caissons, ammunition wagons, and cannons.

Just ahead, on the path the Yankee soldiers were taking, lay a wounded Rebel lieutenant who had been overlooked when the Confederates picked up their wounded the night before. Lieutenant Gregory Downing had been shot twice in the Antietam battle. The first Yankee bullet hit him in the stomach. As he lay there in the meadow, knowing he was slowly bleeding to death, Yankee soldiers came running his way, dodging bullets. Downing pulled his revolver and fired at the closest man in blue. The Yankee went down, and his companions fired several shots at Downing. One of them grazed his head, knocking him unconscious.

Downing had come to sometime during the night, but the darkness was so thick, and he was so weak, he had no choice but to stay where he had fallen. When daylight came, Downing was amazed that he was still alive, though he knew he didn't have long to live. Blood from his abdomen wound was all around him. Not only that, but his pain was almost unbearable. He would rather die than suffer any longer.

The revolver! Where's my revolver? In agony, he twisted his body, searching for the gun. It took only a moment to spot it. It lay no more than the length of his body to his right. All he had to do was crawl a few feet, and he could reach it.

Downing struggled against the pain in his midsection and managed to reach the revolver. He gritted his teeth and rolled onto his back. With trembling thumb, he eared back the hammer. He was about to bring the muzzle to his mouth when he heard a horse blow, followed by the sound of hooves and tramping feet. He strained to raise his head and saw a mass of blue. He blinked and squinted until he brought the marching column of Union soldiers into focus. Out front were some officers on horses.

Why not? They'll put me out of my misery, and this way, I'll take a rotten Yankee officer with me.

Shane Donovan's horse was directly behind the stone-gray stallion that carried Joshua Chamberlain. Shane's mind was on Charly. He knew she would be at work in the factory office right then and wondered if she was thinking of him. His heart ached for her, to see her beautiful face and to hold her in his arms.

Something caught his eye off to the right. Then he saw the movement again. It was a man in gray, on his side, shakily bringing a revolver to bear on Joshua Chamberlain.

"Colonel Chamberlain! Look out!" Shane shouted, whipping out his revolver. He gouged his horse's sides to put himself between the Rebel officer and Chamberlain.

Shane's horse leaped forward and brushed the rump of Chamberlain's mount, startling the stone-gray and making him do an abrupt side-step. At the same time, Downing's revolver fired. The bullet whizzed past Chamberlain's ear.

Shane steadied his gun on the Rebel officer and shouted, "Don't do it!"

But the officer was dogging back the hammer in a desperate attempt to fire another shot. Shane's gun roared. The slug struck Downing in the temple, killing him instantly.

Colonel Ames raised a hand to halt the column behind him and twisted in the saddle to look at Chamberlain. The lieutenant colonel's face was white as baking powder.

"You all right?" Ames said.

"Yes, sir, I'm fine." Chamberlain looked at Shane, who was off his horse, standing over the man he had just killed.

Mike O'Hanlon was off his mount too, dashing toward his best friend. When he got to him, he put an arm on his shoulder and felt Shane's body shaking.

"You all right?" Mike said.

Shane said nothing. He was looking at the dead Rebel officer, biting his lower lip, on the verge of tears.

Just then Chamberlain and Ames drew up. Ames had commanded the rest of the soldiers to hold their ranks. They looked on wide-eyed, as did the men of the other regiments.

"Shane, you saved my life," Chamberlain said.

"And put himself between you and the Rebel, sir," Mike said. "I saw it, Colonel Chamberlain. That's exactly what he did."

"I saw it, too," Tom Chamberlain said, who was now beside Mike.

Ames moved past Chamberlain and said, "Captain Donovan, you just did a wonderful thing. You put your own life at risk to save that of Colonel Chamberlain. We're all very proud of you."

Shane ran a sleeve across his tear-filled eyes and shook his head. Still staring at the man he had just killed, he said, "I'm glad I was able to keep him from shooting you, Colonel Chamberlain, but…it's the first time I've ever taken the life of another human being."

"These other men will have that first time too, Captain," Ames said. "I had mine at Rich Mountain a year ago in June. But you…you have distinguished yourself by an act of pure heroism."

Shane raised his head, looked at Ames, and said, "I'm no hero, sir. I just did what had to be done to save Colonel Chamberlain's life."

"You are a hero, Shane," Mike said. "Just like when you saved little Darlene Brainerd."

Chamberlain squeezed Shane's shoulder and said, "I'll never forget what you did here, Shane. And Fannie and my children will never forget, either. Words are weak vessels at a moment like this, but thank you. If you hadn't done what you did, I'd be lying dead over there on the road right now."

"It's time to go, gentlemen," Ames said. "We've still got a long way to march today."

As the officers of the Twentieth Maine turned and walked back toward the column of soldiers, a loud cheer went up for Captain Shane Donovan. He grinned shyly, his face tinting.

Before any of the officers mounted up, Ames ran his gaze along the line of men and said, "Captain Donovan is the first man of the Twentieth Maine Regiment to fire a shot in the Civil War. In so doing, he killed an enemy officer at the risk of his own life in order to save the life of his lieutenant colonel."

A louder cheer erupted from the thousand men of the regiment.

The Twentieth Maine, along with the other units, marched through Sharpsburg, Maryland, and onto the north bank of the Potomac River, where they set up camp for the night. General Morell's warning for his men to stay alert for Rebel troops was well-spoken. The Rebels were dug in on the south bank of the river, right across from where the Union troops were setting up camp. The river was wide and shallow there and a favorite spot for crossing into Virginia. The Confederates would stay hidden until the Federals showed if they were going to pursue General Lee and his battered troops. If they started across, the Rebel guns would open up.

When morning came, the Confederates watched as all units but one marched away, heading north up the bank. What would the remaining unit do? The Rebels were outnumbered, but they had their orders from General Lee. They must not allow the Yankees to cross the river.

They did have some advantages, however, if the Union troops started across. They were well-hidden in heavy brush and trees. They would have more protection than the Yankees. And they would have the element of surprise.

Colonel Ames had explained to his men before the other troops marched away that General Butterfield had sent orders for the Twentieth to remain and wait for further instructions. He had plans for them, but had to get them approved by General McClellan. It would take a day or two.

Ames sent men to patrol the north bank of the Potomac and to keep a sharp eye for any suspicious activity across the river. He didn't trust the Confederates. They might do just as General Morell had said.

Colonel Ames then had a private conference with his lieutenant colonel, advising Chamberlain that he was going to recommend Shane Donovan for a Presidential Commendation. His act of unselfishness and heroism in saving Chamberlain's life must be recognized. Chamberlain was voicing his agreement when one of the men who had been sent on patrol came toward them, eyes wide.

"Colonel, I saw movement across the river! It was a gray uniform amongst the trees, and I'm sure I saw the mouths of a couple howitzers hidden in the brush!"

"Any of the others on patrol see anything?" Ames asked.

"I don't think so, sir. The instant I saw the Rebel uniform and the cannons, I came here."

"You didn't run, I hope."

"No, sir. I just slowly left the edge of the river and came straight here."

Ames told Chamberlain to send two men downriver till they were out of sight past the bend. They were to cross the Potomac and move up on the Confederate position from its blind side. If they confirmed that the Confederates were there, the Twentieth Maine would cross the shallow spot in the river and attack at dawn.

Chamberlain chose Buster Kilrain and Alex Cowbray for the mission. Before sundown, Buster and Alex returned to report that the man on patrol was indeed correct. They counted four howitzers and a unit of about two hundred men.

Word spread among the Mainers that they were going to make a surprise attack on the Rebel position at dawn. Ames met with the officers, explaining his plan, and the officers took the plans to their units. There was great excitement in the ranks of the Twentieth Maine as they prepared for their first confrontation.

SIXTEEN

I t was mid-afternoon on Thursday, September 18, 1862. Charolette Donovan looked up from her desk and saw Fannie Chamberlain and Ashley O'Hanlon come through the office door. Charolette could tell both of them had been crying.

"Fannie…Ashley…what's wrong?" she asked, rising from her chair as they drew up.

Fannie's lips quivered. "I can tell you haven't heard."

"Heard what?"

"News came over the wire at the newspaper about forty-five minutes ago that the Twentieth was involved in a horrible battle yesterday at Sharpsburg, Maryland. There's no actual count yet, but Washington says it's the bloodiest battle the war has seen. Several thousand were killed, and several thousand more were wounded."

Charolette closed her eyes and prayed aloud, "O dear Lord, help us." A cough broke from her lips. She pulled a hanky from her sleeve and coughed into it, putting the other hand to her chest.

Lewis O'Hanlon emerged from his office looking at some papers in his hand. He was about to say something to Charolette when he saw Fannie and Ashley. He stopped, looked at their wan expressions, then looked at Charolette, who was bracing herself against the desk.

"Ladies…what's wrong?" he asked.

"A wire just came in to the *Brunswick Times,*" Fannie said. "Father happened to be there when it came in. Our regiment was involved in the worst battle since the war began. At Sharpsburg, Maryland. All we know is that several thousand were killed, and thousands more were wounded."

Charolette lowered herself onto her chair, her knees feeling watery. Lewis felt his own knees go weak as he laid a hand on Charolette's shoulder and said, "Would you like a cup of water?"

"I'll get it," Ashley said, and went to a nearby cupboard where a jar of water was kept. Several tin cups were lined up, each bearing the name of an office employee. She filled Charolette's cup and hurried back to the desk.

"Father is calling a special prayer meeting at the church tonight at 7:00 o'clock," Fannie said. "I hope you can be there, Mr. O'Hanlon."

"We'll be there. In fact, I'm going to head home right now and tell Maureen. I hate to have to tell her about the battle, but she needs to know."

Charolette was sipping the water when she choked and began to cough again. Ashley patted her back until the coughing subsided, then Lewis said, "Ladies, this war is a terrible thing. We've only one recourse to this kind of news. We must continue to hold our soldiers before the Lord in prayer and trust Him to take care of them."

"If…if we could only know," Charolette said. "If we could only know that they're all right."

Ashley blinked at the tears in her eyes and said, "All we can do is keep praying and wait for an answer to our letters."

"I can think of one good thing that will come out of this horrible war," Fannie said. "It's going to teach us how to lean on the Lord like we never have before."

Just before dawn on Friday, September 19, Colonel Adelbert Ames had his men spread out along the north bank of the Potomac. Five hundred of them were to cross the river, while the other five hundred remained on the bank to provide cover. Half of the five hundred who crossed the river would close in on the west side, and the other half on the east, leaving the center for a barrage of musket fire when Ames launched the surprise attack. Lieutenant Colonel Joshua Chamberlain was on his horse and would lead the unit going in from the west.

Colonel Ames watched as his men waded across the seventy yard span of water. Dawn was breaking, and they looked like specters moving among the mists that hovered thinly over the surface of the Potomac. When the five hundred were ten feet from the shore, Ames gave his signal, and the soldiers on the far bank opened fire. It took the Rebels several minutes to begin firing back, so successful had been Ames's surprise attack.

The barrage went on for nearly half an hour. Suddenly Ames saw Joshua Chamberlain riding into the river, waving his cap and shouting, "Cease fire! Cease fire!"

Ames shouted for the men to stop firing as Chamberlain splashed up on his horse and said, "They took off, Colonel. We'd have had to shoot them in the back to stop them, and I couldn't give that kind of an order."

"You did right, Chamberlain. Anybody get hit?"

"Not on our side, sir. There are some dead Rebels in the brush. Maybe four or five. They took their wounded with them."

"All right. Let's get our men back over here."

For the six weeks that followed the Antietam Battle and the Twentieth Maine's skirmish on the Potomac, the regiment was used to guard some of the Potomac's fords. During that time they were drilled, trained, and toughened by Colonel Ames.

The first day of October brought President Lincoln himself to the banks of the Potomac. He wanted to have a talk with his top general and picked the spot where he could meet with General

George B. McClellan and take a look at the troops. Everyone knew the president was perturbed with McClellan for not pursuing the battered and disheartened Confederate army when he had the men, guns, and full opportunity to overpower them.

Though Lincoln's conference with McClellan was held privately in a field tent, the men of the Twentieth Maine were thrilled to see the president when he reviewed their regiment and others camped nearby. When the president had moved from the Twentieth Maine to another regiment, Joshua Chamberlain commented about Lincoln's drawn features and his deep, sad eyes to the officers who stood by him.

On October 15, mail arrived from home. That evening, as men sat beside the campfires, Shane Donovan was sitting alone by a fire, pouring over four letters that had come from Charolette. He looked up to see his best friend standing over him.

"Mind if I sit down?" Mike said.

"Of course not."

"Well, I figure you might want to be alone with Charly…in the letters, I mean."

"I have been for a while. It's okay."

Mike eased down across the fire from Shane, sitting Indian-style. "How many letters did you get?"

"Four from my parents and four from Charly. You?"

"Three from my folks. Four from Ashley."

"Everything all right?"

"Yeah. Sorry about Charly. Ashley filled me in."

"What do you mean?"

"The cough."

Shane looked at the four letters in his hand, then back at his friend. "You'll have to tell me what you mean, Mike. Charly hasn't even mentioned the cough. I figured it had cleared up."

"Why wouldn't she tell you about it?"

"Doesn't want me to worry, I guess. What do you know about it?"

"Well, Ashley says it's getting worse. The last letter said it's already frosted several times in Maine, but the frost didn't help at all. It's not an allergy."

"I had a strong feeling it wasn't an allergy. Any mention by Ashley or your parents about receiving the letters you've sent them?"

"Nope."

"Not in mine either. Guess the mail we've sent home isn't getting through."

"No surprise. Look, Shane, I'm sorry if I've upset you. Guess I should've kept my mouth shut. I...I just figured Charly was letting you know about herself."

"Don't feel bad. You naturally thought Charly would tell me how she was doing. I don't really blame her, either. She just doesn't want her condition weighing heavy on my mind. She knows if she told me it was worse, it would do exactly that."

"And now that I've shot off my big mouth, it *will* weigh heavy on your mind."

"Hey, it's all right. At least knowing that the cough is worse, I can pray more intelligently about it."

Mike walked around the fire and put an arm around Shane's shoulder. "Why don't we pray right now for her?"

Shane smiled, blinked at the tears that had surfaced, and said softly, "Yes. Let's do that."

Dr. James Holladay stood over Charolette Donovan as she sat on his examining table.

"Do you want me to bring them in and tell them?" he said.

She nodded, biting her lips. A moment later, Garth and Pearl Donovan and Ashley O'Hanlon were seated on straight-backed chairs beside the examining table, deep concern showing in their eyes.

Holladay leaned on the table next to Charolette, looked down at them and said, "There's no question, now. She has consumption. I held out hope that it was something—anything—else, but since she's been coughing up blood these past several days, I can come to no other conclusion. As you know, it was consumption that took her mother in her early thirties."

"What now, Doctor?" Pearl asked.

"Well, she'll have her good days and her bad days. Up to this point, she hasn't missed a day of work, even though she's gone to the factory when she really didn't feel like it. And she's young. The consumption isn't going to go away, but she could get better and have more good days than bad ones."

Garth looked at Charolette and said, "What's Lewis's attitude about this? Will he continue to let you work for him if you should have to ask for a day off now and then?"

"Yes, he told me I could work for him even if I could only come in every other day."

Garth looked at his daughter-in-law with tender eyes. "Charolette, you know that Pearl and I love you as if you were our own daughter."

"Yes. You've shown me that over and over again."

"We've offered to have you come live with us before, and we're offering it again. If it would help, we'd love to have you."

Charolette thought on it for a moment. "Papa Donovan…I love you both so very much, and I appreciate your offer. Maybe the day will come when I'll need to take you up on it. But…our little cottage is where Shane and I started our marriage. I really need to be in the house. I feel so much closer to Shane there. Can you understand that?"

"Yes, of course. Just know that you're welcome at our place at any time should you change your mind."

"Thank you."

Ashley took hold of Charolette's hand. "I don't want to push myself on you, Charolette, but if it would help for me to stay with you on weekends, I'll be glad to do it. We can ride back and forth to church together on Sundays."

"Ashley, you're already doing far more than you should, giving me your nights. I can't ask you to—"

"You didn't ask. I volunteered. And to make it easier for you, I'll come to your house every time rather than you coming to my house every other night during the week. I know that will take some load off you."

"But, Ashley—"

"Ah, ah, ah! There will be no argument. It's a settled matter. Then…if the day comes when you decide to move in with your in-laws, I'll step out of the picture."

Tears filmed Charolette's eyes. She opened her arms, and the two of them embraced.

After a few seconds, Charolette said to Ashley and her in-laws, "I don't want Shane to know that it's consumption. Not now, I mean. He's got enough on his mind as it is."

"But, honey," Pearl said, "he has a right to know. He's your husband."

"Pearl's right," Garth said. "We'll be glad to write him if you say it's okay."

"Well, we don't even know if our letters have reached Shane and Mike," Ashley said. "Even if you wrote to him, you wouldn't know if he got it."

"All we can do is try," Pearl said. "How about it, Charolette? May Garth and I write and tell him?"

"Maybe I could find him and tell him," came a familiar voice from across the room.

All eyes turned to see John Calhoun Chamberlain standing at the clinic door.

"Hello, John," Garth said. "How long have you been there?"

"We've been here long enough to learn that Charolette's been di- agnosed with consumption," Fannie said, stepping around her brother-in-law. "John arrived just this morning on a little furlough. We were across the street at Strother's buying him some new clothes when I saw all of you come into the office."

Fannie moved toward the table and took Charolette in her arms. "O Charolette, I'm so sorry to hear this."

"John, you said maybe you could find Shane and tell him," Garth said. "Are you going where the Twentieth is?"

"Yes, sir. I have to leave tomorrow. I've been up in Brewer visiting my parents and stopped by to see Fannie and the children just for today."

"Do you know about the Twentieth?" Pearl asked. "I mean, how it went for them at Sharpsburg?"

"No, ma'am, I don't. The Christian Commission has had me at Washington up until a week ago working with the wounded soldiers. I tried to see if any of the Twentieth Maine had been wounded at Sharpsburg, but couldn't find out a thing. I do know they're assigned somewhere along the Potomac River, but that's all. I'm going back to Washington two days early so I can find Tom and Joshua. If any of you want to send letters along with me, I'll be glad to take them."

"John," Ashley said, "if you get there and…and find out that Mike and Shane are all right—or if…well, you know. Is there a way you can notify us?"

John shook his head. "Afraid not. The wire service is strictly for military and newspaper use. All I can do is write to you, but things are pretty hectic down there. Looks like it's going to get worse before it gets better. The mail isn't getting through very well."

"We've found that out," Fannie said. "None of us has heard a thing since those men of ours left nearly two months ago."

"Well, you get those letters written," John said, "and I'll do my dead-level best to deliver them."

Charolette looked at Pearl and Garth and said, "I'll write a letter and send it with John. You're right. I hate to worry Shane, but he has a right to know how I am. I certainly would want to know if it was the other way around."

***

On the afternoon of October 30 (the same day Charolette Donovan learned she had consumption), orders came from General McClellan for the Fifth Corps to march south into Virginia to a spot on the north bank of the Rappahannock River, eight miles south of Warrenton. It would be a full four days' march, and the weather was turning cold. Coats were issued to the entire Fifth Corps.

General McClellan stipulated in his orders that 450 men of Colonel Ames's Twentieth Maine Regiment were to remain in Maryland to continue guarding the fords of the Potomac. Though it was hard to separate from their comrades, the other 550 men of the Twentieth Maine, along with the rest of Fifth Corps, marched south along the east side of the Blue Ridge by the light of the setting sun. Shane Donovan, Ellis Spear, Mike O'Hanlon, Tom Chamberlain, and Buster Kilrain were among those who marched. They marched until midnight, then under a clear, starlit sky and a full moon, they pitched their tents.

As the men of the Fifth Corps lay down for the night, they knew the grounds for war had become even more intense. No longer was the war waged only to preserve the Union and confine slavery to the areas where it existed; now there was a new dimension. Only a few days after the battle of Antietam, President Lincoln had declared his intention to issue on January 1, 1863, his Emancipation Proclamation. This edict would declare the slaves in the Confederate States "thenceforward and forever free." The message had come, along with their marching orders, that Lincoln was going to enforce the edict as planned on New Year's Day. This act would infuriate the Southerners.

The next day found the men of First Division, Fifth Corps, skirting the base of Loudoun Heights and proceeding south through Loudoun Valley. Untouched so far by the war, the valley was one of the most beautiful and fertile in Virginia. As the Union soldiers marched in long blue columns, they kept a sharp eye on the Blue

Ridge Range to their right. General Morell had warned that there could be Confederate troops hiding in the shadows of the mountains.

After three more days of marching, First Division arrived without incident at its designated spot on the bank of the Rappahannock River.

The next day, November 4, the men of the Twentieth Maine were busy about their tents. Some shaved, others washed their clothes in the cold waters of the Rappahannock, still others wrote letters, hoping they would somehow arrive at their destination before Christmas.

Shane Donovan and Mike O'Hanlon were hanging their long underwear on a rope stretched between two trees and talking to Joshua Chamberlain. Suddenly Mike's attention was drawn to a familiar face coming toward them.

"Hey, Colonel! Look who's here!"

"John!" Chamberlain exclaimed, dashing to his brother.

The Chamberlain brothers hugged and pounded each other on the back, then John shook hands with Mike and Shane.

"I sure am glad to see you fellows alive! I heard about the Twentieth being in the Sharpsburg battle, but there was no way to find out if you came through it. What about Tom?"

"He's fine too," Joshua told him. "Right now, they have him leading a guard patrol downriver. He'll sure be glad to see you."

"And me him. Mercy me, I had a hard time catching up with you guys. Good thing I had a horse. I was wondering even then if I'd ever catch up to you."

"Where you coming from?" Mike asked.

"Home." John let a wide smile capture his face. "And I've got some mail, too."

There was elation in the hearts of the three officers as John removed envelopes from his coat pocket and gave two to each of them.

"See you guys later," Shane said, holding his letters close to his heart. "I'm going to find a private spot under a tree somewhere and devour these."

"Me too," Mike said. "See you gentlemen later."

John Chamberlain watched Shane and Mike move away in opposite directions, then said to his brother, "Charolette's letter is going to tear him up, Josh."

"What do you mean?"

"Well...I guess you've known about her cough."

Joshua studied his brother's face. "Don't tell me she's got consumption."

"I'm afraid so."

"Her mother died of consumption while still a young woman. This is going to shake Shane hard. I'll give it a few minutes, then go talk to him."

Shane walked quickly to an old oak tree that stood by itself on the riverbank. He sat down, leaned against the tree, and opened the envelope from his parents. There were two letters inside, one from each. Soon he was wiping tears as he read precious words from his parents. He read both letters twice, then slipped them back in the envelope, anticipating Charolette's letter with a pounding heart.

"Hey, Captain! When did the mail arrive?"

Shane grinned up at a young corporal who was passing by with two others. "This isn't army mail, Corporal Todd. It was delivered personally by Colonel Chamberlain's brother."

Todd snapped his fingers and said, "Oh, to be an officer! They have all the good fortune!" The other corporals agreed in a lighthearted way and moved on.

Shane opened Charolette's envelope. His fingers trembled a little as he unfolded the four handwritten pages and began to read.

Ten minutes later, Joshua Chamberlain and Mike O'Hanlon drew near the tree. They could see Shane sitting at the base of the trunk, his knees pulled up and his arms resting on them. His head lay on his arms. They could hear him weeping and talking softly. They both picked up the word *Lord* and agreed silently to wait.

Soon the talking stopped, but the weeping continued. Chamberlain nodded to Mike, and together they moved up beside him.

SEVENTEEN

Shane…" Joshua Chamberlain said softly.

Shane Donovan raised his head. "Yes, sir?"

"We know about it. John told us."

Shane struggled to bring his voice under control. "I was afraid all along that it was consumption. I just wouldn't let myself believe it."

Mike knelt down and said, "I know you don't need me to tell you this, but God can heal her."

Shane nodded. "He can do anything. I know that. It's just that her mother died of the same disease at a young age, and I…"

"Hey, you're only human. The Lord is aware of that, too. Shane, I can't say that I understand how you feel, because I've never been where you are right now. But I want you to know my heart aches for you, and I'll be praying for both you and Charolette more than I have before."

"So will I, Shane," Joshua said. "And if there's ever anything I can do for either of you—I mean *anything*—don't you hesitate to ask."

Shane met the lieutenant colonel's gaze. "Do you really mean that, sir?"

"I sure do."

"Then, Colonel Chamberlain, Charly needs me right now. And I need to see her. Would you talk to Colonel Ames for me? See if he'll grant me time to go home?"

Chamberlain rubbed his forehead. "That will be quite irregular, but I'll give it a try. You and Mike wait here. I'll be back shortly."

When Chamberlain walked away, Mike said, "Shane, let's pray and ask the Lord to move on the colonel's heart. Charly needs you."

Chamberlain returned ten minutes later. He explained that Colonel Ames had gone into Warrenton with Generals George Morell and Dan Butterfield, who were ordered to a meeting with Abraham Lincoln's general-in-chief, Henry W. Halleck. General Fitz John Porter, commander of Fifth Corps, and General George McClellan himself would also be meeting with them. Morell, Butterfield, and Ames wouldn't be back for several hours. Chamberlain would talk with the colonel as soon as he returned.

Shane said that a meeting with General Halleck had to mean something important was going on. Chamberlain agreed.

With hope that the Lord would do His work in the colonel's heart, Shane went about his daily routine, his heart heavy for Charolette.

The sun went down just before mealtime, and a cold wind swept across the valley. The troops ate supper in their small tents to protect themselves from the biting wind. The nights had been growing colder of late.

Shane and Mike were eating together in Shane's tent when they heard footsteps approach. "Captain Donovan," came a familiar voice.

Shane stuck his head out of the cramped space. "Yes, Colonel Chamberlain?"

"Just wanted to let you know that Colonel Ames is back, and I'll be talking to him as soon as I possibly can."

"Thank you, sir. I'll be right here."

Over an hour later, Chamberlain returned. Shane and Mike saw by the light of a nearby fire that the lieutenant colonel was smiling.

"I explained the situation to the colonel," Chamberlain said, "and he said you can have four days, starting at dawn in the morning. He figures there won't be any fighting within that time. He said to see Sergeant Fillmore tonight. He's the one in charge of the horses. Colonel Ames is right now making arrangements for you to use one."

Shane lifted his eyes heavenward. "Thank You, Lord!"

"You can ride the horse to Washington, leave it at an army camp there, and take the train. That's only going to give you about a day with your Charly."

"That's all right, sir," Shane said. "At least I'll get to see her."

Chamberlain reached into his coat pocket and pulled out two slips of paper. "Here's a map to show you how to find the right camp. And this other paper is to show that Colonel Ames authorized you to leave camp and return home. Has his signature on it. Just show it to the officer in charge of the Washington camp, and any military authority who might question you."

"All right, sir," Shane said as he took the papers.

"You'll note that the dates of your leave are specified in the letter. You must be back here by midnight next Saturday, the eighth. You'll be in deep trouble if you're not."

"I understand, sir. I'll not be late."

"Colonel," Mike said, "did you learn what the meeting in Warrenton was about?"

"Only that General Morell is now meeting with the commanders of all regiments here and that every regiment is going to be addressed by its commander before bedtime. We should be ordered to assemble shortly."

The order came just over a half-hour later.

Several fires burned in the area to give off light. Colonel Ames stood in the cold wind with his cap pulled low and his overcoat collar up and announced to his regiment that President Lincoln had relieved General George Morell of his command of First Division in order to place him at the head of another division stationed further east. Morell was being replaced by General Dan Butterfield, effective immediately.

There was more news. General-in-Chief Henry Halleck had informed the officers that President Lincoln, out of patience with General McClellan's long failure to seek out the enemy and take the fight to him, had relieved him of his command and replaced him with Major General Ambrose Burnside, who had distinguished himself in the battle at Sharpsburg. This change in command would take place the next day, November 5.

By the same directive, Lincoln had ordered McClellan's right-hand-man and commander of the Fifth Corps, Major General Fitz John Porter, removed from his position, with Major General Joseph Hooker placed in his stead.

Colonel Ames then said, "Before we dismiss, men, there's one more thing. Since he is now commander of First Division, General Butterfield is going to introduce to us a bugle tune—one he composed himself—that will be played every night at lights out. It will also be used when we bury men of our division who are killed in battle."[1]

"Colonel Ames..." said a young soldier who stood near the front of the ranks.

"Yes?"

"Did General Butterfield put words to the tune?"

"I don't know, soldier."

"Aye, he did, sir," Buster Kilrain said. "General Butterfield calls it 'Taps.' I heard about it from an Irish lieutenant named O'Leary that I met when we were camped up on the banks o' the Potomac. The words are fittin', Colonel, both for soldiers beddin' down at night and for those laid to rest in their graves."

"And what are those words, Sergeant?"

Kilrain rubbed the back of his neck, pressing his memory for the words. "Let's see...'Day is done, sinks the sun. And the stars all appear one by one. Rest in peace comrades dear, God is near.'"

Ames nodded, then said to the brigade, "All right men, when you hear the bugler tonight, you'll know what he's playing and the words that go with the music. Regiment dismissed!"

Shane Donovan arrived at Brunswick, Maine, just short of twenty-eight hours after riding out of camp at 4:00 o'clock on Wednesday morning, November 5. He had changed trains in Boston, and upon arriving in Portland, had rented a horse and headed for Brunswick at a full gallop. He wanted to catch Charolette at home before she left for work. It was 7:35 when he slid from the saddle in front of the little cottage and headed for the door.

Not wanting to frighten Charly, he decided to knock rather than walk in. He tapped on the door, his heart pounding wildly, and braced himself. There were light footsteps, followed by the rattle of the doorknob. The door swung open, revealing a thinner Charly with gray circles under her eyes. She was dressed and ready for work. When she saw the face of her husband, her mouth flew open.

"Shane! Oh, you're alive…and all in one piece!"

They embraced, kissed, and embraced again. Charolette clung hard, weeping, and Shane held her tight, shedding his own tears.

"I guess you haven't received any of my letters," he said.

"No."

"I've received five from you. It was the last one that told me about…your sickness. I just had to come and see you."

"Oh, I'm so glad you could come! We heard about the Sharpsburg battle in September, but we couldn't find out anything about your regiment. There's been no way for us to find out if any of you survived. What about Mike? Ashley's been beside herself with worry, just like I have."

"Mike's fine. So is Colonel Chamberlain and Uncle Buster. Tom's okay, too. We didn't actually get into the battle at Sharpsburg, so no one was even scratched. We had a skirmish with some Rebels right after that, but still nobody was hurt. We're camped on the Rappahannock in Virginia now. When your letter came, I asked Colonel Chamberlain if he would try to get me a leave so I could come and see you. He did it in a hurry."

"Well, how long—" she turned her head, covered her mouth, and coughed. "Excuse me. How long can you stay?"

"They gave me a little less than four days. It took me almost twenty-eight hours to get here. I have to report in by midnight Saturday, so I'll have to ride for Portland in the morning at ten."

Charolette looked over his shoulder and said, "Here comes Mr. O'Hanlon."

Lewis O'Hanlon was ecstatic to see Shane and to learn that Mike was alive and well. He gladly gave Charolette the day off, saying she didn't have to come to work on Thursday either. He was going to head home and tell Maureen that their son was fine.

Shane explained that the Twentieth had not yet seen combat, so Lewis could spread the word that everyone in the regiment was all right. He asked Lewis to swing by his parents' house and tell his mother he was home. He wanted to spend a few minutes alone with Charly, then they would come to the house.

There was a sweet reunion with Shane's mother, then Shane told her they were going to see Dr. Holladay. Pearl invited them for supper and said she would invite Ashley, too.

Shane sat with Charolette in the doctor's office and questioned Dr. Holladay thoroughly. The doctor explained that consumption worked differently with different people. Charolette could linger for years with it, or it could end her life in a few months, as it had her mother's.

Shane and Charolette went back home and spent the rest of the day alone. They read the Bible and prayed together, asking God to take the disease from her body. Charolette tried to encourage her husband by staying optimistic.

That evening, a precious time was enjoyed at the Donovan home. When Ashley and Shane saw each other, they embraced, and Shane gave her a letter Mike had hastily written to take to her. She was thrilled to receive it and handed one to Shane to take to Mike. Garth led in special prayer for Charolette and for Shane as he returned to the war. He also prayed for Mike and the others who were known and loved by the O'Hanlon family.

Charolette had a coughing spell right after the prayer. She coughed up pink foam, but hid it from Shane.

Later that evening, Shane and Ashley hugged each other good-bye. She asked him to tell Mike she loved him with all her heart and was looking forward to the day he came home to her. Shane assured her he would convey the message.

The next morning, Garth and Pearl came by to tell Shane good-bye, then left to give him and his wife their final hour together alone.

At ten o'clock, Charolette walked Shane to the front porch of the cottage. The horse was tied to a hitching post, saddled and ready to go. It nickered when it saw them.

Charolette did her best to maintain her composure. As they clung to each other, she said, "Darling, please don't worry about me. I'm in the Lord's hands. We are in His hands. I must trust Him to bring you back safe and sound. You must trust Him to have me waiting here when you come home."

Shane's chest felt as though it were on fire as he battled for composure. He held her at arm's length and said, "The real soldier in this family is you."

They kissed long and lingering, then Shane swung into the saddle. Charolette wiped tears and coughed as she watched him ride away. When he reached the end of the block, he reined in, waved, then rounded the corner and was gone.

Upon reaching the Union camp on the Rappahannock, Shane Donovan learned that the Army of the Potomac's new commander, General Ambrose E. Burnside, had announced that he was planning to move his army south to take Fredericksburg. He would then march to the Confederate capital and take it. When Richmond was in Union hands, the war would be over.

In order to accomplish his objectives, General Burnside reorganized his army. Changes in command followed as he formed three

"Grand Divisions" of two corps each. Burnside appointed General Joseph Hooker to command Center Grand Division, consisting of Second and Fifth Corps. The other four corps formed the Right and Left Grand Divisions. General Dan Butterfield was made commander of Fifth Corps, and Brigadier General Charles Griffin became commander of First Division in his place.

In late November, Burnside deviated from a plan assented to by General-in-Chief Henry W. Halleck and President Lincoln and marched his army southward down the Rappahannock to Falmouth, opposite his first target, Fredericksburg.

Burnside had agreed with his superiors to cross the river above Fredericksburg, occupy the loftiest point behind the town, known as Marye's Heights, and establish a supply base north of the river. Instead, Burnside resolved to cross the Rappahannock on pontoon bridges directly in front of Fredericksburg. When his army was gathered at Falmouth, Burnside decided not to occupy Marye's Heights, believing it was not necessary. He would have the city in hand before the Confederates would know what hit them.

Then things began to go wrong. General Lee was notified that the Federals were making moves to take Fredericksburg. Lee's army had licked its wounds from the whipping at Sharpsburg and had been reinforced. Lee led his army from Richmond with two of his most formidable generals, James Longstreet and Thomas J. "Stonewall" Jackson.

The pontoons failed to arrive as scheduled, and as the days passed, Lee and his Army of Northern Virginia moved in and set up their defensive positions. General Longstreet's division occupied Marye's Heights with artillery and infantry. General Jackson's division set up barriers at ground level.

Panic was building in Burnside. He wired Washington, asking where his pontoons were. There had been a misunderstanding as to when the pontoons would be needed. A rush was put on, and they finally arrived on December 10, more than a week late. By this time, Lee's forces were well-established.

When Lee saw the pontoons from his position on Marye's Heights, he sent a message down to General Jackson to place snipers in buildings along the riverbank to pick off the Federals as they began to connect the floating bridges. Lee then called for Fredericksburg to be evacuated. The Union army had stationed artillery on the heavily forested hills across the river, and he knew bombardment would come. He wanted all civilians out of the city. The command was given late afternoon on December 10, and the evacuation was done on Thursday morning, December 11, under a thick fog.

A four-inch snow had fallen on December 8, followed by freezing cold. None of it had melted off. Fredericksburg's citizens made their way out of the city in a pitiful procession into the foggy forests and fields and set up camps in the snow.

The Twentieth Maine Regiment was sent to the river bank to fire at Stonewall Jackson's snipers, who in spite of the fog were making life miserable for the Union engineers. The Twentieth Maine had excellent cover from which to fire and was able to fend off the Rebel snipers, giving the Union engineers freedom to work.

The pontoon bridges were in place by noon, though the fog had grown thicker. Burnside would now soften up the enemy by bombarding the city. The command was given, and 150 pieces of Union artillery—including several of their largest cannons—opened their iron mouths with a terrific roar, hurling a tempest of destruction upon the city.

Colonel Ames and his Twentieth Maine stood in the icy weather, along with thousands of other men in blue, and listened to the bombardment. The air shook and the ground trembled with the deafening cannonade. Curiously, there was no return fire from Longstreet's guns on Marye's Heights, nor from Jackson's troops on ground level. Rebel soldiers in the city scattered for cover amid the howling of solid shot, the bursting of shells, the crashing of missiles through roofs and walls, and the dull sound of houses and commercial buildings collapsing.

As the bombardment continued, Mike O'Hanlon turned to Joshua Chamberlain and said, "Sir, I don't get it. Why aren't the Rebels shooting back?"

"I don't know. I'm sure Colonel Ames could tell you."

"I'm right here." Ames had been slowly making his way among his men, talking to them in quiet tones. "I couldn't make out the question, but I probably already know what it is. Everybody's asking the same thing. You want to know why Lee isn't firing back."

"Yes, sir," Mike said. "I'd think he'd be retaliating."

"It's quite simple, Lieutenant. General Lee knows we're set up strong enough to take out the city, no matter what he does. So he's waiting to take us on when he can see us and try to make every shot count."

"How soon will we be crossing the bridges, sir?" Chamberlain asked.

"I think General Burnside will put us across under cover of darkness. However, if the fog stays this low and thick, he may start putting us across before dark."

Shane stood next to Mike. "What's the general's purpose in destroying the town, Colonel? Ruining homes and businesses won't shorten the war, will it?"

"No, Captain. If I understand his thinking correctly, it's because the town is full of Rebel soldiers. It's them he's after. He gave the citizens time to evacuate before starting the bombardment. It's too bad, but civilians do suffer in a time of war. And we must remember, the Southerners fired the first shot."

Shane thought of the gospel-preaching churches in Fredericksburg and hated to think of their buildings being destroyed.

The horrible din lasted until after noon. Burnside readied a great number of his troops to cross the bridges even though the fog was breaking up. By one o'clock, the sun was shining through the clouds, revealing the smoking ruins of the city. Many houses, commercial buildings, and churches were on fire.

General Lee stood on Marye's Heights with General Longstreet and watched as the long lines of men in blue crossed the river on the bobbing pontoon bridges. Stonewall Jackson's sharpshooters were firing at them from the west bank of the river, but they were hindered by Union riflemen firing back.

Darkness fell, and the snipers' rifles went silent. A quarter of Burnside's army was on the west bank of the Rappahannock.

December 12 started with heavy fog, making it difficult for the Yankees to cross the bridges. Slowly, however, they made their way across, line after line of them. Burnside's force was massive—130,000 men. It would take time to get them all across. The fog was one hindrance. The Confederate sharpshooters were another.

Lee's army was much smaller…some 78,000 men. They had an advantage, however. General Burnside's decision to ignore Marye's Heights and the delay of his pontoon bridges gave the Confederates the high ground and time to establish bulwarks at ground level.

The road to Richmond, a sunken road some twenty-five feet wide, ran along the base of Marye's Heights. A long, shoulder-high stone wall ran the length of the hill's base, a perfect entrenchment for 2,500 of Longstreet's riflemen. Furthermore, Longstreet had positioned his artillery atop the heights so that the ground in front of the wall would be vulnerable to a murderous crossfire.

Lee, Longstreet, and Jackson were ready for the big battle that lay ahead of them.

December 13 came with fog once again covering the valley. Burnside now had the bulk of his army on the west side of the Rappahannock. Part of the Union's Fifth Division, including the Twentieth Maine, was kept in reserve in the dense forest on the east side.

Just before ten o'clock, the fog began to lift. From their position on the east bank of the river, Colonel Ames and his lieutenant colonel waited with their 550 men. They agreed that waiting in reserve was harder than being first into battle.

At precisely ten-thirty, the battle erupted. First there was firing in the city, as Union and Confederate soldiers collided, then the artillery units of both sides cut loose. Soon Longstreet's cannons on the heights and his infantry behind the stone wall were firing into brigades of men in blue as they swarmed across the level ground toward the wall and the high hill behind it.

From across the river, the men of the Twentieth Maine waited and watched in horror and fascination. To observe the deadly action and not be able to go to the aid of their comrades was a trial for all of them.

Shane Donovan's mind left the battle from time to time, though his eyes were fixed on it. He thought of Charly and found himself praying for her and wishing he could be with her.

Mike O'Hanlon's line of sight remained steadily on the fierce combat, but like his friend, his mind traveled back to Maine and the auburn-haired woman he had loved for so long. If only he could hold Ashley in his arms and whisper words of love into her ear.

The day ended with the Fifth Corps still in reserve. But before the men of the Fifth laid down for the night, they were told they would all see action the next day. Burnside's forces had been whittled down frightfully by the deadly crossfire that came from Marye's Heights and from behind the stone wall. Tomorrow the Union troops would storm the wall, climb the hill, and overpower Longstreet's artillery with overwhelming numbers.

A common grave was dug on the plain, and "Taps" was played in the light of a clear-edged moon as hundreds of Union soldiers were laid to rest.

There was only light fog on Sunday morning, December 14. The weather had warmed considerably, and what had been frozen ground was now slushy mud.

The battle began just after sunup and raged as violently as it had the day before. The Twentieth Maine watched several regiments that had been in reserve with them cross the river and enter the fight. Their nerves were stretched to the limit knowing that at any time they were going to face enemy guns.

Buster Kilrain found Shane and Mike talking to Joshua Chamberlain.

"Ye blokes ready to get into it?" he asked.

"More than ready," Chamberlain said.

"What's it like to know you're out there charging at men who are bent on killing you, Uncle Buster?" Mike asked.

"Well, son, there really isn't a way to describe it. You'll know soon enough, I'm sure."

Colonel Ames's voice cut the air. "All right, Twentieth Maine! We just got orders to cross the river! Let's go!"

Mike looked at Shane. "Let's stay close to each other, okay?"

"Sure. I can't blame you young boys for wanting a mature man fighting alongside you."

Mike grinned and punched Shane's arm. As they hurried toward the bridges together, he said, "Shane..."

"Yeah?"

"If you should make it and I don't—"

"Stop that kind of talk!"

"We have to be realistic. If I don't make it and you do, tell Ashley I died loving her with all my heart. Okay?"

"I said don't talk that way."

Cannonade thundered and rifle fire rattled as the Twentieth Maine reached the west side of the Rappahannock. Colonel Ames was there to give orders. They were to stay in close ranks and charge across the open plain along with two other regiments—the Sixteenth Michigan and the Eighty-third Pennsylvania—that were collected and ready to go. Their assignment: Charge the wall, kill the riflemen, then climb the hill and wipe out the Confederate soldiers manning the cannons.

Three other regiments—the Twelfth, Seventeenth, and Forty-fourth New York—had gone before them that morning and been repulsed. Hundreds of them lay dead on the field in front of Marye's Heights. The survivors were standing by, ready to join the new reinforcements in a fresh charge as they moved in long blue lines across the open plain.

After the New York Regiments closed ranks with the new ones, the sharp command to charge was given. Thousands of Union soldiers bolted across the open field toward the Confederates who waited at Marye's Heights. As they drew within two hundred yards, the sprawled and crumpled bodies of men who had died in the day's first charge grew thicker, and they had to weave around them or hop over them.

There was no time for fear as they drew near the wall, behind which Longstreet had positioned better than three thousand riflemen. The Confederate artillery opened up, and black muzzles spit fire all along the top of the wall. Cannonballs exploded into the charging swarm of blue, throwing bodies every direction.

The Twentieth Maine was green, but the discipline and hours at drill were paying off. The men who followed Ames and Chamberlain into the storm did not falter.

The gallant Union soldiers came within thirty paces of the stone wall, but encountered such a fire of canister and musketry that they had to fall back. Colonel Ames led his men toward a series of ditches where they could reload in relative safety. He cast a glance at many of his men who had fallen.

"Pure carnage!" he shouted at Chamberlain.

"We should have taken those heights when we had the opportunity!" Chamberlain shouted back.

"General Burnside will have some explaining to do," Ames said as the two of them dropped into a ditch.

Shane and Mike were running side by side toward a section of ditch. Shane could always outrun his best friend. As he began pulling ahead of him, he looked over his shoulder and shouted, "Come on! Only another thirty yards!"

"You run pretty fast for an old man!" Mike called in return. "But one of these days, I'm going to—"

Shane looked back and saw Mike go down. "Mike!" he cried, whirling and running toward him.

"Don't do it!" a soldier of the Sixteenth Michigan yelled as he came running past. "He's dead!"

"He's my best friend!" Shane shouted.

Shane would not believe Mike was dead. How could that soldier know? While hot lead whizzed all around him and men ran past him, he picked Mike up, cradling him in his arms, and ran to the nearest ditch. He lowered Mike gently into the ditch, then eased down beside him, keeping his head low.

Then he saw it. A bullet had hit Mike in the back of the head. The Michigan soldier was right. Mike was dead.

In solemn quietness, General Burnside's soldiers buried their dead by bright moonlight in a common grave dug hastily in a field a mile from Marye's Heights. Joshua Chamberlain and Buster Kilrain flanked Shane Donovan as he held Mike O'Hanlon's lifeless form in his arms, hesitating to lower it into the deep hole along with the other bodies. A bugler stood near, ready to blow "Taps" when the last body was placed in the ground.

Tears streamed down Shane's cheeks. Chamberlain laid a hand on his shoulder.

"One consolation, Shane."

"Yes, sir. I'll see him again in glory."

"The Christian's hope. Thank God for it."

Shane nodded, then looked into Mike's pale, stone-like face.

"I'll tell her, Mike. I'll tell her."

---

[1] All of us are acquainted with the haunting refrain known as "Taps." The song is connected in our minds with death and burial, but General Dan Butterfield composed it to *save* lives.

During the Civil War, just about every event in army life was ordered by bugle calls. Military burials, however, were conducted with a volley of rifle shots.

On June 25, 1862, Union and Confederate armies came together on the peninsula at Seven Pines, Virginia, in what was to become known as the Seven Days' Battle. The battle produced forty-three thousand casualties, and bodies were strewn for miles over the rolling, densely-wooded land. General Butterfield and his soldiers were forced by the terrain to camp within firing range of the Confederate forces. When they attempted to bury their dead and fired a volley of shots over the fresh graves, the Confederates thought they were under attack and immediately retaliated. Union soldiers were being killed just for attending the burial of their fallen comrades.

Determined that his dead soldiers would be buried with proper ceremony, General Butterfield composed a short tune for his buglers. He called it "Taps" and ordered it played in the place of the customary rifle volleys. The tune saved the lives of many Union soldiers of the Third Brigade, and it soon was used for "lights out," also. General Butterfield then put words to his tune that in his mind befit either occasion.

When he began to use "Taps" for the entire First Division upon becoming its commander, the tune caught on and spread throughout the Union forces. Before the Civil War was over, the Confederates were using it, too. Our American military has used it ever since.

EIGHTEEN

ajor General Ambrose E. Burnside called for a meeting of his officers following the burial ceremony. He wanted to launch another attack on Lee's army at dawn the next morning. Burnside had not perceived that the losses were so heavy that his officers and their troops were ready to back away from Fredericksburg.

Stonewall Jackson's men had fought like tigers, taking losses but killing a higher number of Yankees. The worst onslaught, however, had come from James Longstreet's artillery atop Marye's Heights and the infantry behind the stone wall. Together they produced a deadly crossfire that had killed thousands of Union troops.

The officers protested another attack; their commands had already sustained severe losses and had accomplished nothing. A great part of Fredericksburg had been reduced to rubble, but Lee's army was still intact and in control. General William B. Franklin was brazen enough to remind Burnside that he had deviated from the plan approved by President Lincoln and Henry Halleck, and that his most grievous mistake was not occupying Marye's Heights immediately. Other officers, including Daniel Butterfield, argued that to continue to assault the Confederates in their strong defensive positions would destroy the Union army.

Such strong arguments from his military leaders shook Burnside's resolve, and he ordered the final withdrawal of the Army of the Potomac back across the river. Upon the Union army's return to the camps at Falmouth, the disaster at Fredericksburg weighed heavily on the minds of the soldiers who had left so many of their comrades behind in the common graves.

Though the losses of the Twentieth Maine Regiment were heavy (153 dead and 47 wounded seriously enough to be sent to Washington for medical attention), Colonel Ames was well pleased with his regiment's performance under fire. After the volley of heavy artillery and musketry that had driven them back to the ditches, they had charged the wall again. Though repulsed once more, they had taken a measurable toll on the Rebels.

Ames was convinced his regiment had performed better than any other and had earned that day a reputation for fighting tenacity. The fierce battle had taught his officers and men the value of the hard-learned discipline acquired in seemingly endless hours of drill and instruction. A strong and united fighting unit had emerged from a band of green volunteers.

On the whole, however, the Army of the Potomac was in a low state of mind. Men of every division felt they had been foolishly and needlessly sacrificed by attacking an enemy so well fortified that victory was impossible.

Before January 1863 passed into history, President Lincoln, realizing that Burnside had lost the respect and confidence of his army, replaced him with Major General Joseph Hooker. Dan Butterfield was made Hooker's chief of staff, and George Meade was made commander of Fifth Corps in his place. Hooker did away with the Grand Divisions and reorganized the army, retaining the corps structure. Charles Griffin commanded First Division, and T. W. B. Stockton was made commander of Third Brigade, which still contained the Twentieth Maine Regiment.

Ames went to Meade, requesting that the other segment of his regiment that had been left behind to guard the Potomac fords be brought to Falmouth. He needed them to bolster the numbers of the Twentieth Maine after their heavy losses at Fredericksburg. Meade gladly obliged, and within a week the Twentieth was all together again.

There was relative quiet for the Twentieth Maine in the following weeks. Joshua Chamberlain, concerned that the Twentieth had lost so many men, asked Ames if he could return to Maine to talk to the new governor, Abner Coburn, about recruiting more volunteers.

On February 4, Chamberlain approached a field tent occupied by Shane Donovan. It was a cloudy, cold, blustery day. Buster Kilrain was standing near with his head bent into the wind, in conversation with two young soldiers.

"Good mornin', Colonel," Kilrain said, breaking off his conversation.

"Captain Donovan in his tent?" Chamberlain asked.

"Yes, sir. He's talkin' to Benny Wilson. But I'm sure he won't mind if you interrupt."

Chamberlain was about to call to Shane when the flap came open.

"I heard you ask if I was in here, Colonel," Shane said. "Come on in."

Chamberlain knew Corporal Wilson, who was from Winthrop, Maine. Wilson was eighteen years old and had gone through the Fredericksburg battle. As Chamberlain ducked his head and stepped into the tent, he saw Wilson thumbing tears from his eyes.

"Good morning, Benny."

Wilson smiled through his tears. "It sure is, sir. It's the best morning of my life! I just got saved!"

"Wonderful!" Chamberlain exclaimed. "What brought this about?"

"I've talked to Benny on a few occasions about becoming a Christian," Shane said. "He showed some interest, but that was about it. Well, Fredericksburg put a scare into him. He realizes he could've been killed, and he wouldn't have gone to heaven if he had. It's been eating on him. Or I should say the Holy Spirit has been working on him. He came to me an hour or so ago, wanting to know more about it. Just a few minutes ago he acknowledged to the Lord Jesus that he's a sinner in need of salvation, and called on Him to come into his heart and save him."

Chamberlain shook Wilson's hand. "You just took care of the biggest issue in your life, young man."

"Yes, sir, I know…thanks to Captain Donovan here."

"Well, I hate to interrupt this happy occasion, Wilson, but I need a few private moments with Captain Donovan. So if you'll excuse us…"

"No problem, sir."

When Wilson stepped out of the tent, the first thing he did was tell Buster Kilrain he had received Christ. Buster rejoiced with him.

Shane smiled at Chamberlain and said, "What can I do for you, sir?"

"It's what I can do for you, Shane. How would you like to go home and see Charly?"

The winter sunlight was shining through the bedroom windows, giving ample light, as Charolette Donovan sat in front of the mirror, brushing her long black hair. She was still in her robe, though it was nearly ten o'clock. She heard a knock at her front door. She stood up, laid the brush on the dresser, and wondering who was at the door, took a brief look at her pale features and the dark circles under her eyes.

She crossed the small parlor and could see the shadow of a tall man through the curtains that covered the window in the door. Her heart leaped in her breast. Could it be Shane? She pulled the collar of her robe up around her neck and opened the door.

"Hi, beautiful lady!" said the smiling soldier.

Charolette made a tiny squeal, took his hand, and pulled him inside. Shane shut the door and folded her in his arms.

After several minutes of sweet reunion, he said, "I went to the factory, but Darrell told me you weren't working today."

"Well, I...I haven't been working every day, darling. I just can't do it anymore. I'm...well, I'm just not strong enough. I've been working three days a week."

Shane ushered her to an overstuffed chair, sat her down, then knelt in front of her and took both hands in his.

"O honey, I'm so sorry. Have you seen Dr. Holladay about the loss of strength?"

"He says it just goes with my disease. He says I might take a turn for the better one of these days, and maybe go back to working full time. Ashley's working in my place."

The mention of Ashley sent a cold chill through Shane. He was going to have to tell her about Mike. The government had no system of notifying families of soldiers' deaths. It would fall on him to tell Mike's parents also.

"Honey, listen. Maybe you shouldn't work at all. Maybe it's time you go and live with my folks."

"No. Not yet. I want to work, Shane. It's therapy for me. And...and living in this house keeps me closer to you."

"All right. I just want what's best for you."

"Shane, we all heard about the Fredericksburg battle. It must have been awful. Oh, it's so horrible when I don't know whether you're dead or alive...or maybe alive but wounded. How were you able to come home this time...and how long can you stay?"

Shane told her that Joshua Chamberlain had obtained permission to come to Maine to recruit more volunteers for the Twentieth. Chamberlain had asked Shane if he wanted to come home with him for a couple of days. He had already obtained permission for Shane to take the leave.

"So you'll be here two days?" Charolette asked.

"Colonel Chamberlain and I are scheduled to take the 11:15 train from Portland day after tomorrow."

Shane took a deep breath and said, "Honey—"

A knock at the door cut him off.

"Expecting anybody?" he asked, heading for the door.

"No."

Shane swung the door open, and his heart leaped to his throat at the sight of Ashley O'Hanlon. The way the mid-morning sun struck her hair made it look like burnished copper.

"Hello, Shane," she said. "Darrell told me you were back. I don't mean to interrupt, and I'll only stay a minute, but I just had to hurry over. I knew you could tell me how Mike is."

"Come in," Shane said, praying silently for God's help.

Charolette spoke from her chair, "Hi, Ashley. Colonel Chamberlain was coming to Maine to talk to the governor and invited Shane to travel with him."

"That's wonderful!" Ashley said.

"Take your coat off and come sit down," Charolette said.

"Oh, no. Your time together is too valuable to have an intruder. I just wanted to hear about Mike, and I'll be on my way."

"Go ahead and take the coat off, Ashley," Shane said. "I…have something to explain to you. It'll take some time."

"Something's wrong, Shane," she said, her voice shaky. "What *is* it?" She removed her coat and scarf and laid them on a chair.

"Sit down, Ashley. Here. Next to Charly."

Ashley dropped into the chair, her eyes never leaving Shane's face.

"Shane, what is it? Something's happened to Mike, hasn't it? Is he…is he hurt? Bad?"

Ashley studied Shane's eyes. Her throat was frozen with fear. She waited for him to speak. Charolette rose to her feet and moved to her best friend. She laid a hand on Ashley's shoulder, set her tired eyes on Shane, and waited to hear whatever was coming.

After long seconds of painful silence, Shane knelt in front of Ashley, drew an uneasy breath, and said, "Ashley…Mike was killed at Fredericksburg."

Charolette sucked in a sharp breath, then leaned over and wrapped her arms around Ashley's shoulders. Ashley's face went the color of gray stone. Charolette could feel her go stiff. Tears welled up in Ashley's eyes. Her lips parted, but she couldn't speak. She sat transfixed, unable to move.

"We...the Twentieth...were attacking a Rebel fortification behind a stone wall. There was heavy artillery unleashing on us from the top of a hill behind the wall. They had us in a crossfire, and our commander signaled for us to retreat. We...we were running across an open field for safety." Shane choked up, bit his lips, and felt tears fill his eyes. "Mike was a few steps behind me. A...a bullet took his life, Ashley. Instantly. He never felt it. He didn't suffer."

Ashley stared at the floor. Her lips quivered. "Where is he...buried?"

"In a field outside of Fredericksburg. Along with hundreds of other Union soldiers."

"I'll never even get to see his grave."

Ashley suddenly burst into tears, wrapping her arms around Charolette. She sobbed as if her very soul would wrench itself from her body. Charolette held her and spoke soft words of understanding and comfort.

Shane and Charolette went with Ashley to inform Mike's family of his death. They left Ashley with her in-laws and went to Shane's family and told them. The next stop was the parsonage of First Parish Congregational Church to tell Dr. and Mrs. George Adams.

The day Shane was to head south with Joshua Chamberlain was a Saturday. Some twenty minutes before Chamberlain was to pick him up, Shane took his wife in his arms and said, "Darling, I can't stand this. It's tearing me up to go off and leave you when you're doing so poorly. I'm going to ask Colonel Chamberlain to get me out of the army. You need me, and I need to be here with you."

Charolette stroked his cheek. "Sweetheart, a lot of people are praying for me. You especially. The Lord doesn't always answer in a hurry. I still have hopes that He will touch me, and I'll take a turn for the better. Besides, Shane, you're a soldier of the United States Army. You must go back. Our country is at war. Thousands of others are making great sacrifices for the Union. Can we do any less?"

Shane bit hard on his lower lip, then said, "No. We can't. It's my duty to help bring this horrid war to an end."

They clung to each other, savoring the precious minutes, then Joshua Chamberlain pulled up in the rented buggy.

As the buggy pulled away, Shane looked back and waved. Charolette waved back, tears streaming down her cheeks. When the buggy reached the corner, the last thing Shane saw was Ashley O'Hanlon hurrying up to Charolette and the two women throwing their arms around each other.

When Joshua Chamberlain and Shane arrived back at the Falmouth camp, they learned that the Army of the Potomac was being ordered back to a camp near Washington.

On March 29, President Lincoln appeared at the camp for a Grand Review. He was pleased to see the rejuvenated fitness and morale of his troops under the leadership of Joseph Hooker. When the Review was over, Lincoln addressed the troops. He spoke words of encouragement and optimism that the Union was going to be victorious. The men in blue cheered, and Lincoln was thrilled with their response.

Before dismissing the army, the president announced that the commanding officers of three regiments had submitted the names of three soldiers who had displayed unusual courage during the battle at Fredericksburg. He was going to present them with Presidential Commendations for their unselfish and gallant deeds.

The names were called out, and Captain Shane Donovan was surprised to hear his name among the three. The recipients were asked to come to the platform.

Lincoln already had the regiment commanders ready to meet the soldiers on the platform. Colonel Ames smiled broadly at Shane when their eyes met. Shane stood beside his colonel as the commanders of the other regiments told the crowd of soldiers of the brave deeds done by their two men.

After both men had received their written commendations from the president, Colonel Ames was called to speak. Ames explained that he had submitted a written statement of Captain Shane Donovan's act of courage on September 18, 1862, near Sharpsburg, Maryland. Donovan had hazarded his own life to protect Lieutenant Colonel Joshua Chamberlain from a Confederate officer's bullet and had killed the enemy officer in the process.

Eyewitnesses had also told Ames that at Fredericksburg, Captain Donovan had picked up a fallen fellow officer under heavy fire and carried him to safety, not knowing the officer was already dead.

For these two deeds of courage and heroism, Shane Donovan was given the Presidential Commendation by Abraham Lincoln while thousands of his fellow-soldiers cheered and applauded.

April came to Washington, and with it spring warmth. During the first week of April, the Twentieth Maine was given the job of protecting Union telegraph lines in northern Virginia.

Since things were quiet, Shane approached Joshua Chamberlain about getting another leave so he could go home and see Charly. Chamberlain was able to talk Colonel Ames into it, but on the same day, some seventy-five men of the Twentieth Maine fell ill. The entire regiment had been inoculated for smallpox two days earlier, and it was discovered that the seventy-five had been given defective vaccine. The regiment was pulled off telegraph line duty and quarantined until late April. Thirty-eight of the seventy-five died.

When the quarantine was lifted, Shane was making ready for a trip to Maine when things heated up with the Confederates. A battle was about to take place at Chancellorsville, Virginia. Shane's leave was canceled.

The battle started on May 2 and lasted until May 4. After making a promising beginning to his campaign, Joseph Hooker was outmaneuvered by Robert E. Lee and his bold subordinate, Stonewall Jackson. Hooker had started the campaign confident of victory, then was forced to withdraw the army to its Falmouth camps.

The spirits of the Union troops were deflated by the unexpected defeat. They had entertained such high hopes of victory under Hooker's leadership. Though President Lincoln was disappointed with Hooker's performance, he left him in charge of the army.

On May 20, Colonel Ames was promoted to brigadier general and transferred to the Union's Eleventh Corps. Much to the elation of the Twentieth Maine, Joshua Chamberlain was promoted to full colonel and given the Twentieth as his command.

On May 23, 120 new men arrived in response to Chamberlain's request to Governor Coburn for fresh recruits. Among them was Rex Carden, a young man who had worked with Shane at the lumber mill in Brunswick. Though a likable person, Carden had always been a bit "devil-may-care" and unruly.

Shane took Carden aside and warned him that he would have to toe the line in the army, or pay the consequences. Carden assured him that he had changed. Shane had often talked to Carden about the Lord, but the unruly young man had no time for God. When Shane asked him if he had also changed in that way, Carden chuckled nervously and said he had thought about their talks and even recalled some of the Scriptures Shane had quoted him. He would give it some consideration.

On June 1, Colonel Strong Vincent, a native of Pennsylvania, was made commander of the Third Brigade. A robust and handsome man, Vincent was an 1859 graduate of Harvard College and had just passed his twenty-sixth birthday. Vincent was only a year older than Shane, and upon being introduced, they struck an instant friendship.

Shane Donovan rode his horse along the telegraph lines that led through the Virginia hills and valleys to Washington and talked with the men of the Twentieth. None of them had seen any sign of Rebels. So far, Lee hadn't sent any troops to destroy Union communications.

At sundown on June 8, Shane was riding toward the camp, his heart longing for Charly. He hadn't seen her since early February. He had received four letters from her since then, and though she tried to put on that she was doing fine, he knew better. Her handwriting showed signs that she was growing weaker, and she was now living with his parents. Since there was no immediate battle pending as far as he knew, Shane decided to ask Chamberlain for permission to make a quick trip home. When he arrived at the camp, Shane found that Chamberlain had gone to Washington with General Charles Griffin and would not be back for two days.

Strong Vincent looked up as he sat in a canvas-backed chair at the front of his field tent and saw Shane drawing up. Vincent closed the Bible he was reading and stood up.

"Good afternoon, Captain," Vincent said. "What can I do for you?"

Shane eyed the Bible and smiled. "Wonderful Book, isn't it?"

"None like it. A man needs a map to get through this country. Our engineers provide that for us. A man also needs a map to get through this life…and into the next. Our God has provided that for us. This Bible is that map, and Jesus Christ is the Way."

"Amen to that. Man talks like that, makes me think he's a born-again child of God."

"Since October 2, 1860. The young lady who is now my wife led me to Jesus. We were married six months later."

"Thank God for a dedicated Christian young lady."

"That's for sure. She wouldn't date me until I became a Christian. I fought the Lord and His gospel for a while, but finally He broke down my stubborn will. After I received Christ, we had our first date. Things got better, and we finally got married. But let's see...you haven't told me why you came to see me."

"Well, sir, may I take a minute and explain something to you?"

"Certainly. Here's another chair. Sit down."

Shane gave Vincent a brief explanation of Charly's health, without telling him that Charly may be dying, and asked if he could have permission to make a quick trip home to see her. Vincent took it to heart, saying he would go right then to General Hooker and try to persuade him to give leave for Shane to go see his ailing wife.

Shane waited at Vincent's tent. A quarter-hour later the colonel returned, the look on his face conveying that he had bad news.

"I'm sorry, Captain. General Hooker said he wishes he could let you go, but Lee is making moves that spell a big battle in the offing. No leaves are being granted at all."

The denial hit Shane like a club in the chest. "But sir, I can make the trip and be back here in four days. I...I didn't tell you how serious Charly's sickness really is. I'm afraid the Lord is going to take her home. I must see her before that happens. You have a wife that you love with all your heart. Please...put yourself in my place. If you don't feel you can go back and explain this to General Hooker, I'll try to see him myself."

Vincent scrubbed a hand across his clean-shaven face. "Tell you what...I'll take you to him. Maybe my presence will help."

Shane and Vincent were able to see Hooker, but the general still would not grant the leave. He needed every officer he had on hand. Lee was making a move the Union army was going to have to watch. Small units of gray-uniformed troops were moving northward toward Pennsylvania.

Shane walked away from the general's tent with a heavy heart, but he thanked Colonel Vincent for trying.

By June 14, Robert E. Lee was moving his Army of Northern Virginia toward Pennsylvania in large units. This was enough to press

Joseph Hooker into matching Lee in a parallel march. Hooker gathered his Army of the Potomac and began marching northward toward Frederick, Maryland.

Summer had arrived in full, and the hot weather slowed both armies to a snail's pace. They were making only a few miles a day. Many men on both sides were dropping from sunstroke.

On June 25, the heat and humidity were so intense that General Hooker called for a halt in early afternoon. They were at a small creek lined with shade trees, and the entire Union force stopped to take shelter from the sun and to cool off in the creek. Shane Donovan was off his horse and walking beside Buster Kilrain when the news came down the line of General Hooker's order to halt and rest.

"This march to Frederick is going to take a while, Captain," Buster said. "Why don't you talk to Chamberlain and see if he can't get you permission to go see her. Won't hurt to try."

"I'll do it," Shane said. "He's up front of the troops. I'll find him somewhere along the creek and see what he says."

Shane saw a group of soldiers at the head of the Twentieth's lines break rank and make a circle. Suddenly Rex Carden was running toward him, calling, "Captain Donovan!"

Shane handed the reins of his horse to Buster and ran to meet Carden. "What is it, Rex?"

"It's Colonel Chamberlain, Captain! He's passed out!"

Shane hurried toward the spot where Chamberlain's riderless horse stood in the heat of the sun.

Shane Donovan stayed beside Joshua Chamberlain for the rest of the afternoon, dampening his face with water from the creek and using the colonel's cap to fan him. Chamberlain was stretched out on the grass in the shade, and Buster Kilrain sat there, too. From time to time, Chamberlain roused and seemed to be coming to, then he would slip under again.

"Buster, I don't think he's going to come around for a while," Shane said. "I've just got to go to Charly. Looks like I'll have to see if

Colonel Vincent will try to help me convince General Hooker to let me go."

"I'll take care of Joshua. You go on and talk to Vincent."

Strong Vincent's heart went out to Shane Donovan, but he shook his head and said, "Captain, I can't get to General Hooker right now. He and President Lincoln are having some problems between them, and the general is in wire contact with the president a couple of miles from here. I think he's going to be tied up there for some time."

"Well, sir, would you give me the leave? I'm about to come apart inside. I've got to get to Charly."

Vincent used a bandanna to mop his brow. "Captain, I wish I could, but General Hooker would have my neck. He absolutely will allow no leaves at this time. You know something's got to explode between us and the Rebels pretty soon. We need every man—especially every officer—we have. I'm really sorry, but you'll have to stay."

Shane reasoned that it would be at least ten days to two weeks before the two armies would go to battle. But another battle was already raging inside him. Shane loved Charly more than he loved life itself. He couldn't let her die without seeing her again. He did not want to disobey his superiors, nor did he want his fellow-soldiers to think he had run away. But he had to see her.

Tom Chamberlain had found his brother and was seated on the grass under the trees with Buster Kilrain as Shane approached.

"How's he doing?" Shane asked, kneeling down next to Buster.

"Still rallies every once in a while," Buster said, "but goes back under again. He'll be all right by mornin', I'm thinkin'."

"Tom, could I talk to you in private?" Shane said.

The two men moved to a relatively private spot in the shade and Tom asked, "What is it, my friend?"

"Tom, you're an officer, and you're my colonel's brother, so I'll tell you."

"Tell me what?"

"You know Charly is very sick."

"Of course. I pray for her often."

"Thank you. Listen, Tom, I know there's a big battle in the cooker. But from what I can put together, it's not going to happen for at least a couple of weeks or so."

"That's probably true."

"I need to go home and see Charly. I think she's dying. Can you understand that?"

"Yes. Have you talked to Josh about it?"

"I was going to when we stopped for the day."

"How about Colonel Vincent?"

"I tried. He says General Hooker's tied up with the president, and he can't give me leave without the general's permission. He says the general wouldn't do it even if he could talk to him."

"Shane, if you just up and go it will appear to the army as desertion."

Shane Donovan's voice was strained as he said, "I've thought of that. But I'm *not* deserting! As I see it, I would be deserting if I ran during battle. Charly's dying, Tom. I feel it in my heart. There's so little time. I've got to see her before she dies!"

"But Shane, why didn't you just take off? Why tell me you're going?"

"Because I'm not deserting, Tom. I'm only going home to see my wife before she dies. Tell your brother I will be back. Within four days. Please don't let anybody stop me. I'll head out when it gets dark."

Tom Chamberlain sleeved sweat from his brow, nodded, and said, "All right, Shane. I won't alert anyone. You go see Charly. I'll tell Josh when he comes around."

NINETEEN

C ampfires flickered along the creek, and Union soldiers talked in low tones, discussing the rumored problem between General Hooker and the president. They also expressed their opinions as to when and where the big battle would take place.

Tom Chamberlain was alone with Joshua when he came to. The sunstroke had left him weak and a bit nauseated, and Tom waited till Joshua had taken some water and was sitting up against a tree before telling him about Shane Donovan.

"Tom, please tell me you're joking," Joshua said.

"I wish I was, Josh. But he's gone."

"How long ago?"

"About forty minutes."

"As commander of the Twentieth, I'm duty-bound to report him. But since I'm not feeling well, guess I'll have to give it another couple of hours before I'm strong enough to go to the general's tent and turn in the report."

Tom grinned. "For sure."

Shane Donovan rode into Brunswick on the afternoon of June 27, 1863, on a horse rented in Portland. As he drew near his parents' house, he saw his youngest brother, Ryan, who was now nineteen, coming up the street from the opposite direction. Lewis O'Hanlon had talked Ryan into working at the shoe and boot factory upon his graduation from high school in May. Patrick had joined the Christian Commission with John Chamberlain and was somewhere down south serving the Federal cause.

Ryan smiled at his oldest brother as Shane swung from the saddle. They embraced. Shane felt relief when Ryan told him Charolette would be plenty happy to see him. He raised his eyes to the window of the bedroom he knew she occupied, but no face appeared.

At that moment, Shane heard a young female voice cry from the front porch, "Uncle Shane!"

Darlene Brainerd was ten years old now, and when school was out, spent a lot of time at his parents' house. He saw his mother standing on the porch as Darlene ran and threw her arms around him. Pearl Donovan was smiling at him and brushing tears from her cheeks.

"Hello, sweetheart," Shane said, giving Darlene a strong hug. "How are you and the rest of your family?"

"We're doing fine, Uncle Shane. Mama will be glad to know you're home and looking good. Do you have to go back to the war?"

"Yes, I'm afraid so."

"I'll be glad when you can come home for good. Aunt Charolette will too. She's going to be real glad to see you!"

Shane walked toward the porch with an arm around Darlene and kissed and embraced his mother. Pearl told him how glad she was to know he was alive and well. She asked how soon he had to head back, and he said he would have to leave at ten the next morning.

Darlene and Ryan followed Pearl and Shane into the house. Shane headed for the staircase, and Pearl said in a hushed voice, "She's not doing well at all, son. She's thinner than when you saw her in February, and she's awfully weak. In bed most of the time. Sits up in her chair in the mornings, but by early afternoon she's down again." She paused, then said, "She may be asleep, but go ahead and wake her. She'll want every minute with you she can have."

"Dear God," Shane said as he mounted the stairs, "thank You that she's still here."

The door was pushed shut, but not latched. Shane quietly pushed it open and saw that Charolette was asleep. Her raven-black hair lay in wavy swirls on the pillow, and her face seemed as white as the pillow case. Indeed, she was thinner, and the circles around her eyes were darker.

As he tiptoed across the room, the floorboards squeaked and Charly stirred. He stopped a few steps from the bed, and when she opened her eyes, she saw him.

"Shane!" she cried in a husky voice, lifting her arms. "O Shane, is it really you, or am I dreaming?"

Shane dropped to his knees beside the bed and took her in his arms. She clung to his neck. They held on to each other for a long time, then he kissed the tip of her nose and said, "You're not dreaming, precious lady. It's really me. General Hooker is moving the army across Maryland into Pennsylvania. There's going to be one whinging of a battle somewhere soon. I have to hurry back tomorrow morning, but...I just had to take a little side trip and see my wonderful wife."

They held each other for a long time, then talked about Charolette's health. She was a fighter. Giving up was not in her. She was still trusting God to heal her, and talked of how wonderful it would be when Shane came home for good and they could have their life together.

Shane wanted with all his heart to believe it.

"How's Ashley?" he asked.

"The Lord has given her grace. She still talks a lot about Mike and has her crying spells. Bless her heart, Shane, she comes here every day, even on Sundays between church services, to help take some of the load off your mother. She helps me bathe and washes my hair. I...I can hardly handle the stairs anymore. Ashley carries my meals up to me."

"She's not working at the factory?"

"Lewis hired another woman full-time to take my place. But he still sends a check over here with Ashley every week, same as if I were still working for him."

"You told me about that in a letter. I've got to thank him."

"Ashley does some office work for him as he needs her. She's there probably fifteen hours a week."

"Good she can stay busy."

"She does that, all right. When she's here, she always prays with me and *for* me, and for you…and reads the Bible to me."

"Talk about a real friend. You've got it in her."

"You were that kind of a friend to Mike too, Shane."

"Oh, speaking of Mike…there's something I want to show you."

Shane left the room long enough to go to the head of the stairs and call, "Ryan!"

Ryan came into view quickly. "Yes?"

"On that horse outside there's a blue canvas haversack tied behind the saddle. Has something in it I want to show Charly. Would you bring it up to me, please?"

"I already brought it in and put the horse in the shed out back. I'll bring it right up!"

Shortly thereafter, Shane was sitting on the side of the bed, opening a large brown envelope. He took out an official-looking document and handed it to Charolette. Her eyes focused on the document and she gasped.

"Why, Shane! It's a Presidential Commendation signed by Abraham Lincoln—for courage displayed on the battlefield above and beyond the call of duty! Oh, I'm so proud of you!"

"I hope you don't think I'm showing it to you to boast, or anything like that. I just thought a man's wife ought to know something like this."

"Of course she should. And of course I know you're not boasting. Was this given because of what you did when Mike was shot?"

"That and for an incident when I saved Colonel Chamberlain's life. Did you hear about his promotion to full colonel, and that he's now the commander of the Twentieth?"

"Fannie has made sure the whole state knows about it, I think. I'm so glad for him. He deserves it."

"Sure does. He's a wonderful man. I guess you could say he's my best friend now. On earth, I mean."

"Yes, let's not forget that Mike isn't gone. He's just waiting to see you higher up."

Shane felt his chest grow cold. He feared that soon his beloved Charly would be taken there, too. Suddenly they heard excited voices downstairs, followed by rapid footsteps on the stairs. Then Ashley popped through the door, eyes wide and wearing a warm smile.

"Shane! It's so good to see you!"

The old friends embraced and kissed each other on the cheek. Shane thanked Ashley for the way she was caring for Charly. Ashley said she and Charolette were best friends, just like Mike and Shane had been.

The next morning, Shane tied his haversack on the back of the horse, then went upstairs to tell Charly good-bye. She was in her chair, dressed in a white robe that made her hair look blacker than ever. She seemed to look better. He wondered if it was simply because seeing him had given her a lift, or if it was an indication that her illness might be in remission. With all his heart, he hoped it was the latter.

Shane had spent a little time with his parents and brother the night before. They waited downstairs, knowing he needed the time with Charly. When he had stayed till the last possible minute, he knelt beside the chair, held her in his arms, and told her he loved her with all his heart. They prayed together, then Shane kissed the tip of her nose and rose to his feet.

Charly smiled up at him and said softly, "I'll be lots better next time you come home."

"Promise?"

"Promise."

On June 28, the same day Shane Donovan rode toward Portland with his heart bleeding for Charly, vital changes were taking place in the ranks of the Army of the Potomac, even while it marched toward the Maryland-Pennsylvania line.

By orders from President Lincoln through his general-in-chief, Henry Halleck, Joseph Hooker was relieved as commander of the Union army. His hard-headed insubordination toward Lincoln had run its course. Lincoln replaced him with George G. Meade. By Meade's request, George Sykes became commander of Fifth Corps. The other six corps commanders remained the same. Meade requested that James Barnes be made commander of First Division, Fifth Corps. No other division commanders were changed.

Early on the morning of June 29, the front lines of Meade's army crossed the Pennsylvania border. From what Meade's scouts were telling him, it appeared that the opposing armies would converge at a small Pennsylvania town nine miles north of the border, known as Gettysburg.

At the same time, twenty-five miles south, George Sykes and his Fifth Corps were just arriving at Frederick, Maryland. The citizens of Frederick cheered them, as they had the other Union corps that had passed through before them.

In the heat of the early afternoon on July 1, the Fifth Corps crossed the state line into Pennsylvania. Joshua Chamberlain was riding abreast of Strong Vincent when they crossed into Vincent's home state. Just ahead of them, Old Glory waved in the morning breeze.

Vincent pointed to the flag and lifted his cap. "If I die in this battle, Colonel Chamberlain, what death more glorious could any man desire than to die on the soil of old Pennsylvania fighting for that flag?"

Chamberlain only smiled. He would rather die on Maine soil, but he could not wish that the war would reach the rolling hills and forests of his home state.

Just behind the ranks of the Twentieth Maine was the Eighty-third Pennsylvania Regiment. As the men of that unit crossed the border, their color-bearer unfurled the regiment's battered flag, and the fifes and drums struck up "Yankee Doodle." A tremendous shout went up from hundreds of throats. The enthusiasm spread both ways, and men all along the lines began shouting. Soon every drum was beating and every banner flying, including the battle flag of the Twentieth Maine.

General Robert E. Lee had kept his seventy thousand troops west of Meade's and was leading part of them in close-knit columns down the Chambersburg Pike from Cashtown. Meade's ninety thousand men were still strung out southward over thirty miles.

Neither army was ready to enter into full-scale battle on July 1. Lee insisted that no general engagement be started until the rest of his strung-out army was concentrated between Cashtown and Gettysburg. His plan was to engage the enemy in the fields between the towns, but his scouts reported that Meade already had his engineers laying out a defensive line in the ridges just outside of Gettysburg on the west.

Lee had his Third Corps with him, under the command of Ambrose Powell Hill, who was a fierce fighter. But his other two corps were still miles away. First Corps, under the command of Lee's "Old War Horse," James Longstreet, was almost a day's march to the west. Second Corps, commanded by Richard Ewell, was several miles to the north. Ewell had taken Stonewall Jackson's place as commander of Second Corps when Jackson was killed at Chancellorsville. The death of Jackson had left Lee feeling that he had lost his right arm.

While halted at a small creek for water a mile or so north of the state line, Strong Vincent and Joshua Chamberlain stood in what little shade an old elm tree could give them and drank from their canteens. Vincent cast a long look toward the south, and Chamberlain followed his line of sight.

"Looking for something, Colonel?"

"Some*one*. Your Captain Donovan. I'm beginning to wonder if he's coming back."

Chamberlain was silent for a moment. Did Shane find Charolette dead when he got home? Or if she was still alive, would he really come back as he told Tom he would? Aloud, Chamberlain said, "He'll be back unless providentially hindered."

Colonel Vincent had not taken it well when Chamberlain told him of Shane's departure, though Chamberlain had tried to impress on him that either of them might have done the same thing given similar circumstances. Vincent had said only that it would be wrong, no matter who left the camp without permission.

Chamberlain then told Vincent of Shane Donovan's Presidential Commendation, and why he received it. This caused Vincent to grow quiet for a long time, then having difficulty clearing his voice, he repeated that it was still wrong for a soldier to leave camp without permission.

"Colonel," Vincent said, "if Captain Donovan does come back, you understand I have to put him under arrest and hold him for court-martial."

Chamberlain set steady eyes on him, but did not reply.

Vincent frowned. "I hate to do it, Chamberlain. Especially because he's my Christian brother. But it's military law. You know that."

"Yes, sir. Military law."

Late afternoon on June 30, Shane Donovan galloped toward Frederick, following the trail of the Union army. By the condition of the animal droppings along the trail, he figured the tail end of the Union lines was not far ahead.

He slowed his horse as he reached the edge of the city and held it to a slow walk. People on the main street waved and smiled at him. He greeted them in return, then spotted an elderly man who was about to cross the dusty street in front of him. Shane rode up to him and leaned from the saddle.

"Good afternoon sir. I'm part of the Twentieth Maine Regiment, which had to have come through here along with the rest of the Army of the Potomac. When did the last bunch go through?"

"Yesterday afternoon. From what I could pick up, they're headed due north. Looks like there's gonna be a big battle somewhere over the line in Pennsylvania."

"Yes, sir. That's what the army officials told me in Washington. Thanks for the information."

"My pleasure. God be with you, son."

"And you, sir."

Shane had ridden two more blocks when a group of young women in front of the general mercantile store took note of him. As he drew near, they began to smile and wave. He touched the bill of his officer's cap and smiled back. His eye fell on a lovely brunette who strongly resembled Charly.

"God bless you, soldier!" one of them cried.

"Send those Rebels home where they belong, Captain!" said another.

When he was past them, Shane breathed a prayer for the one who was bone of his bones and flesh of his flesh. "O Charly," he whispered, "I love you so much. Please keep your promise. Please be better the next time I come home."

The Fifth Corps pulled off the road some four miles north of the state line shortly before the sun dipped behind the western hills. There were no fires, for General Meade had made it clear they were to leave the Pennsylvania countryside like they found it. They drank water from their canteens and ate beef jerky or salt pork, along with hardtack and dried-out biscuits. As they ate, they heard the sound of artillery and musketry coming from the direction of Gettysburg, some five miles to the north.

Joshua Chamberlain was sitting on the grass in the open field, eating with Tom and Buster Kilrain. Thousands of men in blue surrounded them. The men were quiet, talking little. They were tired, and their minds were fixed on the sounds of the distant guns. Their forward corps were no doubt already in conflict with the enemy. As the sun set, the sounds of battle diminished, then finally went still.

Buster was telling the Chamberlain brothers what he figured Lee had in mind, when Tom looked up and saw two familiar faces coming toward them.

"Josh..."

"Yeah?"

"Shane."

Joshua Chamberlain's head jerked around. Shane Donovan and Rex Carden were walking toward him.

"I knew he'd come back," Buster said almost under his breath.

As Joshua, Tom, and Buster stood up, Rex veered off, saying, "I'll think about it some more, sir."

Other soldiers in the area looked on as Shane halted and said, "Colonel, sir, I caught up to you as fast as I could. They told me at the camp in Washington about the changes in command, and that General Meade had the army moving toward Pennsylvania."

The Chamberlain brothers and Buster made a small half-circle in front of him.

"What about...Charly?" Joshua asked.

Shane removed his cap and ran a sleeve across his brow. "She's not well, sir."

"Worse than when you saw her last?" Buster asked.

Shane nodded. "She's lost more weight, and she spends most of her time in bed."

"Sorry to hear that, Shane," Tom said.

"I'm not giving up hope, though. The Lord can heal her."

"Aye, He can," Buster said.

Joshua's insides were churning. He took a step closer and said, "Shane, I...I have to take you to Colonel Vincent."

"I'm in trouble, aren't I?"

"Yes. I tried to reason with him, even told him about your Presidential Commendation. But he says it's his duty to put you under arrest and hold you until you can face a court-martial."

Shane took a deep breath. "I'll turn myself in."

"I'll go with you."

"Me and Tom will come too, if ye like," Buster said.

"No need. But thanks anyway."

Dusk was on the land as Shane and Joshua Chamberlain drew near Colonel Vincent's field tent. A rider was just galloping off, heading due north. Vincent's back was to them as he watched the rider thunder away.

"Colonel Vincent, sir..." Shane said.

The colonel turned around slowly, glanced at Chamberlain, then set his gaze on Shane Donovan.

"I've come to turn myself in, sir. I fully realize that I left the camp without your permission. Colonel Chamberlain was sick and unable to talk, and you were not available. I did what I thought was right in view of the circumstances, sir, but I am ready to take my punishment."

"Captain Donovan, may I ask about your wife?"

"She's not well, sir."

Vincent nodded silently. "Do you think this may have been the last time you will see her?"

"On this earth, sir. Unless the Lord intervenes."

Vincent took a deep, tremulous breath and let it out through his nostrils. "I'm sorry."

"Thank you, sir."

Vincent looked at Chamberlain again, then back at Shane. "According to military law, Captain, it is my duty to arrest you and hold you for court martial."

"Yes, sir."

The colonel's face was solemn. "I am a graduate of Harvard Law School, as you may have heard."

"Yes, sir."

"It was my dream to one day become a judge. Judges are given the responsibility of interpreting the law, Captain."

"Yes, sir."

"They must take all circumstances into consideration when doing so."

"Yes, sir."

"Military commanders in the field must often act as judges. I'm sure you understand that because you are my brother in Christ, I would like to just forget your deed. But if Christians do wrong, other Christians cannot condone it."

"I understand that, sir."

"Since discussing your case with Colonel Chamberlain, I have been giving it a lot of thought."

"Yes, sir."

"I decided to take it higher."

"Sir?"

"To Generals Barnes, Sykes, and Meade."

Shane swallowed hard. "Yes, sir."

"After listening to their judgment in your case, Captain Donovan, I hereby inform you that as far as the generals are concerned, your little trip to Maine never happened." Even as he spoke, Vincent's lips curved into a wide smile.

Astonishment showed in Shane Donovan's face, followed by great relief. "I...I don't know what to say, Colonel."

"Just thank the Lord. It was His doing. I prayed fervently before I went to the generals."

"I do thank Him," Shane said. "And I thank you, sir. And you!" he added, turning to Chamberlain.

After both colonels told Shane he was welcome, Chamberlain asked Vincent, "Was that messenger from General Meade?"

"Yes. He informed me what the fighting was about at Gettysburg that we heard a little while ago. Our First and Seventh Corps fought a desperate battle with part of the Rebel army. A lot of men were killed on both sides. General Meade wants us to march till midnight. We'll stop, sleep three hours, then march again. The rest of Lee's army is marching tonight, too."

When the Fifth Corps started its march at 3:00 A.M., they were but three miles from Gettysburg. As always, moving troops and equipment was slow. When dawn came, the men in blue began to see evidence of a cavalry battle—trampled grain, broken fences, dead horses, and bodies of Yankees and Rebels strewn in the fields.

Fifth Corps, weary and sleepy, arrived at Gettysburg just before 7:00 on Thursday morning, July 2, 1863. They halted at Wolf's Hill, a mile or so southeast of the town's center. The other six corps of the Union army were already there.

Running north and south three-quarters of a mile west of Gettysburg was Seminary Ridge, rising some forty feet above the surrounding fields. The ridge was crowned by the three-story brick building of the Lutheran Theological Seminary.

Due south of town was its cemetery, which was on a gentle rise that topped out some eighty feet above the town. Cemetery Ridge skirted Cemetery Hill on the south side and curved west, then south. It was about the same height as Seminary Ridge some thousand yards to the west.

Culp's Hill butted up on a portion of the south edge of Cemetery Ridge. The Fifth Corps, having no time for rest nor breakfast, was moved quickly to Culp's Hill. This placed them in the rear of the right of the Union line, which resembled a giant, upside-down fishhook. The hook started with its barb southeast of Culp's Hill, curved north, then ran west to the top of Cemetery Hill. After proceeding around Cemetery Hill, the hook—made up of thousands of Union troops—plunged south along Cemetery Ridge. A half-mile south of Cemetery Ridge stood a granite hill, thick with trees, known as Little Round Top, which stood 170 feet high. Some 500 yards slightly to the southwest of Little Round Top rose the highest prominence in the area, called Big Round Top. It was heavily wooded and cone-shaped and stood 305 feet high.

When the Fifth Corps looked the area over, they were glad to see Union flags atop Cemetery Hill, Cemetery Ridge, both Round Tops, and Culp's Hill. Gaining the high ground was always advantageous. This they remembered from the devastating experience at Fredericksburg. One thing bothered them, however. There was a Confederate flag atop Seminary Ridge. Lee had occupied at least one high spot.

To the west of Little Round Top was a massive jumble of huge granite boulders known as Devil's Den. Beyond Devil's Den toward Seminary Ridge was a large peach orchard. Between Devil's Den and Little Round Top was a marshy, rock-strewn valley. Through it flowed a small stream named Plum Run.

The land that spread out from Cemetery Ridge and the Round Tops south, east, and west contained houses, barns, fields, pastures, and woods of several farms. Fences built from stones cleared from the land ran in several directions across the peaceful terrain, which was about to become a raging, bloody battlefield.

TWENTY

As the sun continued its climb into the Pennsylvania sky, heating up the land as it went, General Robert E. Lee was not yet ready to engage the enemy. He needed to position his troops to assault the Union forces, who had most of the high ground.

At 8:00 A.M., General George Meade met with the officers of Fifth Corps at the field tent atop Cemetery Hill. The way Lee was shifting his army about, Meade knew he had some time before any Confederate assault began. Meade set aside several regiments to be held in reserve. One of those regiments was the Twentieth Maine. Also present for the meeting were Winfield S. Hancock, commander of Second Corps, and Daniel E. Sickles, commander of Third Corps. These men would have some of the reserve regiments at their disposal once the day's battle began. For the time being, the Twentieth Maine was to return to Culp's Hill and wait.

When the meeting was dismissed, Shane Donovan walked a few yards from Meade's tent and in among the tombstones. His heart grew heavy as he read the inscriptions. Was this what he would find when he returned home—Charly's grave with a tombstone coldly declaring the date of her birth and the date of her death?

The tired and hungry men of the Twentieth Maine settled down on Culp's Hill, pulled hardtack, biscuits, salt pork, and beef jerky from their canvas haversacks, and wolfed them down. The temperature was rising, and the air was humid and oppressive. Many took advantage of the wait to doze, while others talked in low tones of the coming battle. Shane and Joshua Chamberlain sat on the sloping hill and read their Bibles together. They were just closing them when Shane saw Rex Carden sitting a few feet away, watching them.

"Hello, Rex," Shane said. "Come join us."

Carden got up and walked to them, then sat down beside Shane.

"So have you been thinking about what we talked about the other day?" Shane asked.

"Yes, sir. But I just don't think I'm ready to get saved."

"We're going into battle, Rex. Are you ready to die?"

The young soldier met Shane's gaze, then looked at the ground. "No."

"Do you remember what the Bible says…that whoever believes in Jesus, God's Son, will not perish but will have everlasting life? All you need to do is call on Jesus, Rex, to put your faith and trust in Him. You can go into battle today knowing that if you should die, you'll spend eternity in heaven. Wouldn't you like to have that assurance?"

"Yes, sir. I'm…just not ready to call on Him, Captain."

"What do you think it will take to make you ready?"

"I don't know, sir. But until I am, I wouldn't mean it if I called on Him."

"Of course I want you to mean it, Rex. But you can put Him off too long and be eternally sorry. He says in this Bible that *now* is the day of salvation. You don't know about tomorrow."

"I know, Captain," said Rex, rising to his feet. "I appreciate your concern…and I'll give what you've said some more thought."

The two armies carefully made plans and positioned their troops and guns as the day grew hotter. Then suddenly at just before 11:00 A.M., a sharp cannonade burst forth from the Confederate guns on Seminary Ridge. The Union artillery answered back, and within minutes, infantrymen were swarming at each other across the open fields. The battle was underway.

By two o'clock, the Twentieth Maine had been moved several times to positions east of Culp's Hill, then near a lumber mill, and finally across a small creek and the Baltimore Pike to a low rise beside the highway. They were expecting to be called into battle at any time. Chamberlain held his men in strict line, ready to go. Colonel Strong Vincent sent a supply wagon, giving twenty rounds of extra ammunition to each man.

Rebel artillery from the north end of Seminary Ridge was concentrating fire on Union artillery and infantry on Cemetery Ridge. From the south end, it was bombarding troops along the west edge of Cemetery Ridge and further south toward Devil's Den, where Meade had placed thousands of men. Meade's artillery pounded them back.

Confederate infantry and cavalry swept through the peach orchard and across a large wheat field to meet the Union infantry and cavalry. Boards of barns, sheds, and houses flew in splinters through the air as cannonballs landed on farm homes. Rock walls shattered, spraying the fields with sharp stone missiles and pelting the fighting men. Exploding shells gouged holes like miniature graves in the earth.

Countless flashes of musket fire began to appear amid the heavy smoke and tongues of flame of the artillery batteries on both sides. Long gray and blue lines came scurrying onto the fields to mix with the battle smoke.

Joshua Chamberlain's regiment sat in the low spot along the Baltimore Pike, waiting, listening. A long, rounded rise just across the Pike blocked their view of the battle that raged less than a mile away. Waiting was harder than fighting. In the quiet of his own mind, a man had time to imagine all kinds of horrible things that could happen to him. In the midst of battle, a man's attention was so riveted he didn't have time for such thoughts. Chamberlain walked among his men and saw the torment written on their sweat-stained faces.

The heat was becoming unbearable. For the most part, the men who waited in reserve along the Baltimore Pike had been born and raised in northern New England. There, summers were comparatively brief and never as hot and humid as what they had found in Virginia, Maryland, and Pennsylvania.

The unseen battle raged on. The Mainers watched the clouds of smoke drift toward the sky on the afternoon breeze—the same breeze that brought them the acrid odor of burnt powder and the unmistakable smell of death.

And death was busy with his grim sickle as the sun slowly ran its course. Men were falling on the ridges, in the peach orchard, on the open fields, and in the small, marshy valley between Little Round Top and Devil's Den. Bodies lay so thick in the valley, men were walking on human flesh to fight each other. Little Plum Run, which ran through the center of the valley, was littered with lifeless forms floating lazily southward in a winding stream of red.

Cannon after cannon along the battery lines of the east and west ridges leaped where they stood as the artillerymen yanked the lanyards, bellowing canister and grape-shot on the enemy.

Still the swarms of fighting men filled the field of battle, advancing under the cries of their leaders. From Gettysburg's south edge all the way to Big Round Top, between the long ridges, stretched an uninterrupted field of conflict. One by one, the reserve regiments on both sides were called into action.

Though the men of the Twentieth Maine waited impatiently, on the battlefield, all sense of time was dulled. The roar of gunfire and the yells of the enemy seemed to fade into the background as impassioned men fought to wipe each other off the face of the earth. Battery men drove deadly charges of canister into a maze of humanity. Cavalrymen charged enemy lines, firing their weapons and thrusting them through with their sabers. Infantrymen fired, reloaded, and fired again, leaving wounded and dying men on the crimsoned grass. Poor, mutilated creatures, some with an arm dangling, some with a leg torn and bleeding, limped and crawled toward the rear.

There was no faltering. Men of blue and gray fought nobly for their cause as the sun, an indistinct ball of fire beyond the smoky mist, began to lower in the western sky.

At the Confederate headquarters atop Seminary Ridge, General Lee and his First Corps commander, James Longstreet, were at odds. Lee had told Lafayette McLaws, a division commander under Longstreet, to pull his division away from First Corps and take up a position at a strategic spot just southwest of Cemetery Hill.

Longstreet, already perturbed at Lee for not capturing the Round Tops before the Union forces arrived at Gettysburg, exploded, telling McLaws to keep his division where it was. Lee lashed back in anger, but his indignation was suddenly interrupted by chest pains. He had to sit down and catch his breath.

In spite of the differences between them, Longstreet loved and admired his commander. He quickly poured Lee a cup of water from a canteen and gave it to him a sip at a time. McLaws stood by, waiting for a final command.

Longstreet was piqued because Lee's arrangements for the complicated battle operations were, in his military mind, incredibly casual. At no time since the Confederate army had converged at Gettysburg had Lee brought together his three corps commanders, upon whose understanding and cooperation the entire campaign depended. During the lull before the battle that morning of July 2, Lee had acted as his own courier, riding back and forth between Longstreet, Ewell, and Hill at a considerate cost of time.

General Lee had been suffering with severe chest pains since March, and to Longstreet seemed "out of sorts" and not thinking clearly.

Earlier that day, two regiments of John Geary's division of the Union Third Corps occupied Little Round Top. As the battle raged, Major General Daniel Sickles ordered Geary to leave a small signal corps on Little Round Top and remove his regiments to a spot at Culp's Hill.

Geary, a Mexican war veteran, knew that signalmen could never hold Little Round Top. If the Confederates occupied it, they would have a distinct advantage over the Union left wing and turn the tide for the South in the entire battle. To hold Little Round Top was crucial.

Hastily, Geary wrote a note, handed it to the courier who had brought the order, and told him to rush it to Sickles. The note conveyed Geary's opinion that keeping a tight hold on Little Round Top was of critical importance.

Sickles shrugged it off, sending back a message that he would attend to Little Round Top in due time. Geary was to obey the order. Geary returned another message urging the Third Corps commander to reconsider. A third message came, commanding Geary to obey or face the consequences. Geary reluctantly led his regiments off Little Round Top, leaving it virtually undefended.

Captain Samuel R. Johnston rushed up to Robert E. Lee's field tent atop Seminary Ridge and peered through the flap opening. "Pardon me, sirs," he said. "I realize I'm interrupting, but what I have to say to General Lee cannot wait."

"Come in, Captain," Lee said.

As Johnston stepped inside, Lee said to McLaws, "General Longstreet is outranked here. You move your division to the position southwest of Culp's Hill as I told you."

"Yes, sir," McLaws said, giving Longstreet an uneasy glance as he hurried from the tent.

Lee turned his attention to Johnston. "What is it, Captain?"

"Sir, the Yankees have just left Little Round Top."

"What? I can't believe that!"

Longstreet frowned. "You mean they've taken every man off it?"

"They left a signal corps, General. Best we can count are maybe a half-dozen men."

"Why would they do that?" Lee said. "That is the key position on this battlefield. It doesn't make sense."

Lee stood to his feet, swayed a bit, and said to Longstreet, "Who have we got that we can thrust to Little Round Top immediately?"

Longstreet stepped to the table where a crude map of the Gettysburg area was laid out. Lee moved up beside him. Longstreet ran a finger back and forth on the map and said, "Colonel Oates's Fifteenth Alabama, sir. He's had several men killed and wounded, but the last I knew, he still had close to eight hundred men. He's with the Forty-Seventh Alabama right now, trying to take Big Round Top."

"That'll take a while," Lee said, turning to Johnston. "Captain, ride hard and find General Law. Tell him I said to cut William Oates and his Fifteenth Alabama out and send them to take and defend Little Round Top...on the double!"

Major General E. McIver Law responded quickly to Lee's order. In addition to the entire Fifteenth Alabama, he added men from the Fourth Alabama and the Fourth and Fifth Texas regiments, making a unit of over three thousand men.

Colonel William C. Oates, an officer known for his valor and courage in battle, pulled away from the fighting at Big Round Top and assembled his eager unit amid the heavy trees at its eastern base. They would make a wild run across the five-hundred-yard saddle that lay between the Round Tops.

Oates was convinced that he and his men held the key to victory in the Battle of Gettysburg. By taking Little Round Top with its height and strategic location, they would possess a Gibraltar that they could hold against ten times their number and turn the tide for the Confederacy in the entire war.

It was 3:40 P.M. as they assembled in a dense stand of trees overlooking the space that led to Little Round Top.

At the same time, the Union's chief topographical engineer and a seasoned veteran of the Mexican War, Brigadier General G. K. Warren, was nearing Little Round Top on an errand for General Meade. Warren was on horseback, sided by his staff officer, Ranald Mackenzie. Warren was to observe the situation at Devil's Den and send Mackenzie back with his assessment of how the battle was going. Warren was to then assess the condition of the Union troops at the peach orchard and return to Meade on Cemetery Hill.

Warren's attention was drawn to the crest of Little Round Top, where he saw a signal corpsman waving two flags; a handful of others stood nearby. He wondered why he saw no artillery, nor anyone to man the cannons. Neither did he see one infantryman. He was about to say something about it to Mackenzie when the lieutenant pointed toward Big Round Top and said, "General! Over there in those trees! Looks like the Rebs are getting ready to plunge out of there and head into the open. Where could they be going?"

Warren saw the glistening of gun barrels and bayonets at the edge of the trees and gasped, "Little Round Top, Ranald! Somebody's pulled our fighting men off and left a few signal corpsmen. Those Rebels can see that as well as we can. We've got to man that hill, or they'll have an advantage we can't overcome!"

"What shall we do, sir?"

"You ride to General Sickles. I'll ride to General Sykes. There's enough canister and musket balls flying in that space to make the going slow for those Rebs, but we've got to man Little Round Top before they get there!"

Ranald Mackenzie found his way to General Sickles's position on the battlefield, but Sickles said he could not spare a man. At the same time, General Sykes saw the urgent situation and assured Warren he would take care of it. Sykes sent immediate orders to James Barnes to rush a brigade to the threatened hill. Warren hurried back to Cemetery Hill to tell General Meade what was going on.

Joshua Chamberlain was pacing back and forth with his hands clasped behind his back as the sounds of battle continued to thunder over the hill. Suddenly there was a rider galloping around the south end of the hill, coming as fast as his horse would carry him.

Buster Kilrain moved up beside Chamberlain and said, "Looks like we're finally gonna get into the fight, Colonel."

"It's Colonel Vincent!" Shane Donovan said.

The men of the Twentieth Maine scrambled to their feet as Vincent skidded the lathered animal to a halt.

"Colonel Chamberlain, I need your regiment over at Little Round Top as fast as you can get there!"

He gave a quick explanation of the situation, and rode away as the Twentieth Maine began a hard run in the oppressive heat. The officers rode at a trot ahead of the men, who were eager to get into the fight.

The distance was short, and within minutes, Chamberlain and his troops came near Little Round Top. Three other regiments in Vincent's brigade also had been ordered to the coveted hill—the Sixteenth Michigan, the Forty-fourth New York, and the Eighty-third Pennsylvania.

As the men of the Twentieth looked out over the land toward Devil's Den and the peach orchard, they saw bayonet fighting in one place, musketry spread wide, and cannonade along the ridges. Across the sloping saddle toward Big Round Top, they saw Colonel Oates attempting to lead his swarm of Rebels toward them, but Union artillery hindered them. At times, they had to hit the ground and hunt for cover.

Oates watched with fiery eyes as the Union troops under the leadership of Colonel Strong Vincent ran toward Little Round Top. General Lee's order had come too late.

Confederate artillery some seven hundred yards west of Little Round Top arched whistling cannonballs down on the troops scurrying toward that hill. Men of the New York, Michigan, and Pennsylvania regiments ahead of the Maine regiment were taking a pounding. Those who escaped the shells ran for the hill as fast as they could. Vincent led them behind Little Round Top on the wooded east side to make the climb. The half-dozen signal corpsmen were at the crest on that side, cheering them on.

The cannonade continued as the men of the Twentieth Maine hastily made their way amid bodies of New York, Michigan, and Pennsylvania soldiers who had preceded them. The officers on horseback were almost around to the safer east side when three…four…five shells struck the line of Mainers. Men were blown every direction.

Those who escaped the shelling kept running. Soon the officers reached the massive boulders at the back side of Little Round Top and left their horses with Vincent's orderlies. More deadly cannonballs fell on the Mainers as the rear lines tried to reach the safety of the hill.

Vincent stayed just below the rocky, forested crest of the hill and gave commands; the regiments formed their positions. The Michigan regiment was on the extreme right, facing west. The New York regiment was placed alongside them and told to man the artillery that General Geary's men had left. The New York had plenty of artillerymen, and there was a modest supply of ammunition. The Pennsylvania regiment was positioned to the New Yorkers' left. Their battle line curved around the southwest turn of the hill. Last was Colonel Chamberlain and his Twentieth Maine, who had taken heavy losses in getting to Little Round Top. The regiment faced south and slightly west on the steep and heavily wooded side.

As they were getting positioned, Rex Carden drew up beside Shane Donovan and said, "That was close, wasn't it? We lost a lot of men!"

"Yes," Shane said sadly. "A lot of men."

"And did you see all those bodies in that low spot where that creek runs…this side of all those huge boulders?"

"I saw them."

"I heard one of the Pennsylvania guys say those boulders are called Devil's Den, and another one said General Meade is calling that low spot the Valley of Death." Rex moved closer. "Isn't there a valley of death in the Bible?"

"Well, there's one implied, but there's no place I know of where a valley is called the valley of death. Jeremiah wrote of a valley of slaughter, and Ezekiel wrote of a valley of dead men's bones. Psalm 23:4 is where the valley of death is implied, but it's called the valley of the *shadow* of death. There's a difference. I—"

"Captain Donovan!" one of the men shouted. "We have a man dying over here!"

Shane excused himself and hurried to where a young soldier lay on the rocky ground. Two of his friends hovered over him. Rex followed and looked on as Shane knelt beside the dying man. He had been hit with shrapnel, and his two friends had picked him up and carried him to the top of the hill.

Several yards away, Colonel Vincent and Colonel Chamberlain were talking together.

"Colonel Chamberlain, I learned that the Rebels headed this way from Big Round Top are led by Colonel Bill Oates. He's a real fighter. He'll get the bulk of his men through all that cannonade of ours soon."

"My men are ready, Colonel."

"Have you had time to make a count?"

"Yes, sir. Best I can come up with, we're down to 386, including me."

"Well, my friend, you're going to find out what your regiment's made of today. Do you understand that you are at the left of the

Union line? By that I mean, the Twentieth Maine is at the extreme left of the entire Army of the Potomac."

"I know that, sir."

"Chamberlain, a desperate attack is coming very shortly. You are to hold this ground at all costs. Do you understand? At all costs."

"I understand, sir. We'll do it."

Vincent reached out and grasped Chamberlain's hand. They stood, hands clasped, looking into each other's eyes.

"I know you will," Vincent said. "The victory in this battle, and possibly the ultimate victory in this whole rotten war, depends in large measure on what you and your men do in the next few hours. If you can break Lee's back here and now, maybe you can go home to that family of yours soon."

"I'd like that, sir."

"I must go, Colonel. May the Lord protect you."

With that, Vincent whirled and disappeared around a huge boulder. Joshua Chamberlain had a strange feeling pass over him, a feeling that he had just seen Colonel Strong Vincent for the last time in this world.

The young soldier with the shrapnel wound died before the eyes of the four men who hovered over him. Rex Carden's face was sheet-white as he walked away beside Shane Donovan.

"Colonel," Rex said, "remember last time you talked to me about repenting of my sin and asking Jesus to come into my heart and save me?"

"Yes."

"And I told you I wasn't ready?"

"Yes."

"Well, I am now."

TWENTY-ONE

"Rex, are you sure you mean it?" Shane's heart quickened pace.

"Yes, sir. Ever since you started talking to me about Jesus, God's been working on me. I'm not going to resist Him any more. I want to be saved."

Shane took his Bible from his haversack, opened it, and quickly went over the Scriptures he had shown Rex Carden many times before. After Rex had humbly called on the Lord to save him, Shane prayed with an arm around his shoulder, asking the Lord to help Rex faithfully serve Him.

Tears filled Rex's eyes and he shook his head in wonderment. "Thank you, Captain. Thank you for caring about me and where I spend eternity. How foolish I was to put Jesus off as long as I did."

Both men heard a noise behind them and turned to see Colonel Chamberlain.

"Captain," Chamberlain said, "the Fifteenth Alabama and whoever else they've got with them are about to hit us. We've got maybe ten minutes."

Colonel Oates found a few moments' lull in the cannonade that hindered his approach to Little Round Top, and when it came, he shouted to his men to charge. They were out in the open, and Oates figured the best thing to do was to take Little Round Top by force. His troops clearly outnumbered Vincent's.

Atop Little Round Top, artillery and infantry were in place. The four regiments of Colonel Strong Vincent's brigade braced themselves for the attack.

At approximately 5:00 P.M., Oates's troops ejected a wild Rebel yell and charged the rocky hill. The wild-eyed Confederates swarmed in on three sides, and the Union regiment commanders shouted for their men to commence fire.

At the bottom of the steep hill, the Fifteenth Alabama and their Texas comrades plunged into the bushes and began crawling over the boulders. Howitzer shells exploded and bullets hissed at them by the hundreds, many of them striking stone and ricocheting away in angry whines.

On the south side of the hill, Joshua Chamberlain stood slightly above his men, sword in one hand and revolver in the other. He saw dozens of Rebels go down in the initial volley unleashed by the Twentieth Maine. But Lee's soldiers meant business. They kept right on coming.

Chamberlain shouted encouragement to his men as he fired his revolver at those Rebels who were climbing closer. He saw Buster Kilrain, below to his left, fire his rifle and drop a charging Rebel, but another took aim at the redheaded Irishman. Just to Kilrain's left, Shane Donovan fired on the Rebel with his revolver. Before the man in gray could squeeze the trigger, Shane's bullet stopped his heart.

Below to Chamberlain's right were his brother, Tom, and Ellis Spear blasting away with their pistols, shouldered on both sides by riflemen. The metallic sound of ramrods punching lead balls into gunpowder rang over the hillside amid the roar of gunfire.

Colonel Vincent's words echoed through Chamberlain's mind: "You are to hold this ground at all costs. Do you understand? At all costs."

The responsibility weighed heavily on Chamberlain's mind and doubled his resolve. If they failed to hold the left flank, the Confederates would gain the rear of the entire Union position where large amounts of supplies and ammunition had been placed. Meade's army would be faced with defeat, resulting in unthinkable disaster to the Union cause. The way to Philadelphia, Baltimore, and Washington would be wide open to a victorious Robert E. Lee.

Chamberlain watched his gallant men carrying the fight to the swarming enemy. These Mainers would do it; they would hold. Most of them were not much more than boys, but they were rugged, disciplined, and tough—veterans of march and battle. They had character, and they knew what they had to do. He remembered their faces as they took their battle positions. There was resolve and courage fixed on each one. And now they were demonstrating it.

Shane Donovan was reloading his revolver when two Confederates pushed through the trees right in front of him, rifles poised to fire. Suddenly there was a staccato of musket fire to his near right. Buster Kilrain and two other men had seen the Confederates and cut them down. Shane grinned and Buster shouted, "Just payin' ye back for an earlier favor!"

Suddenly Buster jerked, hunched, and dropped to the ground, his teeth clenched. Shane punched in the last cartridge with shaky fingers and snapped the cylinder shut. Before he could move, Colonel Chamberlain was beside Buster, calling for a corps medic.

The medic was several yards away, tending to a fallen soldier. He called back that he would be there momentarily, then worked furiously to finish applying a bandage.

The screaming Rebels kept coming through the trees and over the blood-stained boulders and the bodies of their fallen comrades.

Shane fired away keeping Buster in his peripheral vision. Though death was in the air in the form of hot lead, Chamberlain did not leave Buster's side until the medic arrived. As the colonel stood to climb back to his vantage point, Shane called, "How bad is it, Colonel?"

"Got him under the right arm just below the shoulder," Chamberlain called back. "Bullet's lodged somewhere in his chest cavity. He's conscious, but it's not good."

There was no time to go to Buster's side. Colonel Oates's troops were coming too fast and too furious. Rank after rank charged up the slope, taking furious fire from the Twentieth Maine. Bullets buzzed on Little Round Top like hordes of angry hornets, and thick clouds of powder smoke filled the air.

Mainers were dropping here and there, but the real toll was being taken on the brave and determined Rebels. They were falling by the dozens, a mass of torn bodies. Fresh troops appeared from behind the trees and boulders, rushing forward to replace the dead and wounded.

The Mainers tried to find a moment to take a hurried drink from their canteens. Though it was late in the afternoon, the sun's heat was like that of a blast furnace. Chamberlain moved among his men, still bearing his sword and revolver, his entire body soaked with sweat.

"You're doing fine, you bunch of Mainers!" he shouted from time to time. "Keep it up! We're not giving this hill to them! Let them go back to Alabama or Texas and find their own hills!"

Shane was taking a swig from his canteen when a rifleman next to him took a bullet. There was a muffled grunt, and the rifleman fell dead. A swarm of gray uniforms came out of the trees directly in front of him, yelling and firing their muskets on the run.

Mainers unleashed on them, muskets blazing, and Shane fired his revolver as fast as he could snap back the hammer. Rebels went down two and three at a time.

Shane saw four of them who had just fired their muskets stumble over their fallen comrades. Lying flat, each one started to reload his musket. Shane's revolver had clicked on a spent cartridge in the exchange. It was empty.

The other men of the Twentieth were fully occupied with the seemingly limitless reserve of men in gray. There was no time for Shane to reload his revolver. He had to do something before the four Rebels reloaded or came at him with their bayonets. He picked up the musket of the soldier who had just died next to him and leaped to his feet.

"Drop those muskets!" he yelled, charging at them.

The four Rebels looked at him, eyes wide. One of them said, "He can only get one of us, boys! Let's take him!"

"But which one will it be?" Shane said.

From his high perch, Chamberlain peered through the battle smoke and saw Shane standing alone, holding the musket on four enemy soldiers. The Rebels dropped their guns and placed their hands on top of their heads. Shane waved the muzzle at the Rebels and herded them around to the back side of Little Round Top toward one of the massive boulders.

The sight seemed to Chamberlain to be worthy of some rousing song or sonnet that commemorated the deeds of war heroes. But there was no time for sentiment. The battle was hot, and the enemy was determined.

The Confederates kept coming and the battle roared on. When Shane did not appear after a few minutes, Chamberlain bent low and ran to the boulder. When he rounded it, he almost ran into Shane, who was coming his way. Behind Shane, Chamberlain saw the four Rebels on the ground, trussed up to each other, bound hand and foot with their belts.

"That was good work, Captain," Chamberlain said. "It takes some doing for one man to capture four by himself."

Shane looked over his shoulder at his prisoners and said, "Especially with an empty gun, sir."

"An empty gun!" one of them said.

Shane had the hammer of the musket in cock position. He pulled the trigger, and the hammer made only a dry click as it snapped down.

Though the battle continued to rage on the other sides of Little Round Top, there was a momentary lull for the Twentieth Maine. Joshua and Tom Chamberlain and Shane Donovan rushed to Buster Kilrain. The medic was elsewhere, caring for wounded men, but Buster was conscious. Though he was a bit glassy-eyed, he knew them as they bent down around him.

"Are you in a lot of pain, Sergeant?" the colonel asked.

Buster was gritting his teeth. "Not…for a tough ol' Irishman, laddie. I mean, *Colonel*, sir."

"You can call me anything you want, just so you don't let this wound do you in."

"Colonel!" came a sharp cry. "Here they come again!"

Every man hurried to his station. As Chamberlain was returning to his spot, the sergeant in charge of ammunition ran up to him.

"Colonel, sir, we're running low on powder and bullets!"

"We'll have to make sure we use the ammunition from our dead…and from the enemy dead, Sergeant. Pass the word along."

The sounds of the next assault met the ears of the men in blue. The Rebels came yelling and clawing up through the battle-torn bushes, the shattered trees, over and around the bullet-chipped boulders.

"Stand firm, Mainers!" Chamberlain shouted. "Not once in a century are men permitted to bear such a responsibility! We cannot fold! We must keep fighting!"

And fight they did.

The entire regiment was mantled in fire and smoke, which filled their lungs and stung their eyes. Powder blackened their faces as they tore the paper cartridges with their teeth and stuffed powder into the smoking muzzles. Steel ramrods rattled and clanged in hot barrels. Their valor touched Joshua Chamberlain deeply.

The carnage went on. Within half an hour, the men of the Twentieth Maine were virtually out of ammunition. Sergeant Neil Bulkley ran about, taking powder and lead minié balls off the bodies of Yankees and Rebels alike and distributing them along the lines. Soon there was no more to be found.

Colonel Chamberlain carefully fired the last six rounds in his revolver, making sure every one of them counted. He saw Sergeant Bulkley zigzagging his way among the fighting men, heading toward him. He emptied his revolver before Bulkley reached him.

"Sir, we're out of ammunition," Bulkley gasped. "The men are using up their last rounds now! And…we've lost well over a hundred men, sir. I mean, dead. There are about seventy or eighty wounded scattered about. We haven't got more than two hundred left who can fight."

Even while the sergeant was speaking, the Mainers blasted the Confederates with their last rounds. Chamberlain noticed the Confederates fade back down the hill, as if reforming for a final assault. He was about to give a command when he saw Rex Carden running around the rocky crest from the west. Chamberlain had sent Carden to see how the battle was going with the other three regiments.

"Colonel…the news is not good," Carden said, sucking hard for air. "They're taking a real beating over there. Every one of the regiments has lost nearly half their men."

Chamberlain nodded grimly. Then the commander of the Twentieth Maine shouted, "Fix bayonets! We're going to attack!"

There was no hesitation. The distinct rattle of bayonets being fixed to muskets filled the air.

Chamberlain's empty revolver was in his holster. With his sword in hand, he pointed to the right and said, "I want you spread out in this direction in one long line. We'll charge like a giant swinging door. We've got to stop them this time! We won't get another chance!"

From the bottom of the hill came a high-pitched Rebel yell.

Above the screaming Rebels, Chamberlain shouted, "Charge!" He leaped down from the high spot, yelling over and over. "Charge!"

The whole Twentieth Maine, yelling wildly, followed Chamberlain down through the bushes and trees, over boulders and bodies of dead and wounded, going after the enemy with intent to destroy.

The Rebels, who had reached a point about a fourth of the way up, suddenly froze, eyes wide. The two hundred screaming men surging down the slope with their sharply pointed bayonets was enough to strike terror in the hearts of the most courageous men.

A few raised their rifles and fired, then turned and ran. Some of the Mainers fell.

Shane Donovan was about ten yards behind Rex Carden and saw him take one of the bullets. Rex went down head-over-heels, crashed into a tree, and lay still. Shane wanted to stop, but pressed on.

Colonel Oates was already calling for a retreat, and hundreds of men in gray stampeded from the scene. Hundreds of others, afraid they would be shot if they turned and ran, threw their guns down and raised their hands high in the air.

Eventually all firing stopped on the entire battlefield, and the dust slowly settled. The Confederate army gathered behind Seminary Ridge. General Meade saw it all from his vantage point at Cemetery Hill and did not order his army to pursue them. It would be dark soon. He would fight them again tomorrow.

For Colonel Joshua Chamberlain and his valiant regiment, it was over. The battle for Little Round Top was finished.

It was finished for Rex Carden, who lay dead against the tree as Shane Donovan knelt beside the lifeless form.

It was finished for Buster Kilrain, who had bled to death internally while his fellow-soldiers bounded down the hill and vanquished the enemy.

It was finished for Colonel Strong Vincent, who was killed by a Confederate bullet on the west side of Little Round Top as he bravely rallied his troops.

The men of the Twentieth Maine were bunching up their prisoners when someone shouted that Colonel Chamberlain was down. The colonel was sitting with his cap off at the base of Little Round Top, leaning against a boulder. His brother Tom knelt beside him, and Ellis Spear and Shane Donovan knelt on the other side. The corps medic was hunkered down in front of him.

While some of the men kept the prisoners, the bulk rushed to see what had happened to their colonel.

The medic looked up and said, "He's not seriously hurt. He has a bruised thigh where one of those last Rebel bullets hit his scabbard and ricocheted off. He's also got a slight injury to his right foot. He's not sure when it happened, but his instep was cut through his boot. He wasn't aware of it till he started running down the hill and felt some pain. But he'll be fine."

Chamberlain asked his brother and Shane to help him stand, and he addressed his troops. "Men, we've lost many of our comrades today. They aren't here for me to speak to, but I want to say to every one of you that I am proud to be your commander. I'm sure history will record what happened here today. You did what you were called to do, and you did it with courage and dignity. I must say that our enemies were gallant men in this fight, but they can't hold a candle to you."

"I agree wholeheartedly, Colonel Chamberlain!" came the voice of General George Meade as he threaded his way through the weary men. "And I would like to add one more thing. From what I know about your stand here today, I believe you men gained the victory because of the great man who led you!"

A rousing cheer went up for Joshua Chamberlain.

The four Rebels Shane had captured were brought off the hill and placed with their fellow-prisoners. Then they were taken to the top of Cemetery Hill and held at gunpoint.

To secure Little Round Top, General Meade ordered the Twentieth Maine to spend the night on its crest. Meade felt sure Lee's army would be defeated the next day, and he told Chamberlain that after the tremendous battle his regiment had fought, they needed and deserved a rest. They were to stay on Little Round Top tomorrow and fight only if Lee tried to take it again, which he doubted would happen. Both Round Tops were firmly in Federal hands. The Twentieth Maine was resupplied with ammunition, and their wounded were carried away to be treated by the medics. They would not be able to bury their dead until the full battle was over.

On the morning of July 3, General Lee's attacking forces formed their lines in the cover of the woods near the peach orchard at Seminary Ridge. Lee had assembled Major General George Pickett and his division of six thousand men at the forefront. Picket had yet to fight in the battle. His orders were to converge on Meade's headquarters at Cemetery Hill. It was Lee's last-ditch effort to gain the victory at Gettysburg.

Pickett had argued with his commander in Lee's field tent before sunup. With James Longstreet present, Pickett told Lee the best thing to do was pull what was left of the Confederate army out of Pennsylvania and go back to Virginia. There, on home ground, they could heal their wounds and fight Billy Yank once again. Longstreet voiced his agreement, saying that any more fighting at Gettysburg would lead to disaster.

Lee became angry and told Pickett he must take Cemetery Hill and wipe out Meade's troops. Pickett grew silent, knowing he must obey orders. Lee laid them out. While Pickett was charging Cemetery Hill, Longstreet would lead the other Confederate divisions—battered and diminished as they were—in an attack on Federal forces in the open fields.

As Pickett and Longstreet predicted, July 3 was a disaster for the Confederate army. Longstreet's forces were battered severely, and over three thousand men were killed in Pickett's division, including every one of his officers.[1] Under cover of darkness that night, a dejected Robert E. Lee began moving his devastated army toward Virginia, openly admitting that the defeat was his fault.

---

[1] For the rest of his life, General George Pickett grieved for his men lost in the battle on July 3, 1863, and he blamed Robert E. Lee for the disaster. Five years after the war, when Pickett and the Confederate guerrilla leader John Mosby paid a courtesy call on Lee in Richmond, Virginia, the atmosphere was less than cordial. After leaving the Lee house, Pickett launched into a bitter diatribe, saying, "That old man had my division slaughtered at Gettysburg."

TWENTY-TWO

ll was quiet as the sun rose over the battlefield at Gettysburg on the morning of July 4, 1863. The Confederates were gone.

It was an unforgettable scene for the Union troops as they scanned the vast area between the two ridges. Upon the open fields, bodies were strewn everywhere. There were bodies in crevices of the rocks, in ditches, behind fences, trees, and buildings, and in thickets where bloodied soldiers had crept for safety only to die in agony. By stream or hedge or rock wall—wherever they had fought or crawled or their faltering steps could take them—lay the dead.

All around was the wreckage battling armies leave in their wake—overturned wagons, broken-down caissons, lopsided cannons, muskets bent and twisted. Farmers' implements, barns, sheds, fences, and houses were in shambles. And over all, suffocating the land and poisoning the breath of the living, hung the powerful stench of decaying flesh, both human and animal.

Each regiment found a place to bury its dead. The Twentieth Maine found a small area near the base of Little Round Top where the ground was not filled with rocks. One hundred and eighty-two of them gathered to pay respect to their fallen comrades.

Colonel Joshua Chamberlain used a broken tree limb as a cane to make his way to the forefront to stand in front of the long mound of dirt where the bodies of his dead soldiers had been laid to rest in a common grave. Some of the men attending were bandaged, and many were also leaning on broken tree limbs. Every man stood on his feet, eyes fixed on the colonel as he ran his gaze over their weary, saddened faces.

"Men of the Twentieth Maine, once again I salute you. You are the greatest bunch of fighting men any army has ever produced. This war is not over. General Lee will rebuild his army and fight us again. But I don't think he will ever send his army against the Union flag without remembering Little Round Top and the Twentieth Maine and the losses his thousands sustained fighting our two hundred.

"We have gathered here to honor our dead. It is customary that when soldiers are buried, the highest ranking survivor of the battle conduct the memorial service, usually with the help of a chaplain. We have no chaplain, but I have asked Captain Shane Donovan to take my place and the chaplain's and read some appropriate Scriptures. Captain…"

Shane Donovan took a few minutes to pay tribute to the men of the Twentieth Maine who had given their lives for the Union cause since entering the war. He then paid special tribute to the men they had just buried, bringing many a tear to the eyes of his hearers with his touching words.

Shane then opened his Bible and read the Twenty-third Psalm. When he finished, he explained that salvation comes only through the Shepherd Himself, the Lord Jesus Christ. He urged every man there to open his heart to Jesus. He closed by telling them that Rex Carden had opened his heart to the Shepherd only hours before being killed. Shane invited any man who wanted to be saved to see him, Colonel Chamberlain, or Tom Chamberlain. Then he prayed, asking God to bless and help the families of the dead and to draw men who stood before him to Jesus.

The bugler stepped forward and played "Taps" as the men of the

Twentieth stood in silence, shedding tears. When the last sad note died away, Colonel Chamberlain looked up to see General George Meade riding toward them, sided by his aides.

Meade dismounted and stood before the small remnant. With emotion in his voice, he expressed his gratitude to the Twentieth Maine for their courageous stand at Little Round Top. He told them their effort contributed to the Union victory more than any other single unit in the Army of the Potomac. In closing his short speech, Meade said the Twentieth Maine had displayed valor to the ultimate.

Shane's thoughts went to Charly. In his mind, she had shown the greatest valor when she sent him back to the war with death breathing on her heels. Charly...was she yet alive?

When the men were dismissed, several approached Shane and Tom Chamberlain, wanting to receive Christ. By the time General Meade rode away, Shane and Tom had led thirteen men to Christ.

Joshua Chamberlain rejoiced when he was told about it. He then took Shane aside and said, "Captain, I talked to General Meade about you and Charly. He has granted you two weeks' leave to go home. You're to report to Camp Number Seven in Washington on July 18, where we'll be resting up before going back into battle."

Shane blinked at the tears that filled his eyes and embraced his colonel and friend. He thanked him for what he had done, and asked him to thank General Meade for him.

Shane Donovan's heart was in his throat as he rode the rented horse up the street toward his parents' house. There was no sign of life on the entire block, though it was midafternoon, and none at the Donovan house as he reined in and dismounted. He took his blue haversack from behind the saddle and stepped up on the porch. He turned the knob and pushed the door open.

He stepped inside and called in a subdued voice, "Mother!" If Charly was asleep, he didn't want to wake her just yet. He would rather do that while standing over her bed.

He dropped the haversack in the vestibule and proceeded into the parlor and past the staircase toward the kitchen. He called his mother again as he entered the kitchen, keeping his voice low.

The house was perfectly still. All the windows were open, and the curtains fluttered in the warm summer breeze. He smelled the sweet scent of freshly baked oatmeal cookies. His mother always did make great oatmeal cookies. He and his brothers could never get enough of them.

He was moving past the kitchen table to go into the backyard when he spied a note under a salt shaker on the table.

Ryan
Ashley and I have gone downtown shopping. We should be home shortly. There are oatmeal cookies in the cookie jar. Don't eat too many. I want you to eat supper!

I love you!
Mother

Shane walked quickly to the staircase, and his pulse quickened as he mounted the stairs. Charly, are you up there?

The floorboards squeaked as he made his way down the hall toward Charly's room. The door was standing open as he reached it and looked inside. The bed was made up. His mouth went dry, and something cold slid next to his heart.

"Charly!" he whispered.

He entered the room and could see none of her personal things. There was nothing in the room that hinted Charly had ever been there. Suddenly his eyes locked on a white envelope that leaned against the mirror. It had one word written on it: Shane.

Feebly, he moved toward the dresser. He stopped mid-room and took a deep breath. Fear surged through him.

"No!" he gasped, and hurried to the closet. He pulled the door open and saw Charly's dresses and coats hanging in perfect order. Four pairs of her shoes were on the floor, along with some small boxes. He removed the lid of one and found within it the personal items he had expected to see on the dresser.

"No!" he cried again, and dashed to the dresser. He picked up the envelope and found it sealed. With trembling fingers, he opened it. There was a folded note inside. He pulled it out and saw that it was in Charly's handwriting.

My Darling Shane,

I am trusting the Lord to bring you back from that awful war, though I do not know when it might be. This much I know—I'll be gone when you return.

I know I promised to be lots better the next time you came home, and you may think I didn't keep my promise, but I did. I'll be with Jesus when you read this, Shane, so you see, I truly am lots better!

I'm in a better world, darling. There are no battlefields here, not even the personal kind. I'm not coughing any-more, and I have no pain. There is no sickness where I am. I know you will feel pain at my passing, but time and the Lord's hand will heal that. Please don't wish me back in your world, Shane. I've seen the shining face of Jesus now. Your world would be too dark.

One more thing. I know you still carry that special love for Ashley that you knew when both of you were young. She still carries it for you, too. She's so lonely, darling, and I love her so much. And, of course, I love you with all my heart. If you will let Him, I believe the Lord will take that love between you and Ashley and make it what it might have once been.

I want you and Ashley to know that if you find it in your hearts to marry, you have my blessing.

Yours lovingly,
Charly

Shane Donovan's body shook. The letter trembled in his hand. He staggered to the bed, fell on it, and wept for several minutes. Then he ran from the room, leaving the tear-stained note on the wrinkled bedspread. He bounded down the stairs, through the door, and swung into the saddle.

Brunswick's cemetery was on a hillside just outside the city limits on the east. Shane guided the horse up the grassy slope on the small road that led through the cemetery. His eyes roamed among the grave markers, looking for a fresh mound.

Suddenly, there it was, under a weeping willow tree, the afternoon sun casting a long shadow from the marker. He left the horse on the road and walked up the slope.

As he drew near, he saw the grave was decorated with flowers. A strangled moan escaped his lips as his eyes fell on the inscription carved in stone:

CHAROLETTE DONOVAN
"CHARLY"
COURAGEOUS LOVED ONE
JUNE 14, 1839–JULY 4, 1863
Gone to be with Jesus

Shane fell to his knees beside the grave and wept for a long time. "Oh, Charly, I love you! I'll miss you. I'm so sorry I didn't get back in time to say good-bye. I won't wish you back in this dark world, but how I wish I could see you again. I love you, Charly! I love you!"

Shane rose to his feet after more than half an hour, wiped his tears with a bandanna, then stood looking at the grave. Drawing a deep breath, he turned and walked slowly toward the horse. Suddenly he froze in his tracks. There, standing below him beside the horse, was Ashley. Her auburn hair shone like burnished copper in the late afternoon sun. A smile graced her tear-stained cheeks.

Around her neck was a delicate chain necklace of gold. The necklace was adorned with a gold heart-shaped locket, engraved with a male hand and a female hand in a tender grasp of love.

EPILOGUE

T he three-day battle around Gettysburg, Pennsylvania, was the
bloodiest of the entire Civil War. Union casualties totaled
twenty-three thousand and Confederate casualties twenty-
eight thousand.

In his fifty-seventh year as he rode away from the bloody scene,
General Robert E. Lee resembled a man thirty years older. His head
was bent and his shoulders drooped. The lines in his face seemed to
have deepened in the three days he had just endured. Lee knew he
had made several poor judgments in the face of resistance by General
James Longstreet, and he publicly shouldered the blame for the
Confederate loss at Gettysburg.

Within four weeks, Lee asked to be relieved of his command.
President Jefferson Davis refused, unwilling to believe that Lee's tactical decisions at Gettysburg were the cause of the defeat. Lee went on
to serve the Confederacy until the Civil War ended in April of 1865.
He died five years later of heart disease.

On July 4, 1863, a burial detail came upon a dead Union soldier at
Gettysburg whose only identification was an ambrotype of three

young children held in a death-grip in his stiff fingers.

Though there was no formal system within either government for notifying families of men killed in action, the soldiers themselves wanted to identify every man before they buried him. Word of the ambrotype spread among the Union forces. The two boys and a girl in the picture were dubbed "children of the battlefield," and an all-out campaign blossomed among the Union army.

Thousands of copies of the picture were circulated in the Northern states. A fifty dollar prize was offered for the best poem about the incident, and the winning verse was set to music. Its refrain was a prayer:

"O Father, guard the soldier's wife,
And for his orphans care."

In November 1863, a New York woman whose husband was listed as missing recognized the ambrotype. The "children of the battlefield" were hers. She had sent the picture to her husband months before the Gettysburg battle. He was Sergeant Amos Humiston of Company C, 154th New York Infantry.

The story did not end there. Proceeds from sales of the photograph and sheet music were used to establish the Soldiers' Orphans' Home in Gettysburg in 1866. Humiston's widow became its first matron, and his children were educated there.

So many dead were buried at Gettysburg that President Abraham Lincoln declared the hallowed ground a National Cemetery. On November 19, 1863, he traveled to the scene to formally dedicate the cemetery. We have all read his immortal words spoken at the dedication:

Four score and seven years ago our fathers brought forth on this continent, a new nation, conceived in Liberty, and dedicated to the proposition that all men are created equal.
Now we are engaged in a great civil war, testing whether

that nation, or any nation so conceived and so dedicated, can long endure. We are met on a great battlefield of that war. We have come to dedicate a portion of that field, as a final resting place for those who here gave their lives that that nation might live. It is altogether fitting and proper that we should do this.

But, in a larger sense, we cannot dedicate—we cannot consecrate—we cannot hallow—this ground. The brave men, living and dead, who struggled here, have consecrated it, far above our poor power to add or detract. The world will little note, nor long remember what we say here, but it can never forget what they did here. It is for us the living, rather, to be dedicated here to the unfinished work which they who fought here have thus far so nobly advanced. It is rather for us to be here dedicated to the great task remaining before us—that from these honored dead we take increased devotion to that cause for which they gave the last full measure of devotion—that we here highly resolve that these dead shall not have died in vain—that this nation, under God, shall have a new birth of freedom—and that government of the people, by the people, for the people, shall not perish from the earth.

Joshua Lawrence Chamberlain fought in many more battles during the Civil War, and he was promoted twice more—to brigadier general, and later to major general. He was wounded six times and cited for bravery in action four times. For his leadership under fire at Little Round Top, he was thanked by all of his superior officers. Each one stated that the bold and daring stand he took at Little Round Top saved the day for the Union.

Chamberlain recounted soon afterward that the highest praise must go to his regiment. He said not only had the Twentieth Maine immortalized itself, but its conduct was magnificent.

The historian of the Fifth Corps paid this tribute to the regiment's great accomplishment:

> The truth of the history is, that the little brigade of Vincent's with the self-sacrificing valor of the 20th Maine, under the gallant leadership of Joshua L. Chamberlain, fighting amidst the scrub-oak and rocks of Little Round Top on July 2, 1863, saved to the Union arms the historic field of Gettysburg. Had they faltered for one instant—had they not exceeded their actual duty—Gettysburg would have been the mausoleum of departed hopes of the national cause; for the Confederates would have enveloped Little Round Top, captured all on its crest from the rear, and held the key position of the entire battleground.

After the War, Chamberlain was awarded his country's highest veneration, the Congressional Medal of Honor, bestowed on him for his "daring heroism, courage, and great tenacity in holding his position on Little Round Top against repeated enemy assaults."

When General Robert E. Lee surrendered to General Ulysses S. Grant at Appomattox Court House, Virginia, on April 9, 1865, Grant chose Major General Joshua L. Chamberlain to officially command the ceremony of surrender.

In 1866 Chamberlain was elected governor of Maine by the largest majority in the history of the state, and was elected to the office three more times in succession. While still governor of Maine, he was elected president of Bowdoin College in 1871. He remained in that office at Bowdoin until June of 1883, when ill health resulting from his Civil War wounds forced him to resign.

Fannie Chamberlain died from a broken hip on October 18, 1905, at the age of eighty. Joshua died at his Portland, Maine, home on the cold, wintry morning of February 14, 1914, at the age of eighty-five. The cumulative effects of his six war wounds finally took their toll. Two of his children were at his bedside when his soul left the painfully wounded body and made its flight to the arms of the God he served.

The Battle Begins...

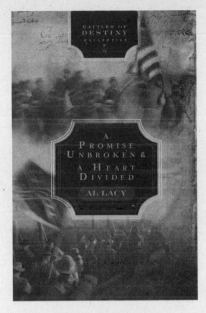

ISBN: 1-59052-945-6

Volume 1

A Promise Unbroken (Battle of Rich Mountain)
As the first winds of Civil War sweep across the Virginia countryside, the wealthy Ruffin family is torn by forces that threaten their way of life and, ultimately, their promises to one another. Mandrake and Orchid, slaves on the Ruffin plantation, must also fight for the desire of their hearts. Heartache and victory. Jealousy and racial hatred. From a prosperous Virginia plantation to a grim jail cell outside of Lynchburg, follow the dramatic story of love indestructible.

A Heart Divided (Battle of Mobile Bay)
Wounded early in the Civil War, Captain Ryan McGraw is nursed back to health by army nurse Dixie Quade. In her tender care, love's seed is sown. But with the sudden appearance of Victoria, the wife who once abandoned Ryan, and the five-year-old son he never knew he had, come threats endangering the lives of everyone involved. Between the deadly forces of war and two loves, McGraw is caught with *a heart divided*.

The Battle Continues...

ISBN: 1-59052-946-4

Volume 2

Beloved Enemy (Battle of First Bull Run)
Faithful to her family and the land of her birth, young Jenny Jordan covers for her father's Confederate spy missions. But as she grows closer to Union solider Buck Brownell, she's torn between devotion to the South and her feelings for the man she is forbidden to love.

Overwhelmed by pressure to assist the South, Jenny carries critical information over enemy lines and is caught in Buck Brownell's territory. Will he follow orders to execute the beautiful spy... or find a way to save his beloved enemy?

Shadowed Memories (Battle of Shiloh)
Critically wounded on the field of battle, one man struggles to regain his strength and the memories that have slipped away from him. Although he cannot reclaim his ties to the past, he's soon caught up in the present and the depth of his love for Hannah Rose.

Haunted by amnesia, the handsome officer realizes he may already be married. And so, risking all that he knows and loves, he turns away to confront his shadowed memories, including those of "Julie"—the mysterious woman he thinks he left behind.

Snakes

Rachel Firth and Jonathan Sheikh-Miller

Designed by Cristina Adami,
Nickey Butler and Neil Francis

Illustrated by John Woodcock

Edited by Gillian Doherty
Consultants: Chris Mattison and Kevin Buley
Managing editor: Jane Chisholm
Managing designer: Mary Cartwright
Photographic manipulation: Roger Bolton and John Russell

SCHOLASTIC INC.
New York Toronto London Auckland Sydney
Mexico City New Delhi Hong Kong Buenos Aires

Contents

 Internet links

Throughout this book there are boxes, like this one, containing Web site addresses. If you have access to a computer with an Internet connection, you can use these to help you continue your snake research on the Internet.

 You will also find symbols like this one next to some of the pictures. Wherever you see this symbol, it means that you can download the picture from the Usborne Quicklinks Web site. For more information on using the Internet, and downloading Usborne pictures see inside the front cover and page 62.

This page: an eyelash viper
Title page: West African green mamba

What is a snake?

There are over 2,500 different species, or types, of snakes. They belong to a group of animals called reptiles. Snakes are very easy to recognize as they have distinctive long, thin bodies and no arms or legs.

In the family

This lizard, called a chameleon, is a relative of snakes.

Snakes are related to crocodiles, lizards and turtles, which are also reptiles. Reptiles have scaly skin and are "cold-blooded". This means that they do not have a constant body temperature. Snakes will often move between sun and shade to help warm themselves up or cool themselves down.

Where do snakes live?

Snakes live in a variety of places, or habitats. Most snakes live either on the ground or in trees. But some spend much of their time underground, and a number of snakes even live underwater, in rivers or in the sea.

This is a rough green snake. It lives in grass and bushes, but it also climbs trees and swims in streams.

Internet links

See the snakes kept in the Reptile House at the Los Angeles Zoo on this Web site.
www.lazoo.org/reptiles.htm

For easy access to this site go to
www.usborne-quicklinks.com

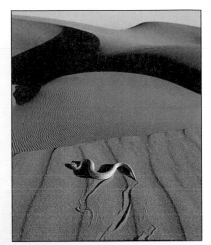

This Peringuey's adder lives in the sandy Namib desert in Africa.

All over the world

Snakes are found in many parts of the world but are most common in warm tropical areas. This is because the heat helps to keep their body temperatures quite high. But snakes can survive in all kinds of places – in deserts, high up on cold mountain rocks and even within the Arctic Circle.

This green palm viper lives in the tropical rainforests of Costa Rica.

All sorts of snakes

Although different kinds of snakes have similar body shapes, they don't all look the same. Some snakes can be five times as long as a person, while others are smaller than a person's foot. Snakes also have a wide variety of patterns on their skins.

Are snakes dangerous?

There are many different types of snakes, but most are harmless to humans. About 400 species have venomous, or poisonous, bites, but only a small number of these could cause serious injuries to people.

This eyelash viper has pointed scales above each eye, which make it look as if it has eyelashes.

Fact: Although snakes are found in most parts of the world, there are none in the wild in either Ireland or New Zealand.

Snake shapes and skeletons

Although you may not be able to tell at first glance, there are important differences in snakes' shapes. By looking at a snake's shape, you can often guess what kind of place it lives in.

Three shapes

Snakes' bodies have three main shapes. Round snakes often live underground. Their shape enables them to move easily through soil and sand. Some flat-bottomed snakes live in trees. Their shape helps them to grip onto rough surfaces, such as bark. Narrow snakes also often live in trees. Their shape helps them to stay rigid as they slither from one branch to another.

Here you can see the three main types of snake shapes in cross-section.

A narrow snake

A round snake

A flat-bottomed snake

This Asian long-nosed tree snake has a thin, light body which enables it to slither over these leaves without bending them.

Thick and thin

Some snakes are much thinner and lighter than others. Many of them live in trees and being light enables them to slither along small branches without breaking them. Others live in open country. They are fast movers and chase after animals for food.

Snakes that are short and thick, such as some vipers and pythons, are usually slow-moving and don't chase animals or climb trees.

Changing shape

Some snakes can change their shapes for a while. For example, European vipers can flatten their bodies. They do this when they are lying out in the sun. By making their bodies flatter, they expose a larger area to the sun. This means that they can soak up heat more quickly.

Internet links

On this Web site, you can discover some of the advantages of being snake-shaped.
www.szgdocent.org/cc/c-long.htm

For easy access to this site go to
www.usborne-quicklinks.com

Fact: Many snakes have only one working lung – their right lung. There isn't enough room inside their bodies for their second, much smaller, left lung to function.

Long organs

Although snakes' body shapes can vary, all snakes are long and thin compared to other animals. Snakes' inside organs, such as their hearts, stomachs, lungs and kidneys, are long and thin too. A snake's inside organs are protected by its skeleton.

This shows what the inside of a snake looks like.

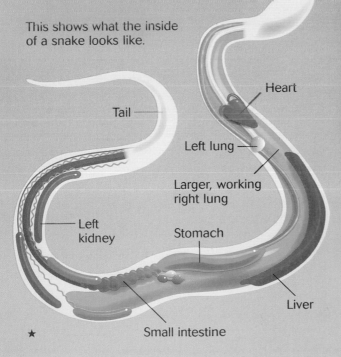

Tail

Heart

Left lung

Larger, working right lung

Left kidney

Stomach

Small intestine

Liver

Snake skeleton

A snake's skeleton is made up of a skull, a backbone and ribs. The backbone is made from lots of little bones called vertebrae. Snakes have more vertebrae than any other type of animal.

The dark area running down the middle of this snake's skeleton is its backbone.

Ribs are curved bones attached to a snake's neck and backbone. Snakes have between 150 and 450 ribs. These help to support the large amount of muscle a snake needs to move around and hunt.

Skin and scales

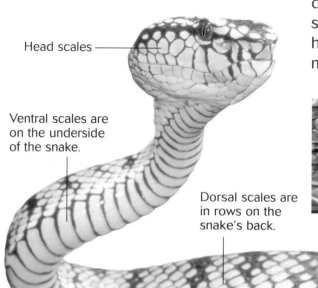

All snakes have scales covering their skin. These scales are of different shapes and sizes depending on where they are on the snake.

Head scales

Ventral scales are on the underside of the snake.

Dorsal scales are in rows on the snake's back.

Subcaudal scales are under the snake's tail.

Smooth and rough

Many snakes have very shiny scales which make them look as if they're wet and slimy. In fact, if you touch a snake, it usually feels dry and smooth. But not all snakes are smooth and shiny. Puff adders, for example, have very rough, or keeled, scales which make them look dull and flaky.

These puff adder's scales are rough, or keeled.

These smooth scales are the dorsal scales of an emerald boa.

These are the dorsal scales of a ratsnake.

Protective scales

Scales form a protective shield around a snake's body. They are hard enough to stop some insects from biting snakes. They also help to prevent snakes from being badly wounded by animals that bite back as a snake attacks them.

This desert horned viper has two special scales behind its eyes that look like two little horns. Scientists aren't sure what they're for.

Keeping water in

Some snakes live in very hot, dry places, where most other animals couldn't survive. Snakes are able to live there because their scales help to keep moisture inside their bodies, stopping them from drying out. Like all animals, if snakes become too dry, they will die.

Shedding skin

When a snake's eyes become clouded, like this ratsnake's eyes, it is about to shed its skin.

Throughout their lives, as snakes grow bigger, they grow new skins. Every time they grow a skin, they have to shed the old one. They do this all at once, usually in one big piece. You can easily spot snakes that have recently shed their skin. Their new skin looks very shiny.

@ ~ Internet links
On this Web site, you can see amazing photographs of a snake shedding its skin.
cyberfair.gsn.org/elanora/repskin.html

For easy access to this site go to
www.usborne-quicklinks.com

The snake begins to shed its skin by rubbing its snout on a rough surface to tear the skin.

Next it begins to wriggle out of the skin. As the skin is pulled off, it is turned inside out.

Once the whole skin is off, the snake can slither away, leaving it behind.

 Fact: Montpellier snakes and some sand snakes "polish" their scales with an oily liquid that comes out of their noses. Scientists aren't sure why they do this.

Slithering snakes

You might think that it would be difficult for snakes to move around without any legs. But, in fact, snakes can get around easily by slithering on their bellies. Indeed, they move in a variety of amazing ways.

S-shaped slithering

Most snakes move by pushing first one side of their bodies and then the other against small rocks or bumps on the ground. As they do this, their bodies form s-shapes. This is called serpentine movement. Snakes move in a similar way when swimming.

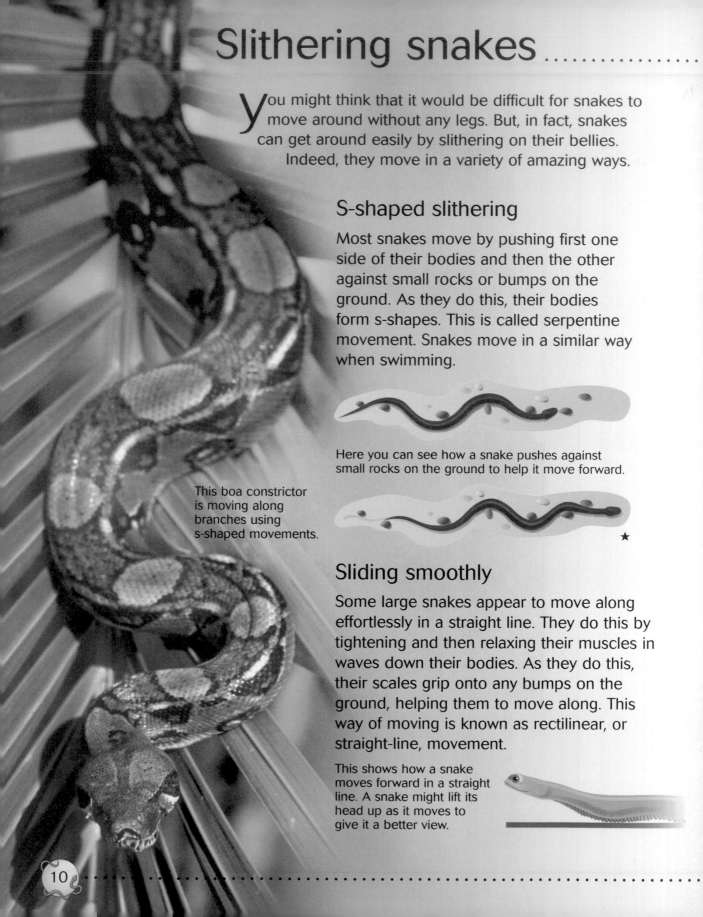

This boa constrictor is moving along branches using s-shaped movements.

Here you can see how a snake pushes against small rocks on the ground to help it move forward.

★

Sliding smoothly

Some large snakes appear to move along effortlessly in a straight line. They do this by tightening and then relaxing their muscles in waves down their bodies. As they do this, their scales grip onto any bumps on the ground, helping them to move along. This way of moving is known as rectilinear, or straight-line, movement.

This shows how a snake moves forward in a straight line. A snake might lift its head up as it moves to give it a better view.

Folding and stretching

When snakes are in narrow spaces, such as tunnels or burrows, they move by folding and then stretching their bodies. By bunching up one half of the body, until it is wedged between the sides of a tunnel, a snake can then push or pull the rest of its body forward. This is called concertina movement.

The snake squashes up its body so that it is tightly wedged against the walls of the tunnel.

Next the snake pushes the front half of its body forward.

Then the snake folds up the front half of its body so that it can pull the back half after it. ★

 Internet links

On this Web site, you can see a desert horned viper sidewinding across the Sahara desert.
www.pbs.org/sahara/wildlife/horned.htm

For easy access to this site go to
www.usborne-quicklinks.com

Sidewinding in the sand

Many snakes find it difficult to move over smooth, loose surfaces, such as sand, because there is little to push against. But desert snakes have a special way of doing this. The snake makes a loop with its body, and then throws its head and the loop forward and to the side. By repeating this action, the snake is able to move sideways across the sand. This is called sidewinding.

As this African viper moves sideways, it leaves behind clear tracks in the sand.

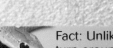 Fact: Unlike many animals, snakes can't move backward. Instead, they have to turn around and slither back the way they came.

Snake senses

Snakes need very keen senses to hunt down food and avoid animals that hunt them. Although they have sight, smell, taste and touch, as we do, they also have some more unusual ways of detecting things in their surroundings.

Snake sight

Many types of snakes have very poor eyesight. For example, snakes that live in burrows underground have small eyes and can only tell the difference between light and dark. But some snakes have far better eyesight. They are good at detecting movement which helps them when they are hunting for animals to eat.

Detecting smells

Snakes can detect smells using their nostrils just as other animals can. But they also have special smell detectors, called Jacobson's organs, in the roofs of their mouths.

Jacobson's organ

Forked tongue   ★

A snake can pick up tiny, invisible particles of scent from the air on its forked tongue. When it pushes its tongue over its Jacobson's organ, it can tell what the scent is. This means it can identify animals nearby, even if it can't see them.

The black circle in the middle of this boomslang's eye is called a pupil. Snakes with such large, round pupils usually have good eyesight.

Snakes with slit-like pupils, like this white-bellied viper's, can usually see much better at night. In the dark, their pupils become larger.

Like all snakes, this grass snake can use its tongue to help it detect smells.

This is a green whip snake's eye. Scientists aren't sure whether its key-hole shaped pupil helps it to see better.

Detecting vibrations

Snakes' ears don't have outside openings as people's ears do and they can't hear many of the sounds that we hear. But they can detect vibrations in the ground made by other animals. When a snake has its lower jaw in contact with the ground, the vibrations travel through the bones in the snake's jaw to its ears.

Mysterious senses

Some snakes have small hollows and pimples on some of their scales. Scientists aren't sure what they are for. Some think that they are sensitive to light and tell the snake which parts of its body are exposed to light and which are safely concealed in the dark.

Heat seekers

Pit vipers, and some species of pythons and boas, are able to detect heat in a way that no other animal on earth can. They have little areas near their mouths called heat pits. All animals give off heat. If an animal approaches a snake, the snake can detect a change in temperature with its heat pits.

The open areas in this green tree python's face are its heat pits. With them, it can detect heat given off by other animals.

When a rabbit sits very still and is hidden by plants, it is very difficult for a snake to see it.

The snake is able to locate the rabbit because of the heat it gives off.

 Fact: Snakes' heat pits are so sensitive to temperature that they can detect changes of 0.002°C (0.8°F), or even less.

 13

Teeth, fangs and jaws

All snakes are predators, which means that they hunt animals for food. They eat their prey (the animals they hunt) whole, even if those animals are much bigger than they are. Snakes' jaws and teeth are specially adapted to help them eat in this way.

Sharp teeth

Some snakes have hardly any teeth and others have a lot. Snakes don't chew or tear at flesh with their teeth. Instead, they use them to grip their prey. Most snakes have extremely sharp teeth that point backward.

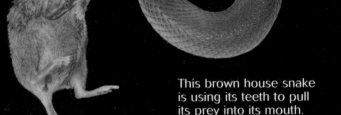

This brown house snake is using its teeth to pull its prey into its mouth.

This is the skull of a viper. You can see its teeth pointing backward into its mouth.

Fearsome fangs

Some snakes have two very sharp, long teeth called fangs. They use them to inject venom, a poisonous liquid, into their prey or, sometimes, into an animal that is threatening them. Once injected with venom, the animal usually dies.

Loose bones

Snakes that swallow large animals have stretchy skin, and skulls with bones that can move apart from one another. These allow them to open their jaws very wide, so that they can fit their prey into their mouths.

Internet links

On this Web site, you will find pictures of different venomous animals, including snakes, to shade in online.
www.enchantedlearning.com/painting/venomous.shtml

For easy access to this site go to
www.usborne-quicklinks.com

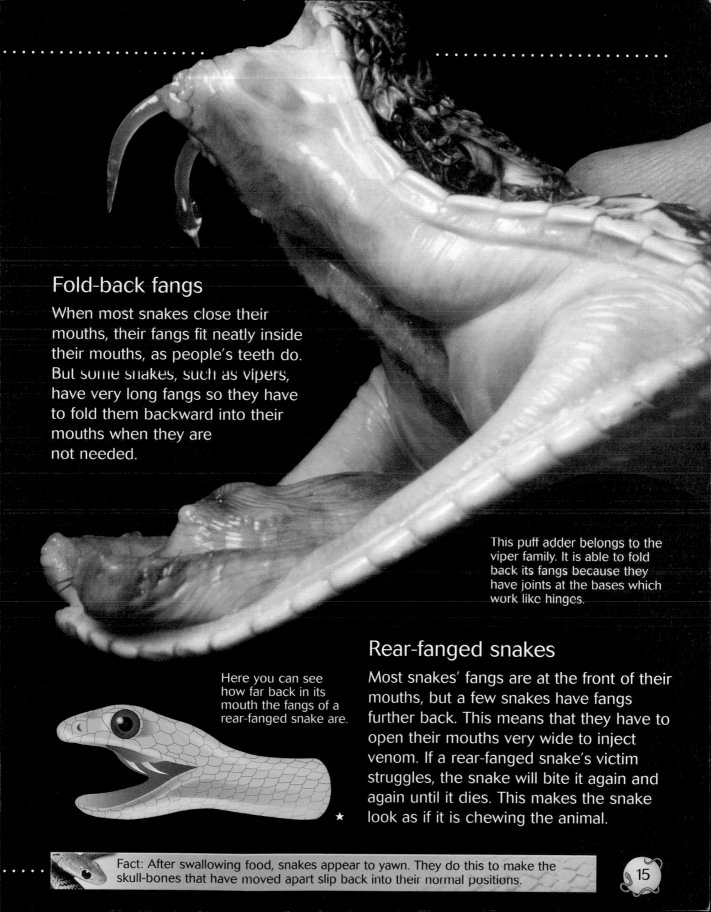

Fold-back fangs

When most snakes close their mouths, their fangs fit neatly inside their mouths, as people's teeth do. But some snakes, such as vipers, have very long fangs so they have to fold them backward into their mouths when they are not needed.

This puff adder belongs to the viper family. It is able to fold back its fangs because they have joints at the bases which work like hinges.

Rear-fanged snakes

Here you can see how far back in its mouth the fangs of a rear-fanged snake are.

Most snakes' fangs are at the front of their mouths, but a few snakes have fangs further back. This means that they have to open their mouths very wide to inject venom. If a rear-fanged snake's victim struggles, the snake will bite it again and again until it dies. This makes the snake look as if it is chewing the animal.

★

Fact: After swallowing food, snakes appear to yawn. They do this to make the skull-bones that have moved apart slip back into their normal positions.

Hunting for food

Many predators chase after their prey when hunting, but this uses up a lot of energy. To save energy most snakes usually lie in wait for their victims. Some snakes also eat prey that is already dead, for example animals that have been run over on roads.

Lying in wait

Snakes usually lie in wait in places their prey often visit. They find these places by detecting the scents animals leave behind. A snake may have to wait many days before an animal comes close enough for it to seize it.

Going for the kill

When an animal finally gets close enough to a waiting snake, the snake suddenly thrusts forward and grabs the animal in its mouth. This is called striking.

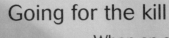

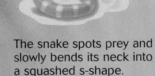

★

The snake spots prey and slowly bends its neck into a squashed s-shape.

Suddenly, it darts its head forward to catch the prey in its mouth.

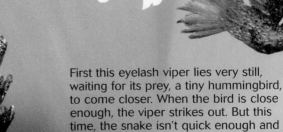

First this eyelash viper lies very still, waiting for its prey, a tiny hummingbird, to come closer. When the bird is close enough, the viper strikes out. But this time, the snake isn't quick enough and the bird escapes.

Chasing prey

A few small, fast snakes do chase after their prey. Green parrot snakes chase tree frogs across the forest floor, relying on good eyesight rather than their sense of smell to detect their prey.

Following prey doesn't always mean moving fast. Some snakes eat snails. They find the snails by following the trail of slime they leave behind.

This ringed snail-eater is carefully watching its prey, a snail.

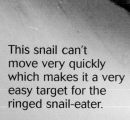

This snail can't move very quickly which makes it a very easy target for the ringed snail-eater.

Tempting tails

Some snakes tempt their prey to come close to them. Young copperheads have brown, patterned bodies, but the tips of their tails are yellow. To attract prey, they waggle their tails. Frogs and lizards mistake the moving tail for a caterpillar, and move close in the hope of catching their next meal. But it's the snake that catches and eats them.

A frog might not realize that it's near to a snake because the snake keeps its body very still as it waits for its prey to come closer.

☺ Internet links

On this Web site, you can find out more about how different snakes hunt for prey.
www.szgdocent.org/cc/c-hunt.htm

For easy access to this site go to
www.usborne-quicklinks.com

Fact: Snakes hunt and eat a wide variety of animals including rats, birds and crocodiles. Some snakes even eat other snakes.

17

Deadly biters

About a sixth of all snake species kill their prey by biting them and injecting poisonous venom into them. They may also bite other animals if they feel threatened by them, to defend themselves. This is usually why people get bitten.

This venomous boomslang can kill humans with its venom.

Hognosed vipers like this one mainly eat frogs and mice. But they can still be dangerous to humans if they feel threatened.

Lethal venom

Snake venom usually has at least one of two main types of poison in it. One type causes paralysis, or stops an animal from being able to move. The animal dies because its heart stops beating. The other sort of poison destroys an animal's flesh from the inside.

Even if a mouse is able to run away, after it has been bitten by a snake, it will still die, because it has been injected with venom.

Strong poison

How poisonous venom is varies from one species of snake to another. Snakes that eat fast-moving animals usually have stronger venom, which kills animals more quickly. If a fast-moving animal is injected with weaker venom, it may be able to escape and run far away from the snake before it dies.

Quick strike

It's important for a snake to bite its victim quickly, so that the animal doesn't have the chance to fight or run away. An animal may not know that a snake is nearby until it has already been bitten. A snake usually checks carefully to make sure that its prey is dead before it eats it. The snake waits a while for the venom to take effect. It then flicks its tongue all over the animal's body.

This coral snake (the snake with a striped pattern) has made sure this crowned snake is dead and is now beginning to swallow it.

Swallowing food

A snake swallows its prey by moving each side of its jaw in turn to pull the animal down its throat. It uses its teeth to hook into the animal's body. Once the animal is in the snake's throat, strong muscles pull it further down into the snake's stomach.

Digesting slowly

As soon as an animal has been bitten, the snake's venom begins to digest it, or break it down, from the inside. In the snake's stomach, juices break the animal down even more. It can take many days for a snake to digest a big meal.

The snake grips a frog in its jaws and begins to swallow it head first.

The frog is in the snake's stomach. You can see its shape.

Now the frog has almost been digested.

Fact: Snake's venom is most effective on the type of animal the snake usually eats. Other animals may be less affected by the venom.

Suffocating snakes

Not all snakes kill their prey by injecting them with venom. Some of them kill animals by squeezing them until they stop breathing. These snakes are known as constrictors.

This anaconda is constricting a cayman (a reptile that's similar to an alligator).

Coiled killer

A constrictor kills its prey by coiling itself around the animal's body. The animal's lungs are then squeezed so that the animal can't take in air. When an animal dies because it can't breathe, this is called suffocation. Sometimes, the pressure of the snake's body stops the animal's heart from beating before it has suffocated.

Swallowing smoothly

If a snake is constricting a large animal, such as a crocodile, it can take several minutes for the animal to die. Once the animal is dead, the snake begins to swallow it whole. It will usually start with the animal's head. If the snake started at the tail end, the animal's legs would be pushed outward as it moved down the snake's throat, making it much more difficult to swallow.

After the snake has constricted its prey, it remains tightly coiled around it.

Next the snake begins to pull the animal head first through its coils and into its mouth.

As the snake swallows more of its prey, it begins to loosen its coils.

Fact: When constrictors swallow very large prey, their ribs move apart so they can fit the animal inside them.

Pushing pythons

Some constrictors, such as Australian woma pythons, hunt animals that live in burrows, often following them down into their burrows. Sometimes, there isn't enough room in a burrow for the snake to coil around its prey. Instead, it pushes the animal against the wall of the burrow until it can no longer breathe.

★

Here you can see how a snake suffocates its prey in a burrow by squashing it against the wall. There isn't enough room for it to coil around its prey.

Internet links

On this Web site, you will find a fact sheet about boa constrictors to print out.
www.enchantedlearning.com/subjects/reptiles/snakes/Boa.shtml

For easy access to this site go to
www.usborne-quicklinks.com

Heavy eaters

Snakes often eat animals that are much bigger than they are. Swallowing a big animal makes the snake very heavy, and it is unable to move very fast after such a large meal. If they are threatened in this state, they are able to bring back their food so that they can slither away more quickly.

A rock python swallowing an antelope

Swallowed alive

Some animals are difficult to kill by constriction. For example, frogs are difficult to constrict. When they are squeezed, they can make their lungs swell up, allowing more air to get into them. This makes it difficult for snakes to suffocate them. Constrictors either avoid eating frogs or swallow them live.

Camouflage and warnings ....

Some snakes are hard to see because the patterns on their skin allow them to blend in with their surroundings. This is called camouflage. Other snakes have bright skin which makes them easy to see. In different ways, both types of skin help snakes to avoid being attacked by predators.

Watch your step

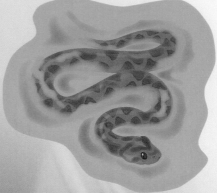

In this picture, a carpet viper is partly buried in sand and so is fairly hard to see.

In Africa and Asia, carpet vipers kill a lot of people. These snakes are very hard to see because they blend in with the dry, rocky areas where they live. Often, people tread on them by mistake and are then bitten. Carpet vipers can also bury themselves by wriggling their bodies and this adds to their camouflage.

Lost in the trees

Many snakes that live in trees, such as the striped palm viper and the white-lipped pit viper, have green skin which helps them to keep well hidden among the leaves.

The vine snake also lives in trees, but looks very different from most tree snakes. This snake is thin and mainly light brown, just like a branch, or vine. When it is perfectly still, it is very hard to spot.

This vine snake can easily disappear from view in a large shady tree.

Fact: All snakes that are born totally white are called albinos. They find it very hard to hide and so become easy prey.

Snake warnings

Some venomous snakes have bright skin which makes them easy to see and warns attackers that they are best left alone. For example, coral snakes are highly venomous and have vivid skin patterns.

This blue Malayan coral snake has bright skin which warns predators that it is very venomous.

Mimicking milk snakes

Some harmless snakes also have bright skin patterns, so that predators think they are a venomous species and will leave them alone. In America, the skin patterns of harmless milk snakes closely resemble those of deadly coral snakes.

It isn't easy to tell which is the harmless snake and which is the venomous one.

Coral snake

Milk snake

Ringneck surprise

Ringneck snakes are able to change their appearance very quickly if they feel threatened.

Usually, a relaxed ringneck snake shows only its dark brown or black topside.

But a ringneck has a red tail which it reveals when it senses danger.

It also has a bright underside and it will roll over to show this if the danger persists.

Staying alive

Snakes are usually very shy and try to avoid trouble by hiding or moving away from danger. But if a possible attacker takes too much of an interest in them, some snakes are able to use unusual tactics to avoid being attacked.

Up for the challenge

When threatened, cobras raise the front parts of their bodies off the ground and stretch the skin on their necks to form a wide hood. To do this, they spread out the flexible rib bones in their necks, so that the skin tightens. They then look much bigger and more threatening.

A relaxed cobra lies flat on the ground, keeping its hood hidden.

When it senses danger, the cobra raises the front of its body and begins to stretch out its hood.

If alarmed, the cobra rises even further off the ground and spreads its hood defiantly.

★

This Indian cobra has risen up high and opened its hood to make itself look more intimidating.

Spitting with rage

Some cobras can spit jets of venom through small holes in the fronts of their fangs when they are threatened. They can hit predators as far away as 3m (9ft).

Cobras rise up off the ground before spitting and aim for the predator's eyes. If venom enters the eyes, it causes great pain and may badly damage eyesight.

This Mozambique spitting cobra is defending itself against a possible predator.

A warning rattle

Rattlesnakes get their name from the rattles at the tips of their tails. These are made of old scales that are left behind each time a snake sheds its skin.

When a rattlesnake vibrates its tail, the old scales rub together and make a rattling noise. The snake uses this as a way of warning animals to keep away.

Playing dead

This grass snake may look dead but it is very much alive and is trying to trick a possible predator.

Rattles are fragile and sections like this one often break off. They are soon replaced by more old scales, every time a snake sheds its skin.

When a predator is near, some snakes, such as grass snakes, turn over on their backs, stick out their tongues and lie very still, as if they are dead. They do this in the hope that the predator will then ignore them and move away.

Fact: Some snakes emit foul smells when threatened. One species, the Chinese stink snake, gets its name from this unattractive habit.

Getting together

Snakes usually live alone. But occasionally they come together to breed, or produce young. All snakes breed by mating with another snake, apart from the brahminy blind snake which can produce babies all by itself.

These two smooth snakes are mating.

Finding a mate

In order to breed, the first thing most snakes have to do is find a mate (a snake of the opposite sex). Usually, it is the male snake that does the searching. When female snakes are ready to mate, they produce a strong smell. By following this smell, a male snake can track down a female.

Mating snakes

In order to produce baby snakes, one of the female snake's sex cells (eggs) has to join up with one of the male snake's sex cells (sperm). By becoming entwined with the female snake, the male snake is able to place some sperm into the female so that the cells can join together. The snakes may remain wrapped around each other for hours.

 Fact: Some female snakes can store sperm inside them for several years, so that they can continue to have babies without needing to mate again.

Fighting for a female

Some male snakes, such as mambas, vipers and rattlesnakes, will fight with each other over a female snake. They rear up and wrap themselves around one another, each trying to push the other to the ground. The snake that wins may mate with the female snake, if she allows it.

These two male mambas may look as if they are being friendly, but in fact they are fighting over a female.

Snake ball

Some snakes don't have to look far for a mate. Large groups of red-sided garter snakes spend the cold winter months asleep in shared burrows. When they wake up, it is time to mate. Up to 100 male snakes all try to mate with the same few female snakes, forming a tangled "mating ball" around the females. Only one male will succeed in mating with each female in the mating ball.

Strange snakes

Brahminy blind snakes are very unusual because they are all female. Each female is able to develop eggs when she reaches adulthood, without needing to mate with a male snake. The eggs contain female snakes which are all exact copies of their mother.

This brahminy blind snake can produce babies without ever needing to mate.

Baby snakes

Some female snakes give birth to live young, but most lay eggs. Their growing babies stay inside the eggs until they are ready to break out, or hatch.

Safe inside

Snake eggs need to be kept at the right temperature, or incubated, for the baby snakes inside to grow and develop. Some female snakes bury their eggs in rotting leaves, or place them under rocks. This stops them from becoming either too cold or too hot.

These python's eggs are kept warm and protected by their mother as she coils around them.

Protective pythons

Although some female snakes stay near their eggs to warn off predators, most leave their eggs after they have laid them. Female pythons are unusual because they coil themselves around their eggs to protect them and incubate them.

Hatching out

About two months after a mother snake lays her eggs, the baby snakes are ready to hatch. Snakes' eggs aren't hard and easy to break like birds' eggs, but are more like strong paper. To hatch, baby snakes tear slits in their shells. They have a special tooth called an egg tooth to help them do this.

Baby snakes make tears in the tough, papery shells of their eggs.

A baby snake begins to slither through the hole in the egg.

★

The baby snake is able to slither off into the undergrowth immediately.

Keeping babies inside

Not all snakes lay eggs.
Some keep their eggs
inside their bodies, where
they are protected and
kept at the right temperature.
When the babies are ready to be
born, they break out of their eggs
while still inside their mother's
body. The mother then pushes
the babies out of her body.

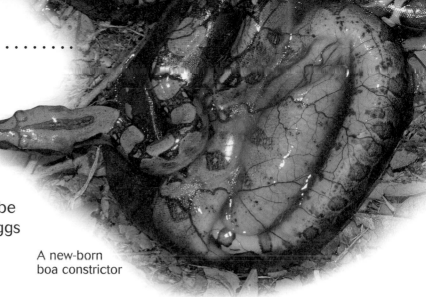

A new-born
boa constrictor

Independent babies

As soon as they have hatched or been
born, baby snakes are able to do
most of the things adult snakes
can do. They know how to protect
themselves and find food without
being shown how by their parents.

A baby snake, such as this
baby green mamba, will
go back inside its shell,
after making the first slit,
if it senses danger.

Fact: Babies that are kept inside female snakes take up a lot of room. This means
that the mother snake can only eat small animals until the babies are born.

Giant snakes

Snakes vary greatly in size. Some are as small as a pencil, while others are as long as a car. But a few are even bigger than that. The very biggest, fattest and longest snakes come from the python and boa families.

The green anaconda these hunters are holding is 5.5m (18ft) long.

Measuring snakes

Finding out the length of a snake isn't as easy as it might sound. Snakes tend to coil their bodies when they are picked up which makes it difficult to measure them. Even when they are dead, it is still hard to be accurate because dead snakes stretch very easily when handled.

Green anacondas like this one can weigh up to 180kg (400lb). That's about the same weight as three adult women.

Getting bigger

Snakes don't stop growing when they become adults, as people do. They continue to grow throughout their lives, although they grow much more slowly as they get older.

Heavy anacondas

Green anacondas are members of the boa family and are the heaviest of all snakes. Their weight slows them down on dry land. But in swamps and rivers, it is supported by water. This means that they can swim much faster than they can slither, and so they spend much of their time in water.

Fact: The New York Zoological Society has offered a cash reward for anyone finding a reticulated python over 9.14m (30ft) long. So far, no one has claimed the reward.

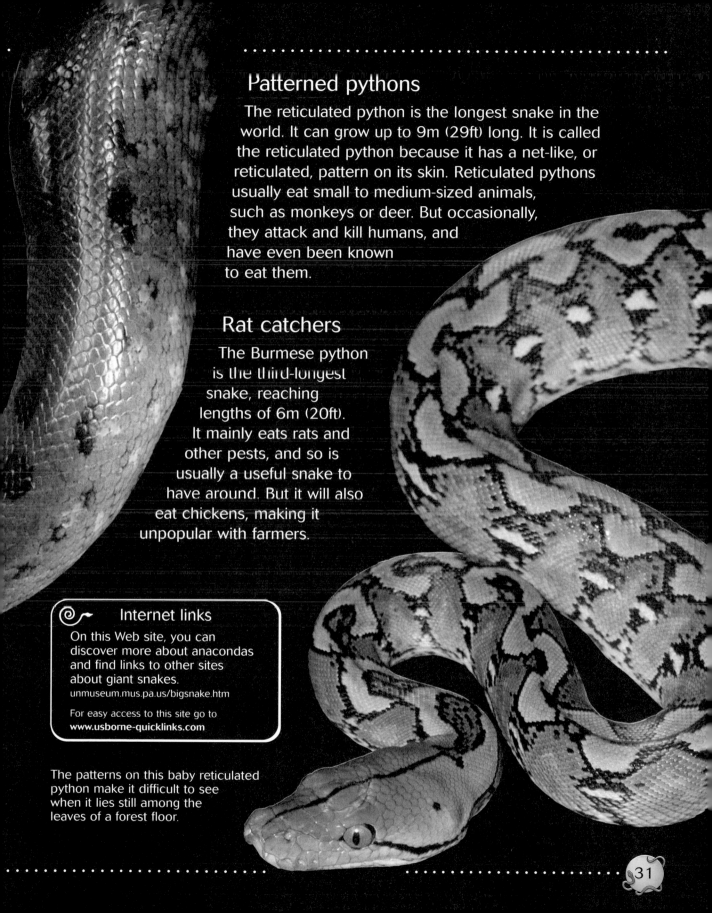

Patterned pythons

The reticulated python is the longest snake in the world. It can grow up to 9m (29ft) long. It is called the reticulated python because it has a net-like, or reticulated, pattern on its skin. Reticulated pythons usually eat small to medium-sized animals, such as monkeys or deer. But occasionally, they attack and kill humans, and have even been known to eat them.

Rat catchers

The Burmese python is the third-longest snake, reaching lengths of 6m (20ft). It mainly eats rats and other pests, and so is usually a useful snake to have around. But it will also eat chickens, making it unpopular with farmers.

◎ ~ Internet links

On this Web site, you can discover more about anacondas and find links to other sites about giant snakes.
unmuseum.mus.pa.us/bigsnake.htm

For easy access to this site go to
www.usborne-quicklinks.com

The patterns on this baby reticulated python make it difficult to see when it lies still among the leaves of a forest floor.

Boas and pythons ....

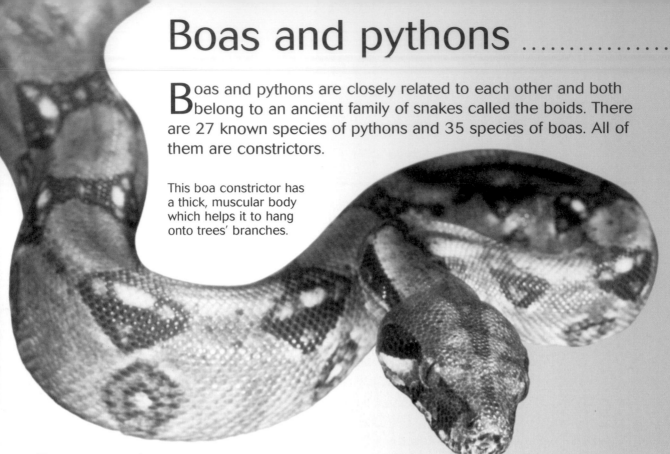

Boas and pythons are closely related to each other and both belong to an ancient family of snakes called the boids. There are 27 known species of pythons and 35 species of boas. All of them are constrictors.

This boa constrictor has a thick, muscular body which helps it to hang onto trees' branches.

Boa constrictors

Boa constrictors, or common boas, are perhaps the best-known snakes. They can grow to be as long as 3m (9ft). This may be why some people think of them as being dangerous to humans. But, in fact, they rarely attack people and certainly wouldn't try to eat anything as big as a person. Instead, they feed on birds and other small animals.

The pattern on this carpet python's skin helps it to stay hidden from predators.

Carpet pythons

Carpet pythons come from Australia. They live in a wide range of places, from dry deserts to tropical rainforests. They are called carpet pythons because of the striking markings on their skin which look a little like the pattern on an oriental carpet.

Green tree python

Green tree pythons live in rainforests. The adult is a stunning shade of bright green, with an irregular pattern of white and yellow blotches down its back. This pattern looks similar to the pattern light makes when it shines through trees.

Green tree pythons, like this one, sleep in trees during the day and hunt at night.

Internet links

On this Web site, you can see pictures of boas and find out more about them.
www.thesnake.org/boas.html

For easy access to this site go to
www.usborne-quicklinks.com

Turning green

Surprisingly, when green tree pythons first hatch out of their eggs, they are bright yellow or, much more rarely, red. After about a year, they turn green. Scientists aren't sure why this happens.

This baby rainbow boa has smooth, shiny scales which appear to shimmer as it moves.

Rainbow boa

Rainbow boas have striking, shimmering scales. They live in rainforests, hunting mainly at night, when they look for bats, mice and other small animals.

Countless colubrids

The colubrid family of snakes contains a huge number of different species. About half of all snakes belong to this family. Most colubrids are totally harmless but a few are venomous and have occasionally killed people.

Boomslangs

All rear-fanged snakes belong to the colubrid family. Most of these pose no threat to humans, but the boomslang is an exception. It has very strong venom and its fangs are near enough to the front of its mouth to bite into a human.

Although boomslangs can be dangerous, they are not usually aggressive. It is easy to tell if one becomes angry or alarmed, because it puffs up its throat.

Boomslangs are graceful movers that live in trees. They have distinctive large eyes and pointed snouts.

Airborne snakes

The five species of flying snakes are part of the colubrid family. Flying snakes can't actually fly but they can glide spectacularly from tree to tree, in the tropical rainforests where they live.

They launch themselves into the air and form their bodies into s-shapes. To help them glide more easily, they spread out their rib bones so that their bodies become flatter and wider.

Internet links

You can see exciting video clips of snakes flying through the air on this Web site.

home.uchicago.edu/~jjsocha/flyingsnake/flyingsnake.html

For easy access to this site go to
www.usborne-quicklinks.com

This picture shows a flying snake forming its body in an s-shape as it launches itself into the air.

Hungry for eggs

There is no mystery about what egg-eating snakes like to eat. Although they are very thin, these snakes can easily swallow eggs that are more than three times the size of their heads.

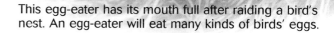

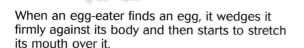

When an egg-eater finds an egg, it wedges it firmly against its body and then starts to stretch its mouth over it.

This egg-eater has its mouth full after raiding a bird's nest. An egg-eater will eat many kinds of birds' eggs.

Hungry for rattlers

Even though rattlesnakes are venomous, they are easy prey for certain kingsnakes. This is mainly because these snakes are not badly affected by their venom. Kingsnakes can overpower rattlesnakes and swallow them while they are still alive.

Once the snake has managed to stretch its whole mouth over the egg, it uses pointed spines in its throat to puncture and crush it.

This Californian kingsnake is starting to eat a rattlesnake it has overpowered.

★

When the egg has been emptied of food, the egg-eater spits the crushed, flattened shell out.

Cobras

Cobras are very distinctive-looking snakes. An alarmed cobra with the hood on its neck spread wide is a dramatic and intimidating sight. There are many different species of cobras, including the longest venomous snake in the world, the king cobra.

The king of snakes

The king cobra's head is as big as a man's hand and its body can reach about 6m (18ft) in length. When alarmed, a king cobra can look a person in the eye, if it raises the front part of its body off the ground.

Internet links

Find out all you need to know about king cobras by clicking on the body of the life-size king cobra on this Web site.
www.nationalgeographic.com/features/97/kingcobra/index-n.html

For easy access to this site go to
www.usborne-quicklinks.com

King cobras are fairly thin snakes and have narrower hoods than most cobras.

Nest builders

King cobras are the only snakes to build nests to protect their eggs. Once a female king cobra has laid her eggs, she guards them until they hatch, 60 to 80 days later. King cobras are not aggressive, but they may attack if they feel that their nest is being threatened.

To make a nest, a female king cobra uses the loops of her body to drag dead leaves into a pile.

Once the nest is complete, the king cobra lays her eggs inside the pile and then rests on top of it.

Weaver eaters

Weaver birds build nests high up in trees away from predators, such as snakes. But these nests offer no protection against South African cape cobras. They can climb to the highest branches and force their way into these nests to feed on baby birds and eggs.

Weaver birds build nests with long entrances to try to stop snakes from getting in.

Back to front

When cobras become alarmed, they rise up off the ground and display their hoods. On the backs of their hoods, many cobras have markings known as eyespots because they look similar to eyes. It is thought that they have them to confuse predators. A cobra can quickly turn around and start to escape, yet still appear to be facing its attacker.

The Indian cobra is known as the spectacled cobra, because the shape of its eyespots looks like a pair of glasses, or spectacles.

 Fact: One bite from a king cobra contains enough venom to kill an elephant.

Sea snakes

Many snakes are good swimmers and will enter water to hide from a predator or to cool down on a hot day. But some snakes spend their entire lives in water. Some of these live in rivers and lakes, but most water-dwelling snakes are sea snakes.

Knotted snake skin

This shows how a sea snake twists its body to help it shed its skin.

Sea snakes shed their skin more frequently than land snakes. Some sea snakes, such as yellow-bellied sea snakes, rub their skin off by rubbing one part of their body against another. Their bodies look very tangled while they do this, and the skin they shed is often knotted into coils.

Coming up for air

Many sea snakes have to stay in water all their lives because they can't move on land and will soon die if washed up onto a beach. But sea snakes can't breathe underwater as fish can. Instead, they have to come up to the surface now and again to take a breath of air.

Once they have taken in enough air, most sea snakes can remain underwater for at least an hour. In fact, yellow-bellied sea snakes are able to hold their breath for over three hours.

Salty snakes

All animals need to drink water to survive. But the only water available to sea snakes is sea water, which is very salty.

Sea snakes can get rid of the salt they don't want using special organs under their tongues, called salt glands. Excess salt collects in the gland until the snake pushes its tongue out to smell. When the snake does this, salty water is pushed out at the same time.

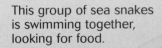

This group of sea snakes is swimming together, looking for food.

Migrating snakes

Some sea snakes make long journeys together in large groups. This is called migration. In many countries there are legends about huge sea monsters. Perhaps what people really saw were hundreds of migrating sea snakes, moving along together. This may have looked like one huge animal.

Deadly snakes

Sea snakes are among the most venomous snakes in the world. Belcher's sea snake is thought to have the most deadly venom. It is around a hundred times more venomous than the most venomous land snake.

Some people used to think there were huge snake-like monsters in the sea like the one shown here.

In and out of the sea

Seakraits are distant relatives of sea snakes. They also live in the sea, but can leave it for dry land. They do this to mate and lay eggs. They also often move onto beaches to lie in the sunshine. The sun's warmth helps to break down food inside their stomachs more quickly.

This is a seakrait. It's not as well adapted to life in the sea as sea snakes are. But, unlike many sea snakes, it can move on land as well as in water.

Fact: True sea snakes give birth to live young in the sea.

Mambas

Mambas are part of the same family as cobras. There are only four species of mambas and all of them live in Africa. Their highly venomous bites have made them both feared and respected by humans.

Green mambas are attractive snakes with bright green skin.

A gathering of greens

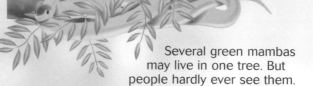

Several green mambas may live in one tree. But people hardly ever see them.

In some parts of Kenya and Tanzania, green mambas are found in very large numbers. Several hundred can live in an area about the same size as a small town park. Sometimes four or five can live in one large tree.

Green mambas

There are three different species of green mambas. They spend most of their time in woodland and forests where their green skin makes them very hard to see. Although they are highly venomous and have killed people, green mambas are not aggressive and prefer to move away from danger rather than attack.

Fact: Without medical treatment, mamba bites can cause death within a few hours, or even just a few minutes.

Internet links

Find out more about mambas, and see other
pictures of them on this Web site.
www.thesnake.org/elapidae.html#gmamba

For easy access to this site go to
www.usborne-quicklinks.com

Fast snake

Black mambas are the fastest of all
snakes, reaching speeds of 20kph
(12mph) or more when they are on the
attack. Even when moving quickly, they
can keep their necks and heads off the
ground, ready to make a sudden attack.

Not so black mambas

Black mambas are rarely, if ever, black.
They are usually a light chocolate-brown,
but they get their name from the black
lining of their mouths. Black mambas
are the longest venomous snakes
in Africa, reaching 4m (12ft) in
length. They are also greatly feared
because they are quite nervous
and will attack if threatened.

Although black mambas
spend much of their time
on the ground, they are
also good at climbing trees.

Home sweet home

Black mambas sometimes like to find
a special place where they can regularly
take shelter. They tend to choose holes
in trees, rock crevices, and even the
thatched roofs of houses.

More elapids

Cobras, sea snakes and mambas all belong to the elapid family. There are about 300 species of elapid snakes and many of them live in or near Australia. They vary greatly from one species to another. But one feature they all share is that they have highly poisonous venom.

Deadly taipans

Taipans are large elapid snakes that live in Australia and New Guinea. Inland taipans are the most venomous of all land snakes. A single bite from one would inject enough venom to kill 12 adult men.

Inland taipans, such as this one, are very dangerous to humans. But they are rare and few people have been bitten by one.

Death adders

Death adders don't belong to the same family as other adders (see pages 44–45). They are, in fact, another type of elapid. Like carpet vipers, they bury themselves under leaves, or in sand, to lie in wait for prey. This makes it easy to tread on them by mistake. Without fast treatment, a bite from a death adder can kill a person.

This northern death adder, like other death adders, is unusually heavy and wide compared to most other elapid snakes.

 Fact: Death adders are unusual for elapids because they give birth to live young rather than laying eggs as other elapids do.

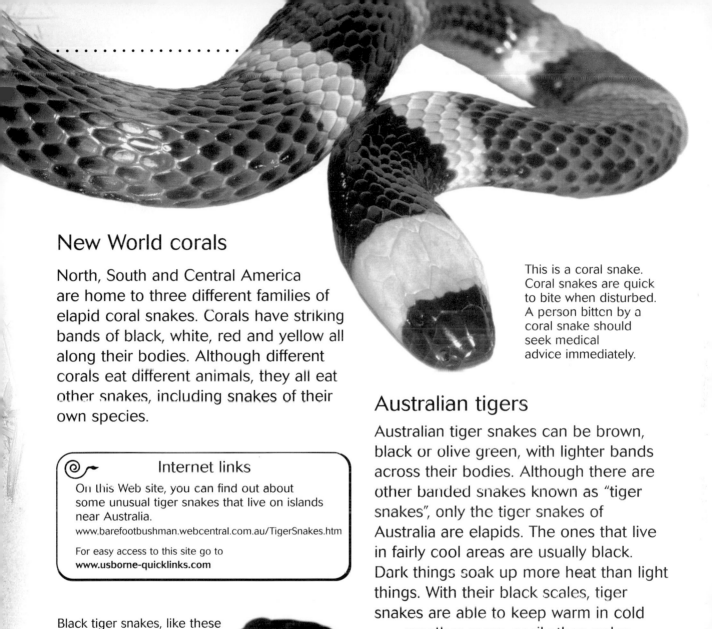

New World corals

North, South and Central America are home to three different families of elapid coral snakes. Corals have striking bands of black, white, red and yellow all along their bodies. Although different corals eat different animals, they all eat other snakes, including snakes of their own species.

This is a coral snake. Coral snakes are quick to bite when disturbed. A person bitten by a coral snake should seek medical advice immediately.

╭─────────────────────────────────────╮
ⓔ～   Internet links

On this Web site, you can find out about some unusual tiger snakes that live on islands near Australia.
www.barefootbushman.webcentral.com.au/TigerSnakes.htm

For easy access to this site go to
www.usborne-quicklinks.com
╰─────────────────────────────────────╯

Australian tigers

Australian tiger snakes can be brown, black or olive green, with lighter bands across their bodies. Although there are other banded snakes known as "tiger snakes", only the tiger snakes of Australia are elapids. The ones that live in fairly cool areas are usually black. Dark things soak up more heat than light things. With their black scales, tiger snakes are able to keep warm in cold weather more easily than paler snakes can.

Black tiger snakes, like these two, are better able to survive in colder places than many other snakes.

Vipers and adders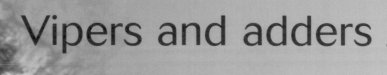

There are over 200 different types of vipers (some of which are called adders) living all over the world. Many are well camouflaged and some are highly venomous.

Worldwide snake

The northern viper, or adder, lives in a wide range of places. It can be found in western Europe and Russia and it is the only snake living within the Arctic Circle. It is also the only venomous snake in Great Britain.

Adders, like this one, can tolerate cold conditions. This enables them to live in places where other snakes can't survive.

Sheltering snakes

During the winter months, adders hibernate, or rest, to avoid the cold harsh weather. When they do this, they sometimes group together in sheltered underground burrows or dens.

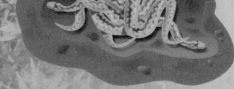

This picture shows a group of adders hibernating in an underground den.

Puffed-up snake

Puff adders get their name from their habit of puffing up their bodies when alarmed. They do this by quickly sucking in air. This makes them look bigger and more intimidating. As they let out the air, they make a loud hissing noise which is also meant to warn off predators.

 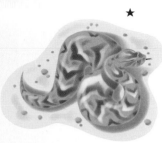

A puff adder has a fat, chunky body and a flat, wide head.

When alarmed, a puff adder sucks in air and becomes even fatter.

 Internet links

Visit this Web site to watch a video clip of a puff adder moving along the ground. You can see video clips of other snakes on this site too.
www.safaricamlive.com/wildlife_and_underwater_videos.htm

For easy access to this site go to
www.usborne-quicklinks.com

Patterned viper

The gaboon viper has brown, beige, white and black skin and is a very distinctive-looking snake. The patterns on its skin allow it to blend in with the floor of the tropical forests where it lives. It can conceal itself so well that even alert prey, such as monkeys, come close enough to be bitten.

This gaboon viper is partly hidden in a pile of dead leaves.

Pit vipers

Pit vipers are part of the viper family, but they have something in common with some boas and pythons – they have heat pits on their faces. This is how they get their name.

Heat pits

This shows where a heat pit is on a palm viper's head.

Cottonmouth

The cottonmouth is an aggressive and dangerous snake from the swampy areas in the southeast of the U.S.A. It gets its name from the skin inside its mouth, which reminds people of white cotton. Cottonmouths are easily angered, but luckily they give warning signals before they attack.

While boas and pythons have many heat pits on their heads, pit vipers have just two. They are located on either side of the snake's face, between its eyes and nostrils. Heat pits help pit vipers find prey if they are hunting at night.

This angry cottonmouth is trying to scare off a possible predator.

To scare off a predator, a cottonmouth opens its mouth and displays the white skin inside.

The cottonmouth also shakes its tail violently. If the predator doesn't move away, the snake may attack.

This fer-de-lance has caught a whiptail lizard and is injecting it with venom.

South American killer

The fer-de-lance belongs to a group of snakes called lanceheads. These snakes get their name from their triangular, pointed heads which look like the tips of lances, or spears.

The fer-de-lance lives in South America and is feared by workers on coffee and banana plantations. These deadly snakes hunt for rats and mice on plantations, and workers are sometimes bitten by them.

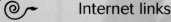

℮ Internet links

To see close-up pictures of fer-de-lance snakes and learn more about them, visit the reptile section of this Web site.
www.animalsoftherainforest.com/frames.htm

For easy access to this site go to
www.usborne-quicklinks.com

Tail beaters

Bushmasters are large venomous snakes from the rainforests of Central and South America. To scare off predators, they beat the tips of their tails on dead leaves on the forest floor. This makes a loud rustling noise and warns animals to keep away.

A bushmaster snake coiled up on the forest floor

Fact: The Himalayan pit viper lives at 5km (3 miles) above sea level, in the Himalaya mountains in Asia. No other snakes live at such a height.

Rattlers

Rattlesnakes are one of the best-known species of snakes. They are part of the pit viper family and are only found in North, Central and South America. All rattlesnakes are venomous, and a few are potentially deadly to humans.

The Santa Catalina has one old scale on the tip of its tail instead of a rattle.

Getting rattled

When rattlesnakes sense danger, for example if a large animal is about to tread on them, they use the rattles on the ends of their tails to make a loud buzzing noise (see page 25). This warns nearby animals to keep away from them.

When a rattlesnake becomes alarmed, it raises its head off the ground and makes the front part of its body into an s-shape.

At the same time, the rattlesnake starts to shake its tail rapidly to make as loud a buzzing noise as possible.

Once the danger has passed, the rattlesnake lowers its head, stops vibrating its tail, and is able to relax once again.

Rattlesnake without a rattle

Santa Catalina rattlesnakes are the only rattlesnakes without rattles. On the island of Santa Catalina where these snakes live, there are no big animals, so they don't need rattles to warn them off. Without rattles they can also wait silently in bushes for lizards and birds to come close enough to bite.

Internet links

Why not test out your rattlesnake knowledge by trying the trivia quiz at the American International Rattlesnake Museum Web site?
www.rattlesnakes.com/core.html

For easy access to this site go to
www.usborne-quicklinks.com

Fact: Rattlesnakes are greatly feared in the U.S.A., but, on average, they kill only 12 people a year. That's fewer than the number of people killed by lightning.

Deadliest rattlers

The aggressive mojave rattlesnake is the most venomous rattlesnake in North America, being almost twice as deadly as its nearest rival. The venom from just one of its bites could kill as many as 15,000 mice.

A few species of tropical rattlesnakes from South America, such as the cascaval, are even more deadly. They are known as "neck breakers" because a bite from one of them can cause a person's neck muscles to become rigid or frozen.

Mojave rattlesnakes live in rocky places and deserts.

Rattlesnake round-ups

These hunters are about to spray a jet of gas into a rattlesnake den.

In some parts of the U.S.A., people organize rattlesnake hunts, or round-ups. Hunters spray chemicals into burrows to drive snakes out into the open, where they are caught and then killed. The chemicals are very poisonous and kill many other animals living in the same habitat, such as foxes and skunks.

Underground snakes

Many species of snakes can burrow, or dig tunnels, and some spend most of their lives underground. The snake families with the largest number of burrowing snakes are blind snakes and thread snakes.

Bodies for burrowing

You might think that it would be difficult to dig without arms or legs. But burrowing snakes have developed special features to help them. They usually have perfectly round bodies and smooth scales, which help them move through soil easily.

Strong skulls

Many burrowing snakes have stronger, heavier skulls than other snakes. They need strong skulls to help them force their way through the soil.

★

Strong skulls enable blind snakes to push their way through soil without hurting themselves.

Heads and tails

Some burrowing snakes, such as blind snakes, have heads that are the same shape as their tails. At first glance, it isn't always easy to tell which end is the head and which end is the tail.

Can you tell which end of this blind snake is its tail and which end is its head?*

*The snake's head is at the bottom of the picture.

This shiny-scaled sunbeam snake hunts other burrowing animals for food.

Occasional burrowers

Underground, snakes' eggs are better protected from predators than they would be on the surface.

Borrowing burrows

Some snakes don't dig their own tunnels. Instead, they use ones made by other animals. They hunt underground for small burrowing animals, such as rats and even other snakes.

Short-sighted snakes

Most underground snakes have very small, simple eyes, compared to other snakes. They have poor eyesight and some may even be totally blind. But underground there isn't enough light to see by, so they don't need to have good eyesight. Instead, they rely on their sense of smell to help them find food.

Snakes that live mainly above ground also burrow from time to time. For example, ratsnakes and kingsnakes burrow if the temperature on the surface becomes too hot. Other snakes, such as pine snakes, make chambers underground and lay their eggs there.

This western thread snake has tiny eyes and very bad eyesight.

Fact: Some blind snakes can produce a smell which stops the ants they are hunting from trying to bite them.

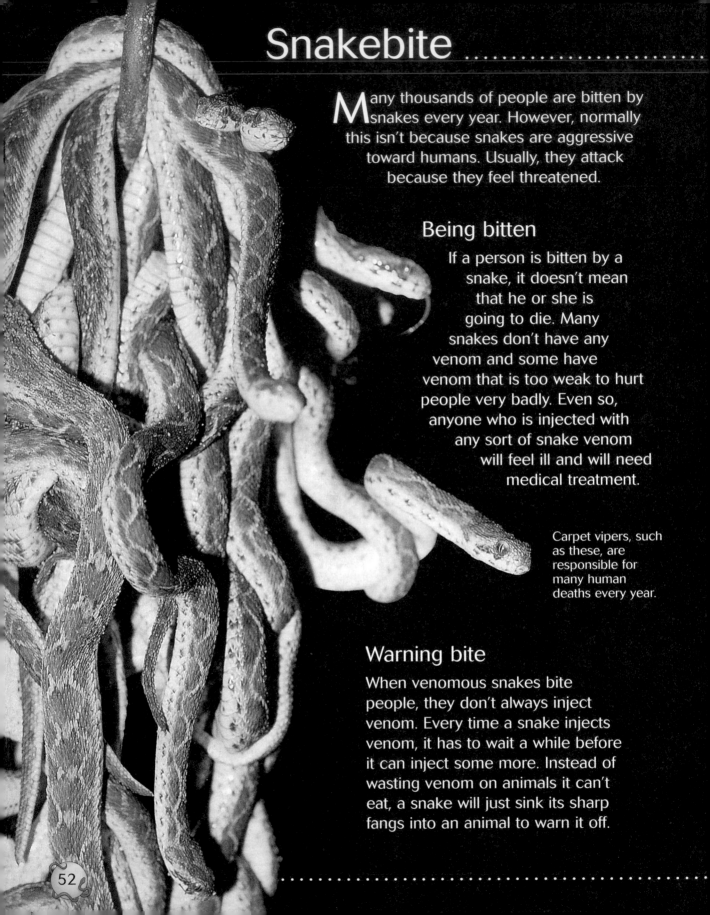

Snakebite

Many thousands of people are bitten by snakes every year. However, normally this isn't because snakes are aggressive toward humans. Usually, they attack because they feel threatened.

Being bitten

If a person is bitten by a snake, it doesn't mean that he or she is going to die. Many snakes don't have any venom and some have venom that is too weak to hurt people very badly. Even so, anyone who is injected with any sort of snake venom will feel ill and will need medical treatment.

Carpet vipers, such as these, are responsible for many human deaths every year.

Warning bite

When venomous snakes bite people, they don't always inject venom. Every time a snake injects venom, it has to wait a while before it can inject some more. Instead of wasting venom on animals it can't eat, a snake will just sink its sharp fangs into an animal to warn it off.

Surviving snakebites

About fifty species of snakes inject venom that can kill humans. But a person will not usually die from a bite, if treated quickly. Scientists have developed medicine called antivenom, which is made from snakes' venom. If enough antivenom is given to someone soon after they have been bitten, they usually survive.

Different cures

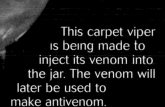

This carpet viper is being made to inject its venom into the jar. The venom will later be used to make antivenom.

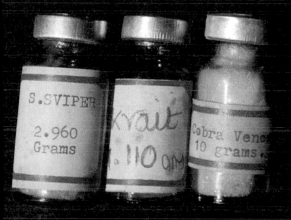

S.SVIPER
2.960
Grams

Krait
.110 gm

Cobra Venom
10 grams

The antivenom in these bottles can save the lives of people who have been bitten by snakes.

Because venoms from different snakes have different sorts of poisons in them, scientists have to make different antivenoms to treat different sorts of snakebites. So, if someone is bitten by a snake, it's very important to find out what sort of snake it was, so that doctors can give the patient the right antivenom.

Don't get bitten!

Of course, it's much better not to get bitten by a snake in the first place. Here are a few precautions you can take if you are walking in areas where there might be snakes:

- Leave snakes alone! If you leave them alone, they will leave you alone.

- Always cover up your legs and wear sensible shoes, and avoid walking through long grass.

- Never pick up a snake, even if it looks as if it is dead. It may just be injured or stunned, or even "playing dead".

Fact: About 25,000 people die from snakebites each year.

Snakes at stake ....

Many people fear snakes because of their deadly reputations. But, in fact, snakes have more reasons to fear people. Snakes are hunted for their skin, their habitats are frequently destroyed, and many are killed by cars and trucks as they try to cross busy roads.

Threatened forests

Rainforests are home to many types of snakes, but millions of rainforest trees are cut down every year for their wood or to make way for farming.

As their habitats are wiped out, snakes suffer because their hiding places are destroyed and their prey is driven away. Snakes can't travel long distances, so they are unable to escape and many die.

Activities such as tree felling do vast amounts of damage to snakes' habitats.

Milos vipers are only found on a few Greek islands, including Milos, from which they get their name.

Skin trade

Over a million snakes are killed each year, so that their skin can be used to make handbags, wallets and boots. Some countries, such as India, have banned the exportation of snakeskin in order to discourage the hunting of snakes.

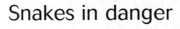

This snakeskin bag has a cobra's head on the front.

Snakes in danger

The numbers of some species of snakes are falling rapidly. For example, there are only about 2,500 Milos vipers left. They have been badly affected by the mining industry, forest fires and also by people running over them on roads. The Greek government is under a lot of pressure to help protect the Milos viper before it becomes extinct.

Road kill

Many snakes are killed by cars and trucks. This is because roads are often built through areas where snakes live. Most snakes are slow movers and find it hard to get out of the way of a fast-moving vehicle.

 Internet links

Visit this Web site to find out how you can help to protect the world's forests and the wildlife living in them.
www.worldwildlife.org/forests/

For easy access to this site go to
www.usborne-quicklinks.com

 Fact: Since 1800, almost half of the world's total area of tropical rainforest has been destroyed.

Rituals and legends

For many thousands of years, snakes have been viewed as mysterious, even magical, creatures. They have often been a part of ancient legends and tales, as well as religious rituals and beliefs.

Snake temple

Venomous Wagler's pit vipers, like this one, live around the pillars and statues of Penang's snake temple.

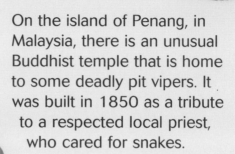

On the island of Penang, in Malaysia, there is an unusual Buddhist temple that is home to some deadly pit vipers. It was built in 1850 as a tribute to a respected local priest, who cared for snakes.

Local people say that on the day the temple was completed, a number of snakes came out of the jungle to live in the temple. These days, the temple is a tourist attraction and snakes are taken from the wild to keep it well stocked.

Snake monster

In ancient Greek mythology, there was a monster called Medusa, whose hair was made of real snakes. Just one glimpse of her face was supposed to turn a person to stone. According to the myth, she was killed by the hero Perseus, who chopped off her snake-covered head.

A sculpture of Medusa's head from a museum in Rome, Italy

Dancing with snakes

A Native American people called the Hopi think that snakes are messengers of the gods. Until recently, they used to hold nine day rituals, where they caught rattlesnakes and washed them. On the ninth day, they danced with the snakes, holding them between their lips. Then the snakes were released. The ritual was to ensure a good harvest and heavy rains.

This is a picture of one of the Hopi people wearing ceremonial clothing.

Charming snakes

Snake charming is an ancient but dangerous art. It involves a charmer playing a flute to a snake, often a deadly cobra, just a few feet away. As the charmer moves the flute from side to side, the snake sways to and fro, as if moving with the music. But as snakes have poor hearing, it is more likely to be following the movement of the flute because it thinks the flute may attack it.

Snake charmers, like this one, can be seen in India.

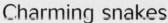

Fact: Most snake charmers look after their snakes, but some, afraid of being bitten, sew up the snakes' mouths or remove their fangs.

Snake facts

Snakes are intriguing animals and there is so much you can find out about them. Here are some fascinating facts for you to explore.

A deadly Russell's viper

🐍 The sharp-nosed viper is also known as the "hundred-pace snake". This is because it is said that a person can only walk 100 paces after being bitten by this snake before dropping down dead.

A baby king cobra

🐍 In parts of Asia, king cobras were once believed to be sun gods, who had power over the weather. Today, they are still highly respected there and are closely associated with the religions of Hinduism and Buddhism.

🐍 Baby snakes have bites that are just as venomous as adult ones. In fact, because baby snakes are often much more aggressive than their parents, they can be particularly dangerous.

🐍 Russell's vipers are among the world's most dangerous snakes. Every year, their bites are responsible for the deaths of at least 10,000 people.

🐍 The Antiguan racer is one of the world's rarest snakes. It is only found on small islands off the coast of Antigua in the Caribbean Sea. It is thought that there are fewer than 100 of these snakes in the wild.

🐍 The jumping viper from Central America gets its name from its habit of sometimes leaping almost 1m (3ft) off the ground when it launches an attack.

🐍 All snakes have long, large stomachs. But some have stomachs that take up a third of the length of their bodies.

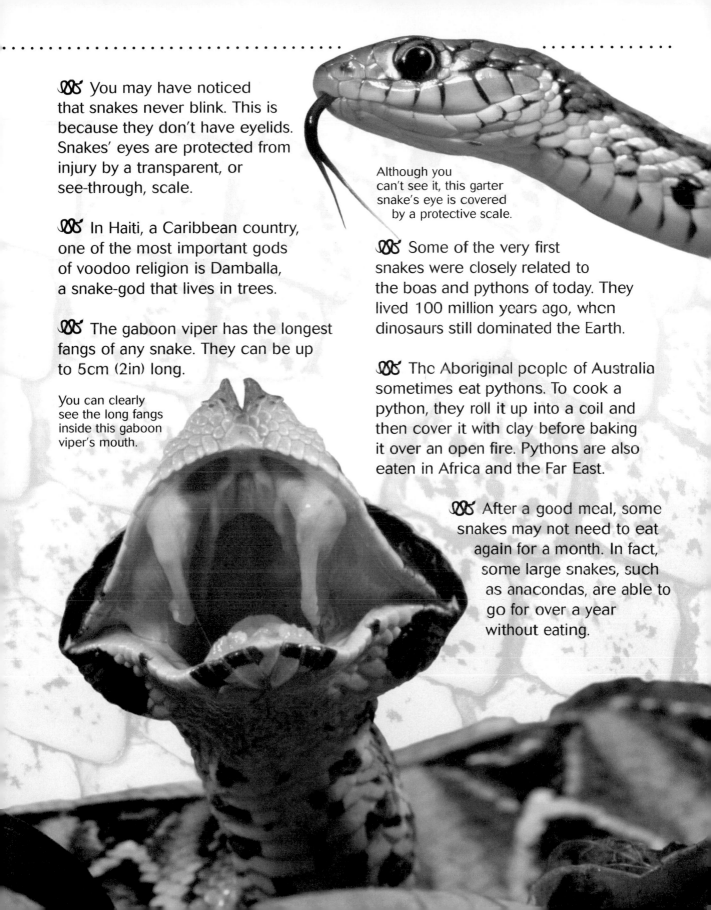

∞ You may have noticed that snakes never blink. This is because they don't have eyelids. Snakes' eyes are protected from injury by a transparent, or see-through, scale.

∞ In Haiti, a Caribbean country, one of the most important gods of voodoo religion is Damballa, a snake-god that lives in trees.

∞ The gaboon viper has the longest fangs of any snake. They can be up to 5cm (2in) long.

Although you can't see it, this garter snake's eye is covered by a protective scale.

You can clearly see the long fangs inside this gaboon viper's mouth.

∞ Some of the very first snakes were closely related to the boas and pythons of today. They lived 100 million years ago, when dinosaurs still dominated the Earth.

∞ The Aboriginal people of Australia sometimes eat pythons. To cook a python, they roll it up into a coil and then cover it with clay before baking it over an open fire. Pythons are also eaten in Africa and the Far East.

∞ After a good meal, some snakes may not need to eat again for a month. In fact, some large snakes, such as anacondas, are able to go for over a year without eating.

Glossary

This glossary explains some of the words you might come across when reading about snakes. Words in *italic* type have their own entries elsewhere in the glossary.

antivenom Medicine used to treat someone who has been bitten by a venomous snake. It can reverse the effects of *venom*.

aquatic Living in water.

arboreal Living in trees.

breed To produce young.

camouflage Markings on an animal's body that help it to blend in with its natural surroundings. These markings make it difficult to see the animal.

cold-blooded Having a body temperature that varies with the temperature of the surroundings. Cold-blooded animals are not able to produce their own body heat. They have to lie in sunshine to warm up.

concertina movement A way of moving along by bunching up the body and then stretching it out again. Snakes may move like this when they are in tunnels.

conservation Protection and preservation of our surroundings and the plants and animals living in them.

constrictor A snake that kills animals by squeezing them until they can't breathe any more.

egg tooth A special tooth which some baby animals have to help them break out of their eggs.

endangered Under threat. An endangered *species* is a type of animal or plant that is in danger of dying out.

environment The natural surroundings in which plants and animals live.

extinction When all the members of a *species* die out.

eyespot A marking which resembles an eye on the back of some cobras' heads.

fang A long, very sharp tooth. Snakes can use their fangs to inject *venom* into other animals.

front-fanged snake A snake with *fangs* near the front of its mouth.

habitat The place where a group of plants or animals lives.

hatch To break out of an egg.

heat pit An area near some snakes' mouths which is used to detect changes in the temperature of their surroundings.

herpetology The study of reptiles.

hibernate To sleep for a long period of time, often in the cold winter months.

hood A flap of skin covering cobras' ribs near their heads.

immune Resistant to a poison, such as venom, or a disease.

incubate To keep eggs at the right temperature for the babies inside to grow and develop.

Jacobson's organ A special organ in the roof of some animals' mouths which they can use to detect smells.

mate (noun) One of a pair of animals that *breed* together.

mate (verb) To come together to *breed*.

mating ball A tangled group of male snakes that are all trying to mate with a few female snakes.

migrate To make a long journey to look for food, or to find warmer surroundings.

predator An animal that hunts other animals for food.

prey An animal that is hunted for food.

protected species A type of animal that it is prohibited to hurt or kill because it is in danger of becoming *extinct*.

rainforest Very damp, hot forest, located in the *tropics*.

rattle Old scales at the tip of a rattlesnake's tail that make a sound like a rattle when the snake shakes its tail.

rattlesnake round-up An organized hunt for rattlesnakes.

rear-fanged snake A snake with *fangs* near the back of its mouth.

rectilinear movement A way of moving forward in a straight line.

reptile A *cold-blooded* animal with scaly, waterproof skin.

serpentine movement A way of moving by following an s-shaped path. Most snakes usually move in this way.

sidewinding A way of moving by repeatedly throwing the body to the side in a loop. Some desert snakes move like this.

species A type of plant or animal.

sperm Male sex cells.

strike To dart out to attack an animal.

subterranean Living mainly underground.

suffocate To stop an animal from breathing until it dies.

tropics Warm, wet areas, near to the Equator, an imaginary line around the middle of the Earth.

venom A poisonous liquid that some snakes inject into their prey.

warm-blooded Having a body that is able to produce its own heat. Animals that are warm-blooded can keep warm, even if their surroundings are cold.

Using the Internet ....

This page contains more information about Internet links, and guidelines to help you find your way around the Internet safely and efficiently. You can find more tips and information on the inside of the front cover.

Usborne Quicklinks

The best way to access the sites recommended in this book is to go to **www.usborne-quicklinks.com** and follow the simple instructions there. In Usborne Quicklinks you will find links that you can click on to take you straight to the recommended sites, and to the free downloadable pictures from this book that you can print out for your own personal use. You can use these pictures in your homework or projects, but they must not be copied or distributed for any commercial purpose.

Help

For general help and advice on using the Internet, go to the Usborne Quicklinks Web site and click on Net Help. To find out more about how to use your Internet browser, click on its Help menu and choose Contents and Index. You'll find a huge searchable dictionary containing tips on how to find your way around the Internet easily. For more up-to-the-minute technical support for your browser, click on Help and then Online Support. You'll be taken to the browser manufacturer's Web site.

Computer viruses

A computer virus is a program that can seriously damage your computer. A virus can get into your computer when you download programs from the Internet or in an attachment (an extra file) that arrives with an e-mail. You can buy anti-virus software at computer stores or download it from the Internet. It is quite expensive, but costs less than repairing a damaged computer. To find out more about viruses, go to Usborne Quicklinks and click on Net Help.

Internet safety

Very rarely, an unsuitable site might be accessed accidentally by typing in an address wrongly. To avoid this possibility, we strongly recommend that the Web sites listed in this book are accessed via the Usborne Quicklinks Web site rather than by typing in the addresses listed in the boxes. When using the Internet, you should always follow these guidelines:

- Check with your parent, teacher, or the owner of the computer that it is all right for you to connect to the Internet. They can then stay nearby if they think they should do so.

- If you use a search engine to search the Internet, read the description of each suggested site to make sure it is what you want before clicking on the address.

- If you find that a site isn't what you were looking for, click on the Stop button on your browser's toolbar to stop the page downloading, then on the Back button to go back to the previous page.

- Never give out personal information, such as your real name, address or phone number.

- Never arrange to meet someone that you come across on the Internet.

> For quick and easy access to all the Web sites in this book, go to
>
> **www.usborne-quicklinks.com**